The Cardinal's Blades Omnibus

The Cardinal's Blades
The Alchemist in the Shadows
The Dragon Arcana

PIERRE PEVEL

Translated by Tom Clegg

This omnibus first published in Great Britain in 2021 by Gollancz
an imprint of The Orion Publishing Group Ltd
Carmelite House, 50 Victoria Embankment
London EC4Y 0DZ

An Hachette UK Company

3 5 7 9 10 8 6 4 2

The Cardinal's Blades original text
Copyright © Pierre Pevel/Editions Bragelonne 2007
The Cardinal's Blades English translation
Copyright © Tom Clegg/Editions Bragelonne 2009
The Alchemist in the Shadows original text
Copyright © Pierre Pevel/Editions Bragelonne 2009
The Alchemist in the Shadows English translation
Copyright © Tom Clegg/Editions Bragelonne 2010
The Dragon Arcana original text
Copyright © Pierre Pevel/Editions Bragelonne 2011
The Dragon Arcana English translation
Copyright © Tom Clegg/Editions Bragelonne 2011

Map copyright © Pierre Pevel/Editions Bragelonne 2009

A CIP catalogue record for this book is
available from the British Library.

ISBN (Mass Market Paperback) 978 1 473 22833 7

Typeset at The Spartan Press Ltd,
Lymington, Hants

Printed in Great Britain by Clays Ltd,
Elcograf S.p.A.

www.gollancz.co.uk

Contents

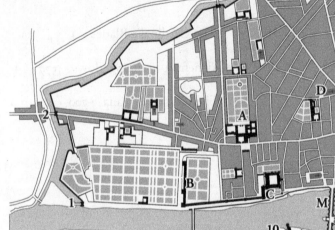

1. Porte de la Conférence
2. Porte Saint-Honoré
3. Porte de Richelieu
4. Porte Montmartre
5. Porte de la Poissonnerie
6. Porte Saint-Denis
7. Porte Saint-Martin
8. Porte du Temple
9. Porte Saint-Antoine
10. Porte de Nesle
11. Porte de Buci
12. Porte Saint-Germain
13. Porte Saint-Michel
14. Porte Saint-Jacques
15. Porte Saint-Marcel
16. Porte Saint-Victor
17. Porte de la Tournelle

A. Palais-Cardinal
B. Palais des Tuileries
C. Louvre
D. Église Saint-Eustache
E. Les Halles
F. Cimetière des Saints-Innocents
G. Le Châtelet
H. Abbaye Saint-Martin
I. Enclos du Temple
J. Place Royale
K. La Bastille
L. Arsenal
M. Pont-Neuf
N. Place Dauphine
O. Palais
P. Hôtel-Dieu
Q. Notre-Dame
R. Les Écailles
S. Hôpital de la Charité
T. Abbaye de Saint-Germain-des-Prés
U. Foire Saint-Germain
V. Palais du Luxembourg
W. Place Maubert
X. Abbaye Saint-Victor
Y. Jardin des Plantes
Z. Val de Grâce

PARIS

THE YEAR OF OUR LORD
1633

The Cardinal's Blades

*This book is dedicated to Jean-Philippe,
my brother who fled too soon.*

A Call to Arms

Long and high-ceilinged, the room was lined with elegantly gilded and bound books which shone with a russet gleam in the half-light of the candle flames. Outside, beyond the thick red velvet curtains, Paris slept beneath a starry sky and a deep tranquillity had settled on the dusky streets which penetrated even here, where the scratching of a quill barely troubled the silence. Thin, bony and pale, the hand which held the quill traced fine, tight writing, delicate yet steady, making neither mistakes nor blots. The quill paused regularly to take a fresh load from the inkwell. It was guided with precision and, as soon as it returned to the paper, continued to scratch out an unhesitating thread of thought. Nothing else moved. Not even the scarlet dragonnet which, curled in a ball, its muzzle tucked under its wing, slept peacefully by the thick leather blotter.

Someone knocked at the door.

The hand wrote on without pause but the dragonnet, disturbed, opened one emerald eye. A man entered wearing a sword and a fitted cape of red silk blazoned, on each of its four panels, with a white cross. His head was respectfully uncovered.

'Yes?' said Cardinal Richelieu, continuing to write.

'He is here, Your Eminence.'

'Alone?'

'As you instructed.'

'Good. Send him in.'

Master Saint-Georges, Captain of His Eminence's Guards, bowed. He was about to withdraw when the cardinal added:

'And spare him the guards.'

7

Saint-Georges understood, bowed again and took care to close the door silently as he left.

Before being received in the cardinal's apartment visitors normally had to pass through five rooms throughout which guards were stationed on continuous watch, day and night. Each carried a sword at their side and pistol in their belt, remaining alert to the slightest hint of danger and refusing let anyone pass without a direct order to that effect. Nothing escaped their scrutiny, which could shift at a moment's notice from merely probing to actively threatening. Wearing their celebrated capes, these men belonged to the company of His Eminence's Guards. They escorted him everywhere he went, and wherever he resided there were never less than sixty men to accompany him. Those not on duty in the corridors and antechambers killed time between their rounds, their short muskets always near to hand. And the Guards were not the only troops detailed to protect Richelieu: while they ensured his safety inside, a company of musketeers patrolled outside.

This constant vigilance was not a simple, ostentatious show of force. They had good reason to guard him; even here in the heart of Paris, in the ornamental palace the cardinal had built just a few steps from the Louvre.

At forty-eight years old, Armand-Jean du Plessis, Cardinal de Richelieu was one of the most powerful men, and one of the most threatened, of his time. A duke and peer of the realm, member of the Council and principal minister to His Majesty; he had the ear of Louis XIII – with whom he had ruled France for a decade. That alone accounted for the numerous adversaries he reckoned with, the least of whom only plotted to disgrace him, while others made detailed plans for his assassination – for if the cardinal were forced into exile he could still act from abroad, and if imprisoned there was always the possibility of his escape. Such plots had come close to succeeding in the past, and new ones were no doubt being prepared. Richelieu had to guard himself against all those who hated him out of jealousy, because of his influence over the king. But he also had to be wary of attacks orchestrated by the enemies of France, the first and foremost being Spain, and her Court of Dragons.

It was about to strike midnight.

The sleepy dragonnet heaved a tired sigh.

'It's very late, isn't it?' the cardinal said, addressing the small winged reptile with an affectionate smile.

He looked drawn himself, both from fatigue and illness, on this spring night in 1633.

Normally he would have been in bed soon. He would sleep a little if his insomnia, his migraines and the pain in his limbs allowed it. And especially if no one woke him with urgent news requiring orders to be drawn up hastily, or worse still, a meeting in the dead of night. No matter what occurred, he rose at two in the morning and was promptly surrounded by his secretaries. After quick ablutions, he would eat a few mouthfuls of broth and then work until six o'clock. Then perhaps he would allow himself one or two hours of additional sleep, before beginning the most challenging part of the day – the rounds of ministers and secretaries of state, ambassadors and courtiers. But tonight, Cardinal Richelieu had not yet finished with the affairs of France.

Hinges squeaked at the other end of the library, then a firm step sounded against the parquet floor, followed by a clatter of spurs, as Cardinal Richelieu reread the report he intended to present to the king concerning the proposed policies against Lorraine. Incongruous at this hour and echoing loudly beneath the library's painted ceiling, the growing noise woke the dragonnet. Unlike its master, it raised its head to see who had arrived.

It was a gentleman, his features marked by long service in times of war.

Large, energetic, still strong despite his years, he had high boots on his feet, and carried his hat in his hand and his rapier at his side. He wore a grey doublet slashed with red and matching hose the cut of which was as austere as the fabric itself. His closely trimmed beard was the same silver-grey as his hair. It covered much of his severe-looking face, rendered gaunt by battle and long hours of riding, and perhaps also by old regrets and sadness. His bearing was martial, assured, proud, almost provocative. His gaze was that of a man who would never look away first. And he wore a tarnished steel ring on his left hand.

Letting a silence settle, Richelieu finished his perusal of the report while his visitor waited. He initialled the last page, sanded it to help the ink dry, and then blew the grains away. They rose into the air, tickling the dragonnet's nostrils. The little reptile sneezed, raising a smile on the cardinal's thin lips.

'Apologies, Petit-Ami,' he murmured to it.

And finally acknowledging the man, he said:

'A moment, if you will?'

He rang a small bell.

The chimes summoned the faithful and indefatigable Charpentier, who had served His Eminence in the capacity of private secretary for twenty-five years. Richelieu gave him the initialled report.

'Before I present it before His Majesty tomorrow, I want Père Joseph to read it and add those biblical references which His Majesty likes so much and serve the cause of France so well.'

Charpentier bowed and departed.

'The King is very pious,' the cardinal explained.

Then, speaking as if his guest had only just arrived:

'Welcome, Captain La Fargue.'

'Captain?'

'That's your rank, isn't it?'

'It was, before my commission was taken from me.'

'We wish that you return to service.'

'As of now?'

'Yes. Did you have something better to do?'

It was an opening sally, and Richelieu predicted that there would be more to follow.

'A captain must command a company,' said La Fargue.

'Or a troop, at the very least, which may be more modest in size. You shall reclaim yours.'

'It was dispersed, thanks to the good care and attention of Your Eminence.'

That comment raised a spark in the cardinal's eye.

'Find your men. These letters, intended for them, are ready to be sent.'

'They may not all answer the call.'

'Those who respond will suffice. They were the best, and they should still be. It has not been so long . . .'

'Five years.'

'. . . and you are free to recruit others,' Richelieu continued without permitting an interruption. 'Besides, my reports indicate that, despite my orders, you have not severed all of your connections with them.'

The old gentleman blinked.

'I see that the competence of Your Eminence's spies has not faltered in the least.'

'I believe there are few things concerning you of which I am unaware, captain.'

His hand poised on the pommel of his sword, Captain Etienne-Louis de La Fargue took a moment to think. He stared straight ahead, over the cardinal's head who, from his armchair, observed him with patient interest.

'So, captain, you accept?'

'It depends.'

Feared because he was influential and all the more influential because he was feared, Cardinal Richelieu could ruin a destiny with a stroke of his quill or, just as easily, propel a career towards greatness. He was believed to be a man who would crush all those who opposed him. It was a significant exaggeration but as he himself was fond of saying, 'His Eminence has no enemies other than those of the State. But towards them, he is utterly without mercy.'

Cold as marble, the cardinal hardened his tone.

'Is it not enough for you, captain, to know that your king recalls you to his service?'

The man unflinchingly found and held the cardinal's gaze.

'No, monseigneur, it is not enough.'

After a pause, he added:

'Or rather, it's not enough any more.'

*

For a long moment, nothing but the hissing breathing of the dragonnet could be heard beneath the rich panelling of the Palais-Cardinal's great library. The conversation between the two men had taken a bad turn, with one of them still seated and the other standing, each taking the measure of the other, until La Fargue gave in. But he did not lower his gaze. Instead he lifted it, looking straight ahead again and focusing on a precious tapestry behind the cardinal.

'Are you demanding guarantees, captain?'

'No.'

'In that case, I'm afraid I do not understand you.'

'I want to say, monseigneur, that I demand nothing. One does not demand that which one is due.'

'Ah.'

La Fargue was playing a dangerous game, opposing the man said to be in greater command of France than the king himself. His Eminence knew that not all battles were won by force of arms. As the old soldier stood at unwavering attention, no doubt ready to be incarcerated in the deepest, grimmest prison for the remainder of his days, or swiftly dispatched to fight savages in the West Indies, Richelieu leaned on the table and, with a gnarled index finger, scratched the dragonnet's head.

The reptile closed its eyes and sighed with pleasure.

'Petit-Ami was given to me by His Majesty,' said the cardinal in a conversational tone. 'It was he who named it, and it seems these creatures become accustomed very quickly to their nicknames . . . In any case, it expects me to feed it and care for it. And I have never failed in that, just as I have never failed to serve the interests of France. Nevertheless, if I suddenly deprived it of my care, it would not take Petit-Ami long to bite me. And this, without any consideration for the kindnesses I had lavished upon it previously . . . There's a lesson to remember here, don't you think?'

The question was rhetorical. Leaving the dragonnet to its slumber, Richelieu sank back into the cushions of his arm-chair, cushions which he piled on in a vain attempt to ease the pangs of his rheumatism.

He grimaced, waiting until the pain lessened before continuing.

'I know, captain, that not so long ago I let you down. You and your men served me well. In view of your previous successes and your value, was your disgrace justified? Of course not. It was a political necessity. I grant you that your efforts were not entirely unworthy and that the failure of your delicate mission during the siege of La Rochelle was in no way your fault. But considering the tragic turn taken by the events in which you were involved, the French Crown could do nothing but disown you. It was necessary to save face and condemn you for what you had done, secretly, by our order. You had to be sacrificed, even if it heaped dishonour upon the death of one of your men.'

La Fargue agreed, but it cost him to do so.

'Political necessity,' he said in a resigned tone while his thumb rubbed the steel signet ring against the inside of his fist.

Suddenly seeming very tired, the cardinal sighed.

'Europe is at war, captain. The Holy Roman Empire has known nothing but fire and blood for the last fifteen years, and France will no doubt soon be drawn into the fighting there. The English threaten our coasts and the Spanish our borders. When she is not taking up arms against us, Lorraine welcomes all the seditious elements in the kingdom with open arms while the queen mother plots against the king from Brussels. Revolts blossom in our provinces and those who foment and lead them are often placed at the highest levels of the State. I shall not even mention the secret factions, often funded from abroad, whose intrigues extend all the way into the Louvre.'

Richelieu looked La Fargue firmly in the eye.

'I cannot always choose the weapons I employ, captain.'

There was a long silence, and then the cardinal spoke again:

'You seek neither fortune nor glory. And in truth, I can promise you neither. You can rest assured that I am as ready now as yesterday to sacrifice your honour or your life if reasons of State demand it . . .'

This frank admission surprised the captain, who raised a sceptical eyebrow and returned Richelieu's gaze.

'But do not refuse the hand I extend to you, captain. You are not one of those who shirk their duty, and soon the kingdom will have great need of a man like you. A man capable of gathering together and commanding honest, courageous and expert swordsmen, adept at acting swiftly and secretly, and above all, who will kill without remorse and die without regret in the service of the king. Captain, would you still be wearing your signet ring if you were not the man I believe you to be?'

La Fargue could not answer, but for the cardinal the business had been settled.

'You and your men liked to call yourselves the "Cardinal's Blades", I seem to recall. The name was never whispered lightly amongst the enemies of France. For that reason, among others, it pleased me. Keep it.'

'With all the respect that I owe you, monseigneur, I have not yet said yes.'

Richelieu stared at the old man for a long time, his thin angular face expressing only coldness. Then he rose from his armchair, opened a curtain a little to look outside and said carelessly:

'And if I said it could affect your daughter?'

Suddenly growing pale, and visibly shaken, La Fargue turned his head towards the cardinal who seemed absorbed in the contemplation of the night-time garden.

'My . . . daughter? . . . But I don't have a daughter, monseigneur—'

'You know very well that you do. And I know it as well . . . But don't be alarmed. The secret of her existence is one guarded by a few trustworthy people. I believe that even your Blades are unaware of the truth, is that not so?'

The captain surrendered, abandoning a battle he had already lost.

'Is she . . . in danger?' he asked him.

At that moment Richelieu knew he had won. His back still turned to La Fargue, he hid a smile.

'You shall understand soon,' he said. 'For now, gather your Blades in preparation to receive the details of your first mission. I promise you that these shall not be long in coming.'

And at last rewarding La Fargue with a glance over his shoulder, he added:

'Good night, captain.'

2

Agnès de Vaudreuil woke with a scream in her throat, her eyes wide and filled with the terrors which haunted her every night. She had sat up in a panic, and remained dazed for a moment watching the shadows around her bed. She was forced to wait while the furious pace of her heart slowed. Wait until her breathing, almost panting, finally calmed. Wait for the sour sweat to dry on her skin.

The terror left her little by little, with regret, like a pack of dogs frustrated not to have triumphed over their wounded yet tenacious prey.

The young woman sighed.

A peaceful silence reigned inside as much as it did without, a clear shimmering light falling from the cloud-flecked sky and through the open window as far as the four-poster bed. Elegant and spacious, the room was richly furnished, decorated with heavy hangings, valuable miniatures, delicately painted woodwork and gilded mouldings. A certain disarray disturbed this tableau of luxury, however. A chair had toppled over. A man's hat perched at a jaunty angle atop an antique statuette. Candles had burned down into wax stalagmites clinging to the candlesticks. The remains of a fine supper stood on an inlaid table and an assortment of clothes were strewn across the carpet.

Leaning forwards, Agnès pulled her knees up under the bedclothes, leaned her elbows on them and slid her fingers through her thick hair, running them from the front to the back of her skull. Then she slowly raised her head, letting the palms of her hands smooth her cheeks. She felt better but the fear was only postponed, not gone for good. The pack would return, always hungry and perhaps more ferocious than ever. There was nothing to do but accept it.

And live.

Agnès pulled herself together.

She rose without disturbing the man sleeping beside her, pulling a rumpled sheet with her and wrapping herself in it. Taller and considerably thinner and more muscular than her peers, who took care to remain plump in order to entice men, she was not, however, without charm. She had an elegance of gesture, a nobility of movement, and a severe and savage kind of beauty, provocative and almost haughty, which promised failure to any who attempted to conquer her. Thick with ample curls, her long black hair framed a slender but forceful face and underlined her paleness. Her full, dark lips seldom smiled. Nor did her emerald green eyes, in which burned a cold flame. Had they shown any sign of joy, she would have been, all in all, absolutely radiant.

Her left fist holding the cloth tight against her chest, Agnès trampled over the dress and the ruffled underskirts she had worn the day before. Her white stockings still sheathed her long legs. With her free hand she lifted and shook a number of wine bottles before finding one that wasn't empty. She poured the dregs into a glass and carried it to the window, letting the warm May breeze caress her. From the first floor she had a view over the courtyard of her manor and the surrounding countryside, reaching as far as the distant glimmer of the Oise river.

Agnès sipped her wine and waited for dawn to come.

By daybreak the sheet had slipped a little, revealing a mark on her shoulder blade – a mark which worried some of her lovers and prompted a few to comment that Agnès had something of a witch about her. Remaining at the window, she toyed distractedly with a signet ring she wore around her neck. The jewel, set in tarnished steel, was etched with a Greek cross with arms capped by fleur-de-lys, and crossed by a rapier. Agnès heard the man rise from the bed behind her. She released the ring and thought of covering her shoulder but didn't turn as he dressed and left the room without a word. She saw him appear in the courtyard and wake the coachman sleeping beneath the harnessed carriage. The whip cracked, the horses snorted, shaking their heads, and the vehicle of this already-forgotten gentleman was soon nothing more than a cloud of dust on the stony road.

Life soon began to stir in the manor, as the surrounding village bell-towers signalled the first mass of the day. Agnès de Vaudreuil finally left the window when she saw a valet taking orders from the ostler outside the stable. She performed a rapid toilette and hastily braided her long hair. She changed her stockings, did up her breeches, pulled on a wide-collared shirt and, over it, an old red leather corset. She chose her best riding boots, then belted on the baldric and sheathed rapier which hung by the door.

The blade had been made for her especially, forged in Toledo from the best steel. She unsheathed it to admire its perfect straightness, its beautiful shine, its suppleness and keen edge. She sketched a few feints, parries and ripostes. Finally, with her thumb, she made a spike as long as her hand spring from the pommel, fine and sharp-edged like a Florentine dagger, which she admired with an almost loving gleam in her eye.

3

On its completion, the Palais-Cardinal would comprise a splendid main building, with two long wings, two courtyards and an immense garden which stretched between rue de Richelieu and rue des Bons-Enfants. But in 1633, it was still little more than the original Hôtel d'Angennes, acquired nine years earlier, although its new, illustrious owner, determined to have a residence in Paris appropriate to his station, was busy having it enlarged and embellished. He was so determined, in fact, that when he was put in charge of the city's new fortifications he seized the opportunity to extend his domain into the vast area which the old ramparts had occupied, rebuilding the walls further to the west from the Saint-Denis gate to the new gate of La Conférence. The capital gained as much as the cardinal from this enlargement: new streets were laid out and new districts were born where only wasteland and ditches had existed before, including the creation of a renowned horse market and the beginnings of the neighbour-hoods of Montmartre and Saint-Honoré. But Richelieu was condemned to live with the builders a while longer in the Hôtel d'Angennes. The imposing façade of his palace, on rue de Saint-Honoré, would still take years to complete.

Thus it was that, at eight o'clock in the morning, Ensign Arnaud de Laincourt entered the Palais-Cardinal by passing beneath a large scaffold which was already loaded with work-men. The musketeers who had just opened the wrought iron gates recognised him and gave him a military salute to which he responded before entering the guard room. This area, with its one hundred and eighty square metres of floor space and its monumental chimney, was where ordinary visitors waited to be summoned. There were already a score of them in attendance, but above all the room was crawling with men in red capes, as it was here that guards who had ensured the safety of His Eminence all night were relieved by those who, like Laincourt, had arrived to take their shift. Rows of muskets – loaded and ready to fire – were arranged on the racks. The light fell from high south-facing windows and conversations blended into a hubbub which echoed beneath the wainscoting.

Slender and athletic, Arnaud de Laincourt was approaching thirty. He had dark eyebrows, crystalline blue eyes, a straight nose, smoothly-shaven cheeks and pale skin. His fine features had a strange charm, youthful yet wise. It was easier to imagine him studying philosophy at the Sorbonne than wearing the uniform of the cardinal's horse guards. Nevertheless, he carried the plumed felt hat and the white gloves, and wore the cape blazoned with a cross, along with the sword hanging from the regulation leather baldric which crossed his chest from his left shoulder. Moreover, as an ensign he was an officer – a junior officer according to the military hierarchy then in force, but an officer nonetheless, and one who was promised a lieutenancy, so highly did Richelieu regard him.

He was saluted again and, as was his habit, he courteously returned the salute with a personal reserve which discouraged idle chatter. Then he took one of the small books known as sextodecimos from his russet-red leather doublet and, intending to read, went to lean against a pillar close to two guards sitting by a pedestal table. The youngest, Neuvelle, was only just twenty-six and had not been with the guards for more than a few weeks. His companion, on the other hand, was turning grey. He was called Brussand, was a good forty years of age, and had served with the Cardinal's Guards since the formation of the company seven years earlier.

'Still,' said Neuvelle in a lowered voice, 'I would love to know who the man His Eminence received in such secrecy last night was. And why.'

When Brussand, leaning on the card table, did not react, the young man insisted:

'Think about the fact that he did not pass through the

antechambers. The musketeers who guard the little gate were ordered to do nothing but announce his arrival, and not ask questions. All the other guards were kept away. And it was Captain Saint-Georges in person who escorted him to the cardinal's apartments and accompanied him back!'

'Our orders' Brussand finally replied, without raising his eyes from his game of patience, 'were to be deaf and blind to all that concerned this gentleman. You should not have watched the doors.'

Neuvelle shrugged.

'Pff . . . What harm did I do? . . . And anyway, I only caught a brief glimpse of a silhouette in the corner of a very dark corridor. He could have shook hands with me without my recognising him.'

Brussand, still absorbed by his game, smoothed his salt-and-pepper moustache without comment, then with an air of satisfaction laid the wyvern of spades, which had appeared at the opportune moment, upon the previously troublesome knave of hearts.

'All these mysteries intrigue me,' Neuvelle blurted.

'They shouldn't.'

'Really? And why is that?'

Although he gave no sign, Brussand, unlike his young companion, had noticed Laincourt's discreet arrival.

'Would you explain it to him, monsieur de Laincourt?'

'Certainly, monsieur de Brussand.'

Neuvelle watched Laincourt, who turned a page and said:

'Accept that there are secrets into which it is better not to pry, nor even to pretend to have stumbled across. It can prove to be harmful. To your career, of course. But also to your health.'

'You mean to say that—'

'Yes. I mean to say exactly that.'

Neuvelle mustered a weak smile.

'Go on! You're trying to frighten me.'

'Precisely. And for your own good, believe me.'

'But I'm a member of the Guards!'

This time, Laincourt lifted his eyes from his book.

21

And smiled.

Neuvelle wore his scarlet cape with a mixture of confidence and pride, convinced, not without reason, that he was protected to the same degree that he had been promoted. Because he entrusted his life to them, Richelieu chose all his guards personally. He wanted them to be gentlemen of at least twenty-five years in age, and required most of them to have served for three years in the army. Perfectly trained and equipped, subjected to an iron discipline, they were a company of elite horsemen. The cardinal preferred them by far to the company of musketeers – foot soldiers – that he also maintained and which recruited professional soldiers from the ranks of ordinary folk. And he rewarded his guards for their devotion by extending his protection to them in turn.

However . . .

'To be in the Guards, Neuvelle, is an honour which particularly exposes you to dangers that the common run of people do not even suspect – or which they exaggerate, which amounts to the same thing. We are like the fire-dogs before a hearth which holds an eternal flame. This blazing fire is the cardinal. We defend him, but if you draw too near, you risk being burned. Serve His Eminence faithfully. Die for him if circumstances require it. Nevertheless, only listen to what he wishes you to hear. See only that which you are given to see. Guess only at what you are supposed to understand. And be quick to forget the rest.'

His tirade complete, Laincourt peacefully returned to his reading.

He believed the matter was settled, but still Neuvelle persisted.

'But you—'

The ensign frowned.

'Yes?'

'I mean . . .'

Searching for words, Neuvelle's eyes implored for help from Brussand, who rewarded him with a black look in reply. The young guard suddenly understood that he had ventured into territory which was delicate, if not dangerous.

He would have given a great deal to have been suddenly transported elsewhere and was very relieved when Laincourt chose another target.

'Monsieur de Brussand, have you spoken to monsieur de Neuvelle about me?'

The interested party shrugged his shoulders, as though excusing himself.

'We're often bored, when we're on guard.'

'And what have you said?'

'On my word, I said what everyone says.'

'Which is?'

Brussand took a breath.

'Which is that you had intended to become a lawyer, before the cardinal noticed you. That you joined the ranks of his personal secretaries. That he soon entrusted you with confidential missions. That on one of these missions you left France for two years and, when you returned, you took the cape and the rank of ensign. There. That's everything.'

'Ah . . .' said Arnaud de Laincourt without betraying any emotion.

There was a silence in which he seemed to reflect on what he had heard.

Finally, with a vague glance, he nodded.

Laincourt returned to his reading while Neuvelle found other things to do elsewhere and Brussand began a new game of patience. A few minutes passed, and then the veteran guard blurted out:

'To you, and you alone, Laincourt, I would say—'

'What is it?'

'I know who His Eminence received last night. I saw his outline as he was leaving, and I recognised him. His name is La Fargue.'

'This name means nothing to me,' said Laincourt.

'At one time, he commanded a troop of highly trusted men and carried out secret missions on the cardinal's behalf. They were called, in a whisper, the Cardinal's Blades. Then there was some nasty business during the siege of La Rochelle. I don't know the details but it brought about the disappearance of the Blades. Until last night, I had believed they were permanently disbanded. But now—'

Arnaud de Laincourt closed his book.

'The same prudent advice I gave to Neuvelle also applies to us,' he said. 'Let us forget all of that. Without doubt we shall be better off for having done so.'

Brussand, thoughtful, nodded.

'Yes. You are right. As always.'

At that moment, Captain Saint-Georges summoned Laincourt. Cardinal Richelieu wished to go to the Louvre with his entourage, and his escort needed to be prepared. Saint-Georges was taking command and Laincourt, in his capacity as an officer, was to watch over the cardinal's palace during his absence.

4

Two coaches sat at some distance from each other in a
meadow by the road to Paris. Three elegant gentlemen surrounded the marquis de Brévaux by the first coach while, by
the second, the vicomte d'Orvand paced alone. He went
backwards and forwards, sometimes stopping to watch the
road and the horizon as he nervously stroked his thin, black
moustache and the tuft of hair beneath his lower lip and
sent impatient looks towards his coachman, who remained indifferent to the entire proceedings but was beginning to feel
hungry.

At last, one of the gentlemen detached himself from the
group and walked towards d'Orvand, passing through the
soft, damp herb grass with a determined step. The vicomte
knew what he was going to hear and struck as appropriate an
attitude as possible.

'He's late,' said the gentleman.

'I know. I'm sorry, believe me.'

'Will he come?'

'I believe so.'

'Do you even know where he is, right now?'

'No.'

'No?! But you're his second!'

'Ah . . . well, that is to say . . .'

'A quarter of an hour, monsieur. The marquis de Brévaux
is willing to be patient for a little longer – for another quarter
of an hour, by the clock. And when your friend arrives, if he
arrives, we—'

'Here he is, I believe . . .'

*

A richly decorated coach arrived. Drawn by a splendid team of horses, it stopped in the road with a spray of dust and a man climbed out. His doublet was entirely undone and his shirt hung half out of his breeches. His hat in his right hand and his left resting on the pommel of his sword, he kept one boot on the footplate in order to embrace a pretty young blonde leaning towards the open door. This spectacle did not surprise d'Orvand, who did, however, roll his eyes when he saw another farewell kiss exchanged with a second beauty, a brunette.

'Marciac,' murmured the vicomte to himself. 'You never change!'

The gentleman charged with conveying the marquis de Brévaux's complaint returned to his friends while the luxuriously gilded coach made a half-turn in the direction of Paris and Nicolas Marciac joined d'Orvand. He was a handsome man, attractive despite, or perhaps even because of, the disorder of his attire. He was in need of a razor and he bore a wide grin on his face. He tottered only slightly and was the very image of a society-loving rake enjoying his evening, entirely heedless of the morrow.

'But you've been drinking, Nicolas!' exclaimed d'Orvand, smelling his breath.

'No!' insisted Marciac, shocked . . . 'well . . . a little.'

'Before a duel? It's madness!'

'Don't alarm yourself. Have I ever lost before?'

'No, but—'

'All will be well.'

By the other coach, the marquis de Brévaux was already in his shirtsleeves and executing a few feints.

'Good, let us finish it,' Marciac declared.

He removed his doublet, threw it on the vicomte's coach, greeted the coachman and asked after his health, was delighted to learn it was excellent, caught d'Orvand's gaze, adjusted his shirt, unsheathed his sword and set out towards Brévaux, who was already walking to meet him.

Then, after a few steps, he changed his mind, turned on his

heel without fear of further exasperating the marquis, and pitched his words for his friend's ear alone:

'Tell me just one thing . . .'

'Yes?' sighed d'Orvand.

'Promise me you will not be angry.'

'So be it.'

'Well then, I have guessed that I am to fight the man in his shirtsleeves who is watching me with that rough gaze. But could you give me some idea as to why?'

'What?' the vicomte exclaimed, rather louder than he had intended.

'If I kill him, I should know the reason for our quarrel, don't you think?'

D'Orvand was initially lost for words, then pulled himself together and announced:

'A gambling debt.'

'What? I owe him money? Him too?'

'Of course not! Him! . . . It's he who . . . Fine. Enough. I shall cancel this madness. I shall tell them you are unwell. Or that you—'

'How much?'

'What?'

'How much does he owe me?'

'Fifteen hundred livres.'

'Good God! And I was going to kill him . . . !'

Light-heartedly, Marciac continued to walk towards the furious marquis. He assumed a wobbly *en garde* stance and declared:

'I am at your disposal, monsieur le marquis.'

The duel was speedily concluded. Brévaux took the initiative with assertive thrusts which Marciac nonchalantly parried before punctuating his own attack with a punch that cut his adversary's lip. Initially surprised, then enraged, the marquis returned to the fray. Once again, Marciac was content to merely defend, feigning inattentiveness and even, between two clashes of steel, stifling a yawn. This offhandedness left Brévaux crazed with anger. He howled, struck a foolish two-handed blow with his rapier and, without understanding how, suddenly found himself both disarmed and wounded in the shoulder. Marciac pressed his advantage. With the point of his blade, he forced the marquis to retreat to his coach, and held him there.

Pale, breathless and sweating, Brévaux clutched his shoulder.

'Very well,' he said. 'You win. I'll pay you.'

'I am afraid, monsieur, that a promise is not enough. Pay me now.'

'Monsieur! I give you my word!'

'You have already promised once, and you see where we are now . . .'

Marciac tensed his arm a little and the point of his rapier approached the marquis's throat. The gentlemen of Brévaux's retinue took a step closer. One of them even began to draw his sword while d'Orvand, worried, came forward and prepared to assist his friend if necessary.

There was a moment of indecisiveness on both sides, but then the marquis removed a ring he wore on his finger and gave it to Marciac.

'Are we now even?'

He took it and admired the stone.

'Yes,' he said, before sheathing his sword.

'Damned Gascon!'

'I hold you in high esteem as well, monsieur. I look forward to seeing you again.'

And as he turned towards d'Orvand, Marciac deliberately added:

'Splendid day, isn't it?'

5

In a small study to which she alone possessed a key, the very young, very blonde and very charming vicomtesse de Malicorne removed the black silk cloth protecting the oval mirror before which she sat. With only two candles burning, one to either side of the mirror, the room was shrouded in a half-light.

In a low voice, with her eyes closed, the vicomtesse chanted words in the ancient, dread language of the Ancestral Dragons, the language of magic. The surface of the precious silver mirror rippled, moving like a puddle of mercury disturbed by movement deep within it, then solidified again. A dragon's head appeared in the ensorcelled mirror – all blood red scales, gleaming black eyes, a bony crest and pale, large and prominent fangs.

'Greetings, my sister.'

'Greetings, my brother.'

Someone, thousands of leagues distant, had answered the vicomtesse's call. Wherever he was, he must have been human in outward form. But the mirror did not lie: the images it portrayed were an accurate reflection of the true nature of those who used it, so that the pretty young woman also presented a draconic appearance to her faraway contact. For although neither of them were Ancestral Dragons, they were both descendants. In their veins ran the blood of a race which had evolved over centuries and millennia, a race which had given up the superior draconic form to become part of mankind. But their race was no less feared for having changed, and with good reason.

'There is some concern about your progress, my sister.'

'Who is concerned?'

'I am, in the first instance. But there are others as well who, unlike me, are not favourably inclined towards you. Not everyone within the Black Claw is your ally.'

'I would have thought the Black Claw would be delighted by the prospect of my forthcoming success. A success which shall also, incidentally, be theirs.'

'Here, in Spain, there are brothers who are jealous of your foreseeable triumph. You will prevail where some of them have failed—'

'Should they not be reproached for that, rather than blaming me?'

The dragon in the mirror seemed to smile.

'Ah, my sister. You are not so naïve—'

'Certainly not!'

'You're aware that failure shall not be forgiven.'

'I shall not fail!'

'Under the pretext of assuring themselves of this, certain Masters of the Grand Lodge have decided to assign one of their initiates of the first order to assist you. A certain Savelda. You know of him?'

'Enough to guess that his mission is less to help me than it is to keep count of every conceivable error. So that if I do fail, my enemies are as well armed as possible to denounce me . . .'

'At least you know what awaits you. Savelda is already on his way and shall present himself to you soon. His duplicity with respect to you is certain, but the man is capable and he has the interests of the Black Claw at heart. Politics is likely to be of no importance to him. Employ him advisedly.'

'So be it.'

A ripple crossed the surface of the mirror and, as the vicomtesse struggled to focus her will, the phantom dragon head facing her began to waver.

'You are tired, my sister. If you wish to continue this later—'

'No, no. It will pass . . . Continue, please.'

In the dark close room, the young woman nimbly wiped away the black droplet that had beaded on her nostril.

'We have,' said the dragon, 'introduced a spy into the upper levels of the Palais-Cardinal.'

'I know. He—'

'No. It's someone other than the spy who keeps you informed. As yet, you do not know of the spy of whom I speak. Or, at least, not in this capacity. He is one of your future initiates.'

The vicomtesse was visibly surprised.

The Grand Lodge of Spain had an agent close to the cardinal, an exclusive agent, of whose existence she had only just learned. It was common practice for the Black Claw, and the Grand Lodge in particular, to proceed in this manner. The Spanish Lodge had been the very first to be founded and it traditionally predominated over the other lodges of Europe, welding together an empire of which it became all the more jealous as its authority began to be questioned. It was rightly criticised for being stifled by the crushing weight of tradition and guided by masters primarily concerned with preserving their privileges. Against its influence, in the very heart of the Black Claw, there was a growing plot involving dragons who secretly dreamed of renewing – if not cutting down – the old idols. The vicomtesse de Malicorne was one of these ambitious rebels.

'So?' she said.

'Our spy has informed us that the cardinal has a project afoot to recall one of our old enemies. Given the time it took this news to reach us in Spain, it is perhaps already done.'

'One of our old enemies?'

'La Fargue.'

'La Fargue and his Blades.'

'Without a doubt, yes. I don't know if their sudden return relates to your business, but guard yourself against these men, and especially against their captain.'

6

Jean Delormel's fencing school was situated on rue des Cordières, close to the Saint-Jacques gate. It could only be reached by entering a small courtyard which was unevenly but solidly paved, and was almost entirely concealed by the foliage of an apple tree which grew up from its centre. At the bottom to the left the beautiful main building met the stable, which was adjoined at a right angle to a small forge. The feet and gaze of visitors, however, were naturally drawn towards the house on the right, which could be recognised for what it was by the traditional sign which decorated the threshold – an arm holding a sword.

Sitting on a stone bench under the apple tree, a small six-year-old girl was playing with a doll – its body made of rags and with a painted wooden head – when Captain La Fargue arrived on horseback. Neatly dressed and with curly red hair, little Justine was the youngest child of Delormel, the fencing master, and one of seven offspring his wife had given him, three of whom survived. As an old friend of the family, La Fargue had witnessed Justine's birth just as he had witnessed the births of her elder siblings. But during his lengthy absence the infant had become a pretty child, full of seriousness, who listened more than she spoke, and thought even more. This metamorphosis had seemed sudden to the captain, the evening before, on his return after five years. Nothing showed the passage of time better than children.

Rising, Justine dusted down the front of her dress in order to offer a most formal curtsey to the rider, who had just got his feet on the ground and, to tell the truth, took little notice of her now as he walked towards the stables.

32

'Good morning, monsieur.'

Reins in hand, he stopped.

His cold glance, severe expression, grey beard and patrician neatness, the austere elegance of his attire and the proud assurance with which he carried his sword, all impressed adults and intimidated children. This little lady, however, did not appear to fear him.

Somewhat disconcerted, the old captain hesitated.

Then, very stiffly, he greeted her with a nod of his head and the pinch of his thumb and index finger to the rim of his hat, before walking on.

Busy in the kitchen, Justine's mother had observed the scene through an open window in the main building. She was a young woman, pretty and smiling, whose successive pregnancies had done surprisingly little to enlarge her slender waistline. Her name was Anne, and she was the daughter of a renowned fencing master who gave lessons on Ile de la Cité. La Fargue also greeted her as he approached, this time doffing his hat.

'Hello, madame.'

'Good morning, captain. A beautiful day, isn't it?'

'Indeed. Do you know where your husband is?'

'In the practice room. He's waiting for you, I believe . . . Will you dine with us?'

It was common to breakfast in the morning, dine at midday and eat supper in the evening.

'With pleasure, madame. I thank you.'

La Fargue tethered his mount to a ring in the stable when he heard:

'Monsieur, my papa is going to scold you.'

He turned and saw Justine, who loitered right at the threshold of the stable but did not enter, almost certainly because she was forbidden to approach the horses.

Intrigued, the old gentleman's brow wrinkled. It was difficult to imagine anyone 'scolding' a man of his temper. But, the little one was still at the age when a daughter would not for a moment doubt the invincibility of her father.

'He will scold me? Truly?'

'My father was very anxious. So was my mother. They waited for your return until very late last night.'

'And how do you know this?'

'I heard them talking.'

'Were you not in your room?'

'I was.'

'And weren't you asleep at that hour, as is appropriate for young ladies of your age, if they are well-behaved?'

Caught out, Justine paused for a moment.

'Yes,' she said.

La Fargue stifled a smile.

'Very well then, you were asleep in your room, yet you heard my friend your father speaking . . .'

The little one replied in a flash:

'I happen to have very good ears.'

And, full of dignity, she turned on her heel.

La Fargue left the stable a few moments later.

Beneath the apple tree, Justine was only interested in her doll, with whom she seemed to be arguing. The morning was over. The sunshine was warm and the thick foliage gave the courtyard a pleasant freshness. From here the bustle and racket of the Paris streets were just a distant murmur.

In the practice room, La Fargue found Martin – a young man, the eldest son and senior instructor in Delormel's school – dispensing a private lesson while a valet gave the earthenware floor a thorough scrubbing. The room was almost empty, with bare walls and furnished with nothing but three benches, a rack of swords and a wooden horse for teaching students mounted swordplay. There was a gallery which could be reached by a staircase on the right, from which one could comfortably observe the action below. The fencing master was at the balustrade. He adopted an air of great satisfaction on seeing the captain enter. La Fargue climbed the steps to meet him, exchanging a friendly smile with Martin on the way, the young red-haired slender man beating time for his pupil's movements by striking the ground with a large stick.

'Glad to see you, captain. We've been waiting for you.'

In spite of events, Delormel had never ceased to address La Fargue by his rank. Out of habit, no doubt. But also to make the point that he had never acknowledged that La Fargue had been stripped of his commission.

'For most of the night, yes, I know. The news reached me. I am sorry.'

Delormel was astonished.

'That news reached you? How?'

'Your daughter. The youngest.'

The fencing master smiled affectionately.

'The little devil. Nothing gets past her . . .'

Tall and broad across the shoulders, Delormel was a fencing master who had been a soldier and who regarded fencing as more of a practical experience than a science. A thick scar scored his neck; another traced a pale furrow down his face. But what one noticed first was his thick russet-red hair, which he had inherited from his father and passed on to all his children: a Delormel was a redhead, or they weren't a Delormel. Well-groomed, he wore a modestly cut and perfectly pressed doublet.

'However,' said La Fargue, 'you are more correct than you believe in addressing me as "captain".'

'I beg your pardon?'

'The cardinal has secretly returned my rank to me. He wants the Blades to return to service. Under my command.'

'All of them? That is: all of the Blades?'

The captain shrugged.

'All those who are left and would like to serve, at least. And for those who do not, I have no doubt that the cardinal shall find some persuasive leverage. Letters summoning them have already been sent out.'

Reading the concern on La Fargue's face, Delormel hesitated, and then asked:

'And this isn't good news?'

'I've yet to form an opinion on the subject.'

'Come, captain! The Blades are your life! And here you are! Soon those five years will be—'

But he did not complete the sentence.

Suddenly nervous, he looked to the left and right and then murmured:

'I beg you, do not tell me you said no to the cardinal! No one says no to the cardinal, do they? Nobody. Not even you, eh?'

La Fargue had no reply.

His eyes flicked toward Martin and his student below and he said:

'I thought you only opened your practice room after dinner.'

'It's only a private lesson,' specified Romand. 'That braggart you see there pays in gold.'

Calling him a braggart spoke volumes. The old gentleman, however, asked:

'And how is he doing?'

The fencing master made a disdainful face.

'He can't tell his right from his left, holds his sword like a shovel, believes he knows everything, understands nothing and constantly complains, claiming that everything is badly explained to him.'

'His name?'

'Guérante, I believe. If I was Martin, I would have slapped him ten times by now.'

'And you would have lost your client.'

'No doubt, yes . . .'

La Fargue did not take his eyes from Martin's student. He was a young man, very richly dressed and everything about him, especially his attitude, indicated that he was a wealthy scion with a head swollen by his family's title and fortune. He lacked patience as much as he lacked talent, became irritated over nothing, and found a thousand excuses for his awkwardness. He was out of place here, where serious, practical fencing was taught; fencing which demanded hard work without sparing the ego.

36

'I didn't say no,' the captain suddenly announced. 'To the cardinal, last night. I did not say no to him.'

Delormel's face split into a broad smile.

'Praise be! You are never truly yourself unless you're serving the king and, no matter what you think, you never served him so well as you did during the years when you commanded your Blades.'

'But to what end? One death, and the treachery of a friend—'

'You are a soldier. Death comes with war. As for treason, it comes with life.'

La Fargue nodded, but it lacked the vigour that would suggest he truly agreed.

Clearly anxious to change the subject, Delormel took the captain by the elbow and, limping a little because of an old wound, drew him away from the balustrade.

'I do not ask you what your mission is, but—'

'You can,' interrupted La Fargue. 'At the moment, all we have to do is arrange, with all speed and without attracting too much attention, the recall of the Blades. And perhaps find others . . . It seems clear that the cardinal has precise plans, which I shall soon learn. But why is he recalling the Blades? Why them, when he does not lack other devoted agents? Why me? And most importantly, why now, after all these years? There is a mystery behind all of this.'

'These are troubled times,' suggested Delormel. 'And contrary to what you said, perhaps His Eminence does lack men capable of doing the things you and your Blades have achieved in the past . . .'

Below them there was a sudden outburst which drew them, surprised, back to the balustrade.

Guérante had just fallen, entirely through his own fault, and, furious, he hurled insults at the younger Delormel. Pale, the other withstood the outburst without responding: he was only a commoner while his student was of the nobility, and therefore both protected and permitted to do as he pleased.

'Enough,' said La Fargue after a moment. 'That will do.'

He walked down the staircase with a determined step while the gentleman struggled back to his feet and continued to howl. La Fargue seized him by the collar, forced him out of the room ignoring his thrashings, dragged him across the courtyard in front of Justine, who watched with huge round eyes, and threw him out into the street. Guérante measured his length in a patch of mud through which one would hesitate to walk, to the great delight of passers-by.

Livid, stinking and dripping with muck and urine, the braggart pushed himself up and would have stripped off his soiled outer layers ready to fight. But La Fargue froze him in place with a movement of an index finger, pointing at Guérante's chest.

'Monsieur', he said to him, in too calm a voice not to be threatening. 'I am a gentleman and therefore do not have to put up with either your whims or your poor temper. If you would draw your sword, do so, and you shall learn with whom you speak.'

Guérante hesitated, changed his mind, and returned the two inches of steel he had drawn in the heat of the moment to their scabbard.

'Another thing, monsieur,' added the captain. 'If you are religious, pray. Pray that my friend Delormel does not come to any misadventure. Pray that no one bothers either his clients or his family. Pray that petty thieves do not come in the night and plunder his school or his home. Pray that he does not receive a beating on a street corner . . . Because I shall learn of it. And without any further consideration, I shall find you and I shall kill you, monsieur de Guérante. Do we understand each other?'

Mortified and covered in slurry, the other made an effort to recover his dignity. There were spectators watching and mocking him, and he did not want to lose face entirely.

'This business,' he promised, puffing himself up . . . 'This affair does not end here.'

'It does,' La Fargue shot back, harsh and inflexible.

'We shall see!'

'This business is finished here and now if you do not draw your sword, monsieur . . .'

His terrible gaze plunged Guérante into the deepest pit of fear.

'Well?' he demanded.

Delormel and his son waited for La Fargue in the courtyard. His wife, pale and worried, watched from the threshold of the main building, Justine pressed against her skirts.

'Let's eat,' said the captain, as he returned.

His rapier had never left its scabbard.

7

In the kitchen of the Vaudreuil manor, a woman in an apron and a large serge skirt scrubbed a series of copper saucepans.

Her name was Marion.

Sitting at the end of a large oak table worn smooth by old age and hard use, she turned her back to the hearth where small flames gently heated the blackened bottom of a pot. Drying herbs, a string of garlic and some earthenware pots decorated the chimneypiece. A door which stood open onto the courtyard allowed tiny dust particles to enter which, carried by a light breeze, sparkled in the spring air. Pieces of straw were scattered on the floor as far as the threshold.

A horse could be heard approaching at a fast trot. It frightened the hens, which squawked and fluttered their wings, and when it neighed a dog responded excitedly, barking from the end of its chain. Iron-shod boots struck the hard earth with a jingle of spurs. Steps approached and Agnès de Vaudreuil ducked her head as she came through the low door.

Seeing the young baronne arrive, Marion greeted her with a warm smile and a disapproving glance, a subtle combination which she had perfected through long practice over the years. Dressed for riding, her rapier thumping against her thigh, Agnès was covered in dust from her riding boots to the top of her breeches, and she was still wearing that infernal red leather corset which, rough and waxed and buckled on tight like armour, was as much a warrior's talisman to her as an item of clothing. Her face glistened with sweat. As for the heavy braid which fell from the nape of her neck, it only managed to confine half of her hair, allowing the rest to hang free.

'I have left Courage tethered outside,' the young woman said breathlessly.

Marion nodded to show that she was listening.

'I pushed him a little in the lower valley and I really believe he is perfectly recovered from his injury.'

The maidservant had no reply to that either.

'Damnation! I'm dying of thirst.'

Agnès went over to the brass water tank which, set up at an angle, released water through a small tap. She leaned over it, cupping the palms of her hands, and splashing water over the stone floor slabs as she drank. Then she grabbed a crusty heel of bread lying on the sideboard and, ripping it open with her fingers, proceeded to nibble at its soft interior.

'Have you eaten anything today?' asked Marion.

'No.'

'I'll make you something. What would you like?'

She was about to rise, but the young woman halted her with a gesture.

'Don't trouble yourself. I'm fine.'

'But—'

'I said I'm fine.'

The servant shrugged and returned to her work.

Standing up, leaning against door to the salting room and putting a foot up on a bench, Agnès looked at Marion. She was still attractive, with an ample bosom and small greying locks of hair twisting themselves free between the nape of her neck and her linen bonnet. At one time she had been much courted by men, and she continued to be on occasion. But she had never married, a fact that intrigued other local inhabitants of this area of the Oise valley.

A silence settled over the room, and lingered.

Finally, when she could restrain herself no longer, Marion said:

'I heard a coach leave early this morning.'

'Good. Then you're not deaf.'

'Who was it?'

Agnès threw the piece of bread, reduced to no more than an empty crust, onto the table.

'What does it matter? I remember only that he was well built and knew what he was doing between the sheets.'

'Agnès!' Marion exclaimed.

But there was more sadness than reproach in her voice. With an air of resignation, she gently shook her head and started to say:

'If your mother—'

'None of that!' interrupted Agnès de Vaudreuil.

Suddenly frosty, she became absolutely rigid. Her emerald green eyes gleamed with contained anger.

'My mother died giving birth to me and it's futile for you to tell me that she might say this or that. As for my father, he was a pig who shoved himself between every pair of thighs he could snuffle out. Including your own, as I well know. So do not preach to me about the way in which I occasionally fill my bed. It's only in such moments that I feel even remotely alive, ever since . . .'

Trembling, with tears in her eyes, she couldn't finish the sentence.

Marion was visibly shaken by this outburst, and returned ashen-faced to her scrubbing with more energy than was strictly necessary

Now in her forties, Marion had witnessed Agnès' birth and the accompanying agony of her mother, who had lain in labour for five days. After fighting at the side of the future King Henri IV during the Wars of Religion in France, the baron de Vaudreuil was always too busy serenading the beautiful ladies at the royal court or stag hunting with the French monarch to interest himself in the fate of his spouse. And upon learning that the child was female, he had not even bothered to attend his wife's funeral. Entrusted – or rather abandoned – to the care of Marion and a rough soldier by the name of Ballardieu, it was seven years before the little girl met her father. This occurred during a brief stay on his domain, when he had also dragged Marion into his bed. Although she might have offered herself freely to him, if she had had any say in the matter. But the baron was not one to brook refusal from a servant, and would have dismissed her without further ado if denied. Marion could not bear the thought of being separated from Agnès, who adored her and had almost no one else in the world to look after her. The baron had been highly amused to discover that his latest conquest, although by no means a young woman, was still a virgin. Delighted, after it was done he left her to go sleep elsewhere, saying that he deserved her gratitude.

Calmer now and beginning to feel ashamed of herself, Agnès walked around the table to stand behind the woman who had raised her, and bent to embrace her, resting her chin against Marion's head.

'Forgive me, Marion. I'm mean and stupid . . . Sometimes, I think I'm going mad . . . But it's not you who's making me so angry. You realise that, don't you?'

'Yes. But who is it, then?'

'I think . . . I'm angry at myself. All these memories I have, that I would just as soon forget. Things I've seen and done . . . And things which were done to me . . .'

She straightened up, sighed, and added:

'One day, perhaps, I shall tell you all.'

8

As they travelled back to Paris by coach, Nicolas Marciac and the vicomte d'Orvand enjoyed a light red wine designed to sharpen their appetites. A wicker basket filled with food and some good bottles of wine stood between them on the bench. They drank from small engraved silver goblets, half-filled so that the bumps and jolts of the road, which shook them violently and without warning, soaked neither their chins nor their laps.

'You hadn't been drinking,' said d'Orvand, referring to the duel.

Marciac gave him a wicked, amused glance.

'Just a mouthful for my breath. Do you take me for a complete idiot?'

'Then why this comedy?'

'To make sure Brévaux was overconfident and lowered his guard.'

'You would have defeated him without that.'

'Yes.'

'Moreover, you could have let me in on it—'

'But that would have been much less fun, wouldn't it? If you could have seen your face!'

The vicomte could not help but smile. His friendship with the Gascon had accustomed him to this kind of joke.

'And who were the two charming ladies whose coach you borrowed to make your entrance?'

'Now, vicomte! I would be the very lowest of gentlemen if I told you that.'

'In any event, they seemed to have a great deal of affection for you.'

'What can I say, my friend? I am well liked— Since you are so curious, then know that one of them is the very same beauty upon whom the marquis de Brévaux, it seems, has set his sights. I'm sure he recognised her . . .'

'You are reckless Nicolas. No doubt the marquis's anger grew and his skill as a fencer proportionately decreased when he saw you kiss the woman. But by doing so you gave him a reason to demand another duel. Not content to defeat him, you had to humiliate him. For you it's a game, I know. But for him . . .'

Marciac thought for a moment about the prospect – which had not crossed his mind until now – of a second duel against the marquis de Brévaux. Then he shrugged.

'Perhaps you're right . . . We shall see.'

And extending his empty goblet, he added:

'Before we start on the pork, it would be my pleasure to drink a little more of your wine.'

As d'Orvand poured for his friend, risking his clean, beautifully cut breeches in the process, Marciac held the prize he had won from the marquis up to the light. Admiring the ruby, he slid it onto his finger, where it came to rest against a signet ring. But it was the signet ring itself which caught the vicomte's eye – made of tarnished steel, it was etched with a rapier and a Greek cross capped with fleur-de-lys.

'There,' said Marciac admiring the shine of the stone, 'that should keep Madame Rabier satisfied.'

'You borrowed money from La Rabier?' exclaimed d'Orvand in a tone of reproach.

'What else could I do? I have debts and it is necessary that I honour them. I am not the marquis de Brévaux.'

'Still, La Rabier . . . Borrowing money from her is never a good idea. I would have been happy to advance you a few écus. You should have asked me.'

'Asked you? A friend? You're joking, vicomte!'

D'Orvand slowly shook his head in silent reproof.

'All the same, there is one thing that intrigues me, Nicolas . . .'

'And what would that be?'

'In the nearly four years during which you have honoured me with your friendship, I have often seen you impoverished – and even that word is a poor description for it. You have pawned and redeemed your every possession a hundred times over. There were times when you were forced to fast for days, and you would doubtless have let yourself die of hunger if I hadn't invited you to my table under one pretext or another. I even remember a day when you had to borrow a sword from me in order to fight a duel . . . But never, ever, have you agreed to be separated from that steel signet ring. Why is that?'

Marciac's gaze became vague, lost in the memories of the day when he first received the ring, until a sudden bump in the road jolted the two men perched on their stuffed leather bench.

'It's a fragment of my past,' replied the Gascon. 'You can never be rid of your past. Not even if you pawn it . . .'

D'Orvand, who found that melancholy did not suit his friend, asked after a moment:

'We will soon be in Paris. Where would you like to stop?'

'Rue de la Grenouillère.'

The vicomte paused a moment, then said:

'Did you not have enough of duelling for one day?'

Marciac replied with a smile, and muttered, almost to himself:

'Bah! . . . When I die, I want to be certain at least that I have truly lived.'

9

Paris at midday was packed with working, bustling and gossiping people, but in contrast, at the Palais-Cardinal, the guards on duty seemed to be sentries of some luxurious necropolis. Accompanied by his large entourage of advisors and his armed escort, Richelieu was at the Louvre, and in his absence, life at his residence carried on slowly, almost as though it was night. Men in capes were barely to be seen. More lowly servants moved along dark corridors without haste or noise, carrying out routine menial tasks. The crowd of supplicants had thinned out considerably when they heard that the master of the palace had left, and only a few persistent souls decided to wait for his return, making do with an improvised repast on the spot.

Alone in a small study, Ensign Arnaud de Laincourt made use of this lull in activity to carry out a task which came with his rank: filling out the log-book of the Cardinal's Guards. The rule was that the officer on duty must scrupulously record all the day's events, whether they were ordinary or unusual, from the hour when guards were relieved at their posts to possible lapses in discipline, and detailing every occurrence or incident which might affect His Eminence's security. Captain Saint-Georges consulted the log at the end of each shift, before communicating anything noteworthy to the cardinal.

'Enter,' said Laincourt, on hearing a knock at the door.

Brussand entered.

'Monsieur de Brussand. You're not on duty . . . Would you not be better off at home, resting after your long night on watch?'

'Of course, but . . . Would you grant me a minute?'

47

'Just allow me to finish this task.'

'Certainly.'

Brussand sat down in front of the desk at which the young officer was writing by candlelight. The room had only a high, bevelled window opening onto a light well into which the sun barely peeped. There were, without a doubt, dungeons in the Bastille or in the château de Vincennes that were better lit.

Laincourt finished his report, checked it, wiped his quill on a rag and then slipped it between the pages of the thick log-book before he closed it.

'There,' he said. 'I'm all yours.'

And turning his crystal blue eyes upon Broussard, he waited.

'I have come to assure myself,' said the other, 'that you do not hold anything against me.'

'Regarding what?'

'Regarding confidences about you that I repeated to young Neuvelle. Concerning your past. And the circumstances under which you joined the Cardinal's Guards.'

Laincourt gave an amiable smile.

'Did you say anything slanderous?'

'Certainly not!'

'Anything untrue?'

'No. At least, not unless I've been misled myself.'

'Then you have nothing to reproach yourself for. And therefore, neither do I.'

'Of course. But . . .'

There was a silence during which the officer's smile did not waver.

His courteous mask, ultimately, proved to be a perfect defence. Because it expressed nothing but polite interest it left others to carry the conversation, so that, without any effort on his part, they little by little became less self-assured. Rarely failing, this strategy was proving particularly effective against Brussand, who was growing more embarrassed by the moment.

But the old guard was a soldier, and rather than remain exposed in this manner, he instead charged forward:

'What can I say? There are certain mysteries surrounding you that encourage rumours—'

'Indeed?'

'Your famous mission, for example. The one which, it is whispered, detained you for two years in Spain. And for which, no doubt, you were promoted to the Cardinal's Guards with the rank of ensign . . . Well, you can imagine what is said about all that, can't you?'

Laincourt waited without making any reply, the same indecipherable smile on his lips.

Then, a clock sounding half past one, he rose, picked up his hat and tucked the heavy log-book under his arm.

'Forgive me, Brussand, but duty calls.'

The two men walked together to the door.

As he allowed the officer to go first, Brussand said to him in a conniving tone:

'Strange country, Spain, isn't it?'

Laincourt walked on, leaving Brussand behind him.

With the air of a man who knows exactly where he is going, Arnaud de Laincourt strode through a series of salons and antechambers, paying no heed to either the servants or the guards on duty who snapped to attention as he passed. Finally, he entered an empty service corridor and, at its intersection with another, paused a few seconds before turning right towards the cardinal's private apartments.

From that point, he moved as quickly and silently as possible, although taking care not to appear furtive: there was no question of making his way on tip-toe, or hugging the walls, or glancing anxiously around. If someone was to surprise him, it was best to behave in a manner unlikely to arouse suspicion. His rank and his cape, certainly, protected him. But then, suspicion was the rule in the Palais-Cardinal.

He soon pushed open a door which, seen from the room within, merged seamlessly with the decorated wooden panels. This was the study where monsieur Charpentier, Richelieu's secretary, normally worked. Functionally but elegantly furnished, it was filled to the point of overflowing with papers.

Daylight filtered in through the closed curtains, while a candle guttered weakly. It was not there to provide light, but its flame could be transferred to numerous other candles at hand, and thus, in an emergency, fully illuminate the study in the middle of the night if required. Just one of the many precautions taken by those in the service of His Eminence, who demanded readiness at all times of the day or night.

Laincourt set the log-book down.

He drew a key from the pocket of his doublet and opened a cupboard. He had to be quick, as every minute now counted. On a shelf, a box sat between two tidily bound manuscripts. This was the object of his search. Another key, a tiny one, opened its secrets to him. Inside were letters waiting to be initialled and sealed by the cardinal. The ensign thumbed through them impatiently, and took out one which he perused more closely.

'That's it,' he murmured.

Turning, he brought the letter closer to the candle and read it twice in order to memorise its every comma. But as he refolded the document, he heard a noise.

The squeak of a floorboard?

The ensign froze, heart thumping, with all his senses alert.

Long seconds passed . . .

Nothing happened. No one entered. And, almost as if it had never occurred, the sound was not repeated.

Pulling himself together, Laincourt replaced the letter in the box and the box in the cupboard, which he relocked with his key. He assured himself that he had disturbed nothing, and then departed silently, taking his log-book with him.

But Laincourt had barely gone when someone pushed open another door, left ajar and hidden behind a wall hanging.

Charpentier.

Returning in haste from the Louvre to fetch a document which Cardinal Richelieu had not thought he would need, he had seen everything.

10

Having saddled his horse, La Fargue was strapping on the holsters of his pistols when Delormel joined him in the stable, amidst the warm smell of animals, hay and dung.

'You'll come see us again soon?' asked the fencing master. 'Or, at least, not wait another five years?'

'I don't know.'

'You know you are always welcome in my home.'

La Fargue patted his mount's neck and turned round.

'Thank you,' he said.

'Here. You left this in your room.'

Delormel held out a small locket on a broken chain. The old gentleman took it. Worn, marked, scratched and tarnished, the piece of jewellery seemed worthless, lying there on his big gloved hand.

'I didn't know you still kept it after all this time,' added the fencing master.

La Fargue shrugged.

'You can't give up your past.'

'But yours continues to haunt you.'

Rather than answer, the captain made to check his saddle.

'Perhaps she didn't deserve you,' Delormel commented.

His back turned, La Fargue went rigid.

'Don't judge, Jean. You don't know the whole story.'

It wasn't necessary to say anything more. Both men knew they were speaking of the woman whose chipped portrait was to be found inside the locket.

'That's true. But I know you well enough to know that something is eating at you. You should be delighted by the prospect of reuniting the Blades and serving the Crown once again. So I'd guess that you only accepted the cardinal's proposal under duress. You yielded to him, Étienne. That's not like you. If you were one of those who yielded easily, you would already be carrying a marshal's baton—'

'My daughter may be in danger,' La Fargue said suddenly.

Slowly, he turned to face Delormel, who looked stunned.

'You wanted to know the whole truth, didn't you? There, now you know.'

'Your daughter . . . ? You mean to say . . .'

The fencing master made a hesitant gesture towards the locket which the captain still held in his fist. La Fargue nodded:

'Yes.'

'How old is she?'

'Twenty. Or thereabouts.'

'What do you know of the danger she's in?'

'Nothing. The cardinal simply implied there was a threat against her.'

'So he might have lied to you in order to secure your services!'

'No. I doubt he would have played this card with me without good reason. It is—'

'—despicable. And what will you say to your Blades? These men give you their blind trust. Some of them even look on you as a father!'

'I shall tell them the truth.'

'All of it?'

Before mounting his horse, the old captain admitted, at some cost:

'No.'

11

Fiddling distractedly with his steel signet ring before returning it to the third finger on his left hand, Saint-Lucq watched the everyday drama on display in the crowded tavern.

Located on a miserable-looking courtyard in the Marais neighbourhood, tucked away from the beautiful private mansions with their elegant façades being built in the nearby Place Royale, *The Red Écu* was a cellar tavern whose poor-quality candles gave off more soot than light, in an atmosphere already poisoned by sweaty bodies, bad wine-soaked breath, tobacco smoke and a potent whiff of the muck picked up by shoes walking the streets of Paris. Here, everyone spoke loudly and forced others to raise their voices in turn, creating an infernal uproar. The wine being drunk had something to do with this. Loud laughter burst out, as did the occasional sharp quarrel. A hurdy-gurdy played songs on demand. From time to time, cheers and applause greeted a lucky throw of the dice, or the antics of a drunkard.

Saint-Lucq, without appearing to do so, kept a close eye on all.

He observed who entered and who left through the small door at the top of the stairs, who used that other door normally reserved to the tavern keeper and the serving girls, who joined someone else and who remained alone. He stared at no one, and his gaze slid away whenever it met that of another. But those present barely took any notice of him. And that was exactly as he liked it, in the shadowy corner where he had chosen to sit. He was constantly on the lookout, keeping track of any anomalies that might indicate a threat. It could be anything: a wink between two people who otherwise

53

pretended not to know one another, an old coat concealing new weapons, a faked fight designed to distract attention. Saint-Lucq was always wary and watched for such things automatically, out of sheer force of habit. He knew that the world was a stage filled with deception, where death, disguised in everyday rags, could strike at any moment. He knew this all the more, for it was often he who delivered the mortal blow.

Upon his arrival, he had ordered a jug of wine, none of which he drank. The young woman who served him offered to keep him company, but he declined the offer with a calm, cold, definitive 'No'. She went off to talk with the other two serving girls, who had watched her approach the new customer. From their reaction, it was obvious that they found Saint-Lucq both attractive and intriguing. He was still young, well-dressed, and a handsome man in a dark way which hinted at sinister and exciting secrets. Was he a gentleman? Perhaps. In any case, he wore his sword naturally, his doublet with elegance, and his hat with a quiet, gallant confidence. His hands were exquisite and his cheeks freshly shaven. Of course, his boots were muddied, but despite that they were made from excellent leather, and who could go unsullied by the disgusting muck of Paris, unless they travelled by coach? No, clearly, this cavalier dressed in black had plenty of pleasing assets. And then he had those curious spectacles with red lenses perched on his nose, which concealed his eyes and rendered him still more mysterious.

Since Saint-Lucq had turned away a slim brunette, a busty blonde tried her luck. And met with the same lack of success. The serving girl returned to her friends, irritated and disappointed, but she shrugged and said to them:

'He just left a brothel. Or he has eyes only for his mistress.'

'I think he prefers men,' added the brunette, with a pout which betrayed her hurt feelings.

'Perhaps . . .' the third trailed off. 'But if he does not touch his glass and he is not seeking company, what does bring him here?'

The other two agreed, in any case, that there was little point in persisting with their advances, and Saint-Lucq – who was watching their debate out of the corner of his eye – was led to hope that they would now leave him in peace.

He returned to his surveillance.

A little after midday, the man Saint-Lucq had been expecting to appear entered the tavern.

He was tall and badly shaven, with long greasy hair, a sword at his side and a surly air about him. He was called Tranchelard and, as was his habit, he was accompanied by two scoundrels, no doubt hired for their brawn rather than their brains. They picked a table – which emptied as they approached – and did not have to order the wine jugs the tavern keeper brought to them with an apprehensive look.

The third serving girl, whose eyes had remained fixed on Saint-Lucq, chose this moment to act.

She was red-haired and pale-skinned, very pretty, no more than seventeen and knew – from experience – the effect that her green eyes, rose-coloured lips and young curves had on men. She wore a heavy skirt and, beneath her bustier, her open-necked blouse left her shoulders bare.

'You do not drink,' she said, suddenly standing in front of Saint-Lucq.

He paused before replying:

'No.'

'No doubt because you don't care for the wine you have been served.'

This time he said nothing.

'I could bring you our best.'

Silence again.

'And at the same price.'

'No thank you.'

But the girl wasn't listening. Adolescent pride dictated that, after the unsuccessful attempts of her two colleagues, she could not fail.

'In return, I shall ask you only to tell me your name,' she insisted with a smile full of promise. 'And I shall give you mine.'

55

Saint-Lucq held back a sigh.

Then, expressionless, he slid his red spectacles down his nose with an index finger and gazed back at the young girl . . .

. . . who froze when she saw the reptilian eyes.

No one was unaware of dragons, of the fact that they had always existed, that they had adopted human form, and that they had been living among men for centuries. To the misfortune of all of Europe, a great number of them were now to be found within the royal court of Spain. And their distant racial cousins, the wyverns, served men as winged mounts, while the tiny dragonnets made valued pets and companions. Despite that, a half-blood always made a powerful impression. They were all born of the rare love between a dragon and a human woman, provoking a malaise which became hatred in certain people, horror in others, and in the case of a few men and women, an erotic fascination. Half-bloods were said to be cold, cruel, indifferent and scornful of ordinary human beings.

'I— I'm sorry, monsieur . . .' the serving girl stammered. 'Forgive me . . .'

She turned on her heel, her lower lip trembling.

Saint-Lucq pushed his spectacles back to the top of his nose and interested himself anew in Tranchelard and his bodyguards. As they had only come to drink a glass of wine and extort their protection fee from the tavern keeper, they soon left. The half-blood drained his glass, rose, left a coin on the table and followed them out.

Tranchelard and his men moved steadily through the packed streets where their ill manner alone was enough to open a path for them. They chattered and laughed, unaware of any danger. The crowd protected them, although it also provided cover for Saint-Lucq as he tailed them discreetly. As luck would have it, they soon turned off into a winding alley, as rank as a sewer, which offered a shortcut to the old rue Pavée.

It was too good an opportunity to miss.

Suddenly pressing forward, Saint-Lucq caught up with them in a few strides and took them totally off-guard. They barely had time to hear the scrape of the steel leaving its scabbard. The first man fell at once, knocked out by a blow from Saint-Lucq's elbow which also broke his nose, Tranchelard was held immobile by the caress of a dagger blade at his throat, and the third man had barely moved his hand towards his sword when a rapier point, an inch from his right eye, froze him in mid-gesture.

'Think twice,' the half-blood advised in a quiet voice.

The man did not delay in taking to his heels, and Saint-Lucq found himself alone, face-to-face with Tranchelard. Continuing to threaten him with the dagger, Saint-Lucq pressed him back up against a grubby wall. They were so close that their breaths blended together; the street thug stank of fear.

'Look at me carefully, my friend. Do you recognise me?'

Tranchelard swallowed and nodded slightly to the man with red spectacles, sweat beading at his temples.

'Perfect,' Saint-Lucq continued. 'Now, open your ears and listen . . .'

12

As his feet touched ground in the courtyard of a beautiful mansion recently built in the Marais quarter, near the elegant and aristocratic Place Royale, the gentleman entrusted his horse to a servant who had rushed up at once.

'I'm not staying,' he said. 'Wait here.'

The other nodded and, reins in hand, watched out of the corner of his eye as the marquis de Gagnière climbed the front steps with a quick and supple step.

Sporting a large felt hat with a huge plumed feather, he was dressed in the latest fashion, with such obvious care for his appearance that it bordered on preciousness: he wore a cloak thrown over his left shoulder and held in place beneath his right arm with a silk cord, a high-waisted doublet of grey linen with silver fastenings, matching hose decorated with buttons, cream lace at his collar and cuffs, beige suede gloves and cavalier boots made of kid leather. The extreme stylishness of his manner and attire added to the androgynous character of his silhouette: slender, willowy, and almost juvenile. He was not yet twenty years old but seemed even younger, his face still bearing a childish charm and softness which would take a long time to mature, while the blond hair of his moustache and finely trimmed royale beard preserved a silky adolescent downiness.

An ancient maître d'hôtel greeted him at the top of the steps and, eyes lowered, accompanied him as far as a pretty ante-chamber where the marquis was asked to wait while he was announced to the vicomtesse. When the servant finally returned he held a door open and, with a bow, ushered the marquis through. Remaining by the door, he again avoided

meeting the young man's gaze as though something dangerous and troubling emanated from him, his elegance and
angelic beauty nothing but a façade disguising a poisonous
soul. In that respect, the young marquis resembled the sword
which hung from his baldric: a weapon whose guard and
pommel had been worked in the most exquisite manner, but
whose blade was of good sharp steel.

Gagnière entered and found himself alone when the maître
d'hôtel closed the door behind him.

The luxuriously furnished room was plunged into shadow.
Drawn curtains shut out the daylight and the few scented
candles that burned here and there created a permanent
twilight. The room was a study for reading. Shelves full of
books covered one wall. A comfortable armchair was installed
next to a window, by a small side table which bore a
candelabrum, a carafe of wine and a small crystal glass. A
large mirror in a gilded frame hung above the mantelpiece,
looming over a table and an old leather-backed chair with a
patina of age.

Upon the table in the middle of room, supported by a
delicate red and gold stand, reposed a strange globe.

The gentleman approached it.

Black, gleaming and hypnotic, it was as though the globe
was filled with swirling ink. It seemed to absorb the light
rather than reflect it. One's eye soon became lost in its deep
spirals.

And with it, one's soul.

'Don't touch it.'

Gagnière blinked and realised he was leaning over the
table, his right hand stretched out towards the globe. He
pulled himself back and turned, feeling perturbed.

A young woman dressed in black and purple had made her
appearance through a concealed door. Elegant yet severe in a
gown with a starched bodice, her low neckline was trimmed
with lace and decorated with a grey mother-of-pearl brooch
representing a unicorn. She was beautiful; blonde and slender,
with a small sweet face that seemed to have been designed to
be adorable. Her sparkling blue eyes, however, showed no

sign of any warm emotions, any more than her pretty, but unsmiling, lips.

The vicomtesse de Malicorne took a slow but assured step towards the gentleman.

'I . . . I'm sorry,' he said, '. . . I have no idea what—'

'There is no need to reproach yourself, monsieur de Gagnière. No one can resist it. Not even me.'

'Is it . . . Is it what I think it is?'

'A *Sphère d'Âme*? Yes.'

She spread a square of brocaded golden cloth over the ensorcelled globe, and it was as though an unhealthy presence had suddenly deserted the room.

'There. Isn't that better?'

Straightening up, she was about to continue when the marquis's worried expression stopped her.

'What is it?'

Embarrassed, Gagnière pointed a hesitant finger towards her, and then indicated his own nose:

'You have . . . there . . .'

The young woman understood, touched her upper lip with her ring finger and found its tip fouled by a blackish fluid that had leaked from her nostril. Untroubled, she took an already-stained handkerchief from her sleeve and turned away to press it to her nose.

'Magic is an art which the Ancestral Dragons created for themselves alone,' she said, as though that explained everything.

She faced the large mirror above the mantelpiece and, still dabbing at her lip, spoke in a conversational tone:

'I recently charged you with intercepting a covert courier between Brussels and Paris. Have you done as I required?'

'Certainly. Malencontre and his men have undertaken the task.'

'With what result?'

'As yet, I don't know.'

Her pretty face now clean of all foulness, the vicomtesse de Malicorne turned from the mirror and, with a half-smile, said:

'Allow me to enlighten you then, monsieur. Despite all the

opportunities he has had to lay an ambush, Malencontre has already failed twice. First at the border, and then close to Amiens. If the rider he pursues continues at the same pace, Malencontre's only hope of catching him is at the staging post near Clermont. After Clermont, he will proceed straight on to Paris. Is it truly necessary to remind you that this letter must under no circumstances reach the Louvre?'

The gentleman didn't ask how she knew so much: the globe, with all the secrets it deigned to reveal to any who sacrificed part of themselves to it, was sufficient explanation. He nodded in reply:

'I remain confident, madame. Malencontre and his men are quite used to these missions. They shall succeed, no matter what the cost to themselves.'

'Let us hope so, monsieur le marquis. Let us hope so . . .'

With a gracious, urbane gesture the vicomtesse invited Gagnière to take a seat and took one herself, opposite him.

'Right now, I would like to speak with you on an entirely different matter.'

'Which is, madame?'

'The cardinal is about to play a card of great importance, and I fear that he means to play it against us. This card is a man: La Fargue.'

' "La Fargue"?'

'An old captain and one of the king's most faithful swordsmen. Believe me, his return does not bode well for us. Alone, this La Fargue makes a formidable opponent. But in the past he commanded the Cardinal's Blades, a secret company of devoted and reliable men, capable, with La Fargue, of achieving the impossible. If they have been reunited . . .'

Pensive and worried, the young woman fell silent.

'Do you know the cardinal's intentions?' Gagnière asked cautiously.

'No. I merely guess at them . . . Which is why I want you to make inquiries into this matter. Speak with our agent in the Palais-Cardinal and learn everything you can from him. Can you meet him soon?'

'Yes.'

'Perfect.'

Having received his orders, and believing the interview to be over, the gentleman rose.

But the vicomtesse, looking elsewhere, continued:

'All this comes at the worst possible moment. We are about to achieve everything the Black Claw has been so desperate to accomplish for so long: to firmly establish itself in France. Our Spanish brothers and sisters have long since concluded that this goal is impossible, and although we are but a few hours from proving them wrong, I know that the majority are still doubtful. As for those who no longer doubt us, they already envy our forthcoming success – which amounts to saying that they too secretly hope for our failure.'

'You think that—'

'No, no . . .' said the vicomtesse, her hand brushing away the theory the marquis was about to propose. 'Those who are envious will not try to harm us . . . But they will not forgive the slightest shortcoming on our part and will seize any pretext to speak ill of us, of our plans and of our competence. They will be only too happy to claim they would have succeeded where we might still fail . . . These envious persons, moreover, have already begun to set their pawns in motion. I have been informed of the imminent arrival of a man sent to us by the Spanish lodge.'

'Who?'

'Savelda.'

From the corner of her eye, the vicomtesse de Malicorne detected Gagnière's dubious grimace.

'Yes, marquis, I share the sentiment. I've been told that Savelda comes to help us put the finishing touches to our project, but I know that his true mission is to observe us and take note of our mistakes, in case someone wishes to reproach us—'

'We should keep him in the dark, then.'

'Absolutely not. But we shall be beyond any reproach . . . Now you understand why it essential that we foresee and fend off every blow the cardinal might like to strike against us, don't you?'

'Indeed.'

'Then start by catching that courier from Brussels. Then we shall take on the Cardinal's Blades.'

13

Located at the entrance to a hamlet, which had no doubt risen up in its shadow, the inn was a typical example of the staging posts to be found across the country. In addition to the main building capped with red tiles it comprised a stable, a barn, a forge, a hen house, a loading area for coaches and a small pig pen, all of which was enclosed by a high wall whose grey and white stones were warmed by the afternoon sun. A river flowed past nearby, turning the wheel of a small mill. Beyond, the meadows and fields where cattle grazed stretched away to the east until they met the edge of a verdant forest. The weather was splendid, and the light from the great clear sky shone so brightly that one was obliged to squint.

A dog barked as a rider arrived.

Hens were pecking away in the courtyard, where the wheel of a stagecoach was being changed. Once it was repaired the coach would be harnessed with fresh horses and reach Clermont by evening. The coachman was lending the blacksmith and his assistants a hand while the passengers watched or took advantage of this opportunity to stretch their legs. Coaches generally offered a reliable and rapid service, barring accidents and taking into account the state of the roads – for the most part dust tracks in summer and turning boggy after the first autumn rains. Passengers had to put up with the unpleasantness of travelling in a jouncing and noisy vehicle, open to the wind, squeezed together in fours on opposing wooden benches, shoulder to shoulder and knees pressed together.

As soon as he dismounted, Antoine Leprat d'Orgueil held out the reins to a stable boy, no more than twelve years old, who was dressed in rough serge and ran around barefoot.

'Groom him and feed him with good oats. But don't let him drink too much. I leave again in an hour.'

The rider spoke like a man accustomed to being obeyed. The child nodded and headed towards the stables leading the horse behind him.

Indifferent to the sidelong glances sent in his direction, Leprat spied a water trough into which, his hat in hand, he plunged his head. Then he rubbed his face and the back of his neck with fresh water, rinsed his mouth, spat, smoothed back his chestnut hair, and finally replaced his black hat with its grey plume and rim raised on the right-hand side. His dust-covered doublet, worn open over his shirt, had seen better days but it was made of fine cloth. His riding boots, dirtied and softened by use, also seemed to be well made. As for the rapier, ensconced in its scabbard which hung from his leather baldric, it was of a kind that no one, here or anywhere else, could boast of ever having seen the like. He carried it on the right, being left-handed.

Leprat slowly climbed the steps to the main building, fronted by a gallery with ivy clinging to its beams. Having pushed the door to the building open he stood on the threshold for a moment, silence falling within the room as he looked over the ordinary travellers seated at several tables, and they observed him in return. Tall, well-built, with stubbled cheeks and a stern gaze, he exuded a masculine charm which was reinforced by the warlike garb of a weary courier. A first glance suggested that here was a man who smiled little, spoke less, and did not seek to please others. He was between thirty-five and forty years old. His face had the lined features that indicate the iron will of a man of honour and duty who can no longer be moved or upset by anything, because he has already witnessed all the evils of this world. He did, however, spare a brief but tender look for a little girl who was sitting on her mother's knee, dipping her chubby fingers into a bowl and smearing herself with jam.

Leprat let the door close behind him. Conversations picked up again as he came inside, his iron-tipped boots thudding against the rough floor with a rattle of spurs. As he passed, a few noticed the sword he carried at his side. Only the pommel and guard could be seen above the scabbard, but they seemed to be carved from a solid block of a material which shone like polished ivory.

A white rapier.

That was enough to be intriguing, even if no one knew exactly what it implied. Elbows were nudged discreetly, and uncertain expressions were exchanged with looks of puzzlement.

Having chosen a small empty table, Leprat sat with his back to a window through which, with a mere glance over his shoulder, he could cast an eye over the courtyard. The landlord, with greasy hair and a stained apron wrapped around the curve of his enormous belly, hastened towards him.

'Welcome, monsieur. How can I be of service?'

'Wine,' said Leprat, placing his hat and sheathed rapier on the table.

Then, eyeing the bird roasting on a spit over the hearth, he added:

'And the chicken, there. And bread.'

'Immediately, monsieur. Hard travelling in this heat, isn't it? You'd think it was already summer!'

'Yes.'

Understanding that the conversation would go no further, the landlord passed his order to a serving girl.

Quickly served, Leprat dined without lifting his eyes from his plate. He had not unsaddled his horse since the previous evening and found himself more famished than tired. In fact, he did not even feel the aches and pains plaguing his back until he was finally sated. He had been riding hard on the road between Brussels, which he had left in the middle of the night almost three days previously, and Paris, where he hoped to arrive that very evening.

The dog that had welcomed him barked again.

Turning his head towards the window, Leprat saw the riders arrive in the courtyard. He'd thought he'd succeeded in leaving them behind in Amiens, after the first ambush which

66

he had eluded on the border between France and the Spanish Netherlands.

Evidently, he had been mistaken.

He summoned the serving girl with a calm gesture. An overly plump brunette of about twenty, she resembled the innkeeper so strongly she had to be his daughter.

'Monsieur?'

'Could I ask that you close the window curtains, please?'

The young girl hesitated as the window in question was the only source of light in the room.

'If you please,' Leprat insisted.

'Certainly, monsieur.'

She closed the curtains, blocking all view of the new arrivals who were dismounting outside. Inside the inn, there was some surprise at being suddenly pitched into shadow. But seeing who had made this request to the serving girl, all those present held their tongues.

'There, monsieur.'

'Now, do you see the woman with the white bonnet? The one with the little girl on her knee?'

'Yes.'

'Take them both out of here, without delay. Whisper in the mother's ear that they are in danger, and tell her she must leave for her own safety and that of the child.'

'Excuse me? But, monsieur—'

'Do it.'

The young woman obeyed, looking worried. Leprat watched while she spoke quietly with the woman in the white bonnet. The woman frowned, and although she displayed some signs of concern, she seemed disinclined to move . . .

. . . at least, not until the door opened.

On seeing who it was, she hurried ahead of the serving girl into the kitchen, her little girl in her arms.

Relieved, Leprat edged his chair back without rising.

The freebooters entered with a swagger, as thugs everywhere enter a room when they are certain they are danger personified. Armed with rapiers and wearing thick leather doublets, they were grubby, sweaty, and stank of the stable. A tall thin man with long flaxen hair was in the lead – he wore a leather hat and had a scar across the corner of his lips which drew them into a strange, smiling rictus. The other three, each with a sinister bearing, escorted him closely and had the almost ordinary faces of conscienceless mercenaries who would cut a throat for a mouthful of bread. And then the last of the riders entered, and with his appearance alone managed to congeal the already apprehensive silence. He was a drac: a member of a race spawned by the dragons in order to serve them, known for its cruelty and violence. A grey drac, as it happened. Fine slate-coloured scales covered his jowled face, and his clawed hands had four fingers. He, too, was dressed as a hired killer.

Dumbstruck, the patrons in the inn made a show of paying no attention to the freebooters, as if this ploy could somehow dispel their menacing presence. The innkeeper hesitated over whether or not to go up to them, hoping against all odds that they would desire neither food nor drink. In the end, his courage deserted him entirely and he decided to remain close by the door leading to the kitchen.

The mercenaries slowly swept the room with inquisitorial gazes as their eyes adjusted to the half-light. When they saw Leprat, sitting with his back to the window and its closed curtains, they knew that they had found their man.

They approached him without crowding one another and took up position before his table. The drac remained by the door, and when customers tried to rise discreetly in order to leave, he was content to simply turn his head towards them. His vertical, membranous eyelids closed briefly over his expressionless reptilian eyes. Everyone resumed their seat.

The flaxen-haired man settled himself at Leprat's table, sitting opposite him, without provoking any reaction.

'May I?' he asked, pointing a finger at the chicken Leprat had been eating

Without waiting for permission, he tore a wing from the plump carcass, bit into it and gave a sigh of satisfaction.

'This is truly an honour,' he said conversationally. 'Now I can say I have shared a meal with the famous Antoine Leprat, chevalier d'Orgueil . . . Because that's who you are, are you not? No, no, don't answer. Seeing that is proof enough.'

With his chin he indicated the white rapier lying, in its scabbard, on the table.

'Is it true that it was carved in one piece from the fang of an ancient dragon?'

'From the point to the pommel.'

'How many others like that do you think there are in the world?'

'I don't know. Perhaps none.'

The mercenary chief put on an admiring expression that might have been quite sincere. Half turning, he called out:

'Innkeeper! Wine for the chevalier and I. Be sure it's your best!'

'Yes, monsieur. At . . . at once.'

The two men locked eyes until the innkeeper came to serve them with a trembling hand, then scurried away leaving the wine jug. Leprat remained impassive as the other lifted his glass; upon seeing that his gesture was not imitated, the mercenary shrugged and drank alone.

'And me. Do you know who I am?'

The chevalier eyed him with contempt and did not reply.

'I am called Malencontre.'

Leprat smiled faintly.

Malencontre.

In other words: mishap. Or ill met.

Yes, that name did indeed fit this character.

14

'Do I know enough?'

'You will always know enough, if your adversary knows less than you.'

'But would you say I've progressed?'

Having counted up his meagre salary, Almades tightened the strings of his purse and raised his eyes towards the very young man who, still sweaty and out of breath from his latest fencing lesson, was watching him anxiously. He knew that look. He had seen it often in the past year, and he was astonished that he was still moved by it.

'Yes, monsieur. You have indeed made progress.'

It was no lie, considering that a week earlier the man had never held a sword in his life. He was a law student, who had come one morning to this inn, located in the outlying district – known as a *faubourg* – of Saint-Antoine, seeking the courtyard where Almades received his clients. He had a duel to fight, and wanted to learn how to cross blades. Time was short. But wasn't it said that this backyard, where the Spaniard taught, was a better school than the finest fencing halls in Paris? Paid for in coin, no doubt a few lessons, properly learnt and applied, would suffice. After all, he only needed an unstoppable flurry of two or three clever thrusts to kill his man, didn't he?

Almades frequently asked himself, when faced with students like this, if these young men truly believed in the existence of such 'deadly thrusts' which, once their secrets were mastered, were capable of guaranteeing success without any need for fencing talent. And even if there were such a thing, did they imagine this mysterious knowledge could be had for a mere fistful of pistoles? But it was highly likely that this student, terrified by the prospect of risking his life, sword in hand, would want to believe it to be true. Like all the others, he would be led by honour, pride, or stupidity to the meadow tomorrow. He was afraid and, now that he was committed to this duel, hoped for salvation from a miracle worker.

Almades had carefully explained that in the time available to them he could not do more than impart the basic rudiments of fencing, that the greatest swashbuckler ever born was never certain to carry the day, and that it was always better to renounce a bad duel than one's life. But faced with the student's insistence he had accepted taking him on as a pupil, for a week, on condition that he paid the greater part of the agreed fee in advance. Experience had taught Almades that novices, put off by the difficulty of actually learning to fence, were quick to abandon their lessons, and with them, payment of any tuition.

This one, however, had not yet given up.

'I beg you, monsieur, tell me if I am ready,' the young man pleaded. 'I must fight tomorrow!'

The fencing master stared at him for a long while.

'Above all else,' he finally said, 'what truly matters is whether you are ready to die.'

His full name was Anibal Antonio Almades di Carlo. He was tall and thin, clearly of a naturally slender build, but had grown gaunt due to long periods of hunger. He had dark eyes and hair with a pale complexion and a grizzled but still tidy moustache. His doublet, his shirt and his shoes were clean, although discreetly patched in places, and the lace at his collar and cuffs had seen hard use. His hat was missing its plume and the leather of his fold-over boots was unpolished. But even if he had nothing but rags to wear, Almades would have worn them well. Old Andalusian blood ran in his veins, nourishing his entire being with a haughty austerity which shone forth from him.

Brutally confronted by the prospect of his own death, the student blanched.

'Your duel,' asked the fencing master to lessen the blow, 'Is it to first blood?'

'Yes.'

'Well, that's for the best. Rather than employing this science to kill your adversary, use it to ensure you're only slightly wounded. Stay on the defensive. Take breaks to conserve your strength and catch your breath. Wait for a mistake; it's always possible that your adversary will make a clumsy move. But don't be in too much of a hurry to finish him off, as you risk exposing yourself. And hold your left hand high enough to protect your face if necessary: it's better to lose a finger than an eye.'

The young man nodded.

'Yes,' he said . . . 'Yes, I will do exactly as you say.'

'Goodbye, monsieur.'

'Goodbye, master.'

They parted with a handshake.

Leaving the gloom of the inn, Almades went out into the open courtyard at the rear, a simple square of beaten earth where he supervised the exercises of his rare students. Hens squawked nearby; a horse neighed; a cow could even be heard lowing in the distance. The faubourg Saint-Antoine was a recent addition to the city, still very rural in character, made up of new dwellings and manors whose façades along both sides of the dusty roads converging on Paris hid the surrounding farms, fields and pasture land from travellers' sight. The faubourg began in the shadow of the Bastille, just beyond the Saint-Antoine gate and the city's defensive moat, and the buildings progressively thinned out as one moved away from the capital and its stink.

At a table which had been left outside, exposed to the elements, Almades took out the rapier he kept for his clients' use. Along with the sword which hung at his side, this comprised his sole teaching aid, and his entire fortune. It was an iron rapier of poor quality, doubtless too heavy, and in danger from rust. Sitting on a wooden stump, he began to patiently clean the notched blade with an oiled rag.

Footsteps could be heard in the courtyard. A group of men approached him, stopping a few metres away, remaining silent and waiting to be noticed.

Almades examined them from beneath the brim of his hat.

There were four of them. A provost and three apprentices. The first was armed with a sword, while his seconds carried iron bars. And they had all been sent by a fencing master who maintained a school close to the Bastille, and who simply could not bear the thought of anyone benefiting from fencing lessons illegally dispensed by the Spaniard.

His iron rapier across his knees, Almades raised his head, squinting in the sunlight. He observed the four men with an inscrutable expression, and as he did so, idly fiddled with the steel signet ring he wore on his left finger, twisting it around three times.

'Monsieur Lorbois, isn't it?' he said to the provost with a slight accent.

The other nodded and announced:

'Monsieur, my master has warned you a number of times to cease laying any claim to the title of "fencing master", without which the practice of teaching fencing is illegal. You have persisted in spite of those warnings. My master has sent us today to assure ourselves that you will leave Paris and the surrounding area within the hour, never to return.'

Like any other trade, that of fencing masters was regulated. Formed in 1567 under the patronage of Saint Michel, the guild of Parisian fencing masters organised and oversaw the practice within the capital, and the status of its members was confirmed by letters of patent. None who lacked such a letter could instruct another in the art of fencing.

Almades rose, the iron rapier in his left hand.

'I am a fencing master,' he said.

'In Spain, perhaps. But not in France. Not in Paris.'

'Spanish fencing is as worthy as French.'

'Do not force us to deal with you, monsieur. There is to be no question of a duel here. We are four, and you are alone.'

'Then let us even the odds.'

Under the gaze of the provost, who did not understand the

73

implications of this sentence, Almades placed himself in the centre of the courtyard, still holding the old iron rapier in his left hand . . .

. . . and unsheathed his own steel rapier with his right.

'I await you, messieurs,' he said, whipping both his blades around and up to the vertical three times.

Then he placed himself *en garde*.

The provost and his three apprentices deployed themselves in a semi-circle and pressed their attack at once. In a single flurry Almades pierced the shoulder of the first apprentice, the thigh of the second, ducked to avoid the iron bar of the third, straightened up and slashed the armpit of this last assailant while turning, and completed his move by crossing his rapiers to seize the provost's throat in the scissors formed by his two sharp blades.

No more than a few heartbeats had passed. The apprentices were out of the fight and their provost found himself at the Spaniard's mercy, paralysed by shock and fear, hesitating to even swallow with the blades placed against his throat.

Almades allowed a handful of seconds to pass and allow the provost to take full stock of the situation.

'Tell he who sent you that he is rather a poor fencing master and that what I've seen of his science, as displayed by your performance, makes me laugh . . . Now, get out.'

The humiliated provost retreated from the courtyard, along with his entourage of apprentices, one of whom, his thigh drenched in blood, had to be supported by the other two. The Spaniard watched them limp away, sighed, and heard a voice behind him say:

'My congratulations. The years have not dulled your skills.'

He turned to discover captain La Fargue standing there.

A twitch of the eyelid was the only sign that betrayed Almades's surprise.

They took a table in the near-empty inn. Almades ordered and paid for a jug of wine, which would deprive him of dinner later, then filled their glasses, pouring three times in each case.

'How did you know where to find me?' he asked.

'I didn't.'

'The cardinal?'

'His spies.'

The Spaniard swallowed a mouthful of wine while La Fargue slid a letter towards him. Richelieu's seal was stamped into the red wax seal.

'I have come,' said the Captain, 'to bring you this.'

'What does it say?'

'That the Blades have returned to the light of day and they wish for your return.'

Almades took in the news with a slight movement of his head.

'After five years?'

'Yes.'

'Under your command?'

The captain nodded.

Almades mulled this over, keeping his silence while twisting his signet ring around, over and over, in series of threes. Memories, not all of which were happy, flooded into his mind. Then he gave his current surroundings a long sweeping glance.

'You'll need to buy me a horse,' he said finally.

15

In Paris, the vicomte d'Orvand's coach left Marciac, as he requested, on rue Grenouillère, or more precisely, in front of a small, cosy house which had no real distinguishing features compared to the rest except that it was known to locals as *Les Petites Grenouilles* ('The Little Frogs'). Being familiar with the neighbourhood, the Gascon knew he would find the front door closed at this hour of the afternoon. So he went around to the rear and climbed over a wall, before crossing an attractive garden and entering the house through a low door.

He walked soundlessly into the kitchen where a very plump woman dressed in a skirt, apron and white bonnet had her back turned to him. He approached her on tiptoe and surprised her with a sound kiss on the cheek.

'Monsieur Nicolas! Where did you spring from? You almost scared me to death!'

'Another kiss, to win your forgiveness?'

'Be off, monsieur. You know very well that I have passed the age where such gallantries—'

'Really? And what about that handsome, strapping carpenter who curls his moustaches on the doorstep every time you go to the market?'

'I don't know of whom you speak,' replied the blushing cook.

'Now, now . . . Where are the young ladies?'

'In the next room.'

Moments later Marciac made his appearance in a bright and elegantly furnished room, where he immediately attracted the notice of four pretty young ladies who were sitting about in casual dress. The first was an ample blonde; the second a slim brunette; the third was a mischievous redhead; and the last was a Jewish beauty with green eyes and dusky skin. The blonde read from a book while the brunette embroidered and chattered with the other two.

Armed with his most roguish smile, Marciac bowed, doffed his hat with a flourish and exclaimed:

'Greetings, mesdemoiselles! How are my charming little frogs?'

He was welcomed with fervent cries of joy.

'Monsieur Nicolas!'

'How are you—?'

'It's been so long—!'

'Do you know how much we've missed you—?'

'We were worried—!'

The eager young women, relieving Marciac of his hat and sword, made him sit on a divan.

'Are you thirsty?' asked one of them.

'Hungry?' asked another.

'Desire anything else?' asked the most daring of the lot.

Marciac, delighted, accepted both a glass of wine and the demonstrations of affection that were lavished upon him with such good grace. Teasing fingers roamed over his chest and toyed with his shirt collar.

'So, monsieur Nicolas, what do you have to recount for us after all this time?'

'Oh, not much, I'm afraid . . .'

The young women made a show of profound disappointment.

'. . . merely that I fought a duel today!'

This news produced rapture.

'A duel? Tell us! Tell us!' the redhead cried, clapping her hands.

'Before anything else, I must describe my adversary, because he was rather formidable—'

'Who was he? Did you kill him?'

'Patience, patience . . . If memory serves me, I believe he was almost four measures tall.'

A measure was equal to two metres. They laughed.

'You're mocking us!'

'Not at all!' Marciac protested in a joyful tone. 'He even had six arms.'

More laughter.

'And to complete his portrait, I should add that this demon came straight from hell, had horns and breathed fire from both his mouth and his ars—'

'And just what is going on here?' demanded a voice which rang with authority.

A heavy silence fell. Everyone froze, while the temperature in the room seemed to fall by several degrees. Marciac, like some Levantine pasha in the midst of his harem, found himself caught with one little frog on his right, one to his left, another kneeling at his feet and the last perched on his knee. He attempted a smile, which only worsened the delicate situation in which he had been surprised.

Gabrielle had just made her entrance.

She had shimmering strawberry-blonde hair and was one of those women who are less striking for their beauty – however great – than for their imperious presence. A gown of silk and satin emphasised the perfection of her skin and the spark of her royal blue eyes. Tiny wrinkles had begun to appear at the corners of her eyelids over the passing years – lines which usually denote experience, as well as a certain penchant for laughter.

But Gabrielle neither laughed, nor even smiled.

Icily, she took in each detail of the Gascon from head to toe, as though he were a muddy dog who threatened to ruin her carpets.

'What are you doing here?'

'I came to pay my respects to your little frogs.'

'Have you?'

'Uh . . . yes.'

'Then you can go. Goodbye.'

She turned on her heel.

Marciac extricated himself, not without difficulty, from the divan and its little frogs. He caught up with Gabrielle in the corridor and detained her by the elbow, but, when skewered by her deadly stare, promptly released his hold.

'Gabrielle, my beauty, please . . . One word—'

'Don't you dare speak to me. After that nasty trick you played, I should have you beaten! . . . Ah, actually, that's an idea.'

She called out:

'Thibault!'

A door – leading into the front hall through which visitors to the house normally passed – opened. A giant dressed as a lackey appeared, who seemed at first astonished and then delighted to see Marciac.

'Hello, monsieur.'

'Hello, Thibault. How is your son, the one who broke his arm in a fall?'

'He has recovered, monsieur. Thank you for your concern, monsieur.'

'And your littlest one? How is she?'

'She cries a great deal. She's teething.'

'Just how many children do you have, exactly?'

'Eight, monsieur.'

'Eight! Well, well, you know your business, my lusty chap!'

Thibault blushed and dropped his gaze.

'Have you finished?' Gabrielle asked in a frosty voice. 'Thibault, I am not pleased.'

When he looked at her without comprehension she had to explain:

'He waltzed in here as though we live in a barn!'

Thibault turned towards the front hall and the main entrance.

'But he didn't. The door is shut tight and I swear to you I never left my stool. Although I wouldn't say no to a cushion, due to the pains which—'

Marciac made an effort not to laugh.

'That's enough, Thibault,' Gabrielle decreed. 'Return to your stool and your tightly shut door.'

And, catching sight of the little frogs peeping at them from the salon door, she ordered:

79

'And you! Off with you! Now! And close the door.'

Swiftly obeyed, but still dissatisfied, she added:

'Well, there's never a moment's peace in this house. Come.'

Marciac followed her into an antechamber, one adjoining her bedroom, whose delicious pleasures he remembered well. But the door to that retreat remained closed and Gabrielle, standing very stiff with her arms folded, prompted him:

'You wanted a word with me? Very well. Go ahead, I'm listening.'

'Gabrielle,' the Gascon began in a conciliatory tone—

'There. A word. You've said it. Now, goodbye. You know the way . . . And do not make me ask Thibault to accompany you.'

'Under these circumstances,' Marciac said contritely but gamely, 'I wager that even a chaste kiss would be too much to ask—'

'A kiss from Thibault? I'm sure you can arrange that.'

His shoulders lowered, Marciac made a show of leaving. Then he turned and proffered, as a peace offering, the ring won in his duel against the marquis de Brévaux.

'A gift?'

Gabrielle made an effort to remain unmoved. In her eyes, however, there was a gleam with the same sparkle as the ruby in its setting.

'Stolen?'

'You wound me. Handed over willingly by its former owner.'

'Before witnesses?'

'Yes. D'Orvand. You can ask him.'

'He no longer visits me.'

'I'll make him come see you again.'

'It's a man's ring.'

'But the stone is still beautiful.'

She softened somewhat.

'That's true.'

'And it has no regard for gender.'

With a shrug of her shoulders, Gabrielle took the ring with

80

a swift gesture and, pointing her finger menacingly, she snapped:

'Don't believe that all is forgiven because of this!'

Marciac, now happy and seeking to endear himself further, gave her a knowing look and replied:

'But it's a start, no?'

16

Inside the inn on the road to Clermont, no one had dared to speak or move since the five mercenaries had entered.

'Malencontre,' their leader repeated, tucking his flaxen hair behind his ear. 'It's a memorable name for a warrior, isn't it?'

He was still seated at Leprat's table and, having ordered wine, made conversation in a tone that was too self-confident to be at all innocent. Three of his men gathered together behind him while the last of the band, the drac with slate grey scales, guarded the door and kept an eye on everything.

'And yet,' continued Malencontre, 'My name means nothing to you. Do you know why?'

'No,' said Leprat.

'Because all those who have heard it from my mouth, without being my friends, soon met their end.'

'Ah.'

'That doesn't worry you?'

'Hardly.'

Malencontre scraped the scar at the corner of his mouth with a fingernail, and forced himself to smile.

'You're right. Because you see, today, I happen to be in a merciful mood. I am ready to forget the numerous difficulties which you have created for us. I am even disposed to forgive you for the two bodies you left on the bridge at the border. Not to mention that trick you played on us in Amiens. But . . .'

'But?'

'But you have to give us what we seek.'

The mercenaries scented victory. They were five against a single adversary who had no hope of reinforcements. They smiled, anticipating the moment when they would draw swords and let blood spill.

Leprat appeared to take stock of his situation, and then said:

'Understood.'

He slowly plunged his left hand into his dusty doublet and withdrew a letter sealed with a blob of red wax. He placed the document on the table, pushed it in front of him, and waited.

Malencontre watched this, frowning.

He made no move to pick up this missive which had already cost two lives.

'That's all?' he said in surprise.

'That's all.'

'You simply comply? Without even making a show of resistance?'

'I've already done enough, it seems to me. I will no doubt be held accountable for my actions, but it does not serve me at all if, in the end, you pluck a piece of paper from my corpse, does it? In any case, I must have been betrayed for you to have found me so quickly. Someone told you which route I would follow. I believe that this authorises me to take a few liberties as far as my masters' orders are concerned. One owes nothing to those who prove unworthy of one's trust.'

When the other continued to hesitate, Leprat insisted:

'You want this letter? Take it. It's yours.'

In the shadowy room, lit only by the faint red flames of the hearth, the silence grew as it does just before the fall of an executioner's axe, when the upraised blade catches a ray of sunlight and the crowd holds its breath.

'So be it,' said Malencontre.

Slowly, he extended a dirty-nailed hand towards the letter.

And if he glimpsed, at the last moment, a gleam awaken in Leprat's eye, he was too slow to react to it.

The mercenaries were caught short by their leader's screams: Leprat had nailed his hand to the table with the greasy knife he had used to slice up the fowl. Malencontre freed his tortured hand and spat:

'KILL HIM!'

On his feet, Leprat had already seized his sheathed rapier.

With a violent blow from his heel, he propelled the table into his attackers' legs and added to the confusion by forcing them to spread out before they could draw their swords. Malencontre, his bloody hand held tight against him, jostled them in order to reach the drac who was coming to his rescue. Backed against the curtained window, Leprat was forced to retreat. But he still had enough space to fight. Calmly, he slashed the air with his sword and managed to dislodge its scabbard, which slid across the floor.

Then he placed himself *en garde*.

And waited.

The tables around them finished emptying in a clatter of moving furniture. Silent and anxious, the inn's patrons huddled tight against the walls or on the steps of the staircase leading to the first floor. No one wanted to receive an ill-judged blow. But they all wanted to watch. The innkeeper himself had taken refuge in the kitchen. It seemed he lacked the stomach for this type of entertainment.

In a corner, the drac wrapped up Malencontre's hand with shreds torn from the first handy piece of cloth. The other three, finally untangled and ready to fight, prudently deployed themselves in a semi-circle. Without taking his eyes off them, the chevalier d'Orgueil allowed them to approach.

Closer.

Much closer.

In reach of a blade.

That should have worried them, but they realised it too late.

Leprat suddenly thrust his right hand behind him and pulled open the curtains. Brilliant daylight burst into the darkened room, clearly revealing his dark silhouette and striking the mercenaries in the face. Without waiting, he struck. The ivory rapier found one blinded freebooter's throat and produced a scarlet spurt which the villain tried in vain to staunch with his fingers. He fell, blood bubbling from his mouth and nostrils. Leprat broke off his attack immediately and dodged a clumsy lunge from another mercenary, who was still protecting his eyes from the sun with his elbow. Leprat doubled him up with a blow from his knee and sent him smashing, head first, into the mantelpiece. The man's skull cracked. He fell face-first into the hearth and began to burn; the smell of scorched hair and cooking meat quick to impregnate the room. The third brigand, who could now see better, was already charging him from behind, brandishing his sword. Leprat didn't turn. In one movement he reversed his sword and wedged it beneath his armpit, took a step back and dropped to one knee, allowing his attacker to impale himself on the ivory blade. The man stiffened, arm raised, face incredulous and lips dribbling pink spit. Leprat slowly returned to his feet, pivoted and finished driving his blade into the body, up to the hilt. He stared deeply into the dead man's eyes, and then pushed the corpse away, to fall backward to the floor.

Less than a minute had passed since he had opened the curtain, and three assassins were already lying dead beneath blows from the chevalier d'Orgueil. He was well known in Paris, in the Louvre as well as in all the fencing schools, as one of the best swordsmen in France. Evidently his reputation was not undeserved.

Malencontre was in no state to fight, but the drac was still waiting to enter the fray.

Leprat sized him up. He snapped out a sharp movement with his rapier which spattered the floor with red droplets, drew a dagger from its sheath over his kidney with his left hand, and resumed the *en garde* position. The drac seemed to smile. In his turn, he crossed his arms before him and simultaneously drew a straight sabre and a dagger.

He would also fight with two weapons.

The duel was furious from the very first exchange. Tense and concentrated, the drac and Leprat exchanged attacks, parries, counterattacks and ripostes without holding back. The reptilian understood who he was fighting and the chevalier quickly realised the worthiness of his opponent. Neither seemed to have the upper hand. When one of them retreated a few paces, he was quick to reclaim the advantage. And when the other was forced to parry a flurry of blows, he always managed to take the initiative with his next attack. Leprat was an experienced and talented swordsman, but the drac had greater strength and endurance: his arm seemed indefatigable. Steel against ivory, ivory against steel, the blades spun and clashed together faster than the eye could see. Leprat was sweating, and could feel himself tiring.

He had to finish it quickly.

Finally daggers and swords crossed at the guards. Pushing one against the other the drac and Leprat found themselves nose-to-nose, their arms extended above them like a steeple. With a mighty bellow, the drac spat a mouthful of acid into the chevalier's face, who replied with a powerful head butt. He managed to stun his opponent and, seizing the moment, wiped his burning eyes on his sleeve, but the drac was already rushing at him with foaming mouth and bloody nostrils. It was a weakness of dracs: they were impulsive and quick to abandon themselves to blind rage.

Leprat saw an opportunity that wouldn't present itself a second time.

With one foot, he slid a stool into the drac's path. The reptilian stumbled but continued his charge, half running, half falling as he came. His attack was fierce but inaccurate. Leprat stepped aside and pivoted towards the left as the reptilian passed him on the right. He managed to turn and slash, arm extended horizontally.

The ivory rapier sliced neatly through its target.

A scaly head spun and, at the end of a bloody arc, bounced against the floor and rolled a considerable distance. The decapitated drac's body fell, releasing a thick jet of liquid from its neck.

Leprat immediately looked for Malencontre. He didn't find him, but heard cries and the sound of hoof beats out in the courtyard. He rushed to the door in time to see the man escaping at a gallop, watched by those who had remained outside and were only now emerging from their hiding-places.

Stained with the blood of his victims, the remains of the acidic reptilian spit still clinging to his cheeks, Leprat went back inside the inn. He was the focus of attention of all those present, whose reactions wavered between horror and relief. So far no one was inclined to move, and certainly not to talk. The soles of nervous feet scraped against the raw wooden floor.

Weapons in hand, Leprat contemplated the carnage and disorder with a tranquil air. Amidst the upturned furniture, the broken plates and the trampled food, three bodies lay in thick pools of blood, while the fourth continued to burn in the hearth, the greasy flesh of his face crackling in contact with the flames. The smell, a mixture of blood, bile and fear, was appalling.

A door creaked open and the innkeeper came out of the kitchen brandishing an antique arquebus before him. The fat man wore a ridiculous-looking helmet on his head and a breastplate whose straps he was unable to fasten. And due to the trembling of his limbs, the barrel of his weapon – gaping open like an incredulous mouth – seemed to be following the erratic path of an invisible fly.

Leprat almost laughed, but succeeded only in smiling wearily.

It was then he saw the blood running from his right hand and realised that he had been wounded.

'All's well,' he said. 'In the king's service.'

17

'What?' exclaimed a merchant. 'That Amazon with the flying hair who galloped past us this morning? A baronne?'

'God's truth!' confirmed the old soldier. 'Just as I told you!'

'It's beyond belief!' blurted another merchant.

'And yet,' added a pedlar who knew the region well. 'Nothing could be truer.'

'And since when did baronnes carry swords, around here?'

'Why, since it pleased them to—'

'It's simply extraordinary!'

'The baronne Agnès de Vaudreuil . . .' sighed the first merchant dreamily.

'It's said she's of excellent birth,' said the second.

'Old nobility of the sword,' declared the veteran of the Wars of Religion. 'The best. The true . . . Her ancestors went on the crusades and her father fought beside King Henri.'

This exchange took place at *The Silver Cask*, a village hostelry on the road to Paris. The two merchants had stopped there after concluding their business at an excellent market in Chantilly, which explained their shared good humour. Two more men had invited themselves to join their table. One was a quaint, garrulous local, an old soldier with a wooden leg who lived on a meagre pension, passing the greater part of his days drinking, if possible at someone else's expense. The other was a pedlar who seemed not at all eager to resume his rounds, carrying his heavy wicker pannier on his back. It was an hour after dinner and, with the afternoon rush over, the tables had quickly emptied. With the aid of wine, the conversation rolled along freely and vigorously.

'She seemed very beautiful to me,' said a merchant.

'Beautiful?' repeated the veteran. 'She is more than that . . . Her firm tits. Her long thighs. And her arse, my friends . . . that arse!'

'The way you speak of her arse I would swear you'd seen it?'

'Bloody hell! I've not had that good fortune . . . But others have seen it. And felt it. And enjoyed it. For it's a very welcoming arse, indeed . . .'

The drinkers were talkative, the subject ripe for discussion and the wine pitchers quickly emptied, all to be replaced immediately. However, the prospect of a handsome profit was not enough to gladden the heart of master Léonard, owner of *The Silver Cask*. Anxious, but not daring to intervene, he kept an eye on another customer sitting all alone at a table, visibly fuming.

The man wore sagging funnel-shaped boots, brown leather trousers and a large red velvet doublet left open over his bare chest. His body was of a robust build but weighed down with fat − large thighs, broad shoulders, and a thick neck. He might have been fifty-five years old, perhaps more. Beneath a close-cut beard, his lined face was that of an old soldier who had grown soft over the last few years, and interlacing crimson veins − which would soon blossom into blotches − decorated his cheeks. Nevertheless, his eyes remained sharp. And the impression of strength which emanated from his person was unmistakable.

'And where are they, these happy arse-samplers?' gaily demanded the most cheerful, and most drunk, of the merchants. 'I would like to hear more from them!'

'They're all about. This beauty is not shy.'

'It's said she kills her lovers,' interjected the pedlar.

'Nonsense!'

'You might better say that she exhausts them!' corrected the veteran with a bawdy wink of the eye. 'If you know what I mean . . .'

'I see, yes,' nodded the merchant. 'And I say, myself, that there are worse deaths than that . . . I'd gladly flirt with her myself, the naughty wench!'

Hearing that, the man who had been listening to them unnoticed rose with the air of someone resolved to carry out a necessary task. He advanced with steady steps and was half-way to the table when master Léonard nimbly barred his path, a somewhat courageous act, since he was two heads shorter and only half the other man's weight. But the safekeeping of his establishment was at stake.

'Monsieur Ballardieu, please?'

'Don't be alarmed, master Léonard. You know me.'

'Precisely. With respect . . . they've been drinking. No doubt, too much. They don't know what they're—'

'I tell you, there's no cause for concern,' the man said with a friendly and reassuring smile.

'Just promise me you won't start anything,' begged the innkeeper.

'I promise to do everything possible to that end.'

Master Léonard stepped aside with regret and, wiping his damp hands on his apron, watched Ballardieu continue on his way.

On seeing him, the veteran with the wooden leg turned pale. The three others, in contrast, were taken in by his easy manner.

'Please excuse me, messieurs, for interrupting you . . .'

'Please, monsieur,' replied a merchant. 'What can we do for you? Would you care to join our table?'

'Just a question.'

'We're listening.'

'I would like to know which of your four heads I shall have the honour of breaking first.'

18

A sound disturbed the drowsing Saint-Lucq.

It was a repeated, irregular scratching, which sometimes seemed to have stopped only to promptly begin again. A scrape of a claw. Against wood.

The half-blood sighed and sat up under the bedclothes. The afternoon was drawing to a close.

'What is it?' asked the muffled voice of the young woman lying beside him in bed.

'You can't hear it?'

'I can.'

'What is it?'

'Nothing. Go back to sleep.'

And she turned over, pulling the bedcovers round her.

Having two or three hours to kill during the day, Saint-Lucq had approached her on rue de Glatigny, an alley in the city where ladies of pleasure had plied their trade since the Middle Ages. He had offered to pay her handsomely on the condition that he could also take rest in her dwelling. The deal concluded, she had led him into the little attic room where she lived, close to the law courts. 'You're not my first', she had said, on seeing the half-blood's reptilian eyes.

Then she'd undressed.

An hour later, she was asleep. As for Saint-Lucq, he had remained awake for a moment, looking at the stripped plaster ceiling. He had no preference for the company of prostitutes but their bought hospitality had its advantages – one being that, unlike hoteliers, they did not keep a guest register.

The scratching continued.

Saint-Lucq rose, put on his breeches and his shirt, listened carefully, and drew back the nasty brown rag which served as a curtain to the sole window. The sound was coming from there. Daylight entered, and the silhouette of a black dragonnet was clearly visible behind the pane of glass.

The half-blood was still for a moment.

'Is he yours?'

The young woman – she claimed to be called Madeleine, 'like the other Magdalene' – sat up and, squinting in the light, grumbled:

'No. But it seems to think so . . . I made the mistake of feeding it two or three times. Now it won't stop coming here to beg for more.'

Truly wild dragonnets had almost disappeared in France. But those that were lost, had escaped or been abandoned by their masters, lived in the cities like stray cats.

'Find me something to feed him,' ordered Saint-Lucq as he opened the window.

'Oh, no! I want to persuade him to go elsewhere. And it's not—'

'I'll pay for it as well. Surely you have something he'll eat?'

Madeleine rose, naked, while the half-blood watched the dragonnet and the dragonnet watched the half-blood, with equal wariness. The reptile's scales shone in the light of the waning sun.

'There,' said Madeleine, bringing in a cloth tied together at the corners.

Saint-Lucq untied the linen and found a half-eaten dried-up sausage.

'That's all?'

'That's all,' confirmed the young woman, already back in bed. 'But there's a roast-meat seller on the street corner, if you like . . .'

Hand held flat, the half-blood presented a morsel of sausage to the dragonnet. The animal hesitated, sniffed, took the food in at the tip of its pointed muzzle, and seemed to chew it with some regret.

'You prefer your victims to be alive and fighting, don't you?' murmured Saint-Lucq. 'Well, so do I . . .'

'What are you saying?' asked Madeleine from the bed.

He didn't reply, and continued to feed the dragonnet.

A wyvern – which, ridden by a royal messenger, was returning to the Louvre – passed high above them, giving voice to a hollow cry from the skies. As though responding to the great reptile's call, the black dragonnet suddenly spread its leathery wings and was gone.

Saint-Lucq shut the window, swallowed the remains of the sausage and finished getting dressed.

'You're leaving?' asked Madeleine.

'So it would seem.'

'You have a meeting?'

'Yes.'

'Who with?'

The half-blood hesitated, then offered a truth so incredible it might as well be a lie.

'With the Grand Coësre.'

The prostitute laughed loudly.

'Oh, really! Say hello for me. And to the entire Court of Miracles, while you're at it . . . !'

Saint-Lucq simply smiled.

A minute later, he buttoned his doublet, hung his sheathed sword from his belt and fitted his strange spectacles with their crimson lenses. Then, from the attic room's threshold, the door already half-open, he turned and threw two pieces of silver on to the bed.

The gesture astonished Madeleine since she had already been paid for her services.

'That's a lot for a little bit of sausage,' she teased him.

'The first coin is for you to feed the dragonnet if it returns.'

'Done. And the second?'

'It's so you don't forget what the first is for.'

19

Arnaud de Laincourt lived on rue de la Ferronnerie which ran between the neighbourhoods of Sainte-Opportune and Les Halles, extending rue Saint-Honoré, skirting the Saints-Innocents cemetery and linking up with rue des Lombards, thus creating one of the longest routes through the capital. Broad, at almost four metres across, and heavily used, it was a place of sad memories: it was here that Ravaillac had stabbed Henri IV when the royal coach was halted by the busy street traffic. But this detail aside, Laincourt's address was quite commonplace. He rented accommodation in a house similar to many others in Paris: tall and narrow, crammed in between its neighbours, with a small shop on the ground floor – a ribbon seller, as it happened. Next to this establishment, a door for residents opened onto a corridor which passed through the building and led to a lightless staircase. From there, the top floors could be reached by following a shaky wooden banister up through the fetid air well.

Laincourt had his foot on the first step when he heard the squeak of hinges behind him in the shadowy corridor.

'Good morning, officer.'

It was monsieur Laborde, the ribbon seller. He must have seen him arrive, just as he saw everyone who came and went. In addition to the shop, he rented the three rooms on the first floor for himself and his family, as well as one poor, tiny room on the second floor for their maid. He was the principal lodger in the house. Because of this, he collected the rent and claimed to keep an eye on everything, puffed up with pride, jealous of the trust placed in him by the landlord, and very concerned about the respectability of the place.

Laincourt turned to greet him, suppressing a sigh.

'Monsieur Laborde.'

Like most members of the petty bourgeoisie, the ribbon seller evinced a fearful hatred of the popular masses, despised anyone poorer than himself, envied his equals and deemed them all to be upstarts, was quick to abase himself before those with power and always felt he needed to wriggle into the good graces of representatives of authority. He dreamed of being able to count Laincourt, an ensign with His Eminence's horse guards, amongst his customers.

'I invite you to do me the honour of passing by my shop sometime, monsieur. I have received some swathes of satin which, if I am to believe my wife, would look quite wonderful on you if made up into a doublet.'

'Ah.'

'Yes. And you know as well as I do how the ladies have an eye and a taste for such things.'

Laincourt could not stop himself from thinking of Laborde's wife and the metres of coloured ribbons which adorned the least of her dresses, although in all honesty none of these could be described as 'the least' once one had seen the imposing dimensions of the lady in question.

'True elegance is in the detail, isn't it?' insisted the tradesman.

Detail. Another word which sat poorly with the enormous madame Laborde, who raised her little finger when she sipped her chocolate and gobbled up pastries as though eating for four.

'No doubt,' said Laincourt with a smile which said nothing. 'Good day, monsieur Laborde.'

The ensign climbed as far as the second floor and, passing in front of the garret door where the ribbon seller's maid slept, he entered his own rooms. His apartment was made up of two very ordinary rooms, that is to say: cold and gloomy ones, where the air circulated poorly. But he didn't have much reason to complain as each had a window – even if one looked onto a dirty courtyard and the other into an alley so narrow that one could touch the opposing wall with an outstretched arm. His furniture was meagre: a bed and a chest for clothes in the bedroom; and a table, a rickety sideboard and two chairs in the second room. This furniture, moreover, did not belong to him. With the exception of the chest, they had all been there when he arrived and would remain there when he left.

In order not to compromise the impeccable cleanliness of his rooms, Laincourt's first care was to remove his stained boots, promising himself he would soon clean off the black and stinking muck they had acquired from the Parisian streets. Then he hung his belt from the same nail which held his felt hat with its white plume, and took off his cape.

There were writing implements on the table and Laincourt set to work at once. He had to re-transcribe the letter he had read at midday in Charpentier's – Richelieu's secretary – tiny study. He copied it out from memory, only he used Latin vocabulary combined with Greek grammar. The result was a text which, while not entirely undecipherable, could not be read by anyone without a perfect knowledge of both languages – which remained the province of scholars alone. The ensign didn't hesitate even once as he filled a page with lines of cramped writing, and he didn't release the quill until he had penned the final full stop.

He was waiting, motionless and impassive, for the ink to dry, when someone knocked on the door. Laincourt turned his head towards it, frowning.

As the knocking was insistent, he resolved to go and open the door. When he did, he saw the Labordes' servant, a nice girl with pink cheeks who nursed a secret crush on the young ensign of the Cardinal's Guards.

'Yes?'

'Good morning, monsieur.'

'Good morning.'

'I don't know if you know, but a gentleman came here.'

'A gentleman.'

'Yes. He asked some questions about you.'

'Questions to which monsieur Laborde no doubt zealously replied . . .'

The servant nodded, embarrassed, as if a little of her master's abject nature reflected on her.

'Did he give his name, this gentleman?' asked Laincourt.

'No.'

'How did he look?'

'He was tall, slightly handsome, with black hair. And he had a scar on his temple . . . He did not give any cause for alarm, but he was . . . frightening.'

The ensign nodded, inscrutable.

At that moment, madame Laborde called out for her maidservant, who made haste to answer the summons.

'Thank you,' said Laincourt, as she took leave with a brief curtsey.

Having closed the door again, he returned to his writing table and slipped the transcription of the letter into a thin leather envelope. He carried it to the chair, lifted the rug, dislodged a floorboard and hid the secret document before returning everything to its normal place.

Or almost.

As he saw at once, a corner of the rug remained rolled up: an obvious discrepancy which was at odds with the perfect order of the room.

The ensign hesitated for a moment, then shrugged and prepared to leave. He pulled his fouled boots back on, strapped on his belt, took his hat and threw his folded cape over his shoulder. In the distance, the Sainte-Opportune bell-tower tolled the half-hour, almost immediately followed by the Saints-Innocents church.

20

At *Les Petites Grenouilles*, Marciac woke sated and happy in a very rumpled bed, and leaned on an elbow to watch Gabrielle as she brushed her hair, sitting half-naked in front of her dressing table. This sight made his joy complete. She was beautiful, the folds of cloth which barely covered her had all the elegance of the drapery of ancient statues, and the light of the setting sun shining through the window made the loose strands of hair at the nape of her slender neck iridescent, flattered her pale round shoulders, and outlined the curve of her satiny back in amber. It was one of those perfect moments when all the harmony of the world is combined. The room was silent. Only the faint sound of the brush caressing her smooth hair could be heard.

After a moment, Gabrielle caught her lover's gaze in the mirror and, without turning, broke the spell:

'You should keep the ring.'

The Gascon saw the prize that he had won in the duel. Gabrielle had removed it from her finger and placed it near her jewel case.

'I gave it to you,' said Marciac. 'I shall not take it back again.'

'You need it.'

'I don't.'

'Yes, you do. To repay La Rabier.'

Marciac sat up in bed. Gabrielle, her back still turned to him, continued to brush her hair, saying no more.

'You know about that?' he said.

She shrugged.

'Of course. All secrets are known in Paris. All you have to do is listen . . . Do you owe her much?'

Marciac didn't reply.

He let himself fall back onto the bed, arms opened wide, and contemplated the canopy above his head.

'As much as that?' said Gabrielle in a quiet voice.

'Yes.'

'How did you let it come to this, Nicolas?'

There was both reproach and commiseration in the tone of her voice – a tone which was, ultimately, very maternal.

'I played, I won, I lost triple,' explained the Gascon.

'Mother Rabier is a vicious woman. She can harm you.'

'I know.'

'And the men she employs have blood on their hands.'

'I know that as well.'

Laying her brush down, Gabrielle turned in her chair and fixed Marciac with a clear and penetrating gaze.

'She should be paid. Would this ring be enough?'

'It would be enough to make a start.'

'Then it's decided.'

They exchanged a smile. A smile full of affection from her, and one full of gratitude from him.

'Thank you,' he said.

'Don't mention it.'

'I should consult you over every decision I make.'

'If you merely do the opposite of whatever your whim dictates, all will be well.'

Smiling easily, Marciac rose and began to dress while his mistress drew on her stockings, another spectacle of which he missed nothing.

Then, without preamble, Gabrielle said:

'A letter arrived here for you.'

'When?'

'Today.'

'And as you were still furious with me,' guessed the Gascon while lacing his breeches, 'you burnt it.'

'No.'

'Not even tore it up?'

'No.'

'Nor crumpled it?'

'You're infuriating, Nicolas!' exclaimed Gabrielle.

She had almost shouted, and then, stiffening, stared straight ahead.

As they had often teased each other like this, he couldn't explain her reaction. His chest bare, he watched the woman he loved and detected her anguish.

'What is it, Gabrielle?'

With her index finger, she discreetly wiped a tear from the corner of her eye. He approached her and, leaning over her from behind, held her gently.

'Tell me,' he murmured.

'Forgive me. It's for you.'

Marciac took the letter she held out to him, and understood her distress when he saw the emblem stamped into the red wax seal.

It was that of Cardinal Richelieu.

'I thought . . .' said Gabrielle in a strangled voice, 'I thought that this period of your life was over.'

He had thought so too.

21

The sun was still high when Agnès de Vaudreuil arrived in sight of the village. Her doublet open and her sheathed rapier beating against her thigh, she was covered in the dust raised by her galloping horse's hooves since she left the manor with all speed. She had pink cheeks and her face shone with sweat. Thrown into disarray by the ride, her long plait was now a mess of loose braids barely held together at their ends, with many full black curls having already escaped completely. Her face, however, still expressed a combination of relentless determination and contained anger. And her gaze remained fixed on the objective towards which her foaming mount progressed without flagging.

From a mere hamlet, the village had grown up around its church at the crossroads between two roads which wound between wooded hills. It was still only a staging post on the Chantilly road and it owed its incipient prosperity to *The Silver Cask*, an inn renowned for the quality of its cellar and kitchen, and the amiable company of its serving girls. Local people went there for a glass of wine on occasion and well-informed travellers would happily sleep there – on their outward journey if their business did not require them to be in Chantilly at daybreak, or else upon their return.

Agnès slowed as she passed the first houses. In the streets her horse trod the same beaten ground as on the road, and she guided it into the heart of the village at a trot. In front of *The Silver Cask*'s porch, the villagers were dispersing. They smiled and chattered with one another, sometimes making grand gestures. One of them climbed on to a mossy stone bench and raised a laugh by miming blows and vigorous kicks up the arse. All of them seemed delighted, as though they were leaving a theatre where they had seen an exceptionally funny farce. Agnès guessed who might be behind this festive mood, which didn't bode well. Just because the spectators were delighted did not mean that the spectacle itself had been pleasant. In these times, crowds gathered to witness the public punishment of condemned criminals, and were greatly amused by the many howls and twitches of the unfortunates being thus tormented.

On seeing the horsewoman pass, some of them doffed their caps, and the clown climbed down from his bench.

'Who is that?' asked someone.

'The baronne de Vaudreuil.'

'Our Lady!'

'As you say, my friend. As you say . . .'

The Silver Cask was a picturesque sight with its crooked buildings, its old and beautiful grey stone, its façades covered with ivy and its red-tiled roofs.

Agnès dismounted just beyond the porch, her spurs jingling as the heels of her riding boots touched the cobblestones of the courtyard. She wiped her shining face with the back of her sleeve, unbound her hair and shook her head to make her heavy black curls fall into place. Then, dishevelled, dusty and yet heedless of anyone's glance, she looked around.

She recognised the innkeeper standing in front of the main building, trying to calm the impatience, if not the anger, of several patrons. Nervous and agitated, they were vying with one another for the chance to roundly scold the man, punctuating each angry point with jabs of their index fingers at his chest. The innkeeper made appeasing gestures expressing his most fawning respect, all the while preventing anyone from entering the building. But his efforts proved unsuccessful. His customers would not be soothed, and Agnès noticed that the appearance of a few of them – if not quite as disorderly as her own – left something to be desired. One had the right sleeve of his doublet, torn at the shoulder, tightly wrapped around his elbow; another, shirt hanging out from his breeches, was pressing a wet cloth against his face; a third was wearing a badly dented hat, and his lace collar hung down miserably.

Finally, remarking on her arrival, the innkeeper excused himself from the gentlemen. They grumbled while he hastened to greet Agnès. On his way, he hailed a stable boy, who abandoned his bucket and pitchfork to busy himself with the baronne's horse.

'Ah, madame! Madame!'

She walked towards him with a firm step. And as she neither slowed her pace nor changed her course when they met, he was forced to make an abrupt about-turn and trot along at her side.

'What has he done now?' asked Agnès.

The innkeeper was a small, dry, thin man, although sporting a pot-belly as round as a balloon. He wore a short waistcoat over his shirt, and his figure was squeezed by the belt of his apron, which fell to his thighs.

'Thank the Lord, madame. You're here.'

'Rather than heaven, thank the boy you sent to warn me, master Léonard . . . Where is Ballardieu? And what has he done?'

'He's inside, madame.'

'Why are all these people waiting outside?'

'Because their coats or bags are still within, madame.'

'Then why don't they collect them?'

'Because monsieur Ballardieu will not let anyone in.'

Agnès halted.

Caught unawares, the innkeeper was two steps past her before he followed suit.

'Pardon me, master Léonard?'

'It's just as I said, madame. He threatens to shoot anyone who opens the door in the head, unless it is you.'

'Is he armed?'

'Only with a pistol.'

'Is he drunk?'

Master Léonard had the air of a man who was not quite

certain he understood the question and was afraid of committing a faux pas.

'Do you mean: more drunk than usual?'

The baronne gave an aggravated sigh.

'Yes, that's exactly what I mean.'

'Then yes, madame. He is drunk.'

'Plague on the old toss-pot! Can he not indulge within reason?' she said to herself.

'I believe he never learned how, madame. Or else he has no desire to do so—'

'So how did all this start?'

'Ah, well,' the innkeeper hesitated . . . 'There were these gentlemen . . . Please note, madame, that they had enjoyed an excellent meal and that it was more the wine than themselves that was talking . . .'

'I see. And then?'

'A few of their comments displeased monsieur Ballardieu—'

'—who, in his way, let them know it. Very well, I understand. Where are they, these gentlemen?'

The innkeeper was astonished.

'They're still inside, madame!'

'So who are those three over there, covered with bumps and bruises?'

'Just those who attempted to intervene.'

Agnès raised her eyes to the sky then continued to walk towards the inn and, in addition, towards those standing outside it. Master Léonard hurried ahead of her to open a path.

Seeing that she was about to enter, an elegant officer who had only remained to be entertained by the comedy of the situation, said to her:

'Madame, I advise you against opening this door.'

'Monsieur, I advise you against preventing me,' the baronne replied in a flash.

The officer drew back his shoulders, more surprised than annoyed. Agnès suddenly understood that he had only meant to be gallant. She softened.

'Never fear, monsieur. I know the man conducting the siege inside.'

'What?' interrupted the man with the dented hat. 'You know that raving madman?'

'Have a care with your remarks, monsieur,' said Agnès de Vaudreuil glacially. 'He of whom you speak began some work upon you which I could easily complete. And it would cost you a little more than a hat.'

'Would you like me to accompany you?' the officer insisted politely.

'No, thank you, monsieur.'

'Know, nevertheless, that I shall be ready if needed.'

She nodded and entered.

Low-ceilinged and silent, the room had been thrown into an upheaval of fallen chairs, toppled tables and shattered crockery. Splatters of wine stained the walls where jugs had been broken. Several panes of glass were missing from a window. A serving platter had been cracked. In the hearth, the spit was only held up by one forked support and the counterweight mechanism designed to keep it turning clicked uselessly.

'Finally!' exclaimed Ballardieu in the tone of someone welcoming a long-hoped-for visitor.

He was enthroned in triumph in the middle of the chaos, sitting on a chair, one foot leaning against a supporting beam to balance himself. His red velvet doublet was open over his massive chest, hairy and sweating, and his smile was huge, seeming full of reckless joy despite – or perhaps because of – his split lip and swelling eye. Ballardieu was one of those who took delight in a good brawl.

He held a wine bottle in one hand and, in the other, something which looked like a wooden skittle.

'Finally?' Agnès was astonished.

'Of course! We've been waiting for you!'

' "We"? Who is this "we"?'

'These messieurs and myself.'

Tearing her incredulous gaze away from the old soldier

with great difficulty, Agnès observed the men. They were all a sorry sight to see, having received a severe chastising.

Two very richly dressed men – merchants no doubt – were piled up one on top of the other, either unconscious or pretending to be. Another – most likely a pedlar – had scarcely fared better: he was sitting with his arms and chest pinned inside a large wicker basket through the bottom of which his head had burst, the latter now swaying woozily on his neck. Lastly, a fourth member of the party was huddled up at Ballardieu's feet, and his cringing manner indicated that he feared another thump. This one the baronne knew by sight at least: he was a veteran who had lost a leg in the Wars of Religion, and henceforth, hobbling around, dedicated his days to a tour of the local inns.

'You've left them in a pretty state,' commented Agnès.

She noticed that the veteran was missing his wooden peg-leg, and suddenly realised it was the skittle-shaped object with which Ballardieu was playing.

'They deserved it.'

'Let us hope so. Why have you been waiting for me?'

'I wanted this man, right here, to offer you his apologies.'

Agnès looked at the unfortunate one-legged man who, trembling, was protecting his head with his forearms.

'Apologies? For what?'

Ballardieu suddenly found himself extremely embarrassed. How could he explain, without repeating the vulgar and abusive comments that had been made about her?

'Uhh . . .'

'I'm waiting.'

'The important thing,' continued the old soldier waving the wooden peg-leg like a sceptre . . . 'The important thing is that this lout offers his apologies. So, lout, speak up! The lady is waiting!'

'Madame,' groaned the other, still seeking about for his prosthesis, 'I beg you to accept my most sincere and respectful apologies. I have ignored all my obligations, which not even my poor nature, my neglected education and my deplorable habits can justify. I promise to mind my conduct and manners in future and, conscious of my faults, I deliver myself to your goodwill. I add that I am ugly, have a mouth like an arse and that it is difficult to believe, having seen me, that the Almighty made Adam in his own image.'

The man had recited this act of contrition in a single breath, like a practised speech, and Ballardieu had followed the tirade with regular shakes of his head and the synchronous movements of his lips.

The result appeared to satisfy him.

'Very good, lout. Here, take back your leg.'

'Thank you, monsieur.'

'But you forgot to mention your ugly mug, which is—'

'—so foul it turns milk into piss. I'm sorry, monsieur. Should I start again?'

'I don't know. Your repentance seems sincere to me, but . . .'

Ballardieu questioned Agnès with a look.

She simply stared at him, dumbstruck.

'No,' he said again. 'Madame la baronne is right: that will suffice. The punishment must be just and not cruel if it is meant to be a lesson.'

'Thank you, monsieur.'

Ballardieu rose, stretched, emptied his flagon of wine in two swallows and threw it over his shoulder. At the end of a beautiful arc through the air, the aforementioned flagon bounced off the pedlar's head, who was still sitting imprisoned in his wicker pannier.

'Good!' cried Ballardieu joyfully, rubbing his hands together. 'Shall we go?'

Behind him, the stunned pedlar tipped over onto his side like an overturned basket.

22

Alerted by her son, the woman appeared on the threshold of the thatched cottage to see the rider who had just arrived. With a word, she ordered her son to go and bring her something from inside. He was quick to obey, returning with a wheel-lock pistol which he handed to his mother.

'Go and hide, Tonin.'

'But mother—'

'Go and hide under the bed and don't come out unless I call you.'

The afternoon was drawing to close, with a faint warm breeze in the air. There were no other dwellings anywhere around the cottage for as far as the eye could see. The nearest village was a good mile away, and the road leading there passed by some distance away. Even pedlars and sellers of almanacs only rarely stopped off to visit them. In this lonely corner of the French countryside, the inhabitants were by and large abandoned to their own devices.

Remaining at the door alone, the woman checked that the pistol was loaded and that the gunpowder in the chamber was dry. Then she let the weapon hang at the end of her arm, slightly behind her body, out of the rider's sight as he entered the yard where a few hens pecked at the brown sun-beaten ground.

She barely nodded when Antoine Leprat greeted her from his mount.

'I should like to water my horse. And I would be glad to pay you for a glass of wine.'

She studied him for a long while without saying a word.

Badly shaven, grimy and bedraggled, he seemed exhausted

and hardly inspired either confidence or fear. He was armed: pistols were tucked in the holsters on his saddle and a curious white rapier hung at his side — his right side, as though he were left-handed. His night-blue doublet was open over a sweat-stained shirt and its sleeve, up by the shoulder, had a nasty gash through which a recent bandage could be glimpsed. Fresh blood had trickled over his hand, a sure sign that his wound had reopened.

'Where are you going?' asked the woman.

'To Paris.'

'By these roads, you won't reach Paris before nightfall.'

'I know.'

She continued to study him.

'You're wounded.'

'Yes.'

After his battle with Malencontre and his hired killers, Leprat had not immediately realised that he was bleeding. In the heat of the action, he had not noticed which of his adversaries had cut his arm. Nor had he felt any pain at the time. In fact, the wound had only begun to trouble him when he saw the threads of blood running from his sleeve and making his right hand sticky. It wasn't particularly dangerous, but the gash deserved medical attention. Leprat had simply applied a makeshift bandage and immediately returned to the road.

'An unlucky encounter,' he explained.

'With brigands?'

'No. Assassins.'

The woman didn't blink.

'Are you being followed?'

'I was being followed. I don't know if I still am.'

Since leaving the staging post Leprat had followed the minor roads which, although not the shortest route, reduced the risk of being ambushed. He travelled alone and his wound made him easy prey for ordinary brigands. But also he feared there was another ambush laid for him along the Paris road, set by those who had put the mercenaries on his trail.

'I will see to your wound,' said the woman, no longer

making any effort to conceal the pistol she held. 'But I don't want you to stay.'

'I ask only for a bucket of water for my horse and a glass of wine for myself.'

'I will see to your wound,' she repeated. 'I will look after you, and then you will leave. Come in.'

He followed her into the house, whose interior consisted of one large, dark and low-ceilinged room, poor but clean, with a few pieces of furniture on the hard-earth floor.

'You can come out now, Tonin,' the woman called.

While her son climbed out from beneath the bed and offered a timid smile to the stranger, she prepared a basin of water and clean linen cloth, all the while keeping the pistol close at hand.

Leprat waited until she pointed him to a bench before sitting down.

'My name is Leprat,' he said.

'Geneviève Rolain.'

'And I'm Tonin!'

'Hello, Tonin,' said Leprat with a smile.

'Are you a gentleman?' asked the boy.

'I am.'

'And a soldier?'

'Yes.'

'My father was a soldier, too. Of the Picardy regiment.'

'A very old and very prestigious regiment.'

'And you, monsieur? In which regiment do you serve?'

Predicting the reaction he would provoke, Leprat announced:

'I serve in a company of His Majesty's mounted musketeers.'

'With the King's Musketeers?' Tonin marvelled. 'Really? Did you hear, mother? A musketeer!'

'Yes, Tonin. You're shouting quite loudly enough for me to hear you —'

'Do you know the king, monsieur? Have you ever spoken to him?'

'A few times.'

'Go and water monsieur the musketeer's horse,' Geneviève interrupted, placing a basin of water on the table.

'But mother?'

'Now, Antoine.'

The boy knew it was never a good sign when his mother switched from 'Tonin' to 'Antoine'.

'Yes, mother . . . Will you still tell me about the king, monsieur?'

'We'll see.'

Delighted by this prospect, Tonin left the house.

'You have a lovely little boy,' said Leprat.

'Yes. He's at that stage where they dream of nothing but glory and adventure.'

'It is a stage which does not always pass with the coming of manhood.'

'And thus his father died.'

'I'm sorry to hear that, madame. He fell in battle?'

'Soldiers are quicker to die of hunger, cold or disease than a thrust from a sword . . . No, monsieur, it was the ranse which took my husband during a siege.'

'The ranse,' Leprat murmured, as though evoking an old and dreaded enemy . . .

It behaved like a virulent disease, and originated from dragons and their magic. The dragons – or more accurately their distant descendants of human appearance – suffered little from it, but the men and women who frequented their company for too long a period were rarely spared. The first symptom was a small mark on the skin, scarcely more alarming than a beauty spot, and which often went unnoticed in an age when people did not wash and never took off their shirts. The mark grew, becoming purplish in colour and rough to the touch. Sometimes it would slowly develop black veins and begin to crack open, oozing pus, while deeper tumours would develop underneath. This was known as the 'Great ranse'. Then the patient became contagious and felt the first pains, the first lumps, the first deformities, and the first monstrosities . . .

The Church saw this as clear proof that dragons were evil

incarnate, to the extent that they could not even be approached without mortal danger. As for seventeenth-century medicine, it was impotent to either fight or prevent the ranse, whether great or small. Remedies were sold, to be sure, and new cures appeared in the apothecaries' dispensaries and the smooth-talking vendors' stalls almost every year. But most of these were nothing but the work of more or less well-intentioned charlatans or practitioners. As for allegedly more serious medications, it proved impossible to measure their effectiveness objectively because those afflicted were not all equally susceptible to the ranse. Some passed away after two weeks, while others lived for a long time after the appearance of the first symptoms and suffered little. Meanwhile, you could still encounter other unfortunate victims in the final stages of the disease who, having been transformed into pitiable monsters, were reduced to begging on the streets to survive. They were obliged to wear a red robe and announce their presence by shaking a rattle, when they were not forcibly incarcerated in the recently founded Hospice des Incurables in Paris.

Shrugging away her bad memories, Geneviève helped Leprat remove his doublet. Then she unwound the bandage he had hastily wrapped around his bicep, over his shirt sleeve.

'Your shirt now, monsieur.'

'Rip the sleeve, that will suffice.'

'The shirt is still good. You just need to have the tear sewn up.'

Leprat reflected that the price of a new shirt was not the same for a gentleman as for a countrywoman forced to make economies.

'It is,' he admitted. 'But please, close the door.'

The woman hesitated, with a glance at her pistol, but finally went to shut the door which still stood open to the yard. Then she lent a hand to the musketeer, who was stripping to the waist, and understood immediately when he bared his muscular back.

Large, coarse and purplish splotches of the ranse spread across it.

'Do not fear, madame. My illness has not yet reached a

point where it could affect you. But it's a sight that I'd rather spare your son.'

'Do you suffer?'

'Not yet.'

23

Sitting at a table in an empty tavern whose keeper was sweeping the floor at the end of a very long day, the Gascon was glowering into the bottom of his glass when he realised someone was standing nearby.

'Captain.'

'Good evening, Marciac.'

'Please, take a seat.'

'Thank you.'

La Fargue pulled a chair towards him and sat down.

A second glass, as clean as one might hope for in such an establishment, was placed on the table. Marciac took and filled it for the old man.

It was the dregs of the jug. Barely a mouthful.

'Sorry, captain. It's all that's left.'

'It will do.'

La Fargue didn't touch his glass and, while the silence stretched out, noticed the crumpled letter which the Gascon had received in rue de la Grenouillère.

'The Blades are recalled to service, Marciac.'

The other nodded, pensive and sad.

'I need you, Marciac.'

'Mmh.'

'The Blades need you.'

'And who are they?'

'The same as before. Other letters have been sent. They will be arriving soon.'

'The same as before. That's to say: those who still live.'

'Yes.'

The silence fell again, thicker than before.

Finally, Marciac burst out:

'I have a life now, captain.'

'A life which pleases you?'

They exchanged a long glance.

'Which pleases me well enough.'

'And where is it leading you?'

'All lives lead to the cemetery, captain. What matters is to make the path pleasant.'

'Or useful.'

'Useful? Useful to whom?'

'We serve France.'

'From the sewers.'

'We serve the king.'

'And the cardinal.'

'It's the same thing.'

'Not always.'

Their conversation, sharp and delivered like a lethal clash of blades, ended with these words. Averting his eyes, Marciac drained his glass and asked:

'Will we be justly rewarded?'

'With neither honour nor glory, if that's your idea. In that respect, nothing has changed.'

'Let us speak of finances instead. If I accept I want to be paid handsomely. Very handsomely. On the day and hour specified. At the first delay, I hang up my sword.'

La Fargue, intrigued, blinked slowly.

'Agreed.'

The Gascon allowed himself a few moments of further thought while he examined his steel signet ring.

'When do we start?' he asked.

24

There were a dozen courts of miracles in Paris. All of them were organised according to the same hierarchy, inherited from the Middle Ages: they consisted of an enclosed area where the communities of beggars, criminals and other marginal elements could congregate. Scattered through the capital, they took their name from the professional mendicants – the kind with fake diseases and fake mutilations – who were 'miraculously' restored to good health after a hard day of begging, once they were far from the inquisitive eyes of outsiders. Cour Sainte Cathérine was one such refuge, situated in the Saint-Denis neighbourhood; another was to be found on rue du Bac; and a third near the Saint-Honoré market. But the most famous court, the one which had earned its status as the Court of Miracles – with capital letters and without further reference – was the one on rue Neuve-Saint-Sauveur, near the Montmartre gate.

According to a chronicler of the times, it was located in 'the worst-built, the dirtiest and the most remote district of the city' and consisted of a vast courtyard dating from the thirteenth century. It was rank, muddy, surrounded by sordid, rickety buildings, and hemmed in by the tangled and labyrinthine alleys behind the Filles-Dieu convent. Hundreds of beggars and thugs lodged here with their women and children, so that there were at least a thousand inhabitants in all, ruling as absolute masters over their territory, permitting neither intrusions nor strangers nor the city watch, and ready to repel them all with insults, thrown stones and bludgeons. When, eight years earlier, a new street was supposed to be laid nearby, the workers were attacked and the project had to be abandoned.

Jealous of its independence, the insubordinate little world of the Court of Miracles lived according to its own laws and customs. It was led by one man, the Grand Coësre, who Saint-Lucq was waiting to meet this afternoon. Through the slimy glass of a first floor window, from behind his red spectacles, he observed a large, sorry-looking and at this hour almost deserted cul-de-sac – it would only become animated at nightfall when the thugs and beggars returned from their day of larceny and mendicity in Paris. The décor had something sinister and oppressive about it. Those who ventured here unawares would sense that they were in enemy territory, and being spied upon, just before the inevitable ambush.

The half-blood was not alone.

An old woman dressed entirely in black kept him company, sitting in her corner she nibbled on a wafer like a rabbit chewing a chicory leaf, clasping it between the fingers of her emaciated hands, her eyes lost and vague. Tranchelard was there too, the thug Saint-Lucq had threatened earlier. The man endeavoured to make the atmosphere as unpleasant as possible with a heavy silence and a fixed black glare directed against the visitor, his hand on the pommel of his sword. Back turned, Saint-Lucq was unaffected. Minutes passed in this room, where the mottled and stained appearance of the floor, the walls and the door frames contrasted with the motley collection of luxurious furniture and carpets stolen from some mansion or wealthy bourgeois house. Nothing but the old woman's chewing disturbed the silence.

Eventually, preceded by a severe-looking individual with a noticeably receding hairline, the Grand Coësre arrived.

Slender and blond, the Grand Coësre was no more than seventeen years old, an age when one was already reckoned an adult in these times, but he seemed rather young to be leader of some of the toughest and most frightening members of the Parisian underworld. He nevertheless displayed all the self-assurance of a feared and respected monarch, whose authority was never disputed without blood and tears flowing from the challenge. His right cheek carried the scar from a badly-healed gash. His clear eyes shone with cynicism and intelligence. He was unarmed, certain that that no harm would befall him in his own stronghold where a mere glance on his part could condemn another to death.

While the Grand Coësre settled himself comfortably on the high-backed armchair reserved for his use, the man who had held the door for him moved to his side, standing straight and expressionless. Saint-Lucq knew him. His name was Grangier and he was an *archisuppôt*. Within the strict hierarchical organisation of the Cour des Miracles, archisuppôts ranked just below the Grand Coësre, along with the *cagoux*. The latter were responsible for organising the troops and training new recruits in the arts of picking pockets and eliciting compassion – and money – from strangers. The archisuppôts, in contrast, were often highly educated judges and advisors. A defrocked priest, Grangier had his master's ear due to his formidable perspicacity.

Saint-Lucq bowed his head, but did not remove his hat.

'I must admit you're not lacking in courage,' the Grand Coësre observed without preamble. 'If anyone but you behaved like this, I would think I was dealing with a cretin.'

The half-blood didn't respond.

'To come here after having manhandled two of my men and threatened to cut poor Tranchelard's throat—'

'I had to be sure he would not forget to pass on my message.'

'You realise that he now speaks of nothing but disembowelling you?'

'He's of no importance.'

Tranchelard bristled, visibly itching to draw his sword. As for his undisputed master, he burst out laughing.

'Well! You can always boast later of how you piqued my curiosity. Speak, I'm listening.'

'It concerns the Corbins gang.'

At hearing these words, the Grand Coësre's face darkened.

'And?'

'Recently, the Corbins have seized certain goods. Precious, fragile merchandise. Merchandise of a kind which, up until now, had never interested them. Do you know what I am referring to?'

'Perhaps.'

'I would like to find out where they stash their goods. I know the place is not in Paris, but nothing more than that. You, on the other hand . . .'

The master of the Cour des Miracles paused for a moment without speaking. Then he leaned towards Grangier and said a few words to him in *narquois*, a language which was incomprehensible to the uninitiated. The archisuppôt replied in the same idiom. Without reacting, Saint-Lucq waited for their secretive discussion to end. It was brief.

'Supposing I have the information you seek,' the Grand Coësre said to him. 'Why should I tell you?'

'It's information for which I'm willing to pay full price.'

'I'm already rich.'

'You're also a bastard without faith or morality. But above all, you are a shrewd man.'

'Which is to say?'

'The Corbins are making inroads into your territory. Because of them, your influence and your business revenues are shrinking. But, in particular, they don't take their orders from you.'

'This problem will soon be resolved.'

'Really? I can resolve it for you now. Tell me what I want to know, and I will deliver the Corbins a blow from which they will have trouble recovering. You can even take the credit if you want . . . We don't like one another, Grand Coësre. And no doubt, one day or another, blood will be spilt between us. But in this matter our interests coincide.'

The other stroked his well-trimmed moustache and goatee thoughtfully, although they were still not so much hair as down.

'This merchandise is precious to you, then?'

'To you, it's worth nothing.'

'And for the Corbins?'

'It is worth the price they have been offered. I think they are only hirelings in this business and soon they will deliver the goods to their employers. For my purposes, it will be too late to act once that occurs, and you will have lost a beautiful opportunity to give them a taste of their own medicine. Time is short.'

'Allow me an hour to consider it.'

The man and the half-blood exchanged a long glance, in which each delved into the heart of the other.

'One hour, no more,' Saint-Lucq stipulated.

Once Saint-Lucq had gone, the Grand Coësre asked his archisuppôt:

'What did you make of that?'

Grangier took a moment to reflect.

'Two things,' he said.

'Which are?'

'To begin with, it is in your interest to help the half-blood against the Corbins.'

'And then?'

Rather than replying, the archisuppôt turned towards the old woman who, he knew, had followed his chain of thought. Between nibbles of her wafer, her gaze still directed straight ahead like someone either blind or indifferent to the world, she said:

'The following day, he will have to be killed.'

25

Within the Cardinal's Guards, the troops received their pay every thirty-six days. This occasion demanded a roll call, which was also an opportunity to take a precise count of the Cardinal's manpower. The guards lined up. Then the captain or his lieutenant walked past with a list in hand. Each man in turn called out his name, which was immediately ticked off the list. Each ticked name was then copied out onto a list which was certified and signed by the ranking officer. This document was given to the paymaster, and the guards would go – in good order – to receive their due at his office.

Today, it had been decided that roll call would take place at five in the afternoon, in the courtyard of the Palais-Cardinal, since His Eminence was currently residing there. Unless they were excused, all the guards not currently on duty thus found themselves collected here. They were impeccably turned out – boots polished, capes pressed and weapons burnished. They waited to be called to attention and chattered amongst themselves, enjoying the idea of soon being a little richer. They might have been gentlemen in social rank, but most of them lacked fortunes of their own and lived on their pay. Happily, the cardinal paid well – fifty livres for a guard and up to four hundred for a captain. But above all, he paid punctually. Even the prestigious King's Musketeers were not remunerated so regularly.

Sitting by himself on a windowsill, Arnaud de Laincourt was reading when Neuvelle joined him. The young man, delighted to be taking part in his first roll call, was beaming.

'So, monsieur Laincourt, what will you do with your hundred-and-fifty-four livres?'

It was the pay grade of an ensign with the Cardinal's Guards.

'Pay my landlord, Neuvelle. And also my debts.'

'You? You have debts? That's not like you. Don't take this the wrong way, but I can't imagine you burning through money . . .'

Laincourt smiled amiably without replying.

'Let's see,' continued Neuvelle. 'I have observed that you don't drink and you scorn the pleasures of the table. You don't gamble. You're not vain. Do you have a hidden mistress? Rumour has it that you give all you have to good works. But you can't run into debt through acts of charity, can you?'

'My debts are with a bookseller.'

Neuvelle made a face while curling up the tips of his slender moustache, between his thumb and index finger.

'Myself, I read nothing but monsieur Renaudot's *Gazette*. You can always find a copy of it lying about somewhere. The news is sometimes a little dated, but I always find myself rather well informed.'

Laincourt nodded, his blue eyes expressing nothing other than an amiable and patient reserve.

It had been two years since Théophraste Renaudot began to produce – with royal dispensation – a highly popular news journal which was hawked on the streets. Every week his *Gazette* comprised thirty-two pages and two slim volumes – one dedicated to 'News from the East and the South', the other to 'News from the West and the North'. It also contained information pertaining to the French court. To this was added a monthly supplement which summarised and then enlarged upon the news from the preceding weeks. It was common knowledge that Cardinal Richelieu exerted tight control over everything which was printed in the *Gazette*. He had, on occasion, even taken up a pen himself and contributed to it under his own name. And, surprising as it seems, even the king did not scorn to comment on events which related closely to him in the *Gazette*.

'What are you reading at this hour?' asked Neuvelle to make conversation.

Laincourt offered him his book.

'Goodness!' said the young guard. 'Is that Latin?'

'Italian,' explained the officer, abstaining from further comment.

Like most gentleman of the sword, Neuvelle was almost illiterate. However, he could not hide his admiration of Laincourt's learning:

'I've heard that in addition to Latin and Greek you understand Spanish and German. But Italian?'

'Well, yes . . .'

'And what does this work speak of?'

'Draconic magic.'

A bell-tower, and a few others nearby, sounded three quarters of the hour, indicating to the assembled guards it was time to prepare for the roll call. Neuvelle returned the book as though it were some compromising piece of evidence and Laincourt slipped it beneath his cape and into his doublet.

At that moment, a lackey wearing the cardinal's livery walked towards them.

'Monsieur Laincourt, the service of His Eminence calls you before monsieur de Saint-Georges.'

'Now?' Neuvelle was astonished, seeing the troops being formed up.

'Yes, monsieur.'

Laincourt reassured the young guard with a glance and followed the lackey inside.

After climbing a staircase and a long wait in an antechamber, Arnaud de Laincourt saw, without real surprise, who awaited him beneath the high carved ceilings of the captain's office. The room was vast and impressive in length, its gold and its woodwork burnished to a high gleam in the daylight which shone in through two enormous windows in the rear wall. These windows opened onto the main courtyard and through them came the sound of roll call, now almost over.

Stiff and impassive, six guards renowned for their loyalty stood at attention, three to the right and three to the left, opposite each other, as though showing the way to the grand desk at which captain Saint-Georges was sitting with his back to the light. Stood close to him, and slightly further back, was Charpentier.

The presence, in this place and under these circumstances, of Richelieu's private secretary could only signify one thing, and Laincourt realised this immediately. He waited until the lackey had closed the door behind him, then took one slow step forwards between the guards. Old Brussand was one of their number and seemed to be struggling with his emotion; he stood more stiffly than the others and was almost trembling.

As all present held their breath, Laincourt pulled himself together and saluted.

'By your order, monsieur.'

Saint-Georges, his gaze severe, rose and walked around his desk.

And holding out his hand before him, he ordered in an irrevocable tone:

'Your sword, monsieur.'

At the same moment, the beat of a drum outside announced the end of the roll call.

26

'You know that it's not your fault, don't you?'

Agnès de Vaudreuil jumped as though she'd been poked in the kidneys with a blazing poker. She had been dozing and, startled by the voice, dropped the book which had been lying open on her lap. A feeling of surprise tinged with fear took hold of her, but a second was enough for her to realise that she was alone. Besides, the voice that she had heard or dreamed could only have been speaking from beyond the grave.

As soon as she returned from the inn with Ballardieu she had shut herself away in her favourite room in the manor, a very long hall almost devoid of furniture, where, when it fell, the silence seemed greater than anywhere else in the house. On one side, old suits of armour on their pedestals alternated with panoplies and racks of mediaeval weaponry. On the other side, through four tall windows with stone mullions, daylight fell in oblique rays – against which the armour seemed to be mounting a resolute guard. Two large chimneys opened their blackened brick mouths at each end of the hall originally intended to host banquets. But the chairs and the immense table had been removed, and the great iron chandeliers now looked down on empty flagstones.

Agnès was drawn to this room when times were bad, either alone or with Ballardieu. She liked to take refuge here to read, reflect or simply to wait until another day, or sometimes another night, was over. For this purpose she had arranged an area for her use around the one fireplace which could still serve against the early frosts. There was an old leather-covered armchair there, a table polished by age and use, a worm-eaten old chest, some shelves where she stored her treatises on fencing, and an old quintain.

Her entire world was here.

On this afternoon, Agnès was taking her ease with a book. She had hung her belt over the quintain, removed her boots and her thick red leather corset, and then she had ensconced herself comfortably in the armchair, legs stretched out and ankles crossed on the chest before her. But she was clearly more tired than she had thought. Sleepiness had won as she thumbed through a chapter dedicated to the comparative merits of quadruple and sextuple parries against a point lunge delivered by an adversary with the advantage of a longer reach.

Then there came the voice:

'You know that it's not your fault, don't you?'

Agnès' gaze fell on the quintain.

Before reaching the ultimate disgrace of becoming a porte-manteau, it had served as training mannequin for fencers for a long time. Its horizontal arms had been shortened by two-thirds and its bust – firmly fixed to a solid base which no longer allowed it to pivot – was covered with notches, the number of which increased in proportion to their proximity to the heart symbol engraved on the wood. It was Ballardieu, the soldier to whose care Agnès had been abandoned by her father, who had brought this worm-eaten device in from the field where it had then been serving as a scarecrow. At the time, still a child, the future baronne had to struggle, with both hands, in order to lift a rapier that was almost as tall as she. But she had refused to use any other.

The cry of a wyvern nearby tore through the silence.

Agnès pulled on her boots, rose, laced up her leather corset which fastened at the front, and, with her baldric slung over her shoulder and her sheathed rapier crossing her back, she headed for the courtyard on which the first shadows of the evening were beginning to encroach.

The wyvern rider was already climbing down from his white mount, its broad leathery wings now folded against its flanks. The beast's colour and the man's livery were unmistakable: he was a royal courier. He had evidently come straight from the Louvre.

After he had assured himself of the identity of the baronne de Vaudreuil and had saluted respectfully, the wyvern rider held out a letter drawn from the great reptile's saddle bags.

'Thank you. Is an immediate response expected?'

'No, madame.'

Seeing Marion appear on the kitchen threshold, Agnès directed the royal messenger to her so that he could partake of a glass of wine and whatever else he desired before setting out again. The man thanked her and left Agnès in the company of his wyvern which, calm and docile, twisted its long neck around to observe its surroundings with a placid eye.

Agnès broke the wax seal showing the Cardinal Richelieu's arms and, without expression, read the contents.

'What is it?' asked Ballardieu coming over for news.

She didn't reply at once, but turned her head and stared at him for a few moments.

And then, finally, for the first time in a very long while, she smiled.

27

That evening three riders passed through the Buci gate – or Bussy, as it was written then – entering the vast and peaceful faubourg surrounding Saint-Germain abbey. They rode down rue du Colombier at a slow walk, soon reached rue des Saints-Pères, passed Les Réformés cemetery and, in front of La Charité hospital, turned into rue Saint-Guillaume.

'Here we are,' said La Fargue, stepping down from his horse.

Marciac and Almades shared the same expression as they looked towards the huge gates before which they had stopped – these were massive and gloomy, with two carved, rectangular wooden panels fixed in place with large round-headed nails. They also dismounted and, as their captain rapped the wrought iron knocker three times, they observed the tranquil street which forked halfway along its length towards rue de Saint-Dominique. There were only a few people walking on its filthy paving stones beneath the golden and crimson skies at sunset, and its tradesmen were packing away their stalls. The vague odour of cooking mingled with the excremental scent of Parisian muck. Not far away, a fistful of knotted hay served as a sign for a local tavern.

'It's barely changed,' said the Gascon.

'No,' the Spanish master at arms replied laconically.

A door for pedestrians had been cut into one of the great panels of the carriage gate. This door was pushed open slightly and, from within, a voice inquired:

'Who's there?'

'Visitors,' replied La Fargue.

'Are they expected?'

'Their presence has been called for.'

This curious exchange made Marciac smile with nostalgia.

'Perhaps we should change the passwords,' murmured Marciac to Almades. 'It's been five years, after all . . .'

The other made a face: right now, all that mattered was whether the door would open for them. And it did.

La Fargue going first, they passed through the small door one by one, leading their mounts by their bits to make them lower their heads. As soon as they crossed the threshold the horses' shoes clattered loudly against the paving stones, filling the courtyard into which they emerged with echoes.

It was a massive old residence built in a severe architectural style, entirely out of grey stone, which a strict Huguenot had commissioned according to his specifications, following the massacre on the feast day of Saint-Barthélemy in 1572. It evoked the ancient fortified manors which still survive in some parts of the French countryside, whose walls are veritable ramparts and whose windows can be used as embrasures. A high wall separated the courtyard from the street. To the right, as one entered, rose the scabby, windowless wall of the neighbouring building. Opposite the gates were two coach doors leading into the stables, which were topped by a hay loft. Finally, to the left, the main building stood at an angle. Flanked by a turret and a dovecote, it comprised a tier of tiny attic windows embedded in its slate rooftop, two rows of stone-mullioned windows looking on to the courtyard, a protruding study and a ground floor which could be reached by a short flight of steps.

Abandoning his horse Marciac climbed these steps, turned towards his companions who had remained behind, and declared with affected pomposity:

'And so we have returned to Hôtel de l'Épervier, the House of the Sparrowhawk which, as you can see, has lost none of its charms . . . Damn!' he added in a lower tone. 'This place is even more sinister than I recalled, which I hardly believed possible . . .'

'This house has served us well in the past,' declared the

captain. 'And it will serve again. Besides, we are all familiar with it.'

Having closed the pedestrian door again, the person who had granted them admission now came to join them.

The old man limped on a wooden leg. Small, skinny, dishevelled, he had bushy eyebrows and his bald head was surrounded with a crown of long thin yellowish-white hair.

'Good evening, monsieur,' he said to La Fargue, holding a large bunch of keys out to him.

'Good evening, Guibot. Thank you.'

'Monsieur Guibot?' interrupted Marciac, coming closer. 'Monsieur Guibot, is it really you?'

'Indeed, monsieur, it's me.'

'I thought I recognised your voice but . . . have you really been guarding these sorry stones for the past five years?'

The man reacted as though someone had insulted his family:

'Sorry stones, monsieur? Perhaps this house is not very cheerful and no doubt you will find, here and there, a few cobwebs and some dust, but I assure you that her roof, her structure, her walls and her floors are solid. Her chimneys draw well. Her cellars and stables are vast. And of course, there is always the small door at the bottom of the garden which leads to a dead-end alley which—'

'And her?' Almades interrupted. 'Who is she?'

A young woman in an apron and white bonnet hovered on the threshold to the main building. Plump and blonde, with blue eyes, she smiled timidly while wringing her hands.

'This is Naïs,' Guibot explained. 'Your cook.'

'What about madame Lourdin?' inquired Marciac.

'She passed away last year, monsieur. Naïs is her niece.'

'Is she a good cook?'

'Yes, monsieur.'

'Can she hold her tongue?' asked La Fargue, who had his own sense of priorities.

'She is, so to speak, mute, captain.'

'What do you mean, "so to speak"?'

'She is so timid and bashful that she almost never utters a word.'

'That's not exactly the same thing . . .'

Naïs hesitated to approach, and La Fargue was about to beckon her closer when the knocker on the carriage gate was heard again. It took everyone by surprise and even made the young girl jump.

'It's him,' Guibot announced with a hint of worry in his voice.

The captain nodded, his silver hair touching the collar of his grey doublet.

'Let him in, monsieur Guibot.'

' "Him"?' asked the Gascon while the porter obeyed. 'Who is "he"?'

'Him,' said the captain lifted his chin towards the gentleman who entered the courtyard leading a bay horse by the bridle . . .

Somewhere between forty-five and fifty years old, he was tall, thin and pale, patently smug and self-assured, dressed in a crimson doublet and black breeches.

Marciac recognised him even before he caught sight of the man's well-groomed moustache and the scar on his temple.

'Rochefort.'

28

As was his habit, the young marquis de Gagnière dined at home, early and alone. An immutable ritual governed even the tiniest details of the meal, from the perfect presentation of the table to the silence imposed on the servants, as they presented a series of dishes prepared by a famous and talented rôtisseur who was accustomed to the tastes of the most demanding of his customers. The crockery laid out on the immaculate linen tablecloth was all made of vermeil, the glasses and decanters were all crystal, the cutlery silver. So luxuriously dressed that he would dazzle at court, Gagnière ate with a fork according to an Italian fashion which had not yet become commonplace in France. He cut small, equal pieces which he chewed slowly, emotionless and stiff, his gaze always directed straight ahead, and pausing between each dish he placed his hands flat to either side of the plate. When he drank he took care to wipe his mouth and moustache in order to avoid dirtying the edge of the glass.

He had finished a slice of pheasant pie when a lackey, taking advantage of one of the pauses between dishes, murmured a few words into his ear. The marquis listened without betraying any emotion or moving a muscle. Then he nodded.

A little later, Malencontre entered.

His manner was defeated; he was filthy and bedraggled, stank like a stable, had his hair stuck to his face and his left hand trussed up in a grimy bandage.

Gagnière accorded him one clinical glance.

'I gather,' he said, 'that all did not go according to plan.'

A stuffed quail was placed before him, which he proceeded to meticulously carve up.

'Your men?' he asked him.

'Dead. All of them. Killed to a man.'

'By one man?'

'Not just any man! It was Leprat. I recognised his rapier.'

Gagnière lifted a morsel of quail to his mouth, chewed, and swallowed.

'Monsieur Leprat,' he said to himself. 'Monsieur Leprat and his famous ivory rapier . . .'

'A musketeer!' insisted Malencontre as though that justified his failure. 'And one of the best!'

'Did you think the king would entrust his secret dispatches to comical lackeys . . . ?'

'No, but—'

'The letter?'

'He still has it.'

The marquis finished his quail while Malencontre watched his expressionless young face in silence. Then, having crossed his fork and spoon on his plate, he rang a small bell and said:

'You can go, Malencontre. And take proper care of your hand; you'll be less useful to me without it.'

A lackey entered to serve him and the assassin, in leaving, passed a servant who carried a sealed missive on a plate. He presented it to Gagnière, who carefully unsealed and opened it.

It was written in the vicomtesse de Malicorne's hand.

Your man has failed. The courier will arrive at the Saint-Denis gate before midnight. The letter must not reach the Louvre.

The marquis refolded the paper and allowed himself one last mouthful of wine.

At the same moment Leprat, travelling alone, was riding into the sunset on a dusty and empty road.

Lying against his heart, in the folds of his shirt, beneath his dust, sweat and dried blood stained doublet, he carried a secret piece of diplomatic mail which he had sworn to defend even at the cost of his life. Exhausted and wounded, weakened by the illness which patiently ate away at him, he galloped towards Paris and nightfall, unaware of the dangers which awaited him.

The Spanish Chevalier

1

Huge torches lit the Saint-Denis gate when the chevalier Leprat d'Orgueil arrived there an hour after nightfall. Tired, grimy, his shoulders slumped and his back in torment, he was scarcely in a better state than his horse. As for that poor beast, its head drooped, it was struggling to put one foot in front of the other, and was in danger of stumbling with every step.

'We're here, my friend,' said Leprat. 'You've certainly earned the right to a week's rest in the stable.'

Despite his own fatigue he held his pass out with a firm hand, without removing his plumed felt hat or dismounting. Distrustful, the city militia officer first lifted his lantern to take a better look at this armed horseman with a disturbing, dangerous air: unshaven cheeks, drawn features and a hard gaze. Then he studied the paper and upon seeing the prestigious signature at the bottom, he displayed a sudden deference, saluted and ordered the gate opened.

Leprat thanked him with a nod of the head.

The Saint-Denis gate was a privileged point of access to the city of Paris. Pressed up against the new rampart and fortifications to the west that now encircled the older faubourgs, it led into rue Saint-Denis which crossed the entire width of the city's Right Bank from north to south, stretching as far as Le Châtelet and the Pont au Change bridge. During the day this almost straight arterial road teemed with turbulent, noisy life. Once twilight fell, however, it became a narrow trench that was quickly filled with mute, menacing shadows. Indeed, all of Paris offered this dangerous visage to the night.

Leprat soon realised that he was being watched.

His instincts warned him first. Then the peculiar quality of an expectant silence. And, finally, a furtive movement on a rooftop. But it was only when he drew level with La Trinité hospital that he saw the barrel of a pistol poking out between two chimneys and he suddenly dug heels into his mount.

'YAH!'

Startled, his horse found a last reserve of energy to surge forward.

Gun shots rang out.

The balls whistled past, missing their targets.

But after a few strides at full gallop, the horse ran straight into an obstacle which slammed into its forelegs. Neighing in pain the animal fell heavily, never to rise again.

Leprat freed himself from the stirrups. The shock of impact was hard, and a sharp pain tore at his wounded arm. Grimacing, he got to his knees—

—and saw the chain.

Parisian streets had capstans at either end which made it possible to stretch a chain across the roadway – an old mediaeval device designed to obstruct the passage of the rabble in the event of a riot. These chains, which could not be unwound without a key, were the responsibility of officers of the militia. They were big and solid, too low to stop a rider but high enough to oblige the horse to jump. And in the darkness, they had been turned into a diabolical trap.

Leprat realised then that the gunmen's main objective had not been to shoot him, and that this was the true ambush, on the corner of rue Ours, not far from one of the rare hanging lanterns lit by the city authorities at twilight, which burned until their fat tallow candles were extinguished.

Three men emerged in the pale glow and more were arriving. Gloved and booted, armed with swords, they wore hats, long dark cloaks and black scarves to hide their faces.

Leprat got to his feet with difficulty, unsheathed his ivory rapier and turned to face the first of the men charging towards him. He dodged one and let him pass, carried on by his momentum. He blocked the second's attack and shoved the third with his shoulder. He struck, pierced a throat, and recoiled *in extremis* to avoid a blade. Two more masked killers presented themselves. The chevalier d'Orgueil broke away and counterattacked at once. He seized one of his new assailants by the collar and threw him against a wall while continuing to defend himself with his sword. He parried, riposted and parried again, endeavouring to set the rhythm of the engagement, to repulse or elude one adversary in time to take on the next. Although being left-handed gave him a small advantage, the reopened wound on his arm handicapped him and his adversaries had the advantage of greater numbers: when one faltered, another took his place. Finally, he skewered the shoulder of one and with a violent blow of his pommel, smashed in the temple of another. This attack earned him a vicious cut to his thigh, but he was able to step back as the combatant with the wounded shoulder fled and his partner fell dead on the muddy pavement.

The two remaining assassins paused for a moment. They moved prudently, with slow gliding steps, to corner the chevalier. He placed himself *en garde*, his back to the wall, careful to keep both of them in his field of vision. His arm and thigh were giving him pain. Sweat prickled in his eyes. As the assassins seemed unwilling to take the initiative, Leprat guessed that they were expecting reinforcements, which were not long in arriving: three men were coming down rue Saint-Denis at a run. No doubt the same men who had fired on him from the rooftops,

Leprat could not afford to wait for them.

He altered his guard slightly, pretending to attack the adversary to his left and thereby offering an opening to the one on the right, only to abruptly change his target. The ivory caught a ray of moonlight before slicing cleanly through a fist which remained clenched around a sword hilt. The amputee screamed and beat an immediate retreat, clutching his stump which was bleeding in vigorous spurts. Leprat promptly forgot him and pivoted in time to deflect a sword thrust aimed at his face. Parrying twice, he seized an over-extended arm, pulled the man towards him and head butted him full in the mouth, then followed it with a blow of the knee to his crotch and finally delivered a reverse cut with his sword that slit the man's throat.

Letting the body fall into the blood-soaked mud, the chevalier snatched a dagger from its belt and made ready to face the three latecomers. He deflected the first thrust with his white rapier, the second with the dagger and dodged the third which, rather than slicing through his eye as far as his brain, merely left a scratch across his cheek. Then he shoved one brawler away with a blow from his boot, succeeded in stopping the blades of the two others with a high parry, and with the ivory grating beneath the double bite of steel, heaved them both back and to the side, forcing their blades downward. His dagger was free: he stabbed it into one assailant's exposed flank three times. Pressing his advantage, Leprat planted a foot firmly on a boundary stone and, spinning into the air, decapitated the man he had just kicked away before the latter managed to fully recover his balance. A bloody scarlet spray fell in a sticky rain over the chevalier d'Orgueil and his third, final opponent. They exchanged a number of attacks, parries and ripostes, each advancing and retreating along an imaginary line, mouths drawn into grimaces and exchanging furious glares. At last the assassin made a fatal error and his life came to a swift end when the slender ivory blade slid beneath his chin and its stained point exploded from the back of his head.

Drunk from exhaustion and combat, weakened by his wounds, Leprat staggered and knew he was in a bad way. A violent retch doubled him over and forced him to lean against a door as he vomited up long strands of black ranse phlegm.

He believed the fight was over, until he heard a horse approaching at a slow walk.

Keeping one hand against the wall at whose foot he had vomited, Leprat peered to one side, his tired eyes straining to make out the rider advancing towards him.

He was a very young and very elegant gentleman with a blond moustache, mounted on a lavishly harnessed horse.

'My congratulations, monsieur Leprat.'

All his limbs in agony, the chevalier made an effort to

straighten up, although he felt as if even a breath of wind would knock him over.

'To those with whom I am unacquainted, I am "monsieur le chevalier d'Orgueil".'

'As you wish, monsieur le chevalier d'Orgueil. I beg your pardon.'

Leprat spat out the remains of blood and bile.

'And you. Who are you?'

The rider offered a sympathetic smile and levelled a loaded pistol at the chevalier.

'It is of very little importance, monsieur le chevalier d'Orgueil, if you carry my name with you to your grave.'

The chevalier's eyes flared.

'A man of honour would face me with his feet on the ground and draw his sword.'

'Yes. No doubt he would.'

The marquis de Gagnière took aim and shot Leprat with a pistol ball straight to the heart.

2

In bed a little earlier than usual, Armand Jean du Plessis de Richelieu was reading when he heard the scratch at the door. Candles were burning and on this cold spring night a huge, greedy log fire burned in the hearth. Of the three secretaries who shared the cardinal's chamber, always ready to take down a letter by dictation or to provide the care which their master's failing health required, two slept on trestle beds arranged against the walls while the third stayed awake on a chair. This one rose, and after a nod from His Eminence, opened the door slightly, then wider still.

A Capuchin monk in his fifties entered. Dressed in a grey robe and shod in sandals, he silently approached the grand four-poster bed in which Richelieu was sitting, his back propped up against pillows to allay the pain in his back.

'This missive has just arrived from Ratisbonne,' he said, presenting a letter. 'No doubt you would like to read it before tomorrow.'

Born François-Joseph Leclerc du Tremblay, and known to the world as Père Joseph, he was of a noble family and had received a solid military education before joining the Capuchins at the age of twenty-two, by religious vocation. A reformer of his order and also founder of the Filles du Calvaire congregation of nuns, he had distinguished himself through his zeal and his sermons to the royal court. But above all, he was the famous 'Grey Eminence', the most intimate and influential of Richelieu's confederates, to whom His Eminence was prepared to entrust certain affairs of state. He sometimes took part in the deliberations of the king's Council and later became a minister of the Crown in his own right. A sincere friendship, a mutual high esteem and a shared view on the policies needed to counter Habsburg influence in Europe united the two men.

Closing his copy of Plutarch's *Lives*, the cardinal took the missive and thanked him.

'There is one other thing,' said Père Joseph.

Richelieu waited, then understood and ordered his secretaries out. When the one who was on duty had wakened and accompanied his colleagues into the next room, the monk took a chair and the cardinal said:

'I'm listening.'

'I would like to speak to you again about your . . . Blades.'

'I thought this matter was settled between us.'

'I yielded to you without being persuaded by all of your arguments.'

'You know that men of such temper will soon be necessary to France—'

'There are other men beside these.'

Richelieu smiled.

'Not so many. And when you say "these", you're thinking "him", aren't you?'

'It is true that I have little love for monsieur de la Fargue. He is inflexible and has disobeyed you too often.'

'Really?'

Père Joseph launched into a rapid inventory, ticking each item off on his fingers.

'To refresh your memory: in Cologne, in Breda, and in Bohemia. And I've not even mentioned the disaster at La Rochelle—'

'If La Rochelle was torn from the bosom of France to become a Protestant republic, I do not think that the responsibility can be laid at Captain La Fargue's door. After all, if the dam we built had resisted the force of the ocean tides for a few more days, the outcome would be quite different today . . . As for the other events you mention, I believe that La Fargue only "forgot" his orders when doing so increased the chances of his mission's success.'

'He will always be headstrong. He is one of those men who never change.'

'I certainly hope so.'

Père Joseph sighed, reflected a moment, and then returned to his argument:

'And what do you think will happen when La Fargue uncovers the secret motives behind the task we are about to confer on him? He will feel deceived and, in view of his grievances against you, he could be tempted to ruin everything. If he stumbles across the comte de Pontevedra's true identity—!'

'He would have to stumble across the comte's existence first.'

'He will, without question. Your Blades are spies as much as they are soldiers. They have no end of craftiness and imagination, and we have seen them unravel far more complicated knots than this.'

It was His Eminence's turn to utter a sigh.

'If it comes to that, we shall take the necessary measures . . . For the moment, what matters is that this mission is vital for France. And for reasons with which you are well acquainted, the Blades are the ones best able to carry it out successfully – as well as the ones who must be prevented from learning about this cabal . . .'

'A curious paradox.'

'Yesterday I told the captain that I do not always have a choice of weapons. It's very true. In this business, the Blades are the weapon which I must employ. Spain has set her conditions. I have preferred to give her some degree of satisfaction rather than seeing her harm us.'

Père Joseph nodded resignedly.

'You're tired,' continued the cardinal in a solicitous, almost affectionate, tone. 'Take some rest, my friend.'

In the Palais-Cardinal the monk's chamber was next to Richelieu's. Père Joseph glanced at the door leading to it.

'Yes,' he said. 'You're right.'

'And if it helps you sleep, remember that we are speaking of a ship that has already set sail and cannot be recalled to port.'

Père Joseph look puzzled.

'At this very moment,' explained the cardinal, 'Rochefort is briefing La Fargue on the details of his assignment.'

'So the dice are thrown.'

3

'Thank you,' Marciac said to Naïs as she placed a bottle of wine on the table. 'You should go and lie down, now.'

The pretty young servant thanked him with a smile and, looking truly tired, took her leave accompanied by an admiring glance from the Gascon.

He and Almades were in the main room of the Hôtel de l'Épervier, where Naïs had just served them an excellent dinner. The remains of their meal and several empty bottles stood on the long oak table around which the Blades used to meet and, so it seemed, would be meeting once again. For the time being, however, there were only the two of them and the immense room seemed bleak. The fire in the hearth was not enough to brighten it, any more than it was enough to warm it. It crackled, sang, groaned and seemed to throw itself fiercely into a battle already lost against the advancing shadows, and the silence and the cold of the night.

'She's lovely, that girl,' offered Marciac, to make conversation.

The Spanish master at arms didn't respond.

'Yes, quite charming,' Gascon tried again.

Less carefree than he wished to appear, he drew a pack of cards from his pocket and proposed:

'Shall I deal you a hand?'

'No.'

'Name your game. Or a throw of the dice?'

'I don't play.'

'Everyone plays!'

'Not me.'

Discouraged, Marciac fell against the back of the chair, which creaked ominously.

'You've always been dreadful company.'

'I am a master of arms. Not an exhibitor of bears.'

'You're an entirely dismal individual.'

Almades drank three small sips of wine.

'Always in threes, hmm?' said the Gascon.

'Excuse me?'

'Nothing.'

With a heavy sigh, Marciac rose and walked around the room.

He was one of those men whose roguish charm and nonchalance is emphasised by their neglect of their appearance. His cheeks bore a three-day stubble a shade darker than his blond hair; his boots were in need of brushing and his trousers of ironing; his unbuttoned doublet gaped open over his shirt; and he carried his blade with a studied but unforced nonchalance that seemed to say: *Don't be fooled, old chap. I have a good friend at my side whose weight is so slight that she's no burden to me, and upon whom I can always rely.* His eyes, finally, glittered with laughter combined with a mocking intelligence; the eyes of a man no more easily deceived by himself than by life's great comedy.

Almades, on the other hand, was severity incarnate. Fifteen years older than the Gascon, black-haired and with a grizzled moustache, he was as economical with his gestures as he was with his words, and even at the best of times his long angular face expressed nothing but an austere reserve. He was neatly dressed despite wearing an old mended doublet; the feather was missing from his hat, while the cuffs and collar of his shirt bore lace that had seen better days. It could thus be guessed that he was poor. But his state of destitution in no way altered his dignity: it was simply one more test in life that he faced with a stoicism as proud as it was unshakeable.

While Marciac paced fretfully, the Spaniard remained like marble, head lowered, his elbows on the table and his hands clasped together around the tin beaker he was turning round and round and round.

Three turns, then a pause. Three turns, a pause. Three turns . . .

'How long have they been in there, do you reckon?'

The fencing master directed a dark, patient eye towards the Gascon. With a thumb, Marciac indicated the door behind which La Fargue and Rochefort were closeted together.

'I don't know.'

'One hour? Two?'

'Perhaps.'

'I wonder what they're saying. Do you have any idea?'

'No.'

'And it doesn't intrigue you?'

'When the time comes, the captain will tell us everything we need to know.'

Marciac, thoughtful, ran his nails up his stubbled cheeks.

'I could press my ear against the door and listen.'

'No, you couldn't.'

'Why not?'

'Because I forbid you from doing so, and I shall also prevent you.'

'Yes, of course you would. That's an excellent reason.'

The Gascon returned to his chair like a scolded schoolboy.

He drained his glass, refilled it and, rather than say nothing, asked:

'So what were you doing, during the past five years?'

Perhaps with the intention of diverting Marciac's attention from the door, Almades made an effort to reply.

'I practised my trade. In Madrid to begin with. Then in Paris.'

'Ah.'

'And you?'

'The same.'

'Because you have a trade.'

'Err . . . In fact, no,' the Gascon admitted.

But he added quickly:

'That's not to say I have not been very busy!'

'I don't doubt it.'

'I have a mistress. That can keep you occupied, a mistress.

Her name is Gabrielle. I shall introduce you to her when she stops hating me. Very beautiful, nevertheless.'

'Prettier than little Naïs?'

Marciac was known for his many amorous adventures.

He caught the allusion and, a poor loser, shrugged his shoulders.

'The one has nothing to do with the other.'

A silence fell beneath the dark ceiling, which the sound of the fire was barely able to fill.

'They don't care much for one another,' said the Gascon finally.

'Who?'

'La Fargue and Rochefort.'

'No one likes Rochefort. He does the cardinal's dirty work. A spy, and no doubt also an assassin.'

'And what are we, then?'

'Soldiers. We fight in a secret war, but it's not the same thing.'

'Nevertheless, there's a feud between those two which goes far beyond the ordinary quarrel.'

'You think so?'

'I'm sure of it. You've seen the scar Rochefort bears on his temple?'

Almades nodded.

'Well, never mention it in front of Rochefort when the captain is present. Rochefort could take it as a mocking reference. He might think you know how it got there.'

'And you . . . you know?'

'No. But I act as though I do. It gives me a certain air.'

The Spaniard let this remark pass without comment, but said:

'I'd like you to shut up now, Marciac.'

The door opened and Rochefort crossed the room without sparing a glance for either of them. La Fargue appeared behind him. He walked to the table, sat down astride a chair and, preoccupied, began to pick at the remaining food on the plates.

'So?' asked Marciac innocently.

'So we have a mission,' replied the veteran of numerous wars.

'Which is?'

'Briefly put, it is a question of serving Spain.'

Spain.

The sworn enemy of France: Spain, and her Court of Dragons.

The news fell as heavily as an executioner's axe on the block, and even the exceptionally reserved Almades raised a wary eyebrow on hearing it.

4

Armed with the information that the Grand Coësre had given him, Saint-Lucq waited for dawn before springing into action.

The location proved to be perfect for his purpose: discreet, hidden from the road by the wood that surrounded it and less than an hour from Paris. It was on the farthest fringe of the faubourg Saint-Jacques, a short distance from a hamlet whose presence was indicated by a silent bell-tower. An old mill, whose large waterwheel no longer turned, had been built on the bank of the river. Its stones stood firmly in place, but its roof – like those of the other buildings in the vicinity: a woodshed, a granary, a miller's house – had suffered from years of exposure to the weather. A solid wall still enclosed the abandoned property. Its front porch opened on to the only road which passed by, not much travelled since the mill had stopped working.

How did the Grand Coësre know the Corbins – the Crows – had established one of their hideouts in this place? And how did he know that Saint-Lucq would find what he wanted here? Perhaps it was of minor importance. All that mattered, in the end, was that the information was accurate. The reasons that had persuaded the king of the Cour des Miracles to help the half-blood remained shadowy and unclear. Certainly, it would be in his interest if Saint-Lucq's plan succeeded and he made some mischief for the Corbins. The gang had held sway over the province and the faubourgs for the past two years and their attention had now turned to the capital. A battle for territory was brewing, which the Grand Coësre no doubt wished to forestall. But above all he feared that the Corbins' activities, even indirectly, would harm him to some greater or lesser extent in the long term. These highwaymen plundered, raped, were quick to use torture and often murdered. They terrorised the population and infuriated the authorities, who would ultimately react brutally and instinctively, mobilising a regiment out of necessity and erecting dozens of gibbets. The Corbins were running to their own destruction. However, not all of the blows directed against them would strike the gang. The Court of Miracles would also suffer the consequences and its leader wished to avoid them. Nevertheless, Saint-Lucq had played a dangerous game in going to find him in his fiefdom on rue Neuve-Saint-Sauveur and demanding information in such a challenging manner. Time was running short, to be sure, and the half-blood would stop at nothing to achieve his objectives. But one day he would pay the price for his audacity. The Grand Coësre's hand could not be forced with impunity.

A man was dozing in a chair in front of the miller's house, his sword hanging from the back of the chair and his pistol resting across his thighs. His hat was tipped down across his eyes, and he was wrapped up in one of the big black cloaks which were the gang's distinctive sign. He had been on guard, shivering in the cold, all night.

Another Corbin left the house. Dressed in leather and coarse cloth, he stretched, yawned, scratched his side with one hand and the back of his neck with the other, and then shook his accomplice by the shoulder. The guard sat up and stretched in turn. They exchanged a few words and then the man in leather walked away, undoing his belt as he went. He went into the woodshed where the horses were stabled, pulled down his trousers, squatted, urinated loudly with a sigh of ease and had begun to defecate when Saint-Lucq garrotted him from behind.

Unable to call for help, the brigand tried to seize the thin strap which bit into his flesh and stood up abruptly. The half-blood matched his movement without reducing the pressure on the strap and drew his victim with him as he backed up two steps. The Corbin's ankles were trapped inside his dropped breeches. His arms thrashing, he tipped over

backwards but could not fall as Saint-Lucq held him suspended halfway to the ground, strangling him under his own
weight. The man fought, struggling as much as he could. His
heels frantically dug into the urine-saturated ground. A death
rattle was torn from his chest as his face turned crimson. His
fingernails scratched deeply into his tortured throat, clawing
uselessly at the leather garrotte. Then he tried to strike back,
his fists furiously pummelling the air in front of the half-
blood's face. Saint-Lucq, impassive and focused, simply drew
his shoulders back. Terror emptied the remaining contents of
the unfortunate man's bowels. Brown, sticky faeces stained his
thighs before falling to the ground with a soft squelch. With
a final spurt of effort, the Corbin searched desperately for a
foothold, for some support, for a rescue which was not coming. His struggles weakened. Finally, his windpipe collapsed
and his sex released its last, smelly dregs. His tongue hanging
out, his eyes rolling up, the man slowly collapsed into his own
excrement, still held by his torturer.

The horses had barely stirred.

Dropping the soiled corpse, Saint-Lucq rewound his garrotte and pushed his red spectacles further up his nose before
going to look outside.

The brigand on guard duty was still at his post. Legs
stretched out and ankles crossed, fingers interlaced over his
stomach and his hat covering his eyes, he was dozing in a
chair, its back tipped against the wall of the house.

The half-blood drew his dagger and, advancing with a
determined step which he meant to be heard, walked towards
the man. The other heard his approach but mistook it for the
return of his companion.

'So? Feeling better?' he asked without raising his nose.

'No.'

The Corbin jumped with a start and dropped the pistol
resting across his thighs. Swiftly, Saint-Lucq slapped a hand
against his mouth to both silence him and force him back
down into his chair, and struck with his dagger, upwards
from beneath his chin. The blade went home with a dry
thump, pierced the brigand's palate and dug deep into his

brain. He died in an instant, his eyes wide-eyed and full of pain.

The half-blood dried the dagger on the Corbin's shoulder and left the body slumped limply on the chair, its arms hanging. He had counted six horses in the woodshed. Six minus two. Four men remained.

He went to the front door and pressed an ear to it before gently pushing it open. Inside, two brigands who had just risen were talking while eating a frugal meal. Both had their backs turned to him, with one sitting on a small upturned barrel and the other on a wobbly stool.

'We'll be running out of wine soon.'

'I know.'

'And bread. And you wanted to feed him—'

'I know, I know . . . But we'll be finished with this business today.'

'You said that yesterday.'

'Today, I tell you. They can't be much longer.'

Saint-Lucq entered silently. As he passed, he picked up a poker which had been abandoned on the mantelpiece above a long-unused fireplace.

'In any case, I'm not spending another night in this ruin.'

'You'll do as you're told.'

'We'll see about that!'

'No, you'll see. You remember Figard?'

'No. I never knew him.'

'That's because he disobeyed an order before you arrived.'

Saint-Lucq was on them quicker and more silently than any ordinary assassin. The first collapsed, his skull split by the poker. The second only just had time to rise before falling in turn, his temple shattered.

Two seconds, two blows. Two deaths. No cries.

The half-blood was on the point of letting the bloody poker fall onto the stomach of one of the dead bodies when he heard the squeak of hinges.

'So, lads?' someone said. 'Already busy stuffing your faces, are you?'

Saint-Lucq about-turned and flung out his arm.

The poker hummed as it whirled through the air and drove itself, hook first, between the eyes of the Corbin who, hatless and dishevelled, had so casually entered the room. Stunned, the man staggered backward and crumpled onto the floor.

Four and one made five – the count was still short.

His right hand tightening around the hilt of his sheathed rapier, Saint-Lucq slipped into the room the dead brigand had just come from.

Makeshift beds had been set up in there and, Saint-Lucq found the last surviving Corbin lying on one of them, paralysed by absolute terror. He was young, an adolescent of perhaps fourteen or fifteen years old. His lip sported no more than blond fuzz and bad acne ate at his cheeks. Woken with a start, he seemed unable to tear his gaze from the corpse and the wrought iron rod embedded in its face. The poker began to tip over very slowly, its point spattered with viscous fluid and lifting up a piece of skull bone which tore through the skin. With a final cracking sound, it toppled and fell to the floor with a clatter.

The sound made the adolescent quiver all over and he suddenly directed his attention towards the half-blood wearing red spectacles. Looking deathly pale and distraught, his eyes already filled with tears, he vainly tried to force out a few words, vigorously shaking his head – a quiet, desperate supplication. Rising from his bedcovers, he retreated until his hands and heels touched the wall. He wore nothing but a shirt and a pair of breeches, breeches that were now stained with urine.

'Mer . . . Mercy—'

Saint-Lucq took a slow step towards him and drew his sword.

Lucien Bailleux shook with fear, cold and exhaustion. He wore nothing but a nightshirt and the hard ground on which he was lying proved as chilled as the stones against which he sometimes leaned.

It had been three nights since he had been surprised, unsuspecting, in his sleep at home, in the apartment where he lived above his notary's office. They had gagged him before pulling a hood over his head and knocking him senseless. What had they done with his wife, who had been sleeping at his side? He had woken here, bound hand and foot, in a location he could only guess at due to the hood. He was attached to a wall by a short, heavy chain that ran around his waist. He had no idea on whose authority he was held. All he knew for sure was that he was no longer in Paris, but somewhere in the countryside. The noises from his present surroundings, which also allowed him to keep track of the passing days, had made that much clear to him.

Initially believing he had been abandoned he had chewed away his cloth gag and shouted, yelling until his voice broke. He'd finally heard a door open, the footsteps of several men in boots approaching and a voice, at last, saying to him:

'It's just you and us, here. No one else can hear you. But your shouting annoys us.'

'What . . . what do you want with me?'

Rather than answering him, they had beaten him. In the stomach and kidneys. A kick had even dislodged one of his teeth. He'd swallowed it, as his mouth filled with blood.

'Not the head!' the voice had said. 'We must deliver him alive.'

After that, the notary had done nothing to draw attention to himself. And the hours and the nights had dragged by, filled with anguish and uncertainty about his fate, and without anyone troubling to give him something to eat or drink . . .

Someone pushed the door open and entered.

Bailleux cowered reflexively.

'I beg you,' he mumbled. 'I will give you everything I have.'

His hood was removed and, once he grew used to the light, he saw a man squatting close beside him. The stranger was dressed as a cavalier, with a sword at his side and strange red glass spectacles covering his eyes. Something dark and threatening emanated from him. The notary grew even more frightened.

'Don't hurt me, please . . .'

'My name is Saint-Lucq. The men who abducted you are dead. I've come to free you.'

'Me . . . To free me . . . Me?'

'Yes.'

'Who . . . who sent you?'

'It's not important. Did you talk?'

'I'm sorry?'

'You've been beaten. Was it to make you talk? Did you tell them what you know?'

'Good Lord! What is this all about?'

The half-blood sighed and patiently explained:

'You recently discovered and read a forgotten testament. The testament indicated where a certain document could be found.'

'So, this is about . . . that?'

'Well?'

'No. I didn't say anything.'

Saint-Lucq waited.

'I swear to you!' the notary insisted. 'They didn't ask me a single question!'

'Good.'

Only then did the half-blood unfetter Bailleux, who asked:

'And my wife?'

'She is well,' replied Saint-Lucq, who in truth had no idea.

'Thank God!'

'Can you walk?'

'Yes. I am weak but—' There was the sound of a horse neighing in the distance and they heard hoof beats approaching. Leaving the notary to complete the task of freeing his ankles, Saint-Lucq went to the door. Bailleux took note of his surroundings. They were on the ground floor of a disused, dusty old water mill, close to the enormous grindstone.

Having risked a glance outside, the half-blood announced:

'Six horsemen. No doubt those to whom you were to be delivered.'

'Lord God!'

'Do you know how to fight? Or at least how to defend yourself?'

'No. We are lost, aren't we?'

Saint-Lucq spotted an old, worm-eaten wooden staircase and raced up the steps.

'Up here,' he said after a brief moment.

The notary followed him to the next floor, where the central driveshaft, attached to the hub of the huge waterwheel, joined the vertical axle which, passing through the floor, had formerly powered the grindstone.

The half-blood forced open a skylight.

'We have to slip out through here and let ourselves drop into the river. The current will carry us away. With a little luck, we won't be seen. Although it's a shame, because I had horses waiting for us in the wood.'

'But I can't swim!'

'You'll learn.'

5

That morning, reclining on a long, low seat, the vicomtesse de Malicorne was savouring the tranquillity of her flowering garden when the marquis de Gagnière was announced. The strange globe filled with its shifting darkness was next to her, on its precious stand, and she caressed it nonchalantly – as she might have stroked the head of a sleeping cat. The turbulent interior of the Sphère d'Âme seemed to respond to each stroke. Gagnière, arriving on the terrace, made a conscious effort to look elsewhere. He knew the dangers that the soul sphere represented. He also knew the use to which it was destined to be put, and the casual manner with which the young woman was treating this relic, entrusted to her by the Masters of the Black Claw, both worried and astonished him.

'Good morning, monsieur le marquis. What have you come to tell me at such an early hour?'

'Leprat is dead.'

'Leprat?'

'The messenger Malencontre and his men failed to stop between Brussels and Paris. Using your information I laid an ambush for him yesterday evening, near the Saint-Denis gate.'

'Monsieur Leprat . . .' sighed the young woman with a thoughtful look. 'Is that so?'

'One of the King's Musketeers,' Gagnière hastened to explain.

'And formerly one of the Cardinal's Blades. I told you you would be hearing more about them, didn't I?'

'Indeed. However—'

'You killed him?'

'Yes. With a pistol ball to the heart.'

'My congratulations. And the letter?'

The elegant marquis took a deep breath.

'He didn't have it.'

For the first time since their conversation began, the vicomtesse lifted her gaze to look at her visitor. Her angelic face remained unreadable, but her eyes burned with fury.

'Excuse me?'

'He did not have it on him. Perhaps he never had it at all.'

'So he was simply playing with us while the true messenger travelled discreetly, by a different route and without mishap?'

'I believe so.'

'Yes,' said the vicomtesse de Malicorne, contemplating her garden anew. 'It's certainly possible, after all . . .'

They were silent for a moment and Gagnière did not know what to do with himself; his perfect manners forbade him from taking a seat without invitation so he was forced to remain standing, ill at ease, his beige deer-skin gloves in his hand.

'If the letter is at the Louvre—' he began.

'That indicates that the king and the cardinal now know we represent a threat to France,' finished the pretty young woman. 'I'll wager that the prospect of facing the Black Claw within their kingdom does not enchant them.'

From the little smile she displayed, however, one could guess that this development, upon reflection, did not truly displease her.

'It's no use crying over spilt milk,' she concluded. 'For the moment we have other matters to attend to . . .'

She suddenly rose and, taking the arm of the marquis, asked him to stroll with her in the garden. This initiative surprised Gagnière, until he realised that the vicomtesse wished to be out of range of any listening ears. Even here, in her own home.

'You will recall,' she said at last, 'that our Spanish brothers and sisters promised to send us a trustworthy man. And so they have: Savelda is here in Paris.'

'I still think we should not let him know of our plans.'

'Impossible,' interrupted the vicomtesse. 'On the contrary,

give him a warm welcome. Do not hide anything from him and employ him as usefully as possible. If it is understood, between you and I, that Savelda's mission is to keep us under surveillance, then we should not reveal our suspicions. We must show ourselves to be grateful of the honour the Grand Lodge of Spain does us by placing a man of his worth at our disposal . . .'

'Very well.'

This matter being settled, the vicomtesse turned to another subject:

'When will you capture Castilla?'

'Soon. Tonight, even.'

'And the girl?'

'Castilla shall lead us to her and we will abduct her.'

'Charge Savelda with the task.'

'What—!'

'It will keep him busy. And that will leave us with a freer hand to prepare our first initiation ceremony. Once that has taken place, a Black Claw lodge shall exist in France and our Spanish brothers, jealous as they may be, shall not be able to do anything against us.'

'You will then take the rank of Master.'

'And you, that of First Initiate . . . but do not cry victory just yet. Many have failed because they were too quick to believe they had succeeded and did not see danger coming. In our case, I do foresee that there is danger.'

At the bottom of the garden, in a verdant nook, was a stone bench. The vicomtesse took a seat, and indicated to Gagnière that he should join her.

'There is one matter,' she murmured, 'about which Savelda and our masters must be kept in ignorance: one of our agents at the Palais-Cardinal was caught yesterday.'

'Which one?'

'The best. The oldest. The most precious.'

'Laincourt!'

'Yes. Laincourt . . . I still don't know how it was done, but it has happened. Monsieur de Laincourt was unmasked. He is under arrest now, no doubt waiting to be interrogated.'

'Where?'

'Le Châtelet.'

'Laincourt won't talk.'

'That remains to be seen. You will need, perhaps, to make sure of it.'

6

A long night had gone by since Captain Saint-Georges had solemnly requested his sword and in so doing indicated to Laincourt that he was under arrest for treason. The prisoner had then been led to Le Châtelet under a firm escort, where his last personal effects were removed before he was anonymously locked up. In the eyes of the world, he might just as well have vanished into the bowels of the earth.

He no longer existed.

In 1130, Louis VI had ordered a small fortified castle – or *châtelet* – built to defend the Pont au Change, which connected the Right Bank of the Seine to Ile de la Cité. Rendered useless by the construction of King Philippe Auguste's ramparts, the Grand Châtelet – as it was sometimes called to distinguish it from the Petit Châtelet built on the Left Bank at the mouth of the Petit Pont – lost its military function. But King Louis IX enlarged it, Charles IV remodelled it and Louis XII restored it. In the seventeenth century, Le Châtelet was the seat of the legal courts under the jurisdiction of the provost of Paris, while its dungeon housed the prison cells. These cells, located on various levels, were given nicknames. On the upper level were the common halls where prisoners were packed together: Beauvoir, La Salle, Barbarie and Gloriette; below that, there were three areas with individual cells: La Boucherie, Beaumont and La Griesche; lower still: Beauvais, another communal hall; and finally, in the very foundations of the place, were the worst of all, without air or light: La Fosse, Le Puits, La Gourdaine and L'Oubliette.

Laincourt had been accorded the honour of La Gourdaine, where he was forced to endure its rotting straw overrun with vermin. At least he had been spared the horror of La Fosse, a pit into which the prisoner would be lowered through a trap door, on the end of a rope. The bottom of that most infamous gaol cell was swimming in stagnant water and took the shape of an inverted cone, so that a prisoner could neither lie nor sit down, and was even denied the relief of something to lean against.

Since the door had been closed on Laincourt, the hours had passed, stretched out and silent, in absolute darkness. In the far distance he heard the echo of a scream, that of a prisoner gone mad in solitude or of some poor wretch being subjected to torture. There was also the sound of water falling slowly, drop by drop, into deep brackish puddles. And the scratching of rats against the damp stone.

And then suddenly, in the morning hours, a key scraped in the lock. A gentleman with a greying moustache entered, with whom the gaoler left a lit lantern before closing the door again.

Laincourt stood and, blinking his eyes, recognised Brussand.

'You shouldn't be here, Brussand. I'm in solitary confinement.'

'For you,' replied the other, handing him a flask of wine and a piece of white bread. The former ensign of the Cardinal's Guards gladly accepted the victuals. He tore into the bread but forced himself to chew slowly. Then, having swallowed a mouthful of wine, he asked:

'How were you able to get in here?'

'The officer in charge of admissions owed me a favour.'

'Was the favour you did him as big as this one?'

'No.'

'So now you are in his debt . . . That is regrettable and entirely unnecessary on your part. Nevertheless, you have my thanks . . . Now go, Brussand. Go before you compromise yourself completely.'

'Our time is short, in any case. But I want you to tell me something.'

Beneath his unshaved cheeks and drawn features, Laincourt gave a faint, pale smile.

'I owe you that much, my friend.'

'Just tell me that all this is untrue,' the old guard demanded. 'Tell me they've made a mistake on your account. Tell me that you are not the spy they accuse you of being. Tell me that and, in the name of our friendship, I will believe you and defend you!'

The prisoner stared at the old guard for a long time.

'I don't want to lie to you, Brussand.'

'So it's true?'

Silence.

'My God!' Brussand exclaimed. 'You . . . ? A traitor . . . ?'

Demoralised, disappointed, misled, and still incredulous, he retreated a step. Finally, like a man resigned to facing the inevitable, he took a deep breath and cried out:

'Then talk! Talk, Laincourt! Whatever happens, you will be judged and condemned. But spare yourself being subjected to questioning . . .'

Laincourt searched for the right words and then said:

'A traitor betrays his masters, Brussand.'

'So?'

'I can only swear to you that I have not betrayed mine.'

7

He woke up washed and bandaged in the room that he rented under the eaves of a house on rue Cocatrix, and he recognised the familiar décor as soon as he opened his eyes.

'So you have finally returned to us,' said a deep male voice.

Although he was rather modestly dressed, the gentleman sitting at his bedside had a natural elegance that signalled his superiority to common mortals from a hundred paces. He carried a sword, had laid his hat down close to hand and was holding a book which he now closed. He looked to be forty years old and he served in the King's Musketeers.

'Good morning, Athos,' said Leprat.

'Good morning. How are you feeling?'

Leprat sat up against the pillows with caution and took stock of his wounds. His arm was carefully bandaged, as was, beneath the sheets covering his naked body, his thigh. He was not in much pain, felt rested and had a clear mind.

'Surprisingly well,' he replied. 'The letter?'

'Don't worry, it has reached its destination. The duty officer at the Saint-Denis gate, to whom you so prudently entrusted it on your arrival in Paris, made no delay in delivering it to monsieur de Tréville . . . Are you hungry?'

'Yes.'

'That's an excellent sign.'

Athos picked up a basket which he placed on the bed between them and lifted the red-and-white chequered cloth to reveal sausage, cheese, a pot of pâté, half a round loaf of bread, a knife, two glasses and three bottles of wine.

'And so,' said Leprat while the other spread a thick layer of pâté on a slice of bread, 'I am alive.'

'Indeed. Here, this is for you, eat.'

The patient bit into the slice and found it only stimulated his appetite more.

'And how is it that I am still for this world?'

'Thank the heavens in the first instance. And monsieur de Tréville in the second . . . But start by telling me what you remember.'

Leprat searched his memories.

'Yesterday evening, after nightfall . . . it was yesterday evening, wasn't it?'

'Yes.'

'So, yesterday evening, after nightfall, I was caught in an ambush at the corner of rue Saint-Denis and rue aux Ours. I beat off most of my attackers, but the last, a gentleman, got the better of me. I remember that he shot me with a pistol ball to the heart, and after that – nothing.'

'Did you know your would-be assassin?'

'No. But from now on, I would recognise him amongst a thousand others.'

Athos nodded, thoughtful. He knew neither the details nor the heart of this mission and, being a discreet man, refused to pose any questions on the subject. He suspected that the chevalier knew little more than he did. He twisted around on his chair, unhooked Leprat's baldric from its back and said:

'This is why you should thank the heavens in the first instance. They made you left-handed.'

Leprat smiled.

'Because you are left-handed, you carry your sword on your right. The baldric comes over your left shoulder, protected the left-hand side of your chest and stopped the ball which was meant to pierce your heart. It was the force of impact alone that knocked you down, and senseless.'

'Thank God my assassin did not aim for my head . . .'

'Such are the fortunes of war. They are not always against us.'

The wounded man nodded in agreement and accepted the proffered glass of wine. He had sufficient experience to know that those in battle often owed their lives to luck.

'Although I can guess at the reason,' he said as their glasses clinked together, 'now tell me why I must thank monsieur de Tréville.'

Athos drained his glass before replying.

'Despite being alerted by the sounds of your fight, the clowns who were guarding the Saint-Denis gate only reached you at the moment when you were shot. Their arrival forced the assassin to flee. Naturally they believed you were dead at first, but then realised that you were not – or not quite. Thanks to the pass you had shown at the gate they knew you were a musketeer; one of them ran to find monsieur de Tréville while the others carried you to a doctor. Monsieur de Tréville rushed to you at once, rescued you from the claws of that quack, brought you back here and entrusted you to the good care of his own surgeon. And that's all.'

'That's all?'

'That's all.'

'But how does that explain why you now play nurse-maid?'

Athos shrugged.

'I was on duty last night,' he explained.

Cutting the discussion short, he rose, picked up his hat, and announced:

'And now I must leave you.'

'Are you returning to rue du Vieux-Colombier?'

'Yes.'

'With your permission, I'll come with you.'

'Really?'

'I believe I'm fit enough and monsieur de Tréville is no doubt waiting to hear my report . . . Just give me time to dress.'

'Very well. I shall wait for you in the corridor.'

Antoine Leprat lived on Ile de la Cité.

Dressed in clean clothes but sporting an ugly three-day beard, he was quick to rejoin Athos but begged him to permit a short stop with a barber. The other accepted all the more readily as he would also benefit from the barber's attentions. Monsieur de Tréville required that his Musketeers be – at the very least – presentable. A barber on rue de la Licorne left their cheeks clean-shaven and furnished them with the opportunity to relax and talk a little more.

'One thing intrigues me,' said Athos.

'What is that?'

'You only remember the cavalier who shot you, is that right? But the archers posted upon the Saint-Denis gate spoke of seeing a second cavalier . . . A rider dressed in light grey or in white, on a horse with a white caparison, who sat facing the first while you lay sprawled on the ground. To hear them speak, this latecomer was almost ghostly in appearance . . . And he lingered no longer than the other to be recognised.'

'I told you everything I can remember, Athos.'

Later, around ten o'clock, they crossed the Petit Pont. Like most of the bridges in Paris, the Petit Pont was built up; on either side of the narrow roadway stood a row of houses which could in no way be distinguished from those on an ordinary street and which made it possible to cross the Seine without ever catching a glimpse of the river. On the Left Bank, they followed rue de la Harpe and then rue des Cordeliers as far as the Saint-Germain gate, where they were slowed by an impatient, agitated crowd. But such delays in passing through the city gates were an unavoidable ordeal for anyone wishing to leave Paris or reach its faubourgs.

The capital was indeed fortified in its fashion. Punctuated by turrets topped with conical 'pepper pots', the mediaeval walls measured over four metres in height and overlooked a series of ditches. They were supposed to protect the city in times of war, whether domestic or foreign. However, these defences did not seem at all warlike in this period. One would search in vain for the smallest cannon. The ditches were filled with rubbish. And the ramparts were falling into ruin despite the best efforts of the city authorities to rebuild them. Parisians, who could not be fooled, said that their walls were made of nothing more than potter's clay and that one shot from a musket could create a breach, while a drum roll would be enough to bring them tumbling to the ground. Nevertheless, it was not possible to enter Paris except through one of these gates. They were large buildings as outmoded as they were dilapidated, but they accommodated the Paris tax collectors, as well as the city's militia. The first levied taxes on all merchandise entering the city while the second examined foreigners' passports. Both groups carried out their duties zealously, which did nothing to speed the flow of traffic.

Once they reached the faubourg Saint-Germain, Athos and Leprat passed before the church of Saint-Sulpice and, taking rue du Vieux-Colombier, entered the gates to the Tréville mansion.

Monsieur de Tréville being the captain of the King's Musketeers, this building was more like a military encampment than a great man's residence. It was filled with a jostling crowd and one ran a constant risk of bumping shoulders with some proud gentleman of no fortune but with a murderous eye. Although lacking in wealth, all of His Majesty's Musketeers had hot blue blood. All were ready to draw swords at the first provocation. And all of them, whether they were on duty or not and whether they wore the blue cape with its silver fleur-de-lys cross or not, tended to congregate here in their captain's house. They gathered in the courtyard, slept in the stables, mounted guard on the stairs, played dice in the antechambers and, on occasion, even joyfully crossed blades in the hallways for entertainment, training or the demonstration of the excellence of a particular series of moves. This picturesque spectacle that visitors found so striking was by no means extraordinary. In these times, most soldiers were recruited only when war loomed and then dispersed, for reasons of economy, once their services were no longer required. As for the few permanent regiments that existed, they were not barracked anywhere . . . due a lack of barracks. As members of the king's own prestigious military household, the Musketeers were among these few troops who were always available and not disbanded in peacetime. Nevertheless, no particular arrangements were made for housing them, equipping them, or supplying their daily needs: the pay they received from the king's Treasury, as paltry and irregular as it was, was supposed to suffice for these provisions.

Within the Hôtel de Tréville, everyone had heard about the ambush into which Leprat had fallen. Rumour had said that he was dead or dying, so his return to the fold was warmly greeted. Without participating in the effusive cries of joy and other virile manifestations of affection, Athos accompanied Leprat as far as the great staircase littered with musketeers, servants and various seekers of favour. There, he took his leave.

'Remember to conserve your strength, my friend. You've received a hard knock.'

'I promise you I will. Thank you, Athos.'

Leprat was announced and did not have to wait long in the antechamber. Captain de Tréville received him almost immediately in his office, rising to greet him when he entered.

'Come in, Leprat, come in. And have a seat. I am delighted to see you, but I did not expect to see you on your feet again so soon. I was even planning to come and visit you at home this evening.'

Leprat thanked him and took a chair, while monsieur de Tréville sat down again at his desk.

'First of all, how are you?'

'Well.'

'Your arm? Your thigh?'

'They both serve me once again.'

'Perfect. Now, your report.'

The musketeer began, recounting how he had initially overcome Malencontre's henchmen but allowed the leader himself to escape.

'"Malencontre", you say?'

'That's the name he gave me.'

'I'll make a note of it.'

Then Leprat quickly outlined the ambush on rue Saint-Denis and the mysterious gentleman who had shot him down without a second thought. When he finished his recital the captain rose and, hands behind his back, turned towards the window. It offered a view of the courtyard of his private mansion, a courtyard full of the musketeers he adored, protected and scolded like a father. As undisciplined and unruly as they were, there was not one of them who was not prepared to risk a thousand dangers and give his life for the king, for the queen, or for France. Most of them were young and, like all young men, they believed they were immortal. But that was not enough to explain either their fearlessness or their extraordinary devotion. Although they might not look like much, they were an elite force equal to the Cardinal's Guards.

'You should know, Leprat, that the Louvre is well pleased with you. I saw His Majesty the king this morning. He remembers you and sends his compliments . . . Your mission has been a success.'

Turning his gaze from the courtyard, Tréville faced Leprat again.

'I have been charged with sending you on leave,' he said in a serious tone.

'Thank you.'

'Don't thank me. It is to be an unlimited leave of absence.'

The musketeer stiffened in shock and disbelief.

A few days or weeks of leave were a reward. But unlimited leave signified that, until given new orders, he was to hang up his cape.

Why?

8

Entering Paris through the Richelieu gate, a two-horse coach descended the street of the same name between the Palais-Cardinal gardens and Saint-Roch hill, followed the quays of the Seine and crossed the river over a recently built wooden toll bridge: the Pont Rouge, so-called because of the red lead paint with which it was daubed. And so the coach reached the faubourg Saint-Germain which was prospering in the shadow of its famous abbey and almost constituted a city in its own right.

A new neighbourhood had sprung up, just at the far end of the Pont Rouge. Before Queen Marguerite de Navarre decided, at the beginning of the century, to make the Pré-aux-Clercs her domain the area had been nothing but a muddy riverbank and a vast empty ground. Now it comprised a new quay, a luxurious mansion, a large park and the convent of Les Augustins Réformés. The queen, who was Henri IV's first wife, had borrowed money to finance her projects and had even gone as far as to misappropriate funds – from which, it was said, came the name of Malaquais quay, meaning 'badly acquired'. Upon her death in 1615 she left behind a magnificent property, but also 1,300,000 livres in debts and a host of creditors who were still anxious to collect. To satisfy them, the domain was put up for auction and sold off in lots to various entrepreneurs who laid out new streets and started building.

Guided by the sure hand of a solidly built grey-haired coachman who chewed at the stem of a small clay pipe, the coach followed the Malaquais quay and then took rue des Saints-Pères. At Hôpital de la Charité he turned the coach onto rue Saint-Guillaume and soon came to a halt before a large and sombre looking nail-studded door.

Within the coat of arms, worn away over time, a bird of prey carved from dark stone presided on the pediment above the gate.

Sitting at the bottom of the steps to the Hôtel de l'Épervier, Marciac was bored and playing dice against himself when he heard the heavy thud at the coach door. He lifted his head to see monsieur Guibot hobbling on his wooden leg across the courtyard to see who was knocking. At the same time, Almades leaned out of an open window.

A moment later a woman entered through the pedestrian gate. Very tall, slender, dressed in grey and red, she wore a dress whose skirt was hitched up on her right side to reveal male hose and the boots of a cavalier beneath it. Her wide-brimmed hat was decorated with two large ostrich feathers – one white and the other scarlet – and a veil which hid her face while protecting it from the dust to which anyone undertaking a long coach journey on the terrible roads was exposed. But the shape of her mouth could be discerned: pretty, with full, dark lips.

Without taking any interest in Marciac, who approached her, she looked up at the private mansion as if she were considering buying it.

'Good day, madame.'

She turned towards him, looking at him haughtily without replying.

But her mouth smiled.

'How may I help you?' the Gascon tried.

From the window, Almades chose that moment to intervene.

'You have a very poor memory, Marciac. You don't even recognise your friends.'

Disconcerted, Marciac shrugged and wrinkled his brow, then went from puzzlement to sudden joy when the baronne de Vaudreuil lifted her veil.

'Agnès!'

'Hello, Marciac.'

'Agnès! Will you permit me to embrace you?'

'I will allow that.'

They hugged in a friendly fashion, although the young woman had to restrain a hand that had gone wandering down the small of her back before they separated. But the happiness which the Gascon displayed on seeing her again seemed sincere and she did not want to spoil it.

'What a delight, Agnès! What a delight . . . ! So, you too, you're back in the game?'

Agnès indicated the steel signet ring she wore over her grey leather glove.

'By my word,' she said. 'Once in . . .'

'. . . always in!' Marciac completed for her. 'Do you know how many times I have thought of you over the past five years?'

'Really? Was I dressed?'

'Sometimes!' he exclaimed. 'Sometimes!'

'Knowing you, that's a very pretty compliment.'

Almades, who had left the window, emerged from the front door of the main building.

'Welcome, Agnès.'

'Thank you. I'm very pleased to see you. I've missed your fencing lessons.'

'We can continue them at your pleasure.'

During these effusions, Guibot had toiled to open the two great doors of the carriage gate. This done, the coach entered, driven by Ballardieu who jumped down from the seat and, pipe between his teeth, smiled broadly. Once again, the greetings were jubilant and noisy, in particular between the old soldier and the Gascon: these two shared quite a few memories of bottles emptied and petticoats lifted.

They had to unhitch the coach, tow it into the stables, unload the luggage and settle the horses in their stalls. This time everyone lent the porter a hand, all the while forbidding Agnès from lifting a finger to help. She wasn't listening, but happily made acquaintance with the charmingly shy Naïs who had been drawn from her kitchen by the sound of raised voices.

La Fargue, in his turn, arrived.

Without entirely putting a damper on their joyful mood, his presence did cause them to lower their tone slightly.

'Did you have a good journey, Agnès?'

'Yes, captain. We hitched up the horses upon receiving your letter and we have burned our way through the staging posts getting here.'

'Hello, Ballardieu.'

'Captain.'

'It's still a sad place,' said the young woman, indicating the sinister grey stones of the Hôtel de l'Épervier.

'A little less now,' said Marciac.

'Is that everyone, captain?'

Looking stern and proud, girded in his slate-grey doublet and with his hand resting on the pommel of his sheathed sword, La Fargue blinked slowly and paused before replying, his gaze drifting towards the carriage gate.

'Almost, now.'

The others turned and immediately recognised the man standing there, with a white rapier at his side, smiling at them in a way which might have been melancholic or simply sentimental.

Leprat.

9

On Sundays and feast days, when the weather was fine, Parisians were happy to travel beyond the capital for their pleasure. Once past the faubourgs the country villages of Vanves, Gentilly and Belleville, and the market towns of Meudon and Saint-Cloud offered hospitable inns where all could drink, dance, play bowls beneath the trees, or simply partake of the cool shade and fresh air. The atmosphere was joyful and people took liberties or, in the eyes of some, indulged in scandalous licence. And it is true that spontaneous revels of love-making at times took place there in the evenings, enlivened by wine and a desire to taste all of life's pleasures. There being fewer customers during the week, these establishments then became retreats which were visited mainly for their tranquillity and the quality of their table – such as *Le Petit Maure*, in Vaugirard, renowned for its peas and strawberries.

Saint-Lucq and Bailleux had temporarily found refuge in one of these inns. Having jumped into the river through a window in the water mill where the notary had been held captive, they successfully escaped the cavaliers who had come to collect their prisoner but were also carried far from their horses by the current. Rather than turn back towards their enemies Saint-Lucq had decided they would continue on foot. They therefore walked for several hours through woods and across fields, scanning the horizon on constant lookout for signs of pursuit, and arrived, exhausted, at a village with a hostelry standing by its entrance.

For the time being Lucien Bailleux found himself alone in a room on the first floor. Sitting at a table laid for the purpose, he ate with a ferocious appetite born of three days' captivity, poor treatment and fasting. He was still in his nightshirt – the same one he had been wearing when he was dragged from his bed in the middle of the night. But at least he was clean, after his forced bath in the river. Thin, his face drawn and his hair falling across his eyes, he looked exactly what he was: a survivor.

He gave a sharp, worried glance towards the door when Saint-Lucq entered without knocking. The half-blood brought a package of clothes which he threw onto the bed.

'For you. They belonged to a guest who left without paying.'

'Thank you.'

'I also found us two saddled horses,' continued Saint-Lucq, risking a quick glance out of the window. 'Can you ride?'

'Uh . . . Yes. A little . . . You think the cavaliers are still after us?'

'I'm sure of it. They want you and they've not given up the fight . . . The bodies of the brigands I killed at the mill were still warm when they arrived and as a result, these cavaliers know they only missed us by a tiny margin. And if they found the horses I had planned to use in our flight, they also know there are two of us, and that we are on foot. They are no doubt scouring the countryside for us at this very moment.'

'But we'll escape them, won't we?'

'We'll have a chance if we don't delay. After all, they don't know where we're going.'

'To Paris?'

'Not before we've reclaimed that document. Not before we've put it in a safe place. Get dressed.'

A little later, Bailleux was just finishing dressing when he broke down. He dropped onto the bed, put his face in his hands and burst into sobs.

'I . . . I don't understand,' was all he managed to say.

'What?' said the stone-faced half-blood.

'Why me? Why has all this happened to me . . .? I've led the most orderly of lives. I studied and worked with my father before inheriting his position. I married the daughter of a colleague. I was a good son and I believe I am a good husband. I'm charitable and I pray. I conduct my business with honour and honesty. And in return, I have asked for nothing but to be allowed to live in peace . . . So why?'

'You opened the wrong testament. And, what is worse, you let that fact be known.'

'But it was my duty as a notary!'

'Undoubtedly.'

'It's not fair.'

To that, Saint-Lucq did not reply.

From his point of view, there was no fairness in life. There were only strong men and weak ones, the rich and the poor, the wolves and the sheep, the living and the dead. That was how the world was, and how it would always be. Anything else was merely fiction.

He approached the notary in the hope of encouraging him to get a grip on himself. The notary rose suddenly and hugged him hard. The half-blood braced himself as the other spoke:

'Thank you, monsieur. Thank you . . . I don't know who you are, in truth. I don't know who sent you . . . But without you . . . My God, without you . . .! Believe me when I say that you have my eternal regard, monsieur. There is nothing, from now on, that I could refuse you. You saved me. I owe you my life.'

Slowly but firmly, Saint-Lucq moved away from him.

Then, his hands resting on Bailleux's shoulders, he gave him a shake and ordered:

'Look at me, monsieur.'

The notary obeyed and the crimson spectacles returned his gaze.

'Do not thank me,' continued Saint-Lucq. 'And do not trouble yourself any further with the question of who employs me, or why. I do what I do because I'm paid to. If I had been required to kill you, you would be dead. So never thank me again. My place is neither in sensational novels, nor in the chronicles of our times. I'm not a hero. I'm only a swordsman. Contrary to your opinion, I do not deserve anyone's esteem.'

Initially incredulous, Bailleux was visibly hurt by this declaration.

Finally, still looking dazed, he nodded and pulled on the beret the half-blood had brought him.

'We should hurry,' concluded Saint-Lucq. 'Each minute that passes is a minute lost.'

The notary left the room first and while he climbed gracelessly into the saddle in the courtyard the half-blood paused inside for a moment to pay the landlord and slip a few words into his ear. The man listened to his instructions attentively, then nodded and pocketed an additional piece of gold.

Less than half an hour after Saint-Lucq and Bailleux left, armed riders arrived. The landlord was waiting for them on the doorstep.

10

In the dining room of the Hôtel de l'Épervier, the Cardinal's Blades finished their lunch.

Seated at the head of the rough oak table, La Fargue spoke very seriously with Leprat and Agnès. Marciac listened, close by, and occasionally made an interjection but otherwise contented himself with rocking back and forth on his chair and shuffling a deck of cards which, inevitably, then turned out to have all four aces on top. Almades, silent, waited. As for Ballardieu, he digested his lunch while smoking a pipe and sipping the last of the wine, not without casting longing glances at Naïs' backside as she cleared the table.

'Pretty girl, isn't she?' Marciac said to him, seeing the old soldier ogling the comely young woman.

'Yes. Very.'

'But not very talkative. Almost mute.'

'I see an advantage there.'

'Really? What a strange idea . . .'

They had all been somewhat apprehensive of this meal, which, following the immediate and genuine rejoicing of their initial reunion, would force them to take the true measure of their friendship. What remained of the people they had been? One never knows what friends lost from sight for a long time may have become and the circumstances which led to the disbanding of the Blades during the siege of La Rochelle had laid a mournful veil over the memories of its members. This veil, however, soon lifted and the previous ties between them were quickly re-established.

As was entirely natural, the distribution of the Blades around the table indicated their affinities as well as the resumption of old habits. Thus the captain presided over the table, in close council with Agnès and Leprat whom he consulted with ease, the musketeer even acting as a lieutenant within the very informal organisation of the Blades. Marciac, remaining somewhat aloof, was one of those who knew their own value and abilities but preferred to stay on the margins, never showing himself to be unworthy and who would consider it an insult if he were ordered about. Serious and reserved, Almades waited to be called upon. And Ballardieu, accustomed to long preludes before battle, took advantage of any moment of peace.

Only three Blades, out of the original band, were missing. One of them had vanished as if the twisted shadows from which he had emerged had engulfed him once again after La Rochelle. The other had been a traitor and no one, yet, had dared to speak his name. And the last one, finally, had perished and his loss was a wound which continued to bleed in the memories of all present.

As Naïs left the room with the last plates, Agnès glanced with a question in her eye at La Fargue, who understood and nodded. The young woman rose and said with deep feeling:

'I believe, messieurs, that the time has come to raise our glasses in honour of he whom only death could keep from being here.'

They all stood, glasses in hand.

'To Bretteville!' said La Fargue.

'To BRETTEVILLE!' cried the others in chorus.

'To Bretteville,' Agnès repeated in a strangled voice, as if to herself.

The Blades re-seated themselves, divided between the joy of having known Bretteville, the pride of having loved this man and the sorrow of having lost him at the last.

'We have a mission,' La Fargue said after a moment.

They listened.

'It is a matter of finding a certain chevalier d'Ireban.'

'What has he done?' Agnès inquired.

'Nothing. He has disappeared and there is concern for his life.'

'People who have not done anything do not disappear,' Almades declared in a neutral voice.

'A Spaniard?' Marciac was surprised.

'Yes,' said the captain.

'So Spain will be busy trying to find him!'

'That is precisely what the Cardinal wishes to avoid.'

La Fargue rose, walked around his chair and leaned against the back, his hands folded.

'The chevalier d'Ireban,' he repeated, 'is the heir to a Spanish grandee. A secret and unworthy heir to the title. A corrupt young man who, under an assumed name, has come to Paris to spend his coming fortune.'

'What is his real name?' asked Almades.

'I don't know. It seems Spain would like to keep it a secret.'

'No doubt for fear of a scandal,' Ballardieu guessed. 'If his father is a grandee—'

'"If"!' Marciac interrupted. 'Should we take everything Spain says at face value?'

La Fargue silenced the Gascon with a glance and continued:

'His father is not well. He will soon be dead. And Spain has been seeking the safe return of the son since she first realised he had disappeared. Ireban seems to have vanished suddenly and it is feared he has met with some mishap in Paris.'

'If he was leading a life of debauchery,' noted Agnès, 'that's probable. And if he was keeping bad company, and they realised who he really is—'

'Once again, "ifs",' Marciac emphasised in a low voice.

'Via a special emissary,' La Fargue went on, 'Spain has explained the situation, her concerns and her intentions to our king.'

'Her "intentions"?' queried Ballardieu.

'Spain wants Ireban returned and to this end, not to mince words, she is threatening to send her agents into our kingdom if France is not prepared to do what is necessary. That is where we become involved.'

Leprat's self-restraint finally wore away.

Unable to hear any more he rose and paced a hundred steps in livid silence, his expression hard and a fire in his eyes. Firstly, he was displeased that Spain was imposing conditions upon France. But secondly, and more importantly, he had not intended to hang up his musketeer's cape only to discover, on the very same day, that he had done so in order to serve another country.

An enemy country.

La Fargue had been expecting this reaction from his Blades.

'I know what you're thinking, Leprat.'

The other stopped his pacing.

'Really, captain?'

'I know because I think just like you. But I also know that Richelieu is seeking a rapprochement with Spain right now. France will soon be at war in Lorraine and possibly in the Holy Roman Empire. She cannot allow herself to come under threat from the Pyrenees border at the same time. The cardinal needs to please Spain and so he's offering her tokens of friendship.'

Leprat sighed.

'Very well. But why us? Why recall the Blades? The cardinal does not lack for spies, as far as I know.'

The captain didn't respond.

'The mission is delicate,' Agnès began . . .

'. . . and we are the best,' added Marciac.

But as agreeable as this was to say and to hear, these explanations did not satisfy anyone.

It was a mystery which filled each of their minds.

The silence stretched out, until at last the Gascon said:

'We don't even know this chevalier d'Ireban's real name and Spain is unlikely to tell us anything more about him. Suppose he lives. Suppose he is in hiding or being held prisoner. The fact remains that there are some five hundred thousand souls in Paris. Finding one, even a Spaniard, will not be easy.'

'We have a trail to follow,' announced La Fargue. 'It is thin and no doubt cold, but it has the merit of existing.'

'What is it?' Agnès asked.

'Ireban did not come to Paris alone. He has a companion in vice. A gentleman of means, also a Spaniard. An adventurous duellist when it suits him and a great connoisseur of Paris at night. The man goes by the name Castilla. We shall begin with him. Almades, Leprat, you'll come with me.'

Those he'd named nodded.

'Marciac, stay here with Guibot and make an inventory of everything we're missing. Then this evening you will make the rounds of all the cabarets and gambling houses that Ireban and Castilla are likely to frequent.'

'Understood. But there are a lot of them in Paris.'

'You will do your best.'

'And me?' asked the baronne de Vaudreuil.

La Fargue paused for a moment.

'You, Agnès, must pay a visit. See to it.'

She already knew what he meant and exchanged a glance with Ballardieu.

Later, La Fargue went to see Leprat who was saddling horses in the stable.

'I know what this costs you, Leprat. For the rest of us, a return to service with the Blades is a benefit. But for you . . .'

'For me?'

'Your career with the Musketeers is well established. Nothing forces you to give it up and if you want my advice . . .'

The captain didn't finish.

The other man smiled warmly, obviously touched, and recalled what monsieur de Tréville had said on relaying the orders for his new mission:

'You are one of my best musketeers. I don't want to lose you, especially not if you wish to keep your cape. I will take your side. I will tell the king and the cardinal that you are indispensable to me, which is the simple truth. You could stay. You have only to say the word.'

But Leprat had not said the word.

'This mission does not inspire confidence in me,' La Fargue

continued. 'Spain is not being frank with us in this business. I fear that she intends to use us for her benefit alone, and perhaps even at the expense of France . . . At best, we shall gain nothing. But you, you have a great deal to lose.'

The former musketeer finished tightening a strap, and then patted his new mount on the rump. The animal was a beautiful chestnut, a gift from monsieur de Tréville.

'May I speak freely, Etienne?' he demanded of La Fargue.

He only spoke to the captain so personally in private.

'Of course.'

'I am a soldier: I serve where I'm told to serve. And, if that is not enough, I am a Blade.'

11

For Ballardieu, the moment of his true reunion with Paris took place on the Pont Neuf. For if the market at Les Halles was the city's belly and the Louvre was its head, then the Pont Neuf was the heart of the capital. A heart that pumped blood, giving the city life and movement, animating the great populous flow that ran through its streets. Everyone, after all, used the Pont Neuf. For convenience, primarily, since it permitted people to travel directly from one bank to the other without passing through Ile de la Cité and its maze of mediaeval alleyways. But also for the sake of entertainment.

The bridge was originally intended to support houses, as was only to be expected in a city where the tiniest building space was already utilised. But this plan was abandoned to avoid spoiling the royal family's view of the Cité from the windows of the Louvre. Of this original plan only two wide platforms survived, both six steps high and running the entire length of the bridge, on either side of the paved roadway. These platforms became pavements, the first in Paris, from which it was possible to admire the Seine and enjoy the fresh air without fear of being run over by a coach or a horse rider. Parisians soon grew to like going for a stroll there. Street artists and traders set up shop along the parapets and in the half-moon-shaped lookout points, and the Pont Neuf soon became a permanent fair, filled with jostling crowds.

'God's blood!' Ballardieu exclaimed, taking a deep breath. 'I feel like my old self again!'

More reserved, Agnès smiled.

They had come through the Nesle gate on foot and passed

in front of the Hôtel de Nevers before arriving at Pont Neuf. It was the shortest route to the Louvre, their destination.

'It is good to be here!' added the delighted old soldier. 'Don't you think?'

'Yes.'

'And nothing has changed! Look at that buffoon, I remember him!'

He pointed to a tall thin fellow in a moth-eaten cloak, mounted on the back of a poor old nag who was as gaunt as he was, boasting of a miraculous powder which he claimed would preserve your teeth. The fact that he had only one remaining tooth in his own mouth did not seem to weaken his conviction or bother his audience.

'And over there! Tabarin and Mondor . . . ! Come on, let's go hear them.'

Tabarin and Mondor were famous street entertainers who each had their own stage at the entrance to Place Dauphine. At that moment one of them was singing a bawdy song while the other, armed with an enormous enema bag, was playing at being a quack and offering all comers the chance to have 'their arseholes washed all clean and pink!' Their spectators were bursting with laughter.

'Later,' said Agnès. 'On our way back.'

'You've no sense of fun, girl.'

'You do remember that I am a baronne?'

'A baronne I knew when she had neither tits nor an arse, who rode on my shoulders and who I made drink her first glass of *eau-de-vie*.'

'At eight years old! What a handsome feat . . . I remember puking my guts out the whole night after.'

'That helps forge character. I was only six when my father did the same for me as I did for you, madame la baronne de Vaudreuil. Have you some objection about the education that my father saw fit to give me?'

'Come on, you old beast. Move along, now . . . On the way back, I tell you.'

'You swear?'

'Yes.'

The traffic of carriages, horses, wagons and handcarts on the roadway was so dense that one could barely advance, while the sidewalks were crammed solid with gawking pedestrians. Charlatans, traders, tumblers, exhibitors of trained dragon-nets, teeth pullers ('No pain! And I replace the one I pull!') and street minstrels all put themselves on show or touted their wares to the crowd in Italian, Spanish, and even Latin or Greek to appear more learned. There were numerous book-sellers, offering wrinkled, dog-eared and torn volumes at low prices, among which there were sometimes buried treasures to be found. Each of them had their own stand, hut, tent or stall. Places were dear and bitterly disputed. Those who had no right to a spot on the bridge put up signboards giving their names, addresses and specialities. Others – flower sellers, second-hand hatters and *eau-de-vie* vendors – hawked their goods loudly as they made their way from one end of the bridge to the other, carrying a tray on their bellies or pushing a cart before them. Anything could be bought or sold on the Pont Neuf. A lot was stolen there, too, for thieves like nothing better than an idle crowd.

Agnès was passing in front of a famous bronze horse – which, standing on its marble pedestal, would wait almost two centuries before being finally mounted by Henri IV – when she realised she was walking on her own. Retracing her footsteps, she found Ballardieu halted before a Gypsy woman playing a tambourine and dancing lasciviously with a metallic wriggling of her sequined skirt. Agnès dragged the old man away by his sleeve. He followed her backwards at first and tripped on the scabbard of his sword, before pricking up an ear at the call:

'*Hasard à la blanque!* With three tries, you can't miss! For one sou, you'll get six! *Hasard à la blanque!*'

The fellow who was shouting this at the top of his lungs was luring passers-by to place bets on the game of *blanque*, that is to say, the lottery. He was turning a wheel, while the prizes to be won were spread before him: a comb, a mirror, a shoehorn, and other ordinary bric-a-brac which wouldn't be nearly so attractive if anyone looked them over twice.

Ballardieu tried his luck, won, and took away a snuffbox with a lid that was only slightly chipped. He was endeavouring to show this prize to the increasingly impatient young baronne when a fanfare of trumpets resounded.

Intrigued and murmuring, the people in the crowd craned their necks uncertainly, seeking the source of the noise.

On the Left Bank, soldiers belonging to the regiment of French Guards were arriving to clear the bridge. They herded coaches and horse riders from the road across the bridge, pushed the pedestrians back onto the pavements and formed three rows on the steps, standing to attention with their pikes held straight up or with muskets on their shoulders. A line of drummers beat out a steady rhythm as the regiment's vanguard marched forward, followed by a group of elegant riders – officers, lords and courtiers. Pages dressed in royal livery came next on foot, while the famous hundred Swiss mercenaries with their halberds accompanied them on either side. Then came the golden royal coach, drawn by six magnificent horses and surrounded by an escort of gentlemen. Was it really the king whose profile could be glimpsed as it passed? Perhaps. Kept at a distance by the hedgerow of pikes and muskets, the people did not applaud or cheer. They remained respectful and silent, with bared heads. Other coaches went by. One of them lacked any coat of arms, and was pure white, like the team of horses harnessed to it. This coach belonged to the abbess of the Order of the Sisters of Saint Georges – the famous 'White Ladies' who for the past two centuries had protected the French royal court from the draconic menace.

Agnès had stopped, like everyone else on the bridge, standing speechless and hatless as the procession went by.

But the royal coach interested her far less than the immaculate white one from which she was unable to tear her eyes the moment she saw it. When it drew level with her, a gloved hand lifted the curtain and a woman's head appeared. The abbess did not need to search for what she sought. She immediately found Agnès' eyes and stared straight into them. The moment stretched out, as if the white coach had somehow slowed down, or time itself was reluctant to interrupt the silent exchange going on between these two beings, these two souls.

Then the coach passed on.

Reality reasserted itself and the procession moved away with a clattering of hooves on paving stones. In perfect order, the French Guards relinquished control of the pavements and marched off the bridge. The usual frantic activity resumed on the Pont Neuf.

Only Agnès, looking towards the Louvre, remained still.

'Now that was a pair of eyes I would not like to have staring at me,' said Ballardieu from nearby. 'And as for staring right back . . .'

The young woman gave a fatalistic shrug.

'At least now I don't have to go to the Louvre.'

'You won't speak with her?'

'Not today . . . What would be the point? She knows I'm back. That's enough.'

And determined to put the matter behind her, Agnès smiled at the old soldier.

'So?' she asked him. 'Shall we go?'

'Where?'

'But to listen to Tabarin and Mondor, of course!'

'Are you sure?'

'I made you a promise, didn't I?'

12

They arrived at the chapel in the middle of the afternoon

It sat in the middle of the countryside at a spot where a deserted road crossed a pebble-strewn track. A flock of sheep grazed nearby. A windmill whose sails turned slowly in the breeze looked out over a landscape of green hills.

'Here we are,' said Bailleux from the edge of the wood.

He and Saint-Lucq were side by side on horseback, but rather than watch the chapel the half-blood watched their surroundings.

He had just caught sight of a cloud of dust.

'Wait,' he said.

The cloud was approaching.

He could just make out riders trotting up the road. There were four, or perhaps five, of them, all armed with swords. It was not the first time that Saint-Lucq and the notary had spotted them since leaving the inn. Them, or others like them, in any case. But all of them had only one thing in mind: laying their hands on Bailleux and ripping his secret out of him.

'We'll let them go by,' said the half-blood, very coolly.

'But how could they know . . . ?' Bailleux worried.

'They don't. They're searching, that's all. Calm yourself.'

The riders halted for a moment at the crossing with the track. Then they split up into two parties, each taking a different direction. A short while later they had all disappeared off into the distance.

'There,' said Saint-Lucq before spurring his mount.

Bailleux caught up with him as they descended a grassy slope at a slow trot.

'I think the baptism was held here. That's why—'

'Yes, of course,' the half-blood interrupted.

They soon dismounted on a patch of ground in front of the chapel and then entered the building. It was low-ceilinged, cool, bare of decorations and the air was laden with dust. No one seemed to have visited for quite some time, although perhaps it served occasionally as a refuge for travellers caught in bad weather.

Saint-Lucq took off his spectacles in the dim light and rubbed his tired eyes with his thumb and forefinger before surveying their surroundings with a slow circular gaze. Almost at once, the notary pointed to a statue of Saint Christophe standing on a pedestal, in a niche.

'If the testament speaks truly, it's there.'

They approached and examined the statue.

'We'll need to tilt it,' said Bailleux. 'It won't be easy.'

The weight of the painted statue would indeed have posed a difficulty if Saint-Lucq had desired to preserve it intact. But he braced himself, pushed and simply tipped the effigy of Saint Christophe over, to fall heavily onto the flagstones and break into pieces. Bailleux crossed himself at this act of sacrilege.

Someone had slipped a slender document pouch beneath the statue, and the cracked leather now lay exposed on the pedestal. The notary took it, opened it, and carefully unfolded a page torn from an old register of baptisms. The parchment threatened to come apart at the folds.

'This is it!' he exclaimed. 'This is really it!'

The half-blood held out his hand.

'Give it to me.'

'But will you tell me, finally, what this is all about? Do you even know?'

Saint-Lucq considered the question, and reached the conclusion that the notary had a right to this information.

'This piece of paper proves a certain person's legitimate right to an inheritance. One which is accompanied by a ducal coronet.'

'My God!'

Bailleux wished to read the prestigious name which

appeared on the page, but the half-blood swiftly snatched it from him. At first taken aback, the other man decided to be reasonable.

'It's . . . It's no doubt for the best this way . . . I already know too much, don't I?'

'Yes.'

'So it's over now. I won't be troubled again.'

'It will be over soon.'

Just then, they heard riders arriving.

'Our horses!' gasped Bailleux, but keeping his voice down. 'They're bound to see our horses!'

The riders came to a halt before the chapel but did not seem to dismount. The horses snorted as they settled. Inside the chapel the long seconds flowed by in silence. There was no means of exit other than the front doors.

Panicking, the notary could not understand the half-blood's absolute state of calm.

'They're going to come in! They're going to come in!'

'No.'

With one sharp, precise move, Saint-Lucq stabbed Bailleux in the heart. The man died without comprehension, murdered by the man who had initially saved him. Before he died, his incredulous eyes found the emotionless gaze of his assassin.

The half-blood caught the body and laid it gently on the ground.

Then he wiped his dagger carefully and replaced it in its sheath as he walked towards the door with an even step and emerged into broad daylight. There, he put his red spectacles back on, raised his eyes to the heavens and took a deep breath. Finally, he looked over at the five armed riders who waited before him in a row.

'It's done?' one of them asked.

'It's done.'

'Did he really believe we were chasing you?'

'Yes. You played your part perfectly.'

'And our pay?'

'See Rochefort about it.'

The rider nodded and the troop left at a gallop.

Saint-Lucq followed them with his gaze until they disappeared over the horizon and he found himself alone.

13

It was early afternoon when they came for Laincourt.

Without a word, two of the gaolers at Le Châtelet took him from his dungeon cell and led him along dank corridors and up a spiral stairway. The prisoner did not ask any questions: he knew it would be futile. Both his ankles and his wrists had been unbound. Overly confident of their strength, the gaolers were only armed with the clubs tucked into their belts. But escape was not on the agenda as far as Laincourt was concerned.

They reached the ground floor and continued upwards, which told Laincourt that they would not be leaving Le Châtelet. On the next floor, the gaoler walking ahead stopped before a closed door. He turned to the prisoner and gestured to him to hold out his wrists while his colleague bound them with a leather cord. Then he worked the latch and moved away. The other gaoler tried to push him forward, but Laincourt shoved back with his shoulder the moment he felt the other man touch him and entered of his own accord. The door was shut behind him.

It was a cold, low-ceilinged room, with a flagstone floor and bare walls. Sunshine fell in pale, oblique rays from narrow windows, former embrasures now equipped with frames and dirty panes of glass. There was a fireplace, where a fire had just been lit and the heat was still struggling to dispel the prevailing damp. Candles were burning in two large candelabra on the table at which Cardinal Richelieu was sitting, wrapped up in a cloak with a fur collar. Wearing boots and dressed as a cavalier, he had kept his gloves on, while the wide hat he used to remain incognito outside the walls of the Palais-Cardinal was resting in front of him.

'Come closer, monsieur.'

Laincourt obeyed and stood before the table, at a distance which offered no threat to Richelieu's security.

The cardinal had not come alone. Without his cape or anything else that might reveal his identity or his function, Captain Saint-Georges, the commanding officer of the Cardinal's Guards, was standing to the right of his master and slightly behind him, wearing his sword at the side and a look on his face that expressed a mixture of hatred and scorn. One of Richelieu's innumerable secretaries was also present. He sat on a stool with a writing tablet on his lap, ready to transcribe the details of this interview.

'So,' said the cardinal, 'you've been spying on me . . .'

The secretary's goose quill began to scratch across the paper.

'Yes,' replied Laincourt.

'That's not good. For a long time?'

'Long enough.'

'Since your over-extended mission in Spain, I should think.'

'Yes, monseigneur.'

Saint-Georges quivered.

'Traitor,' he hissed between his teeth.

Richelieu immediately lifted a hand to command silence and, seeing that he was obeyed, addressed the prisoner again.

'I would say, by way of reproach, that I have honoured you with my trust but, of course, that is a prerequisite in the exercise of your profession. After all, what good is a spy if one is wary of him . . . ? However, it does seem to me that you have been well treated. So why?'

'There are some causes that transcend those who serve them, monseigneur.'

'So it was for an ideal, then . . . Yes, I can understand that . . . Nevertheless, were you well paid?'

'Yes.'

'By whom?'

'Spain.'

'But more than that?'

'The Black Claw.'

'Monseigneur!' Saint-Georges intervened, seething with anger. 'This traitor doesn't deserve your attention . . . ! Let us hand him over to the torturers. They'll know how to make him tell us everything he knows.'

'Now, now, captain . . . It's true that, sooner or later, their victims will tell an expert torturer everything. But they will also say anything . . . And besides, you can see for yourself that monsieur de Laincourt is not at all indisposed to answering our questions.'

'Then let him be judged, and be hanged!'

'As for that, we shall see.'

Richelieu returned his attention to Laincourt who, throughout this exchange, had remained unperturbed.

'You do not appear to be afraid of the fate that awaits you, monsieur. Yet I assure you that it is an unenviable one . . . Are you are a fanatic?'

'No, monseigneur.'

'Then enlighten me. How is it that you remain so calm?'

'Your Eminence knows the reason, or already guessed it.'

The cardinal smiled, while Saint-Georges could no longer contain himself, taking a step forward, hand on his sword.

'Enough of this insolence! Answer!'

Richelieu was once again forced to dampen his captain's ardour.

'I wager, monsieur de Laincourt, that you have a document that protects you hidden away somewhere safe.'

'Indeed.'

'It's a letter, isn't it? Either a letter or a list.'

'Yes.'

'There is always too much being written down . . . What would you require in exchange for it?'

'Life. Freedom.'

'That is a lot to ask.'

'Furthermore, there will not be an exchange.'

Saint-Georges was dumbstruck, while the cardinal frowned

and, elbows on the table, gathered his fingers to form a steeple in front of his thin lips.

'You won't exchange,' he resumed. 'Will you sell?'

'No, I won't sell either.'

'Then I don't understand.'

'The letter in question will cease to protect me once it is in your hands, and one does not remove one's armour when faced by the enemy.'

'The enemy can promise to make peace . . .'

'The enemy can promise all it likes.'

This time Richelieu lifted his hand even before his captain reacted. The secretary, on his stool, seemed hesitant to take down this retort. A log shifted in the hearth, and the fire gained new strength.

'I want this letter,' the cardinal declared after a moment. 'Given that you are not prepared to divest yourself of it, I could turn you over to the torturer. He will make you reveal where you have hidden it.'

'I have placed it in the care of a reliable person. A person whose rank and birth protects them. Even from you.'

'Such people are rare. Throughout the entire kingdom, they can be counted on the fingers of one hand.'

'A hand wearing a steel glove.'

'English steel?'

'Perhaps.'

'A clever move.'

Laincourt bowed slightly.

'I attended a good school, monseigneur.'

Richelieu dismissed the compliment with a vague gesture, as one might wave away an annoying insect.

'This person of whom we speak, do they know the nature of the paper you have entrusted to them?'

'Certainly not.'

'So what do you propose?'

'Monseigneur, you are misleading when you say you desire to find this letter.'

'Really?'

'Because instead you wish to destroy it, don't you? What

you desire, above all, is that this letter should remain unread by anyone, ever.'

The cardinal sat back in his armchair and signalled to the secretary to stop writing.

'I think I guess your intentions, monsieur de Laincourt. You want your life and your liberty, and in return you would pledge that this overly compromising letter remains where it is. And thus it would continue to guarantee your safety: if I were to incarcerate you for too long, or kill you, its secret would be revealed. But what guarantees can you offer me in return?'

'Nothing will protect me from you if I reveal the secret of this letter, monseigneur. And I know that wherever I go, it will never be far enough to escape you. If I want to live—'

'But do you want to live, monsieur de Laincourt?'

'Yes.'

'In that case, think instead of your masters. Think of the Black Claw. The lever that you employ with me will not work with them. On the contrary, the Black Claw has every interest in seeing the secret that binds us be revealed. So, who will protect you from them? I should even say: who will protect *us* from them?'

'Do not trouble yourself on that account, monseigneur. With respect to the Black Claw, I have also made certain arrangements.'

The cardinal then drew the secretary's attention and indicated the door. The man understood and went out, taking his writing tablet with him.

'You also, monsieur,' said Richelieu addressing Saint-Georges.

The captain at first thought he had misheard.

'Excuse me, monseigneur?'

'Leave us, please.'

'But monseigneur! You cannot seriously think I would leave you!'

'Never fear. Monsieur de Laincourt is a spy, not an assassin. Besides, I only need to call out to have you return, is that not so?'

Regretfully, Saint-Georges left the room and as he was closing the door, he heard:

'You are most decidedly a very prudent man, monsieur de Laincourt. Explain to me what this is all about . . .'

14

'He no longer lives here, messieurs.'

'Since how long?'

'Some time.'

La Fargue and Leprat were questioning the owner of an inn on rue de la Clef, in the faubourg Saint-Victor. While Almades guarded the horses outside, the other two had taken a table, ordered wine and invited the innkeeper to bring a third glass for himself.

'Have a seat, monsieur. We'd like to talk to you.'

The man hesitated for a moment. Wiping his big red hands on his stained apron, he looked around the room, as if making sure that he had nothing better to do. Then he sat down.

La Fargue knew that Castilla, the chevalier d'Ireban's companion in debauchery, had been lodging here. Unfortunately, that was no longer the case.

'Be more precise, if you please. When did he leave?'

'Let me see . . . It was about a week ago, I think. He took his things one night and never returned.'

'In a hurry, then.'

'I believe so, yes.'

'Had he been lodging here long?' asked Leprat.

'About two months.'

'Alone?'

'Yes.'

'No visitors?'

Suddenly wary, the innkeeper moved back in his chair.

'Why these questions, messieurs?'

The other two exchanged a look and La Fargue spoke again.

'Castilla has debts. He owes money, lots of money, to certain people. These people wish to recover what is owed them. They would prefer that their names not be mentioned but they are willing to be most generous. You understand?'

'I understand. Gambling debts, is it?'

'Indeed. How did you guess?'

The innkeeper had the satisfied smile of one who, without saying anything, wants to give the impression of knowing much.

'Bah . . . Just an idea, like that—'

'His room,' Leprat interrupted. 'We want to see it.'

'Well . . .'

'What? Have you let it to someone else?'

'No, but Castilla has paid for the month. Whether he uses the room or not, it is still his. Would you be happy to think I had opened the door to your room for strangers?'

'No,' conceded La Fargue.

'So what do I tell him if he returns tomorrow?'

'You shall tell him nothing. And what's more, you shall send word to me at the address that I shall indicate to you shortly . . .'

The captain drew from his grey doublet a purse – small but full – which he pushed across the table to the innkeeper. It was swiftly snatched up.

'Follow me, messieurs,' said the man as he rose.

They accompanied him upstairs where the innkeeper unlocked a door thanks to a ring of keys attached to his belt.

'This is the room,' he announced.

He pushed the door open.

The room was modest but neat, with walls daubed in beige and an unpolished wood floor. The sole furniture consisted of a stool, a small table upon which was placed a water pitcher and a basin, and a stripped bed whose straw mattress was folded back. A chamber pot was turned over on the sill of the window that opened onto the street.

The place had been tidied up and, perfectly anonymous, awaited a new lodger. The two Blades exchanged glances and sighed, doubting that they would find much of interest here.

Nevertheless, to allow Leprat a chance to inspect the room in peace, La Fargue kept the innkeeper busy in the corridor.

'You didn't tell us if Castilla had any visitors . . .'

'Only one, in truth. A very young cavalier, another Spaniard like him. Castilla addressed him as "chevalier", but they seemed to be close friends.'

'Do you remember his name?'

'Something like . . . Oberane . . . Baribane . . .'

'Ireban?'

'Yes! The chevalier d'Ireban. That's it . . . Does he also have debts?'

'Yes.'

'That doesn't surprise me. Between those two, it was often a question of whether to visit madame de Sovange. And why would they go to see madame de Sovange, if not to gamble?'

'What did he look like, this Castilla?'

Without shutting it completely, Leprat pushed the door until it was ajar, under the pretext of looking behind it. He then conducted a thorough search of the room.

He did not know what he was looking for, which didn't make the task any easier. He knocked on the walls and floor, looked in corners, prodded the straw mattress and examined its seams closely.

In vain.

The room concealed no secret. If Castilla had ever possessed anything of a compromising nature, he had taken it with him.

The former musketeer was about to give up when by chance he looked out the window and down into the street. What he saw there or rather who he saw there – made him instantly go still.

Malencontre.

Malencontre who, wearing his leather hat and a bandage on his left hand, was being directed towards the inn by a passer-by. He gazed up towards the room's window, stiffened in surprise and promptly turned tail.

'Merde!' swore Leprat.

He knew that he would never catch the hired assassin if he

took the stairs. He shoved open the window, causing the chamber pot to smash on the floor, and jumped out into the air just as La Fargue – drawn by the noise – came into the room.

Leprat landed near Almades in front of the inn. But he had forgotten the wound to his thigh. Pain shot through his leg and he crumpled with a loud yelp that alarmed people in the street. Unable to stand, grimacing and cursing at himself, he nevertheless had the presence of mind to point out Malencontre to the Spanish master of arms.

'There! The leather hat! Quick!'

Malencontre was moving away, almost running, jostling people as he went.

As he set off in pursuit, Almades heard Leprat yelling at him from behind:

'Alive! We need him alive!'

The Spaniard had already lost sight of the assassin when he arrived at the corner of rue de la Clef and rue d'Orléans. He climbed onto a cart that was being unloaded and, paying no heed to the protests he was raising, looked further down the street. He spotted the leather hat just as Malencontre was turning into an alley. He leaped into the crowd, banging his hip into a stall which tipped and spilled its vegetables onto the paving stones. He did not stop, pushing aside anyone who did not get out of his way quickly enough, provoking shouts and raised fists in his wake. Finally, he reached the alley.

It was deserted.

He drew his sword.

La Fargue left the inn with his rapier in his fist, only to find Leprat twisting in agony on the ground, clenching his teeth and holding his thigh with both hands. Some kind souls came over to help him, but they hung back upon seeing the captain.

'Blast it, Leprat! What the hell . . . ?'

'Malencontre!'

'What?'

'Leather hat. Bandaged hand. Almades is after him. I'll explain later. That way! Quick!'

La Fargue took a pistol from the saddle of his horse and dashed off down the street.

Step by cautious step, Almades inched his way through silent alleys as narrow as corridors in a building. He had left the noises of the crowded streets behind him and he knew his prey had stopped running. Otherwise he would have heard his footsteps. The man was hiding. Either to escape from his pursuer, or to set an ambush for him.

Careful . . .

The attack came suddenly, from the right.

Emerging from a recess, Malencontre struck with a log he had taken from a woodpile. Almades raised his sword to protect himself. The log hit the rapier's hilt violently, dislodging the weapon from the Spaniard's grip. The two men immediately shifted to hand-to-hand fighting. Each held the right wrist of the other, grunting as they wrestled, bouncing off the walls of the alley, both of them receiving jarring blows as their backs collided with the rough stone. Then Almades drove his knee hard into the assassin's side. Malencontre lost his hold but succeeded in landing a sharp blow with the log to the temple of his opponent. Stunned, the Spaniard reeled and then stumbled backward. His vision blurred while his ears filled with a deafening buzz. The universe seemed to lurch dizzily about him.

Dimly, he perceived Malencontre unsheathing his rapier.

Dimly, he perceived him preparing to deliver the fatal stroke while he himself slid down the wall to a sitting position on the ground, vanquished.

And as if wrapped in some woolly dream, he scarcely heard the detonation at all.

Malencontre fell in a heap.

At a distance of ten metres, La Fargue was pointing a pistol with a smoking barrel.

15

There were three riders waiting at Place de la Croix-du-Trahoir, which was a modest square in the neighbourhood near the Louvre, where rue de l'Arbre-Sec met rue Saint-Honoré. Silent and still, they sat on their horses near the fountain with an ornamental cross which gave its name to the square. One of them was a tall gentleman with a pale complexion, who had a scar on his temple. Not many passers-by would have recognised the comte de Rochefort, the cardinal's henchman. But his sinister bearing never failed to disturb those who saw him.

Drawn by a handsome team, a coach without any coat of arms pulled up.

Rochefort descended from his horse and gave his reins to the closer of the two other riders, saying:

'Wait for me.'

And then he climbed into the coach which immediately drove off.

The leather curtains were lowered, so that the interior of the vehicle was bathed in ochre shadow. Two white wax candles were burning in wall holders fixed to either side of the rear bench of the coach. A very elegant gentleman had taken a seat on this bench. With thick long hair and greying temples, he wore a brocade doublet with braids embellished by gold and diamonds. He was in his fifties, a respectable age for these times. But he was still robust and alert, and even exuded a physical charm that was enhanced by maturity. His moustache, as well as his royale beard, was perfectly trimmed. A thin scar marked his cheekbone.

By comparison, the man sitting to his right was rather undistinguished.

Short and bald, he was modestly dressed in a brown outfit with white stockings and buckled shoes. His manner was both humble and reserved. He was not a servant, yet one perceived him to be a subordinate, a commoner who had risen above his state by dint of zeal and hard work. He was perhaps thirty or thirty-five years in age. His features were of a type that did not attract much notice and were easily forgotten.

Rochefort was seated opposite these two persons, with his back to the direction of travel.

'I'm listening,' said the comte de Pontevedra in perfect French.

Rochefort hesitated, glancing at the little man.

'What? Is it Ignacio who worries you? Forget him. He does not matter. He is not here.'

'So be it . . . The cardinal wishes you to know that the Blades are already at work in this matter.'

'Already?'

'Yes. Everything was prepared. It only remained for them to answer the call.'

'Which they did promptly, I suppose . . . And La Fargue?'

'He is in command.'

'Good. What does he know?'

'He knows that he is searching for a certain chevalier d'Ireban, whose disappearance upsets Madrid because he is the son of a Spanish grandee.'

'And that is all?'

'Just as you wished it.'

Pontevedra nodded and took a moment to reflect, the candlelight highlighting his forceful profile from the side.

'La Fargue must remain unaware of the true underpinnings of this affair,' he said finally. 'It is of the utmost importance.'

'His Eminence has seen to that.'

'If he should discover that—'

'Do not be concerned about this, monsieur le comte. The secret you evoke is well guarded. However . . .'

Rochefort left his sentence unfinished.

'Well, what?' said Pontevedra.

'However, you should know that the success of the Blades is by no means certain. And if La Fargue and his men should fail, the Cardinal is anxious to know what—'

The other interrupted:

'It is my turn to reassure you, Rochefort. The Blades shall not fail. And if they do, it will be because no one could succeed.'

'And so Spain . . .'

'. . . will keep its word, come what may, yes.'

Once again, Pontevedra looked away.

He suddenly seemed struck by great sadness, and in his eyes there was a flicker revealing a profound worry.

'The Blades shall not fail,' he repeated in a strangled voice. But rather than asserting a sense of conviction, he seemed to be addressing a prayer to Heaven.

16

By the time they reached the Hôtel de l'Épervier, Leprat was barely hanging on to his saddle and Malencontre was laid over Almades's horse. La Fargue called out, summoning everyone into the courtyard. They took care of Leprat first, Agnès helping him walk while Guibot closed the gate. Then Ballardieu and the Spaniard carried Malencontre into the house. Following the captain's instructions, they stretched him out on an unused bed, tucked away in a windowless cubbyhole.

'What happened?' asked Marciac when he returned from his bedroom with a dark wooden case.

'Later,' replied La Fargue. 'See to him first.'

'Him? What about Leprat?'

'Him first.'

'Who is he?'

'He's called Malencontre.'

'And . . . ?'

'And he must live.'

The Gascon sat down on the bed facing the unconscious wounded man, and set the case down at his feet. Bound in iron, it took the shape of a small chest that could be carried easily using a leather grip nailed to its curved lid. It was a surgeon's kit. Marciac opened it but did not touch any of the sinister-looking instruments – blades, saws, hammers, pincers – it contained. He leaned over Malencontre and began, with a great deal of care, to remove the bloody bandage wrapped about the assassin's skull.

'What happened to him?'

'I fired a pistol ball into his head,' explained La Fargue.

With a smirk, Marciac turned towards the captain.

'And he must live? Would it not have been better to not bash his head in, for starters?'

'He was going to kill Almades. And I wasn't aiming at his head.'

'No doubt that will console him and help him to heal.'

'Do your best.'

Marciac was left alone with the patient.

He rejoined the others in the main room a little later.

'Well?' asked La Fargue.

'He will live. Your pistol ball only scraped across the bone, and the man has a hard head . . . But I don't think he will be up to answering questions for a while. In fact, he still hasn't regained his senses.'

'Merde.'

'Indeed. May I take care of Leprat now?'

The captain nodded, looking troubled and preoccupied.

Leprat had been installed as comfortably as possible in an armchair, with his leg stretched out and resting on a footstool. A large rip in his breeches exposed his wounded thigh, which Naïs was finishing washing with warm water and fresh linen.

'Naïs, let me take your place, please.'

The pretty servant got up, looked at the surgeon's kit curiously and gave the Gascon a searching glance.

'I'm a doctor,' he explained. 'Well, almost . . . It's a long, complicated story . . .'

This revelation astonished Naïs even more. She turned to Agnès, who nodded in confirmation.

As he busied himself examining the wound, the others explained how Leprat managed to reopen it. Then they told him of the pursuit, the fight between Almades and Malencontre in the alley and La Fargue's timely intervention.

'Rest and a crutch,' the almost-doctor prescribed when he finished bandaging the wound. 'This is what happens when a patient plays at being an acrobat.'

'I overdid things a bit,' apologised Leprat.

'I suspect you forgot to think before you leaped . . . For the next few days, I suggest you eat your meat rare and drink a decent quantity of unwatered red wine.'

'So tell us, what the devil got into you?' intervened La Fargue. 'Who is this Malencontre exactly? And what did you want with him?'

They all drew closer to listen, except Naïs and Guibot who left the room, and Ballardieu who remained leaning against a wall nibbling on sugared almonds out of a large cornet that he had purchased on the Pont Neuf. Only Agnès had been invited to share them.

'Until this morning,' said Leprat, 'I was still with the Musketeers. And yesterday, I carried out a secret mission . . . For some time now, the King's couriers have been attacked, robbed and murdered on the roads between Brussels and Paris. The first time it occurred, it was thought the courier had merely run into brigands. But there was a second time, then a third, and finally a fourth, despite changes in the itinerary. It was as if the assassins not only knew when couriers were leaving, but also which routes they would take . . . A diligent inquiry was conducted by the Louvre. In vain. So it was decided to lay a trap for the enemy.'

'And you were the bait,' guessed Agnès.

'Yes. After arriving in Brussels incognito I came back carrying a letter from our ambassador to the Spanish Netherlands. And it worked: I was ambushed on the border, then in Amiens, and finally at a staging post a few leagues from Paris I was caught and attacked by a group of hired assassins. Only one of them escaped me. Their leader. It was Malencontre.'

'And that's all?' asked La Fargue.

'Almost . . . I didn't reach Paris until yesterday, during the night. Since my horse was tired and I wasn't feeling too strong myself, plus as a precaution, I had been taking minor roads. I think Malencontre reached the capital before me. Be that as it may, I rode into an ambush on rue Saint-Denis. And I would have been killed if the pistol ball aimed at my heart had not been stopped by my leather baldric.'

'So where did you acquire the wound to your thigh?' inquired Marciac.

'Rue Saint-Denis.'

'And the one on your arm?'

'At the staging post.'

'And having been fortunate enough to survive a pistol ball, the following day you jumped out of a window . . .'

Leprat shrugged.

'I didn't stop to think . . . Malencontre saw me the moment I saw him. He was already fleeing when—'

He cut himself short and turned to Almades.

'I'm sorry, Anibal.'

Head bare, the Spaniard was holding a cool, damp cloth against his temple.

'I let myself be taken by surprise,' he said. 'It was my own fault. I'm lucky to get away with just this handsome bump . . .'

'Let us return to the matter at hand,' said La Fargue. 'What else do you know about Malencontre?'

'Nothing. I know his name, which he told me. And I know that he works for the enemies of France.'

'Spain,' suggested Marciac. 'Who else but Spain would wish to know the content of France's dispatches from Brussels?'

'The whole world,' retorted Agnès. 'England, the Holy Roman Empire, Lorraine. Perhaps even Holland or Sweden. Not to mention supporters of the Queen Mother in exile. The whole world. Friends or enemies . . .'

'Yes, but the whole world isn't looking for the chevalier d'Ireban . . .' said Ballardieu between sugared almonds.

'Malencontre,' explained Leprat, 'did not find rue de la Clef by chance. He was being pointed in the direction of Castilla's inn when I recognised him. It can't have been a coincidence.'

There was silence, punctuated only by the sound of Ballardieu munching, while each of them reflected on what had been said. Then La Fargue placed his hand on the table and said:

'It is useless to lose ourselves in conjecture. This business is more complex than it seems, that's plain. Let us hope that we learn more from Malencontre when he comes round. But for the moment we have a mission to accomplish.'

'What's the next step?' asked Agnès.

'It all depends on Marciac.'

'Me?' the Gascon was astonished.

'Yes, you . . . Do you know a certain madame de Sovange?'

17

Urbain Gaget was speaking to one of the handlers who worked for his flourishing enterprise when he received word that his merchandise had arrived at the Saint-Honoré gate. The information was transmitted to him by a gangling adolescent who came rushing into the courtyard.

'Finally!' snapped Gaget.

Evening was falling and the Paris gates would soon be closed.

Gaget gave a coin to the boy, went over the final preparations one last time with the handler and called for his lackey. He was trading his shoes for a pair of clean boots to protect his stockings from the ravages of Parisian muck when Gros François joined him.

'Take a stick,' he told him. 'We're going out.'

Thus escorted by a solid-looking lackey armed with an equally solid stick, he hastened to go and make his payment to the tax collectors.

As he had taken care to add a few pistoles to the tax, the formalities were dealt with swiftly. Soon he was watching the heavy cart enter the queue of travellers and suppliers granted permission to enter the capital. A dense crowd blocked the area around the gate and stretched almost as thickly along rue Saint-Honoré. This had been one of the main Paris roads even before the city's recent enlargement. Still as busy as ever, it had now been extended as far as the new fortified city wall – called 'Yellow Ditches' by Parisians because of the colour of the earth that had been dug from the site – and was so full that it was difficult to make any progress here, with a noisy, restless multitude trying to advance up and down the street.

Loaded down with a dozen cages, each of which sheltered a dragonnet, the cart moved forward at a slow but steady pace behind the oxen pulling it. A peasant held the reins; his partner had given his place on the driver's bench up to Gaget and was guiding the beasts forward by their bits while Gros François walked ahead and opened a path through the tightly packed mob with some difficulty. Fortunately, their destination spared them from having to follow rue Saint-Honoré into the twisted, populous maze of the old heart of Paris. Instead, they turned onto rue de Gaillon and continued along the street for almost its entire length until they came to the porch of a building opposite rue des Moineaux. In the shadow of Saint-Roch hill with its windmills, it was one of the most attractive areas on the Right Bank – that is to say, the *Ville*, as it was designated by way of contrast to the *Université* on the Left Bank and the *Cité* on its island between them. This new neighbourhood was still under construction in the spring of 1633, but it had already been divided up and was crisscrossed with regular streets and punctuated by numerous gardens as well as a vast esplanade that served as a horse market. As further proof of its success, many beautiful and prosperous-looking private mansions were now being built there.

If it had been located elsewhere in the capital, Urbain Gaget's property would easily have occupied an entire block. Several stone buildings were arranged around a cobbled courtyard that was strewn with straw. These included a round, slender tower capped with a conical slate roof that was pierced with several rows of semi-circular openings. It resembled a dovecote – an oversized one, for inmates who made meals out of doves. Dragonnets could be heard moving around inside, mewling and sometimes spitting, accompanied by the brusque flapping of wings.

It was thanks to these small winged reptiles that Gaget would soon be a very rich man and was already a very busy one. He had started out with his father's business selling ordinary dragonnets in the city markets. Then he turned his attention to the luxury end of the trade, selling creatures with pedigrees or with spectacular physical characteristics to his wealthier customers. But the idea that would make his fortune only came to him later, when he hit upon a method of using dragonnets for a new purpose: a messenger service. Whereas a homing pigeon could only transport a minuscule roll of paper, a dragonnet was powerful enough to carry letters, or even a small package, faster and further than any bird.

The problem was that while dragonnets could be trained to travel between two given points in the same city, they lacked the predispositions of homing pigeons: they went astray or escaped when the distances they covered became too great. His solution was to take advantage of the females' maternal instinct, an instinct that always brought them back to their egg regardless of the difficulty or length of the journey. Gaget began to displace the females just after they laid their eggs, substituting the real eggs with simulacra when necessary to which the dragonnets would became equally attached and to which they would inevitably return, along with the mail they carried, once they were released. All that was left, after that, was to transport the females back to their point of departure by road.

Without abandoning the retail trade of buying and selling the dragonnets themselves, the breeder was soon able to carry out his new trade with a royal licence granting him a monopoly within Paris and surrounding towns. His messenger service very quickly thrived, linking the capital with Amiens, Reims, Rouen and Orléans. With the help of relay stations, it was even possible to send mail by air as far as Lille, Rennes, or Dijon.

A slender and rather handsome grey-haired fellow, not lacking in charm, Gaget supervised the unloading of the cart and watched as his employees carried the cages into a building where the dragonnets would remain confined and alone for a few days, until they settled down after the stress of their journey and became accustomed to their new environment. The result of a strict selection process, these particular speci-mens were destined to be sold and each one was worth a small fortune. They had to be treated with care, for fear that they might injure one another or damage themselves.

Satisfied, the breeder left his handler to examine the reptiles and returned to his office, where tedious paperwork awaited him. He removed his cloak and his boots, realised that he had gone out without wearing a hat, and then gave a start when he became aware of another presence in the room when he had believed he was alone. His heart beating fast, he gave a sigh of relief when he saw who it was. He had quickly discovered that along with the royal licence he held came the expectation of certain discreet services. He owed his new privileges to the cardinal's intervention and could of course refuse nothing to such a benefactor, especially when he was so honoured to have his trust. Thus the Gaget messenger service became a favoured means of transmitting secret dispatches.

And much else besides.

'I frightened you,' said Saint-Lucq.

He was sitting in an armchair, his hat lowered over his eyes, legs stretched out and crossed and his heels resting on a window sill.

'You . . . You surprised me,' explained the breeder. 'How did you get in here?'

'Does it matter?'

Quickly recovering his composure, Gaget went to lock the door and close the curtains.

'I've been waiting for you to show up for three days,' he said in a reproachful tone.

'I know,' said the half-blood lifting his felt hat.

With a casual air, he began to clean his spectacles with his sleeve. His reptilian eyes seemed to glow in the shadows.

'I received a visit from the comte de Rochefort,' said the breeder.

'What did he want?'

'News. And to tell you that there is some concern about your progress.'

'They are wrong to be concerned.'

'Will you succeed before it is too late?'

Saint-Lucq replaced the spectacles upon his nose and took time to weigh his reply.

'I was unaware that there was any other option . . .'

Then he asked:

'When will you see Rochefort again?'

'This evening, no doubt.'

'Tell him that the business which worries him so greatly is now settled.'

'Already?'

Saint-Lucq stood, smoothed the front of his doublet and adjusted his leather baldric, ready to leave.

'Add that the paper is in my possession and I simply wait to learn who I should deliver it to.'

'That I do know. You are to deliver it in person to the cardinal himself.'

The half blood paused and gave Gaget a curious glance above his red glasses.

'In person?'

The dragonnet breeder nodded.

'As soon as possible, I was told. This very evening, therefore. At the Palais-Cardinal.'

18

The carriage reached the faubourg Saint-Jacques at dusk and followed rue des Postes, to rue de l'Arbalète before passing through the gates of a large private mansion. Although still useless at this hour, torches were burning in the courtyard where, one by one, passengers were already alighting from their coaches while sedan chairs arrived and elegant horse riders left their mounts in the care of stable boys. Three storeys of tall windows were brightly illuminated from within. Guests were conversing with one another on the front steps as they waited to pay their respects to the mistress of the house. The latter, madame de Sovange, smiled and had a pleasant greeting ready for each of them. Dressed in an elegant court gown she made friendly reproaches to those who did not come often enough, complimented others and flattered everyone's sense of vanity with consummate skill.

Then it was Ballardieu's turn to halt their carriage at the bottom of the stairs. A lackey opened the door and Marciac emerged, elegantly dressed and holding out a hand for Agnès. Coiffed, powdered and beautifully attired, the baronne de Vaudreuil was stunning in a gown of scarlet silk and satin. It was a somewhat unfashionable dress, however, as no one here failed to notice. Agnès was also aware of this, but she'd had no time to convert her wardrobe to the current fashion. Moreover, she knew she could count on her beauty see her through, and this faux-pas in fact corresponded with the character she was playing.

'They only have eyes for you,' Marciac murmured as they waited patiently on the front steps.

In fact, she was attracting a number of sideways glances.

Wary and sometimes hostile looks from the women, interested and often charmed ones from the men.

'It's simply justice, isn't it?' she said.

'You are superb. And what about me?'

'You're not embarrassing, at least . . . To be honest, I wasn't sure you knew how to shave . . .'

The Gascon smiled.

'Try not to stand out too much. Remember who you are this evening . . .'

'Do you take me for a debutante?'

They ascended several steps.

'I only see the great and the worthy here,' observed Agnès.

'Only the most worthy. Madame de Sovange's gaming academy is one of the best frequented in Paris.'

'And they let you in?'

'You are cruel. The important thing is, if Castilla's landlord told the truth, the chevalier d'Ireban and Castilla liked coming here often.'

'Who is she, by the way?'

'Madame de Sovange? A widow whose dear departed husband left her nothing but debts and who resolved to support herself by opening her salons to the biggest gamblers in the capital . . . But her house is not restricted to gambling. There is much intrigue as well.'

'Of what kind?'

'Of every kind. Gallant, commercial, diplomatic, political . . . You can't imagine all the things which can be secretly arranged in certain antechambers, between two games of piquet, with a glass of Spanish muscatel in one's hand . . .'

They arrived before madame de Sovange, a dark, plump woman lacking in any real beauty but whose smile and affable manner provoked a sympathetic response.

'Monsieur le marquis!' she exclaimed.

Marquis?

Agnès resisted the temptation to look around for the marquis in question.

'I am delighted to see you, monsieur. Do you know how much we have missed you?'

'I am the first to regret my absence,' replied Marciac. 'And do not think I have been unfaithful to you. Important business kept me far from Paris.'

'Has this business been resolved?'

'But of course.'

'How fortunate.'

Still addressing madame de Sovange, Marciac turned slightly towards Agnès.

'Allow me to present madame de Laremont, a cousin of mine who I am showing around our beautiful capital.'

The mistress of the house greeted the so-called madame de Laremont.

'You're most welcome, my dear . . . But tell me, marquis, it seems that all of your cousins are ravishing . . .'

'It runs in the family, madame.'

'I will speak more with you later.'

Agnès and Marciac passed through a brightly lit vestibule with all its gilded décor and walked on into a series of salons whose communicating doors had been left wide open.

'And so, you are a—'

'My word,' replied the Gascon, 'if Concini was made maréchal d'Ancre, I could very well be a marquis, couldn't I?'

Neither of them took any notice of a very young and very elegant gentleman who was watching them, or rather, was watching the baronne de Vaudreuil – no doubt attracted by the dazzling beauty of this unfamiliar woman. If he had been present, Leprat would have recognised the cavalier who had fired a pistol ball into his heart on rue Saint-Denis. It was the marquis de Gagnière, who was discreetly approached from behind by a valet who whispered a few words into his ear.

The gentleman nodded, left the salons and found his way to a small courtyard used by servants and suppliers. A hired sword waited for him there. Booted, gloved and armed, both his clothes and his hat were of black leather. A patch – also made of leather and covered with silver studs – masked his left eye, but not enough to hide the rash of ranse that spread all around it. He had an olive complexion and angular features. Dark stubble covered his hollow cheeks.

'Malencontre has not returned,' he said with a strong Spanish accent.

'We will worry about that later,' Gagnière decreed.

'So be it. What are your orders?'

'For the moment, Savelda, I want you to gather some men. We will act tonight. This business has already gone on too long.'

The riders reached the old water mill as sunset bathed the landscape in flaming golds and purples. There were five of them, armed and booted, all them belonging to the Corbins gang, although they did not wear the distinctive large black cloaks. They had been riding for some distance since leaving the forest camp where most of the gang was currently to be found and they preferred not to be recognised as they made their way here.

The first body they saw was the lookout's, lying in front of the miller's house, stretched out close to the chair he'd been sitting in when Saint-Lucq had surprised and stabbed him.

One of the riders dismounted and was immediately copied by the others. A stocky man in his fifties, he owed his nickname Belle-Trogne, or 'handsome mug', to his battered, scarred face. He took off his hat, wiped away the sweat beading his completely bald skull with leather-gloved hand and said in a rough voice:

'Search everywhere.'

As the men scattered, he entered the house and found two lifeless corpses close to the fireplace, then a third lying a little further away. They were lying in congealed puddles that offered a feast to a swarm of fat black flies. The smell of blood was mixed with that of dust and old wood. Nothing could be heard except for the buzzing of insects. The evening light came through the rear windows at a low angle that cast long sepulchral shadows.

The Corbins who had gone to inspect the rest of the property soon returned.

'The prisoner has gone,' said one.

'Corillard is with the horses in the shed,' announced another.

'Dead?' Belle-Trogne asked to put his mind at rest.

'Yes. Strangled while he shat.'

'God's blood, Belle-Trogne! Who could have done such a thing?'

'A man.'

'Just one? Against five?'

'There was no fight. They were all murdered in cold blood. First Corillard in the shed, then Traquin in front of the house. After that, Galot and Feuillant in here, while they were eating. And Michel last of all . . . One man could have done that . . . If he were good . . .'

'I don't want to be the one who tells Soral . . .'

Belle-Trogne didn't reply, instead going to squat near the last body he had mentioned. The man called Michel was lying in the open doorway to the room where the Corbins had been sleeping – pallets and blankets attested to the fact. Feet bare, shirt outside his breeches, his forehead had obviously been split open by the poker that had fallen close by.

'It happened early in the morning,' confirmed Belle-Trogne. 'Michel had just woken.'

He stood back up and then something caught his attention. He frowned, counting the pallets.

'Six beds,' he said. 'One of ours is still missing . . . Have you looked everywhere?'

'The kid!' exclaimed one Corbin. 'I forgot all about him, but don't you remember? He insisted on taking part and Soral finally—'

He didn't finish.

Muffled thumps could be heard and the brigands, by reflex, all drew their swords.

The thumping came again.

Belle-Trogne in the lead, the brigands went back into the common room, cautiously approaching a cupboard. They opened it suddenly and found the sole survivor of the massacre.

Gagged, bound, eyes reddened and wet, a boy aged about fourteen looked up at them with an expression that was both imploring and scared.

20

Night had fallen, but at madame de Sovange's house fires and candles provided a warm light that reflected off the gold, the crystal and the mirrors. The women looked radiant in their elaborate attire and the men were almost equally resplendent. All of them were dressed as if making an appearance at the royal court. Indeed, some of those present had come straight from the court, avid for the distractions and conversation that Louis XIII would not tolerate at the Louvre. But here, at least, away from their dull, timid king who only had a taste for the pleasures of the hunt, one could find amusement in agreeable company. It was possible to converse, pay court, laugh, gossip, dine, drink and, of course, gamble.

There were billiard tables upstairs, upon which madam de Sovange's guests tapped at ivory balls with curved canes. Here and there were chess sets, chequers and trictrac boards left at the guests' disposal. Dice were being rolled. But above all, cards were being played. *Piquet, hoc, ambigu, impériale, trente et un, triomphe* – all of these games involved gambling on an ace of hearts, a nine of clubs, a wyvern of diamonds, or a king of spades. Fortunes were lost and won. Inheritances could disappear with an unlucky hand. Jewels and acknowledgements of debts were snatched up from the felt mat, along with piles of gold coins.

Abandoned by Marciac at the first opportunity, the so-called madame de Laremont wandered through the salons for a while, and turned away a few presumptuous seducers before allowing one old gentleman to court her. The vicomte de Chauvigny was in his sixties. He still maintained a handsome bearing but he was missing several teeth, which he tried to hide by holding a handkerchief to his mouth when he spoke. He was friendly, amusing and full of anecdotes. He wooed Agnès without any hope of success for the sole pleasure of gallant conversation, of which he was a master and which no doubt summoned up memories of his many past conquests as a dashing cavalier. The young woman willingly let him continue, as he spared her from having to endure less welcome attentions and was unknowingly providing her with precious pieces of information. She had already learned that the chevalier d'Ireban and Castilla had indeed been made welcome at the Hôtel de Sovange, that Ireban had not made an appearance here for some time, but that Castilla, even if he never remained for long, continued to visit almost every evening.

Trying in vain to catch a glimpse of Marciac, Agnès saw a dumpy little woman whose austere manner, surly glance and plain black gown jarred with the setting. She skulked about, pillaging the plates of pastries, and kept a watchful eye on the proceedings as if she were searching for something, or someone. No one seemed to notice her and yet everyone avoided her.

'And her? Who is she?'

The vicomte followed the glance of his newfound protégée.

'Oh! Her . . . ? That's La Rabier.'

'Who is . . . ?'

'A formidable moneylender. Permit me, madame, to give you some advice. Sell your last gown and embark for the Indies in your nightshirt rather than borrow money from that ghoul. She will suck your blood down to the very last drop.'

'She doesn't look so terrible . . .'

'That is an error in judgment that others have repented from too late.'

'And she is allowed to carry on?'

'Who would stop her . . . ? Everyone owes her a little and she is only cruel to those who owe her a lot.'

Casting a final wary glance over her shoulder, La Rabier left the room.

'Would you like something to drink?' asked Chauvigny.

'Gladly.'

The vicomte left Agnès but was quick to return with two glasses of wine.

'Thank you.'

'To you, madame.'

They clinked glasses, drank and the old gentleman said in a conversational tone:

'By the way, I just saw that Spanish hidalgo you were asking me about a short while ago . . .'

'Castilla? Where?'

'There, at the door. I think he's leaving.'

'Please excuse me,' said Agnès handing her glass over to Chauvigny, 'but I simply must speak with him . . .'

She hurried over to the door and recognised Castilla from the description given by the innkeeper from the rue de la Clef. Slender, handsome, with a thin moustache and very dark eyes, he was descending the front steps, greeting a passing acquaintance in his strong Spanish accent.

Agnès hesitated to accost him. Under what pretext? And to what end?

No, it would be better to follow him.

The problem was that Ballardieu was nowhere to be found and she could not imagine herself trailing Castilla around Paris at night in her slippers and evening gown. If only Marciac deigned to reappear!

Agnès cursed silently.

'Is there a problem?' madame de Sovange asked her.

'No, madame. None at all . . . Isn't that monsieur Castilla who is just leaving?'

'Yes, indeed it is. Do you know him?'

'Would you happen to know where the marquis is?'

'No.'

Masking her anxiety, the young woman returned to the salon, ignoring Chauvigny who smiled at her from afar, searching for Marciac. She passed before a window and caught sight of Castilla, crossing the porch. At least he was on foot . . .

The Gascon, finally, appeared at a door.

Given the circumstances, Agnès paid no heed to the grave expression on his face.

She caught him by an elbow.

'Good grief, Marciac! Where have you been?'

'Me . . . ? I—'

'Castilla was here. He just left!'

'Castilla?' replied Marciac as if hearing the name for the first time.

'Yes, Castilla! Damn it, Marciac, pay attention!'

Eyes closed, the Gascon took a deep breath.

'All right,' he finally replied. 'What do you wish from me?'

'He left the mansion on foot. If no one is waiting for him in the street with a carriage or a horse, you can still catch him. He was dressed as a cavalier with a red plume on his hat. See where he goes. And don't let him get away!'

'Understood.'

Marciac headed off, watched from behind by Agnès.

The young baronne remained pensive for a moment. Then, seized by a doubt, she pushed open the door through which the Gascon had just emerged. It led to a windowless antechamber, lit by a few candles.

Busy nibbling from a plate of almond paste sweets, La Rabier greeted Agnès with a polite, reserved nod of her head.

21

The same night, Saint-Lucq saw Rochefort in an antechamber within the Palais-Cardinal. They exchanged a brief nod of the head, each taking note of the other's presence without further ado. It was a salute between two professionals who knew one another but were otherwise indifferent to each other.

'He's waiting for you,' said the cardinal's henchman. 'Don't bother to knock.'

He seemed to be in a hurry, no doubt on his way to another errand. The half-blood stepped past him, but waited until he was alone to remove his red spectacles, adjust his attire and open the door before him.

He entered.

The room was high-ceilinged, long, silent, sumptuous, and almost completely plunged into shadow. At the far end of the vast study lined with precious books, beyond the chairs, desks and other furniture whose shapes and lacquered surfaces could barely be discerned, the candles of two silver candelabra cast an ochre light over the worktable at which Richelieu was sitting, his back to a splendid tapestry.

'Come closer, monsieur de Saint-Lucq. Come closer.'

Saint-Lucq obeyed, crossing the hall to reach the light.

'It has been a while since we last saw one another, has it not?'

'Yes, monseigneur.'

'Monsieur Gaget is a very capable intermediary. What do you make of him?'

'He is both discreet and competent.'

'Would you say he is loyal?'

'Most men are loyal for as long as they have no interest in betrayal, monseigneur.'

Richelieu smiled briefly.

'Inform me, then, of the progress of your mission, monsieur de Saint-Lucq. The comte de Rochefort is concerned that the days are passing by. Days which, according to him, are running short for us . . .'

'Here,' said the half-blood, holding out the page torn long ago from an old register of baptisms.

The cardinal took it, unfolded it, drew it closer to a candle in order to decipher the faded ink, and then carefully placed it in a leather satchel.

'Have you read it?'

'No.'

'You have succeeded in just three days when I believed the task impossible. Please accept my congratulations.'

'Thank you, monseigneur.'

'How did you manage it?'

'Does Your Eminence wish to know the details?'

'Just the essentials.'

'The Grand Coësre told me where and by whom the notary Bailleux was being held captive. I freed him and led him to believe we were being hunted by those who had ordered his abduction.'

'Which was, strictly speaking, only the truth . . .'

'Yes. But the riders who were searching the countryside in our vicinity and who constantly seemed to be on the verge of catching us, those riders were solely intended to intimidate Bailleux to the point of losing his better judgment.'

'So that was the purpose of the men you requested from Rochefort.'

'Indeed, monseigneur.'

'And the notary?'

'He won't talk.'

On that point, the cardinal demanded no further explanation.

For a moment, he looked at his little dragonnet, which,

inside its large wrought iron cage, was gnawing at a thick bone.

Then he sighed and said:

'I shall miss you, monsieur de Saint-Lucq.'

'I beg your pardon, monseigneur?'

'I made a promise that I must keep. To my great regret, believe me . . .'

Entering discreetly, a secretary interrupted them to whisper a few words into the ear of his master.

Richelieu listened, nodded and said:

'Monsieur de Saint-Lucq, if you would wait next door for a few moments, please . . .'

The half-blood bowed, and by means of a concealed door, departed in the wake of the secretary. Shortly after, La Fargue appeared, in a manner suggesting that he was responding to an urgent summons. Left hand on the pommel of his sword, he saluted by removing his hat.

'Monseigneur.'

'Good evening, monsieur de La Fargue. How does your mission fare?

'It is too soon to say, monseigneur. But we are following a trail. We have learned that the chevalier d'Ireban and one of his close friends frequented madame de Sovange's establishment. At this very moment, two of my Blades are there incognito, gathering information.'

'Very good . . . And what can you tell me about your prisoner?'

La Fargue twitched.

'My prisoner?'

'Today you captured a certain Malencontre with whom monsieur Leprat had a dispute recently. I want this man to be released to my custody.'

'Monseigneur! Malencontre has still not even regained his senses! He has not spoken a word and—'

'Anything this man could tell you would be of no consequence to your business.'

'But how can we be sure? The coincidence would be enormous if—'

The cardinal imposed silence by lifting his hand.

His sentence allowed no appeal, as the ageing captain, with clenched teeth and a furious look in his eye, was finally forced to admit.

'At your command, monseigneur.'

'You are about to discover, however, that I am not a man who takes without giving in return,' Richelieu murmured.

And in a voice loud enough to be heard in the adjoining room, he ordered:

'Ask monsieur de Saint-Lucq to come in.'

22

Castilla led Marciac through dark deserted streets to the nearby faubourg Saint-Victor. They crossed rue Mouffetard and proceeded up rue d'Orléans, passing the rue de la Clef where the Spaniard had so recently been a lodger, before finally turning into the small rue de la Fontaine. There, after glancing around without spotting the Gascon, Castilla knocked three times on the door of a particular house. It opened almost at once and as the man entered, Marciac caught a glimpse of a female silhouette.

The Gascon waited for a moment, and then crept forward. He approached the windows, but with the curtains closed all he could see was that there were lights burning within. He went up the alley to one side of the house and noticed a small window too high and too narrow to warrant such protection. He jumped up, gripped the sill and lifted himself by his arms until he could rest his chin on the stone. While he was unable to hear what they were saying, he could see Castilla and a young woman speaking in a clean and tidy room. The unknown woman was a slender, pretty brunette, wearing her hair in a simple chignon, with soft curls gracing her temples. She wore a rather ordinary dress, of the kind the daughter of a modest craftsman might own.

Castilla and the young woman embraced in such a way that Marciac was unable to decide if they were friends, lovers, or brother and sister. His arms torturing him, he had to finally let go and landed nimbly. He heard a door open on the garden side of the house and then other hinges squeaked. A horse snorted and, moments later, the Spaniard came riding down the alley at a slow trot. Marciac was obliged to flatten himself in a recess to avoid being seen or run over. He then dashed out after Castilla, but his quarry was already disappearing around the corner of rue de la Fontaine.

The Gascon bit back on an oath. He knew that it would futile to try and follow a man on horseback.

So now, what should he do?

Standing guard here all night would probably serve no useful purpose and, besides, sooner or later he would need to report back to the Hôtel de l'Épervier. It would be better to find the other Blades now in order to organise a continual watch on the house and its charming occupant. In any case, La Fargue would decide.

Marciac was about to leave when he detected suspect noises coming from the direction of rue du Puits-l'Hermite. He hesitated, turned back in his tracks and risked taking a peek around the corner of a house. A little further down the street a group of hired thugs had gathered around a rider dressed in black leather and wearing a patch with silver studs over his left eye.

These devils are up to some mischief, Marciac thought to himself.

He wasn't close enough to hear them and he sought in vain a means of approaching them discreetly at street level. He spied a balcony, climbed to it and then up onto the roofs and then, silently, his left hand holding the scabbard of his sword so it would not knock into anything, he passed from one house to another. His movements were fluid and assured. The gaps that he sometimes had to stride across did not frighten him. He crouched down and finally crawled forward before completing his journey at the tiled roof edge.

'It's on rue de la Fontaine,' the one-eyed man with a Spanish accent was saying. 'You'll recognise the house, won't you . . . ? The girl is alone, so you won't run into any problems. And don't forget that we need her alive.'

'You're not coming, Savelda?' asked one of the thugs.

'No. I have better things to do. Don't fail me.'

Without waiting for a reply, the man in black spurred his horse and left, while Marciac, still undetected, abandoned his observation post.

23

Laincourt emerged, dirty and unshaven, from Le Châtelet at nightfall. His clothes, hat and sword had been returned to him, but his guards had relieved him of the contents of his purse. That did not surprise him and he had not sought to make a complaint. Honesty was not one of the criteria in the selection of gaolers. Nor was it demanded of the archers in the city watch or among the lower ranks of those who served the king's justice. Clerks, halberdiers, scriveners, and turnkeys, all of them found ways of supplementing their ordinary pay.

His stay in prison had left him in a weakened state.

His back, his kidneys and his neck ached. A migraine lanced through his temples with each beat of his heart. His eyes glittered in pain. He felt the beginning of a fever coming on and dreamed of finding a good bed. He was not hungry.

From Le Châtelet, he could easily reach rue de la Ferronnerie by walking a short distance up rue Saint-Denis. But he knew that his apartment there had been visited — and no doubt ransacked — by the cardinal's men. Perhaps those assigned with this task even wore the cape. They would have arrived by horseback, broken down the door, made a great deal of noise and alerted the entire neighbourhood to their activities as they kept the curious at bay. No doubt his neighbours were talking of nothing else right now. Laincourt did not fear their attention. There was nothing to attach him to rue de la Ferronnerie anymore, since Ensign Laincourt of His Eminence's Guards no longer existed.

He rented another dwelling in secret, where he kept the only possessions that had any importance to him: his books.

Despite everything, he resolved not to go there at once and, by way of rue de la Tisseranderie, he went to a square near the Saint-Jean cemetery instead. Out of fear of being followed he made various detours, taking obscure passages and crossing a maze of backyards.

This was the ancient heart of Paris, formed of winding alleys where the sun never shone, where the stinking air stagnated and where vermin thrived. There was muck everywhere, and in thicker layers than anywhere else. It covered the paving stones, was smeared on the walls, spattered pedestrians' clothing and stuck to their soles. Black and foul, it was a mixture of turds and droppings, earth and sand, rot and garbage, of manure, of waste from latrines, of organic residues from the activities of butchers, tanners and skinners. It never completely dried, ate away at cloth fabrics and did not even spare leather. According to one very old French proverb, *'Pox from Rouen and muck from Paris can only be removed by cutting away the piece.'* To protect their stockings and breeches pedestrians were forced to wear tall boots. Others travelled by carriage, or in sedan chairs, or, according to their means, on the back of a horse, a mule, or . . . a man. When they did their rounds, the few dustmen in Paris only managed to collect a certain amount before dumping their carts at one of the nine rubbish tips, or *voieries*, situated outside the city. The peasants from the surrounding areas knew the value of Parisian muck, however. They came each day to harvest it and spread it on their fields. Parisians couldn't help noticing that these tips were cleaner than the capital itself.

Laincourt pushed a tavern door open and entered an atmosphere thick with smoke from pipes and poor-quality candles made of tallow. The place was dirty, foul-smelling and sordid. All of the customers were silent and despondent, seeming to be crushed by the weight of the same contagious sadness. An old man was playing a melancholy air on a hurdy-gurdy. Dressed in moth-eaten rags and wearing a miserable-looking hat whose folded brim at the front boasted a bedraggled feather, he had a gaunt, one-eyed dragonnet sitting on his shoulder, attached to a leash.

Laincourt took a seat at a table and found himself served, without asking, with a goblet filled with a vile cheap wine. He wet his lips, refrained from grimacing at the taste and forced himself to drink the rest in order to buck himself up. The hurdy-gurdy man soon ceased playing, to the general indifference of his audience, and came to sit in front of Laincourt.

'You're a sorry sight, boy.'

'You'll have to pay for the wine. I don't have a brass sou to my name.'

The old man nodded.

'How do matters stand?' he asked.

'I was arrested yesterday and released today.'

'Did you see the cardinal?'

'At Le Châtelet, in the presence of Saint-Georges and a secretary who noted everything down. The match has begun.'

'It's a match in a dangerous game, boy. And you don't even know all the rules.'

'I didn't have any other choice.'

'Of course you did! And there may still be time to—'

'You know that's impossible.'

The hurdy-gurdy player stared into Laincourt's eyes, then looked away and sighed.

The dragonnet leaped from his master's shoulder onto the table. It lay down, stretched out its neck and scratched playfully at a pile of wax that had solidified on the grimy wood.

'I see you are determined to see this whole affair through to the end, boy. But it will cost you, believe me . . . Sooner or later, you will be caught between the cardinal and the Black Claw, as between the hammer and the anvil. And nothing you—'

'Who is Captain La Fargue?'

The question caught the old man short.

'La Fargue,' Laincourt insisted. 'Do you know who he is?'

'Where . . . Where did you hear this name?'

'He reappeared at the Palais-Cardinal.'

'Really? When was this?'

'The other night. His Eminence received him . . . Well?'

240

The hurdy-gurdy player waiting before saying, as if with regret:

'It's an old story.'

'Tell me.'

'I don't know all the details.'

Laincourt grew all the more impatient as he didn't know the reasons for such reluctance.

'I'm not in the mood to drag this out of you. You're supposed to keep me informed and serve me, aren't you?'

But the other man still seemed hesitant.

'Tell me everything you know!' ordered the young man, raising his voice.

'Yes, yes . . . All right . . .'

The hurdy-gurdy player drank some wine, wiped his mouth on the back of his sleeve and, giving Laincourt a reproachful look, said:

'A while ago, La Fargue commanded a group of men who—'

'—carried out secret missions for the cardinal, yes. This much, I already know.'

'They were called the Cardinal's Blades. There were no more than ten of them. Some would say they did the cardinal's dirty work for him. Personally, I would say that they were both soldiers and spies. And at times, it's true, assassins—'

' "Assassins"?'

The hurdy-gurdy player made a face.

'The word is perhaps a little strong. But not all of France's enemies fight on the fields of battle, nor do all of them advance to the beat of drum and preceded by a banner . . . I don't need to tell you that wars can also be waged behind the stage and that many deaths take place there.'

'And for there to be deaths, someone has to cause them '

'Exactly. But I remain convinced that the Blades have saved more lives than they have taken. Sometimes you have to cut off a hand to preserve the arm and the man that comes with it.'

'What happened at the siege of La Rochelle?'

Once again surprised, but now on guard, the old man lifted an eyebrow at Laincourt.

'If you're asking that question, boy, then you know the answer . . .'

'I'm listening to you.'

'The Blades were given a mission that, no doubt, was meant to hasten the end of the siege. But don't ask me the nature of it . . . Whatever it was, La Fargue was betrayed.'

'By who?'

'By one of his own men, by a Blade . . . The mission failed and another Blade lost his life there. As for the traitor, he managed to flee . . . And as for the siege, you know how it ended. The dam that prevented the besieged forces in the town from being reinforced by sea suddenly broke, the king had to recall his armies rather than risk the financial ruin of the realm, and La Rochelle became a Protestant republic.'

'And after that?'

'After that, there was no longer any question of the Blades.'

'Until today . . . What do the Blades have to do with the Black Claw?'

'Nothing. Not to my knowledge, at least . . .'

The dragonnet had fallen asleep. He snored softly.

'La Fargue's return no doubt signals the return of the Blades,' Laincourt declared in a low voice. 'It must have something to do with me.'

'That's by no means certain. The cardinal always has several irons in his fire.'

'Be that as it may, I would prefer not to have to watch my flanks as well as my rear . . .'

'Then you chose the wrong path, boy . . . entirely the wrong path . . .'

Later, as Laincourt ventured back out into the night, a black dragonnet with golden eyes discreetly took flight from a roof nearby.

24

La Fargue was galloping through Paris at Almades's side. He had just come out of the Palais-Cardinal and found the master of arms waiting for him with their horses. They rode along the École quay and crossed a deserted Pont Neuf at full speed.

'His Eminence wants Malencontre?' the captain was saying loudly enough to be heard over the hoof beats. 'Very well. I can only bow to his demand. But nothing prevents me from dragging the truth out of the villain before I hand him over!'

'If the cardinal is asking for him, it's because Malencontre is more valuable than we imagined. No doubt he knows a lot. But about what?'

'Or about who . . . ? If we believe the cardinal, whatever Malencontre knows has nothing to do with the affair that concerns us. We'll see about that . . .'

A short distance from Pont Neuf, they were forced to halt at the Buci gate.

They went forward at a slow walk between two crenellated towers, beneath a wide vaulted ceiling which made the horses' hoof beats echo against the paving stones like shots from a musket. The pikemen of the city militia called their officer over, who examined the riders' passes in the lantern light and saw a seal – that of the cardinal – which opened gates everywhere in France.

The portcullis was already raised and the drawbridge lowered. But the enormous doors themselves still had to be opened and the sleepy militia soldiers were taking their time to remove the chains, lift the bar and push the heavy iron-bound panels. They were wasting time that La Fargue knew to be precious.

He grew impatient.

'Hurry UP, messieurs!'

'Malencontre was still doing poorly when we left,' Almades said to him. 'He had barely regained his spirits and wasn't—'

'That doesn't matter . . . I will make him spill what he knows in less than an hour. By force if necessary. Whatever the cost.'

'But, captain—'

'No! I did not agree to hand this devil over in good condition, after all. He doesn't even have to be alive, come to think of it . . .'

At last they were able to pass and spurred their horses on to cross the foul muck-filled ditch before riding quickly through the streets of the faubourg. They burst into rue Saint-Guillaume just as Guibot was closing the gates to the Hôtel de l'Épervier. Almades slowed down, but not La Fargue. He entered at a full gallop, obliging the old porter to jump aside while pushing one of the panels of the coach gate back open. La Fargue's horse had to pull up abruptly in the courtyard as the captain jumped down from the saddle and rushed over to the main building . . .

. . . and found Leprat sitting, or rather sprawled, on the front steps.

Bare-headed, with his doublet open and his shirt untucked, his wounded leg stretched out before him, the former musketeer was leaning back, supported by his elbows against the last step. He was drinking, without thirst, straight from a wine bottle. His rapier, still in its scabbard, was lying nearby.

'Too late . . .' he spat. 'They took him away.'

'Malencontre?'

Leprat nodded.

'Who?' insisted La Fargue. 'Who took him away?'

The other man swallowed a last mouthful, noticed that his bottle was empty and threw it against a wall where it shattered. Then he picked up his rapier and heaved himself up.

'It looks rather as if, in summoning you, the cardinal only wished to draw you away, doesn't it?' he replied in a bitter tone.

'Spare me that, will you? And answer my question.'

'Rochefort and his underlings, of course . . . They just left. They had an order signed by His Eminence. An order that Rochefort seemed particularly pleased to wave under my nose.'

'I couldn't have foreseen that! I couldn't know—'

'Know what?' Leprat flared. 'Know that nothing at all has changed? Know that the cardinal continues to play his own game with us? Know that we are puppets with him pulling the strings? Know that we count for so little . . . ? Go on, captain, did the cardinal even tell you why he was taking Malencontre from us? No, I think not. On the other hand, he was careful not to announce his decision until you were powerless to do anything about it . . . That should wake some familiar memories in you. And it stirs up just as many questions . . .'

Disgusted, Leprat limped back inside the house.

He left La Fargue behind, who was joined by Almades leading their horses by their bridles.

'He . . . He's right,' murmured the captain in a tight voice.

'Yes. But that's not the worst news . . .'

La Fargue turned towards the Spaniard.

'Guibot,' explained Almades, 'just told me Rochefort and his men brought a coach in which to carry Malencontre off. That means the cardinal not only knew we were holding him, but also that he was not in a fit state to ride a horse.'

'So what?'

'We were the only ones who knew that Malencontre was wounded, captain. Just us. Nobody else.'

'Which means one of us is informing Richelieu on the sly.'

25

After making sure the front door was shut, the young woman extinguished all of the lights except one on the ground floor and, candlestick in hand, walked upstairs protecting the wavering flame with her palm. The candle illuminated her pretty face from below and set two golden points aglow in the depths of her eyes, while the creak of the steps was the only sound to be heard throughout the house.

Once she reached her bedroom, she set down the candlestick on a table and, undoing the chignon that held up her long dark hair, went over to close the window which had been left ajar behind the curtains. She had started to undo the lacings of her dress when someone seized her from behind and placed a hand against her mouth.

'Don't cry out,' murmured Marciac. 'I won't harm you.'

She nodded, felt his grip on her relax, and broke free with a vicious blow of her elbow. She rushed to her bedside table and turned around brandishing a stiletto.

Marciac, who suffered less from his painful ribs than from hurt pride, stretched out his hand in an appeasing gesture and, keeping his distance, said in a voice that he also hoped was calming:

'You really don't have anything to fear from me. On the contrary.'

He was worried that she might injure herself.

'Who . . . Who are you?'

'My name is Marciac.'

He stepped cautiously to one side, but the young woman, on her guard, followed the movement with the point of her stiletto.

'I don't know you . . . ! What are you doing in my home?'

'I have been hired to protect you. And that's exactly what I'm trying to do.'

'Hired? Hired by whom?'

The Gascon was willing to gamble here.

'The man who just left you,' he ventured. 'Castilla.'

That name caused the wary gaze directed at Marciac to falter.

'Castilla . . . ? He . . . He said nothing to me.'

'He was afraid of worrying you unnecessarily. He paid me and told me to stay out of your sight.'

'You're lying!'

With a swift gesture, he reached out and seized the young woman's wrist and, without disarming her, forced her to turn around against him. He now had her firmly in his grasp, but he was trying not to hurt her.

'Listen to me closely, now. Time is short. Some hired swordsmen are preparing to abduct you. I don't know who they are. I don't know exactly what they want with you. All I know is that I won't let them have their way. But you must trust me!'

As he said these words, there was a sinister squeak of hinges, coming from the ground floor.

'Do you hear that? They're already here . . . Do you understand, now?'

'Yes,' replied the young woman in a lifeless voice.

He released her, spun her around again and, placing his hands on her shoulders, looked straight into her eyes.

'What's your first name?'

'Cécile.'

'Do you have a weapon, other than this toy?'

'A pistol.'

'Armed and loaded?'

'Yes.'

'Perfect. Get it, and put on a cloak.'

Without waiting, he left the bedroom and went to the stairs. He listened carefully, and could pick out the sounds of men coming up the steps in single file, as silently as possible. He waited until the first arrived on the landing and, emerging from the shadows, struck him a blow full in the face with a stool.

The man tumbled backward, knocking over his accomplices and provoking a debacle. Cries rose as the thugs struggled with one another on the stairs. For good measure, Marciac threw the stool down at them blindly and scored a hit, adding to the confusion.

By now Cécile was there with him, wearing a large cloak with a hood. He led her towards a window which he opened. It looked out over a side alley, less than a metre away from a balcony. The Gascon passed the young woman over to the other side before joining her. From the balcony, he climbed onto the roof just above, then stretched his hand down. Cécile caught hold of it and he brusquely pulled her up just as one of the swordsmen reached the window. The man attempted to seize her dress, but his fingernails only clawed at the fabric. The young woman cried out. Carried by the momentum of his violent heave, Marciac fell backwards and Cécile collapsed on top of him.

'Are you all right?' he asked.

'Yes.'

They picked themselves up.

One of the thugs had already leaped onto the balcony. He was climbing up when the Gascon surprised him with a powerful kick of his boot which smashed his jaw and sent him tumbling six metres to the ground below.

With Marciac keeping hold of Cécile's hand, they fled together across the tangled maze of abutting rooftops. A shot rang out and a pistol ball crashed into a chimney as they disappeared behind it. They heard the assassins hailing one another and organising the pursuit – some on the roofs, some down on the streets. They climbed up to another roof, their figures standing out for a moment against the starry sky and offering a perfect shot to an eager marksman, but Marciac was able to get a general idea of their situation from this vantage point. He knew they would have to come down again eventually. Rather than wait until they were backed up against an impassable drop, he headed towards a deep dark hole that marked the position of an inner courtyard.

There they found an immense scaffold, the vestiges of an abandoned work site, attached to the three storeys of a condemned building. Their pursuers approaching, As Marciac lowered Cécile and let her drop onto the temporary framework a swordsman appeared out of nowhere. The Gascon drew his sword and a duel ensued. The combatants confronted one another on the ridge of the rooftop. As they crossed swords, they moved back and forth to the rhythm of their strikes and counterstrikes between the sky and the waiting depths. The tiles which they dislodged with their feet fell in a cascade and bounced against the scaffolding before shattering in the courtyard, fifteen metres below. At last, parrying a cut and seizing his opponent by the wrist, Marciac attempted to throw him over his shoulder by pivoting suddenly. But his hold was poor and he lost his balance, dragging the thug who still held him along as he fell. The two men rolled and toppled off the roof. Before Cécile's eyes – who stifled a cry of horror – they crashed through the highest catwalk of the scaffold and landed on the next one down. The impact shook the entire structure, which swayed for a long moment. Boards and beams groaned. Cracking noises could be heard, indicating further sinister developments to come.

Although he was still tottering, Marciac was the first one on his feet. He searched for his rapier, realised that it was now at the bottom of the courtyard and, with a kick beneath the chin, finished off his adversary when he had barely begun to rise. Then he told Cécile to join him by sliding down the catwalk that had broken in the middle. He took her hand again, reassured her with a glance and, together, they climbed down several flights of shaky steps, fearing that the old tormented scaffold would come down around their ears at any second.

Finally on the ground, they discovered that the courtyard had only one exit: a shadowy passage from which three thugs suddenly materialised. One of them pointed a pistol at the fugitives. Marciac immediately clasped the young woman by the waist and turned his back to the shooter. The detonation rang out. The ball gashed the Gascon's shoulder, and he clenched his teeth and pushed Cécile behind a cart filled with wine barrels. He rushed over to his rapier which was lying in the mud and, just in time, turned to face his assailants. Concentrated and relentless, he fought without ceding an inch of terrain or letting himself be outflanked, for fear of exposing his young charge to danger. Then, when he seemed unable to press home his advantage against one swordsman without another forcing him to break off his attack immediately, he initiated a lightning counterattack. He slit the throat of his first opponent with a reverse cut, struck the second with a blow of the elbow to the temple, kicked the third in the crotch and then planted his rapier in the man's chest, all the way to the hilt.

He hoped that it was finished, but Cécile called out to him, pointing to the last floor of the rickety scaffold: with rapiers in their fists, two men who had come down from the roofs were venturing onto the platform with cautious steps. At the same time, a latecomer was emerging from the dark passageway and the entire neighbourhood was starting to awaken. Tired and wounded, the Gascon guessed that he was no longer in any condition to eliminate three additional opponents. Would he have the strength and the time to vanquish one before the other two arrived?

He retreated towards Cécile and the two-wheeled cart behind which she had sought shelter. Impassive, he waited as the first swordsman advanced and his two accomplices reached the second storey of the scaffold. Then suddenly, raising his rapier high with both hands, he struck with all his might at the stretched rope which, passing through rings rooted in the paving stones of the courtyard, kept the cart horizontal. Cut clean through, the rope cracked like a whip out of the rings. The cart leaned sharply, lifting its shafts into the air and freeing its pyramid of barrels, which rolled out like an avalanche.

The swordsman in the courtyard hastily backed up and was brought to bay beneath the scaffold, although he managed to avoid being crushed by the barrels. Some of them burst against the wall, releasing floods of wine. But others slammed into the unstable beams that propped up the enormous framework. These beams gave way and the entire three-storey structure collapsed with an incredible racket which drowned out the cries of the unfortunate souls doomed by the huge falling wooden beams. Pieces of masonry were torn off the façade along with wide plaques of plaster. Thick clouds of dust rose into the air, swallowing the entire courtyard and swelling until they climbed up past the surrounding roofs . . .

. . . and then they fell back onto a courtyard which was turned completely white with dust, and to silence.

Marciac was still for a moment, contemplating the disaster. As the neighbourhood began to fill with worried calls from its residents, he sheathed his sword and walked towards Cécile. Covered in dust like him, she was curled up in a corner.

He squatted, turning his back to the wreckage.

'It's over, Cécile.'

'I . . . I . . . Those men,' stammered the young woman . . .

'All is well, Cécile . . .'

'Are they . . . dead?'

'Yes. Here, take my hand . . .'

She seemed to neither hear, nor comprehend.

He insisted in a gentle voice.

'We need to leave, Cécile. Now . . .'

He was going to help her up when he read a sudden terror in her eyes and realised what it meant.

One of the swordsmen had survived.

He could feel the killer's presence behind him, ready to strike. He knew he didn't have time to stand and turn, and still less to unsheathe his rapier.

He looked deeply into the young woman's eyes, praying that she would understand, even thought he saw her give a very slight nod . . . And then he dove to one side.

Cécile lifted her pistol with both hands and fired.

The Sphère d'Âme

1

His legs dangling, the man's entire weight hung from his bound wrists. He swayed gently and his toenails scraped the hard-earth floor. He was wearing only breeches and a torn, bloody shirt. More of the same blood – his own – soaked his tangled hair, spattered his swollen face and glistened on his bruised torso beneath the torchlight. The man still lived, but was barely breathing: a hoarse rasp escaped from the painful depths of his chest and pink bubbles formed at the nostrils of his broken nose.

He was not alone in this cellar that had been converted into an antechamber of Hell. With him was the obese, sweating giant busy torturing him with heavy blows from a chain, delivered in a brutal but skilful manner. Then there was the one-eyed man who spoke to the prisoner, asking questions in Castilian. With olive skin and a sharp-featured face, he was dressed entirely in black leather, including his gloves and a hat which he never removed. A black patch with silver studs masked his left eye but failed to disguise the fact that it was eaten away by the ranse. Indeed, the disease had ravaged the entire area surrounding the socket and spread towards the man's temple and cheek, the tumour extending in a star-shaped tracery of dark violet ridges.

The one-eyed man went by the name of Savelda and served the Black Claw. In a calm voice, he had promised his prisoner a thousand torments if he did not obtain the answers he was seeking.

He had not been lying.

Patient and determined, Savelda conducted the interrogation without ever becoming too concerned about his victim's obstinate refusal to give up his secrets. He knew that time, pain and despair were all working on his side. He knew that the prisoner would talk eventually, just as the most solid of castle walls will eventually crumble under a barrage of cannon balls. It would happen suddenly, with little or no warning. There would be one impact too many and then a great, liberating collapse.

With a gesture, he halted the rain of blows from the chain. Then he said:

'Do you know what never ceases to amaze me . . . ? It is when I see the degree to which our bodies are attached to life.'

Inert but still conscious, the victim remained silent. His swollen lids were half-shut over his glassy, bloodshot eyes. Seeping clots encrusted his ears. Threads of mixed drool, bile and blood ran from between his cracked, puffed lips.

'Take you, for example,' continued Savelda. 'At this very moment, your only desire is for death. You desire it with your entire will, with all your soul. If you could, you would devote your last remaining strength to dying. And yet it won't happen. Life is there, within you, like a nail driven deep into a solid block of wood. Life doesn't care what you might want. It doesn't care what you're suffering, or the service it would do you if it would just abandon your body. It's stubborn, it persists, it finds secret refuges within you. It's growing tired, to be sure. But it will still take some time to dislodge it from your entrails.'

Savelda tugged on his gloves to tighten them, making the leather creak as he clenched and unclenched his fists.

'And that's what I'm depending on, you see. Your life, the life instilled in you by the Creator, is my ally. Against it your courage and loyalty count for nothing. Unfortunately for you, you are young and vigorous. Your will to resist speaking will give up long before life decides to leave you and death carries you away. That's just how things are.'

The victim made an effort to speak, murmuring something. Savelda bent close and heard:

'Hijo de puta!'

At that moment, a hired swordsman came down the stairs

into the cellar. He halted on the steps and, leaning over the railing, announced in French:

'The marquis is outside.'

'Gagnière?' the one-eyed man said in surprise, pronouncing the French name with a strong Spanish accent.

'Yes. He wants to speak with you. He says it's urgent.'

'All right. I'm coming.'

'And me?' asked the torturer. 'What should I do? Shall I continue?'

Shirt open over his wide torso which was streaming with sweat, he rattled the bloody chain. The victim stiffened on hearing the sound.

'No. Wait,' replied the one-eyed man as he went up the stairs.

After the damp warmth of the cellar Savelda welcomed the cool evening breeze that gently blew through the ground floor. He crossed a room where his men slept or idled away the time playing dice and went out into the night to breathe the fragrant air. A flowering orchard surrounded the house.

Extravagantly elegant as always, the handsome young marquis de Gagnière was waiting on horseback.

'He still hasn't talked,' reported Savelda.

'That isn't what brings me here.'

'A problem?'

'That's one way to put it. Your men failed on rue de la Fontaine. The girl escaped.'

'Impossible.'

'Only one of your men returned, with a broken leg and jaw. From his mutterings, we understood that the girl was not alone. There was someone else with her. And this single person sufficed to rout your entire team.'

Disconcerted, Savelda was at a loss for words.

'I will take it upon myself to inform the vicomtesse,' continued Gagnière. 'For your part, do not fail with your prisoner. He must be made to talk.'

'He'll talk. Before tomorrow.'

'Let's hope so.'

The gentleman dug in his spurs and trotted off in the moonlight between two rows of trees, following a path covered with white petals which swirled beneath his horse's hooves.

2

'She's resting,' said Agnès de Vaudreuil as she left the room. 'Keep her company, would you? And come and find me the moment she wakes.'

Shyly avoiding the baronne's eye, Naïs nodded and slipped through the half-open door which she closed behind her without making a sound.

Agnès waited a short while and then, almost groping her way, went to the stairs. She could barely see anything in this gloomy corridor of the equally gloomy Hôtel de l'Épervier. All of it was built from the same bare, funereal grey stone; the windows were low and far between, often occluded by shutters and always defended by stout iron bars. Elsewhere, along the passageways and stairs, there were narrow embrasures, veritable arrow slits, which at this hour only admitted small slivers of the pale glow of dawn. Moreover, it was usual to carry a light when moving about the house at night, rather than allow a flame to burn alone; out of a natural fear of fire, but also for the sake of economy – even tallow, as nasty smelling as it was, cost money, and the better-quality white wax candles were an expensive luxury. But Agnès had left her candle in the room.

She was about to descend the dark stairs carefully when someone called to her.

'Agnès,' said Captain La Fargue.

She had not noticed him standing there, hidden by silence and shadow. Added to the imposing stature of a body that had been hardened by combat and other trials, his patriarchal air demanded respect: his proud martial bearing and grim face whose features had been sharpened by the years, the closely shaven beard and eyes full of wisdom and strength. He was still wearing his boots and his doublet, with the top button undone. But he did not have his sword or his hat and his thick silver hair almost glowed in the dim light.

He approached Agnès, took her gently by the elbow and invited her to sit with him on the first step of the stairs. She agreed, intrigued, understanding that he wished to speak to her before they rejoined the other Blades, whose faint voices rose from the ground floor. The old captain and the young baronne were separated by gender and three decades. And they also had to overcome a natural reserve on his side and a reluctance to confide in others on hers. But a special bond of friendship and mutual respect united them despite their differences and sense of proprieties. A bond almost akin to the love between father and daughter.

'How is she?' asked La Fargue.

He spoke in a low voice, as if they found themselves in the house of someone recently dead.

Looking over her shoulder, Agnès darted a brief, instinctive glance towards the door of the room where the young woman saved by Marciac had just fallen asleep.

'Her adventure last night has severely shaken her.'

'Did she confide in you?'

'Yes, if she is to be believed, she—'

'Later,' La Fargue cut her short. 'For now, I would simply like to know what you make of her.'

Agnès had not yet had time to change and was still wearing the elegant gown of scarlet silk and satin that she had donned before going out with Marciac to madame de Sovange's mansion. With a rustle of skirts, petticoats and hoop, she drew back from the captain to look at him squarely.

'What a strange question,' she remarked.

Leaning forward, elbows on his thighs and hands clasped, he stared out at a distant point in front of them.

'Among other talents, you are better at delving into people's souls than anyone else I know. So what do you make of her?'

Agnès turned away from the captain, sighed and took the time to collect her thoughts and sum up her impressions.

'I believe . . .' she started to say. 'I believe that she lies a little and hides much.'

Inscrutable, La Fargue nodded slowly.

'I would also guess that she was born in Spain,' Agnès continued. 'Or has at least lived there for many years.'

She watched him from the corner of her eye and caught his expression. He frowned, straightened up and asked:

'How do you know that?'

'Her Spanish origins cannot be detected from her inflexions. But a few of her turns of phrase could be directly translated from Castilian.'

He nodded again, this time with a worried, resigned air.

A silence ensued.

'What exactly is it that you want to know, captain?' the baronne finally asked in a quiet voice. 'Or rather, what do you already know . . . ? I was next to you when Marciac returned with the girl. I saw how you reacted. You went completely white . . .'

On her return from the gambling house, Agnès had found the lights still burning at the Hôtel de l'Épervier despite the late hour and the Blades in turmoil following the abduction – at the cardinal's orders – of Malencontre by the comte de Rochefort. Frustrated and humiliated, Leprat in particular would not calm down and drank more than was reasonable. Then Marciac had arrived with a woman he had managed to rescue after an epic struggle and they were suddenly faced with other matters of concern.

'I am not yet sure of anything,' La Fargue said. 'Go rejoin the others, will you? And do not speak to them of our conversation. I will be with you shortly.'

Agnès hesitated, then rose and went downstairs.

Once he was alone, the old captain withdrew a medallion from his doublet, opened the small carved lid and lost himself in the contemplation of a miniature portrait. If it had not been painted twenty-five years earlier, it might have been that of the new, mysterious guest at the Hôtel de l'Épervier.

After removing her gown and washing her face, Agnès joined the rest of the Blades in the main room, where the torches provided more light than the faint glimmer of day that entered through the small lozenge-shaped window panes.

Sitting in an armchair by the fireplace, Leprat, with his wounded leg propped on a stool before him, was silently drinking from a bottle. To one side, Almades was sharpening his rapier with a whetstone – three strokes along one edge, three strokes along the other, over and over. At the table, Ballardieu and Marciac partook of a light but solid repast that Guibot, hobbling about on his wooden leg, had served at their request. They drank, but the Gascon, still excited by his recent adventure, spoke more than he ate while the veteran nodded vigorously and polished off his meal with an appetite that nothing could discourage.

'I thought I was lost,' Marciac was saying. 'But I threw myself to the side, she brandished her pistol with both hands and – bam! – she fired. And her aim was dead on . . . ! The assassin who was about to run me through from behind collapsed with a ball right in the middle of his forehead.'

'That was damned good piece of luck,' Ballardieu commented before washing down a mouthful of *pâté en croûte* with a swallow of wine.

'It was destiny, my friend. Destiny. "*Audaces fortuna juvat!*" '

His lips greasy and his mouth full, the other man looked at him with wide eyes.

'The saying,' Marciac explained 'is more or less borrowed from Virgil: "Fortune smiles upon the brave".'

Ballardieu was about to ask who Virgil was, but held his tongue as the Gascon, seeing Agnès, asked anxiously:

'How is she?'

'Well. She sleeps.'

'I'm glad to hear it.'

'And you? Your shoulder?'

In addition to a girl who was still trembling from fright, Marciac had returned from his eventful evening with the air of a conquering hero, his hair full of plaster, a few bruises and

– not that he paid much notice to it – a nasty wound to the shoulder.

'Oh, it's just a scratch,' he said, with a vague gesture towards the bandage hidden beneath the sleeve of his clean, unwrinkled shirt. 'It scarcely bled at all.'

'You were lucky,' Leprat said from his armchair, with just a hint of bitterness.

'No one succeeds without a bit of luck,' said Agnès as she sat down at the big table.

She took a plate and, after poking around in the dishes, loaded it with cold meats and cheeses, gratefully accepting a glass of wine that Ballardieu poured for her. La Fargue arrived, sat astride a backward-turned chair, and immediately launched a general discussion:

'You first, Marciac. Tell us what you know about this girl.'

'Her name is Cécile.'

'And what else?'

'That's all. I followed Castilla, who Agnès and I spotted leaving madame de Sovange's gaming salons. Castilla led me to Cécile's house in rue de la Fontaine. He did not stay long and left on horseback. By chance, I then came upon some men who I overheard preparing to abduct Cécile – although at the time, I didn't know that was her name. Be that as it may, I told myself that I could not let them succeed in their plan. And there you have it.'

'Who were these men?'

'Just some hired swords, like others of their kind. But they took their orders from a Spaniard, a one-eyed man in black leather who was so sure of their success that he did not remain with them.'

'Would you recognise him?' asked Leprat.

'Of course.'

'But you'd never seen him before.'

'No.'

La Fargue mulled over this information and then turned to Agnès.

'Now you.'

The baronne emptied her glass before speaking.

'She says her name is Cécile Grimaux. Last year she was living with her father and mother in Lyon. Both of them are now dead, the father from illness and the mother from grief, shortly after him. With no other resources, Cécile went to join her elder sister, Chantal, a seamstress who was living modestly in Paris but who was glad to take her in—'

' "Was living"?' Leprat interrupted.

'I'm coming to that . . . she occasionally worked for a glove maker and it was through him that Chantal made the acquaintance of two Spanish adventurers, the chevalier d'Ireban and his friend Castilla. She fell in love with the first and became his mistress. They trysted in secret in a little house in the faubourg Saint-Martin, living their perfect love while hidden from the eyes of the world. It lasted for a few weeks until they both disappeared suddenly. Since then, Castilla has been searching for them and Cécile awaits news. It seems that this ordeal has drawn them together.'

'How closely has it drawn them together?' asked Marciac.

Cécile being a very pretty girl, the others immediately guessed the reason for his interest.

'I believe you have a rival for her affections,' indicated Agnès with a quirk of her lips. 'But no doubt your chivalrous exploits last night plead in your favour—'

'That's not at all what I was thinking about!'

'Come, now . . .'

'That's enough!' La Fargue ordered with a rare display of temper.

But he recovered his calm quickly, pretending not to notice the wary looks being exchanged by the others.

'Nevertheless,' said Ballardieu, 'it's a strange tale.'

'But it matches pretty well with what Rochefort has told us,' noted Leprat almost regretfully.

Resuming the discussion, the Blades' captain asked Agnès:

'What does Cécile know of Ireban?'

'Almost nothing. According to her, her sister was not very forthcoming on the subject.'

'And of Castilla?'

'We hardly spoke of him. I only know that he has taken up

264

residence at the love nest in the faubourg Saint-Martin, in case Chantal or the chevalier shows up there.'

'Do you know where it is?'

'Yes.'

'Give Almades the directions: he will accompany me there in the hope of finding Castilla, who may help us get to the bottom of things. You will stay here, Agnès, and learn everything you can from Cécile once she wakes. As for you, Marciac, you've earned the right to rest for a bit.'

Since it went without saying that wherever Agnès was, one would also find Ballardieu, it only remained to assign Leprat. For a brief moment, out of respect, La Fargue tried to think of a task for him. But the former musketeer came to his rescue:

'Don't trouble yourself, captain. I know that I'll be useless until this blasted leg is healed. Let's just say that I am holding the fort in your absence.'

Everyone nodded, slightly embarrassed, before heading off on their various errands.

As preparations were being made, La Fargue went to his room and wrote a short letter which he carefully sealed. Agnès saw him a little while later, scratching at the door to Cécile's room and exchanging a few words with Naïs through the narrow opening, before giving her the missive. The baronne slipped away unnoticed and went to find Ballardieu.

'Get ready,' she said, once she was sure they were out of earshot of the rest of the company.

'For what?'

'Naïs will be going out, no doubt after the captain and the others have left. I want you to follow her.'

'Naïs? Why?'

'You'll see.'

'Ah . . . right.'

3

Arriving by way of rue Beauregard, the marquis de Gagnière dismounted in front of Notre-Dame-de-Bonne-Nouvelle church and hitched his horse to a ring. It was still very early in the morning and not many people were up and about. But the elegant gentleman still found it prudent to entrust his mount to the watchful eye of one of the vendors of *eau-de-vie* who, in the early hours of the day, went around Paris – crying '*Vi! Vi!* Drink! Drink!' – selling little cups of alcohol which were bought and eagerly drunk on the spot by people of the lower classes before their hard day of labour.

The church was silent, dark, damp and empty. As was usual in churches there were no pews, but chairs were stored in a corner ready to be rented out during services by the porter, who was also charged with ensuring the tranquillity of the premises, chasing away any beggars or stray dogs who attempted to enter with equal zeal. Gagnière advanced between the columns and placed himself in front of the high altar, near a thin young man with smooth cheeks and crystal-line blue eyes. The young man did not react until they stood almost shoulder-to-shoulder. He wore an ochre doublet that matched his breeches, boots, and was carrying a sword at his side. If he was not praying then he seemed at least meditative, with his eyes shut and his hat in his hand.

'I am rather surprised to see you here this morning,' said the marquis after a moment.

'Have I ever missed one of our appointments?' Arnaud de Laincourt replied, opening his eyes.

'No, to be sure. But, until now, you had never been arrested.'

For a few seconds, the former ensign of His Eminence's Guards did not respond.

'So you know,' he said at last.

'Naturally. Did you believe that such news would escape our attention?'

'No, I didn't. But so quickly—'

'We are everywhere, Laincourt. Even at the Palais-Cardinal. You, better than anyone, should know that.'

'And at Le Châtelet, marquis? Are you present there, too?' Gagnière pulled a face.

'The walls there are, shall we say . . . thicker.'

They remained silent for a moment in the sinister refuge of this deserted church where their secret meetings took place, always at dawn.

Notre-Dame-de-Bonne-Nouvelle had begun its life as a chapel, which was destroyed by soldiers of the Catholic League when the king of Navarre – and future Henri IV of France – laid siege to Paris in 1591. The existing church had been built in its place, with the first stone laid by Queen Anne d'Autriche. As the city absorbed its faubourgs, so the church now found itself at the extreme limit of the Saint-Denis district, right by the new city wall; only the narrow width of a newly laid street lined with building sites separated it from the bastions between the Poissonnière and Saint-Denis gates. This was the very edge of Paris.

'I am still a faithful servant of the Black Claw,' announced Laincourt in a calm voice. 'My loyalty remains unchanged.'

'Permit me to doubt that. Your liberation scarcely argues in your favour. By all rights, at this moment you should be locked away in Vincennes castle waiting to be put to the question. But here you are, having been found guilty of treason, free to come and go as you please. You must admit that the extraordinary clemency the cardinal has shown you offers ample grounds for suspicion . . .'

With a conciliatory shrug, Laincourt indicated that he understood. He explained:

'I possess a document which protects me; it contains a secret the cardinal fears will be divulged.'

Perplexed, Gagnière frowned. Then, almost amused, he said:

'A document that you have therefore taken pains not to transmit to us. A shining example of loyalty!'

'I am loyal, but also cautious,' Laincourt replied unmoved. 'I knew that a day like today would come.'

This time it was the turn of the marquis to accept the other's argument: he was forced to recognise that a 'day like today' had indeed come.

'Very well. What is this document?'

'It's a list naming France's secret correspondents in the Spanish royal court. It is in reliable hands and will be released if ever I delay too long in giving signs of life. The cardinal had no choice. He and I agreed that I should remain alive and free as long as this list remained secret.'

'You are very naïve if you imagine Richelieu will be satisfied with such an arrangement for long. He will deceive you at the very first opportunity. He may already be working to do so as we speak. He will find your list and have you murdered.'

'That is precisely why I am turning to you rather than galloping towards the nearest border.'

'Where is this list?'

'In reliable hands, as I told you. And they will remain anonymous.'

Gagnière's tone became menacing.

'It is a secret which we could tear out of you.'

'Not before the list would be brought to the knowledge of all.'

'So? We do not share the cardinal's fears. On the contrary, we would be delighted to see relations between France and Spain deteriorate even further.'

'To be sure,' allowed Laincourt. 'However, information concerning the Black Claw itself would be revealed at the same time. And believe me, this information could be most damaging.'

Gagnière greeted this news calmly, measuring what Laincourt knew about the Black Claw and the danger it might pose.

'Another list?' he suggested.

'Another list.'

'You are playing a very dangerous game, monsieur de Laincourt . . .'

'I have been employed as a professional spy for some time now, Gagnière. Long enough to know that servants of my type are sacrificed just as easily as the foot soldiers on a field of battle.'

The marquis sighed, no doubt annoyed not to have the upper hand.

'Let us cut to the chase. You would not be here if you had nothing to offer me. Speak.'

'I offer to deliver both lists to you as a token of my loyalty. You will destroy the one and do as you see fit with the other.'

'These papers protect you and yet you would separate yourself from them? Doesn't that run contrary to your interests?'

'I will separate myself from them, even though I'll risk incurring the cardinal's wrath. But, in return, I want to be assured of the Black Claw's protection.'

Gagnière was beginning to understand where this was leading, but nevertheless asked:

'How?'

'I want to join the circle of initiates to which you belong. Besides, I believe I have already earned that right on merit alone.'

'It is not up to you to be the judge of that.'

'I know. So take this proposal to the person who is.'

4

Barely distracted this time by the noisy, colourful crowd that milled about on the Pont Neuf, Ballardieu followed Naïs discreetly. He was in a foul mood and, with an angry look in his eye, talked to himself as he pushed through the throng.

'Ballardieu, you're not a complicated man,' he grumbled. 'You're not a complicated man because you don't have very much in the way of wits and you know it. You have loyalty and courage but not much wit, and that's simply the way of things. And you do as you're told, usually without protest. Or without protesting too much, which is the same thing. You are a soldier, even a good soldier. You obey orders. But I know you would greatly appreciate it if someone did you the honour of explaining, just once in a while, for the sole pleasure of breaking with old habit, the orders they gave you . . .'

At this point in his monologue, keeping an eye on Naïs' white bonnet, Ballardieu repeated Agnès' words and his own, hastily exchanged at the Hôtel de l'Épervier.

'"I want you to follow her." "Naïs? Why?" "You'll see." "Ah . . . right." A fine explanation! And what did you reply to it? "Ah . . . right." Nothing else . . . ! Ballardieu, you might have even less wit than you imagine. Because, in the end, there's nothing preventing you from demanding an explanation, is there? Well, granted, the girl had that look in her eye and you know very well that she wouldn't have explained anything at all. But at least you'd have tried instead of meekly following orders . . .'

Now getting himself worked up, Ballardieu shook his head.

'Good soldier! Good faithful dog, more like it . . . ! And where will the first blows land when things go wrong? On the dog, not on the mistress, by God! Because have no doubt about it, Ballardieu, this business will go wrong and it'll do so at the expense of yours truly. No one acts behind the captain's back and gets away with it. Sooner or later, you—'

Lost in his thoughts, he had bumped into a lampoonist who fell backwards in an explosion of printed papers.

'What?' flared Ballardieu angrily and in perfectly bad faith. 'Can't you watch where you're going? Is this the new fashion in Paris?'

The other man, bowled over in both the literal and figurative senses, took some time to recover himself. He was still wondering what had happened to him, and gaped with amazement and fear at this bull of a man who had come out of nowhere and charged into him as he was haranguing the crowd and brandishing his sheets which – as he was unable to blame the king directly – accused Richelieu of crushing the people beneath the weight of taxes. The individual who had so abruptly entered the life of the lampoonist was not someone with whom he would wish to seek a dispute. Without being particularly tall, he was wide, heavy and massive, and in addition to being red in the face and fuming, he was armed with a good-sized rapier.

But Ballardieu, to the great relief of his innocent victim, passed almost at once from anger to compassion and regret.

'No, friend. Forgive me. It's my fault . . . Here, take my hand.'

The lampoonist found himself catapulted upwards rather than simply raised.

'I offer my apologies. You'll accept them, won't you? Yes? Good man! Nothing broken, I hope . . . Good, I would happily pay for the brushing of your clothes but I'm short of time. I promise to buy you a drink when next we meet. Agreed? Perfect! Good day, friend!'

With these words, Ballardieu went on his way, while the other man, still tottering and dazed, an idiotic smile on his lips, bade him farewell with a hesitant wave.

Far ahead of him, Naïs had fortunately taken no notice of the incident and he had to quicken his pace in order not to lose sight of her. After Pont Neuf she followed rue Saint-Denis, then rue de la Vieille-Cordonnerie, came out on rue de la Ferronnerie and went up rue Saint-Honoré, which Ballardieu had never known to seem so long. They passed in front of the scaffolding of the Palais-Cardinal and went as far as rue Gaillon, into which Naïs turned. Recently absorbed by the capital by the construction of wall know as 'Yellow Ditches', this former faubourg was foreign territory to Ballardieu. He was about to discover its layout, its houses and its building sites.

Opposite rue des Moineaux, Naïs crossed a large porch that opened onto a courtyard full of people and animation, overlooked by a strange tower that stood at the end, like an oversized dovecote. A sign hung over the entrance where one could read the words: 'Gaget Messenger Service'.

'"Gaget Messenger Service"?' muttered Ballardieu with a frown. 'What's this, then?'

Seeing a passer-by, he asked him:

'Excuse me, sir, what is this place of business?'

'There? Why it's the Gaget Messenger Service, of course!'

And the man, in a hurry like all Parisians and as lofty as most of them, walked away.

Feeling his temper rise, Ballardieu sucked in his cheeks, took a deep breath in the vain hope of controlling the murderous impulses that had entered his head and caught up with the passer-by in a few strides, gripping him by the shoulder and forcing him to spin round.

'I know how to read, monsieur. But what is it exactly?'

He was breathing hard through his nose, was red-faced again and his eyes were glaring dangerously. The other man realised his mistake. Turning slightly pale, he explained that the company owned by Gaget offered customers a postal service using dragonnets, that this service was both rapid and reliable, although somewhat expensive, and . . .

'That's enough, that's enough . . .' said Ballardieu, finally releasing the Parisian to go about his business.

He hesitated for a moment over whether or not he should enter and then decided to take up a position at a discreet distance in order to wait and to observe – after all, Naïs might go elsewhere next. It wasn't long before the old soldier saw a familiar figure come out of Gaget's establishment.

It was not Naïs.

It was Saint-Lucq.

5

La Fargue and Almades had no trouble finding the house
Cécile had indicated, which stood at the fringe of the faubourg
Saint-Denis where the buildings faded away into open
countryside. It was surrounded by an orchard enclosed by a
high wall, in the middle of a landscape of fields, pastures,
small dwellings and large vegetable gardens. The spot was
charming, peaceful and bucolic, yet was less than a quarter-
league from Paris. There were peasants working in the fields
and herds of cows and sheep grazing. To the east, beyond
some leafy greenery, the rooftops of the Saint-Louis hospital
could be seen.

Along the way they had encountered a band of riders
coming in the other direction at full gallop, forcing them to
draw aside towards the ditches. In normal circumstances they
would have taken little notice of them. But the band was
headed by a one-eyed man dressed in black leather who
strongly resembled the individual Marciac had surprised the
night before, organising the abduction of the young Cécile
Grimaux.

'I don't believe in coincidences of this kind,' La Fargue
had commented as they watched the riders disappear towards
Paris.

And, after a meaningful look in reply from Almades, they
both promptly spurred their mounts in an effort to arrive at
their destination as quickly as possible.

They did not slow down until they reached the gate. It was
opened wide onto the path that led straight through the
orchard to the house.

'Are your pistols loaded?' asked the old captain.

'Yes.'

Riding side by side, all their senses alert, they advanced up the path between rows of blossoming trees. The air was sweet, full of delicate fruity fragrances. A radiant morning sun dispensed a light that was joyfully greeted by birdsong. The foliage around them rustled in the gentle breeze.

There were two men standing in front of the small house. On seeing the riders approaching at a walk, they came forward, curious, craning their necks to see better. They were armed with rapiers and wearing doublets, breeches and riding boots. One of them had a pistol tucked in the belt that cinched his waist.

'Who goes there?' he challenged in a loud voice.

He took a few more steps, while the other stood back and placed the sun behind him. At the same moment a third man emerged from doorway to the house and remained close to the threshold. La Fargue and Almades observed these movements with an appreciative eye: the three men were perfectly positioned in case of a fight.

'My name is La Fargue. I've come to visit a friend of mine.'

'What friend?'

'The chevalier de Castilla.'

'There is no one by that name within.'

'Yet this is his dwelling, is it not?'

'No doubt. But he just left.'

The man with the pistol was trying to appear at ease. But something was worrying him, as if he was expecting something irremediable to happen at any minute. His companions shared his anxiety: they were in a hurry to finish whatever they were doing and wanted these untimely visitors to turn round and leave.

'Just now?' asked La Fargue.

'Just now.'

'I'll wait for him.'

'Come back later, instead.'

'When?'

'Whenever you please, monsieur.'

Almades was leaning forward like a tired rider, his wrists

275

crossed over the pommel of his saddle, hands dangling just a few centimetres from the pistols lodged in his saddle holsters. His glance sweeping out from under the brim of his hat, he observed his potential opponents and knew which of them – taking into account, among other things, the layout of the place – he would have to take on if things went badly. With his index, middle and ring fingers he idly tapped out a series of three beats.

'I would be obliged,' said La Fargue, 'if you would inform the chevalier of my visit.'

'Consider it done.'

'Will you remember my name?'

'La Fargue, was it?'

'That's right.'

The hired swordsman at the doorstep was the most nervous of the three. He kept glancing over his shoulder, seeming to watch something going on inside the house which was likely to be coming out soon. He cleared his throat, no doubt signalling to his accomplices that time was running short.

The man with the pistol understood.

'Very well, messieurs,' he said. 'Goodbye, then.'

La Fargue nodded, smiling, and pinched the felt brim of his hat in farewell.

But Almades sniffed: a suspect, alarming odour was tickling his nose.

'Fire,' he muttered from the corner of his mouth to his captain.

The latter looked up at the chimney of the house, but could see no plume of smoke rising from it. On the other hand, in the same instant he and the Spaniard caught sight of the first curls of smoke obscuring the windows from within, on the ground floor.

The house was burning.

The assassins realised their secret was discovered and reacted instantly. But Almades was faster still, seizing his pistols, extending his arms and firing simultaneously to the right and the left. He killed both the man on the doorstep and the other man who had been hanging back with two balls that drilled into the middle of their respective foreheads. The detonations startled his horse, which whinnied and reared, forcing La Fargue's steed to take a step to one side. The last man had meanwhile drawn his pistol and was taking aim at the captain. But his shot missed La Fargue who, struggling to control his mount, had to twist round in his saddle in order to return fire. He hit his target nevertheless, lodging a ball in the neck of his opponent who collapsed in a heap.

Silence returned to the scene just as suddenly as the previous violence had been unleashed. With La Fargue removing a second pistol from its holster, he and Almades dismounted, taking cover for a moment behind their horses, observing the house and its surroundings for signs of any other enemies.

'Do you see anyone?'

'No,' replied the Spanish master of arms. 'I think there were only three in all.'

'No doubt they stayed behind to make sure the fire took good hold.'

'That means there's something inside that must disappear.'

Rapiers in their fists, they rushed into the house.

Fires had been set at several points and thick black smoke attacked their eyes and throats. But the danger was not yet significant, although it was too late for there to be any hope of extinguishing the conflagration. While Almades rushed up the stairs to the floor above, La Fargue took charge of inspecting the ground level. He went from room to room without finding anything or anyone, until he spied a small, low door, just as the Spaniard came back down.

'There's a room up there with a chest full of clothing for both a man and a woman. And there are theatre face paints.'

'Let's look in the cellar,' decided the captain.

They opened the small door, went down some stone stairs and there, in the dim light, found Castilla half-naked and bloody, still suspended by his wrists, having been left to perish in the blaze that was beginning to ravage the entire house. At his feet lay the heavy chain that had served to torture him.

La Fargue supported his weight while Almades cut him down. Then they carried him, hastily crossing the ground floor where flames were already licking at the walls and attacking the ceilings. They stretched the unfortunate wretch out on the grass at a safe distance from the house.

Castilla was agitated, moaning and mumbling in spite of his weakened state. Something urgent was forcing him to call upon his last reserves of strength. La Fargue leaned over him and brought his ear close to the man's swollen lips.

'What is he saying?' inquired Almades.

'I don't know exactly,' answered the captain, straightening up on his knees. 'Something like . . . "garanegra"?'

'*Garra negra*,' murmured the Spaniard, recognising his mother tongue.

La Fargue shot him an intrigued look.

'The Black Claw,' Almades translated.

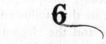

6

It didn't take Saint-Lucq long to spot Ballardieu.

His instinct, initially, had led him to suspect that he was being watched from rue des Moineaux as he left the Gaget Messenger Service. To confirm this, the half-blood entered a bakery nearby. When he reappeared in the street he was nibbling innocently on a little tart, but took the opportunity to survey his surroundings from behind the red lenses of his spectacles. Without seeming to do so, he took careful note of Ballardieu's round, weathered face among the ordinary passers-by.

The presence of the old soldier surprised him but was not a cause for worry. Obviously, Ballardieu had latched onto his trail after following Naïs, the servant from the Hôtel de l'Épervier. This could only be at Agnès' request. All that remained was to find out why.

The previous evening, on returning from a delicate mission, Saint-Lucq had learned both that the Blades had resumed service and that he would be rejoining them under the direct command of La Fargue. The captain, however, had wished to keep the half-blood in reserve and it was agreed that he would await his orders at the Gaget Messenger Service. This idea had not displeased him. It indicated that the captain wished to keep a card up his sleeve, and that he was to be this card. But to be played against whom, and to what end? Did La Fargue mistrust someone within the Palais-Cardinal, or even among the Blades themselves? Saint-Lucq had not deemed it necessary to ask the question. Nevertheless, there was something fishy going on and Agnès de Vaudreuil, evidently, had not taken long to come to the same conclusion. Hence the appearance of Ballardieu on the half-blood's heels.

With La Fargue's letter in his pocket, thanks to Naïs, Saint-Lucq proceeded at a steady, tranquil pace as far as the quays along the Seine, which he then followed upstream. Then, by way of the Pont Neuf and the elegant Place Dauphine he arrived at the Palais de la Cité. He had concluded that he needed to shake Ballardieu from his tail without seeming to do it on purpose, in order not to arouse his suspicions and, above all, those of Agnès, who seemed to be dancing a strange *pas de deux* with La Fargue. The half-blood's loyalty was to his captain first, and the Palais de la Cité was ideally suited for an impromptu game of hide-and-seek. At one time the seat of royal power, it was now, among other things, the most important court of law in the French kingdom, housing fourteen of the twenty-nine jurisdictions in Paris within a jumble of buildings dating back to the Middle Ages.

Saint-Lucq entered via rue de la Barillerie, and then through a gate flanked by two turrets. Beyond were two courtyards to either side of the Sainte-Chapelle. The court-yard on the left was that of the Chamber of Accounts: full of horses, carriages and shops spilling over from the neighbour-ing streets, its walls were hung with signboards displaying the names and portraits of criminals at large. The Mai courtyard lay to the right, giving access to a staircase and then a gallery leading to the Salle des Pas Perdus. This immense, high-ceilinged, dusty and noisy waiting room had been rebuilt in stone after a fire in 1618. It was swarming with people – lawyers, prosecutors and clients who chattered and argued, often shouting and sometimes even coming to blows in a heated atmosphere aggravated by all the legal chicanery. But the plaintiffs and the men of law in their long black robes were not the only individuals haunting the place. It was also invaded by a multitude of curious onlookers and customers of the two hundred and twenty-four shops which occupied the galleries and passageways within the Palais. All sorts of trifles were sold in these small shops whose keepers called out to potential buyers: silks, velvets, lace, bibelots, jewellery, fans, precious stones, hats, gloves, cravats, books and paintings. They were favoured as meeting-places, elegant ladies strolled here and handsome messieurs gave the glad eye to all of them.

Saint-Lucq had little trouble losing Ballardieu in this populous maze. After wandering about in an apparently innocent fashion, he suddenly found a hiding place and watched from afar as the old soldier hurried straight on. The half-blood quickly left the Palais, feeling quite pleased with himself.

He was then free to return to the mission which La Fargue had entrusted to him. He crossed the Seine by the Petit Pont and went to rue de la Fontaine in the faubourg Saint-Victor. There he found a house that he was supposed to first search and then keep an eye on. It was the dwelling of a young woman – a certain Cécile Grimaux – whom the Blades were protecting after some hired swordsmen had tried to abduct her the previous night. Marciac had foiled their attempt, proof that the years had not changed him in the least and that he was still as gifted as ever at playing the valiant knight rescuing demoiselles in distress. Whatever anyone thought of this, such occasions were rare and when they did present themselves, they always seemed to favour the Gascon.

The house was small, modest, and discreet; on the side facing the street, only the shutters and windows distinguished it from its neighbours on this weekday morning. After a quick and unobtrusive look at the place, Saint-Lucq went around to the rear, into the garden and found a window that had already been broken into and left open. He entered cautiously, subjected the ground floor to a rigorous examination, found signs of a fight – or at least a violent upheaval – in the stairway, continued up to the next floor, noted a certain disorder and the wide-open window through which Marciac and his protégée had no doubt made their escape to the rooftops.

Nothing indicated that Cécile's rooms had been searched. Saint-Lucq therefore performed this task with some hope of success, starting with the more obvious hiding places before narrowing his focus. Fortune smiled upon him. In a jewellery box, among various rings, necklaces and earrings of no great value he found a curved nail that caught his interest. He then had only to guess at what this nail might be used to dislodge. As it turned out, it was a small stoneware tile in a corner of the bedroom, beneath a small table which – having been moved too often – had left some faint scuff marks on the floor.

Saint-Lucq sighed upon discovering this cache, half-pleased to exhume the handwritten documents within, half-disappointed by the trivial ease of this paltry treasure hunt.

He was worth better than this.

7

At the Hôtel de l'Épervier, Marciac had slept for less than two hours when he rejoined Leprat in the main room. The musketeer was still sitting in the same armchair near the fireplace, now gone cold, his wounded leg stretched out before him with his foot propped on a stool. Restless from inactivity, he continued to mope, but at least he had ceased drinking. He was still a little inebriated, however, and feeling drowsy.

Marciac, in contrast, seemed full of energy. He smiled, his eyes shone and he displayed a vitality and *joie de vivre* that quickly exasperated Leprat. Not to mention the unkempt – but artfully maintained – state of his attire. The Gascon was every bit the perfect gentleman, dressed in a doublet with short basques and a white shirt, with his sword in a baldric and boots made of excellent leather. But he wore it all in a casual manner that betrayed his blind faith in his personal charm and his lucky star. The doublet was unbuttoned from top to bottom, the collar of his shirt gaped open, the sword seemed to weigh nothing and the boots were desperately in need of a good brushing.

'Come on,' said Marciac in a lively tone as he drew up a chair. 'I need to look at your wound and perhaps change the bandage.'

'Now?'

'Well, yes. Were you expected somewhere?'

'Very funny . . .'

'Grumble as much as you like, you dismal chap. I have sworn an oath that obliges me to treat you.'

'You? An oath . . . ? In any case, my leg is doing quite well.'

'Really?'

'I mean to say that it is doing better.'

'So you aren't downing bottle after bottle to dull the pain . . . ?'

'Haven't you anything better to do than count bottles?'

'Yes. Treat your leg.'

Sighing, Leprat surrendered and with ill grace allowed Marciac to get on with it. In silence, the Gascon unwound the bandage and inspected the edges of the wound, making sure it wasn't infected. His touch was gentle and precise.

At last, without lifting his eyes towards his patient, he asked:

'How long have you known?'

Leprat stiffened, at first surprised and then upset by the question.

'How long have I known what?' he said defensively.

This time, Marciac looked into his eyes. He had a grave, knowing expression that spoke louder than any words. The two men stared at one another for a moment. Then the former musketeer asked:

'And you? Since when have you known?'

'Since yesterday,' explained the Gascon. 'When I first treated your leg . . . I noticed the obatre mixed in with your blood. There was too much for you to be unaware that you have the ranse.'

According to Galen, the Greek physician of ancient times whose theories provided the basis of all Western medicine, human physiology was derived from the equilibrium of four fluids – or humours – that impregnated the organs: blood, yellow bile, black bile and phlegm. The predominance of each of these humours determines the character of an individual, resulting in sanguine, choleric, melancholic and phlegmatic temperaments. Everything is for the best when the humours are present in their proper amounts and proportions within the organism. People fall ill whenever one of these humours is in excess or is tainted. Then it becomes necessary to drain off the malignant humour by means of bleeding, enemas and other purgings.

Avant-gardist for their time, the doctors at the University of Montpellier – where Marciac had studied – believed that the disease transmitted by the dragons came from contamination by a fifth humour peculiar to that race, called obatre. This substance, they claimed, perturbed the balance of human humours, corrupting them one by one and finally reducing victims to the pitiful state observed in terminal cases of ranse. Their colleagues and traditional adversaries at the University of Paris would not hear of any talk about obatre as it was not mentioned by Galen, and his science could not be questioned. And the quarrels between the two schools, although unproductive, went on and on.

'I have been ill for the past two years,' said Leprat.

'Have there been any symptoms of the Great ranse?'

'No. Do you think I would even let you come near me if I thought I was contagious?'

Marciac avoided answering.

'The Great ranse has perhaps not yet set in,' he declared. 'Some people live with the lesser version until their death.'

'Or else it will set in and make me a pitiful monster . . .'

The Gascon nodded sombrely.

'Where is the rash?' he asked.

'All across my back. Now it's beginning to spread to my shoulders.'

'Let me see.'

'No. It's useless. No one can do anything for me.'

As a matter of fact, whether the doctors of Montpellier were wrong or right, whether obatre actually existed or not, the ranse was incurable by any known medicine.

'Do you suffer?'

'Only from fatigue. But I know there will eventually be pain.'

Marciac found he had nothing further to add and redid the bandage on the musketeer's thigh.

'I should be grateful if . . .' Leprat started to say.

However, he did not finish.

The Gascon, standing up, addressed a reassuring smile at him.

'Don't worry,' he said. 'I never actually took the Hippocratic oath, since I never became a physician, but your secret is safe with me.'

'Thank you.'

Then, firmly planted on his legs and smiling again, Marciac declared:

'Well! Now I'll go and make sure that our protégée lacks for nothing. But since Naïs has gone out, I can also make a trip to the kitchen and bring you back anything you like . . .'

'No, leave it. I believe I shall sleep for a bit.'

Upon reflection, Marciac told himself that in fact he was somewhat hungry and went to the kitchen. He found it empty, but searched out a dish of pâté and half a loaf from the bread bin, and made himself a small repast at the corner of the table. Leprat's potentially fatal disease concerned him, but, aware that he could do nothing, he forced himself not to think about it. He could only hope to offer the musketeer some comfort by sharing his secret. If he desired to speak of his illness, he now knew who he could turn to.

The Gascon was drinking straight from a bottle when Cécile entered and greeted him.

'Good morning, monsieur.'

He almost choked, but managed a charming smile instead.

'Good morning, madame. How are you feeling, today? Can I be of service?'

She was looking pale and drawn, but nevertheless remained exceedingly pretty. And perhaps her weakened state and large sad eyes even added to her fragile beauty.

'In fact, monsieur, I was looking for you.'

Marciac hastened to pull out a chair for the young woman and sat in front of her attentively.

'I am listening, madame.'

'I beg you, call me Cécile,' she said in a timid voice.

'Very well . . . Cécile.'

'I want, first, to thank you. Without you, last night . . .'

'Forget that, Cécile. You are now safe within these walls.'

'Indeed, but I know nothing of you and your friends. I

cannot help but ask questions which no one will answer for me.'

She put on a desolate expression that was almost heart-breaking to see.

The Gascon took her hand. She did not withdraw it. Had she leaned forward slightly to encourage him? Marciac presumed so and was amused by this little game.

'By paths I cannot reveal to you without betraying secrets that are not mine to divulge,' he explained, 'my friends and myself have been led to meet you. Nevertheless, rest assured that we are your allies and that your enemies are also our own. In fact, anything that you can tell us will aid your cause, whatever that may be. Have faith in us. And if that is too difficult for you, have faith in me . . .'

'But I have already told madame de Vaudreuil everything,' Cecile replied sulkily.

'In that case, you have no further cause for concern, because we will take care of the rest. I swear to you that if the thing is humanly possible, we will find your sister Chantal.'

'My profound thanks, monsieur.'

'I am entirely at your service.'

'Truly, monsieur?'

He looked deeply into her eyes, this time taking delicate hold of both her hands, with his fingertips.

'Most assuredly,' he said.

'Then, perhaps . . .'

Leaving her sentence unfinished, she turned away, as if she already regretted having said too much. The Gascon pretended to fall into her snare:

'I beg you, Cécile. Speak. Ask what you will of me.'

From beneath her eyelashes, she gave him a timid glance whose effectiveness she had no doubt tested in the past.

'I should like, monsieur, for you to accompany me to my home.'

'Now?'

'Yes. I left there some personal effects that I miss and should like to recover.'

'That would be most imprudent, Cécile . . .'

'Please, monsieur.'

'On the other hand, tell me what you lack and I shall go fetch them for you.'

'It concerns personal effects that a woman cannot go long without . . . Or speak about to a man . . .'

'Ah . . . Well, see about that with the baronne. Or with Naïs . . . Be that as it may, it is out of the question for you to return to your home. The danger is still too great.'

The young woman realised that she would not win this argument. Defeated, she nodded sadly and said:

'Yes. No doubt you are right.'

'And I'm sincerely sorry, Cécile.'

She rose, thanked him one last time, indicated that she was returning to her room and left the kitchen.

Marciac remained pensive and still for a moment.

Then he asked:

'What do you make of that?'

Agnès emerged from behind the door where she had been standing for some time now. She had witnessed the conversation without being seen or heard by Cécile. But the Gascon had noticed her presence, she knew.

'She almost tried everything,' Agnès said. 'For a moment, I even thought you might fall for it.'

'You do me an injustice.'

'Nevertheless, the demoiselle seems most promising.'

'What do you think she wants to collect from her home?'

'I don't know, but I shall go and see.'

'Alone?'

'Someone needs to stay here, and neither Leprat nor old Guibot will prevent Cécile from giving us the slip.'

'At least take Ballardieu with you.'

'He's not here.'

'Wait for him.'

'No time.'

8

Wearing a blue silk and satin gown, with a grey mother-of-pearl unicorn pinned close to her neckline, the vicomtesse de Malicorne was amusing herself by feeding her dragonnet. From a vermilion and silver plate, she was tossing bloody shreds of meat one by one to the little reptile, who plucked them out of the air from his perch and gulped them down. It was a superb animal with gleaming black scales and shared an intimate bond with its mistress. She had sometimes been seen talking to it as if it were an accomplice, a confidant, perhaps even a friend. But the strangest thing was that the dragonnet understood her, a glow of intelligence would pass through its golden eyes before it flew off with a flap of its wings, usually on some nocturnal mission.

When the marquis de Gagnière entered the salon, the young and pretty vicomtesse set down the plate of meat, licking – delicately but with relish – the tips of her slim fingers. She did not accord much attention to the visitor, however, pretending to be interested only in her sated pet.

'Savelda has just returned from the little house in the orchard,' Gagnière announced.

'The refuge of the so-called chevalier d'Ireban?'

'Yes. Castilla finally talked.'

'And?'

'Our Spanish brothers were mistaken.'

The young woman's glance shifted from the dragonnet to the elegant marquis. The news he had just delivered obviously delighted him: a satisfied smile caused his thin lips to quirk upwards.

Among all the more or less well-intentioned individuals

who served the Black Claw, rare were those who did so knowingly. Those who did were known as affiliates. But, generally unaware of the exact nature of their missions, they took their orders from initiates, who occupied the highest rank to which anyone without the blood of dragons running in their veins might aspire. An aristocratic adventurer without land or fortune, Castilla was one of these affiliates whose loyalty had not yet been firmly established. Therefore he had hitherto only been given missions that one wished not to see fail, but which did not require full knowledge of their purpose to be carried out. Intelligent, competent and capable of taking initiatives, he had never given cause for complaint.

At least until he had suddenly gone missing.

'"Mistaken", marquis? What do you mean by that?'

'I mean that Castilla was not running away from the Black Claw.'

Castilla's disappearance had been worrying. Had he betrayed them, and if so, had he taken with him enough secrets to harm the Black Claw? They needed to find him in order to shed light on this affair and, if need be, eliminate him. Their spies discovered that Castilla had left Spain by ship and that he had disembarked at Bordeaux in the company of a certain chevalier d'Ireban – or at least the latter had signed the ship's register under that name. Had they met during the crossing or were they fleeing together? It mattered little in the short run, for the Black Claw then lost trace of them. From Bordeaux, they could just as easily have travelled by sea to another continent as gone by road to a neighbouring country. But they were soon seen again in Paris. Without delay, the Black Claw in Spain had demanded that madame de Malicorne do everything in her power to track them down. In a capital of five hundred thousand souls, that was all the more difficult as she had other business at hand. Nevertheless, she was in no position to refuse and, against all expectations, she had succeeded where some had perhaps hoped she would fail, her first exploits in France having already provoked jealousy in Madrid.

Castilla being too frequent a visitor to a certain Parisian

gambling house, he was the first to be located. Then it was the turn of a young woman he often met, who proved to be none other than the dashing chevalier d'Ireban. No doubt in an effort to remain discreet, she still sometimes disguised herself as a cavalier. But whenever she wore a woman's dress, she had invented for herself the identity of a modest orphan from Lyon. As soon as it was possible, Gagnière – who also had much else to do – organised the capture of the couple with the assistance of Savelda, a henchman recently arrived from Spain. But the young woman escaped, thanks to a miraculous rescue, while Castilla was taken and tortured.

'Come to the point, marquis. And tell me what secrets Savelda extorted from Castilla last night.'

'As we suspected, Castilla and the lady were lovers. However, it was not the Black Claw they wished to escape by fleeing Spain, but the demoiselle's father.'

'Am I to understand that we have spent all this time and effort to find two eloping lovers?'

'Yes.'

'And that Castilla never sought to harm us?'

'Never. And perhaps not even to abandon us.'

The vicomtesse stifled a laugh.

'In other circumstances,' she said, 'I would be furious. But here we have the means of putting our Spanish brethren in their place and, if necessary, teaching them a lesson in humility. Besides, they won't be able to deny it when it is their own envoy, Savelda himself, who uncovered the full facts behind this story.'

'I doubt that the more jealous of our rivals will appreciate the irony when the news reaches Madrid,' said Gagnière in an amused tone.

'Henceforth, they will appreciate whatever we choose to serve them.'

Smiling with pleasure, the young vicomtesse de Malicorne dropped into an armchair.

'But who is this father that Castilla wanted to flee from so badly, even when it meant incurring the wrath of the Black Claw?'

'That's the best part of the story, madame. The father is none other than the comte de Pontevedra.'

The young woman's eyes sparked with sudden interest.

Pontevedra was a foreign aristocrat with a troubled past who, in less than two years after appearing at court, had become a friend of the comte d'Olivares and a favourite of King Felipe IV, thus winning both fortune and renown in Spain. The man was influential, powerful and feared. And he was presently in Paris, on a mission as an ambassador extraordinary. For the past week he had been engaged in secret negotiations at the Louvre, no doubt with the aim of fostering a rapprochement between France and Spain.

A rapprochement that the Black Claw did not want at any price.

'Everything now becomes clear,' said the vicomtesse. 'At least until the Cardinal's Blades entered the scene . . .'

Gagnière forced himself to contain his scepticism on the subject.

His associate's obstinate tendency to see Richelieu's agents everywhere was becoming worrisome. Granted, her magic might be informing her of more than she was telling. But it was almost as if there were an old dispute between her and the Blades that obsessed and blinded her.

'Madame . . .' he started to say in a reasonable tone. 'Nothing indicates that—'

'And just who, according to you, rescued Pontevedra's daughter last night?' she interrupted. 'Her saviour did not fall from the Moon, so far as I know. . And he was able enough to carry her off in the face of numerous opponents . . . ! Courage, audacity, valour: the very mark of the Blades . . . What? You still have doubts . . . ?'

She had become uselessly worked up, as the gentleman's cautious silence made her realise. In order to calm and perhaps reassure herself, she opened a precious-looking casket set on a table beside her. It contained the Sphère d'Âme, which she caressed with the tips of her fingers, her eyelids half-closed.

She drew in a breath and then carefully explained:

'Do me the favour of thinking the matter through. You are the comte de Pontevedra and you know that your daughter has fled to Paris – where she is perhaps under threat from the Black Claw. Now, there is nothing that France would refuse you, given the importance of the negotiations that you are conducting with her. Would you not seek help from the cardinal? And would you not demand that he mobilise his very best men?'

'Yes,' Gagnière admitted reluctantly.

'The very best, meaning the Blades.'

'I believe you.'

'It's about time . . . ! But what a shame that Pontevedra's daughter managed to evade us! What a lever she would have provided us against him!'

'All is perhaps not lost on that score. I sent Savelda to the girl's house, in rue de la Fontaine. He may find something there and, if not, it will at least keep him busy.'

'Excellent initiative. We will thus have our hands free to prepare the ceremony this evening. Is everything ready at the castle?'

'We are applying ourselves to the task.'

'Nothing must disturb our very first initiations, marquis. The Grand Lodge will not forgive us if there is the slightest sour note.'

'I know that. However . . .'

Gagnière, hesitant, left his sentence unfinished.

But as the vicomtesse was looking at him with a frown on her face, he continued:

'We need now to discuss a delicate case, madame.'

'Which is?

'Laincourt.'

9

Agnès de Vaudreuil cursed between her teeth when she discovered the empty cache in the bedroom floor.

Suspecting that Cécile wanted to recover something compromising from her home, Agnès had quickly and discreetly gone there to search the small house from top to bottom. To do so, she had hailed an empty sedan chair that was passing on rue des Saints-Pères and asked the bearers to carry her to rue d'Orléans in faubourg Saint Victor, by way of rue de la Fontaine. She had paid in advance, climbed into the little cabin through the door at the front, between the two handles, and, as soon as the curtains were drawn, felt herself being lifted before she let herself be cradled by the steady rocking of the bearers' walking pace. As they passed along rue de la Fontaine, she had opened a curtain slightly to identify the house Marciac had described and inspect its surroundings without being seen. She had seen nothing disquieting. Descending from the vehicle in rue d'Orléans, she had circled round to enter the premises from the rear, through the garden, remaining out of view of any watchers.

And now Agnès had to face up to two obvious facts. Firstly, she had indeed guessed correctly about Cécile's intentions: she had been hiding something in her bedroom, something valuable enough to her that she wanted to return to the house despite the danger, even attempting to use her charms on Marciac to convince him to accompany her. And secondly, someone had pipped Agnès at the post and seized the prize before her.

But who?

The same men who had tried to abduct Cécile, no doubt . . .

Makeshift as it was, the cache in the floor was not large and offered no clues as to what it had contained. The best thing to do, therefore, would be to seek information from the principal interested party, Cécile herself. In any case, Agnès felt that the Blades – at La Fargue's request – had been too gentle with her. Granted, the young woman had been the victim of a brutal attempt to kidnap her and she did not seem prepared to face this sort of adventure. But the gratitude which she displayed towards her new protectors did not extend as far as laying her true cards on the table. Now convinced of Cécile's duplicity, Agnès was determined not to tolerate it any longer.

To set her mind at rest, she continued to search the entire house. In vain. And when she pushed open the little door leading to the garden, Agnès suddenly found herself standing nose-to-nose with an armed, one-eyed man in black who – initially as surprised as Agnès – smiled at her in a sinister manner.

'Well, well!' he exclaimed with a strong Spanish accent. 'So the little bird has returned to its nest . . .'

Agnès immediately understood.

She wore a plain dress, a thin brown coat and a matching short cape with a hood. The modesty of her attire had been calculated: not knowing that she would have the luxury of making her journey in a sedan chair, the young baronne had left the Hôtel de l'Épervier thinking that she would have to walk to her destination, then loiter near the house while she scouted the surroundings. She had thus wished to go unnoticed and, to that end, the best thing was to seem neither too rich nor too poor. But Cécile could very well have been dressed in similar fashion. She and Agnès also had their beauty, their long, dark hair and their youth in common, being only a few years apart. If the one-eyed man had never met either of them and had been given only a brief description of Cécile, he was entirely likely to mistake one woman for the other.

Agnès promptly adopted a fearful attitude, as one would

expect of a defenceless young woman who had just fallen into the hands of a menacing enemy. Besides, the one-eyed man was not alone. Some hired swordsmen with an evil look accompanied him.

'As Heaven is my witness,' said the Spaniard, exhibiting the cruel signs of the ranse that had destroyed his eye and was ravaging his cheek, 'I could never have hoped for so much in coming here . . . My name is Savelda, Cécile.'

'What do you want from me?'

'I don't know what's wanted of you and it isn't for me to decide. I can only promise that no harm will come to you if you follow us without making a struggle or noise. So, Cécile? Will you be reasonable?'

'Yes.'

A few minutes later, Agnès found herself back on rue de la Fontaine, closely hemmed in by the hired swordsmen, with Savelda leading the way. It was there that she saw and recognised Saint-Lucq; wearing dark clothing and a sword at his side and discreetly positioned at the entrance to an alley-way, he observed the scene from behind his ever-present red spectacles.

Agnès' astonishment was such that she almost betrayed her emotion. All they needed was the half-blood for the Cardinal's Blades to be complete, but La Fargue had not announced his recruitment to anyone. Yet . . . his presence here could not be mere chance? No doubt he was watching the house. Perhaps it had even been Saint-Lucq who had searched the premises and emptied the cache inside. It was ironic that it was her own fault they had missed one another: he could not have guessed that she was in the sedan chair that had passed by in the street and then she had entered the house by the rear while he had been keeping his eye on the main façade out front.

Seeing Agnès being led away, Saint-Lucq was already taking a step towards her and reaching for his sword – if he hadn't lost any of his skills the matter would doubtless be quickly settled. Only Savelda could perhaps pose a problem.

But the false captive stopped the half-blood in his tracks with a glance that she hoped he would comprehend.

Sometimes, throwing yourself into the lion's jaws was the only means of finding its den.

10

La Fargue and Almades returned around noon covered in sweat, soot and blood, the hooves of their horses suddenly filling the walled, cobbled courtyard with loud echoes that woke the Hôtel de l'Épervier from its sad torpor. They turned the care of their mounts over to old Guibot, who came hurrying as quickly as his wooden leg would allow, while they dashed up the front steps.

'War council, now!' shouted the captain as he burst into the main room of the house.

Leprat, trapped in his armchair by his wounded leg, was already there. Marciac joined them and for a brief moment there was expectant silence. Obviously, there had been an urgent new development, about which Leprat and the Gascon were both anxious to learn the nature, while La Fargue paced back and forth before finally asking:

'And the others?'

'Agnès has gone out,' said Marciac.

'Ballardieu?'

'Here,' announced the old soldier, entering the room.

He had just arrived himself – he had even seen La Fargue and Almades pass him in the street at a rapid trot as he was returning from Palais de la Cité, where Saint-Lucq had shaken him off his tail.

' "Gone out"?' asked the captain, thinking of Agnès. 'Gone out where?'

Receiving the same questioning look as Marciac, Leprat shrugged his shoulders: he didn't know anything about it.

'She's gone to search Cécile's house,' explained the Gascon.

'Alone?' inquired Ballardieu in a worried tone.

'Yes.'

'I'm going over there.'

'No,' ordered La Fargue, visibly upset. 'You stay.'

'But, captain . . .'

'You're staying right here!'

Ballardieu was going to protest further but Almades placed a reassuring hand on his shoulder.

'Agnès knows what she's doing.'

Reluctantly, the old man subsided.

'Marciac,' said La Fargue. 'The doors.'

Nodding, the Gascon closed all the exits to the room and when he finished the captain announced:

'We found Castilla. Tortured and left for dead.'

'Is he dead now?' Leprat wanted to know.

'No. But he's hardly better off for being alive. His tormenters spared him nothing. Almades and I rescued him at the last minute from a fire set to make him vanish. We took him straight to the Saint-Louis hospital which, fortunately, was close by.'

'Did he speak?'

'Two words only,' interjected Almades. '*Garra negra*. The Black Claw.'

Everyone went quiet: they all knew what that meant.

The Black Claw was a secret society that was particularly powerful in Spain and its territories. It was not secret in the sense that its existence was unknown, but in that its members did not reveal their identities. And for good reason. Directed by dragons who were avid to acquire power, the society stopped at nothing to further its ends. For a time, it had been thought to serve Spain. However, even although its most active and influential lodge was to be found in Madrid its ambitions were not always in harmony with those of the Spanish crown. Sometimes they were even opposed. The masters of the Black Claw in truth wanted to plunge Europe into a state of chaos that would aid their plans to institute an absolute draconic regime. A state of chaos that, in the end, would not spare the Spanish Court of Dragons.

Tentacular in nature, the Black Claw was nowhere as

powerful as it was in Spain. It was nevertheless at work in the Netherlands, in Italy and in Germany where it had established lodges which remained subordinate to the oldest and most dreaded of them all, the Grand Lodge in Madrid. As for France, so far she had eluded the society's clutches. Although the Black Claw sometimes hatched schemes within the French kingdom, it had never succeeded in implanting a lodge there.

'If the Black Claw is involved,' said Leprat, 'it explains why the cardinal suddenly called us back to service. It also means that the danger is great. And imminent.'

'So this whole affair could just be a pretext to put us on the trail of the Black Claw?' ventured Marciac.

'I doubt that,' answered La Fargue. 'But the cardinal may know more than he has let on.'

'So what are we to believe? And who?'

'Ourselves. We only believe in ourselves.'

'That's a tune I've heard sung before . . .'

'I know.'

'Back to the matter at hand,' prompted Leprat, seeing that the company was rehashing its shared bad memories. 'If the Black Claw is, like us, searching for the chevalier d'Ireban, it is no doubt because he is something more than the debauched son of a Spanish grandee.'

'That much, we already guessed,' interjected Marciac.

'So then, who is he?'

'Perhaps he and Castilla belonged to the Black Claw. If they betrayed it, they had every reason to flee Spain and seek refuge in France, where the Black Claw still enjoys little influence.'

'If the Black Claw were after me,' observed Almades in a grim tone, 'I would not stop running until I reached the West Indies. And even then, I would stay on my guard.'

'Castilla and Ireban might have less good sense than you, Anibal . . .'

'I'll grant you that.'

'We still need to know,' said Leprat, 'what information the Black Claw wanted from Castilla and whether or not they obtained it.'

'If he hadn't talked we would have found a dead body,' asserted La Fargue. 'Judging by his sad state, he resisted as long as he could. He therefore had some important secrets to hide.'

'Perhaps he was trying to protect Ireban.'

'Or Cécile,' suggested Ballardieu, who until then had remained quiet.

His remark gave rise to a pause. To some degree or other, all of them had noticed the curious attitude La Fargue seemed to have adopted with regard to the young woman. Anyone else in similar circumstances would have been closely questioned by the Blades. But it was as if the captain wished to spare her for some obscure reason.

La Fargue understood the silent reproach being directed at him by his men.

'Very well,' he said, assuming his responsibilities. 'Where is she?'

'As far as I know,' said Marciac, 'she's still in her room.'

'Fetch her.'

The Gascon was leaving by one door when Guibot knocked at another. Almades opened it for him.

'Monsieur de Saint-Lucq is waiting in the courtyard,' said the old man.

11

There was a coach in the courtyard of the Hôtel de Malicorne, waiting to depart, when Gagnière arrived at a gallop.

'Madame!' he called out as the vicomtesse, dressed in a travelling cloak with a short cape, was about to climb through the coach door held open for her by a lackey. 'Madame!' Surprised, the young woman paused. She had the casket containing the Sphère d'Âme under her arm. She proffered it to a man sitting inside the vehicle, of whom the marquis saw no more than his gloved hands, saying:

'Don't open it.'

Then turning to Gagnière, she asked:

'Where are your manners, marquis . . . ?'

The gentleman dismounted, and unsure who was inside the coach, said in a confidential tone:

'I beg you to forgive me, madame. But circumstances demand that I forgo the usual formalities.'

'I am listening, monsieur.'

'We have Pontevedra's daughter.'

Gagnière's eyes shone with excitement. The vicomtesse, on the other hand, manifested nothing more than a cautious wariness.

'Really?'

'She fell into our hands by returning to her home at the very moment when Savelda happened to be there as well. The souls of the Ancestral Dragons are watching over us, madame!'

'No doubt, yes . . . Where is she at present?'

'With Savelda.'

The vicomtesse winced.

As the ambassador extraordinary of the king of Spain, the comte de Pontevedra was negotiating a rapprochement with France which the Black Claw opposed. With that in mind, his daughter constituted a choice prey. A prey that should be preserved intact.

'When the Grand Lodge of Spain learns that Pontevedra's daughter is in our hands,' said the young woman, 'it will lay claim to her. We must therefore hide her in a secure place, outside Paris; somewhere no one will be able to reach her without passing through us.'

She thought for a moment and decreed:

'Have Savelda conduct her without delay to the Château de Torain.'

'Today?' asked Gagnière, alarmed. 'But, madame—'

'Do it.'

The man in the coach then spoke up, still without revealing himself:

'It was at Pontevedra's express request that the cardinal called up the Blades . . .'

The vicomtesse smiled.

She privately reflected that it was in her power to, sooner or later, wreck Pontevedra's diplomatic mission by threatening his daughter's life. But the same means could be used to a different, more immediate, end. It would, moreover, be an opportunity to measure the depth of the ambassador's paternal feelings.

'Let us send word to Pontevedra that we hold his daughter and that if he wishes to see her again alive, he must provide us with some tokens of his good will. The first is to persuade Richelieu to recall his Blades as of today. That will remove a thorn from our foot.'

'And who shall carry this news to Pontevedra?' asked Gagnière.

The vicomtesse thought for a moment and an idea came to her.

'Monsieur de Laincourt wishes to be initiated this evening, does he not? Well, let him show his mettle. If he carries out this mission successfully then he shall have what he wants.'

After Gagnière's departure, the vicomtesse climbed into the coach which immediately set out. She sat facing the person the marquis had been unable to see and to whom she had entrusted the precious reliquary.

'It's the Sphère d'Âme, isn't it?' asked the man as she took the casket from him.

'Yes. Without it, nothing that will take place this evening would be possible.'

'I am anxious to see that.'

'I believe you. But the experience is painful. And sometimes, fatal.'

'I don't care!'

Full of confidence in him, the young woman smiled at monsieur Jean de Lonlay, sieur de Saint-Georges . . . and captain of the Cardinal's Guards.

If he survived, there was no question at all that he would become an initiate of the first order in the Black Claw's French lodge.

12

As La Fargue had not informed anyone that he'd recruited Saint-Lucq, the half-blood's entrance on the stage took the others off guard but was not altogether surprising. Firstly, because the Blades could not claim to be complete without him. And secondly, because Saint-Lucq had always been an irregular soldier who was most effective when he was off on his own, operating in the shadows. The news that he brought, moreover, took priority in their minds. He announced it at once, without pausing for preliminaries, in the courtyard of the Hôtel de l'Épervier.

'Agnès has been abducted.'

' "Abducted"?' Ballardieu roared.

Bursting with anger, he took a menacing step towards Saint-Lucq, who did not make any gesture, either to defend himself or to retreat. It took more than this to impress him.

La Fargue, on the other hand, moved to interpose himself between the two Blades.

'Let him explain what happened, Ballardieu.'

Impassive, the half-blood recounted his tale.

'I was watching this house according to your orders . . .'

'Cécile's house,' the captain clarified for the others.

'I suppose that Agnès entered around the back because I didn't see her beforehand. And the same for the men who came out with her and took her away.'

'But what men, by God?!' shouted Ballardieu.

'Hired swordsmen,' replied Saint-Lucq calmly.

'And you did nothing!'

'No. Agnès didn't want me to intervene. She wanted these men to take her away.'

'How do you know that?'

'Agnès saw me in the street. She threw me a glance and I understood.'

'You're very clever . . . !'

'More than you.'

'WHAT?'

Ballardieu, red in the face, seemed to expand in volume. Saint-Lucq looked at him disdainfully, without so much as a quiver, and said:

'You heard me.'

'That's enough!' intervened La Fargue in a loud voice.

Leprat, who had come down into the courtyard despite the wound in his thigh, forced Ballardieu to move back, taking him by the arm. Only Marciac was missing, having gone to find Cécile in her room just as the half-blood was announced.

'Go on, Saint-Lucq. What happened next?'

'Next? Nothing . . . I followed them for as long as I could, but they soon mounted horses. I was on foot.'

'What's going on?' demanded Marciac, coming out of the stables and passing Leprat who was still trying to calm Ballardieu. 'Well! Hello, Saint-Lucq.'

'Agnès has been abducted,' explained La Fargue.

'Oh? By whom?'

'By hired swordsmen led by a one-eyed man afflicted by the ranse,' said the half-blood.

'My one-eyed man with the ranse?' asked the Gascon. 'The one from last night?'

'And the same man as this morning,' added Almades. 'The riders we passed on the road, they were also led by a man whose eye was ruined by the ranse.'

'That means that Agnès is in the hands of the Black Claw,' concluded La Fargue. 'She allowed herself to be taken in order to unmask our adversaries, but she couldn't guess that—'

'I'm afraid I have another piece of bad news to announce,' declared Marciac. 'Cécile has disappeared. She has run away.'

Merde!

The captain's profanity rang out like a musket shot in the courtyard.

The Blades searched the Hôtel de l'Épervier from top to bottom and, when Cécile's disappearance was no longer in any doubt, they gathered in the main room. The young woman had almost certainly slipped out through the garden, where they discovered the gate ajar – from there, she would have had no difficulty losing herself in a maze of alleys and passageways. A wider search would thus have proved futile.

'I think she must have been listening at the door during our meeting,' said Marciac. 'No doubt wishing to avoid answering the questions that we intended to ask her, she preferred to duck out. We were too trusting of her. She wasn't the poor orphan that we believed, mixed up against her will in a dark intrigue. I would even wager that her sister, who supposedly disappeared at the same as the chevalier d'Ireban, never existed.'

'She and Ireban are one and the same,' announced Saint-Lucq, throwing a small bundle of documents on the table. 'I found these in her home. Reading them, you'll discover that Cécile is the daughter of a great Spanish lord, that she and Castilla are lovers, and that they fled Spain together, Cecile disguising herself as a man to fool any spies. You'll also see therein that Cécile and Castilla not only feared the wrath of her father, but also that of another mysterious enemy.'

'The Black Claw,' guessed Leprat.

'Must I remind you that Agnès is in the Black Claw's hands?' Ballardieu interjected in tight voice that barely concealed his contained anger. 'Isn't that the most important thing?'

'Yes,' said La Fargue. 'However, it is perhaps only by getting to the bottom of this whole story that we will find a way to rescue Agnès . . .'

'And I tell you that we need to do everything in our power to save her. Starting right now!'

'Agnès voluntarily placed herself in the lion's jaws,' Leprat reasoned, 'but she may not have known which lion was involved.'

'She passed right in front of me,' Saint-Lucq pointed out. 'I heard the one-eyed man talking to her as they took her away, and by all appearances, they mistook her for Cécile. That won't last. Ballardieu is right: time is running short.'

'Who can help us?' the old soldier asked. 'The cardinal? Castilla?'

'I doubt that Castilla is in any state to talk,' said Almades. 'As for the cardinal . . .'

Silence fell upon them, heavy with worry compounded by a sense of impotence.

'Malencontre,' said Leprat after a long moment.

The others stared at him, while Almades explained briefly to Saint-Lucq who this Malencontre was. That done, Leprat continued:

'Malencontre belongs to the Black Claw; otherwise we would not have surprised him beneath Castilla's windows. And he must know a great deal, or the cardinal would not have taken him from us.'

'But if I follow the chronology of events correctly,' said Saint-Lucq, 'this man can't know where Agnès is being held today, because he was arrested yesterday—'

'He certainly knows enough to put us on the right track!'

'Yes!' exclaimed Ballardieu. 'Yes! That's an excellent idea!'

He turned towards La Fargue and solicited his opinion with a glance.

'The idea is a good one, yes . . . But—'

'But, we don't know were he can be found at present,' Marciac filled in for his captain. 'Moreover, we will not be able to reach him without permission from the cardinal. And, lastly, he won't talk unless we can offer him something in return.'

'Freedom,' said Almades. 'Malencontre knows he is lost. He will not talk in return for anything less than his liberty.'

'We'll persuade Richelieu to offer Malencontre his freedom!' declared Ballardieu. 'If he knows that Agnès' life hangs in the balance . . .'

He wanted to believe it, but the others were less confident. What price did the cardinal currently place on the life of one of his Blades? He had never hesitated to sacrifice them on the altar of political necessity in the past.

'I can arrange a meeting with His Eminence quickly,' proposed Saint-Lucq.

'Then let us try that,' concluded La Fargue.

They all rose and Marciac took the captain to one side.

'With your permission, I would like to go in search of Cécile.'

'Do you know where she went?'

The Gascon smiled.

'If Agnès were here, she would tell you that you do not know women very well, captain.'

'That may be. Go ahead, follow your idea. But we will have need of you soon.'

'I won't be long.'

13

In 1607 Concino Concini, an Italian adventurer who, together with his wife, enjoyed such influence over Queen Marie de Médicis that she made him marquis d'Ancre and a marshal of France, built a vast mansion on rue de Tournon. Greedy and incompetent he was hated by the population, who pillaged his mansion for the first time in 1616 and then again, after his death in 1617. Louis XIII resided there from time to time, and then gave it to one of his favourites, only to buy it back later. From then on, and up until 1748, the beautiful house in rue de Tournon became a residence for visiting ambassadors extraordinary.

The creation of permanent ambassadors was not yet a widespread practice. With rare exceptions, European kingdoms only employed ambassadors extraordinary to conduct particular negotiations or represent their monarchs on grand occasions – princely baptisms, betrothals, marriages, and other important ceremonies. These envoys – always great lords expected to maintain appearances at their own cost – would return to their country once their mission was completed. Diplomacy was yet to become a career.

Thus, in Paris, ambassadors and their retinues were the guests of the king in the marquis d'Ancre's former mansion. Having been appointed by King Felipe IV of Spain, the comte de Pontevedra had been lodging there for several days and would no doubt remain there as long as was necessary to ensure the completion of a mission that was surrounded by the greatest secrecy. What were the comte and Richelieu discussing during the course of their long daily meetings – meetings at which even the king himself made appearances?

The royal court was filled with rumours on this subject and everyone either claimed to know or made educated guesses. The truth, however, went beyond any of their expectations. It involved nothing less than preparing, if not an alliance, then at least a rapprochement between France and Spain. Was such a thing even possible? If it was, it would represent an enduring upheaval in European politics and would affect the destinies of millions of souls.

On this day, the comte de Pontevedra returned rather earlier than usual from the Louvre. He rode in a luxurious coach, surrounded by twenty gentlemen in arms whose role was both to protect him and enhance his prestige with their numbers and their elegance. At the mansion in rue de Tournon he hurried alone to his apartments, sent his servants away and even refused his valet's assistance to remove his brocade doublet and his gold-trimmed baldric. He poured himself a glass of wine and settled down in an armchair. He was preoccupied, eaten away by worry. But it was not the difficulty of the delicate diplomatic negotiations he was engaged in that spoilt his days and haunted his nights.

A door creaked.

The ambassador rose, furious, ready to drive away the unwelcome visitor and then suddenly froze. He glanced around for his sword which, unfortunately, he had abandoned out of easy reach.

'That would be suicide, monsieur,' said Laincourt, emerging from an antechamber. 'I am not an assassin. I am a messenger.'

'Who sent you?'

'The Black Claw.'

In his fifties, tall, dignified, with greying temples and a fine scar decorating his cheekbone, the ambassador was still a handsome man. He was not trembling, but he had grown pale.

'I see,' added Laincourt, 'that you have guessed the reason for my visit . . .'

'Speak, monsieur.'

'We have your daughter.'

Pontevedra remained expressionless.

'You don't believe me,' inferred Laincourt after a moment.

'On what grounds should I believe you? I await your proofs. Can you show me a jewel that could only belong to her? Or perhaps a lock of her hair?'

'Neither jewel, nor hair. But I could return with an eye . . .'

There was another silence, during which the two men exchanged stares, each trying to probe the other.

'What do you want? Money?'

Laincourt gave a faint but amiable smile.

'Why don't you sit down, monsieur? In this armchair. That will place you away from the table you are edging towards and the letter opener that rests upon it.'

Pontevedra obeyed.

In turn, the Black Claw's envoy also took a seat, but one a good distance from the ambassador, while constantly covering him with his pistol.

'Once upon a time,' said Laincourt, 'there was an adventurous French gentleman who became a great lord in Spain. This gentleman had a daughter who, one day, wished to remove herself from his company. The gentleman did not want this to happen. So his daughter fled, crossing the border disguised as a cavalier and finding refuge in Paris. The gentleman received word of this. And he soon learned, through his spies, that one of his most powerful enemies was threatening, or at least also pursuing, his daughter. The gentleman, understandably, became worried . . . What do you think of my story, monsieur? Is it accurate enough that I should continue?'

Pontevedra nodded.

'In that case, I'll go on . . . At the same time, an ambassadorial mission was being prepared in Madrid. Did our gentleman engage in a few little intrigues to have this mission entrusted to him, or did fate serve him by happenstance? It matters little. What does matter is that he was named ambassador extraordinary and came to Paris to negotiate with the king of France and his most eminent minister. His political mission was of the utmost importance, but he merely regarded it as the means of saving his daughter. Using all the influence he was able to wield, he obtained a promise from France, via

Cardinal Richelieu, that she would endeavour to search for his daughter. Or rather, to search for the chevalier d'Ireban, since it was under this name and this disguise that she had secretly reached Paris. Our gentleman gave the chevalier prestigious origins, so that the cardinal might believe that he was rendering a service to the Spanish crown rather than to its ambassador . . . Does my tale still have the ring of truth?'

'Yes.'

'Good . . . This gentleman, in fact, did more than simply demand that France search for his daughter. He wanted France to use her best men for this delicate mission. He wanted the Cardinal's Blades . . . When Richelieu asked him why, he answered that Spain wished to assure herself that France was doing everything in her power to succeed: she would therefore show the best possible goodwill by having recourse to the Blades. Careful not to give offence to Spain on the eve of crucial negotiations, the cardinal no doubt agreed to this demand with fairly good grace. After all, for him it was simply a question of recruiting men who had already demonstrated their worth and could soon prove useful once again. And so it was arranged . . . But I see with regret that my tale has started to bore you . . .'

'It is a tale whose subject matter is already familiar to me.'

'I am coming now to precisely those elements of which you are perhaps ignorant.'

'Very well. Continue.'

'I said earlier, our gentleman was worried that a particular enemy of his was pursuing his daughter. He was indeed worried, but was not surprised by this. It must be said that his daughter had become bound by ties of affection to a handsome adventurer who was in the pay of the enemy in question. That is to say, the Black Claw. The daughter was unaware of this fact. But the gentleman knew. And it was no doubt in seeking to separate her from her dangerous admirer that he provoked her anger and subsequent flight. Because the girl was of an age when people are willing to sacrifice everything for love—'

'You promised to speak of developments that are unknown to me.'

'And here they are: your daughter's lover is dead, but before he died he told us who she is, which we did not know until then. You must recognise that she constitutes a significant prize for us . . . But it remains the case that your manoeuvres have placed the Blades on our trail. This must cease. As of today.'

'What guarantees do you offer me?'

'None. You have persuaded Richelieu to deploy his Blades against us. See that he henceforth employs them for another purpose and your daughter shall live.'

'Richelieu will refuse if he suspects something.'

'Richelieu already suspects something. His suspicions began the instant you demanded he involve the Blades in this matter. Don't forget that he knows who you really are. But does your daughter know? And if she doesn't, do you want her to remain ignorant of the facts?'

14

Escorted by riders, the coach had all its curtains lowered and was travelling at a rapid pace along a dusty, rutted road that subjected its creaking axles to constant torment. Inside, shaken by the bouncing of the cabin, Agnès did not utter a word. She was sitting in front of the one-eyed victim of the ranse who had abducted her. Savelda pretended to pay her no attention, but he discreetly kept his eye on her, watching her slightest movement.

After surprising her at Cécile's dwelling, Savelda and his henchmen had taken Agnès to the courtyard of a nearby inn where their horses were waiting for them. She was placed on the rump of one of their mounts and, still led by the Spaniard, the riders left the faubourg Saint-Victor at a trot, depriving Saint-Lucq of any chance of following them. Their destination was an isolated house where Agnès was kept under guard for a while, no doubt just long enough for news of her capture to be transmitted and for orders to come back. Finally, she had been forced to embark in this coach, which had been on the move ever since. But where was it going?

No one had questioned her yet. For her part she did not speak, remained docile and tried to appear anxious and over-whelmed by all these events. She wanted to lull her guardians into a false sense of security until the moment came for her to act and, until then, she did not wish to say or do anything that risked compromising the misunderstanding that had led to her abduction. These men – Savelda at their head – mistook her for Cécile. Agnès wanted that to last until she was able to discover who she was dealing with and what their motivations were. As they seemed to attach great value to their hostage,

Agnès did not feel actually threatened. But the problem remained that she herself did not know Cécile's true identity. She was playing a dangerous game, trying to impersonate someone about whom she knew almost nothing. The best she could do was to adopt a low profile in order to avoid making any blunders. She didn't fancy her chances if her deception was revealed.

If her story were to be believed, Cécile was an innocent young woman searching for her elder sister who had disappeared at the same time as her lover, the chevalier d'Ireban. Agnès was convinced that she had been lying to the Blades, at least in part. Therefore, Cécile no doubt knew more than she was prepared to say about the hired swordsmen Marciac had saved her from the previous night: she must have some idea what they wanted and why. If it was simply a question of their wishing to eliminate an overly curious sister, then they would have tried to murder her, not abduct her. Rather than merely an awkward witness, she was in their eyes a bargaining token, or perhaps a means of applying pressure on someone.

But for the young baronne de Vaudreuil, the real cause for worry lay elsewhere. She suspected La Fargue knew some of Cécile's secrets. Secrets that he had not shared with anyone.

This was both abnormal and disturbing. It was completely unlike the captain, who, with his frankness and absolute loyalty, had always shown himself worthy of the blind faith invested in him by his Blades. Where had this mistrust come from? Had the years changed him to such an extent? No, time alone did not cause well-tempered souls to bend. But the betrayal of a friend, perhaps . . .

Since Saint-Lucq was also in the game, the Cardinal's Blades were now, arguably, complete. Complete except for two, that is. Those two would never return. One of them, Bretteville, was dead. The other, Louveciennes, had betrayed them. He had been La Fargue's companion-in-arms, his oldest and his best friend, with whom he had founded the Blades and recruited all the others. As brutal as it was unexpected, his treason had first led to the death of Bretteville during the siege of La Rochelle and then brought about the infamous disbanding of the Blades as a whole. La Fargue had witnessed the shattering of his life's work at the hands of a man he had considered as a brother and who, rich from the fortune that this crime had earned him, had found refuge – it was said – in Spain.

The wound was deep. It had probably never healed and no doubt explained why La Fargue distrusted everyone, including the men under his command. Agnès understood this to a certain degree, but her resentment of it remained sincere and profound. The Blades were a citadel in which La Fargue was the central keep. Without the certainty of being able to find refuge there in case of need, Agnès could not imagine herself fighting for long upon the ramparts.

Having almost reached the end of its journey, the coach slowed as it climbed a winding and stony track.

Then it pulled to a halt.

Savelda descended first and, holding the door open, signalled for Agnès to follow him. Beneath a sun which, after the darkness inside the cabin, dazzled her for a moment, she found herself surrounded by the partially crumbled ruins and ramparts of a fortified castle whose imposing keep dominated a courtyard which had long been invaded by weeds and shrubs. Isolated on top of a rocky and wooded height overlooking the Chevreuse valley, the place was a scene of bustling activity at odds with its ancient sleeping stones. Men and dracs were busy planting torches, building woodpiles for bonfires, and erecting three tiers of benches on either side of an open air stage. Wagons loaded with materials were entering the site. Riders came and went. Overseers gave orders and assigned tasks, hurried by a sense of urgency. A wyvern and its rider circled in the sky. A second, saddled, waited in the shelter of a covered enclosure.

Savelda seized Agnès by the elbow and led her into a small building of which only the exterior walls remained standing, its interior being overgrown with brush. He made her descend a stairway carved into the rock, at the bottom of which a hired swordsman was already posted. Upon seeing them he opened

317

a door and Agnès entered an underground chamber filled with dusty debris. There was an old oven for baking bread in one corner. Daylight entered through a small semicircular window which looked out on the courtyard.

A fat woman rose from her seat, abandoning her knitting.

'Keep an eye on her,' Savelda ordered.

Then, turning to the prisoner, he warned her:

'Don't try anything. If you obey us, no harm will be done to you.'

Agnès nodded and the one-eyed man departed, closing the door behind him and leaving her alone with her female guardian. After a moment, as the fat woman did not seem to be overly concerned about her, she went towards the window, whose bars she gripped with both hands in order to raise herself on tiptoe and, while verifying the solidity of the iron, gazed outside.

Something important was about to happen here and, despite the risks she was taking, Agnès knew she had been right to let herself be brought here.

15

Because it was designed to take in plague victims, the Saint-Louis hospital had not only been built outside Paris, it also resembled a fortress. Its first stone had been laid in 1607, after the serious epidemics which the Hôtel-Dieu, the only big hospital the capital possessed at the time, had been unable to cope with. Its four main buildings, each formed of a single storey above a ground floor with taller structures at their centre and extremities, surrounded a square courtyard. Two rings of walls separated it from the rest of the world. Between them, symmetrically distributed, were the dwellings of the employees, nurses and nuns who worked there. The pantries, kitchens, storerooms and bakeries were built against the outer wall. Around them spread the gardens, fields and pastures bordering the faubourg Saint-Denis.

Having shown his pass several times, Marciac received directions to the immense ward where, among the moans and murmurs of the other patients, he found Castilla lying on one of the beds aligned in rows. Cécile was sitting near him. Pale, her eyes red, she caressed his forehead with a light touch. The wounded man was clean and bandaged, but his face was swollen and horribly deformed. He was breathing but showed no reaction to his surroundings.

'Leave me be,' said the young woman on seeing Marciac. 'Leave us both.'

'Cécile . . .'

'That's not my name.'

'It's of little importance.'

'Oh, but it is . . . ! If I wasn't who I am, if he who claims to be my father wasn't who he is, none of this would have happened. And this man here, he would live.'

'He isn't dead.'

'The sisters say he won't live through the night.'

'They don't know anything. I've seen many men survive wounds that were believed to be fatal.'

The young woman did not reply, seeming to forget the Gascon and, leaning over Castilla, continued to caress his brow.

'What should I call you?' asked Marciac after a while.

'Ana-Lucia . . . I believe.'

'You want this man to live, don't you, Ana-Lucia?'

She glared at him with damp eyes, as if this question were the worst possible insult.

'Then you should leave here,' Marciac continued in a gentle voice. 'The men who tried to abduct you are no doubt still after you. And if they find you here, they'll also find him . . .'

She stared at him and a new worry caused her drawn features to look even more distraught.

'You . . . You really think so?'

'I know so, Ana-Lucia. Please come. You will need to be brave. I promise you that we'll return tomorrow.'

Back in Paris an hour later, the beautiful Gabrielle, mistress of a brothel located in rue de la Grenouillère, heard knocking at her door. As no one in the house answered and the knocking continued, she wondered why she bothered paying her porter and, more resigned than angry, leaned from her window.

Outside, Marciac lifted a grave-looking face toward her, which worried her because the Gascon tended to be one who smiled in the face of adversity.

'I need you, Gabrielle,' he said.

He was holding a tearful young woman's hand.

16

The coach picked Rochefort up at Place de la Croix-du-Trahoir and, after a short conversation with the comte de Pontevedra, it left him in front of the scaffolding covering the façade of the Palais-Cardinal. The ambassador extraordinary of Spain had demanded this discreet meeting urgently. He had promised that he had important news and he had not been lying.

La Fargue and Saint-Lucq were waiting in an antechamber of the Palais-Cardinal. They were silent and pensive, aware of what was at stake during the interview His Eminence was about to grant them. Their chances of rescuing Agnès lay with Malencontre, a man Richelieu was keeping locked away and was not likely to give up to them easily – and they had no guarantee of success if he did.

After some considerable hesitation, Saint-Lucq rose from a bench and went to join La Fargue who stood gazing out a window.

'I found this at Cécile's house,' he said in a confidential tone.

He held out an unsealed letter on a yellowed piece of paper.

The old gentleman lowered his eyes to the missive and finally took it with a doubtful air.

'What is it?'

'Read it, captain.'

He read, looking stiff and grim, haunted by old torments that he refuse to show on his countenance. Then he refolded the letter, slipped it into his sleeve, and said:

'You also read this.'

'It was open and I had no way of knowing its contents.'

'Indeed.'

'I haven't said anything to the others.'

'Thank you.'

La Fargue resumed looking out at the cardinal's gardens, where workers were finishing digging the basins. Trees rooted in large sacks of earth were arriving in carts.

'Captain, did you know you had a daughter?'

'I knew it.'

'Why did you hide it?'

'To protect her and safeguard her mother's honour.'

'Oriane?'

Oriane de Louveciennes, the wife of the man who – until his act of treason at the siege of La Rochelle – had been La Fargue's best friend.

Saint-Lucq nodded, impassive behind his spectacles' round, red lenses.

'Why do you think Oriane wrote this letter so many years ago?'

'No doubt so that Anne might one day know who her real father was.'

'Perhaps your daughter came to Paris in the hope of meeting you.'

'Yes. Perhaps.'

A door creaked and Rochefort passed through the ante-chamber with a quick step without seeming to pay them any notice. Unlike them, he did not have to wait before being received by the cardinal.

'I don't like the look of that,' said the half-blood.

In his large and luxurious study, Richelieu was discussing matters with Père Joseph when Rochefort entered and interrupted them. They were speaking of Laincourt, of whom they had heard nothing.

'Please forgive my intrusion, monseigneur. But I have some important news.'

'We are listening.'

'The comte de Pontevedra has just informed me that the chevalier d'Ireban is in Madrid. Although he was thought to have disappeared here in France, in fact he decided to return to Spain by his own means and without letting anyone know.'

The cardinal and Père Joseph exchanged a long look: they did not believe a word of what they had just heard. Then Richelieu settled back into his armchair with a sigh.

'Whether it's true or not,' said the Capuchin monk, 'the mission entrusted to your Blades no longer has any reason to continue, monseigneur . . .'

Richelieu nodded thoughtfully.

He nevertheless took time to reflect before declaring:

'You are right, father. Have Captain La Fargue come in.'

17

Back at the Hôtel de l'Épervier, where Marciac had returned just a quarter of an hour before them, La Fargue and Saint-Lucq found the rest of the Blades gathered together in the main room.

'Richelieu refused,' announced the captain upon entering.

Dismayed, they all fell silent as La Fargue poured himself a glass of wine and emptied it in one gulp.

'Does he know . . .' Ballardieu started to say in a voice buzzing with anger. 'Does he know that Agnès is in danger? Does he know that she is being held prisoner by the Black Claw? Does he know—?'

'He knows!' said La Fargue sharply.

Then he added in a quieter tone:

'He knows all that because I told him.'

'And despite that, he still refuses to return Malencontre.'

'Yes.'

'This time, it has not taken His Eminence long to desert us,' said Leprat whose dark gaze was lost in a limbo where he saw the outline of La Rochelle standing before him.

'But there's more, isn't there?' guessed Almades, standing in a corner where he leaned with his arms crossed. 'Richelieu was not simply satisfied with refusing to allow you to speak with Malencontre . . .'

'No,' admitted the Blades' captain.

He paused for a moment and then said:

'Our mission has been cancelled. The chevalier d'Ireban has supposedly turned up recently in Madrid. Therefore we no longer have any reason to continue searching here in Paris.'

'But Ireban does not exist!' exclaimed Marciac. 'He and

Cécile were always one and the same person! How can he be back in Spain now?'

'Nevertheless, this is the case. At least, if one believes the ambassador extraordinary of Spain.'

'It's absurd!' objected Leprat. 'The cardinal can't be taken in by this lie—'

'It was at Spain's request that Richelieu entrusted us with this mission, and it is once again at her request that he has called us off. The stakes of the negotiations that are currently taking place in the Louvre go well beyond us. It was a matter of pleasing Spain. Now it is a matter of not displeasing her . . .'

'And we are suddenly asked to forget all about the existence of Ireban,' said Marciac. 'And about Malencontre. And about the Black Claw which is scheming in the very heart of the kingdom!'

'Those are our orders,' insisted La Fargue.

'Are we also to forget about Agnès?' Ballardieu demanded.

'There is no question of that.'

Leprat rose and, despite his wounded leg, could not stop himself from pacing back and forth.

'Malencontre remains our best hope of finding Agnès quickly,' he said, thinking out loud.

'The cardinal only deigned to tell us that Malencontre was being held at Le Châtelet, awaiting transfer to the prison in the Château de Vincennes,' indicated Saint-Lucq.

Leprat stopped pacing to and fro.

'I will go and speak with Malencontre,' he declared.

'But he's being held in solitary confinement!' the half-blood pointed out. 'No one can see him without a signed order.'

'I am only on leave from the Musketeers. I can still wear the cape and monsieur de Tréville will not refuse to help me.'

They all fell silent while they considered this idea.

'All right,' said La Fargue. 'Let's suppose that you manage to reach Malencontre. Then what? You have nothing to propose in exchange for his information.'

'Just let me have two words with him,' suggested Ballardieu, balling his fists.

'No,' replied Leprat. 'Malencontre and I are almost old acquaintances by now. Let us do this my way . . .'

Later, while the Blades were getting ready, La Fargue took Marciac by the elbow.

'Did you find Cécile?'

'Yes. At the Saint-Louis hospital, at the bedside of the man she loves, just as I guessed. She was listening at the door when you announced that he was dying there. She fled the house in order to be with him.'

'Is she in a safe place at present?'

'She is in rue de la Grenouillère. No one will go looking for her in a brothel and Gabrielle and the girls will take good care of her.'

'I thought you and Gabrielle had . . . ?'

'A falling out . . . ?' said the Gascon with a grin. 'Yes, we did, for a while . . . Let's just say that she did not particularly appreciate the fact that I was returning to active service under your orders. She remembers how things ended the last time only too well.' He fell silent, thinking, and then with a shrug concluded: 'Bah! She can always marry a haberdasher, if that's what she wants.'

He was turning away in a fairly good mood, when the captain called him back:

'Marciac!'

'Yes?'

'Thank you.'

Puzzled, the Gascon frowned but said nothing.

18

At Le Châtelet, the guards and other personnel were relieved at five o'clock in the evening. Wearing his blue cape with its silver fleur-de-lys cross, Leprat presented himself twenty minutes before the hour at the admissions counter with an authorisation signed by the hand of monsieur de Tréville, captain of His Majesty's Musketeers, and was led to Malencontre's place of detention. The man was being held in Le Puits, or the Well, one of the individual cells in the gaol's lower depths. There reigned a dark and putrid dankness that would have undermined the health and courage of even the most solid of men.

The gaoler left his lantern with Leprat, saying that he would remain within earshot at the other end of the corridor and then shut the door. The light it gave off was dim, barely illuminating the miserable hole, but it sufficed to dazzle the prisoner. Filthy and tired-looking, stinking of urine and refuse, he was sitting on a carpet of rancid straw, back towards the wall to which he was chained by the wrists. His position forced him to keep his arms raised, his long pale blond hair hanging before his face.

'Leprat?' he asked, squinting. 'Is that you, chevalier?'

'It's me.'

'You are very kind to pay me a visit. Would you like some foul water? I think I also have an old crust of bread that the rats haven't carried off yet . . .'

'I came to speak with you.'

The musketeer swept his ivory rapier back, crouched before Malencontre and set the lantern down between them.

'Do you know what awaits you?' he asked.

'I wager that I will soon be asked lots of questions.'

'And will you answer them?'

'If that can save my life.'

'Then talk to me. If you talk to me, I will help you.'

Malencontre stifled a small chuckle and made a grimacing smile that highlighted the scar at the corner of his thin lips.

'I doubt that you have anything to offer me, chevalier.'

'You're wrong. Those who will come after me will ask you the same questions, but in a different manner. Le Châtelet has no lack of torturers . . .'

'The cardinal will not send me a torturer right away. He will first seek to learn if I am disposed to talk. I will reply that I am and I will be treated well. I am no hero, Leprat. I am quite ready to collaborate and only ask for some small consideration.'

His crouching position becoming too uncomfortable due to his wounded thigh, Leprat stood up and, spying a stool in a corner, sat down on it, leaving the lantern where it was.

'You work for the Black Claw,' he said.

'Not really, no. I work for a gentleman who may, perhaps, work for them . . . You serve one master, I serve another.'

'Except that I happen to be free to come and go . . .'

'True.'

'Which gentleman?'

'A very good question.'

'The cardinal's agents will not make the distinction. For them, you belong to the Black Claw.'

'That only increases the value of my modest person, wouldn't you say?'

'You will never see the light of day again.'

'That remains to be seen.'

The musketeer sighed, searching for some means of gaining the upper hand with a man who had already lost everything and to whom he had nothing to offer. If he failed to make Malencontre speak of his own free will, the only solution that remained revolted him.

But the life of Agnès was at stake.

'The cardinal knows nothing of your visit to me, is that not so?' the prisoner remarked. 'So tell me, what brings you here?'

'I am going to offer you a deal that you cannot refuse.'

Outside, in front of Le Châtelet, La Fargue and Almades were waiting. They were on foot, the other Blades guarding the horses a short distance away at the entrance to rue Saint-Denis.

'Do you think Leprat will succeed?'

'Let us hope so.'

Those were the only words they exchanged, both of them anxious as they remained there, keeping track of the time and observing who was coming out of the enormous, sinister-looking building.

As the half hour tolled they saw the large felt hat and cape of a limping musketeer appear at last.

'He's favouring the wrong leg,' noticed Almades.

'What does it matter?'

They hastened to flank Malencontre as closely as possible on either side, without attracting attention.

'You will not be set free until you have told us everything we wish to know,' La Fargue told him in a firm voice.

'And who says that you won't do me an evil turn afterwards?'

'I do. But if you try anything at all . . .'

'I understand.'

They moved quickly towards the other Blades and their horses, fearing that at any moment someone would call after them from the doors of Le Châtelet.

'Who are you?' asked Malencontre. 'And how did you manage this?'

'We took advantage of the changing of the guards,' explained La Fargue taking a discreet look all around them. 'Those who saw Leprat enter were not the guards who let you leave. The hat, the musketeer's cape, the pass from Tréville and the white rapier did the rest. You will return that rapier to me, by the way.'

'And Leprat? Aren't you worried about him?'

'Yes.'

'How will he be freed?'

'It's possible he never will be.'

19

It must have been around eight o'clock in the evening and night was falling.

Still held prisoner, Agnès had seen enough to understand what was going on in the great fortified castle. The preparations were now complete. On either side of the open air stage, the three tiers of benches had been erected and covered with black cloth. On the stage itself, an altar had been placed before a thick velvet cushion. Tall banners had been raised that now floated in the wind, bearing a single golden draconic rune. Torches already illuminated the scene and bonfires waited to be lit. The men and dracs who had installed everything were not workers but hired swordsmen commanded by Savelda and under the direction of a very young and very elegant blond cavalier whom Agnès did not know but who was addressed as marquis: Gagnière. Their task finished, the swordsmen who were not on watch were now gathered around campfires, away from the stage they had set up, near the makeshift stable and the enclosure for the wyverns, and at the foot of the partly collapsed ramparts.

For the past hour, the places along the benches had been filling with men and a few women, most of them sumptuously dressed, whose horses and coaches had been left by the main castle gates. They wore black eye masks embellished with veils of red lace covering their mouth and chin. They waited, visibly anxious and saying little to one another.

Agnès realised why.

She had never taken part in the ceremony that was about to occur, but she had learned something of its nature during her years as a novice with the White Ladies, the religious order devoted to preserving the French kingdom from the draconic contagion. The Black Claw – whose sinister emblem decorated the banners and was even carved into the wood of the altar – was no mere secret society. Led by dragon sorcerers, its power was founded upon ancient rituals that ensured the unfailing loyalty of its initiates by spiritually uniting them with a superior awareness: that of an Ancestral Dragon who came to impregnate their being. A Black Claw lodge was much more than a meeting of conspirators avid for wealth and power. It was the product of a rite that permitted a fanatical assembly to offer itself as the instrument and receptacle of an Ancestral Dragon's soul – thus bringing the dragon back to life through those who had sacrificed a part of themselves, and allowing it to once again exercise power over a land it had been driven from in the distant past. The ceremony could only be performed by a dragon – one who was thoroughly adept in the higher arcana of draconic magic. In addition, it required an extremely rare relic, a Sphère d'Âme, from which the Ancestral Dragon's soul would be freed at the most propitious moment.

A little while before, Agnès had seen a black coach arrive. An elegant woman in a veil, wearing a red-and-grey gown, had descended from it in the company of a gentleman. The latter had paused for a moment to adjust his mask and Agnès, incredulous, had the time to catch a glimpse of his face. It was Saint-Georges, the captain of the Cardinal's Guards. He and the woman had watched the completion of preparations before being joined by Gagnière and Savelda, with whom they exchanged a few words before turning towards the ruin in whose cellar Agnès was being held captive. The prisoner quickly withdrew from the window where she was spying on them and feared for a moment that they would come to see her, but the coach left with all of them except Savelda, driving off in the direction of the keep, which it entered by means of a drawbridge over a ditch filled with bushes.

As she knew that the ceremony would not take place until night, Agnès had resolved to wait until dusk before acting, and thus take advantage of the evening shadows.

*

The moment had come.

In the now darkened cellar, she turned towards the dirty obese woman charged with keeping watch over her, but who in fact almost never lifted her nose from her knitting. The fat woman was the first obstacle Agnès needed to overcome. The next was the closed door and the sentry that Savelda had prudently left behind it.

'I'm thirsty,' she complained, having noticed her guard's red nose, a clear sign of a fondness for drink.

The fat woman shrugged her shoulders.

'Can't we even have a pitcher of wine?' Agnès wheedled in an innocent voice.

The other woman reflected, hesitated, thought about the pitcher and ran the tip of her tongue over her lips, eyes filled with longing.

'I'd give anything for a cool glass of wine. Here, this is for you if you want it . . .'

Agnès removed one of her rings and held it out. In the fat woman's eyes, greed was now combined with longing. But still she hesitated.

'We deserve a little wine, don't you think? After all, we've been shut away down here for hours now.'

Narrowing her eyes, the fat woman licked her lips, her mouth dry. Then she set down her knitting, murmured something that sounded like assent, stood up and went to knock on the door.

'What is it?' ask the sentry on the other side.

'We're thirsty,' grumbled the woman.

'So what!'

'Go find us a bottle.'

'Out of the question.'

'Then let me go find one.'

'No.'

Although furious, the fat woman was about to give up when Agnès approached and showed her the ring again.

'The girl can pay.'

'With what?'

'A ring. Made of gold.'

After a short instant, Agnès heard the bar blocking the door being removed.

And smiled to herself.

'Let me see,' said the man as he opened up.

A few minutes later, Agnès came out beneath a sky of ink and fire, wearing the sentry's clothes and equipped with his weapons. Their owner was lying in the cellar, a knitting needle planted in his eye as far as his brain. The fat woman was stretched out nearby, a second needle sticking out of the back of her neck.

Agnès carefully surveyed the surroundings, pulled the hat down on her skull and, keeping her head slightly lowered, moved away praying that no one would hail her. She saw a masked rider approach who spoke with Savelda without descending from his mount and then spurred the horse towards the keep.

She went in the same direction.

20

Arriving as night fell, Laincourt discovered the old castle lit by torchlight and lanterns. He observed the stage where the first initiation ceremony would take place, had a look at the future initiates – wearing masks like him – waiting there, saw Savelda and directed his horse towards him.

'You're late,' said the Spaniard upon recognising him.

'They must be waiting for me.'

'Yes, I know. Over there.'

Savelda pointed at the impressive keep and Laincourt thanked him with a nod of the head before continuing on his way, not noticing that he was being followed.

If he was late it was because he had, after presenting the conditions set by the Black Claw to the ambassador of Spain, waited in vain for his contact to show up. The hurdy-gurdy player had not appeared at the miserable tavern in the oldest part of Paris where they ordinarily met and, running short of time, Laincourt had been finally forced to leave. Consequently, no one at the Palais-Cardinal knew where he was at present.

The castle keep was in fact made up of three massive towers, joined by ramparts as high as they were and enclosing a steep-sided, triangular courtyard. It was a castle within a castle, to which one gained access by means of a drawbridge, and where there was an immediate feeling of oppression.

Leaving his horse in the courtyard near a harnessed black coach, Laincourt entered the only tower whose embrasures and openings were illuminated. The marquis de Gagnière was waiting for him.

'So the grand evening is here at last,' he said. 'Someone wishes to see you.'

Laincourt still did not know whether or not he was going to be initiated in accordance with his demands.

He nodded before following Gagnière up a spiral staircase that rose up into the tower, its bare walls illuminated by the flames of a few torches. They climbed three storeys filled with flickering shadows and silence to arrive in a small windowless room lit by two large candelabra standing on the floor. The marquis knocked on a door, opened it without waiting and entered ahead of Laincourt. Located at the very top of the tower, the hall within had two other doors and three arched windows looking out over the inner courtyard far below. A curtain closed off an alcove to one side and on a chair in front of more large candelabras sat a young blonde woman, wearing a mask and a red-and-grey gown. She had a superb black dragonnet with golden eyes with her, sitting on the back of her chair. Richly attired, Captain Saint-Georges was standing to her right and Gagnière placed himself to her left, while Laincourt instinctively remained near the closed door at his back, between the two swordsmen on duty as sentries.

He removed his mask in the hope that the woman would imitate him, but she chose not to do so.

'We meet for the first time, monsieur de Laincourt,' declared the vicomtesse de Malicorne.

'No doubt, madame,' he replied. 'I can only say that the sound of your voice is unfamiliar to me.'

'It is rather unfair,' she continued without acknowledging his remark, 'because I know how highly I should regard you. At least if I am to believe monsieur de Saint-Georges . . . And even monsieur de Gagnière, normally so circumspect, tells me that you are, shall we say, a rare find.'

On hearing the compliment, Laincourt placed his left hand on his chest and bowed slightly. But this preamble did not sit well with him. He sensed a threat coming.

'However,' said the vicomtesse, 'your ambitions might seem overweening. Because you are demanding nothing less than to become an initiate, aren't you?'

'My situation is extremely delicate, madame. I believe I have always displayed perfect loyalty and I must now count on the help of the Black Claw against the cardinal.'

Laincourt knew he was risking his all at this precise instant.

'So in a manner of speaking, monsieur, you now wish to be repaid . . .'

'Yes.'

'So be it.'

The vicomtesse made a sign with her hand and Saint-Georges threw open the curtain that had hidden the alcove from view, revealing the hurdy-gurdy player. He was half-naked, covered in blood and possibly even dead. Chained to the wall, his head slack, the old man in his rags was slumped in a squatting position, suspended by his arms.

This vision transfixed Laincourt. In a fraction of a second, he understood that he had been unmasked, that the hurdy-gurdy player had confessed under torture and that the Black Claw no longer believed in the deception Richelieu had created to counter its activities.

A deception of which Laincourt had been the instrument, and now risked becoming the victim.

He smashed the throat of one of the swordsmen with a violent blow of the elbow and suddenly spun to drive his knee into the crotch of the other, then took the man's head between both hands and broke his neck with a brusque twist. Saint-Georges drew his sword and lunged at him. Laincourt avoided his rapier, ducked under his other arm, rose and seized the captain's wrist to bring it high up behind his back, then finished immobilising him by placing a dagger against his throat. The vicomtesse had stood up by reflex and Gagnière protected her with his own body, brandishing a pistol. Irritated, the dragonnet spat and flapped its wings, still gripping the back of the chair.

'I will slit his throat if either of you makes the slightest move against me,' Laincourt threatened.

The young woman stared at him . . .

. . . then invited Gagnière to take a step back. Nonetheless,

337

he continued to keep his pistol aimed at Laincourt and his human shield.

Saint-Georges sweated, trembled and hesitated to swallow. On the floor, the swordsman with the smashed throat finished choking out his series of horrible death rattles. By a common accord, everyone waited for him to die and for silence to settle over the scene.

It seemed to go on for an eternity.

It had all started in Madrid where, already in the service of the cardinal, Arnaud de Laincourt had been appointed private secretary and trusted aide to an expatriate aristocrat through whom France had unofficially communicated with the Spanish crown. An agent of the Black Claw had approached him during this two-year mission and, understanding with whom he was dealing, Laincourt had informed Richelieu immediately by secret dispatch. The cardinal had ordered him to let matters take their course, without compromising himself too seriously: it was better at this stage to let the adversary keep the initiative and move his pieces as he saw fit. Laincourt thus gave a few tokens of goodwill to the Black Claw which, for its part, no doubt out of fear of discouraging a potential and very promising recruit, did not ask him for much. Things hardly went any further until his return to Paris.

Having entered the service of His Eminence's Guards, Laincourt very soon rose to the rank of ensign. He never entirely knew if this swift promotion rewarded his loyalty or was destined to excite the interest of the Black Claw. Whatever the case, after a long silence, the organisation contacted him again through an intermediary: the marquis de Gagnière. The gentleman told him – as if it were a revelation – the nature of those who had been receiving the small bits of information he had shared in Spain. He'd led Laincourt to understand that he had already done too much to back out now. He must continue to serve the Black Claw, but henceforth in full knowledge of his actions. He would not regret it, and he only had to say the word.

With Richelieu's accord, Laincourt pretended to accept and

for months thereafter had provided his so-called masters with carefully selected intelligence, all the while gaining their trust and rising within their hierarchy in the shadows. His objective was to uncover the person behind this dangerous embryo of a Black Claw lodge in France. He was to prevent them from succeeding and also unmask another spy, one who seemed to be working at the highest level within the Palais-Cardinal. As a precaution, Laincourt did not communicate with Richelieu through the habitual secret channels – even Rochefort did not know about him. His only contact was an old hurdy-gurdy player whom he met in a shabby tavern and about whom he knew almost nothing, except that he was trusted by the cardinal.

But this comedy could not continue. Because he was sharing information that always turned out to be less pertinent than it seemed at first, or which hurt France less than it did her enemies, the Black Claw would eventually work out that he was playing a double game. He needed to hurry matters along, and all the more quickly as the French draconic lodge was on the point of being born . . .

Together with Père Joseph, who was also in on the secret, Richelieu and Laincourt sketched out a bold plan. They arranged for the ensign to be caught in the act of spying, and, after that, they allowed a carefully prepared scenario to unfold. Convicted of treason, Laincourt was captured, locked up and then freed on the pretext that he had threatened to reveal explosive documents. These documents did not exist. But they seemed to have enough value to convince the Black Claw to grant Laincourt what he demanded: to become an initiate, as the reward for his work and skills.

The plan, however, did not expect him to actually go this far. The important thing was to identify the true master of the Black Claw in France and learn the date and place of the grand initiation ceremony. He would inform the cardinal as soon as possible, via the hurdy-gurdy player, to allow His Eminence to organise a vast operation to haul in all the conspirators.

But the hurdy-gurdy player had not shown up for the final meeting.

And with good reason . . .

The vicomtesse lifted an indifferent gaze from the dead body of the swordsman and smiled at Laincourt.

'And now?'

Still threatened by Gagnière's pistol, the cardinal's spy hesitated, tightening his hold on Saint-Georges, and then motioning towards the hurdy-gurdy player with his chin.

'Is he dead?'

'Perhaps.'

'Who betrayed him?'

This question haunted Laincourt. Except for himself, only Richelieu and Père Joseph were supposed to know of the role played by the hurdy-gurdy player in this affair. Even the traitorous Saint-Georges had been kept in the dark.

'No one did,' replied the young woman.

'Then how—?'

'I'm not as naïve as you seem to believe, monsieur. I simply had you followed.'

Laincourt frowned.

'By whom?'

'Him.' She pointed to her dragonnet. 'I saw your most recent meeting with the old man. Through his eyes. You can guess the rest . . . By the way, I must thank you for persuading the comte de Pontevedra to keep the Cardinal's Blades away from us. But I'm afraid it will be the last service you ever render us . . .'

Understanding that he could do nothing but try and save his own life, Laincourt used his heel to hook his hostage's ankles out from under him and abruptly shoved him. Saint-Georges tripped forward and collapsed in Gagnière's arms. But the marquis fired at the same time and hit the cardinal's spy in the shoulder as he was rushing out of the room and slamming the door behind him.

Gagnière took some time in untangling himself from his burden and the door resisted him when he sought to launch himself in pursuit of the fugitive. He turned around to address a helpless look at the vicomtesse.

Very calmly, she ordered:

'Let Savelda take charge of searching for monsieur de Laincourt. We three have better things to do. The ceremony cannot be delayed any longer.'

21

Holding a lantern in one hand and his sword in the other, Savelda kicked open the door to an empty, dusty room, dimly lit by the nocturnal glow coming from its sole embrasure. He examined the premises from the threshold, while hired swordsmen came and went behind him on the stairway.

'No one here!' he called out. 'Keep looking. Search the keep from top to bottom. Laincourt can't be far.'

Then he closed the door.

Silence returned and a moment went by before Agnès let herself drop from the ceiling beams she had been clinging to. Stealthily, she went to press her ear to the door and, reassured, returned to place herself at the embrasure. She did not know who this Laincourt was and the news that Savelda was hunting for someone other than her was only a small comfort. Granted, her escape had so far gone undiscovered. But the freebooters combing through the keep were still very much a threat to her.

Outside, in the lower part of the ruined castle, about fifty metres from the keep, the ritual was proceeding.

It had started at moonrise, led by Gagnière who officiated bare-headed, dressed in a ceremonial robe. He chanted in the ancient draconic tongue, a language which his audience did not understand but whose power, beyond its actual meaning, resonated in the depths of their being. Their souls aquiver, the candidates for initiation listened, taken over by a sacred fervour.

Then the vicomtesse, still masked, solemnly entered the

pool of warm light from the torches and bonfires, and took up her place behind the carved altar. There was a heavy silence while Gagnière stepped back to her side and, with lowered head and hands crossed upon his belly, adopted a meditative pose. She then began, also using the draconic tongue, the long litany of Ancestral Dragons, invoking their true names and asking for their protection. This took some time, as each Ancestral Dragon had to be addressed by its title and its closest family ties. And the names she pronounced before each panegyric were moreover repeated by Gagnière in his role as First Initiate, and then taken up in chorus by the entire audience.

Finally, the vicomtesse opened a casket placed on the altar and took out the Sphère d'Âme which she brandished in her outstretched arms. Still speaking in the draconic language, she called upon Sassh'Krecht, the Ancestral Dragon whose primordial essence haunted the globe with its black turmoil. Now, she recited all of Sassh'Krecht's parents and descendants, titles, legendary exploits and, as she declaimed them, the atmosphere around her filled with a presence that was as exalting as it was frightening, originating from the beginning of time and soon to be resurrected in defiance of the laws of nature.

At this point, beginning with Gagnière and with Saint-Georges just behind him, the faithful filed past the altar in good order, each knelt at the vicomtesse's feet, placed their lips upon the Sphère d'Âme which she had lowered to their height and then went to stand in a long row. By their kiss, they had signified their assent. Ready to sacrifice a part of themselves, they waited for Sassh'Krecht to manifest itself and impregnate their soul.

In a trance, the vicomtesse de Malicorne raised the globe towards the moon. She shouted a command. Whirlwinds lifted around her. Above the castle, the clouds in the sky suddenly dispersed, as if driven away by a centrifugal force. Black and grey plumes escaped from the paling Sphère d'Âme. They rose in long ribbons as a dull noise filled the

343

night and, little by little, they formed the shape of a giant spectral dragon which reared up, deployed its wings and occupied an immense span of the sky. Sassh'Krecht had survived death for centuries now, a prisoner of the Sphère d'Âme where all of its power had been concentrated. It gloried in the freedom which it had now almost completely recovered, only its tail still attached to the relic the vicomtesse gripped in her hands, her body traversed by ecstatic shivers. It simply needed to take possession of the souls that its disciples were offering freely.

No one heard the shot, but all of them saw the Sphère d'Âme, now milky white, burst into shatters.

The vicomtesse screamed and collapsed. The entire gathering suffered an enormous shock that left it reeling and Sassh'Krecht emitted a cavernous howl that shook the members of the Black Claw to the core. Detached from the Sphère d'Âme before it had managed to become fully incarnate, the Ancestral Dragon contorted like an animal trapped in a blazing fire that was devouring it.

Gagnière was the first to react.

He rushed over to the unconscious vicomtesse, crouched down, lifted her up slightly, saw that she was still breathing and, at a complete loss, looked about him in an effort to comprehend.

Had the ritual failed?

The skies grew dark. Still howling, the spectral dragon twisted in pain as shreds were torn from its ghostly silhouette like wisps of mist. Stormy rumblings were heard. Gold and crimson flashes ripped through the night sky as Sassh'Krecht liberated energy that had to find an outlet.

Gagnière saw the vicomtesse's dragonnet flapping in the air around them. It hissed at him furiously, and then flew off towards the keep. He followed it with his eyes and saw the thin stream of smoke that filtered from an embrasure.

Pistol still smoking in her hand, Agnès dashed down the steps of the tower from where, both hidden herself and able to observe every detail of the ceremony, she had opened fire. Aware of what was at stake and doubting she would live to see the dawn, she had resolved that as she had nothing to lose she would wreak as much havoc as possible and wait for the ritual to reach its critical point before she intervened.

Now, she had to make an effort to survive and, perhaps, even to escape.

She descended one floor, then two, and had reached the first floor when she heard hurried steps climbing towards her from the ground floor below. She cursed, tore down an old drapery from a wall and hurled it like a fishing net over the first swordsman who presented himself, delivering a kick that broke his jaw. Her victim fell backwards, toppling his comrades who became tangled up with him and the dusty piece of cloth, which they ripped at without managing to free themselves. Those jostling with one another behind them were forced to retreat back down the stairs and Savelda's angry voice could be heard shouting.

Agnès immediately reversed course and climbed the steps two by two. Her only hope was to reach the top of the tower and the walkway along the keep's ramparts. She suddenly came face-to-face with a lone freebooter. She drew her sword to block his blade, violently drove the butt of her pistol upwards into his crotch and sent her opponent tumbling down the stairs, breaking his neck in the process.

With Savelda's men now at her heels, she arrived on the last floor of the tower when a hand on her shoulder drew her behind a wall hanging and through the little doorway which it hid. Agnès found herself in a narrow, shadowy corridor, pressed up against someone who murmured to her:

'Silence.'

She closed her mouth and remained still, while on the other side of the door, the Black Claw's hired swordsmen ran over to the keep's walkway without stopping.

'My name is Laincourt. Don't be afraid.'

'And of what would I be afraid?

At which point, Laincourt felt the nip of a dagger that had reached high up between his thighs.

'I am in the cardinal's service,' he whispered.

'They are searching for you, monsieur.'

'So we have something in common. What's your name?'

'Agnès. I thought I heard a shot just before the ceremony began. Was that you?'

'In a manner of speaking. Come, it won't take them long to figure things out.'

They advanced silently down the dark corridor, passing before a triple-arched window.

'You're wounded,' said Agnès noticing the Laincourt's bloody shoulder.

'I didn't fire the shot.'

'Can you move it?'

'Yes. It's not broken and the pistol ball passed clean through. Nothing serious.'

They pushed a little door open and then followed a passage lit in the distance by some square openings looking out into the courtyard. The ceiling was so low that they could only progress bent double.

'This passage runs beneath the walkway. It will take us to the next tower. They're probably yet not looking for us there.'

'You seem to know the premises well . . .'

'My knowledge is newly gained.'

At the end of the passage they came to another door.

They listened, opened it cautiously and emerged behind a sentry. Laincourt slit his throat and held him as he sagged. They heard a great commotion on the lower floors, found only locked doors and were forced to climb some very steep steps in order to raise a hatch that gave them access to the roof.

They were fortunate it was deserted, although they could see torches and silhouettes moving about on one of the other towers, the one where Savelda and his men were finishing their search. Beyond, in the tormented sky, the spectral dragon had been replaced by a fury of uncontrolled magical energy. The red and golden flashes had redoubled in intensity. Interspersed by thunderclaps, a deep roar rumbled above them that could be felt in the gut and increasingly threatened to unleash itself upon the castle itself.

'Quick!' yelled Laincourt.

Seeking cover behind the crenellations, they took the walkway towards the third tower. They went as fast they could without running upright and started to believe that they might make good their escape when a strident cry rang out nearby: the vicomtesse's dragonnet was beating its wings level with them and giving away their position. Heads turned their way. A hue and cry was raised.

Laincourt brandished his pistol and shot the reptile down with a single ball that ripped off its head.

'A wasted shot,' commented Agnès.

'Not entirely,' replied the cardinal's spy, thinking of the hurdy-gurdy player who had been captured thanks to the dragonnet.

They were halfway between the second and the third tower, towards which Savelda's swordsmen were already hurrying. They ran under sporadic and badly aimed fire, reached the tower before their enemies and tried to open the hatch.

Locked.

'*Merde!*' Laincourt swore.

Agnès took stock of the situation. Savelda and his freebooters were coming towards them from the first tower by the walkway. Others were already emerging from the second tower and blocked any possibility of retreat. The ground was fifty metres below. They did not have time to force the hatch.

They were trapped.

Agnès and Laincourt placed themselves *en garde*, back to back . . . and waited.

Cautious now, the hired swordsmen slowed down and surrounded them, while Savelda, calm and smiling, walked up to them.

A circle of blades closed in the fugitives, who were resolved to die rather than allow themselves to be captured.

'Usually,' Agnès muttered to herself, 'they show up about now . . .'

Laincourt heard her.

'What did you say?' he asked over his wounded shoulder.

'Nothing. Delighted to have met you.'

'Same here.'

And then rescue came from the sky.

22

Outside the keep, the castle was plunged into a state of chaos that was dominated by the roiling storm of energies released by the destruction of the Sphère d'Âme. Sizzling lightning bolts fell from the ragged night sky, igniting trees and bushes, raising sprays of earth, pulverising stones and knocking down sections of wall. One of them split the altar open and set it ablaze as Gagnière fled from it, now rid of his ceremonial robe and carrying the unconscious vicomtesse in his arms. People were screaming and panicked horses whinnied. Followers of the Black Claw and its hired swordsmen were running in every direction, not knowing where to seek refuge or even who or what, exactly, they needed defending against.

Because the Cardinal's Blades had gone on the offensive.

Using Malencontre's information, La Fargue and his men were quietly surrounding the keep when Agnès interrupted the ceremony in such dramatic fashion. As desperate as it was, her initiative proved invaluable in diverting the attention of everyone present to the torments of the great spectral dragon. La Fargue, who was moving alongside a sunken path bordered by a low wall, hastened towards the enclosure where the two wyvern riders, who had been idle since the end of the day, were guarding their beasts. With a pipe in his mouth and a heavy sack slung round his shoulders in a bandolier, Ballardieu climbed to the top of a rampart, broke the neck of a lookout and discreetly took his place directly above the main gate and its sentries. Further off, Saint-Lucq stepped over another sentry's dead body and approached a campfire around which five swordsmen had gathered, all of them gaping up at the extraordinary display taking place in the night skies. At the same time, Marciac was slipping towards the stable.

In the keep, Agnès and Laincourt were moving from one tower to the next in an effort to stay ahead of Savelda's search parties when, outside, the first lightning bolt struck the ritual site. At first paralysed in terror, the Black Claw's followers scattered, ducking their heads as more bolts came down, while the hired swordsmen watching over the ritual finally began to react to the alarm.

Ballardieu judged that this was the right moment to take action. Digging into his bag, he took out a grenade and lit its fuse from his clay pipe before hurling the object blindly over the parapet against which he was crouching. A second and a third immediately followed, their explosions ringing out amidst the screams and the roar of the supernatural storm. He risked a glimpse at the scene below, was satisfied to see the bodies of sentries lying there and then spied a wyvern rising from the enclosure. Standing, he began bombarding the milling crowd with more grenades.

The freebooters gathered around a campfire saw the grenades exploding in the distance, grabbed their weapons and—

—froze.

A man dressed in black, his eyes hidden by red glasses that reflected the flames, was standing before them. He waited and pointed his outstretched rapier at them. He seemed both relaxed and determined. Apparently he had been there for some time. They realised they would have to get past him. And in spite of all their experience of suffering, fighting and massacres, a feeling of dread came over them.

Their guts clenched with fear; they knew for certain that they were going to die.

Panicked by the dazzling flashes of lightning and deafening thunder, the Black Claw's followers and their hired swordsmen were running towards the stable when its doors opened wide to reveal the fire ravaging the interior and a stampede of horses that Marciac had freed. The terrified steeds knocked down and trampled the first arrivals, and shoved the rest aside, whinnying in fear before they dispersed.

The silhouette of the Gascon was outlined against the blaze as he emerged in turn, gripping his rapier. He rapidly dispatched the few disoriented freebooters who remained, slitting one man's throat, running his blade through the chest of another and splitting open the face of a third.

Taking advantage of a moment's respite, he lifted his gaze to the sky which seemed to have gone mad, and then noticed Saint-Lucq dashing off, barely slowing down to eliminate the men who brandished swords in his path. At the end of one assault, the half-blood turned toward Marciac and pointed to the dark mass of the castle keep, which was where he was headed. The Gascon understood and nodded, thought of following him, but was immediately distracted by defending himself against two more opponents.

Surrounded at the top of the tower, Agnès and Laincourt believed they were doomed when, thrown from above, grenades with blazing fuses bounced among the stupefied swordsmen who were threatening them, provoking panicked pushing and shoving before the missiles exploded one after another in clouds of fiery powder, their burning shards ripping through those who had not been able to retreat towards the keep's walkway.

Rearing up and flapping its wings to slow its approach, a wyvern set down on the tower.

'Captain!' Agnès exclaimed in relief when she saw who was riding the reptile.

'Hurry!' yelled La Fargue.

He held out a gloved hand to her, but the young woman pointed instead to Laincourt.

'He's coming too!'

'What? No! Too heavy!'

'He's coming too!'

It was not the time or the place for an argument: around

them, the hired swordsmen were beginning to rally themselves.

Agnès and Laincourt climbed onto the reptile's rump behind La Fargue, who dug in his spurs to launch the wyvern. The beast took a few lumbering steps towards the parapet. Seeing his prey escaping, Savelda ran towards them, taking aim with his pistol while yelling at his men to move out of the way. He fired and the pistol ball passed through the wyvern's long neck at the very instant when it was taking to the air. The reptile flinched. Its surprise, pain and the over-heavy load on its back toppled it over the edge, and it fell. It opened its wings as the ground approached and La Fargue hauled with all his might on the reins . . . and the wyvern pulled out of its dive at the very last second. Its belly brushed against the cobblestones and its claws scraped over them, raising a spray of sparks. It was moving too fast across the small courtyard to have any chance of climbing again. La Fargue barely succeeded in turning its head towards the keep's gate. The reptile swept at full speed beneath the vault. But its span was too wide and the impact broke its leathery wings. The wyvern screamed. Moving like a rock down a hillside, it crossed the lowered drawbridge, rolled over in a whirlwind of dust and blood, and threw off its passengers before finally crashing into one of the great bonfires that had been lit for the ceremony.

Ballardieu saw the wyvern burst forth from the keep and three bodies flying through the air.

'AGNÈS!' he screamed as the reptile with its broken wings smashed into the flaming pyre and vanished beneath it.

He vaulted over the parapet, landed six metres below and began to run without paying any heed to the pain from a sprained ankle. Two drac swordsmen attacked him. He did not slow down or even draw his sword. Instead, taking his sack, weighed with a few remaining grenades, by its bandolier, he swung it round, crushing a temple and dislocating a scaly jaw. Still running, shoving aside everyone in the terrified crowd who stood in his way, he yelled at the top of his lungs:

'AGNÈS . . . ! AGNÈS . . . !'

He saw La Fargue picking himself off the ground and went to him.

'AGNÈS! WHERE IS AGNÈS?'

The captain, in a daze, was staggering on his feet. He blinked and almost tripped over. Ballardieu had to steady him.

'CAPTAIN! WHERE IS SHE? WHERE IS AGNÈS?'

'I . . . I don't know . . .'

Marciac arrived.

'WHAT'S GOING ON?' he asked, trying to making himself heard over the din of thunder that accompanied the magical lightning bolts.

'IT'S AGNÈS!' explained the old soldier anxiously. 'SHE'S HERE! SOMEWHERE! HELP ME!'

Grimacing, with a dazed look in his eye, Laincourt struggled to drag himself from the ground, remaining for a moment on his hands and knees. He coughed and spat out a mixture of dirt and blood.

Then he stood up.

Around him the chaos of the battle drawing to a close blended with that of the incredible storm above, whose windy moans were rising to a high-pitched screech. The destructive bolts of lightning gained in intensity and the furious roaring shook the entire castle to its very depths, dislodging its stones. No one thought of fighting any longer, only of escape. The surviving followers and mercenaries of the Black Claw pressed toward the gate which Ballardieu no longer defended with his grenades.

Laincourt, too, should have been fleeing without delay.

But he had one last task to accomplish.

Still holding the unconscious vicomtesse in his arms, Gagnière arrived in the courtyard of the keep at the same time as Savelda and his men, coming down from the upper floors.

'We're under attack!' said Gagnière sweating.

'Yes,' replied the one-eyed Spaniard. 'And we've already lost . . . Give her to me.'

Without waiting for a reply, he seized hold of the vicomtesse.

The marquis let him take her, too stunned by the turn of events to even protest.

'We must flee!' he said. 'By the passageway. Quickly, while there's still time!'

'No.'

'What?'

'Not you. You stay.'

'But why?'

'To protect our retreat . . . Against him.'

Gagnière turned around.

Saint-Lucq was entering from beneath the vault, armed with a rapier in his right hand and a dagger in his left.

'You and you, with me,' ordered Savelda. 'The rest of you, with the marquis.'

And, followed by the two men he had selected, he disappeared through a door leaving the gentleman and four swordsmen in the courtyard.

Gagnière went over and tried to open the same door, only to find it had been locked from within. He then stared at the half-blood who met his glance and smiled at him from beyond the row of freebooters, as if they were an insignificant obstacle separating the two of them. This idea wormed its way into the mind of the marquis and he became frightened.

Gathering up a sword from a dead body that had fallen from the walkway above, he cried: 'ATTACK!'

Themselves unnerved by Saint-Lucq's predatory calm, the hired swordsmen flinched and then rushed forward. The half-blood parried two blades with his rapier, planted and then left his dagger in the belly of his first opponent, spun round and slit the throat of the second with a reverse thrust. In one smooth motion he ducked down in front of a drac who was preparing to strike high, slipped under his arm and stood up, throwing the reptilian over his shoulder. The drac fell heavily on his back and Saint-Lucq lunged to pierce the chest of the remaining mercenary, whom he disarmed. Then, completing his murderous choreography, he brought the rapier he had just acquired to a vertical position, and without looking, pinned the drac to the ground with it.

Expressionless, the half-blood turned to stare once again at Gagnière.

There was still a wyvern in the enclosure, although no doubt it would have fled earlier if it had not been chained up. Saint-Georges struggled to saddle it and he already had one boot in the stirrup when, amidst the racket of the storm, he heard distinctly:

'Step back.'

Bruised, wounded, bleeding; Laincourt stood a few metres behind him, pointing a pistol. He was a sorry sight, but there was an almost fanatical light in his eyes.

'Obey,' he added. 'I'm just waiting for an excuse to blow your brains out.'

Without making any sudden moves, Saint-Georges set his foot back on the ground and stretched out his arms. He did not turn round, however. Nor did he move away from the wyvern and the pistols tucked into its saddle holsters. Pistols that Laincourt, behind his back, could not see.

'We can still reach an understanding, Laincourt.'

'I doubt that.'

'I am rich. Very rich . . .'

'Your gold is the reward for your treachery. How many men have died because of you? The latest of your victims were no doubt the couriers from Brussels, whose itineraries you gave to the Black Claw. But before them?'

'Gold is gold. It shines everywhere with same brightness.'

'Yours will be worthless where you're going.'

Saint-Georges suddenly spun about, brandishing a pistol.

A shot rang out.

And Laincourt watched the traitor fall, his eye burst and the back of his skull torn out by the ball.

Then he gazed at the saddled wyvern.

The storm was now at its height. Whirlwinds of energy had formed at ground level and lightning bolts fell from the sky every second, digging craters wherever they landed. The castle looked as if it were being battered by a cannonade that was determined to destroy it.

'OVER HERE!' La Fargue yelled suddenly.

He was crouching near Agnès whom he had just found and was raising her head. The young woman was unconscious. Her hair was sticky with blood at her temple. But she was still breathing.

'IS SHE . . . ?' asked Ballardieu, who had come running, fearing the worst.

'NO. SHE LIVES.'

A rider appeared from a breach in a rampart. It was Almades, who towed the Blades' mounts behind him. They were good warhorses, fortunately, and thus did not panic in the din of battle.

'AGNÈS IS IN NO FIT STATE TO RIDE!' declared La Fargue.

'I'LL CARRY HER!' replied Ballardieu.

A lightning bolt struck nearby and showered them with smoking earth.

'LOOK!' cried the Gascon.

The vicomtesse's black coach was coming from the keep, driven by Saint-Lucq.

'Bless you, Saint-Lucq,' murmured Ballardieu.

The half-blood pulled up the coach in front of them. He had great difficulty controlling the team of horses. They whinnied and reared at each explosion, making the vehicle lurch backward and forward. Marciac seized the animals by their bits to settle them.

La Fargue managed to open the door and saw a form inside.

'THERE'S SOMEONE IN HERE!'

It was Gagnière. Fainted away, after receiving a sword wound in the right shoulder.

'A NEW FRIEND!' joked Saint-Lucq. 'COME ON! HURRY!'

Ballardieu climbed aboard holding Agnès in his arms. La Fargue closed the door for them, then mounted the horse whose reins the Gascon, already in his saddle, held out for him.

'COME ON! ALL HELL IS GOING BREAK LOOSE!'

Saint-Lucq cracked the lunges against the rumps of the harnessed horses. The riders spurred their own mounts and opened the way for the coach and they were all soon moving at a full gallop. Miraculously spared by the explosions whose blasts lashed their faces with various bits of debris, they crossed through the gate just before a violent flash brought it tumbling down. The convoy hurtled down the winding road, pitilessly running down any escapees in their path, leaving the ruined castle behind them in the grip of the full destructive fury of ancestral energies.

There was a second of tremendous silence and then a dazzling force broke forth from the sky. It swept away the last vestiges of the castle in an apocalyptic blast whose brightness drowned out the silhouette of a lone wyvern and its rider winging their way from the scene.

At the same moment, a quarter of a league away, a gate was pushed open in a thicket of undergrowth. Savelda came through first, battling with the thorns, soon followed by the two men carrying the vicomtesse. Drained of the draconic energy which had sustained her youth, she had regained her true age, becoming a haggard and ancient-looking old woman: her face was hollow and wrinkled, her complexion had lost its freshness and beauty, her long blonde hair had shrivelled into grey locks and her pretty lips had dried and thinned. A thick black bile ran from her mouth and nostrils, and she breathed with difficulty, moaning and hiccupping.

But she lived.

IV

A New Day

IV

A New Day

Two days went by and then, in the morning, Rochefort came seeking La Fargue. Less than an hour later, La Fargue was received alone by Richelieu. Sitting at his desk, elbows placed on the arms of his chairs and his fingers gathered into a steeple against his lips, the cardinal stared at the impassive old captain for a long while.

Finally he said:

'Monsieur de Tréville displayed great kindness in liberating monsieur Leprat from Le Châtelet, did he not? If it were up to me . . .'

Sitting stiffly and keeping his gaze fixed straight before him, La Fargue did not reply.

'If one is to believe monsieur de Tréville,' Richelieu continued, 'the man known as Malencontre duped your man, stole his things and escaped his prison cell in disguise, taking advantage of the changing of the guards. If monsieur Leprat were not the man that he is, this might be believable . . .'

'No one is infallible, monseigneur.'

'Without a doubt, indeed . . . Naturally, the most regrettable aspect, beyond monsieur Leprat's hurt pride, is the loss of Malencontre. Do you have any idea of where he is to be found?'

'None at all. But it seems to me that the capture of the marquis de Gagnière compensates for his loss. Malencontre served Gagnière. And the master always knows more than his creature.'

'So we have come out ahead in this exchange.'

'Yes, monseigneur. Considerably.'

'We shall see . . .'

The cardinal turned his gaze to the window.

'How is the baronne de Vaudreuil?'

'She is recovering.'

'And the others?'

'They're all in the best of form. These last few days of rest have been very beneficial for them.'

'Good, good . . . But there still remains the fact that I ordered you not to interfere.'

'That's true.'

'Père Joseph warned me about your insubordination. Do you have anything to say in your defence?'

'Yes. I believe that Your Eminence did not wish to be obeyed.'

'Really?'

'I believe that Your Eminence knew that I would not abandon one of my . . . one of your Blades. I believe that Your Eminence had foreseen that I would be led to confront the Black Claw. Finally, I believe that Your Eminence could not do other than to give me the orders that he gave me, out of fear of displeasing Spain. But despite all that, Your Eminence wanted me to pursue matters.'

'And from where do you draw this sentiment, captain?'

'First of all, from the concern you have for the welfare of France, monseigneur.'

'Very well. And then?'

'Nothing obliged you to tell me where Malencontre was being detained. In doing so, you gave me the means to take the next step without risk of annoying the ambassador extraordinary of Spain. Thus, appearances were saved.'

The cardinal smiled. His eyes crinkled and shone with an unspoken satisfaction.

'You will understand, captain, that I can only deny all this.'

'Indeed, monseigneur.'

'Know then that I condemn your initiative . . .'

La Fargue nodded.

'. . . and that I congratulate you.'

The old gentleman betrayed a hint of a sly smile.

He realised that he would probably never know what

Richelieu had or had not known since the beginning of this affair, what he had chosen to say or had preferred to keep silent, or what he had pretended to believe or had secretly guessed. The Blades were a weapon that the cardinal used as he pleased.

Richelieu rose and, a signal honour, accompanied La Fargue to the door.

'I should like, captain, for you to reflect on the proposal that I am about to make to you . . .'

'Monseigneur?'

'It concerns a certain young man of great worth who has served me well. Unfortunately, things turned out in a manner that prevents him from regaining his position among my Guards. Nevertheless, I do not wish to lose him. But if you should deign to accept him among the Blades . . .'

'His name?'

'Laincourt.'

'Is he the man who—'

'One and the same, captain.'

'I promise you that I shall think upon it, monseigneur.'

'Excellent. Think upon it. And give me your accord soon.'

2

'It's me,' announced Leprat after knocking on the door to Agnès' bedroom.

'Come in.'

The young woman was still in her bed, more out of laziness, however, than necessity. She looked well and the scratches on her face would not spoil her beauty. The platter Ballardieu had brought her was set down next to her. Leprat noticed with satisfaction that it was almost empty.

'I came to see how you were feeling,' said the musketeer.

Then pointing to a chair:

'May I?'

'Of course.'

Agnès closed her book, looked at Leprat as he sat down, taking care with his wounded leg, and waited.

'So?' he asked after a moment.

'So what?'

'Are you feeling well?'

'As you can see . . . I'm resting.'

'You deserve it.'

'I believe I do, yes.'

There was an awkward silence during which Agnès became amused by Leprat's embarrassment.

But she finally took pity on him and said:

'Go ahead. Say it.'

'You were reckless in letting yourself be abducted by those men.'

'I didn't know who they were, in fact, and that was precisely what I was counting on finding out. Furthermore, there were five or six of them and I was unarmed.'

'Nevertheless. When you saw Saint-Lucq in the street, you could have . . . Between the two of you, with surprise on your side . . .'

'I know.'

'Things could have turned out very badly.'

'Yes. The Black Claw could have established a lodge, here, in France.'

'That's one way of looking at it. But why did you go there, to begin with?'

'To Cécile's house?'

'Yes.'

'You know very well. To find out what she was hiding there. To find whatever Saint-Lucq managed to find before me, acting on his secret orders from the captain. If I had known that . . .'

Leprat nodded, with a distracted gaze.

Agnès narrowed her eyes and leaned forward to look at him squarely.

'That's what you've come to speak to me about, isn't it?'

'He's changed. He's not the same as he was . . . I . . . I think he's distrustful of us.'

And with an ill-tempered gesture, his voice vibrant with impotent anger, Leprat added:

'Of us, damn it! Of his Blades!'

The young woman, sympathising with him, laid her hand upon his wrist.

'We have Louveciennes to blame for that. When he betrayed us at La Rochelle, he might as well have stabbed La Fargue in the heart. He was his best friend. His only friend, perhaps . . . And that's not even including the death of Bretteville and the shameful dissolution of the Blades. That memory must be branded by a red-hot iron in his mind, and it burns him still.'

Leprat stood up, limped towards the window and let his gaze wander over the rooftops of the faubourg Saint-Germain.

'The worst part . . .' he finally admitted, 'the worst part is that I think he's right to be wary of us.'

'What?'

'Of one of us, in any case.'

'Who?'

'I don't know.'

He turned towards Agnès and explained:

'We were the only ones to know that we were holding Malencontre. But that didn't prevent Rochefort from coming to claim him after a few hours. So the cardinal knew we had him as well. Who told him?'

Sensing a feeling that she did not like at all come over her, the young baronne played devil's advocate:

'There's Guibot. And Naïs, who we don't know from Adam and Eve, after all . . .'

'And you really believe that?'

'Do you suspect me?'

'No.'

'So then, who? Saint-Lucq? Marciac? Almades? Ballardieu . . . ? And why couldn't it be you, Leprat?'

He stared at her without anger, looking almost hurt:

'It's anyone's guess . . .'

3

The comte de Rochefort was waiting in one of the confessionals in the Saint-Eustache church when, at the appointed hour, someone sat down on the other side of the opening occluded by tiny wooden crossbars.

'His Eminence,' Rochefort said, 'reproaches you for not having warned him about La Fargue's plans.'

'What plans?'

'The ones that permitted Malencontre to escape from Le Châtelet.'

'I didn't know about them.'

'Really?'

'Yes.'

'That's difficult to believe. So where is Malencontre hiding?' the comte demanded.

'La Fargue gave him his liberty in exchange for the information that allowed them to rescue Agnès. And, in the process, to strike a blow at the Black Claw. If he has an ounce of good sense, Malencontre has already left the kingdom.'

'That's regrettable.'

'I had rather imagined that defeating the Black Claw would be cause for rejoicing . . .'

'Don't be clever with me. That's not what we're paying you for . . . Did you know that this so-called Cécile was in fact La Fargue's daughter?'

There was an eloquent silence.

'No,' the man said finally.

'Well, now you do. His Eminence wishes to know where she is.'

'In a safe place.'

'That's not what I asked you.'

'Cécile, or whatever her name may be, is simply a victim in this whole affair. She deserves to be left in peace.'

'No doubt. But you haven't answered my question.'

'And I won't answer it.' The man's tone led Rochefort to understand that it would futile to insist.

'As you will,' the comte said resignedly. 'But I have to tell you, Marciac, you're hardly earning your wages.'

4

In the courtyard of the splendid Hôtel de Tournon, an escort of gentlemen sat on their horses near a luxurious coach. They were waiting for the comte de Pontevedra, who was about to take the road back to Spain. The secret negotiations had lately taken an unexpected turn, and having been prematurely interrupted, failed to reach any conclusion. It only remained for the ambassador to return to Madrid in order to inform the king and his minister Olivares.

Pontevedra was finishing preparing for his journey when a last visitor was announced. He displayed a certain astonishment on learning his name, hesitated, thinking, and then indicated that he would receive him unattended in a salon.

La Fargue was already standing there when he entered.

The two men stared at one another for a long time. They were roughly the same age, but one had become a gentleman of court and intrigue while the other remained a gentleman of war and honour. It was not, however, the comte de Pontevedra, ambassador extraordinary of Spain and favourite of His Majesty Felipe IV, that the old captain regarded so impassively. It was Louveciennes, his former brother-in-arms and in bloodshed, the sole true friend that he had ever had and the man who had betrayed him.

'What do you want?'

'I came to tell you that Anne, my daughter, is safe and well. It seemed to me that you deserved to know that.'

Pontevedra gave a twisted, mocking smile.

'"Your daughter"?'

'She is my daughter and you know it. Indeed, you have

always known it. As have I. As did Oriane. And now Anne knows it as well. Just as she knows who you are.'

A hateful mask disfigured the ambassador's face.

'What have you told her?' he spat.

'Nothing. I am not that kind of a man.'

'So how does she know?'

'A letter from her mother. Oriane, who you never loved as much as she deserved . . .'

'A reproach that cannot be made of you,' retorted the comte.

He had venom on his lips and a flame in his eyes.

'I have long regretted our conduct that night,' admitted La Fargue.

'A handsome excuse!'

'Oriane also regretted it as well. But that was before La Rochelle, before you revealed your true nature, before you turned traitor.'

'I made a choice. The right one. And to convince myself of that all I need to do is look at you. You have nothing. You are nothing. While as for me . . .'

'You are merely rich. And Bretteville is dead because of you, Louveciennes.'

'I AM THE COMTE DE PONTEVEDRA!' shouted the former Blade.

'We both know who you are,' said La Fargue in a calm voice.

Turning away, he already had his hand on the doorknob, when Pontevedra, crimson-faced, cried out:

'I will find Anne. Wherever you are hiding her, I will find her!'

The captain spared a thought for his daughter, whom he did not know and even dreaded meeting. For now, she was where no one would be looking for her, in rue de la Grenouillère, entrusted thanks to Marciac to the good graces of the beautiful Gabrielle and her comely lodgers.

That, however, could not last.

'No,' declared La Fargue. 'You will not find her. You are going to forget about her.'

The ambassador burst out laughing.

'How are you going to force me? You can't do anything against me, La Fargue! Nothing!'

'Oh, but I can. You have used your post as ambassador to pursue a personal ambition. You have schemed and you have lied. In doing so, you have seriously compromised your mission and betrayed the trust placed in you by your . . . king. You have even, in demanding that the Blades and I search for the so-called chevalier d'Ireban, gathered together men who will soon, no doubt, be a source of complaint for Spain. You wanted us because we are the best? Well, here we are. Do you believe that Richelieu will now wish to deprive himself of our services? No, Louveciennes. The Cardinal's Blades are back, a development that your masters will have cause to regret before long . . . So, think about it. Do you really want this to become known?'

'Don't threaten me.'

'I exchange my silence for my daughter. You have no choice . . . Oh, and one last thing . . .'

'Which is?'

'The next time we meet, I will kill you. Have a safe journey back to Spain.'

La Fargue left without closing the door.

Epilogue

Night had fallen when La Fargue returned to the Hôtel de l'Épervier that evening.

He led his horse to the stable, unsaddled it and carefully rubbed it down, then crossed the courtyard to the main building. The sound of laughter, snatches of song and joyful conversations reached his ears as he went up the front steps. He smiled, entered and, from the shadows in the front hall, watched the spectacle that presented itself to him through a wide open doorway.

The Blades were gathered around a meal that wine and enjoyment had prolonged. They were all there. Ballardieu and Marciac were standing on chairs and singing off key. Agnès, radiant, was laughing. Leprat was clapping his hands and joining in on the chorus. And even the austere Almades could not help laughing at the clowning of the first two, the Gascon playing at being drunk with only a little effort. Sweet Naïs was serving without losing the least bit of their performance. Delighted, old Guibot tapped out the rhythm with his wooden leg.

> *Ô charmante bouteille!*
> *Pourquoi renfermes-tu*
> *Dans un osier tordu*
> *Ta liqueur sans pareille?*
> *Pourquoi nous caches-tu*
> *Sous tes sombres habits*
> *Ton ambre et tes rubis?*

Pour contenter la vue,
Ainsi que le gosier,
Dépouille ton osier,
Montre-toi toute nue.
Et ne nous cache plus
Sous tes sombres habits
Ton ambre et tes rubis.

They seemed happy and La Fargue envied their joy, their carefree attitude and their youth. He could have been the father of most of them and, in a certain sense, he was.

Or he had been.

In former times, he would have joined in. And he was hesitating over whether or not to do so now when Naïs, in order to pass by, shut the door and left the tired old captain plunged in darkness

He preferred to go to his room without being seen or heard.

Once there, far from the noise and the warmth of the party below, he stretched out, still fully dressed, on his bed, crossed his fingers beneath the back of his neck and waited, eyes wide open but staring blankly ahead.

Soon the Saint-Germain abbey bell-tower tolled midnight.

Then La Fargue got up.

From a small casket, whose key he always kept on his person, he took out a precious silver mirror that he placed before him on a table.

In a meditative pose, with lowered eyelids, he quietly recited a ritual formula in an ancient, dread and almost forgotten tongue. The mirror which at first sent back nothing but his own reflection responded to the call. Its surface rippled and, slowly, as if emerging from a layer of living mercury, appeared the slightly translucent head of a white dragon with red eyes.

'Good evening, master,' said La Fargue.

Ballardieu and Marciac's song

Oh charming bottle!
Why do you enclose
In twisted wicker
Your peerless liqueur?
Why do you hide from us
Beneath your dark apparel
Your amber and your rubies?

To satisfy the eye,
As well as the throat,
Shed thy wicker
And bare yourself
No longer hide from us
Beneath your dark apparel
Your amber and your rubies.

The Alchemist in the Shadows

This book is dedicated to Patrice Duvic,
who showed me the path

Prologue

June 1633

It was that uncertain hour just before dawn, when the wind dies down and the mist begins to rise, the morning still a pale promise at the edge of night. A veil of dew already covered the countryside around the solitary manor, standing close to the border between Alsace and Lorraine. A great silence reigned beneath the long tattered clouds which lazed across a sky pricked with fading stars.

An elegant gentleman observed the manor from the edge of the nearby wood, watching the few lights that glowed within it. A mere shadow among the other shadows beneath the branches, he stood straight as a blade, his feet slightly spread, with his thumb tucked into his belt and one hand curled around the pommel of his sword. He was a tall handsome man. His name was François Reynault d'Ombreuse.

And today, in all likelihood, he would either kill a dragon or the dragon would kill him.

Behind the wall which protected the ruined manor and its outbuildings, mercenaries with tired, heavy eyes waited impatiently for the sun to rise. They leaned tiredly on their muskets or held up lanterns as they peered out into the lightening darkness, envying their sleeping comrades. They were soldiers of fortune, part of a band of thirty freebooters, who had fought and pillaged under various banners during the fifteen terrible years of war that had raged throughout the German principalities of the Holy Roman Empire. Now they had been hired to escort a quiet, pale-faced gentleman whose looks and manner impressed them more than they cared to admit. They knew nothing of him except that he paid well. As his entourage, they had crossed the Rhineland without ever pausing for long enough to unsaddle their horses, until they reached this manor. It had been abandoned for some time, but the thick outer wall and solid gate remained defensible. They had been camped here for two days now, at a safe distance from the roads and, most importantly, hidden from the Swedish and Imperial armies currently fighting for control of Upper and Lower Alsace. It seemed they would soon, secretly, cross into nearby Lorraine. Perhaps they would even visit France. But to what end? And why this halt?

François Reynault d'Ombreuse did not turn around when he heard someone come up behind him. He recognised the footstep of Ponssoy, a comrade-in-arms.

'They've even posted sentries out here, in this isolated place,' Ponssoy said after counting the lanterns in the distance. 'That's more than just cautious . . .'

'Perhaps they know we're on their trail.'

'How would they know that?'

Pursing his lips doubtfully, Reynault shrugged.

The two men served in the prestigious company of the Saint Georges Guards. They wore a half-cuirass for protection and were kitted out entirely in black: wide-brimmed black hats with black plumes, black cloth doublets and breeches, black gloves and boots made of tough leather, black belts and scabbards and, last of all, black alchemical stones of shaped draconite which decorated the pommels of their rapiers. The sole exception to this martial mourning attire was the white silk sash tied about Reynault's waist, proclaiming his rank as an officer.

'It's almost time,' Ponssoy finally said.

Reynault nodded and they turned away from the old manor, plunging back into the wood.

In a clearing, the twenty-five guards who formed Reynault's detachment prayed beneath the stars. They each placed one knee on the ground and one hand on the pommel of their sword, the other hand pressing their hat against their heart. They held a rapt silence, gathering their spirits before battle. They knew that they would not all live to see the sun set, but the prospect of such a sacrifice did not weigh heavily upon their souls.

Sœur Béatrice, also on her knees, faced the men. She belonged to the religious order they had sworn to serve, dedicated to defending France from the draconic menace. She was a Sister of Saint Georges, or a *Chatelaine*, as members of the order founded by Saint Marie de Chastel were commonly known. Tall, beautiful and solemn, she was not yet thirty years of age. Although dressed in white, with a veil, her attire looked as much like a young horseman's as that of a nun. The heavy cloth of her immaculate robe concealed sturdy knee-boots and she had a leather belt cinched around her waist. She even carried a rapier at her side.

After a final amen the assembly stood and dispersed, just as Reynault and Ponssoy emerged from the trees. Ponssoy went over to join the guards, who wordlessly busied themselves with their final preparations: checking their weapons, helping one another with the straps of their breastplates, making sure the horses were correctly saddled, adjusting this, tightening that, taking all of the hundred precautions that prudence dictated, but which also served to keep their minds occupied.

Meanwhile Reynault conferred with Sœur Béatrice. They had become well-acquainted with one another over the past month, tracking the man now returning to France with the mercenaries he had recruited in the Holy Roman Empire. Their consultation was brief.

'He must not be allowed, at any cost, to regain his primal form,' the Chatelaine emphasised. 'Because if that happens—'

'If everything goes according to plan, he won't have time.'

'Then . . . may the grace of God be with you, monsieur d'Ombreuse.'

'And with you, sister.'

A coughing fit woke the Alchemist.

Curled up on his straw mattress, he coughed until his lungs were raw. The fit was painful and it was some time before he could finally catch his breath and stretch out on his back, arms extended, his face glistening with sweat. The Alchemist – not his real name, but one by which certain people knew and feared him – felt worn out. His natural form was that of a dragon and his human body was causing him more and more suffering. He was struggling to keep the pain in check. He knew he was a monster, a monster whose flesh was tormented precisely because his true nature was rebelling against it. It was making regaining his primal form almost impossible for him. Each time it was an ordeal, a slow torture that threatened to kill him and whose aftermath left him feeling weaker still.

Outside, dawn was breaking.

The Alchemist sat up in bed, letting the blanket slip down his bony chest.

He was tall and thin, with an emaciated face of a morbid-looking pallor. His eyes were icy grey and his lips were vanishingly thin. He had slept in his clothes, in the room he had taken for his personal use when he and his mercenaries had installed themselves in this abandoned manor. They had already been encamped here for two days and nights, wasting precious time. Through his own fault. Or rather, the fault of the exhaustion and pain which prevented him from riding further. But he had recovered somewhat. Today they would resume their journey, tomorrow they would be in Lorraine and soon after they would reach France where the Alchemist could pursue matters he had left neglected for far too long.

But right now . . .

Wracked by nausea he felt cold, then warm, and started to shiver.

The symptoms of deprivation.

For his apparent recovery was deceptive. He owed it entirely to the abuse of a certain liqueur, which caused him to burn with an evil fire which energised him even as it devoured him from within.

But wasn't the important thing to hold on and endure, whatever the price?

He turned on his side and, leaning on an elbow, stretched out a hand to a casket hidden near his boots, beneath an old rag. He opened it to reveal four large glass and metal flasks, each secured by leather straps. The first flask was already empty. The three others – one of which was already partly consumed – contained the precious liqueur distilled from henbane, a thick substance that resembled liquid gold.

As always, the first swallow was a delight.

The Alchemist let himself fall back onto the bed, a small smile on his lips. Eyes closed, he savoured the moment as much as he could. A warm, gentle feeling of well-being flowed into him, easing his suffering, lulling his soul . . .

But loud cries suddenly broke the spell. The sentries outside had raised an alarm and their comrades were already responding to the threat. The Alchemist rose and went to the window, which was nothing more than a gaping hole that looked out over the manor courtyard and the surrounding countryside.

Horsemen. They were coming up the track leading to the manor at a gallop. Armed horsemen, led by a figure dressed in white.

The Alchemist immediately knew who he was dealing with. He also understood he was trapped in this manor, and it would not resist an assault for long.

He turned to the casket that lay next to the straw mattress.

Three flasks of golden henbane.

Enough to kill a man.

Enough to awaken a dragon.

The guards in black charged flat out, raising a cloud of dust that caught the first rays of the rising sun. The thunder of hooves made the ground shake. Reynault and Sœur Béatrice led the column. They rode side by side, their eyes fixed on the manor ahead, whose defence was being hurriedly organised. There were signs of movement, as hats and musket barrels appeared along the wall enclosing the courtyard. The Chatelaine unsheathed her sword and brandished the shining black blade, a blade made of draconite, high in the air.

The mercenaries shouldered their muskets and took aim. They knew their weapons had a range of one hundred and twenty paces and that it was best to let the enemy draw near before firing. So they waited.

The horsemen came on at a gallop, following the dusty track, three or four abreast. But what would they do when they arrived? They charged as if they saw an open gate before them. Yet both the heavy doors were closed tight and an old cart loaded with barrels full of earth had even been pushed behind them as reinforcement. Nevertheless, the guards came on at the same mad pace.

They were only two hundred paces away. At sixty, the mercenaries would start firing.

A hundred and fifty paces. The track ahead was a straight line. Her black sword still held aloft, the Chatelaine chanted an incantation in the draconic tongue.

A hundred paces. At any moment a hail of lead would mow down the front ranks of riders, felling both men and beasts whose bodies would in turn force those behind them to tumble.

Seventy-five. Sœur Béatrice was still chanting.

Sixty. The mercenaries were about to open fire . . .

But at the very last second, the Chatelaine screamed a word full of power. Her blade shone with a sudden light and the twin doors of the manor gate shattered into splinters. The explosion was tremendous. It shook the walls, made the ground vibrate and flung the cart and its barrels into the air. It killed, wounded or stunned the mercenaries posted to either side of the gate and left the remaining defenders in shock, deafened by the blast and blinded by the cloud of dust.

The riders did not slow. They burst into the courtyard, firing their short muskets. Some of their enemies responded with their longer guns. Musket balls whizzed back and forth, striking their targets. One of them ricocheted off Reynault's breastplate. Another ripped off his hat. He dismounted, drew his sword and shouted curt orders to his troops. All around him, close-quarters combat broke out. Sœur Béatrice remained close by his side.

'Where?' he shouted over the din of yelling men and clashing weapons.

She seemed to search around and then pointed to the main building.

'There!' she cried.

'With me!' Reynault commanded as he leapt forward.

He was immediately followed by Ponssoy and a few others who surrounded the Chatelaine. She knew how to fight, but it was her powers that could save them all as a last resort. Her survival was crucial.

Muskets appeared at the windows of the large manor house and began to blast away. One of the guards crumpled. Despite his loss, Reynault and the rest of his group nonetheless managed to reach the main entrance. It was barricaded shut – they would have to force their way inside. Someone found a beam to use as a battering ram and with each successive blow the twin doors shivered, then began to crack a little more every time. But they still held.

'Faster!' urged the Chatelaine, a fearful expression on her face. 'Faster!'

The doors gave way at last. Reynault and his men rushed inside, charging straight into the mercenaries who greeted them with a murderous volley of musket fire. Several guards fell. Ponssoy was seriously injured and Reynault's thigh was pierced right through, although he paid the wound no heed. A furious melee broke out, in which even the Chatelaine took part. She and Reynault attempted to force a passage through the combatants, until she finally placed a hand on the lieutenant's shoulder.

He turned to her.

'Too late,' she said in a quiet voice which he nonetheless heard perfectly clearly.

A dull rumble came from somewhere within the house. The stone floor slabs in the great manor hall began to tremble.

Reynault realised what was happening.

'Retreat!' he shouted. 'Retreat! Retreat!'

Carrying their wounded and fending off the mercenaries still pressing them, Reynault and his group hastily withdrew. The whole building was now vibrating, as if shaken by an earthquake. Its foundations began to sag. Tiles fell from the roof. The stones in the walls came loose.

Suddenly a whole section of the façade collapsed.

'Lord God, have mercy on us!' the sister murmured.

Around her, guards and mercenaries were locked in a confused mass, all of them speechless with terror.

A great black dragon emerged from the manor amidst a cloud of plaster and a cascade of debris. Immense in size, it reared up and unfurled its leathery wings with a tremendous roar. A surge of power swept through the courtyard, a wave that churned the earth, toppling the men and causing the horses to bolt.

Only the Chatelaine, her white clothing flapping in the storm, managed to stay on her feet. Holding her black-bladed rapier in her right hand she spread her arms wide and began chanting again. The dragon seemed intrigued by the insignificant creature standing before it, somehow capable of summoning a power comparable to its own. It lowered its enormous head to peer at the sister, who continued her incantation without faltering. She chanted words in a language which found an echo in the dragon's brain – a brain dominated by brutal, primitive impulses, but not entirely devoid of intelligence.

Sœur Béatrice knew it was too late. She had failed. Now the Alchemist had recovered his primal form there was nothing she could do to vanquish – or even restrain – the most powerful adversary she had ever encountered.

But there was one last card she could play.

Looking straight into the terrible depths of the dragon's eye, she gathered her remaining strength and plunged into the huge creature's tormented mind. The effort she had to make was both colossal and perilous. But after several false attempts, she finally found what she was searching for. The vision struck her soul like a fist.

For the space of one brief, yet seemingly eternal, moment the Chatelaine could *see*.

She saw the cataclysm threatening France, both her people and her throne, a cataclysm that would soon become a reality played out beneath ragged skies. It left her terrified, awed and gasping, while the dragon – having been defeated in the very core of its being – screamed with rage before taking to the air and escaping with a few mighty beats of its wings.

La Donna

1

Beneath the dripping boughs of a forest which, on this dark night, was being buffeted by the wind and downpour of a violent storm, two young dragonnets were playing. They squabbled as they flew, heedless of the weather, chasing one another, spinning and fluttering in mid-air, improvising virtuoso acrobatics among the branches. The little reptiles were fighting over a small vole they had hunted down together, whose mauled remains were snatched from one mouth to the other in the course of their unruly game. They were brother and sister, both born from the same egg and thus perfectly similar, sharing the same golden eyes, the same scarlet-fringed black scales, the same grey belly, and the same slender, elegant profile.

And the same intelligence, too.

Growing tired of their play, the twins finally settled on a knotty root where they were sheltered from the worst of the rain. They shook themselves, and then folded up their leather wings. Pulling from either side, they tore the rodent in two and devoured it peacefully together. The darkness lay thick around them and, when the thunder ceased, the only sounds in the forest came from the rain, the wind, and the battered foliage. Yet something interrupted the dragonnets' meal. Something only they could perceive. Something that made them rear up sharply and captured their complete attention.

They remained frozen in place for an instant, like a pair of small onyx statues gleaming wet from the rain. They had to be sure they were not mistaken, that there was no danger of misinforming their mistress, and thus risk incurring her anger or, worse still, losing her affection. But there was no mistake.

So they roused themselves and exchanged nervous growls before taking wing, the male vanishing into the shadows of the vast forest while his sister flew towards the source of their interest. She moved swiftly, weaving between the tree trunks and seeming to take pleasure in dodging them at the very last moment, only finally slowing when she recognised the sound of voices. She found herself a comfortable perch in the hollow of a tree . . .

. . . where she did not have very long to wait.

There were riders approaching.

There were three of them, following a muddy trail beneath the rivulets of rainwater cascading down through the forest canopy. Soaked to the skin, they plodded along in the haloes cast by the lanterns hanging from their saddles. These did not shed much light, but at least, between the flashes of lightning, allowed them to make out the puddles disturbed by their horses' heavy hooves.

Saint-Lucq led the way. Behind him, Captain Étienne-Louis de La Fargue endured the rain with perfect stoicism, as it spattered his aging, patriarchal features: pale eyes, handsome wrinkles, martial bearing, grim mouth, closely trimmed beard, and firm jaw. Tall and solidly built, he was wearing a sleeveless vest over his doublet, which was made of leather thick enough to stop a musket ball fired from a distance, or even deflect a clumsy sword stroke. It was black, as were this old gentleman soldier's breeches, boots, gloves and hat. As for the doublet, it was the same dark red as his baldric and the sash tied around his waist, knotted over his right hip.

Black and red . . .

They were, once again, the colours of the Cardinal's Blades, now they had been secretly recalled to service by Cardinal Richelieu.

'Are we even still in France?' Almades asked, with a trace of a Spanish accent.

Anibal Antonio Almades di Carlio, to give him his full name, rode slightly behind and to La Fargue's left, ready to draw level with a dig of his spurs and protect the flank that a right-handed cavalier would have difficulty defending. Thin and austere-looking, he sported a fine greying moustache that he occasionally wiped dry – always thrice each time – with his thumb and index finger. He sat straight in the saddle, his waist snugly fitted into a red-slashed black leather doublet, and he was armed with a Toledo rapier whose guard consisted of a full hemispherical shell and two long straight quillons. Made of tarnished steel, this duelling sword offered no concessions to aesthetic values whatsoever.

'I doubt it,' La Fargue said to the Spanish fencing master. 'What do you think, Saint-Lucq?' he enquired in turn, raising his voice against the din of the wind and the rain in the branches.

He knew the young man had heard him despite the distance between them. Saint-Lucq took the lead precisely because he heard – and saw – better than any common mortal.

Because he was no common mortal.

Saint-Lucq was a half-blood. The blood of dragons ran in his veins. With his slender, supple figure, smooth cheeks and shoulder-length hair, his ancestry endowed him with enhanced senses, superior athletic abilities, and a personal charm that was both seductive and disturbing. He certainly had an allure, but there was also something dark emanating from him, with his silences, his long stares, his slow measured gestures and his proud reserve. This darkness was heightened by the fact that he only wore black and, on him, the colour was associated more than ever with death. He only permitted two exceptions: the thin red feather in his hat and the lenses – also red – of the small round spectacles which hid his reptilian eyes. Otherwise everything, even the fine basket guard of his rapier, was black.

'We are in Spain,' the half-blood declared without turning round.

They were five leagues from Amiens and had already reached the Spanish Netherlands, which began just beyond Picardy, comprising the ten Catholic provinces that had remained loyal to the Spanish Crown when the lands further north controlled by the Calvinists seceded to form the Dutch republic. The province of Artois, along with the towns of Arras, Cambrai, Lille, Brussels, Namur, and Antwerp were thus all part of the territory of Spain, a power that was hostile to France and jealous in her exercise of full sovereignty. Spanish troops were garrisoned there and guarded the border, only a few days' march from Paris.

'This storm works in our favour,' said La Fargue. 'Without it our lights might be seen by a Spanish wyvern rider. They fly over this area every hour, when weather permits.'

'So all we have to do is avoid the ordinary patrols,' Almades observed wryly.

'Let's hope the person waiting for us had the same bright idea,' the old captain replied in a more serious tone. 'Or else we'll have come all this way for nothing.'

Ahead of them, Saint-Lucq slowly turned his head to the left as his horse advanced at the same steady pace. He'd just spotted the dragonnet spying on them from the shadows, and he wanted to leave it in no doubt as to the fact. Intrigued at first, the young female craned her neck to peer out at him from her tree hollow. Keeping her golden eyes fixed on the half-blood as he passed, she tilted her head slowly to one side, then to the other. Could he really see her? Finally, when she was certain that the rider with the strange red spectacles was staring right back at her, she growled at him in hatred and fury before taking flight from her hiding-place.

La Fargue and Almades both reacted to the sound of wings flapping swiftly through the forest and, thanks to a flash of lightning, they caught a brief glimpse of the small reptile as she sped away.

Saint-Lucq, expressionless, turned his gaze back to the trail ahead.

'We're almost there,' he announced, just before the roll of thunder came.

The storm was still in full fury when the trail began to gradually slope upwards and led the riders to the crown of a hill, where a large building could be seen emerging from the treetops, like an island in a sea of tossing boughs. It was a former inn which had been abandoned after being partially destroyed in a terrible fire. The windows were boarded up, the roof tiles rattled, and the inn's illegible sign swung wildly in the gusting wind and rain. An old wall surrounded the courtyard and a well. Only a few charred vestiges remained of the stables, evidently the starting-point of the blaze.

The riders passed beneath a stone arch and crossed the courtyard, halting in front of the inn. They cast wary glances at their surroundings and although they had extinguished their lanterns they still felt exposed out here in the open, beneath the turbulent sky. Remaining in their saddles, all three could see the wavering light coming from behind the boards nailed across a window on the upper floor.

'She's already here,' La Fargue observed.

'I don't see her mount,' Almades replied.

'Neither do I,' added Saint-Lucq.

The old captain stepped down from the saddle into a mud puddle, and gave his orders:

'Almades, with me. Saint-Lucq, keep watch out here.'

The half-blood nodded and turned his horse around. Almades dismounted as La Fargue, always cautious, loosened his rapier in its scabbard. The weapon was well-matched with its owner, being both solid and quite long: a Pappenheimer, named after the German general who had equipped his cavalry corps with it. La Fargue had put its qualities to the test – and had sometimes been tested by it himself – on battle-fields in Germany and elsewhere. He appreciated its robust strength and long reach, as well as the guard with its multiple branches and the openwork shell that protected his hand.

The dark, cluttered ground floor of the inn smelled of old soot and wet wood. It was impossible to move without stepping over pieces of debris or making the floorboards creak alarmingly, as if they might give way at any moment. The wind whistled through the gaps between the planks that had been crudely nailed across the windows. A single lit candle had been placed on the lowest step of the staircase leading to the upper floor, the flame guttering in the draughts.

'Wait here,' ordered La Fargue before climbing the stairs alone.

Obeying with some reluctance, Almades unsheathed his rapier and took up vigil below.

At the top of the stairway, the old gentleman found a long corridor with a second candle burning at the end, placed on the worm-eaten lintel of a half-opened door. Other doors – which led into the bedchambers – also lined this hallway. But the door at the end, in addition to being lit, was the only one which was not closed.

Since the way had been so kindly shown to him, La Fargue advanced towards the light. He trod carefully, however, keeping a cautious eye on each door as he passed, his hand resting on his sword . . .

There were leaks in the ceiling, and in places, he could hear rain pattering in the attic, directly over his head. The roof must have split wide open, although neither he nor his men had noticed this when they arrived, but a section of it was invisible from the courtyard and could have been missing as far as they knew, not having made a point of inspecting it.

La Fargue stopped in front of the door indicated by the candle.

'Come in, monsieur,' said a charming feminine voice.

A scraping could be heard through the racket of the storm, coming from just beneath the rafters. There was a peal of thunder at almost the same instant, but the sound did not escape the keen ears of the captain, who pondered for a moment, understood its meaning, and smiled to himself. And as if to confirm his suspicions, he then detected the clinking of a chain.

He entered.

This room had been spared by the fire, but not by the ravages of time. Dusty and decaying, it was lit by a dozen candles placed here and there. A large bed, of which only the frame and cabled columns remained, took up almost the entire space. At the rear was a door whose outer corner was bevelled to fit against the sloped ceiling just beneath the roof. Tattered curtains swayed before a window with broken panes. Planks had been nailed across it from within, but one of them had been ripped away recently. La Fargue understood why when he saw a dragonnet wend its way into the room from outside.

After shaking its dripping wings dry the small reptile leapt onto the wrist held out by a beautiful young woman who, turning to the old gentleman, greeted him in a friendly fashion.

'Welcome, monsieur de La Fargue.'

She was perfectly poised and elegant, wearing a grey hunting outfit composed of a jacket that clasped her waist prettily and a heavy skirt that was hitched up on the right to allow her to ride in a saddle like a man. Her attire was completed by a pair of hose, a hat tilted coquettishly over one eye and gloves that matched her fawn leather boots.

'Madame.'

'You can't imagine, monsieur, my pleasure in meeting with you.'

'Really?'

'Of course! Do you doubt it?'

'Yes. A little.'

'And why is that?'

'Because my orders could be to arrest you and bring you to France to be tried. And in all likelihood, be convicted.'

'Are those your orders, monsieur?'

La Fargue did not reply. Impassive, he simply waited.

He was nearly sixty years old, a more than respectable age in a century when anyone over forty was considered elderly. But if ordeals, battles and grief had turned his hair white and left his eyes dull from lost illusions, time had not yet stripped him of his vigour and personal aura. Tall and wide-shouldered, with a proud, confident bearing, the old gentleman remained impressive in both his figure and in the strength that emanated from him – and he knew it. He deliberately resorted to silence rather than words to impose his will on others.

Standing before him, the young woman seemed small and fragile. She met his eyes for a moment, without blinking, and then, quite casually, pointed to a small table and two stools.

'I wager that you have not supped. You must be famished. Sit, please. You are my guest.'

La Fargue took a stool and, as she busied herself with preparations, he was able to look more closely at this woman playing the role of hostess. She was a pale-skinned, red-headed beauty with delicate features, finely drawn lips, a charming smile, and dark, lively eyes. But the old gentleman was aware of the danger lurking behind this pretty face and innocent air. Others before him had learned that lesson to their bitter cost. The she-devil was cunning and had few scruples. And she was said to be a mercenary at heart.

With her dragonnet perched on her shoulder, she brought over a heavy wicker basket, removed the cloth covering it to dress the table, and arranged various victuals between the captain and herself, setting a porcelain plate, a fine-cut glass, and a knife with a mother-of-pearl handle before each of them.

'Would you pour the wine?' she proposed.

Readily enough, La Fargue took the bottle he saw poking from the basket, removed the wax stopper and tipped the layer of oil that protected the wine from contact with the air out onto the floor.

'What should I call you?' he asked as he filled the glasses.

The young woman, who was amusing herself by feeding titbits to her dragonnet, paused and gave La Fargue a puzzled glance.

'I beg your pardon?'

'What is your name, madame?'

She shrugged and smiled as if he were jesting with her.

'Come now, monsieur. You know who I am.'

'To be sure,' allowed La Fargue. 'But of all the names you have employed in the service of France, England, Spain and the Pope, which do you prefer?'

She stared at him for a long moment and her eyes grew cold.

At last, she replied:

'Alessandra. Alessandra di Santi.' She nodded with her chin at the glass which the old gentleman had not yet raised to his lips. 'Aren't you drinking? The wine is from Beaune, and I believe it to be to your liking.'

'Indeed.'

'So?'

La Fargue gave a drawn-out sigh of restrained impatience.

'Madame, a short while ago you asked about my orders. Here they are: I am to hear you out and then report your words to His Eminence. So speak, madame. My men and I rode for ten hours, almost without a break, in order to meet you here, now. And I am anxious to leave again soon. Even in Artois, the Spanish climate does not suit my health . . .'

And having said this, he lifted his glass and drained it in a single gulp.

Then he added:

'I am listening, madame.'

Thoughtful for a moment, Alessandra watched the old gentleman who was proving so immune to her charms. She knew he found her ravishing, yet her beauty inspired him with no need to please her in return. It was unusual in a man, and merited further study.

Outside the storm continued to rage. The intervals between lightning flashes and the resulting thunder seemed to be diminishing.

'I see that you have a poor opinion of me, monsieur de La Fargue,' the young woman said in a provocative tone.

'My sentiment towards you is of no importance, madame.'

'Come now, captain. What do you think of me? In all frankness.'

La Fargue paused for a moment, aware that Alessandra was trying to control their conversation. Then he said:

'I know that you are both intelligent and skilful, madame. But I also know that you are venal. And lacking in scruples.'

'So you don't believe I am capable of loyalty . . .'

'Only if you use the word in the plural form. Because your loyalties, madame, have been many in number. No doubt they still are, even if none of them will ever force you to act against your own interest.'

'So in short, you don't believe me worthy of confidence.'

'That's correct, madame.'

'And what if I were to tell you that I have some knowledge of a plot?'

La Fargue raised an eyebrow.

'I would ask you whom this plot threatens, madame.'

The pretty redhead smiled. She raised her glass to her charming lips, took a sip of wine, and then declared with utmost solemnity:

'I have knowledge of a plot, monsieur. A plot that threatens the throne of France and whose scale goes beyond anything you can conceive.'

The old captain gazed directly into Alessandra's eyes, which remained quite calm. She did not blink, not even when lightning struck so close that the inn shook.

'Do you have so much as a shred of proof to support your claim?' he asked.

'Obviously. However—'

'What?'

'However, I'm afraid I cannot proceed any further without some guarantees . . . from the cardinal.'

'What do you want?'

'I demand His Eminence's protection.'

La Fargue stared impassively at the young woman before rising to leave.

'Goodbye, madame.'

Alessandra leapt to her feet.

'Wait! Monsieur, wait!'

Was that a hint of fear in her eyes?

'I beseech you, monsieur . . . Do not take leave in this manner. Grant me just one more moment . . .'

La Fargue sighed.

'Is it truly necessary, madame, to inform you that the cardinal is as miserly in giving his protection as he is in giving his trust, that he only grants them to those who are deserving of them, or that you would need to provide much more than this if you wish to become one of their number? Come now, madame, think! Remember who you are! And ask yourself—'

At that moment a second dragonnet, identical to the first, entered by way of the missing plank at the window. Very nervous, it shook its wings and emitted a series of piercing cries intended for its mistress.

She listened to them, and then spoke quickly:

'We must part now, captain. Riders are approaching along the same path by which you came. They shall be here soon, and it would be best if they did not find me.'

'Who are these riders?'

'You shall make their acquaintance soon enough. They are one of the reasons that press me to demand the cardinal's protection.'

'Abandon this foolish notion, madame. His Eminence will never—'

'Give him this.'

She removed a thick sealed letter from her sleeve and held it out to La Fargue.

'What is this?'

'Take this letter to the cardinal, monsieur. It contains . . . It contains the shred of proof you just demanded . . . When the cardinal opens it, he will see I am not inventing tales but that the throne of France is truly under threat.'

They heard Almades call from below.

'Captain!'

La Fargue opened the chamber door a crack and saw the Spanish fencing master coming up the stairs at the far end of the corridor.

'Riders, captain.'

'How many?'

'According to Saint-Lucq, at least five.'

Behind La Fargue's back, the dragonnet uttered a brief hoarse cry. Already, whinnying could be heard outside.

'Seven,' Alessandra informed them in a calm voice. 'There are seven of them.'

'Stay right here!' the old gentleman commanded over his shoulder.

He left the chamber, closing the door behind him, and entered a neighbouring room where Almades joined him. Through a gap between the planks in the window, they saw seven armed riders come charging into the courtyard.

'Where is Saint-Lucq?' asked La Fargue.

'Down below. He's the one who saw the riders coming.'

'Damn it all!'

Leaving the Spaniard standing there, he returned to the chamber at the end of the corridor.

It was empty.

'Merde!'

But the little door at the rear was standing half-open.

Behind it, some very steep stairs led to the attic. La Fargue climbed them and, pushing through a trap door, he rose up into the deafening fury of the storm. As he had guessed, a portion of the roof was missing leaving the attic open to the sky, directly exposed to the weather. And there he saw Alessandra, already in the saddle, struggling to force a wyvern to turn towards this exit. Its wings spread to keep its balance, the great reptile was resisting, digging its two clawed feet into the floor. It was frightened by the storm.

'This is madness!' the old gentleman shouted.

Keeping a firm grip on the reins that ran along the wyvern's neck to the bit in its mouth, the young woman smiled confidently at the captain.

'Worry instead about the plot and plead my case with His Eminence! You must believe me and, in turn, the cardinal must believe you . . . Be persuasive! The future of France depends on it!'

'Renounce this matter, madame!' La Fargue insisted, just before a blast of wind almost knocked him over.

Lightning was striking ever closer. Not far from the inn, a tree had burst into flame.

'Inform the cardinal. We shall meet again soon, in Paris.'

'Where? How?'

They could barely hear one another, even shouting at the top of their lungs.

'Tomorrow evening. Don't worry. I know how to find you.'

'Madame!'

Alessandra's wyvern launched into the air and was already

404

flying away into the storm, trailed by the fluttering silhouettes of the twin dragonnets.

La Fargue cursed, powerless to stop her. Then, remembering the riders, he went back down into the inn. Almades followed in his wake as he passed. They reached the ground floor and emerged into the courtyard that was now one immense, slippery mud puddle beneath the deluge of rain.

His back to the door, Saint-Lucq was facing seven horsemen who, forming an arc, had dismounted and drawn their swords. Clearly expecting trouble, they were dressed for combat, wearing wide hats, thick leather doublets, rough breeches, and riding boots.

Beyond that, they were not human.

They were dracs, La Fargue realised, as a flash of lightning gave him a glimpse of the nightmarish scaly, jowled faces beneath the dripping brims of their hats. Worse still, they were black dracs.

Dracs had been created long ago by the Ancestral Dragons to serve and fight for them. In time they had freed themselves from the tutelage of their creators, but they remained cruel, brutal beings who were rightly to be feared. Dracs enjoyed violence. They were stronger and tougher than men. And black dracs were even stronger and tougher than the ordinary kind.

'We're here, Saint-Lucq,' said La Fargue from the doorway, moving forward.

Without turning round or looking away from the dracs, the half-blood took two steps to his right. The captain occupied his place while Almades covered their left. The trio had their swords in hand, but still waited before placing themselves *en garde*.

La Fargue noticed that the dracs stood in a pool of black mist that rose to their ankles and did not disperse.

Sorcery, he thought to himself.

'The woman!' the drac facing him snarled in a hoarse whistling voice. 'We want the woman!'

He was the biggest and most muscular of the seven, which had no doubt earned him the right of command. His face was marked with bright yellow lines that followed the contours of certain facial scales to form complex, symmetrical patterns that La Fargue recognised.

'Impossible,' he declared. 'She is no longer here.'

'Where is she?'

'Gone. She flew away.'

'What?'

While La Fargue devoted his attention to the leader, Saint-Lucq and Almades were watching the six others. The dracs were tense and nervous, obviously making an effort to contain the desire for battle that consumed them. They were almost quivering, like starved dogs forbidden from throwing themselves upon a scrap of bloody meat. Only their fear of their chief held them back. They waited for the order, gesture, or pretext that would unleash them.

'She had a wyvern,' La Fargue explained. 'You brought the wrong mounts.'

'Who are you?'

'Someone hunting the same game as you. But I arrived too late.'

'You lie!'

Saint-Lucq had his eye on one drac – younger and more impetuous than the rest – who was struggling to control his aggressive impulses and twitched with each peal of thunder. The half-blood imagined the desire to hurt and to kill eating away at him like acid. The tiniest thing, probably, would suffice to . . .

'Do you really think so?' La Fargue replied to the drac leader. 'Do you believe this woman only has one enemy?'

'Who do you serve?'

'That's none of your business. Even so, I could answer if you tell me who your master is . . .'

The young drac who had attracted Saint-Lucq's attention could by now barely contain himself. His head was drawn in, his jaws were clenched, and he was breathing hard. His glance crossed that of the half-blood, who, with a thin smile on his lips, dipped his own head slightly to stare directly at him above his red spectacles.

'There are seven of us, old man,' the drac leader observed. 'And only three of you. We can kill you all.'

'You can try, but you shall be the first to fall. And for what? For a woman who is long gone, if the storm hasn't already brought her wyvern down . . .'

As if hypnotised, the young drac couldn't take his eyes off Saint-Lucq. He was filled with a boiling rage and the dracs to either side of him were aware of it. They didn't understand the cause but they, too, started to become agitated.

Then the half-blood supplied the final trigger: a discreet wink and a blown kiss.

The young drac screamed with rage and attacked.

Saint-Lucq easily dodged him, inflicting a nasty sword cut to the face as his opponent charged past. That could have been the signal all had been dreading or hoping for. La Fargue and Almades took a step back and placed themselves *en garde*, while the dracs were about to launch forward when their chief barked out an order that froze them in place:

'Sᴋ'ᴇʀsʜ!'

For a few long seconds, no one dared to move. Bodies remained fixed in martial stances beneath the pitiless downpour. Only eyes shifted, looking left and right, watchful for the first threatening gesture.

'Sᴋ'ᴇʀsʜ!' the drac leader repeated in a lower tone.

Little by little, muscles relaxed and breathing resumed.

Blades were not replaced in their scabbards, but they were pointed back down at the sodden ground. His mouth bloody, the drac Saint-Lucq had wounded ruefully regained his place among his comrades.

Then their leader advanced slowly but resolutely towards La Fargue, who had to wave Almades back before he intervened. The black drac drew so close that they touched chests, allowing him to sniff at the captain's face from below.

He did so for some time, with a mix of avid hunger and animal curiosity.

La Fargue endured this examination without flinching.

Finally, the drac stepped back and promised:

'We shall meet again, old man.'

The dracs retreated in good order and soon vanished at a gallop into the night and the howling rain, taking their black mist with them.

'What now?' Saint-Lucq asked after a moment.

'We return to Paris,' the captain of the Cardinal's Blades replied. 'I don't know what's going on, but His Eminence must be warned without delay. The king's life may be in danger.'

2

Cardinal Richelieu was preparing to take his leave with the other members of the Council when King Louis XIII called him back:

'Cardinal.'

'Yes, Sire?'

'Stay for a moment.'

Lifting a red-gloved hand to his chest, Richelieu indicated his obedience with a silent nod and drew away from the door through which ministers and secretaries of state were departing. They passed one by one, without lingering or looking back, almost cringing as if they feared the sudden touch of an icy breath on the back of their necks.

Draughts were not uncommon in the Louvre, but in this warm month of June 1633 the only ones to be truly feared were the result of a royal cold spell. Such cold spells did not cause noses to drip, aggravate rheumatism, or force anyone to stay in bed, but they could provoke an illness serious enough to ruin destinies and finish careers. The members of the Council were well aware of this and were particularly wary of contagion. And they had all felt a distinctly wintry blast this morning when His Majesty had joined them with a brisk step and, upon sitting down and without greeting anyone present, curtly demanded that the order of the day be read.

The king held his Council every morning after breakfast and did not hesitate to summon its members again later in the day if the affairs of the realm warranted further attention. In this he followed the example of his father. But in contrast to Henri IV, who conducted his meetings so freely that they sometimes took place during strolls outside, Louis XIII –

more reserved, more cautious, and more attached to proper etiquette – required formal deliberations, around a table and behind closed doors. At the Louvre, the Council met either in the chamber on the ground floor traditionally reserved for its use, or – as today – in the Book Room. This was no less formal a setting than the Council chamber but, as Richelieu had noticed, the king preferred its use whenever he was anxious to ensure the complete confidentiality of debates or foresaw the need for a discreet one-to-one conversation at the conclusion of the Council's session. Then he only needed to detain the person with whom he desired to speak for a few moments, and everything could be said in the time it took the other Council members to reappear in public.

The cardinal had therefore guessed that something was in the air when he arrived at the Louvre and was directed to the Book Room. The slight delay in His Majesty's arrival, and his manifest dissatisfaction during the meeting, had confirmed his suspicions and forced him to ponder. He was obliged to pay careful heed to the moods of the man who had raised him to the heights of power and glory, as the same man could just as easily precipitate his fall. No doubt Armand-Jean du Plessis, Cardinal Richelieu, deserved to exercise the immense responsibilities that Louis XIII conferred upon him. And no doubt he had demonstrated his exceptional abilities as a statesman over the past ten years since his recall to the Council and appointment as chief minister. But personal merits and services rendered counted for little without royal favour, and the cardinal could not afford to let the favour he enjoyed run cold. He had far too many enemies for that – ambitious rivals who were jealous of his influence and adversaries hostile to his policies alike – and all of them, in France and elsewhere, were eager to see his star wane.

To be sure, the king's esteem and affection for his chief minister were not likely to disappear overnight. As close as the Capitol might be to the Tarpeian Rock, Richelieu did not believe himself likely to fall victim to a royal whim. Nevertheless, Louis XIII was a grim, temperamental, and secretive monarch, who suffered from an inability to express his emotions and was often difficult to understand. The cardinal himself was often forced to make concessions to appease his authoritarian master whose reactions could still surprise him on occasion. Taciturn by nature, the king would spend much time ruminating over his decisions which he would then divulge suddenly and without explanation, or else explain badly. He was also rancorous in more private matters. Sensitive, he never forgave a slight completely and would nurse grudges that ripened, quietly and patiently, without the knowledge of those close to him. Then came the clumsy word, the indelicate gesture, the ingratitude, or some other small fault that finally proved too much for him to bear. When this occurred, Louis XIII gave way to cold angers which he expressed by way of stern reproaches, cruel humiliations, or even brutal punishments and disgraces.

It was one of these angers that the members of the Council sensed was imminent, and which – despite being great lords and high officials of the Crown for the most part – they had each dreaded they would bear the brunt of, right up until the moment when, to their immense relief, His Majesty had finally released them.

All in all, notwithstanding the king's awful mood, the Council meeting had proceeded almost as usual. Louis XIII had sat alone at the head of the long rectangular table around which the others had taken their places, ready to explain official business or read dispatches. Then the moment had arrived for debate and deliberations, during which each member had to defend or justify his advice. These deliberations were often fairly free discussions, which would become lively when views diverged, with the king insisting that everyone should express their convictions within his Council. This morning, however, no one really desired to stand out, to such a degree that Louis XIII soon became irritated and, wishing to have an opinion on a precise point, he questioned one secretary of state rather sharply. Muddling his papers in surprise, the man had stammered out a confused answer that the king had received with arctic coldness: he himself was afflicted with a slight stammer that he controlled by force of will. At that instant, all those present believed that the king's wrath would fall unjustly upon the poor man, but nothing ensued. After a long silence, a semblance of debate resumed and the king dismissed the Council an hour later.

But not before asking the cardinal to remain behind.

If Richelieu had only lent a distracted ear to the actual debates, he had been observing the proceedings closely, waiting to see which matter, when it was presented, would provoke a reaction – however restrained or disguised – from the king.

In vain.

Yet there was no lack of reasons for concern. There was the war being prepared against Lorraine, the hegemonic ambitions of Spain and its Court of Dragons, the intrigues of England, and the string of military successes by Sweden in its campaign within the Holy Roman Empire which risked upsetting the fragile balance of power in Europe. Within France's borders there were rumblings from the people due to the crushing weight of taxes, the Catholic party showed no signs of disarming, several Protestant towns were demanding the same privileges as La Rochelle, which the city had only obtained by victoriously withstanding a siege five years earlier, and plot after treasonous plot continued to be hatched, even in the very corridors of the Louvre. Lastly, in Paris itself, churches were burning and there was an increasing threat of rioting against the Huguenots and the Jews, who were blamed for starting the fires.

But none of the foreign or domestic affairs that the Council had discussed appeared to be the cause of the rage Louis XIII was struggling so hard to contain. Since the king was very pious, could it be those reports, still confidential, indicating a disturbing revival of sorcerous activity in the capital? Did the king know something that his chief minister did not? The very idea was enough to worry the cardinal, who endeavoured to know everything in order to foresee everything and, if necessary, to prevent anything from happening.

The last Council member to leave was the marquis de Châteauneuf, Keeper of the Seals. Carrying with him the finely wrought casket containing the kingdom's seals which he never let out of his sight, he bade farewell to Richelieu with a respectful nod of the head.

A footman shut the doors behind him.

Agnès de Vaudreuil returned from her morning ride in the outskirts of Paris at around ten o'clock.

Travelling along rue du Chasse-Midi at a fast trot, she barely slowed when she reached the Croix-Rouge crossroads, despite the fact that it was very busy at this hour. The young baronne expected people to make way for her and make way they did, sometimes grumbling and more often railing after her. She followed rue des Saints-Pères as far as rue Saint-Dominique and – now in the heart of the faubourg Saint-Germain, a few streets away from the magnificent abbey which gave it its name – she turned into the very narrow rue Saint-Guillaume. Here she was finally forced to slow her horse to a walk to avoid bowling over some innocent passer-by, street hawker, trader at his stall, goodwife haggling over the price of a chicken, or miserable beggar shaking his bowl.

People watched as she came to a halt before the Hôtel de l'Épervier. She had a wild, austere beauty that was striking to behold, with a slender figure, a proud bearing, a pale complexion, green eyes, full dark lips and long black hair whose heavy curls inevitably escaped from her braid. But the observers were even more surprised by her thigh boots, black breeches, and the red leather corset she wore over a white shirt. It was a daring outfit, to say the least. And not content with publicly displaying herself in this manner, without even covering her head, she also wore a sword and rode her horse like a man. It was scandalous . . .

Indifferent to the discreet commotion she was causing, Agnès swung down from her horse and into the noxious mud that covered the streets of Paris. She would have liked to spare her boots this indignity, but that meant ringing the bell and waiting for someone to come open up one of the great studded doors of the carriage gate. She preferred to push open the smaller, inset pedestrian door that was only locked at night and, leading her horse by the bridle, entered the paved courtyard where the iron-clad hooves clattered and echoed like musket shots.

Coming from the stable, André hurried to greet the baronne de Vaudreuil, respectfully taking the reins from her hands.

'You should have rung the bell, madame,' said the stableman. 'I would have opened for you.'

There was a touch of both reproach and regret in his voice.

A very dark-haired man who was going prematurely bald on the top of his head, although sporting a tremendous moustache on his upper lip, he had the frustrated look of someone who was prevented from doing the right thing but had decided to bear with this in silence.

'It's quite all right, André . . . Thank you.'

While André took her tired, muddy horse to the stable, Agnès removed her gloves and looked at her surroundings with a resigned air.

She sighed.

The Hôtel de l'Épervier was a decidedly sinister place. Austere and uncomfortable, it was a vast residence with thick walls and narrow windows which had been built for a Huguenot gentleman after the Saint-Barthélemy massacre. Now it served as headquarters for the Cardinal's Blades, a clandestine elite unit commanded by Captain La Fargue under direct orders from Cardinal Richelieu. Agnès de Vaudreuil didn't like this mansion, where the nights seemed longer and darker than elsewhere. But she had no choice. Lacking lodgings of her own in Paris, she was obliged to live here, immediately available for the service of His Eminence. An order for an urgent mission could arrive at any time from the Palais-Cardinal.

Ballardieu, coming out onto the front steps of the main building, interrupted Agnès's train of thought. Massively built, with greying hair, he was a former soldier who had put on weight over the years thanks to his fondness for food and drink. His cheekbones were reddened by broken veins but his eye remained sharp and he was still capable of felling a mule with one blow of his fist.

'Where on earth have you been?' he demanded.

Restraining a smile, Agnès walked up to him.

Having raised her as best he could, dandled her on his knee, and taught her how to use her first rapier, she was always prepared to forgive Ballardieu's tendency to forget that she was a baronne and no longer eight years old. She knew he loved her, and that he was still awkward when it came to showing his affection. She also knew that he disliked it if she was absent for too long and fretted until she returned. As a child she had once disappeared for several days in troubled circumstances she no longer recalled, but it was an incident which had evidently marked Ballardieu for life.

'I went as far as Saint-Germain,' she explained nonchalantly as she passed him and went into the front hall. 'Any news from La Fargue?'

'No,' replied the old man from the porch. 'But it might interest you to hear that Marciac has returned.'

She halted and turned round, now wearing a radiant smile.

Marciac had been sent off alone on a mission to La Rochelle three weeks earlier and had stopped sending news soon after. The Gascon's silence had been worrying her for several days now.

'Really?'

'God's truth!'

Marciac was bent over a basin of cold water, splashing his face and neck with both hands, when he heard a voice behind him:

'Good morning, Nicolas.'

He interrupted his ablutions, blindly grabbed a towel, then stood up and turned towards Agnès as he dried his cheeks. She stood on the threshold of his bedchamber, with her arms crossed, one shoulder leaning against the wall, eyes shining and a faint smile on her lips.

'Welcome home,' she added.

'Thank you,' Marciac replied.

He was still wearing the boots and breeches in which he had ridden, but he had stripped down to his shirt and rolled up his sleeves in order to wash. His doublet – an elegant blood-red garment cut from the same embroidered cloth as his breeches – lay on the bed next to an old leather travelling bag. His hat was hanging on the wall, along with his rapier in its scabbard and his baldric.

'How are you?' asked Agnès.

'Exhausted.'

And as if to prove these words, he fell into an armchair, with the towel still around his neck and damp locks clinging to his brow. He did seem tired.

But delighted nonetheless.

'I was in such a hurry to get here,' he explained, 'that I barely slept three hours last night. And the sun! The dust . . . ! Lord, I'm dying of thirst!'

At that very moment, sweet, timid Naïs arrived from the kitchen bearing a platter, a jug of wine, and two glasses. Agnès had to step aside to let her pass. Seeing the servant girl, Marciac joyfully leapt to his feet.

'It's a miracle. Naïs, I adore you. Will you marry me? Do you have any idea how much I thought of you, during my exile?'

The young woman set down her platter, and eyes cast downward, asked:

'Would you like me to make up the bed, monsieur?'

'How cruel! Asking me that, when I dream only of un-making it with you . . .'

Blushing, Naïs giggled, curtseyed, and quickly withdrew.

'Keep on singing, you handsome blackbird!' Agnès said mockingly. 'You shall never pluck that fruit . . .'

Marciac was indeed handsome, fair-headed and full of charm. His hair was always in need of a comb, his cheeks could benefit from a razor, but he was endowed with a natural elegance that was perfectly suited to such neglect. He was more or less Gascon, more or less a gentleman, and more or less a physician. Above all, he was a formidable swordsman, an inveterate gambler, and an unrepentant seducer; a man who had lost count of his duels, his debts, and his conquests.

Shrugging his shoulders, he filled the glasses and handed one to Agnès. They clinked to mark their reunion.

Then Agnès perched on the window ledge while Marciac

returned to his armchair. He would have offered his seat to any other woman, but the baronne de Vaudreuil did not expect such attentions from her brothers-in-arms.

'Now, tell me everything that's happened here,' said the Gascon. 'First off, who's the fellow who took my horse on my arrival? I go away for a few days, and there are new faces when I get back.'

'That's our new groom, André. Formerly of the Picardy regiment, I believe.'

'I suppose we've made quite sure that—'

'Yes,' interrupted Agnès. 'The man is quite trustworthy. He was a stableman at the Palais-Cardinal before he was . . . recommended to us.'

'Good . . . And what about the others?'

'Others?'

'La Fargue, Saint-Lucq, Leprat . . . You remember them? We all formed a band before I left. Damn! Have I been gone even longer than it seems?'

Since the jest was deserved and good-humoured, the young woman accepted it with good grace.

'Leprat is in Paris,' she informed him, 'but he tends to spend his mornings at monsieur de Tréville's house. As for Saint-Lucq and Almades, they are off on a mission with La Fargue. If all goes well, they should be back today.'

Marciac merely cocked an inquisitive eyebrow at this news.

Agnès rose to close the chamber door, leaned against it for a moment, and then in a hushed tone she said:

'Lately, someone has been sending a few discreet signals to the cardinal. This individual claims to have very valuable information and proposed a meeting to discuss how this information might be—'

'Sold?'

'Negotiated.'

'And His Eminence assigned La Fargue to meet this mysterious person.'

'As a matter of urgency.'

'My word, this individual must really be someone. Who are we talking about, exactly?'

417

' "La Donna".'

'Ah . . . now I understand.'

La Donna was the nickname given to an adventuress well known in all the courts of Europe. A clever schemer, a mercenary spy and an expert seductress, she made her living from the secrets she discovered for her own benefit or on behalf of others. Beyond her beauty and intelligence, she was best characterised by her lack of scruples. She was venal, and her excellent services came at a high price. She always had several irons in the fire and was adept at playing them off against one another, making hers an exciting but highly dangerous existence. All those who became acquainted with this woman predicted a violent, premature death for her, but these same people did not hesitate to call upon her talents when needed. It was murmured that her ultimate loyalty lay with the Pope. Others claimed she belonged to a secret society of dragons. All such surmises, however, overlooked her independent spirit and appetite for personal gain.

'But doesn't the cardinal have some grievance against her?' Marciac wondered aloud upon reflection. 'Remember that business at Ratisbon . . . ?'

Agnès shrugged. Putting her hand on the doorknob, she said:

'What do you want me to say? There are some cases in which a grievance might be more harmful to the one who nurtures it than to the one who causes it . . . Well, I must go now.'

Out of politeness, the Gascon rose from his chair. The young baronne was about to leave the room when, without warning, she went over and took him in her arms.

Not knowing the reason for this sudden display of emotion, Marciac let her embrace him.

'We were worried,' she murmured in his ear. 'Don't expect the others to tell you so, but you frightened us all. And if ever again you leave us for so long without sending news, I'll scratch your eyes out. Understood?'

'Understood, Agnès. Thank you.'

She left him standing there, but from the stairs she called back:

'Get some rest, but come down as soon as you're ready. I'm sure Ballardieu has planned a feast in your honour.'

With a smile, the Gascon closed the door.

He remained thoughtful for a moment, then gave a huge yawn and turned longing eyes towards the bed.

A slender, nimble, forked tongue woke Arnaud de Laincourt by tickling his ear. The young man groaned, weakly pushing the scaly snout away, and turned over in his bed. But the dragonnet was stubborn.

It switched ears.

Come on, boy . . . You know him well enough by now to realise that he isn't going to leave you in peace . . .

Giving up on sleep, Laincourt sighed heavily and opened his eyes.

'All right, Maréchal. All right . . .'

Pushing back the sheet, he rose up on his elbows and gave the gaunt old dragonnet an unhappy look. Sitting there with its wings folded and its tail wrapped around its feet, the small reptile seemed to be waiting for something.

He's hungry.

Of course he's hungry, Laincourt replied without speaking. *He's always hungry. In fact, I'm starting to wonder how it is that he eats so much and yet remains so thin.*

Then out loud, he told Maréchal:

'Do you know what a sorry sight you are?' The dragonnet tipped its head to the left. 'Yes, you are . . .'

Laincourt looked over at the big cage with bars as thick as fingers that sat in a corner of the room. It was standing open, as it was every morning, even though he had locked it before going to bed, as he did every evening.

He sighed again.

'Back in your cage!' the young man ordered, clapping his hands. 'Go on! You know the rules! Into your cage!'

Don't be too hard on him . . . When he was mine, he was never locked up.

Slowly, and with obvious reluctance, Maréchal turned around and waddled away. Then with a hop and a flap of his wings, he returned to his prison, closing the door with an insolent swipe of one clawed foot. As it clanged shut, the latch fell into place. The old dragonnet did not appear to be worried by this. Laincourt couldn't help smiling.

He was a thin brown-haired young man, with crystalline blue eyes. He was intelligent, cultivated, calm and reserved. Some found him to be distant, as he was in some ways. Others judged his reserve to be a sign of arrogance. They were mistaken. The truth was that, while Laincourt looked down on no one, he simply didn't much care for his contemporaries, asking only that they leave him peace and feeling no need to please them. He detested hollow platitudes, conventional opinions and polite smiles. He disliked being forced into conversation. He preferred silence to small talk and solitude to futile company. When confronted with someone he found tiresome he smiled, nodded, said nothing, and excused himself as quickly as possible. For him, politeness consisted in saying 'good day', 'thank you', 'goodbye', and enquiring only about the health of those he truly cared for.

As soon as he got out of bed and had pulled on his breeches, Laincourt went to close the window of his bedchamber. He had left it open to enjoy the night's cool breeze, but now it was letting in the heat as well as the stink and noise of Paris.

You've slept late again, boy.

So it seems.

That's a bad habit you've picked up since you've been idle and spent your nights reading.

Reading is not the same as being idle.

You are no longer employed.

I no longer have a master.

You will soon be in need of money.

Laincourt shrugged.

He lived on the second floor of a house in rue de la Ferronnerie, not far from the Saints-Innocents cemetery, between the neighbourhoods of Sainte-Opportune and Les Halles. Barely four metres wide, this street was very busy since it prolonged rue Saint-Honoré and crossed rue Saint-Denis at a right angle, thus linking two of the principal traffic routes in Paris. The flow of passers-by, traders, horse riders, sedan chairs, carts, and coaches went by without interruption from morning till night.

Do you see him, boy?

Laincourt glanced out at the street.

At the entrance to a narrow passage between two houses, a gentleman dressed in a beige doublet was waiting, one hand holding his gloves and the other resting on the pommel of his sword. He was calm and did not appear to be hiding. On the contrary, Laincourt had the impression that he wished to be seen, and recalled having previously noticed his presence, here and there, in recent days.

Of course, he replied to the invisible presence.

I wonder who he is. And what he wants.

I couldn't care less.

A month ago, he would have cared.

A month ago, he would have immediately taken steps to have the man in the beige doublet followed, identified, and no doubt neutralised. But he no longer belonged to the Cardinal's Guards. At the end of a mission that had cost him his red cape and his rank as an ensign, he had turned the page on secrets, intrigues, lies, and betrayals in the service of His Eminence.

After washing with the remaining water in the pitcher, Laincourt dressed and found something in the pantry to calm Maréchal's hunger. Then he decided to go out and have a bite to eat himself. He would then visit his bookseller, Bertaud, in order to return two books for the price of one.

He had just put on his baldric and hung his sword from it when he saw that the old dragonnet had once again escaped from his cage and was now standing near the door, holding his collar and chain in his mouth. The young man promised himself that he would buy a padlock on his way to the bookseller but, being a good sport, he extended his fist to Maréchal.

'All right,' he said. 'I'll take you, too.'

Outside in the street, the gentleman in the beige doublet had vanished.

*

The comte de Tréville, captain of the King's Musketeers, stood at his office window and sought to distract himself by looking out over the courtyard of his house on rue du Vieux-Colombier in the faubourg Saint-Germain. It provided a picturesque spectacle which he enjoyed, arousing nostalgia for the time when he was still a companion-in-arms to Henri IV. As usual, several dozen musketeers were to be found loitering on the cobbled courtyard strewn with fresh straw. Not all of them wore the cape – blue with a silver fleur-de-lys cross – as some were not on active duty. But all of them had their sword at their side and were ready for any opportunity to draw it. They walked or stood about, talking, laughing, playing dice or cards, demonstrating various fencing techniques, reading the gazettes together and commenting on the latest news, while keeping a watchful eye on the comings and goings on the great staircase and in the antechambers, which they also occupied.

'D'Artagnan!' Tréville suddenly called out in a loud voice.

Almost immediately, a door opened behind him . . .

'Monsieur?'

'Tell me, d'Artagnan, isn't that the chevalier d'Orgueil I see near the stables?' Tréville asked without turning round.

The musketeer approached in order to peer over his captain's shoulder.

'It is indeed, monsieur.'

'Ask him to come up, please.'

'Monsieur, they're already queuing at your office door . . .'

In fact, starting in the early hours of the morning, Tréville's days were marked by the unceasing flow of visitors he received at his mansion, when the king's service did not demand his presence elsewhere.

'I know, d'Artagnan, I know . . . Tell my secretary to have them wait, will you?'

'As you command, monsieur.'

'Thank you, lieutenant.'

Alone once again, the captain of the Musketeers uttered a sigh and, regretfully turning away from the window, sat down at his desk. The sheets and ledgers piled there drew his tired glance. Useless paperwork . . . Tréville picked up a small box, opened it with a little key, and drew out an unsealed letter that he placed before him.

Then he waited.

'Come in!' he called, as soon as he heard a knock at the door.

A gentleman entered, wearing a crimson doublet with black buttons and slashes. He was tall, carried himself with impeccable posture, and advanced with a firm step. It was easy to see that he was – or had once been – a military officer. He was thirty-five to forty years of age, with sharp features and the confident gaze of someone who knows they have not faltered, and never will, in fulfilling their duties. He was armed with a rapier that had become famous. Entirely white, made of ivory, it had been carved from tip to pommel from a single dragon's tooth. He wore it on his right side, being left-handed.

Antoine Leprat, chevalier d'Orgueil and a former member of the King's Musketeers, removed his hat to salute the captain.

Tréville welcomed him with a smile.

'Good morning, Leprat. How are you?'

'Very well, monsieur. Thank you.'

'And your thigh?'

'Completely healed, monsieur.'

It was a somewhat excessive claim. But in the King's Musketeers men quickly acquired the habit of minimising the gravity of a wound and exaggerating the speed of their recovery, out of fear of being passed over when the next mission was assigned.

'But it was a rather nasty wound . . .'

'It wasn't before I hit on the notion of jumping out of a window,' Leprat replied with a smile.

'And what a strange notion that was . . .'

'Indeed.'

The two men, separated in age by more than fifteen years, exchanged an amused, knowing glance.

But Tréville's expression became clouded.

'Yesterday,' he said, 'I received a letter from your father.' He pointed to the missive he had placed on the table before Leprat entered. 'He is worried about you. He has become anxious since he heard that you left the Musketeers.'

'My father the comte fears, above all else, that I will harm his reputation. By meeting an ignoble death while carrying out a clandestine mission, for example. I would be a source of pride to him if I died on the field of battle, wearing the cape of a true Musketeer, monsieur. But as far as posterity is concerned, there is nothing for him to gain if I serve under the orders of Captain La Fargue . . . The comte's only concern is for the glory attached to his name,' Leprat concluded.

'Perhaps he is also worried about the glory attached to yours . . .'

The former musketeer smiled bitterly.

'If the comte were to hear my body had been found lying in the gutter, my death would bother him less than the state of the gutter.'

Saddened, Tréville rose and returned to the window.

He remained there for a moment, hands behind his back, silent and troubled.

'All the same, chevalier, you will always be free to rejoin the Musketeers. As you know, you are only on leave of absence. Unlimited leave, to be sure, but a leave of absence nonetheless. Say the word, and I will reinstate you.'

'Thank you, monsieur.'

Tréville turned his back to the window and looked directly into Leprat's eyes.

'You know the esteem in which I hold Captain La Fargue. I have no wish to force you to choose between two loyalties. But you would also be serving the king by wearing the Musketeers' cape. So please keep yours, chevalier. And think on the matter. There will always be time and opportunity to change your mind.'

Cardinal Richelieu emerged, extremely preoccupied, from his interview with Louis XIII. But he did not let his feelings show and decided to make an appearance in the Great Hall of the

Louvre, where ministers and courtiers, officers and parasites, beautiful ladies and great lords were all gathered together. He seemed unruffled, smiled, engaged in conversation, and patiently endured the demands of his hangers-on, supplicants, and flatterers. To complete his pretence of normality, he envisaged paying a visit to the queen in her apartments. But was that a wise idea?

It was vital that he allayed the suspicions of anyone who was already worried, or would soon be, over why the king – in an extremely ugly mood, moreover – had detained his chief minister at the end of the Council meeting. The decisions that Louis XIII had made and the irrevocable orders he had issued during their tête-à-tête could put the kingdom to fire and to the sword. When the moment came they would have to strike quickly, forcefully, and accurately – and without showing so much as an ounce of mercy. That moment was fast approaching. But until it came, the only way to avoid a fatal conflagration was to keep the king's plans an absolute secret. And a secret was best preserved when everyone remained unaware of its importance.

Hence the cardinal would try to behave as if nothing was amiss. Today he planned to attend all of his meetings and ensure that the number of messengers leaving the Palais-Cardinal did not significantly increase. To all appearances, he would keep to his ordinary routine.

Richelieu knew he was being watched.

His role as a statesman meant that even the least important of his visits – those he paid and the ones he received – were noticed, reported, and discussed. There was nothing extraordinary about this. He was a public figure, after all. But amongst those who took an interest in his activities there were some who harboured sinister projects. The cardinal had many enemies. First there were the enemies of the king, not all of whom were foreign. Then there were the enemies of his policies, including the Catholic party. And lastly there were his personal enemies, who hated him because they envied his success or were jealous of his influence on Louis XIII, an influence that was greatly exaggerated but whose legend conveniently permitted the minister to be blamed for the faults and violent acts of his king.

There were two women to be found among Richelieu's most bitter personal opponents. The first was the queen mother, Marie de Médicis, Henri IV's widow: humiliated and unable to forgive her son for preferring to entrust the conduct of the kingdom's affairs to the cardinal rather than to her, she continued to hatch schemes from her refuge in Brussels, and stoked the fires of every revolt that took place in France. The second woman was the beautiful, intelligent, urbane, and very dangerous duchesse de Chevreuse who, for the last fifteen years, had taken a hand in every plot, but was protected by her birth, her fortune, and her friendship with the queen, Anne d'Autriche.

These two women never disarmed, even if at times they were only accomplices of the cabals that were invented and led by other enemies of the cardinal. Enemies who might be Catholic or Protestant, Frenchmen or foreigners, humans or dragons, but who all had eyes and ears inside the Louvre, and none of whom could be allowed to get wind of what was now being set in motion.

Let us not give these people any cause for concern, Richelieu thought to himself.

And so he resolved, in the end, to go and present his respects to the queen.

Marciac awoke still dressed. He had barely found the strength to remove his boots before lying down and had immediately gone to sleep. Rising up on his elbows, he looked around his chamber with bleary eyes and yawned. Then he sat on the edge of the bed, stretched, yawned again, and scratched his neck while at the same time rubbing his belly, realising that he was famished

And thirsty. He was thirsty, too.

How long had he been asleep?

Not long enough to ease the stiffness after his swift and arduous ride from La Rochelle, in any case. By coach the journey took at least eight days. The Gascon, on horseback, had completed it in less than five, which could not be accomplished without some sore muscles . . .

Grimacing, Marciac stood up and, with a heavy step, went to the window. It was open but the curtains were drawn shut. He spread them apart and then squinted, his eyes dazzled by the sun that was beginning to descend in the sky.

It was already the afternoon, then.

Still muzzy from sleep, the Gascon enjoyed the view for a moment. His bedchamber was on the second floor of the Hôtel de l'Épervier. Oriented towards the east, it offered a vantage point over the roofs of the Charité hospital in the foreground, and behind it the splendid abbey of Saint-Germain-des-Prés. With its abundant greenery, fresh air, and scattering of elegant buildings, the faubourg Saint-Germain was definitely a very pleasant neighbourhood.

The ringing of a bell tower succeeded in dragging Marciac out of his daydreaming and informed him of the time.

It was two o'clock.

He turned away from the window and went to wash, wetting and rubbing his blond locks over the basin. Finally feeling refreshed, he addressed a wink at his reflection in the small mirror hanging on the wall. He pulled on his boots, grabbed his hat and his baldric in case of an emergency, and went downstairs with his shirt hanging outside his breeches and his hair still damp.

One of the rare advantages of living in the Hôtel de l'Épervier was that the house was cool in summer. Otherwise it was a particularly sombre and austere place. On the ground floor, Marciac almost knocked down monsieur Guibot who was standing at the bottom of the stairs. Small, thin, and scruffy-looking, the old concierge hobbled about with a wooden leg. He had bushy eyebrows and the bald top of his head was surrounded by a crown of long dirty blond hair. Guibot had served the Blades before they were disbanded and he had kept a jealous watch over their headquarters, which he inexplicably adored, until their return.

While Marciac barely avoided colliding with him in the

front hall, the old man was busy clearing a path for two kitchen boys, dressed in pumps, white stockings, breeches, shirts, and aprons, who were arriving in the courtyard carrying a litter which held a large pâté in a circular pastry crust whose little chimney still steamed and filled the air with an appetising fragrance.

'Good afternoon, monsieur Marciac ... Make way, please ... Begging your pardon ... Watch the step, you two! And mind the door ... ! There ... Gently, gently ... It's this way ...'

His mouth already watering, the Gascon followed the procession through the house and out into the garden.

The garden was in fact merely a square of nature which, left untended, had reverted to its wild state. The grass was high and brush had accumulated at the foot of the walls. A chestnut tree offered some welcome shade. At the rear, a little door opened onto a narrow alley. And right in the middle, beneath the tree, was an old wooden table that was never taken inside. It had gone white from weathering and some intrepid bindweeds climbed up its cabled legs.

Sitting at one end of this table on mismatched chairs, Leprat, Agnès, and Ballardieu were joking and laughing over glasses of wine, sometimes getting up to replenish their drinks from one of the bottles left to cool in a tub of water, or to scrounge a bite to eat from a plate. Absorbed in their amusement, they paid little attention to shy Naïs who was busy setting out dishes on a tablecloth already loaded – in addition to the tableware – with cold meats, a roast goose, cheese, a pie, and a fat round loaf of bread. But the young servant girl always seemed to be forgetting something, forcing her to make further trips back and forth between the garden, the kitchen, the pantry and the cellar. And each time, she scolded herself in a soft voice.

'Useless girl, do you have nothing but sawdust for brains?' she groused as she hurried past Marciac.

'Ah! At last!' cried Ballardieu when he saw who and what was arriving.

Then the old soldier spied Marciac and welcomed him with equal enthusiasm.

Space had to be made for the steaming pâté. Monsieur Guibot wanted to direct the manoeuvre, but Ballardieu, domineering, promptly took control of operations. The pâté left its litter undamaged and the two boys were sent off to the kitchen to have a drink before returning to their master, a pastry cook in rue des Saints-Pères.

'Slept well?' Leprat asked.

'Wonderfully,' replied Marciac as he sat down.

'I'm glad to see you again, Marciac.'

'I'm glad to be back. The captain hasn't returned?'

'Not yet. Nor have Saint-Lucq and Almades, of course.'

'Here,' said Agnès, passing a glass of wine to the Gascon. 'Your health, Nicolas.'

Marciac was touched by the gesture and he smiled.

'Thank you very much, baronne.'

'You're welcome.'

Naïs returned with a bowl of butter, which at first she didn't know where to put on the crowded table.

'Naïs,' Ballardieu called to her. 'Is there anything missing, would you say?'

The old soldier was no ogre, but his deep voice and red face caused the young servant girl to become flustered. She thought it was a trick question and hesitated, looking around the table several times with a panic-stricken look on her face.

'I—'

'Well, I say there's nothing missing,' Ballardieu answered for her. 'You can therefore come and sit down.'

Naïs did not understand. Was she being invited to sit at the masters' table?

'I beg your pardon, monsieur?'

'Sit down, Naïs! And you too, monsieur Guibot . . . Come on, hurry up! The pâté is growing cold.'

The concierge did not need to be asked twice.

The servant girl, on the other hand, sought further advice. She looked to Leprat, who nodded in approval to her. That reassured her. Leprat was a gentleman, and moreover a former member of the King's Musketeers. And the baronne de Vaudreuil seemed not to care at all. So, if they saw no impediment to her sitting at the table . . . Her nervousness settling somewhat, she timidly placed one buttock on the edge of a rickety stool, praying that they would all forget she was present.

'And André?' Ballardieu persisted. 'He should share in this feast, shouldn't he? Somebody should tell him to come. Guibot, go fetch him, would you?'

The concierge, who was already holding out a plate, grumbled under his breath but obeyed willingly enough. He went off on his wooden leg, avoiding the molehills.

Leprat passed a hunting dagger to Marciac.

'Go ahead,' he said. 'Do the honours.'

The Gascon rose before the enormous *pâté en croûte* and looked around at the company seated at the table. Some of his best friends were here and had arranged this meal for him. He felt good, happy inside.

He was even in the mood to say a few words expressing his feelings.

Agnès guessed as much.

'Marciac,' she said, 'if the next thing you say isn't: "Who wants this handsome slice?" I swear I shall make mincemeat out of you.'

He burst out laughing and planted the blade in the golden crust.

The three riders arrived in Paris by the Montmartre gate.

Weariness from their travels had left them with drawn faces and great rings under their eyes. And they were all dirty and in need of a shave. They still wore the same clothing they had on when leaving Paris the previous day, having ridden more than forty leagues in under twenty-four hours to meet La Donna and then return as quickly as possible. Indeed, only the fear of killing their mounts had kept them from galloping the whole way back.

They soon parted ways.

While Saint-Lucq continued straight ahead down rue

Montmartre, La Fargue and Almades took rue des Vieux-Augustins instead and then rue Coquillière, before almost immediately turning left. At last, not far from the palace Cardinal Richelieu was having built for himself, they halted before a tavern in rue des Petits-Champs.

Its sign boasted an eagle daubed in scarlet paint.

The tavern's façade was set back from those of the other buildings on the same street, behind a mossy stone archway and a few feet of uneven paving. There were men occupying this space, glasses in hand, some of them standing around three barrels which served as a table, others leaning beside the tavern's wide-open windows conversing with those inside. Almost all of them were dressed as soldiers, wearing swords, striking dashing poses and bearing scars that left no doubt as to their profession. Moreover, they addressed one another as much by rank as by name, and even the names were often a *nom de guerre*.

Having dismounted, La Fargue entrusted the reins of his horse to Almades and went inside.

The *Red Eagle* was one of the places in Paris most frequented by the musketeers serving His Eminence. Two companies of soldiers served the cardinal directly: the Guards on horseback and the musketeers on foot. The Guards wore the famous red cape. They were all gentlemen, protected His Eminence's person, and accompanied him everywhere. As for the musketeers, they were commoners. Ordinary soldiers, they only signed up for three years and carried out less prestigious duties. Still, they were excellent fighters and were bound together by a strong *esprit de corps*. The best of them could have joined the Guards if they had been of more noble birth.

From the threshold, La Fargue caught the eye of the person he knew to be the owner of the establishment, a tall red-headed man who was still relatively fit despite the incipient bulge of his belly. His name was Balmaire and he walked with a slight limp ever since a wound had forced this former cardinal's musketeer to hang up his sword. He wore an ample shirt, brown breeches, and had an apron tied around his waist. But instead of the usual white stockings and pumps he wore a pair of worn funnel-shaped boots, indicating that his role as tavern keeper did not define him entirely.

Recognising La Fargue, Balmaire addressed a silent salute to him from afar. The old captain responded in the same fashion and went across the taproom to a door giving onto a corridor and a narrow staircase. He climbed the stairs and, upon reaching the first landing, entered a dusty room with peeling walls, cluttered with some crates, old furniture and chairs in need of repair.

Leaning forward, a tall, thin gentleman was gazing out the window at the street. The small, diamond-shaped panes of glass were filthy and had in places been replaced with pieces of carton, so that they blocked more light than they let through.

'You're late,' said the comte de Rochefort without looking around. He stood up straight and slowly turned away from the window. He was close to fifty years of age. He had a haughty face with a pale complexion, dark eyes, and a penetrating gaze. There was a small scar decorating his temple, where he had been grazed by a pistol ball.

'I've come all the way from Artois,' La Fargue retorted. 'And you?'

The old captain waited, silent and impassive.

'I was about to leave,' Rochefort lied.

'I need to see the cardinal.'

'When?'

'As soon as possible. Today.'

Rochefort nodded as if he were weighing up the pros and cons of this request.

It was said of Rochefort that he was His Eminence's damned soul. In fact, he was the henchman who took charge of the cardinal's dirty work and was therefore feared and hated. But he was perhaps Richelieu's most loyal servant and he was certainly the least scrupulous. A man who obeyed his master blindly and did not burden himself with moral considerations. Thus, while he would sometimes commit unspeakable acts when ordered to do so, he would only do so upon receiving the order.

'Did you meet with La Donna, captain?'

'Yes. Last night.'

'And?'

'And now I need to see the cardinal.'

The glances of the two men clashed for a moment, before Rochefort smiled joylessly and said:

'We don't like one another at all, do we?'

'No.'

La Fargue and Rochefort despised one another. Unfortunately the service of the cardinal forced them to work together once again, now that the Blades had reformed. The captain only took his orders from Richelieu. And he answered to him alone for his actions. But the comte was a necessary intermediary.

'I can't guarantee,' Rochefort said, adjusting his baldric, 'that the cardinal will receive you soon.'

He donned his hat, preparing to depart.

'La Donna claims to know something of a plot against the king,' La Fargue revealed.

Rochefort raised an eyebrow.

'Well, now . . .'

'And she is willing to reveal the details if certain of her demands are met.'

'So La Donna is making demands . . . What are they?'

'She asks for His Eminence's protection.'

'Nothing else?' the cardinal's henchman said with amusement.

'What does it matter, if she's telling the truth?'

'No doubt, no doubt . . . But do you believe that she is?'

La Fargue shrugged.

'Who knows? But she gave me something that will perhaps help the cardinal form an opinion.'

The old captain held out a stained and dog-eared letter that seemed to have got wet at some point. It was the letter La Donna had entrusted to him before fleeing into the storm on the back of her wyvern.

'This comes from La Donna?' Rochefort enquired.

'Yes.'

He took the document and examined it with a casual air. Then he placed it in his pocket and walked to the door.

'I'm expected at the Palais-Cardinal,' he declared from the threshold. 'Then I will join His Eminence at the Louvre.'

'Very well,' replied La Fargue, who himself went over to glance out the window. 'But time is running short. La Donna promised to make contact this evening and before I meet her again I need to know what the cardinal has decided with regard to her. Moreover, she is being pursued by a band of dracs who I'm sure will give her no respite. And if they find her before we do—'

'Dracs? What dracs?'

'Black dracs, Rochefort. Mercenaries. Judging by the markings on their leader's face, I would swear they are former soldiers from the Irskehn companies.'

In the drakish tongue, Ir'Skehn meant black fire, and the Irskehns were cavalry companies levied by Spain and composed solely of black dracs. Although they were unreliable on a battlefield due to their inability to control their fury, these cavaliers had no equals when it came to marauding, harassing, and plundering. They were held responsible for several particularly horrible civilian massacres. The mere rumour of their arrival was enough to empty whole areas of the countryside.

Rochefort's eyes narrowed as he took this detail into account.

'And who else would privately hire Irskehns—' he started to say.

'—other than the Black Claw,' La Fargue concluded for him.

Gripping the back of the chair and craning his neck, Maréchal was leaning far over his master's shoulder to observe the trictrac board. The old dragonnet was keeping a rapt eye upon the dice, which he loved to see roll across the flat surface. As for Laincourt, he sat unmoving with a blank gaze, his mind elsewhere.

'Come now, Arnaud! Are you going to play?'

The young man raised his head, forcing Maréchal to straighten up, and looked over at his opponent in bewildered surprise. Amused, the other man smiled at him, arms crossed, in a slightly mocking fashion but with an affectionate gleam in his eye. He was a bookseller called Jules Bertaud, about fifty years old. He'd known Laincourt for almost a year now, and already nurtured paternal feelings for him. They shared a taste for knowledge, for books, and more particularly, for treatises on draconic magic which were a discreet speciality of Bertaud's bookshop. Lastly, they were both from Lorraine, which had helped to forge a bond between them.

'It is your turn, Arnaud . . .'

Once a week, Laincourt and Bertaud convened at the latter's establishment to talk and play trictrac. Since the weather was fine today, they had installed themselves in the pleasantly sunlit rear courtyard of the bookshop, which was located on rue Perdue in the neighbourhood surrounding Place Maubert, where booksellers and printers abounded.

'Oh yes . . .' said Laincourt, returning to the game. 'It is my turn, to be sure. I need to roll, don't I?' he asked as he seized the dice cup.

His gesture immediately drew Maréchal's full attention.

'No,' Bertaud replied impatiently. 'You've already rolled—'

'Really?'

'Really!' called another voice.

In addition to the gaunt old dragonnet, the match had acquired another spectator: Daunois, a ruddy-faced man in his forties, with the physique of a stevedore and a rather sinister-looking face. In his case, however, appearances were deceiving. A printer by trade, Joseph Daunois possessed a fine wit that was intelligent, cultivated, and sometimes cruelly ironic. He and Bertaud were good friends who nonetheless could never resist trading barbed insults with one another.

The printer stood at the threshold of his workshop, and behind him one glimpsed workers busy with their tasks. But above all, one heard the creaking of the big hand presses and smelled the paper and fresh ink which rather effectively countered the city stinks that had worsened in the hot weather.

'Yes, really,' Bertaud confirmed. 'And you rolled a seven.'

'Seven,' repeated Laincourt.

'Yes, seven.'

'Since he's telling you so!' interjected Daunois as he came over to join them.

His massive body cast a shadow over most of the small square table.

'Just give me a few moments to think,' Laincourt begged, leaning over the trictrac board.

He said nothing, but it took him a few seconds to recall that his pieces were the white ones.

And to discover that he was in serious difficulty.

'That's right,' the printer said jokingly. 'Think it over . . . We wouldn't want to you to make some hasty mistake—'

'You know,' added Bertaud, 'it's no good having me abandon my bookshop and customers to play with you if you take no interest in the game . . .'

The young man made to reply, but Daunois beat him to it, in a sarcastic tone:

'Yes, because don't you know, Arnaud, that Bertaud's bookshop is positively packed? There's an impatient mob milling at the door and threatening to break through the windows. They're beating them away with sticks, riots are breaking out, and the city watch will soon be turning up to restore order. It's a right state of panic—'

The truth was that, even if Bertaud was not facing financial ruin, his shop was not well patronised.

'Have you already spoiled all the paper delivered to you this morning?' retorted the bookseller. 'Don't you have some handsome inkblots to inspect? Some botched print you need to perfect? But perhaps I'm being a trifle unfair, seeing as in your shop, you press more fingers than pages . . .'

He had risen as he spoke and, since he was rather small, did not make nearly as impressive a figure as Daunois standing before him. But he held himself firm and his gaze did not waver.

'Your witticisms only amuse yourself, bookseller!' replied Daunois, swelling his chest.

'And you, printer, bore everyone with your remarks!'

Their voices rose while Laincourt, not paying the slightest

heed to their altercation, studied his pieces, wondering how to obtain as many points as possible. A trictrac board closely resembled that used for backgammon, with the same division into two sides and the same series of twenty-four black and white long triangles along which one moved the counters. But trictrac was a game with complex rules, where the aim was not simply to remove your counters as quickly as possible. Instead, players earned points as they progressed in order to accumulate a pre-determined score.

Laincourt lent an ear to the discussion just as Daunois was growling:

'Is that so? Is that so?'

'You heard me!'

'So how is it, then, that people say what they do?'

'And what, pray, are people saying?'

'Quite simply, that—'

'Papa?'

A pretty girl of sixteen, with dark hair and green eyes, had just opened the door leading to the room at the rear of the bookshop. The quarrel immediately ceased and its cause was forgotten.

'Good afternoon, Clotilde,' said the printer with a kind smile.

'Good afternoon, monsieur. And good afternoon to you, monsieur de Laincourt.'

'Good afternoon. How are you?'

'Very well, monsieur,' the girl answered with a blush.

'Well, my girl?' queried Bertaud. 'What is it?'

The bookseller's only daughter said in a faint voice:

'There is someone in the shop, papa. A gentleman.'

Bertaud, who had leaned down to listen to Clotilde, straightened up triumphantly.

'Excuse me,' he said, his words directed so ostensibly at Laincourt that he could only be in fact aiming them at Daunois, 'but I must attend to my business. Unlike some, I cannot spend all day idling about while others do my work for me.'

Daunois, of course, could not let this pass by unanswered:

'Allow me to bid you good day, Arnaud. I must return to my workshop, where there are some delicate operations awaiting that cannot be carried out without my supervision.'

And thereupon, the printer and the bookseller, both draped in a theatrical air of dignity, turned on their heels and went their separate ways. Pretty Clotilde, however, did not follow her father back inside. She lingered for a moment within the frame of the doorway until, embarrassed when the eyes of the former Cardinal's Guard did not shift from the trictrac board, she finally withdrew. No doubt any man other than Laincourt would have perceived the sentiments she felt for him. But this young man, so skilled at detecting lies and dissembling in a thousand different clues, was unable to read the heart of a young girl in love.

Bertaud returned after a few minutes.

He sat back down, observing with pleasure that his opponent had finally made his move.

'So?' asked Laincourt. 'This customer?'

'Bah! He only came in to browse. He didn't even know what he was looking for . . .'

The young man nodded knowingly.

'Slender, elegant, with a blond moustache?' he guessed.

'Yes,' the bookseller replied in astonishment. 'But how—?'

'And wearing a beige doublet?'

'Precisely! Do you know him, then?'

'Slightly,' said Laincourt, holding out the dice cup. 'It's your turn, Jules. This game is certainly dragging on.'

Upon leaving the *Red Eagle,* following his interview with Rochefort, La Fargue rejoined Almades and together they returned to the Hôtel de l'Épervier on their exhausted mounts.

They chose the shortest route, which is to say, they took the Pont Rouge. Thus named because of its coating of red lead paint, the wooden bridge had been built the previous year. Like the Pont Neuf, it allowed Parisians to cross the Seine river directly, but there was a toll to be paid, making it less popular.

On the Left Bank, La Fargue and the Spaniard rode up rue

de Beaune, through a neighbourhood that had only recently sprung up from the ground in the Pré-aux-Clercs, the former domain of Queen Marguerite de Navarre. Beyond it, they finally reached the faubourg Saint-Germain. Rue de la Sorbonne led them to the right-angled crossing with rue des Saints-Pères, which they followed alongside the façades of La Charité hospital before passing in front of Les Réformés cemetery and turning into the small rue Saint-Guillaume.

They arrived at their destination and, despite the questions about La Donna and the alleged plot against the king that still nagged at him, the old captain could only think of finding a bite to eat and then going to bed. He rang the bell at the entrance to the Hôtel de l'Épervier without dismounting, and waited for someone to open one of the great rectangular doors of the carriage gate. It was not monsieur Guibot but André, the new groom, who hurried over. Once inside the courtyard, La Fargue and Almades handed him the reins of their horses.

They found the others in the garden.

Agnès, Leprat, and Marciac were chatting away beneath the chestnut tree at one end of the old table, where the meal had not yet been cleared away. Looking happy and thick as thieves together, they sipped wine and conversed for the sole pleasure of enjoying one another's company. The heat was bearable out here in the garden. The air was fresher and a relaxed hush reigned which was only slightly disturbed by the regular snores from Ballardieu, asleep in an armchair.

The old soldier had drunk a fair amount of wine and he merely stirred in his sleep when the others greeted the new arrivals. He groaned and smacked his lips without opening his eyes as La Fargue and the Spanish fencing master sat down and took their ease, removing their hats and baldrics, downing a few glasses of wine, and attacking the remains of the repast.

While polishing off the last quarter of the *pâté en croûte*, the captain of the Blades recounted his meeting with La Donna. He reported what she had told him and what she was demanding in exchange for the information she claimed to possess. Then he described the confrontation with the dracs, without omitting any details. Almades, meanwhile, remained

439

silent as usual, eating little, controlling his urges despite his hunger and thirst.

'Can we believe what this woman says?' Leprat wondered aloud. 'Isn't she a schemer and a spy of the worst possible kind?'

'As far as scheming and espionage go,' observed Marciac, 'the worst possible kind is also the best . . .'

'To be sure. But all the same . . . A plot against the king!'

'What is she like?' asked the young baronne de Vaudreuil. 'They say she is very beautiful. Is she?'

'Yes,' the captain answered. 'She is.'

'And what impression did she make on you?' Agnès persisted.

'I found her to be intelligent, determined, skilful—'

'—and dangerous?'

'Certainly.'

'If we know anything about La Donna,' Leprat commented, 'it is that she only acts out of self-interest. So what does she gain from exposing this purported plot?'

'The cardinal's protection,' Marciac reminded him.

'A protection that she must truly need,' Agnès emphasised.

'True,' agreed the Gascon. 'You are thinking of the dracs—'

'Yes. La Donna is not only being hunted, but the pack chasing her is a ferocious one—'

'And snapping at her heels.'

'Black dracs and an unnatural black mist,' noted Leprat. 'I don't know about you, but to me all this reeks of the Black Claw . . .'

Marciac and Agnès both nodded.

Led by power-hungry dragons who would stop at nothing to achieve their ends, the Black Claw was a secret society which was particularly strong in Spain and her territories, including the Spanish Netherlands within whose borders La Donna had waited for La Fargue. Its most ancient, influential, and active lodge was to be found in Madrid. But although there were close links between it and the Court of Dragons, the Black Claw's goals were not always in accord with those of the Spanish Crown. Its ultimate aim, in fact, was to plunge Europe into a state of chaos that would permit the establishment of an absolute draconic reign. A reign that would spare no dynasty.

No human dynasty, that is.

'If La Donna is being pursued by the Black Claw,' surmised the Gascon, 'one can certainly understand her eagerness to find a powerful protector . . . I would not like to be in her shoes—'

'And yet you are,' Agnès said in an amused tone. 'Do you suppose that the Black Claw has forgotten the defeat we recently inflicted upon its agents?'

'But in my case, I have you,' Marciac responded. 'Whereas La Donna has no one.'

The young baronne smiled.

'But why would the Black Claw be after La Donna?' Leprat wanted to know.

'Perhaps . . . ,' Agnès started to suggest, 'perhaps the Black Claw is the origin of the plot against the king. Perhaps La Donna somehow got wind of the secret, perhaps the Black Claw knows this, and now wants to silence her . . .'

'All right,' granted the former musketeer. 'Or perhaps the Black Claw is seeking La Donna for some other reason, and she has concocted this tale in the hope that the cardinal will protect her, at least for a while . . . What do you think, captain?'

In the heat of their discussion, Leprat, Marciac, and Agnès had forgotten the presence of La Fargue.

Turning their faces in unison, they saw Almades lifting an index finger to his lips in warning . . .

The captain was fast asleep in his chair.

Aubusson leaned back in his chair and considered the painting with a weary eye. It seemed to be resisting him today. Any further effort was useless. His mind was elsewhere and he could produce nothing worthwhile on the canvas.

'I might just as well go for a walk,' he grumbled to himself as he put down his brushes and his palette.

Like all artists, he occasionally had black days and now had no trouble recognising the signs.

Nearly sixty years old, he had more than four decades of experience as a painter. Starting as an apprentice he had followed the ordinary course demanded by his guild. He rose to the rank of journeyman and finally – after completing a piece his peers judged to be of superior quality – that of master. Acquiring this title was essential for him to open his own studio. Aubusson could then accept commissions and earn a living from his work. He became one of the best portrait painters of his generation. Perhaps the very best of them, in fact. His renown had spread across borders and the courts of Europe vied for his services as he spent years roaming the roads of France, Germany, Italy, England, Spain, and even travelled as far as Hungary and Sweden. He reached the very height of his glory when Marie de Médicis, widow of Henri IV and mother of Louis XIII, had sent him to Madrid to produce a faithful likeness of the Infante Doña Ana Maria Mauricia, the future Anne d'Autriche, queen of France. It was said that even the Grand Turk himself had requested that Aubusson portray him.

These days, Aubusson no longer travelled.

Lacking a wife and children, he had retired to a charming country manor and was wealthy enough to take his rest following a career that had proved far more adventurous than he could have dreamed. He still painted, however. Landscapes mostly. But sometimes portraits when he chose to accept a commission. These tended to be rare now. Aubusson lived in such reclusion that many believed him dead or in exile, when in fact he resided only eight leagues northeast of Paris. His days passed peacefully near the village of Dammartin, with a couple of elderly domestic servants and a tall adolescent valet as his sole company.

This valet was grinding colours in a mortar when Aubusson decided to abandon his painting for the day.

'You will wash my brushes, Jeannot.'

'Very good, master.'

And thereupon, the artist left his studio, leaving its clutter, its golden light, and its intoxicating odours of paints behind.

Outside, the afternoon sun dazzled him as he crossed the courtyard. He hurried, the panels of his large sleeveless vest flapping against his thighs, his buckled shoes raising dust which then clung to his stockings, the hand shading his eyes pushing back the cloth cap on his head. He was quite tall. He had not gained weight as a result of age or retirement, and he remained a handsome man with a firm profile and a thick head of hair which was the same white as his carefully trimmed beard. Women were still attracted to him, although not nearly so many as in his prime. Back then, he had collected mistresses, sometimes selected among those whose portraits he painted at the expense of an overly trusting father or husband.

The big manor was silent.

In the front hall, at the bottom of the stairs, Aubusson washed his hands in a basin of clean water waiting for him. Then he took off his cap and the vest that he only wore when painting, exchanging them for a doublet hanging from the back of a chair. He had finished buttoning it when old Mère Trichet, who had heard him from the kitchen where she busied herself, brought him a glass of newly drawn wine, as she always did when he returned from the studio.

'Have you already finished for the day, monsieur?'

'My word . . . It seems to be one of those days when nothing goes right.'

Mère Trichet – a woman in her fifties with a thick waist and a round face – nodded as Aubusson drained his glass and returned it to her.

'Thank you. Is the signora in her bedchamber?'

'No, monsieur. She is out at the back, with her monstrous beast . . .'

The painter smiled but did not respond to this.

'I will sup alone this evening,' he said as he left.

'Very good, monsieur.'

Once out in the backyard where hens were pecking grain and a tired old hound was snoring, Aubusson went round the stable until he came to an enclosure. Here, beneath a sloping roof made of poorly joined planks, he found a chained wyvern asleep, its energy no doubt sapped by the heat. Crouched beside it, with her head bare and her long red hair sparkling in the sunshine, the beautiful Alessandra di Santi was stroking the great scaly head.

Leaning on the fence, Père Trichet was watching the scene with eyes squinted beneath the brim of his old battered hat, a lit clay pipe in his mouth. He was an elderly man, with a gnarly body hardened and worn from a life of labour. He spoke little, and when Aubusson joined him, he moved off with a visible shake of the head, his way of expressing utter disapproval of proceedings while washing his hands of the matter.

Even when domesticated and trained, wyverns remained carnivorous creatures powerful enough to tear off an arm with a single bite. And if one avoided approaching a horse from behind, one needed to take similar care with these winged reptiles, as placid and good-natured as they might seem. Elementary rules, known to all, or almost all . . . and which La Donna evidently chose to ignore . . .

Standing up, she turned her back to the wyvern as she left the enclosure and, showing no fear of the beast behind her, said to the painter:

'The poor thing is exhausted. I must say I've hardly spared her strength these past few days . . .'

Smiling and serene, she wore a hunting outfit that looked delightful on her, very similar to the one she had worn the night before, in Artois, when she had met La Fargue.

'And you?' enquired Aubusson in a tone where concern outweighed reproach. 'You promised me you would rest a while.'

'I shall rest this evening,' said Alessandra.

The painter helped her shut the gate to the enclosure.

'You must take good care of her,' she added, looking over at the wyvern.

'I promise you I shall.'

'She has truly earned it. Last night, for my sake, she faced a terrible storm and did not falter until she brought me here safely, despite—'

'I shall give up my own bed to her, if that will reassure you . . . But am I permitted to have some care for you?'

The Italian spy did not respond, instead turning round to sweep the surrounding area with a slow scrutinising gaze.

'What is it?' asked Aubusson worriedly, in turn searching around them.

'I'm wondering where my little dragonnets, Scylla and Charybdis, might be.'

'Bah! No doubt they're off hunting some poor field mouse, which they will deposit half-devoured in front of my door . . .'

Taking Alessandra by the elbow, the painter led her towards a table placed in the shade provided by an arbour. They sat down and, once they were face-to-face, Aubusson gently squeezed the young woman's hands in his own and sought to capture her gaze.

'There's still time to abandon this course of action, you know that?'

Touched, La Donna gave him a smile full of tenderness. She felt troubled by this man so imbued with paternal instincts towards her. He was the only man she never made an effort to seduce.

'No,' she said. 'It's too late to turn back. And it has been too late for quite some time . . . Besides, I've already made all my arrangements for this evening. The important thing is not to deviate from the plan. Remember, I shall no doubt be taken to La Renardière.'

'I know. I'll scout out the domain tomorrow. And I shall return there during the night to make sure I will be able to find the path to the clearing, whatever happens.'

'The domain is vast, but well guarded. Don't let them arrest you.'

'If necessary, I shall say that I was out strolling and became lost . . . But what if you're taken elsewhere?'

'Knowing the cardinal, that's highly unlikely.'

'Nevertheless.'

'Then I shall send you a warning by means of Scylla and Charybdis.'

'And if you're someplace where you can't be reached?'

'For example?'

'Le Châtelet? Or the Bastille? Or in a cell at the château de Vincennes?'

Irritated, Alessandra stood up.

'You always take the blackest view of things!'

Aubusson rose to his feet as well.

'Your plan is too full of risks!' he exclaimed. 'It will be a miracle if—'

He did not finish, feeling upset and embarrassed by his outburst.

With a smile and a knowing glance up at his face, the Italian adventuress indicated that she was not angry with him.

'You're forgetting one thing,' she said.

'And what is that?'

'Even if they do not realise it, I shall have the Cardinal's Blades on my side.'

The tavern was located in rue des Mauvais-Garçons, not far from the Saint-Jean cemetery. Like the surrounding neighbourhood, it was dark, filthy, smelly and sinister. Although its dirt floor was not strewn with the same unhealthy muck that spattered the paving stones outside, the air stank of the smoke from pipes and the cheap yellow tallow candles, as well as the sweating, grimy bodies of its clientele. The *One-Eyed Tarasque* was a place where people came to drink themselves senseless, drowning their pain and sorrows in the sour wine. One such drunkard could be seen mumbling to himself in a corner. Not so long ago, a hurdy-gurdy player had performed his melancholy airs here in the evening. But he would be coming here no more.

Arnaud de Laincourt, however, still came.

He was sitting alone at a table upon which Maréchal, roaming as freely as his little chain would allow, was scratching at old wax incrustations in the wood. With a grey stoneware pitcher and a glass before him, the cardinal's former spy had a lost, distant expression on his face.

And a sad one.

Despite himself, he was thinking of all the sacrifices he had agreed to make in His Eminence's service, and the little thanks he had received in return. He was thinking back on all the years he had spent living amidst lies, suspicion, betrayal, intrigue, and murder. He was thinking of that deceitful world where rest was never permitted, and which had little by little eaten away at his soul. He was thinking of all those who had lost their lives there. And in particular, of an old hurdy-gurdy player who had left nothing behind but a decrepit dragonnet.

Don't torment yourself on my account, boy.

Can't I at least shed a tear for you?

Of course you can. But I won't have you blaming yourself for my death. You know it wasn't your fault that I perished.

But I'm still alive. While you—

So what?

Laincourt looked at the empty stool in front of him.

It was the very same stool on which the hurdy-gurdy player used to take a seat during each of their clandestine meetings. The young man imagined that it was occupied once again. He had no trouble at all envisioning the old man, wearing his filthy rags and carrying his battered instrument on a strap around his neck. He was smiling, but his face was bruised and bloody. Laincourt could no longer remember him any other way than this, the way he had seen the hurdy-gurdy player for the very last time.

I've seen the man in the beige doublet again. The one who's been following me around these last few days and doesn't seem to care if he's seen. He was on the Pont Neuf. And I know he came by Bertaud's bookshop later . . .

You can't avoid meeting him much longer.

Bah!

Just because you've finished with intrigues doesn't mean they've finished with you. The world doesn't work that way . . . And besides, you were wrong.

447

Wrong?

Wrong to spurn the cardinal's offer.

The cardinal did not offer me anything.

Come now, boy! Do you think La Fargue would have proposed your joining his Blades without, at the very least, His Eminence's approval . . . ? You should not have refused him.

Suddenly weary, Laincourt looked away.

To the others present in the tavern, he was just a young man whose dragonnet was patiently waiting for him to finish his drinking.

To travel from the Louvre to the Palais-Cardinal, all that was necessary was to take rue d'Autriche, then turn left on Saint-Honoré and follow to Richelieu's official residence.

A first obstacle, however, was posed in leaving the Louvre itself, which had been a mediaeval fortress before it became a palace. Its courtyard therefore had only one public exit: an archway so dark that one winter morning a gentleman had jostled King Henri IV there without even realising it. Twelve metres long, this archway led out to the east. It was the main access to the palace, the one used by royal processions, but also by a crowd of people that gathered before it from morning till night. Flanked by two old towers, it overlooked a nauseating ditch which could only be crossed by means of a narrow bridge defended by a massive fortified gate, known as the Bourbon gate.

Having left the Louvre through this gate, however, other obstacles still lay ahead. The gate opened onto rue d'Autriche, a lane running perpendicular to the Seine, between the École quay to the south and rue Saint-Honoré to the north. In Paris, the narrowness of the city's streets made the passage of traffic difficult everywhere. But the very modest rue d'Autriche was the place where all those seeking to enter the Louvre crossed paths with all those leaving the palace. To make matters worse, its pavement was always filled with coaches, since carriages were denied permission to enter the precincts of the palace, except in the case of certain grand personages, foreign dignitaries, or for reasons of health. Thus the resulting jams, collisions, and confusion were a permanent feature of rue d'Autriche, where people spent more time shuffling in place than advancing in the midst of a great din of shouts, insults, whinnying, hoof beats, and creaking axles.

It was therefore with a certain amount of relief that, on the way to the Palais-Cardinal, it was finally possible to escape from rue d'Autriche and turn left onto rue Saint-Honoré. This street, although one of the longest in the capital since Paris had been extended westwards, was not much wider than the others. Heavily frequented, it too had its share of daily traffic jams. But here at least, there was a more ordinary level of unruliness and bother. And here at least, travellers were no longer subjected to the stench from the stagnant waters in the ditches surrounding the Louvre.

Here at least, one could progress at a walking pace.

Bearing his magnificent coat-of-arms, Cardinal Richelieu's coach left the Louvre with the curtains drawn. It entered rue d'Autriche at a slow walk, moving towards rue Saint-Honoré where a horse escort would open the way for it until it arrived at the Palais-Cardinal.

The heavy curtains were intended to protect His Eminence from both the dust and public view. Nothing could be done, however, about the heat or the stink. Paris had been baking all day beneath a pitiless sun and the excrement and muck that covered its pavement had become a cracked crust from which escaped powerful, acrid, and unhealthy exhalations.

The cardinal held a handkerchief imbibed with vinegar to his nose and sat deep in thought, his face turned towards the window of the passenger door and the curtain that blocked it. Now that he had found refuge in his coach he was no longer obliged put on an act for the ever-present spies at the Louvre. And although he remained in perfect control of his emotions, his severe expression and distant gaze betrayed the extent of his preoccupation. He considered the arrests he would have to order in conformity with the king's will, the interrogations that would then need to be conducted, and the truths that would emerge from them. Disturbing, embarrassing, scandalous truths. Truths that might very well compromise Queen Anne's honour and become a grave affair of State.

The queen, after all, was Spanish . . .

The cardinal sighed and, almost as a means of distracting himself, asked:

'Any news of Captain La Fargue?'

Then he slowly turned his head to look at the gentleman who had been sitting across from him, silent and still, ever since the coach first moved off.

'He returned today,' replied the comte de Rochefort.

'Did you speak to him?'

'Yes, monseigneur. He asks to be received by Your Eminence as a matter of urgency.'

'Impossible,' Richelieu declared.

In order to confound any possible suspicions on the part of his adversaries, he had decided to maintain the pretence that today was an ordinary day, just like any other. He would, therefore, not receive the captain of his Blades. Not even discreetly, or secretly. For if someone happened to catch even a fleeting glimpse of La Fargue in the corridors of the Palais-Cardinal, the most astute observers would be sure to make a connection with the tête-à-tête which Louis XIII had so brusquely held with his chief minister that morning, after the meeting of the Council. A connection that had no basis in fact, as it happened. But it would be dangerous, nevertheless.

Rochefort did not insist.

'La Fargue met with La Donna last night,' he said. 'She claims to have knowledge of a plot threatening the throne of France. She offers to reveal it in return for—'

'How much?'

'She is not demanding money, monseigneur.'

The cardinal quirked an eyebrow.

'Is La Donna no longer venal?'

'She demands your protection.'

'My protection. Meaning that of France . . . What does she fear? Or rather, who does she fear?'

'If one is to believe La Fargue, La Donna is being hunted by the Black Claw,' Rochefort said dubiously.

'Ah,' replied the cardinal, beginning to understand. 'Naturally. That would explain a number of things,' he added in a thoughtful tone. 'Such as the lady's eagerness in seeking to contact me.'

'She asked that this letter be delivered to you.'

Richelieu looked at the letter held out to him, but at that instant the coach, which had previously been advancing very slowly along rue Saint-Honoré, came to a complete halt. Rochefort placed his hand on his rapier. Intrigued, the cardinal lifted the curtain of the coach door and called out:

'Captain!'

The young Captain de La Houdinière drew up aside the coach on his horse.

'Monseigneur?'

'Why aren't we moving?'

'A tarasque, monseigneur.'

Tarasques were enormous reptiles with hard shells. They had three pairs of very short legs. Heavy and slow, they possessed colossal strength and could easily knock over a wall by accident or pass right through a house without changing pace. As stupid as they were placid, they made excellent draught animals. They could also be readily harnessed to hoist machinery at building sites.

And there was no lack of building sites in the vicinity of the Palais-Cardinal.

'Do the best you can,' said Richelieu before letting the curtain fall back into place.

But he had no illusions: there was simply no way of hurrying a tarasque when it crossed a street.

The cardinal considered the letter that Rochefort still held in his hand. Stained and dog-eared, it seemed to him thicker than a simple missive. No doubt there was something inside.

He did not touch it.

'Open it, please.'

The comte undid the seal and unfolded the letter with a certain degree of apprehension. The threat of a possible attempt against Cardinal Richelieu's life was never far from his mind. And poisons existed – born of draconic alchemy –

which, reduced to a very fine powder, could kill the first person who breathed them.

The letter from La Donna presented no such danger. On the other hand, what it actually contained prompted Rochefort to recoil in an instinctive, superstitious manner.

His reaction could not fail to interest the cardinal.

'Well, then?'

'Monseigneur, look . . .'

Richelieu lowered his eyes to peer at the object the other man was showing him, lying in the hollow of the unfolded letter. Still attached to the torn corner of a sheet of parchment, it was a seal in black wax stamped with the sign of the Grand Lodge of the Black Claw.

'Monseigneur . . . Is that what I think it is?'

The cardinal took his time to examine it closely, and then nodded firmly.

'Most assuredly, Rochefort.'

'But how could La Donna have obtained it?'

'That would be a very interesting question to put to her, wouldn't it?'

And as his coach started to move again, Richelieu turned back to the closed curtain of his coach door, as if absorbed by some spectacle that only he could perceive.

452

3

Rochefort came by the Hôtel de l'Épervier in the early evening. Upon entering the courtyard, he leapt from his saddle, threw his horse's reins to André, and dashed up the front steps of the mansion.

Inside, at the bottom of the great staircase, he came across Leprat who, after La Fargue, was probably his least favourite of the Blades. To make matters worse, the former musketeer couldn't bear to see Rochefort walk into the house as if it were his own. He was not one of the Blades and never would be. Leprat therefore gave him a silent, icy welcome.

The cardinal's henchman, in a hurry, paid no heed to this.

'Where's La Fargue?' he demanded.

Leprat pointed towards the main hall on the ground floor, which the Blades had converted into a fencing room. It was a long, high-ceilinged chamber, decorated with gilt but now almost empty of furnishings, whose windows overlooked the garden. La Fargue was in discussion with Agnès and Marciac when Rochefort found him. Their conversation ended at once and all eyes converged on the intruder.

'We need to talk,' Rochefort announced.

La Fargue considered him for a moment.

Then he nodded and with his chin indicated the door of an antechamber, towards which Rochefort briskly led the way. Once the door closed behind them, Agnès and Marciac, both looking intrigued, turned to Leprat who was watching from the threshold.

'La Donna?' guessed the young baronne.

Leprat shrugged, before glancing over his shoulder to see Saint-Lucq approaching.

Although he had returned from the mission at the same time as La Fargue and Almades, the half-blood had vanished and only now was making his reappearance. No one dreamt, however, of asking him where he had been or what he had been doing. Agnès noticed that his clothes – black and perfectly tailored, as usual – were clean and freshly pressed. They were certainly not the same ones he had been wearing on the journey to Artois with La Fargue. But his boots were somewhat dusty, suggesting that he had ridden along a dirt road since he had changed.

'Good evening,' he said without addressing anyone in particular.

The others, preoccupied, answered him vaguely but their offhand greeting didn't offend him.

'Whose horse is that in the courtyard?' he asked.

'Rochefort's,' answered Marciac. 'He is in conference with the captain right now. He seemed to be in a hurry.'

'What's it about?'

'La Donna, no doubt.'

'I see.'

The Gascon was seated at a small table, where there was some food, wine glasses, and bottles. Saint-Lucq joined him and, while he stood there and poured himself a drink, he asked:

'And La Rochelle?'

Marciac pursed his lips and shrugged.

The half-blood drained his glass, peered at the Gascon through his red spectacles, nodded briefly, and went to sit in an alcove window that looked out onto the garden.

Marciac smiled.

It had been three weeks since they had seen one another. Three weeks during which Marciac, on his solo mission, could very well have been killed. But he knew that as far as welcomes were concerned, he could expect no more from Saint-Lucq.

The door of the antechamber opened and Rochefort, without glancing at anyone, departed as quickly as he had arrived. As for La Fargue, he took his time in emerging. He went over to the Blades and accepted the glass Leprat held out to him.

'So?' Agnès asked.

'So, La Donna has somehow managed to achieve her goal. I don't know why, but the cardinal is taking her very seriously. He believes this plot she claims to have discovered does in fact exist, and he charges us with unravelling the whole affair . . .'

'And how are we to do that?' enquired Leprat.

'Obviously, first we need to find our lady spy again.'

'Preferably before the dracs, who are also hunting for her,' added Marciac.

'Yes . . . The trouble is, we have no idea how to find her.'

'Didn't she say she would make contact this evening, in Paris, captain?' recalled Agnès.

'Yes,' La Fargue admitted.

'Then let's hope she doesn't delay too long before keeping her promise.'

'And for now, captain?' Marciac wanted to know.

'For now,' the old gentleman replied, 'we wait.'

'Ah—'

'What? Do you have other plans?'

'Yes. Two of them. And both have very beautiful eyes.'

His dragonnet perched on his shoulder, Arnaud de Laincourt returned home from the *One-Eyed Tarasque* slightly drunk. He arrived at his house in rue de la Ferronnerie just as night was falling and found someone waiting outside for him. It was the man in the beige doublet who seemed to take great pleasure these past few days in dogging his footsteps without openly showing himself.

'Good evening, monsieur,' said the gentleman.

'Good evening. You were waiting for me, I see . . .'

'Indeed.'

'In vain, I fear.'

Without seeming to, Laincourt watched the darkening shadows around them carefully. Although there were still people travelling along rue de la Ferronnerie at this hour, it was never too early to carry out a well-executed ambush in Paris. Prudence was thus called for, until he knew exactly what the man in the beige doublet wanted from him. But the cardinal's former spy – for whom being alert to the slightest hint of danger was second nature – could detect no cause for alarm. And Maréchal, the old hurdy-gurdy player's dragonnet, remained placid.

'In vain? Could you not hear me out, before chasing me away?'

'I am not chasing you away, monsieur.'

'Grant me just a few moments of your time. I only ask that you listen to me.'

Laincourt was silent for a long while, examining the mysterious gentleman with an impassive eye. He was probably approaching forty years of age. Trim, fair-haired, with a well-kept moustache and royale beard, he was dressed elegantly but not ostentatiously. He had a frank and kindly demeanour, and his friendly eyes made no attempt to evade Laincourt's searching gaze.

'With your permission, it is time we had a certain conversation,' the gentleman insisted.

A window opened above them. It was done discreetly, but not so quietly that Laincourt failed to hear it. No doubt it was monsieur Laborde, the ribbon seller who possessed a shop on the ground floor and resided on the first floor with his family . . . unless it was his wife, or both of them, pressed together and lending a curious ear to the proceedings below. Laborde was the principal lodger in the house. Enjoying the landlord's complete trust, he collected other lodgers' rent and made it his business to maintain the respectability of the entire house. When Laincourt was still an ensign in His Eminence's Guards, the ribbon maker had sought his good graces by fawning over him. But now the young man had returned his cape – and done so under such troubling circumstances that it had even started rumours – matters had changed.

Still hesitating over whether he should allow the gentleman a hearing, Laincourt wondered what advice the hurdy-gurdy player would have provided in such a situation.

I would advise you not to have this conversation on the front doorstep. Especially not with that fat Laborde eavesdropping . . .

'Very well,' the former spy decided. 'Let's go inside.'

'Thank you, monsieur.'

Laincourt preceded the gentleman into a corridor that was both narrow and unlit, then led him up a staircase lacking both air and light. As they climbed, they kept a tight hold on the rickety banister, the former Cardinal's Guard cautioning the other man to be careful on the treacherous steps. Reaching the second floor, and allowing himself be guided by habit, Laincourt found his door in the dark. He opened it with his key and left it wide open to assist the mysterious gentleman, who was still groping his way forward. A shadowy grey light filled the small apartment and outlined a faint, irregular patch of the landing.

Having arrived home, Laincourt remained faithful to certain routines. First of all he detached the leash from Maréchal's collar. Then he made the dragonnet enter his cage, before striking a flame to light a candle. Those tasks accomplished, he filled the small reptile's bowl with water, removed his hat, hung up his baldric, and only then turned his attention to the gentleman who, hat in hand, was looking about him.

Laincourt's apartments consisted of two badly ventilated rooms. Very modest and poorly furnished, devoid of any personal note, they were nevertheless clean and tidy – obviously the abode of a bachelor who had never let himself slide into sloth.

'Monsieur,' said Laincourt, 'I only have one chair to offer you. Take it, I shall use this stool.'

'No need, monsieur. I shall not trouble you for long.'

'As you wish.'

'Permit me to introduce myself. I am the chevalier de Mirebeau and—'

'Just one thing, monsieur, before you continue.'

'Yes?'

'Speak softly. If anyone were to bother to listen, they would hear everything through this wretched floor,' indicated Laincourt, tapping his heel.

He imagined the Laborde couple below being showered with dust.

'I understand,' the gentleman replied in a lower tone.

'So what is it you want, monsieur de Mirebeau? I have spotted you, here and there, for the past week.'

'Forgive me, sir, but it has only been four days since I began observing you.'

'Six days. During the first two, you were trying to hide.'

Mirebeau admitted defeat:

'That's right.'

Laincourt didn't care if he was right or wrong.

'So? What do you want from me?'

'I have been charged with informing you, monsieur, that a certain party is surprised by the injustices that have been heaped upon you. This party is saddened to learn that you are alone and unemployed, and worries about your future.'

'So, I have a guardian angel looking out for me . . .'

'Your merits have not gone unnoticed, monsieur. Only a few weeks ago you wore the cape of His Eminence's Guards. You held the rank of ensign and you seemed destined for a lieutenancy. Without ever showing yourself to be unworthy of it, this cape was taken from you. Your name was then quietly cleared of any charges, but without the return of your cape, your rank or the honours that were your due. And then you were abandoned to your fate without further ado . . .'

Laincourt studied the gentleman's eyes and tried to read the truth hidden within them. What did he know, exactly? Was he aware of the circumstances under which Laincourt had been arrested and then dismissed from the Cardinal's Guards? Did he know of the dangerous double role the spy had played with the Black Claw's agents? Of the sacrifices he had been forced to make to complete his mission successfully? Laincourt had accepted the assignment knowing the consequences full well. And he had been aware that it would require forsaking his rank and his uniform, because he was familiar with the rules of the game.

But in him Mirebeau only saw a loyal servant, dismissed out of ingratitude or negligence, whose legitimate ambitions had been shattered.

And, therefore, he had come to offer Laincourt a new master:

'You know how the world works. One cannot get very far or rise very high without a benevolent protector. The person I serve would very much like to count you as a friend. I said that your merits have not gone unnoticed. Your virtues are also known. As are your talents, which would finally be appreciated at their true value. Your Spanish is excellent, I believe. And you are perfectly familiar with Madrid . . .'

Laincourt did not react to this. After all, it was no secret that he had spent two years at the Court of Dragons.

What he had actually been doing there, on the other hand . . .

'To be perfectly frank,' he finally replied, 'I don't believe I wish to offer my services to anyone . . .'

Mirebeau's face took on a kindly expression.

'Would you like to think it over? I understand, and I shall not insist.' He drew forth a note with a stamped seal from his sleeve. 'But at least do me the favour of paying a visit to . . . to your guardian angel. Here. Go to rue Saint-Thomas-du-Louvre. Present yourself on the day and the hour of your choosing and show them this. You shall be received.'

'All right,' said Laincourt, taking the note.

'I bid you a good evening, monsieur.'

The cardinal's former spy answered with a noncommittal smile, then watched the gentleman take his leave. He rose, went to the window, and soon saw Mirebeau come out into rue de la Ferronnerie and follow it east toward the Saint-Honoré neighbourhood. Without even thinking about it, Laincourt invoked the presence of the hurdy-gurdy player who approached to look over his shoulder.

You're not going to examine the seal on the letter, boy?

I don't need to see it to know at whose door I would be knocking.

No, of course not. There are only two noteworthy dwellings on rue Saint-Thomas-du-Louvre, after all.

Laincourt nodded as, with narrowed eyes, he continued to watch Mirebeau walking away into the distance.

One of them is the mansion of the marquise de Rambouillet. It's said she hosts a literary salon of the highest quality in her home.

True. But the other is the Hôtel de Chevreuse, and I rather think that is where your guardian angel is hoping to see you . . .

That night at the Hôtel de l'Épervier there reigned an atmosphere similar to the eve of battle. The Blades, assembled in the fencing room, found ways to quietly kill time in the candlelight. Leprat and Marciac played dice on a corner of the table. Ballardieu was balancing slowly back and forth on a tilted chair facing one of the windows, watching the night sky while he drank a glass of wine. Agnès was leafing through a treatise on fencing. Lying on a bench with his eyes shut, one knee bent, and his hands gathered on his chest, Saint-Lucq might have been asleep. And Almades was sharpening his rapier, giving it three long strokes with the whetstone before turning the blade over.

Three strokes along one edge . . .

. . . three strokes along the other.

Three strokes along one edge . . .

Naïs and monsieur Guibot had gone to their beds. Only the Blades remained, along with André who was guarding the saddled horses in the stables, and La Fargue who had retired to his office.

. . . three strokes along the other.

Three strokes along one edge . . .

All of them were booted and armed, ready to spring into action as soon as their captain gave the word for their departure. They only needed to seize their hats, jump into their saddles, and spur their mounts with their heels. Within the hour, they could be anywhere in Paris. Patiently, they awaited the order.

. . . three strokes along the other.

How would La Donna make her presence known? And, above all, when? Midnight was approaching. The Blades had been waiting all evening for a message or signal. The beautiful spy knew she was being hunted. She would have to be extremely careful. Would she use some indirect means to reestablish contact? But in that case, which one? The dragonnets? Yes, one of the twin dragonnets to which she seemed so attached could deliver a message. Here at the Hôtel de l'Éper-vier. Or at the Palais-Cardinal. Or even at the Louvre . . .

Three strokes along one edge . . .

. . . three strokes along the other.

'You win,' Leprat said to Marciac after a last unlucky roll of the dice.

'Another game?'

'No, thank you.'

The musketeer stood up.

'As you like,' the Gascon said. 'But you'll need to make up for lost ground eventually. Don't forget, you already owe me Piedmont and the duchy of Cleves.'

It was a game between the two of them. It started one day when, neither of them having even a sou in their pocket, they divided Europe up equitably between them and started betting with their territories. Whether they had subsequently come into funds or not, they had continued to play for these imaginary stakes ever since, keeping a careful account of their losses and gains.

Three strokes along one edge . . .

. . . three strokes along the other.

'Never fear, I won't forget,' said Leprat. 'No more than I shall forget winning the bishopric of Munster from you.'

Giving Marciac an amused smile, he went to knock on La Fargue's half-open door.

La Fargue had arranged for his personal use a small private office that communicated with the fencing room by a door and with the upper floors by means of a tiny spiral staircase, hidden behind a moveable wooden panel. Here he received visitors, meditated, and wrote reports to His Eminence. But he rarely shut the door.

This evening, like the Blades, he too waited in a silence measured out by the long, regular strokes of Almades's whetstone. Booted and armed, he was leaning back in his armchair with his crossed ankles up on his worktable. Pensive, he played with a small pendant that he normally wore around his neck, winding the chain around his index finger – first in

461

one direction, then the other. It was a worn, scratched, tarnished piece of jewellery which had a cover to protect the miniature portrait within. That of a woman La Fargue had loved long ago, but which also resembled closely the daughter they had produced together.

Grown into a young woman, that daughter had recently made a reappearance in his life. She had been in danger and he had been forced to take steps to protect her, putting her beyond the reach of both the Black Claw and Cardinal Richelieu's agents. But it had meant he was separated from her once again. He did not even know where she was now, as prudence dictated. But at least his mind was at rest, knowing there was nowhere his daughter would be safer than in the hands into which he had entrusted her.

La Fargue lifted his head and closed his fist over the pendant when he heard Leprat knock at his door.

'Yes?'

The musketeer entered.

'I'm afraid nothing is going to happen this evening,' he said.

'So am I.'

'It will soon strike midnight.'

'I know.'

'Should I order the horses unsaddled?'

'Let's give La Donna another hour to manifest herself.'

'Very well.'

At that same instant, Almades ceased sharpening his rapier. Leprat turned and saw André arriving, a letter in his hand.

'Where's the captain?' asked the groom.

The Spaniard pointed in the direction of the small private office. André crossed the fencing room, watched attentively by the whole company, as La Fargue and his lieutenant walked out to meet him. Agnès, Marciac, and Ballardieu rose to their feet. Almades sheathed his blade, now sharp as a razor. Saint-Lucq remained stretched out on the bench, but had turned on his side, his head propped up by one elbow.

'Captain,' said André, 'a rider just delivered this.'

'Thank you,' replied La Fargue, taking the letter from him.

The seal was Cardinal Richelieu's. The old captain split it open and unfolded the letter amidst a deep silence.

Everyone waited.

La Fargue read the contents, and then announced:

'La Donna presented herself at the Palais-Cardinal an hour ago.'

The others looked at him without understanding.

'She came to offer herself up as a prisoner,' he explained with a faint, ambiguous smile. 'And when you think about it, it's a clever move on her part . . .'

4

It was not the most well-known of the sixteen gates of Paris. It was not the most frequented, or the best defended. And once night fell, and the thick doors between the two massive towers were closed, it became a dark, silent edifice whose sinister calm would – ordinarily – go undisturbed until the following morning.

The dracs arrived shortly after midnight, their mounts walking in the black ground-hugging mist that accompanied them.

There were eight in all.

Seven vigorous black dracs and one other drac with pale scales, the colour of dirty bone. The black dracs were riding calm, powerful warhorses. Wearing gloves and boots, they were dressed like hired swordsmen. Wide leather belts were cinched around their waists and they had solid rapiers at their sides.

The other drac was unarmed. But he carried a large carved staff hung with various small fetishes: tiny bones, teeth, feathers, old scales. Dressed in stinking, filthy rags encrusted with what looked like dried blood, he rode bareback on a giant salamander whose belly grazed the black mist and whose slow, steady step set the pace for the whole group. The drac was very old. He was missing some teeth and his back was bent. His yellow eyes, however, gleamed with a lively spark. And a particularly virulent and baleful aura emanated from him.

The dracs drew to a halt on the narrow stone bridge that crossed over the fetid ditch before the gates. They waited, as the mist beneath them stretched out dark tendrils that snaked their way beneath the city gate in order to accomplish their task on the far side. The task did not take long. The tendrils immediately withdrew.

The old drac raised his staff in one gnarly hand, tipped with jagged yellow claws, and pointed it at the door.

He mumbled a few words in the drakish tongue.

The sound of scraping and several dull thuds could be heard inside.

And then the heavy doors opened, while the portcullis lifted with a clanking noise.

The archway, long and empty, was only lit by two sputtering torches. The dracs passed through it slowly, without sparing a glance for the dying pikeman who staggered out of the guards' lodge and stretched out an arm, trying to cry for help before he collapsed. He died, his body convulsing, retching up a black bile that ran from his mouth, nostrils and eyelids.

The dracs emerged from the gate and melted, one by one, into the shadowy streets of Paris.

II

La Renardière

Alessandra di Santi, also known as La Donna, had been awake since dawn. She rose carefully from her bed, trying not to disturb the two dragonnets still curled up asleep. Silently she went to sit by the window, half naked, with an old Italian song on her lips, methodically combing her hair. She was pale and beautiful, caressed by the dawn sunlight that warmed her long red tresses.

The young woman had a view of the garden and the entire domain of La Renardière – the name of the small castle where she had dwelt for the past five days – from her bedchamber. It was a hunting lodge, quite similar to the one which had just been finished for the king in Versailles. It comprised a central pavilion with two wings framing a courtyard, and to the front, beyond a dry moat crossed by a stone bridge, stood a forecourt flanked by the servants' quarters. Although in truth it lacked for nothing, La Renardière only provided the basic comforts. But the place was both discreet and peaceful, only an hour's ride from Paris, a short remove from the road to Meudon, and practically invisible behind some dense woodland.

In short, it was a perfect retreat.

Having combed her hair, Alessandra shook a little bell to warn the chambermaid – who had been graciously put at her disposal, along with an elegant wardrobe – that she wished to wash and dress. The clear tinkling sound attracted first Scylla, the female of the pair of black dragonnets and then her brother Charybdis, who followed close behind. The twins vied playfully for their mistress's affections. They jostled one another, craning their necks for a caress and rubbing their snouts against La Donna's throat and cheeks. She laughed, pretending to repel the small reptiles' assaults and gently scolding them for being such impudent little devils. An involuntary swipe of a claw scratched Alessandra's shoulder, but the wound closed almost immediately and the single drop of blood that had welled up slid down her perfectly healed skin.

The chambermaid's knock at the door interrupted their frolics.

She had been at La Renardière for five days. Five days of being taken, each morning, to Paris to be interrogated. Five days of being treated with a mixture of courtesy, wariness and resentment.

'This is your room, madame. And this is your key. At night please avoid leaning too far from your window. Someone might fire a musket at you by mistake.'

When she had presented herself at his door and made herself his prisoner the beautiful spy had placed the cardinal in an extremely delicate position. The Parlement of Paris – which was the kingdom's most important court of justice – had recently convicted her in absentia on several charges of corruption, blackmail and theft. And, for the most part, they were quite right in doing so. But Richelieu did not want her to be punished for these crimes: firstly, because the Pope was unlikely to allow her to be executed; secondly, because she was in a position to reveal State secrets which no one in Europe wished to see divulged; and thirdly, most crucially, because she claimed to have knowledge of a plot against Louis XIII and was demanding, before she would say more, that her life and liberty be guaranteed. But the Parlement was jealous of its authority and if it learned the truth, it would call for La Donna's immediate arrest. Once that happened, whatever was subsequently decided, the legal and political complications would accumulate – and as for the plot against His Majesty, they would be forced to wait until it was set in motion to discover its nature and scope . . .

Happily, the members of Parlement could not be displeased by things of which they remained ignorant. It was thus in greatest secrecy that Alessandra spent her mornings with a magistrate at Le Châtelet, where she was asked questions which she answered graciously, while always endeavouring not to say too much. She stayed at La Renardière the rest of the time, protected by musketeers. There were a dozen of them, who patrolled the grounds and occupied a small wooden pavilion in the woods by the entrance to the hunting lodge's grounds. But the young Italian woman was not fooled: the musketeers were there to keep a watch on her as much as they were to protect her, just as the domestic servants in the residence were there to spy on her as much as to serve her. All of them were Richelieu's people, as was the gentleman who acted as her bodyguard.

That one was a Cardinal's Blade.

Seated at her dressing table, Alessandra was finishing arranging her hair and attire to her satisfaction when there was a knock at the door.

'Come in, monsieur!'

It was Leprat. Freshly shaven, wearing boots, breeches, gloves, and a doublet, he was dressed in red, black and grey. His spurs jingling at each step, he entered the room with his hat in hand and his sword at his side.

'Good morning, monsieur le chevalier,' La Donna greeted him, her eyes on the mirror which the chambermaid slowly moved around her. 'Did you sleep well outside my door?'

'No, madame.'

The young woman pretended to be concerned. She turned theatrically in her seat and placed a hand to her throat.

'Did you sleep poorly, monsieur? Are you feeling ill?'

'No, madame.'

Alessandra went from worry to pouting anger, still play-acting.

'Then you must have slept elsewhere. That's very poor on your part. You abandoned me and I could have been assassinated. I'm very upset with you. I was happier when I thought you were ill . . .'

Leprat smiled.

'I was at your door, madame. But I didn't sleep. And I feel quite well.'

'Well, thank goodness on both counts! I am doubly reassured.'

Returning her attention to her toilette, La Donna continued to inspect her reflection in the mirror.

'Madame, would you be so good as to make haste. Your breakfast is served, and monsieur de La Houdinière will no doubt arrive soon.'

Irritated, La Donna snatched the mirror from the chambermaid's hands.

'Monsieur de La Houdinière shall have to wait,' she said. 'And in Paris, inside that depressing Châtelet where he insists on receiving me, monsieur de Laffemas can also wait. And, if necessary, the cardinal can wait too!'

'Madame. If you please . . .'

Alessandra caught Leprat's eye in the mirror.

She smiled at him, adjusted a curl of hair for form's sake, returned the mirror to the servant, and then rose to turn towards the former musketeer. She looked ravishing, in a snugly fitting but otherwise fairly plain brown-and-cream dress which nevertheless enhanced her pale skin, her red hair, and her pretty bosom. She seemed to be waiting for a compliment, but Leprat limited himself to a brief nod of approval.

The beautiful Italian woman had to satisfy herself with that and accepted the arm offered to her before passing into the antechamber.

Kh'Shak, the huge black drac, hesitated for a moment before opening the door and descending the stairs with a cautious step, almost on tiptoe, holding the scabbard of his rapier to keep it from knocking into anything.

The cellar was silent and warm, stingily lit by fat yellow candles whose flames gave off acrid wisps of smoke. The place reeked, filled with strong odours that would turn a human stomach but which were pleasant to drakish nostrils: the smell of blood, offal, and meat both fresh and spoiled.

The old pale-scaled drac was sitting cross-legged on the dirt floor. He was wearing the dirty, smelly rags that were his sole clothing, and his ceremonial staff – the big carved stick with its feathers, bones, scales, teeth, and coloured beads – was resting across his meagre thighs. Eyes shut, he sat completely still, hardly breathing at all. The gutted body of a small white goat lay before him. Other remains were rotting here and there, mutilated and half-devoured.

Halting at the bottom of the steps Kh'Shak hesitated again, as if afraid to enter the cellar completely and set foot on the spattered, blood-soaked floor where he knew awful rituals had been carried out. Yet he was by no means a coward. His courage and fierceness had earned him his position as chief.

But when it came to magic . . .

'Saaskir . . .' he ventured in a hoarse voice.

Saaskir. A drakish word meaning both priest and sorcerer, two notions that were blurred together in the dracs' tribal culture.

'Yes, Kh'Shak?' answered the old drac. 'What is it?'

The black drac cleared his throat. Still unmoving, his eyes still closed, the other had his back towards him.

'Have you found her, saaskir?'

'No, my son,' said the sorcerer in the calm, patient tone that one usually employed with small children. 'I haven't found her yet. La Donna has concealed herself behind seven veils. I rip one away each night, and soon, she will be revealed in full nudity beneath the Eye of the Night Dragon. Then I shall see and, after me, you will be the first to know . . .'

'Thank you, saaskir.'

Kh'Shak was about to turn away, still troubled, when the old drac called out to him:

'You're worried, aren't you?'

The great black drac wondered how he should reply. He opted for the truth.

'Yes, saaskir.'

'That's good. You are a chief. It is your role to worry about things others do not care about, to think of things which others forget, to see what others ignore . . . But as the days pass, your warriors are growing restless, and you're afraid you won't be able to restrain them for much longer.'

Was the saaskir casting doubt on his authority? Kh'Shak's blood began to boil.

'My warriors fear me and respect me! They shall obey!'

The old drac sorcerer gave a faint smile that the other could not see.

'Of course, of course . . . So, all is well?'

'Yes,' Kh'Shak was obliged to concur. 'All is well.'

A silence ensued, during which the black drac did not know what to do. Finally, the old sorcerer's sugary voice came again:

'Now, Kh'Shak, you must leave me. I need to rest.'

La Donna was finishing her cup of chocolate while a servant cleared away the remains of her breakfast. Sitting in an armchair, she eyed Leprat who was looking out of a window. He was watching the track that emerged from the woods and then ran in a straight line, crossing the forecourt between the servant quarters to the bridge over the dry moat.

Antoine Leprat, chevalier d'Orgueil.

One of Captain La Fargue's Blades, therefore. And a former member of the King's Musketeers, it would seem. Calm, reserved, courteous, and watchful. Probably incorruptible. In a word: irreproachable. Tall, dark-haired and grimeyed. Attractive, to those who liked mature men whose faces had been marked by the years, and by their ordeals. He had a brutal side to him. This Leprat knew how to fight and had no fear of violence. His muscular body was doubtless covered with scars . . .

Alessandra di Santi's glance must have been too intense in the silence, because Leprat felt it and turned to her. She did not make the mistake of suddenly averting her eyes, which would have been a tacit admission of a guilty sentiment.

Instead, cleverly, she chose to conceal the motive of her interest.

'Where did you acquire that strange sword, chevalier?'

As always, Leprat had his white rapier at his side, a single piece of ivory carved, from tip to pommel, out of an Ancestral

Dragon's tooth. It was an extraordinary, formidable weapon, lighter and yet more resilient than even the best Toledo blade.

'It was entrusted to me.'

'By whom? Under what circumstances?'

The former musketeer smiled and turned his head back to the window without answering. His eyes drifted towards the tree line.

'Come now, monsieur,' the beautiful spy insisted. 'We've shared this roof and most of our waking hours for several days and I still know almost nothing about you.'

'Just as I know almost nothing about you. No doubt it's best that way.'

Alessandra rose and walked slowly up to Leprat, approaching him from behind as he continued to gaze outside.

'But I only desire that you know me better, monsieur le chevalier. Ask me questions, and I'll answer them . . .'

'I leave the task of questioning you to monsieur de Laffemas.'

'Would a little chocolate soften you? There's some left.'

Turning from the window, Leprat suddenly found himself in close proximity to La Donna. She had drawn so near they were almost touching. Shorter than him, she looked up at him over the rim of the cup, which she held against her moist half-opened lips.

Her eyes were smiling.

'Do you like chocolate, monsieur le chevalier?'

'I . . . I don't know.'

'You've never tasted it?'

'No.'

Not widely known previously in France, chocolate now enjoyed some slight notoriety since Queen Anne d'Autriche, who had acquired a taste for it during her childhood in Spain, asked that it be served to her in the Louvre. Still reserved for the rich elite, chocolate was, curiously enough, sold by apothecaries.

'It's delicious,' murmured Alessandra. With both hands she raised her cup to Leprat's mouth. 'Here, try some . . .'

Their glances met, hers seductive, his troubled.

For an instant that slowly stretched between them, the former musketeer almost gave in to temptation . . .

. . . but the chambermaid – knocking and then immediately entering the room – broke the spell. She brought La Donna's gloves, cloak, and hat. Having surprised Leprat, who quickly drew back, she acted as if she had seen nothing.

'Bah!' said Alessandra, shrugging and turning away. 'It's gone cold now, in any case . . .'

Leprat found La Renardière's maître d'hôtel already on the front porch, waiting as usual.

'Monsieur.'

'Good morning, Danvert.'

Together they watched a coach pass over the dry moat and enter the courtyard. Twelve cavaliers escorted the vehicle, all of them Cardinal's Guards armed with swords and short muskets, although they did not wear the cape. Monsieur de La Houdinière rode at their head. He was the company's new captain and the successor to sieur de Saint-Georges, who had died a month earlier under circumstances which were so infamous that they remained secret, to the satisfaction of all concerned.

The coach drew to a halt at the bottom of the steps. La Houdinière leapt down from his saddle and went over to Leprat. They shook hands like men who held one another in esteem but who could not permit themselves to fraternise – for the first belonged to His Eminence's Guards, while the second remained, even if he had momentarily hung up his cape, a member of His Majesty's Musketeers. There was a traditional rivalry between these two corps, and a lively one: it was a rare fortnight which passed without a guard and a musketeer engaging in a duel for one reason or another.

La Houdinière and Leprat, however, were on good terms.

Their acquaintance had begun when they fought together the previous year, when Louis XIII had marched on Nancy for the second time – and before he had to for a third – at the head of his army to persuade Duke Charles IV of Lorraine to show better sentiments towards the king of France. On the 18th of June, a cavalry regiment from Lorraine had been holding one of the crossings over the Meuse river, close to the small town of Saint-Mihiel and not far from the king's quarters. Hostilities had not really commenced yet – in fact, Charles IV was continuing to parley – but Louis XIII was determined to strike a lightning blow as a demonstration of force. A unit of elite soldiers drawn from the Navarre regiment, the gendarmerie, the light cavalry, the King's Musketeers, and the Cardinal's Guards had therefore been placed under the comte d'Allais's command. La Houdinière – who was then still a lieutenant – and Leprat had been among this elite. Surprised, trapped in their trenches, and soon stricken by panic, Lorraine's forces had suffered a terrible defeat. It had been a massacre which few had survived.

Later the two men's paths had often crossed, but they had not worked closely together again until now. They shared the responsibility of guarding La Donna, Leprat here at La Renardière and La Houdinière during her daily journeys to Le Châtelet, where the spy was interrogated. They thus met twice a day, when the one relieved the other.

'Is everything all right?' asked La Houdinière.

'Yes,' replied Leprat. 'Any orders from the Palais-Cardinal?'

'None.'

And that was everything that needed to be said.

Wearing her cloak and hood, Alessandra soon made her appearance, smiling and unruffled. Ever a gentleman, La Houdinière opened the coach door for her and lent her his hand as she climbed into the passenger compartment. Then he remounted his horse and, after a final salute to Leprat, gave the signal to depart.

The former musketeer stood for a moment watching the coach and its escort move off. He was tired but could not rest just yet.

He turned to Danvert, the maître d'hôtel, who was waiting patiently.

'Let's go,' he said, returning inside. 'We have much to do.'

The old woman was sitting in a peaceful, sunny garden in one of the numerous convents in the faubourg Saint-Jacques.

She spent the better part of her days here, when the heat was bearable, reading and biding her time in an armchair that was brought out from her bedchamber for her. Otherwise she shared the ordinary life of the nuns, punctuated by prayers and meals. She was not obliged to do so, but it suited the character she had invented for herself, that of a rich, pious widow, weary of the world and desiring to pass the last years of her life in retreat from it. Within the convent she was known as madame de Chantegrelle. Only a month earlier, however, she had been the vivacious vicomtesse de Malicorne and, thanks to magic, had looked less than twenty years old. An age which was scarcely more deceptive than the one her present appearance suggested. For her true age was a number of years which stretched far beyond the ordinary span. Ordinary for human kind, that is.

But she was a dragon.

The so-called madame de Chantegrelle lifted her eyes from her book and sighed as she considered both the garden and the life that was hers at present. She had loved being the vicomtesse de Malicorne. She'd possessed youth, beauty, wealth, and power. All of Paris had courted her and vied for her favours. What a shame to have been forced to abandon that role! Officially, the vicomtesse had perished in a fire that had left nothing of her but a charred, unrecognisable corpse – in point of fact, that of some wretched woman taken from the gutter. It was a tragic loss but an almost banal event in Paris, where fire was the cause of many fatal accidents . . .

The truth was, the ritual intended to mark her triumph had instead brought about her ruin. Anyone but her would not have survived the ordeal, no doubt. But that did not assuage her regrets. And it did nothing to diminish the desire for revenge that burned inside her. If not for Cardinal Richelieu, if not for Captain La Fargue and his cursed Blades, today she would have been at the head of the first Black Claw lodge ever founded in France . . .

The sound of a light footstep on the gravel garden path drew madame de Chantegrelle's attention. A nun approached her and, after making sure she wasn't asleep, whispered a few words in her ear. The old woman nodded before turning her head to look at her announced visitor, who stood a short distance away beneath a stone arch covered with climbing roses in flower. A fleeting expression of surprise and fear passed across her face, but she greeted her visitor with a polite smile and extended a hand to be kissed.

The man was dressed as a gentleman, in grey and black, with a sword at his side. He might have been fifty or fifty-five years of age. He was an intimidating figure: tall, rather thin, and hieratic in bearing. He had an emaciated oval face with strangely smooth skin, as if it had been stretched a little too tight over the ridges of his face, and a morbid, sickly pallor. His icy grey eyes crinkled up whenever he coughed – with a dry, brief, guttural sound – into the handkerchief which he dabbed at his fine, livid lips.

Like the woman he now joined, he was a dragon. He had borne many names, some of which she had learned. But the one he preferred was a *nom de guerre*: the *Alchimiste des Ombres*, the Alchemist of the Shadows. Where had it originated, exactly? She didn't know. In any case, it was by this pseudonym – or sometimes merely by a sign featuring an 'A' and an 'O' intertwined – that the Black Claw designated one of its best independent agents.

A novice having brought him a chair, the Alchemist sat down with a nod – not so much in thanks but rather in acknowledgement of the chair being placed at his disposal, as a matter of course.

'I have known of your setbacks for some time, madame. But I have only now had the opportunity to pay you a visit. Please forgive me.'

'My "setbacks",' noted the old woman. 'How kindly put—'

'I will add, in my defence, that it was hardly easy to find you.'

'What can I say? Madame de Chantegrelle is far more discreet than the vicomtesse de Malicorne. And who would concern themselves with a dying old lady living out her final days in a convent, surrounded by sisters whose affection for her was ensured by bequeathing to them what remains of her fortune?'

The Alchemist gave one of his rare smiles, which barely lifted the corners of his thin lips. Like all dragons, he was amused by human religions and the shortcomings of their representatives. His race had no other form of worship than that of ancestors, no other divinities than the Ancestral Dragons whose existence, even in times immemorial, was not subject to doubt.

'Do you lack money, madame?'

'No, thank you. But I am touched by your concern, although it does seem to me that your visit cannot be one of pure courtesy.'

'Madame, I—'

'No, monsieur. Don't defend yourself on this subject; you would only be lying, after all . . .' She sighed. 'I am indeed most ungrateful in reproaching you. Since . . . since my setbacks, visitors have been rare. The Black Claw is quick to forget anyone who can no longer serve it. I do not regret that – I'm happy to still be alive. I imagine I owe it to my birth, to my rank. And perhaps because they believe I've been rendered harmless once and for all—'

'I wager that they are mistaken on that point.'

'Do you really think so?'

The former vicomtesse looked at the Alchemist.

'Yes,' he said, returning her gaze without wavering.

It meant nothing, she knew that.

Nevertheless, she chose to believe that he was sincere.

'I just need to rest, hence my self-imposed retreat here. And then one day, when I have recovered some semblance of my past power—'

She broke off, eyes shining and lost in the distance . . .

The Alchemist waited for her to return from her dreams of restored glory. But perhaps those dreams had carried her too far away. After a moment, he heard her murmuring, as she nodded her head vaguely:

'Yes . . . Some rest . . . I only need some rest . . .'

*

The inn, a little way from Vincennes on the road to Champagne, was full of soldiers going to join their regiment at Châlons-sur-Marne. Swords, daggers and pistols lay on all the tables; muskets and halberds leant against the walls. The noisy, mixed-up, indistinct, but warlike conversations reverberated around the common room where a golden light poured in through the windows. Mocking sallies were thrown above heads wreathed in pipe smoke. Other jests answered them and loud laughter erupted.

Captain La Fargue entered and, from the inn's threshold, where his impressive silhouette was outlined against daylight and blocked the exit, he surveyed the assembly with a slow glance. Eyes narrowed, he did not find the person he was looking for, while ignoring the curious looks that were being warily cast in his direction. Anyone but him would no doubt have drawn some remark that would have started a fight. But none of the soldiers present were stupid enough or drunk enough to pick a quarrel with a man like La Fargue.

A rare kind of man, intimidating and dangerous.

Entering in turn, Almades approached the captain from behind and said in his ear:

'Round the back.'

La Fargue nodded and, accompanied by the Spaniard, went out into the sunny back yard. There he found the comte de Rochefort, who was playing skittles with a group of gentlemen.

Seeing who had arrived, the cardinal's henchman took his time to aim, launched the ball, and managed a fairly good throw. Satisfied, he rubbed his hands together while his playing companions congratulated him. He thanked them, excused himself, finally nodded to the captain of the Blades, and went to recover his doublet which he had removed in order to play more comfortably. Putting it back on, he invited La Fargue to sit with him at a small table beneath a tree. There was a glass and a jug placed upon it. Rochefort drank from the glass and La Fargue, provocatively, from the jug.

'Please, help yourself,' said the cardinal's man ironically.

The old gentleman soldier gazed at him steadily. And for

481

good measure, without blinking, he wiped his mouth with the back of his hand and smacked his lips.

'How very elegant . . .'

'What do you want, Rochefort? I have better things to do than watch you play skittles.'

The comte nodded vaguely. He glanced distractedly at their surroundings, and then took a deep breath as he collected his thoughts. Finally, in an almost casual tone, he asked:

'What do you make of La Donna?'

La Fargue sighed and leaned back in his chair.

'My opinion of her has not changed,' he replied in a weary voice. 'I believe we cannot trust the woman. But I also believe she has come to us with a story that forces us to give her allegations serious consideration. For even if it were the duchesse de Chevreuse herself claiming to denounce a plot against the king . . .' At these words, Rochefort raised an eyebrow, but the captain was not deterred. 'Even if La Donna were La Chevreuse, I say, we would have to lend her an attentive ear.'

'The cardinal is of the same mind as you. Moreover, there is this . . .'

Rochefort discreetly pushed something across the table to La Fargue, an object which looked very much like a jewel case made of precious wood. The captain took it, opened it, and saw a black wax seal inside, still attached to the torn corner of a sheet of parchment.

'That was in the packet La Donna gave you, not long ago, to deliver to His Eminence. Do you know what it is?'

La Fargue sat up in his chair.

'Yes. This is a Black Seal. Each of them contains a drop of dragon's blood, used by the Black Claw to seal its most precious documents . . .' He returned the case, and Rochefort pocketed it immediately. 'So the Black Claw is a player in this game.'

'In one fashion or another, yes.'

'What does La Donna say on this matter?'

The cardinal's man grimaced.

'Not much . . . neither on this matter nor, indeed, on any

other. According to Laffemas she has no equal when it comes to answering a question without saying anything . . .'

For several days now, the beautiful Alessandra di Santi had been transported in secret to a room in Le Châtelet and interrogated, also in the greatest secrecy, all morning. Monsieur de Laffemas conducted these sessions. Beginning his career as an advocate in Parlement, then a master of petitions, he had since been appointed a state councillor. He enjoyed the confidence and esteem of Richelieu, to whom he owed a great deal. Now, at the age of fifty, he was the lieutenant of civil affairs at Le Châtelet, that is to say, one of the two magistrates – the other being the lieutenant of criminal affairs – who worked as deputies to the provost of Paris. An honest, rigorous and devoted man, Isaac de Laffemas was in charge of State prosecutions and therefore the object of enduring hatred due to his role in the great trials ordered by the cardinal.

Thinking about the man's difficulties with La Donna, La Fargue couldn't prevent himself from letting a smile show. Rochefort saw it and also smiled, adding:

'To top it all, without a doubt, is the fact that Laffemas always comes out feeling quite pleased with himself. It is only when he reads the minutes of his interrogation that he realises how, every time, La Donna has not answered the question, or only very partially, or she has merely repeated information she has already given him, and which wasn't worth very much to begin with. She mixes truth and falsehood, all the while cleverly wielding allusion, innuendo, digression, hollow phrases and misleading revelations. She knows how to play at being naïve, foolish, forgetful and charming by turn. Poor Laffemas is losing his wits as well as his sleep over her. And yet, he still returns each morning determined not to let her get the best of him—'

Rochefort was interrupted by the skittles players, applauding an able bowler.

'Very well,' said La Fargue. 'La Donna is leading Laffemas around by the nose. But it's only fair . . . After all, she promised to tell us what she knows of this plot on the condition that

483

she is protected. That means a pardon, without which she will always be persecuted in France. In accordance with the sentences passed by the Parlement, her proper place, right now, is in prison. She knows this full well and, unless she is subjected to torture, she will remain silent on the essential question until she receives her guarantees.'

'The cardinal is not in a position to offer her such guarantees right now. And time is running out. Not simply because we believe the date of execution of the plot against His Majesty is fast approaching. But also because each day that goes by increases the chances that La Donna's presence will be discovered. And when it reaches the ears of the members of the Parlement—'

'The king can annul a ruling by the Parlement, in his Council. He has that power.'

'Certainly. But will he want to use it?'

La Fargue raised an astonished eyebrow.

'Do you mean to say that His Majesty does not know what is going on?'

Rochefort ignored the question:

'Whenever the king annuls a ruling it's always a very unpopular decision. The Parlement protests loudly, everyone gets stirred up, and there are inevitably a few brave souls ready to stoke the people's anger and cry tyranny . . . And kings dislike it when there are rumblings among the people. Especially on the eve of a war.'

'Lorraine.'

'Yes, Lorraine . . . You see, La Fargue, to succeed without making too many waves, these sorts of affairs have to be carefully arranged. Public opinion has to be prepared, some loyalties have to be bought in advance, favourable pamphlets have to be written, suitable rumours propagated . . . It's much easier than you probably think, but it demands care, money and, above all, time. And time is what we lack most . . .'

La Fargue was starting to take full stock of the problem: a spy who would or could not talk, a plot threatening the king looming on the horizon, and an hourglass whose sands were already funnelling downwards.

After a brief moment of reflection, he asked:
'What are His Eminence's orders?'

Holding the door, Leprat waited patiently while Danvert gave
Alessandra di Santi's bedchamber a final but thorough glance.

This had been their routine since La Donna came to stay at
La Renardière. Each morning, as soon as the coach which took
her to Le Châtelet departed, they visited her apartments.
Leprat supervised, although his presence was not truly necessary. The domestic servants the cardinal had so graciously
assigned to serve the lady spy knew their business. They did
not content themselves with observing her every deed and
gesture and making daily reports. They also inspected her
bedchamber and antechamber with a fine-tooth comb, under
the maître d'hôtel's keen eye, and he – rather than Leprat –
directed their search and ensured that nothing was overlooked.

Danvert was alert and gave precise orders, but otherwise
said little. He was about fifty years old. With his trim figure,
grey hair and the naturally hale complexion of Mediterranean
folk, he had devoted his life to providing perfect service. He
was gifted with all the qualities of the best maîtres d'hôtel,
whose duty was to ensure the smooth running of a household
and to manage the domestic staff. That is to say, he was
discreet, intelligent, honest, attentive, and foresighted. But he
also had a flaw that was very common in his profession: a type
of arrogance inspired by the sense – often well-founded – of
being indispensable.

In practice, he was the true master of La Renardière.
Assisted by a staff which was at his beck and call, he kept the
premises in readiness to welcome any guest on short notice,
even in the middle of the night, to stay for any length of time
from a few hours to days or even weeks on end. He was aware
of the exceptional nature of the guests the cardinal received
here. It seemed he was never surprised by anything, did not
ask to know any more than was necessary, and performed
his duties with zeal without ever becoming emotional about
his work. Leprat quickly took his measure and came to rely

on him, in the same way that a good officer would rely on an experienced sergeant. It was a decision that the former musketeer was not given cause to regret, and on which he congratulated himself the first time he witnessed the servants' systematic search of La Donna's apartments: Danvert clearly knew what he was doing.

'A problem?' asked Leprat when the maître d'hôtel hesitated.

Only the two of them remained in Alessandra's antechamber.

Danvert was chewing on his lower lip, a certain sign of perplexity. He did not answer, and, acting on an impulse, he went over to the cage where Alessandra's dragonnets were cooped up. One of the twins – no doubt the male, Charybdis – growled at him when he checked the padlock securing the little door.

That done, the maître d'hôtel finally decided to leave and, in passing, gave Leprat an apologetic look for making him wait. But the Blade gave him a reassuring glance in return.

'It would be simpler if we knew what we were looking for, wouldn't it?'

'Indeed, monsieur. We can never be too careful.'

Leprat closed the door, turned the key twice in the lock, and the two men walked away.

'I'm going to get some sleep,' announced the former musketeer, stifling a yawn. 'Wake me if you need me.'

'Very good, monsieur.'

The dragonnets waited for the voices and the sound of footsteps to fade away in the distance.

Once calm was restored to the deserted bedchamber, Scylla's eyes sparkled and the padlock opened with a click. Charybdis immediately pushed the little door open with a clawed foot. The twins escaped from their cage and swooped up the chimney flue. They emerged into the sunlight in a puff of soot that went unnoticed below and which – even had it been seen – would have had no clear cause. For although they were not invisible the two dragonnets had become translucent, looking as if they were made of a very pure water that barely disturbed the passage of light.

After some joyful and expert aerial acrobatics, Scylla called her brother back to their duties and they sped off towards Paris together.

2

At the Hôtel de l'Épervier, they were waiting for La Fargue.

The Blades were gathered in the garden, in the shade of the chestnut tree, around the weather-bleached old table whose legs were tangled in the tall weeds. Agnès and Marciac were playing draughts while Ballardieu watched the game, sucking on his unlit clay pipe. Saint-Lucq, sitting casually nearby, as impassive as ever behind his red spectacles, juggled with a dagger. And Almades, leaning back against the tree trunk with his arms crossed, simply waited. Leprat was missing, and for good reason: he had orders not to leave La Renardière where La Donna was due to return early in the afternoon, under close guard. Glasses of wine and a bowl of juicy fruit attracted buzzing insects to the table, standing in the dappled sunlight which filtered through the chestnut tree's leaves.

La Fargue finally arrived. He took a seat – turning a chair until its back was against the table, and straddling it – and they all listened to his words closely.

'Here's what it's all about,' he began. 'You know that since she gave herself up La Donna has been interrogated in secret at Le Châtelet every morning, by the Paris provost's lieutenant for civil affairs.'

'Monsieur de Laffemas,' Agnès noted.

'Laffemas, yes. He is both honest and tenacious. He can be difficult at times, but he's hardly the monster that some people claim. In any case, he's smart and not easily fooled. In short, he seemed to be the perfect man to worm information out of La Donna—'

'But?' Marciac interrupted.

'But La Donna is causing problems. Without her smile ever

faltering, she deceives, lies, and evades him. Days have passed without her saying very much about what she has done or learned since she began her career as a spy.'

'And concerning the plot?' asked Saint-Lucq.

'On that subject,' the old gentleman answered, 'she hasn't even pretended to respond. She simply repeats, over and over, that the cardinal knows the price of that information. Laffemas has tried to learn a little more with indirect questions and falsely innocent allusions to the matter, but in vain. So far, La Donna has always seen straight through Laffemas's game and she's played her own cards marvellously.'

'She's a crafty bitch,' the half-blood said. 'But then, no one succeeds in her line of work by being an imbecile—'

'Or ugly,' added Marciac. 'Is she as beautiful as they say? Could I relieve Leprat? He must be getting bored out there, all alone at La Renardière—'

Agnès gave a ringing laugh, and Saint-Lucq smiled at the crudeness of this manoeuvre.

'Out of the question,' said La Fargue with absolute seriousness.

'But—'

'I said no.'

'All right!'

The Gascon shrugged his shoulders and, sulking a little, poured himself a glass of wine. The young baronne de Vaudreuil gave him a sympathetic pat on the back.

Then she declared:

'On this point at least, La Donna has never been mysterious: she has always said that she will reveal the details of the plot against the king in exchange for the cardinal's protection. But she's still waiting to receive that protection. How can we reproach her for remaining silent on the subject? What could she possibly hope to gain by speaking before she obtains her guarantees? She's not an idiot—'

'But that's where the shoe pinches,' said La Fargue.

'How's that?' asked Ballardieu in his loud voice, frowning.

'The cardinal cannot give La Donna his protection while she's considered to be a criminal, which is what she will continue to be until she's acquitted of the crimes she's been convicted of. Or until the king pardons her.'

'But we're taking about La Donna!' Agnès exclaimed. 'Clearing the name of the adventuress would require a rehabilitation trial that would be a parody of justice!'

'And for that same reason, the king cannot pardon her with the stroke of a quill without risking a scandal,' La Fargue acknowledged. 'In short, La Donna is asking for something she knows is impossible—'

'Let's not forget . . .' added Almades in a flat tone which nonetheless drew everyone's attention, 'Let's not forget that time is against La Donna as well as us—'

'What?' said the Gascon, astonished.

'Let us suppose that there is in truth a plot against the king. A plot about which she has some vital intelligence. What will happen if the plotters make their move while La Donna is still at His Eminence's mercy?'

Agnès understood:

'The cardinal will be merciless.'

'And La Donna will be lucky if this adventure doesn't end in a noose,' concluded Marciac.

The Spanish fencing master nodded.

'So what game is she playing at?' the baronne de Vaudreuil wondered.

'That is precisely what the cardinal wants us to discover,' declared La Fargue with enough authority to retake control of the debate and nip any further idle speculation in the bud.

The others all turned back to him and waited for him to continue.

'Let's start by finding those black dracs who are hunting La Donna. They know more about her than we do, and if we could learn why they are tracking her . . . Besides the cardinal would be pleased to hear they have been prevented from doing any further mischief.'

'How do we find them?' enquired Saint-Lucq.

'They are somewhere in Paris. They arrived five days ago.'

This piece of news aroused surprise. Then Ballardieu, who read the gazettes avidly, recalled that the previous week the guards at one of the Paris gates had been found dead without any clues as to who had killed them. The authorities had quickly removed the bodies. Was there a connection between the dracs' arrival in the capital and the deaths of these unfortunate men?

'Yes,' La Fargue asserted. 'One of the guards survived a few days in a delirious state. He spoke of dracs and of a "creeping black death". The cardinal's master of magic thinks it's the same black mist that accompanies our dracs . . . By the way, Agnès and Marciac, you will be seeing him this afternoon.'

'The master of magic?' asked the Gascon.

'The cardinal believes he can be useful to us.'

'Good,' said Agnès.

The old captain then turned to Saint-Lucq:

'As for you—'

'I know,' replied the half-blood. 'If the dracs have been in Paris for five days without being spotted, there is only one place they can be . . . Do you have any special instructions?'

'No. Find them, that's all. And don't get yourself killed . . . For my part, I will be meeting a man Rochefort claims knows La Donna well, who might be able to help us pin her down.'

'Who?' Marciac asked distractedly, observing bitterly that the bottle of wine was empty.

'Do you remember Laincourt?'

'The man Richelieu wanted us to recruit last month? The one who refused?'

Listening to the Gascon, one might wonder which crime, in his eyes, weighed more heavily against the former Cardinal's Guard: having almost become a member of the Blades out of favouritism, or having declined the offer?

'The very same.'

Marciac pulled a face.

'He saved my life at risk of his own,' Agnès said in a conciliatory tone.

'So what?' the Gascon retorted in perfectly bad faith. 'We save each other's lives all the time and we don't make a song and dance out of it—'

The captain clapped his hands and stood:

'Get going!' he cried. 'Into your saddles!' And then, in an almost paternal manner, he added: 'And watch out for yourselves.'

The group of people in the service of any great personage formed his 'household'. Thus one might speak of the king's household, or those of the queen, the duc d'Orléans and the marquis de Châteauneuf. As social customs required that everyone lived in a manner befitting their birth and rank, some households could have as many as two thousand servants all of whom had to be paid, fed, dressed, lodged, and looked after as needed. This applied especially to the king's household, but also to that of Cardinal Richelieu. And it cost fortunes.

Numerous, prestigious, and particularly onerous to maintain, the cardinal's household was commensurate in size with the rank of the public figure it served. It was composed of a military household and a civil household. Devoted to the protection of His Eminence, the military household comprised a company of horse guards, a company of musketeers and a third unit of gendarmes, which was generally deployed in military campaigns. In practice, the right to maintain a military household amounted to possessing a small private army. It was thus a privilege the king rarely granted. But the numerous plots aimed at Richelieu had made it necessary in his case, as well as a mark of the trust which Louis XIII accorded his chief minister.

The cardinal's civil household encompassed all those who were not men of war. In addition to the multitude of domestic servants, kitchen boys, and stable hands, along with other minor employees occupied with necessary but largely anonymous tasks, it included: a high almoner and master of the chamber who filled the role of general superintendent and thus controlled the household's purse strings; a confessor; three auxiliary almoners; secretaries; squires and gentlemen servants, all well-born, the first looking after the cardinal's horses and teams, the second accompanying him about his duties or carrying out delicate missions on his behalf; five valets who commanded the lackeys in livery; a maître d'hôtel who reigned over the ordinary staff and dealt with suppliers; a bursar; three chefs, each assisted by their own cooks; four wine stewards; a bread steward; two coachmen and four postillions; a mule driver; and porters.

To which list, one could add a physician, an apothecary, and two surgeons.

Plus one master of magic.

Every great household had to have one. Of course as the practice of draconic magic was against the law, masters of magic were not themselves magicians. Or, at least, they weren't supposed to be. But their knowledge of dragons and associated arcana was much sought after in order to detect and thwart any possible threats. Some of them called themselves astrologers or seers; others were doctors or philosophers; some were even men of the Church. Many were simply charlatans or incompetents. However, for a select few scholars, draconic magic was an object of serious study which required a reasoned approach.

The cardinal's master of magic was named Pierre Teyssier. He possessed a brilliant and original mind and although Richelieu rarely called on his services he did finance Teyssier's research and publications, in his capacity as a patron and friend of the sciences.

Teyssier lived in rue des Enfants-Rouges, and he was expecting a visit from the Cardinal's Blades.

Agnès and Marciac, accompanied by Ballardieu, decided to go to rue des Enfants-Rouges on horseback and thus spare their boots from contact with the foul Parisian muck, which – in addition to being sticky and smelly – was corrosive and ruined even the best leathers. They would also be able to breathe more easily, with their heads above the crowds in the streets which would soon become oppressive in this heat. Indeed, they made a detour in order to take the Pont Neuf across the Seine, more to benefit from the breeze from the river than from the lively street entertainers performing there. This bridge, unlike others in the city, was not lined with houses, making it possible to enjoy the open air, as well as the unique view of the capital's river banks.

Having travelled along the quays, however, they were finally forced to return to the stuffy, noisy, and polluted atmosphere of the city's streets. With Ballardieu bringing up the rear, the three Blades crossed the narrow, populous Place de Grève, in front of the Hôtel de Ville, without even glancing at the bodies rotting on the gallows. Next they took rue des Coquilles and rue Barre-du-Bec, tiny mediaeval alleys where passers-by were tightly squeezed, then rue Sainte-Avoye and rue du Temple, until they reached their destination.

Located in the northeast of the capital, rue des Enfants-Rouges was named after the hospital of the same name, a hospice for orphans whose little inmates were dressed in red. The neighbourhood was peaceful, still dotted with cultivated fields and dominated by the hulking donjon that rose in the Enclos du Temple. Surrounded by a crenelated wall, this former residence of the Templar knights now belonged to the Order of the Chatelaine Sisters. Marciac pointed out the house La Fargue had described to them before they left the Hôtel de l'Épervier.

'This one,' he said.

He and Agnès dismounted, knocked at the door, introduced themselves to the old manservant who came to open up, and followed him inside. Ballardieu was left with the horses. There was a stall selling refreshment further up the street and the former soldier, with his eyes shining and his mouth dry, cheerfully envisaged a long wait.

'Don't get drunk,' the young baronne warned him before they parted.

Ballardieu made his promise and went off, leading the mounts by the bridle.

The cool air inside the magic master's dwelling was pleasant.

As they waited in an antechamber Marciac removed his brown felt hat and wiped his brow. Agnès envied the comfortable casualness of his attire; she, too, would have liked to go about with her shirt collar wide open and her doublet unbuttoned, although in honesty she had little cause for complaint. True, the thick leather corset that cinched her waist was a little heavy, but her riding outfit – with breeches and boots – was far more practical than the starched dresses that polite society would have normally imposed on her given her gender and rank. Polite society which the baronne Agnès Anne Marie de Vaudreuil blithely chose to ignore.

'What?' asked the Gascon, noticing her watching him out of the corner of her eye.

'Nothing,' she said at first. Then she added impishly, 'That's a pretty doublet.'

They were standing side by side, looking straight ahead, in an antechamber which was almost devoid of furnishings.

'Are you mocking me?' asked Marciac warily.

He feigned nonchalance, if not indifference, towards his clothing, but was in fact quite careful of the image that he presented and even fastidious in his own fashion.

'No!' Agnès protested, hiding a smile.

'Then, thank you,' he retorted, without looking at her.

The doublet in question was a crimson garment that Marciac had not been seen wearing before his long, solitary mission to La Rochelle. The cloth was of quality and the cut elegant. It must have been expensive, yet all of the Blades knew full well that the Gascon chased after two things in life: money and skirts. And he was only ever lacking for money.

'A gift?' Agnès persisted.

'No.'

'I deduce, then, that you have funds. Did the cards smile on you?'

The Gascon shrugged and said modestly:

'Yes they did, rather . . .'

'In La Rochelle?' the baronne asked with some surprise.

La Rochelle had been the Protestant capital of France since the failed siege in 1628 and the withdrawal of the royal armies. Agnès genuinely doubted that gambling dens abounded there, so Marciac was either lying to her or he was hiding something, but she was not given the occasion to ferret out the truth. Someone was coming.

They had expected to see the manservant who had asked them to wait. Instead a young man entered, barely twenty years of age. Perhaps less. He looked like some student from the Sorbonne, with wrinkled clothes, a badly buttoned waist-coat, short but tangled blond hair, a joyful almost impudent air and his hands still damp, as if he had just finished drying himself with a towel after a wash.

One of the master's pupils, no doubt.

'My apologies for keeping you waiting,' he said. 'I know your visit was announced, but . . .'

He did not complete his sentence, but smiled and looked at the visitors.

After a moment of hesitation, Marciac explained:

'We're here to meet with His Eminence's master of magic.'

'Yes, of course,' the young man replied, still smiling.

And as he stood before them in expectant silence, realisation dawned upon the two Blades and they glanced at one another in astonishment.

It was Agnès who guessed first:

'I beg your pardon, monsieur, but would you be—'

'Pierre Teyssier, at your service, madame. How can I be of use to you?'

Laincourt pushed the door open and entered the cool dim interior of the small esoteric bookshop with pleasure. Removing his hat, he mopped at his brow with a handkerchief, only to see Bertaud – after begging another customer to excuse him – come hurrying over.

The bookseller seemed anxious.

'There's someone here, waiting to see you,' he said in a low voice.

'And who would that be?'

Rather than answer, the bookseller instead pointed with his chin at a nook inside the shop. The cardinal's former spy looked over calmly, at the very moment when La Fargue put a book he had been glancing through back on a shelf.

The two men stared at one another without either showing any particular emotion.

Then, not taking his eyes off the old captain, Laincourt said over his shoulder:

'Don't worry, Bertaud. The gentleman and I are already acquainted.'

Turning away from the window, the Alchemist went over to his desk.

He had changed his clothes since his morning visit to the former vicomtesse de Malicorne. He still wore black, but now his attire was that of a member of the bourgeoisie rather than a gentleman. Here, at home, he was a scholar, a master of magic known as Mauduit.

He sat in his armchair with a sigh of mixed relief and discomfort. Maintaining this cursed human appearance was becoming more and more taxing, both physically and emotionally. It caused him fleshly pain, to be sure. But more, he found it an intolerable humiliation that he, a dragon, was forced to wear the outward rags of such an ignoble race.

Stretching a hand towards an elegant liqueur service stowed in a case, he poured himself a small glass of a thick yellow fluid that shimmered like liquid gold. It was golden henbane. Or more precisely, the liqueur distilled from golden henbane, a plant whose cultivation, trade, and consumption were strictly forbidden in France, as it was almost everywhere in Europe, but which permitted the preparation of various potions and brews that were highly prized by sorcerers. For common mortals, however, it was a powerful drug. Particularly sought-after by members of high society in search of thrills, it was sold under the cloak at premium prices.

There was a knock at the door.

The so-called Mauduit closed the liqueur case, sat up straight, and hid his glass before bidding his visitor to enter. But the man who appeared already knew his secrets. He was a hired swordsman with an olive complexion and sharp features. Booted and gloved, his sword at his side, his clothes and hat were made of black leather. A patch – also of black leather, with silver studs – hid his left eye but failed to conceal

497

the smear of ranse that spread around it, across his cheekbone, his temple, and the arch of his eyebrow.

The Alchemist relaxed, recovered his glass, and pointed to the case as the visitor dropped himself into an armchair.

'Do you want some?'

'No,' replied the one-eyed man, who had a strong Spanish accent.

Eyes closed, the Alchemist slowly drank the liqueur and enjoyed every drop. The dragons took great delight in golden henbane. It was not only delicious to their palate but, more importantly, it helped them reclaim their fundamental nature. It was often necessary. If the primeval dragons of long ago had struggled to assume and preserve a human appearance, how many now, among the last-born of their race, were not even capable of maintaining an intermediate draconic form? The Alchemist would have been ashamed to admit it, but the metamorphoses were becoming more and more difficult for him, too. The latest transformation, in Alsace, had proved particularly painful. It had almost killed him. Without the golden henbane it was possible he would not have succeeded at all. And without it, his present sufferings would have been unbearable.

'Really, you're sure?' insisted the Alchemist, pouring himself another dose. 'It's excellent.'

This time the ranse victim contented himself with curt shake of the head.

He called himself Savelda and, like the Alchemist, he served the Black Claw. He was the henchman of the masters of the secret society. Or, rather, a trusted lieutenant. The one the elders of the Grand Lodge sent when the matter was important, the one who carried out their orders without ever questioning them.

'Well?' asked Savelda. 'Your visit to see la Malicorne?'

'She is a spent force.'

'I told you so.'

'I had to be sure . . . In any event, we can expect no help from her. It's a shame. I'm convinced that our projects would have appealed to her. She would have loved to take part in them . . .'

'No doubt.'

The Alchemist waved his hand, as if to dismiss an affair that was definitely closed.

'Where are you with your recruitment?' he enquired.

'Progressing. But finding reliable men at such short notice isn't easy.'

'What can I say? The men I brought back from Germany all perished in Alsace, so do the best you can.' The Alchemist clenched a fist and his eyes blazed. 'Those cursed Chatelaines!' he hissed between his teeth. 'They very nearly had me. If I had failed to assume my primal form . . .'

He rose and, shaking his head, went over to the window.

'Speaking of which . . .' said Savelda after a moment. 'Our masters are becoming alarmed. The Grand Lodge still supports your plan, but the fact that you encountered the Chatelaines on your route has them worried.

'I'm touched by our masters' concern for my well-being . . .'

The one-eyed man ignored his irony.

'What could the Chatelaines know?' he asked.

'Nothing. Those bitches don't know anything.'

'Nevertheless . . .'

The Alchemist spun round and stared into Savelda's eyes.

'They've always been after me,' he asserted. 'Should we have hoped that they would just conveniently give up on the eve of our venture? They recently tried to capture me, just as they've tried in the past and as they shall try again in the future. And that's all.'

'Very well. But let's be twice as prudent, all the same.'

'I am never lacking in prudence, or in determination. So apply yourself to reassuring our masters of the Grand Lodge and remind them that it is only a matter of days now before the destiny of France takes a . . . different turn.'

The Ile Notre-Dame – later known as the Ile Saint-Louis – for a long period had remained in a wild state. Until fairly recently there had been no bridges permitting access to the island, either from the quays along the Seine or from Ile de la Cité, so it was rarely visited except by anglers or, on sunny days, by amorous couples whose rowing boats rocked gently among the tall rushes and beneath the weeping willows' drooping branches. Occasionally, it was the scene of murders. The first dracs settled there during the reign of Henri IV. They built scattered huts for themselves on its banks which soon grew into a village. The king allowed this, against his ministers' advice. He knew that the dracs posed a problem for Western societies that would not be resolved on its own, and he realised that the capital's gates could not shut them out, any more than could the borders of his kingdom. Lastly, he understood that dracs and men were forced to co-exist now that the dracs had freed themselves from the millennial tutelage of the dragons. But Henri IV was also aware of the danger these creatures, with their ferocious, violent nature, represented. So he let them establish themselves on this marshy island, in order to live there by themselves and be contained as far as possible. And when the canons of Notre-Dame protested the king responded by purchasing their island, to do with it as he saw fit.

Under the aegis of Henri IV, the drac village prospered. By 1633, it had been transformed into a neighbourhood built entirely of wood, whose damp lanes, dark alleys, lopsided houses, and shacks built on stilts covered the entire island, which Parisians had renamed as Ile Notre-Dame-des-Écailles, or Our Lady of the Scales. As for the neighbourhood itself, it was nicknamed Les Écailles with a mixture of scorn and fear. Although the king's authority still prevailed there, Les Écailles did not form part of the commune of Paris. It was a faubourg in the very heart of the capital, exempt from municipal taxes and visits from the city watch. During the day, the presence of humans was more or less tolerated, although it was understood that anyone who ventured onto the island did so at their own risk. At night, on the other hand . . .

Between dusk and dawn Les Écailles revealed its true character, that is to say: it was both bewitching and deadly. For at night the neighbourhood became the theatre of a life animated by the primitive energy that heated the blood in the dracs' temples and dug into their bellies. Once night fell, fires were lit; fiery red braziers glowed on street corners; torches sputtered outside tavern doors. Along the winding alleys, dracs jostled one another at almost every step due to their dense numbers. The night air was filled with heady scents. Faint melodies met and became intertwined. Brawls broke out: sudden, violent, and always bloody. Warlike chants rose from smoke-filled cellars. Tribal drums beat and their disturbing rhythms sometimes carried across the Seine to disrupt the sleep of ordinary Parisians. On the island, even the dreams of humans were unwelcome.

Here a human being was a stranger, an intruder, an enemy.

Prey.

But a half-blood?

Night was falling when Saint-Lucq crossed, alone, over the small southern branch of the Seine by one of the three rickety wooden bridges which had been built to link Ile Notre-Dame-des-Écailles to the capital. Four grey dracs were killing time around a big fire. They saw his solitary silhouette arriving and supposed that providence had supplied them with a cheap way to entertain themselves. One of the dracs, urging the others to watch him perform, strutted forth to meet Saint-Lucq and deliberately planted himself in his path with an evil grin on his lips.

The half-blood did not slow down or veer aside by even an inch.

But he halted just before bumping into the drac who surpassed him in terms of height, weight, and strength.

And he waited.

The drac, who until then had been exchanging nods and winks with his companions at a distance behind him, suddenly looked perplexed. This wasn't going as planned. The man should have tried to avoid him while he, by taking successive sidesteps, would have cut off any attempt to advance. And this cruel little game would have continued until his victim became exasperated, fled, or tried to force his way past.

But instead . . .

Because the brim of his hat hid his eyes, Saint-Lucq slowly lifted his head until the grey drac's scaly features were reflected in the scarlet lenses of his round spectacles. The drac's gaze became lost in them, while the half-blood stood there unmoving.

He waited, expressionless, for the reptilian to smell, detect, discern in him the blood of a superior race, a blood that would make the drac's primordial instincts scream out in fear and respect.

As finally happened.

Frightened and ashamed, unable to bear the dumbfounded looks on his comrades' faces, the drac stepped aside, letting Saint-Lucq continue on his way, and then fled down the nearest alley.

The other three members of the band were speechless for a moment. What had happened? Who was this man in black, calmly walking at a steady pace, and now disappearing around a corner to penetrate further into Les Écailles?

After a brief consultation, they resolved to follow him.

And kill him.

The nightmares had stayed at a distance for some time, but tonight the whole baying pack had returned to haunt Agnès's sleep. Awakening with a start, her throat and brow damp with sweat, she knew she would not be able to fall asleep again immediately in the warm night air. She therefore got up and, feeling a slight pang of hunger, decided to find herself something to eat. She would no doubt locate something to nibble in the kitchen, as she waited for sleep to return or for dawn to break. In any event, it was pointless to remain in her bed, surrounded by shadows and at the mercy of her regrets.

Without paying much heed to convention, the young baronne de Vaudreuil dressed in a summary fashion and, barefoot, silently descended the shadowy main staircase. All of the denizens of the Hôtel de l'Épervier were fast asleep . . .

. . . except for one person, already in the kitchen.

It was La Fargue.

Sitting alone in the candlelight, his hat and his Pappenheimer placed beside him, the old gentleman was polishing off a substantial snack.

Upon seeing who had joined him, he smiled and greeted her softly:

'But who have we here? Are you hungry, baronne?'

Agnès cast a longing eye over the appetising victuals on the table.

She yawned.

'Well, yes, as a matter of fact . . .'

'Then sit down,' La Fargue invited her, pointing to the place opposite him.

She took a seat, watching the gentleman cut a piece of bread, butter it, and then spread a thick slice of pâté upon it.

'Here,' he said.

Agnès bit deeply into the tartine, and her mouth was still full when La Fargue, handing her a glass of red wine, asked:

'So? This master of magic?'

She had to swallow with the help of a sip of wine before answering.

'Frankly, the man seemed very young and a trifle . . . whimsical.'

The old captain smiled faintly.

'Sieur Teyssier often gives people that impression.'

'Are you acquainted with him, then?'

'Well enough to know that he is extremely learned. Besides, His Eminence is not in the habit of surrounding himself with mediocrities.'

Still dubious, the baronne de Vaudreuil shrugged and continued to devour her tartine.

'He spoke of the men the dracs killed when they entered Paris that night,' she declared. 'According to him, the poor wretches all died of the ranse.'

The ranse was a terrible disease said to be transmitted to humans by dragons and which, in its final stages, corrupted the soul as much as the body. The process, however, was usually a slow one. Those who fell victim to the disease could live with it for years.

'They succumbed in just a few minutes?' La Fargue queried in astonishment.

Agnès nodded, unable to reply, once again having her mouth full.

She gulped, and added:

'Teyssier had one of their hearts in a jar. It was a black, revolting thing that could have come from the carcass of some old man who'd suffered from the disease for years. But in fact, it belonged to a halberdier on guard that night. The man was not even thirty . . .'

La Fargue grimaced.

'The dracs have a sorcerer,' he said.

'That was Teyssier's opinion . . . Is there any more pâté?'

Agnès had finished her tartine and, with a hungry look, was examining the rest of the food on the table.

'I'll take care of that. Tell me what else Teyssier had to say.'

And while the old gentleman prepared a second tartine for her, Agnès explained:

'Teyssier believes that the dracs have a sorcerer with them, and it's thanks to him they can follow La Donna's trace. He believes they will find her sooner or later, unless they abandon their hunt—'

'—or they are stopped.'

'Yes – not too much butter, please – in all likelihood, if the sorcerer were eliminated, La Donna would no longer be in any great danger.'

'Couldn't another sorcerer take over?'

'That's what I asked. But Teyssier affirms that it is not quite so simple. A bond has to be formed between the sorcerer and his prey, and such bonds are not easily woven.'

La Fargue nodded his head gravely and mulled things over while Agnès started on her second tartine. She respected his silence by chewing as quietly as possible.

'La Donna is hoping that we will rid her of this sorcerer.' La Fargue said.

'Who knows? It's a risky wager, if their trap is gradually closing about her as time passes. As Teyssier puts it, it's a little like a net that the sorcerer tightens each day. Or rather, each night, because drakish sorcery is a nocturnal thing . . .'

'But La Donna was all alone, up until these last few days. Now she has at least twelve musketeers to accompany her wherever she goes. And that's not counting Leprat, who is worth six men alone. I think that, as far as her personal safety is concerned, her situation has improved.'

'So she invented a plot against the king to force us to protect her?'

'No, because she will have to offer a full account soon of what she has already affirmed. But I wager that she has played the card of this plot to her sole advantage . . . I shall go and talk to her tomorrow.'

'And Arnaud de Laincourt? Wasn't he supposed to assist us in this affair? Weren't you supposed to meet him today?'

'According to Rochefort, he knows La Donna well and he could be useful to us. But he refused to give me an answer, even though I saw his eye light up with a strange spark when I mentioned La Donna—'

'I think he would make a fine recruit.'

'Perhaps.'

'And the cardinal thinks so, too . . .'

'True. But I am the sole judge of who does or does not wear this ring.'

La Fargue tapped the steel signet ring he wore on his finger, a ring which all the Blades possessed. Agnès de Vaudreuil carried hers beneath her shirt, hanging on a chain around her neck.

Her hunger satiated, she stifled another yawn and stretched.

'Captain, with your permission I'm going to retire to my apartments and try to get some sleep in the few hours of cool night air that remain.'

'Of course. It's very late.'

The young woman rose.

'And thank you for the tartines,' she said with a smile.

A smile that La Fargue returned in a paternal fashion.

'But now that I think of it . . . ,' he suddenly recalled. 'Where did Marciac get to?'

'He went to gamble at La Souvange's mansion. And I believe he intended to visit Gabrielle tomorrow.'

'Ah . . . ! Good night, Agnès.'

'Until tomorrow, captain.'

At home, in his bed, Arnaud de Laincourt was trying to read by candlelight. But he was finding it impossible to concentrate. He finally gave up, turned his book over on his chest, laced his fingers together behind his neck, and uttered a long sigh.

Then, from the shadows which he haunted, the memory of the hurdy-gurdy player said:

You're thinking about the offer from the duchesse de Chevreuse.

Yes.

The House of Chevreuse is one of the greatest households in France. Under its protection, there is no glory or honour that a man such as you cannot hope to attain after a few years . . . But I sense your trouble: for someone who has served the cardinal so well, joining the duchesse and her party would be almost like going over to the enemy. And then there is La Fargue, isn't there . . . ?

Indeed.

What exactly did he want today?

He wanted my help in a delicate matter involving La Donna.

That sounds rather like the cardinal, calling you back to his service for a time.

No doubt . . .

There was a silence.

Then, just before Laincourt drove him from his thoughts, the hurdy-gurdy player told him:

You will have to make a choice, boy . . . And don't take too long about it, or others will do the choosing for you.

Of the three grey dracs who had followed Saint-Lucq since his arrival on Ile Notre-Dame-aux-Écailles, two were lying dead in the mud, now darkened by their blood, at the end of an alley where they had thought they could easily put paid to their victim – who was armed, to be sure, but also alone and visibly unaware of the danger he was in. As for the third drac, he was currently being held at bay by the point of a rapier that was nicking his larynx, and struggling to comprehend how the human could have surprised and then overcome them. All three dracs had entered the alley with swords in their fists, their senses searching the shadows and the silence, and suddenly death had struck twice.

In the nocturnal darkness, with two small red disks in the place of eyes, Saint-Lucq was no more than a silhouette brandishing his rapier – a rapier which did not so much as tremble as it caught a small sliver of the pale moonlight.

'First, you will listen,' he said in a calm voice, 'and then you will think. And lastly, you will speak . . . Don't speak until you have thought, and above all, don't speak until you have listened carefully. Do you understand? You may answer.'

'Yes,' replied the drac.

'Perfect. This is the moment when you listen. Seven black dracs. Mercenaries. They have been in Paris for five days now, and in those five days no one has seen them. That can only mean one thing: that they have been hiding in Les Écailles for the past five days. I want to find them and I'm counting on you to lead me to them. A mere piece of information or two shall satisfy me. That, and nothing less . . . Have you understood what I just said?'

The drac, still immobilised by the point of the sword threatening to pierce his throat, nodded.

'Good,' said Saint-Lucq. 'Now, this is the moment when you think . . .'

At La Renardière, Alessandra saw the sun rise and knew it was approaching the hour when the chambermaid would knock at her door. The young Italian woman's pallor betrayed her anxious state. Seated in an armchair before her window, with a shawl wrapped around her shoulders and Scylla in her lap, she stared blankly out at the scenery and started whenever she spied signs of movement in the sky.

Charybdis had still not come home.

The two dragonnets had been slipping out of the manor each morning for four days now, and flying to Paris to accomplish a mission whose importance they scarcely understood but whose urgency they nevertheless felt. They returned each afternoon, before their mistress was brought back to La Renardière and her apartment was once again visited.

The previous day, however, Scylla had been alone in the cage when Alessandra returned.

The adventuress was immediately worried, but she had to deal with her most pressing concern first, making sure no one noticed the absence of the male dragonnet. Luckily, Charybdis and Scylla were twins. By leaving their cage open and letting the female come and go freely, all Alessandra had to do was to call 'Charybdis' from time to time in order to convince others that both little reptiles were present, if never together in the same room.

Finally they had all left her alone and La Donna, from her window, had scanned the skies all night, tormented by the long wait. In vain. Dawn had come, and now morning. La Renardière began to stir and Alessandra would soon have to show herself, to endure the hypocritical chatter and attentions of her chambermaid, to put on a brave face with Leprat, and then let herself be taken by coach to see that miserable Laffemas, in his no less depressing Châtelet . . .

Assuming that Charybdis's disappearance wasn't noticed by someone first, would Alessandra be able to maintain the illusion of normality for so long?

She doubted it.

Charybdis and Scylla were far more than pets to her. She adored them and regarded them as her allies, partners whose faithful services she readily employed.

Too readily perhaps.

If anything had happened to Charybdis she would never forgive herself, although she knew she'd had no choice but to use her dragonnets to locate her pursuers' hiding place within Paris. It was in fact the second part of her plan. First, deliver herself up to the cardinal, be held at La Renardière, draw the dracs to Paris, and force them to establish a base in the only area within a radius of ten leagues where no one would notice them: Ile Notre-Dame-des-Écailles. Thus the prey would corner the hunters – concluding the first part of her scheme. Next, discover their lair before they discovered hers. And finally, having achieved all that, carry out the third and last part of a plan that had been carefully thought out in advance . . .

There was a knock at the door.

Surprised, Alessandra leapt to her feet, at a loss for a moment before she recovered her wits. She shut Scylla in the cage, threw the shawl over it and barely had time to slide beneath the bed sheets before the chambermaid came in. It was a typical technique used by domestic servants who were overly curious, either professionally or as a personal vice: knock, open the door, catch sight of something by surprise and, if necessary, excuse themselves, lie, and pretend to have heard permission to enter.

'Get out!' cried Alessandra, feigning to still be half-asleep.

'But, madame—'

'I said, get out!'

'But it's already late, madame!'

'You pest! Leave at once or I shall beat you!'

The chambermaid was in full retreat when La Donna's slipper hit the door.

How much time did I gain? La Donna wondered. *Probably less than an hour. The chambermaid will knock at my door once more, and then it will be Leprat. And I won't be able frighten him away by throwing slippers . . .*

Despondent, Alessandra got up and walked to the window, taking care to remain far enough away so as not to be seen from the garden. Wasn't she supposed to be keeping to her bed out of laziness? Eyes narrowed, she peered up at a sky that was now clear blue . . .

. . . and held her breath when she saw Charybdis.

He was coming back to her.

His flight was erratic, to be sure. But it was her little dragonnet approaching with a great deal of valiant if clumsy flapping of his wings, no doubt too tired to maintain the spell that made his body translucent. Alessandra was unconcerned by that, however. Right now, all that mattered to her was that Charybdis was still alive and, throwing caution to the winds, she opened the window to gather the dragonnet in her arms.

He took refuge there, trembling, exhausted, with a slight wound on his flank, but quite alive.

Moreover, he had succeeded in his mission.

'Yes?' Guibot enquired, opening the pedestrian door within the great carriage gate by a few inches.

'Captain La Fargue, please.'

'Are you expected, monsieur?'

'I believe so. I am Arnaud de Laincourt.'

The little old man, to whom the name meant nothing, nevertheless stepped back to allow him entry. Then, having carefully closed the door behind him, he hurriedly hobbled on his wooden leg to precede the visitor into Hôtel de l'Épervier's courtyard. It was about one o'clock in the afternoon. The sun shone in a cloudless sky and its white heat crushed everything beneath it.

'Might I trouble you to repeat your name, monsieur?'

'Laincourt.'

'This way, monsieur.'

La Fargue received Laincourt in the saddlery, a small room which could only be entered by crossing the stable. He isolated himself there on occasion to work leather with sure, precise gestures, the movements of a conscientious artisan that fully occupied his attention, sometimes for hours on end. Today, sitting on a stool before the workbench, he was re-stitching the seams of an old saddle bag. Without raising his eyes from his task, he asked:

'Do you work with your hands?'

'No,' replied Laincourt.

'Why not?'

'I don't have the skill.'

'Every man should know how to do something with his hands.'

'No doubt.'

'Good artisans know what pace they should work at if they want to do things well. It requires patience and humility. It teaches you about time . . .'

In response to this, the young man held his tongue and waited. He didn't understand the meaning of this preamble and when in doubt he always preferred not to express an opinion.

'There!' La Fargue declared, having assured himself of the solidity of his final stitch.

Rising, he called out:

'ANDRÉ!'

The groom, whom Laincourt had seen in the stable upon arriving, appeared in the doorway.

'Captain?'

'Here's something that could still be useful,' said the old gentleman, tossing him the repaired bag.

André caught it, nodded, and went away.

La Fargue filled a glass with wine from a bottle that was waiting in a bucket of cool water and offered it to Laincourt. It was quite warm in the saddlery. The sun beat down on the roof and the nearby heat of the horses in the stable did not help matters. The two men toasted, Laincourt lifting his glass and La Fargue raising the half-full bottle.

'If you are here,' said the captain, taking a swig from the bottle, 'that means you have come to a decision . . .'

'Yes. I've decided to help you to the extent that I can. But I should like to make it clear that I shall not commit myself to more than that. I want your assurance that no matter what secrets are revealed to me from this moment on, my freedom will be returned to me as soon as I demand it.'

'You have my word on it.'

'Thank you. So, what do you expect from me, monsieur?'

'Follow me.'

Snatching up his baldric and his hat as he passed, La Fargue led Laincourt out of the stable. They crossed the mansion's paved courtyard and passed through the main building to the garden in the rear, where they sat down at the old table beneath the chestnut tree. Sweet Naïs brought them more to drink and a plate of cold meats, and discreetly left them in peace.

La Fargue recounted the whole business that occupied the

Blades at present, from the rendezvous in Artois to their current situation, including the plot which La Donna claimed to have information about and the resistance she was offering to the questions Laffemas put to her.

'La Donna is in the cardinal's power?' Laincourt exclaimed. 'And has been for nearly a week?'

'Yes.'

'Where is she being held? In which prison?'

'She has been given lodging at La Renardière.'

'Under close guard, I hope . . .'

The old gentleman nodded.

'A dozen of the cardinal's musketeers protect the domain. And my lieutenant is lodged under the same roof as La Donna.'

'You can be sure she is doing her utmost to seduce him.'

'Leprat is not a man to let himself fall under some beauty's spell.'

Laincourt did not respond to this. He took a sip of wine and then, after contemplating the weed-choked garden with his quiet gaze, said:

'I still don't know what you expect of me.'

La Fargue paused before saying:

'The cardinal thinks very highly of you, monsieur. And he maintains there is no one in France who knows La Donna better than you. I should therefore like to have your opinion concerning this affair, now that you know the nature of it and all the details.'

The young man allowed himself a few instants of reflection before replying.

'One thing is for certain: La Donna is lying.'

'Why?'

'Because she always lies. And when she isn't lying, she's concealing something. And if she isn't lying or concealing something, it's because she's busy deceiving you.'

'Do you think she is lying about the plot?' asked La Fargue.

'You do realise that this plot comes at exactly the right moment to provide her with protection, just when the Black Claw is, in all likelihood, trying to hunt her down.'

'Nevertheless—'

'Yes, of course. Nevertheless, you cannot afford to be deaf to La Donna's claims. The risks and the stakes are too great.'

'Precisely.'

'I can tell you two things. The first is that if this plot exists, La Donna has only evoked it because doing so serves her own interests. The second is that if she is giving monsieur de Laffemas so much trouble, it is because time is presently on her side. No doubt she is waiting for some event to happen. What might that be? I don't know. And we shall probably only find out once it's too late to do anything about it.'

La Fargue remained silent and thoughtful for a long time, his gaze distant. His meditation, however, was interrupted by Almades who approached, after clearing his throat in warning, and handed him a note.

'This was just delivered,' said the Spaniard before returning from whence he came.

Laincourt watched the old gentleman read the missive before shaking his head in a fashion that expressed both amusement and admiration, a small smile on his lips.

Finally La Fargue asked:

'If you were to meet La Donna, if you had the occasion to speak with her alone, would you be able to disentangle the true from the false in all that she might tell you?'

The cardinal's former spy shrugged his shoulders and pursed his lips.

'Frankly, I don't know . . .' he admitted. 'Why?'

La Fargue handed him the note.

'Because today she has asked to speak with you.'

Delivered with the back of the hand, the slap struck him with full force, reopening the wound on his cheek and provoking general hilarity. Ni'Akt fell over backwards, spilling the meagre contents of his mess kit on the ground, which caused even more laughter. But he immediately got back up and, his eyes shining with fury, he stood before the one who had struck him and was now taking cruel enjoyment from the situation.

They were dracs – more, black dracs – and this was how dracs behaved, as Ni'Akt knew all too well. He was the youngest of the band. It was normal for him to be subjected to taunts and humiliations from the more senior members, until another took his place. But since that famous night in Artois when he had tried to attack that cursed half-blood, he had become a veritable punch-bag who was spared nothing. In fact, his comrades did not reproach him so much for stepping out of line as for the fact that he had been beaten, wounded, and then ridiculed. Dracs did not tolerate weaklings. And the ones taking it out on Ni'Akt, moreover, were feeling bored.

They had been cooped up in the rickety, rotting shack deep in the heart of Ile Notre-Dame-des-Écailles for almost a week now. In the cellar their saaskir, their sorcerer-priest, was performing the necessary rituals to find the woman they had orders to kill. But for the time being they had nothing to do. Their chief, Kh'Shak, had forbidden them to even leave the shack. Under these conditions, tormenting Ni'Akt was welcome entertainment for his five companions.

Simmering with anger, his temples buzzing and his eye aflame, Ni'Akt struggled to restrain himself. Ta'Aresh had struck him while he'd been trying to find an out-of-the-way corner where he could eat in peace what little the others had deigned to leave him. Ta'Aresh, the biggest and strongest of their number, after Kh'Shak. Ta'Aresh who looked down on him and defied him to defend himself.

Ni'Akt hesitated.

The dracs' violent customs allowed him to fight back, just as they generally permitted the use of force to resolve even the slightest problems or differences within the group. However, Ni'Akt did not have the right to fail. If he struck Ta'Aresh, the latter could only save face by killing him. It would force a fight to the death . . .

The young drac preferred to beat a retreat, which only earned him more scornful laughter.

But he had a plan.

This morning, at dawn, he had overheard Kh'Shak conferring with the saaskir after returning from a discreet nocturnal sortie. The chief had learned that a half-blood was looking for them, asking lots of questions and leaving bodies behind him. Evidently, venturing into Les Écailles did not frighten him. In fact, he seemed to arouse a peculiar fear in the dracs he encountered . . .

Like Kh'Shak, who was growing worried, Ni'Akt was convinced this half-blood was the same one they had met on the night when they had almost caught up with La Donna: he had the same black clothing, the same scarlet feather on his hat and, above all, the same round spectacles with red lenses.

To the young drac it seemed as if destiny was offering him a chance to wash away the affront he had received. This evening he would sneak out and, if luck smiled upon him, he would find the half-blood.

And then he would kill him, bring back his head, and drop it into Ta'Aresh's lap.

La Donna's carriage was about to take her back to La Renardière when La Fargue and Laincourt, followed by Almades, arrived in the Grand Châtelet's courtyard at a slow trot.

Le Châtelet was a sombre fortified edifice which had originally been built to defend the Pont au Change, but had since been rendered useless for military purposes following the enlargement of Paris and the construction of new city ramparts by King Philippe Auguste in the 12th century. Massive, sinister, and somewhat deteriorated, Le Châtelet stood on the Right Bank, its main façade looking out over rue Saint-Denis. At present the seat of the law courts under the jurisdiction of the provost of Paris, it possessed several round towers and a large square pavilion, a sort of keep which housed a prison. The sole entrance was an archway flanked by two turrets. Fairly long but narrow, it opened onto a small, foul-smelling courtyard where visitors were immediately struck by the full misery of the place.

From his saddle, monsieur de La Houdinière, captain of the Cardinal's Guards, had already raised his arm to give the departure signal to the coach and its escort. He froze on seeing La Fargue and frowned when he recognised Laincourt, having been his direct superior until the young man had left the company of His Eminence's horse guards. La Houdinière had only been a lieutenant then, and he had not delved into the circumstances behind Laincourt's dismissal. All he knew was that those circumstances were murky.

'You're returning to La Renardière already?' La Fargue observed in surprise as he approached at a walk.

Almades and Laincourt remained behind.

'Yes!' replied La Houdinière. 'Monsieur de Laffemas chose to cut short his interview today as he deemed it to be entirely unfruitful. La Donna's latest whim, it seems, has exhausted his patience.'

'A whim which I believe I know,' said the old gentleman, looking at the coach where a pretty hand had discreetly lifted the window curtain.

The note he had received at the Hôtel de l'Épervier had come directly from Laffemas. La Houdinière, no doubt, did not know its contents.

'Would you allow Laincourt to have a conversation with La Donna, right here?' asked La Fargue.

The other man thought for a moment and then shrugged.

'All right.'

He gave the necessary orders, and Laincourt, after a nod from the captain of the Blades, dismounted. He walked across the uneven paving of Le Châtelet's courtyard and, under the gaze of his former brothers-in-arms, climbed aboard the vehicle. No one heard what was said within, behind the richly padded walls and the thick drawn curtains. But less than half an hour later the coach and its escort moved off, taking La Donna back to La Renardière, while La Fargue, Laincourt, and Almades proceeded to leave Paris by the Saint-Martin gate.

Taking the road to Senlis, then the one leading to Soissons, the three riders passed Roissy and continued at a gallop to Dammartin. There, they needed to ask for directions. The first goodwife they came across in the village square was able to assist them. Everyone living in the area knew the manor belonging to the famous painter, Aubusson.

'Where did you meet La Donna?' La Fargue asked Laincourt as they followed the track that had been indicated to them.

Keeping a watchful eye all about, Almades brought up the rear in silence.

'During my stay in Madrid,' Laincourt replied. 'She was already busy there, hatching schemes.'

'Were you adversaries or allies?'

The young man smiled.

'Frankly I still don't know, to this day. But I would probably not be far wrong to say that La Donna had no true ally but herself, as is always the way with her . . .'

'You seem to be very wary of her.'

'As if she were a salamander on live coals.'

'But she must, for her part, hold you in some esteem. Laffemas has interrogated her for days, practically in vain, and here she is suddenly confiding in you.'

'Don't be fooled, monsieur. I count for nothing in this whole affair. If La Donna spoke to me it is merely because she had already decided to speak, to me or to someone else, in the fullness of time.'

'Then why did she ask for you?'

'Someone constrained by force or a threat to reveal a secret will often offer a final resistance by demanding the right to choose the person they shall finally speak to. It's a way of not surrendering completely, of maintaining some semblance of freedom and control.'

La Fargue nodded.

'And La Donna, according to you, was playing out such a scene.'

'Yes.'

'But why?'

'So that it would seem like she was finally giving in. So that we would be less suspicious of her impromptu revelations. And so that we would not wonder why she chooses to speak now, when in fact that is the only question which should interest monsieur de Laffemas.'

'Why now.'

517

'Precisely. Why now.'

The old captain raised his eyes towards the manor whose red tiled roofs could be seen behind the trees that crowned the hill.

They were getting closer.

'And this Aubusson. Do you know who he is or why La Donna is sending us to him?'

'He is a painter,' said Laincourt, drawing on his recollections. 'A portrait artist who, some years ago, was quite renowned. At present he seems to have retired from the world . . . But I do not know what bonds unite him to Aless— to La Donna. I imagine they met at a princely court somewhere in Europe, when Aubusson still travelled abroad.'

'Perhaps she was his mistress,' La Fargue suggested slyly.

'Perhaps,' said Laincourt impassively.

'And perhaps she still is,' added the old gentleman, watching the other out of the corner of his eye. 'I have heard that she sometimes uses such means to further her ends.'

'We're almost there now.'

Aubusson was reading when his valet came to warn him that three riders were coming up the road leading to the manor. Visitors were rare in these parts. Understanding what was going on, the painter thanked the boy, put his book down, and went to his room to find the thick leather folder that Alessandra had placed in his care the week before. 'You'll know the moment has arrived when a certain Captain La Fargue comes seeking these papers,' she had told him. 'You won't have any trouble recognising him. A white-haired gentleman, but still big, strong, and full of authority. His visit will be the signal.'

From the window of his chamber on the upper floor, Aubusson watched the riders enter the courtyard at a walk, and immediately spotted La Fargue.

Aubusson called back his valet:

'Jeannot!'

'Yes?'

'When the oldest of those three riders tells you his name is La Fargue, I want you to give this to him.'

The boy took the folder, but hesitated.

'The matter has already been settled and he won't ask you any questions,' the painter reassured him.

Jeannot scurried away. He ran down the stairs, crossed the front hall with his heels clattering on the flagstones, burst out onto the front porch, and went with a quick step to meet the visitors.

Without seeking to conceal himself, Aubusson watched the scene from his wide-open window. After exchanging a few words the valet gave the leather folder to La Fargue. The latter untied the ribbon that held it shut, cast a glance at the documents it contained and, without expression, closed it once more.

After which, he lifted his eyes to look up at the painter, as if in search of confirmation.

Is that all? he seemed to be asking.

Aubusson gave him a slow, grave nod, to which the old gentleman responded with a brief salute before giving his companions the signal to depart.

The portrait artist watched the riders head off into the distance at a fast trot and waited for his valet to rejoin him.

'Monsieur?'

'Go to the village and ask the master at the staging post for two saddled horses.'

'Two, monsieur?'

'Yes, two. And don't tarry on the way . . .'

The boy scampered off again.

. . . because it's happening tonight, Aubusson added to himself.

'And now?' Laincourt asked, in loud voice in order to be heard over the beating hooves.

'Here,' replied La Fargue. And without slowing their pace, he handed over the leather folder they had obtained from Aubusson.

The cardinal's former agent hastened to slip it inside his doublet.

'What am I supposed to do with it?' he asked.

'You must take it to rue des Enfants-Rouges, to sieur Teyssier. He is the—'

'—master of magic for His Eminence, I know. But why?'

'So that he can study these documents and determine their authenticity. I will be content with his first impression. Wait until he communicates that to you, and then come and find me at the Hôtel de l'Épervier. Almades and I are going there directly, in case there is news waiting for me there.'

'News from La Donna?'

'Among others, yes.'

'Can you tell me what these documents are, that I'm carrying?'

'If they are in truth what they seem to be, they were stolen from the Black Claw. As for their content, I cannot say. The text appears to be in draconic . . .'

Saint-Lucq tottered backward, leaning against a scabby wall and, eyes closed, waited to recover his breath and his calm. Strength and lucidity returned to him. His heart ceased to beat so furiously. He inhaled deeply and reopened his eyes.

The body at his feet lay in a spreading puddle of black blood. The fight had taken place in a deserted alley in Les Écailles. It did not seem to have drawn anyone's attention, which was a good thing. But someone could turn up at any moment. Night was falling, which meant that Les Écailles would soon be swarming with creatures the half-blood would rather not have to face, especially not with drac blood on his hands.

Saint-Lucq re-sheathed his rapier. Then, crouching, he pushed his red spectacles up onto the bridge of his nose and turned over the body to examine it.

A drac, then.

A black drac. Young. One whose cheek bore a nasty wound that the half-blood abruptly recognised: it was the hired blade he had provoked and wounded that night during the storm, in Artois. Saint-Lucq supposed the young drac had spotted him and been unable to resist the temptation to take immediate revenge. Had he warned his comrades? Probably not. If he had, the half-blood would not have confronted a single impulsive adversary in a hurry to finish him off, but instead a whole group of determined, well-organised mercenaries.

Saint-Lucq stood up again.

He looked around, sniffing at the damp air, and was suddenly convinced that he was close to his goal. It wouldn't be long now before he found the lair of the dracs on La Donna's trail.

Upon their return to Paris, La Fargue and Almades left Laincourt at the entrance of rue des Enfants-Rouges and continued down rue du Temple. They took the Pont au Change, crossed the Ile de la Cité, and then the small arm of the Seine by way of the Pont Saint-Michel. On the Left Bank, they passed through the Buci gate as they returned to the faubourg Saint-Germain and, finally, rue Saint-Guillaume and the Hôtel de l'Épervier. They entrusted their horses to André, and La Fargue immediately summoned his troops. Only Leprat and Saint-Lucq were missing, the former on duty at La Renardière and the latter busy searching Ile Notre-Dame-des-Écailles. So it was therefore Agnès, Marciac, and Ballardieu who joined Almades and their captain in the main hall on the ground floor – their converted fencing room. They all found a seat wherever they could.

La Fargue began by asking if they had received any news from La Renardière, the Palais-Cardinal, the Louvre, or even Le Châtelet. And when they replied no, he proceeded to recount the events of the afternoon. After – and even during – this recital, he had to answer questions about Aubusson, Laincourt, La Donna, and above all, the famous documents they had received from the painter. This took a good hour.

'So,' Marciac summed up, 'having revealed the existence of a plot against the king, La Donna spends almost a week dancing this strange *pas de deux* with monsieur de Laffemas until, one fine morning, she suddenly declares that she will speak to none but Laincourt and, without further ado, sends him to the one person who can provide proofs of her claims.'

'That's right.'

'Am I the only one to find this rather astonishing?'

No one knew how to reply to this, except Ballardieu, who muttered:

'I find this Italian woman very capricious. I say a good spanking would probably suffice to bring her back to sweet reason. The cardinal has coddled her, if you want my opinion.'

The others glanced at one another, thinking there was a certain amount of good sense in the old soldier's words. Marciac, however, was the only one to really imagine the spanking.

'But that's not the most important thing,' said Agnès. 'After all, if La Donna has found some personal advantage in this affair then so much the better, since without it she would have kept the information to herself or else sold it to the highest bidder. What does matter, on the other hand, is the plot itself. Our first duty is to protect the king, the queen, and the cardinal. Not to guess at the secret motives of a foreign spy.'

'Agreed,' said the Gascon. 'So what about these papers found at the painter's home, this Aubusson? Do they even attest to the existence of a plot?'

La Fargue shrugged.

'How can we know? I can only say that if these documents are authentic, their value is immense.'

'Documents belonging to the Black Claw,' Almades reminded them.

'Yes. They will reveal their secrets once they've been translated. It's only a matter of time.'

'To be sure. But isn't time precisely what we lack?' Agnès emphasised.

A silence followed, finally interrupted by monsieur Guibot who knocked, opened the door, and announced Laincourt. The latter was promptly invited to enter. Looking grave, he distributed courteous nods all round, gratified Agnès with a more pronounced salute, and then gave La Fargue a questioning glance.

'Speak,' said the Blades' captain.

'I have just come from His Eminence's master of magic. He cannot yet attest to this formally, but the authenticity of the papers he has studied appears to be borne out. According to him, they are quite definitely Black Claw documents, and may even emanate from the Grand Lodge itself—'

The Black Claw had many lodges throughout Europe, France excepted. The Grand Lodge was that of Madrid. Historically, it was the first to be founded, and it remained the most important and influential of them all.

'—and they have much to do with a certain Alchemist,' Laincourt concluded.

This last revelation had the effect of a thunderbolt in a clear sky. All those present were dumbstruck, as if seized by a superstitious awe. Then, slowly, eyes turned to La Fargue.

His face had turned frighteningly pale.

'What name did you just say?' he asked faintly.

Not understanding the commotion he had just provoked, Laincourt hesitated.

'The Alchemist . . . Why?'

'You say these papers of the Black Claw relate to him. What else?'

'That was all Teyssier said on the subject.'

'Could La Donna have dealings with the Alchemist?'

'Who knows?'

La Fargue rose from his chair with a determined air.

'Almades,' he said. 'Ask André to saddle two horses. You and I are leaving for La Renardière at once.'

'Captain . . .' Agnès objected. 'It will be the black of night by the time you arrive . . .'

But the old gentleman appeared not to hear her.

'Monsieur de Laincourt,' he asked, 'could you be ours until morning?'

When the young man nodded, he went on to say:

'In that case, I want you to return to sieur Teyssier and oblige him, if necessary, to spend all night studying the documents we entrusted to his care. Make sure he knows how important this is. If you wish, Agnès or Marciac will accompany you.'

And turning to those two, he added: 'But I want at least one of you to remain here, to wait for news from either of our two parties. Is that understood?'

Less than a quarter of an hour later, after La Fargue and Almades departed into the dusk, it was decided that Agnès would go with Laincourt to see the cardinal's master of magic.

'It's up to you to guard the fort,' she said to Marciac.

Embarrassed, the latter rubbed a hand over his stubbled cheeks and, drawing the young baronne aside, out of earshot of the others, he murmured to her:

'I have to go somewhere, Agnès.'

'What? Now?'

'Yes.'

'Where?'

'I can't tell you that.'

'Nicolas . . .' Agnès sighed.

'I swear to you it doesn't involve a woman. Or a card game.'

'So what is it then? Or rather, who?'

'I would tell you if I could . . .' Then in a more breezy tone, as if they had already reached an accord, he said: 'Listen, I promise I won't be long. And anyway, Ballardieu will be here. It's not as if I'm abandoning the place to the enemy, is it?'

And after dropping a quick kiss on the young woman's brow, he left her there, making a discreet exit from the mansion through the rear garden. Agnès stood for a moment with a troubled expression on her face, before pulling herself together and quickly dashing up the main staircase to her bedchamber.

Now armed and booted, a leather cord securing the heavy plait of her black hair, Agnès joined Laincourt in the stable, where he was helping André and Ballardieu saddle two more horses.

'We need to make haste,' she said. 'The Paris gates will be closing soon. Need a hand?'

Although its ramshackle walls and muddy ditches were very poor defences indeed, Paris was a fortified city and its gates were closed during the night. The Hôtel de l'Épervier, being located in the faubourg Saint-Germain, lay outside the city's walls, whereas His Eminence's master of magic lived within. To be sure, the Blades all possessed passes signed by Richelieu himself, but persuading the city watch to open up was both a tiresome business and an enormous waste of time.

Laincourt did not answer. He continued to busy himself with the horses as if he had not heard Agnès, and then, with a stony expression, he asked:

'Will you tell me what this is all about?'

The young baronne de Vaudreuil exchanged an embarrassed look with Ballardieu. Then she told herself that the cardinal's former agent no doubt deserved to know the heart of the matter. She sighed and with a resigned air, waved to André and Ballardieu that they should leave.

And once she and Laincourt were alone in the stable she said:

'Go ahead, ask your questions. I will answer if I have the right to do so.'

He had just finished saddling his mount. After tightening a last strap, he stood up and caught the baronne's gaze.

'What happened, just now?' he wanted to know. 'Why did La Fargue react the way he did when he heard me speak the Alchemist's name? And why did the rest of you, at that same moment, seem so worried?'

Agnès wondered where she should start.

'What do you know of the Alchemist, monsieur?'

Laincourt pursed his lips.

'I know what is said about him.'

'Which is?'

'Which is that he is the oldest, the craftiest, and the most formidable of the Black Claw's agents. The very best of them, in fact. But this name – the Alchemist – is all anyone knows of him, and it is, no doubt, a *nom de guerre*. No one knows what he looks like, his age, or even his true gender. He is supposed to have been involved, to a greater or lesser degree, in every important plot and bloody revolt that has taken place. Yet, even if we can detect his presence everywhere, no one has ever caught sight of him anywhere—'

'—to the point that some people doubt his very existence,' Agnès finished for him. 'Yes, I've heard all that before . . . But are you one of these sceptics, Arnaud? If you are, then I urge you to revise your opinion. Because the Alchemist, to our great misfortune, does indeed exist. He was even on the verge of being captured, once. By us, by the Blades, acting on La Fargue's initiative.'

Laincourt frowned.

'I didn't know that,' he confessed.

The young woman's face darkened.

'It was five years ago,' she said.

Night had fallen upon Ile Notre-Dame-des-Écailles when Kh'Shak, returning after an hour's absence, entered a miserable back yard and found his soldiers standing in front of the shack where they had been hiding these past few days. Ready for an expedition, the black dracs were heavily armed and struggling to contain their impatience. Kh'Shak was surprised. He had given no orders to prepare for a sortie before he left in search of Ni'Akt, the youngest member of his unit. Since they had been in Paris, Ni'Akt had suffered more than his fair share of humiliation and insults from his elders and Kh'Shak had feared for a moment that he'd deserted. But guided by rumours, he had quickly found his dead body – already stripped of its possessions – lying in a fresh pool of blood. And then he had come right back.

Kh'Shak walked right through his men without looking at them.

He went into the shack and descended the rotting stairs to the damp cellar filled with its appetising odour of rotting meat. Gutted animal carcasses littered the dirt floor and there were yellow candles burning that produced much smoke in addition to their dim light.

Kh'Shak had expected to find his saaskir cross-legged on the ground in the middle of the room. But the old pale-scaled drac was sitting on a keg, gnawing a haunch of raw, spoiled meat with what remained of his yellowed teeth, finally at the end of his long fast.

'Ni'Akt is dead,' announced the hulking black drac. 'He

went out despite my orders and was killed. I think the half-blood murdered him.'

The other drac nodded but continued to eat.

'That means he will find us soon,' added Kh'Shak. 'He is very close now.'

'It doesn't matter,' said the sorcerer. 'The one we are searching for has finally revealed herself to the Eye of the Night Dragon. I know where she is hiding and I shall lead you there by thought.'

'At last!'

'Did you believe the task was easy?'

'No, but—'

The old drac lifted a thin clawed hand in an appeasing gesture.

'Rejoin your men, Kh'Shak. Find your horses and leave without further delay. If you act quickly and well, La Donna will be dead this very night.'

3

That night, at La Renardière, Alessandra di Santi was reading when she heard riders approaching at a gallop. As her bedchamber only offered a view of the garden paths and the great tree-lined park, she went into the antechamber and, parting the curtains slightly, caught a glimpse of La Fargue and Almades as they jumped down from their saddles and climbed the front steps where they were met by Leprat.

She smiled, withdrew from the window, adjusted her red curls as she passed in front of a mirror, told herself that the soft yellow light of the candles decidedly suited her and, back in her room, returned to her armchair and her book.

The chambermaid soon admitted La Fargue, and lifting her eyes to his, La Donna greeted him with a dazzling smile.

'Good evening, captain. To what do I owe the pleasure of this visit?'

The old gentleman closed the door without replying, turned the key twice in the lock, looked briefly out the window, drew the curtains, and then, looking grave and almost menacing, came to stand before the beautiful lady spy.

'Ah!' she said, putting her book down. 'So this is not a social visit . . .'

'Enough play, madame.'

Serene, Alessandra rose under the pretext of pouring herself a glass of liqueur from a bottle placed on the side table. If she remained seated, she would be permitting La Fargue to dominate her with his massive figure and hold sway over her, something which she detested.

'And what game do you think I am playing, monsieur?'

'I still don't know the rules or the object. But I can affirm that it ends here and now. I am not monsieur de Laffemas, madame. I am a soldier. If you persist in playing games, our conversation will take a most discourteous turn.'

'Are you threatening me monsieur?'

'Yes.'

'And you are a man who is willing to transform your threats into action . . .'

This time, the captain of the Blades was silent.

La Donna met his stare without blinking, returned to her armchair, and invited La Fargue to sit facing her, to which he consented after removing his baldric and his sword.

'It's about the Alchemist, isn't it?' Alessandra guessed.

The old gentleman raised an eyebrow. What exactly did she know about the blows the Alchemist had struck against the Blades?

'Rest assured,' she said as if reading his thoughts, 'I don't know the details of what transpired a few years ago at La Rochelle. I only know the bare essence. But perhaps that is already too much for your taste?'

La Fargue gave La Donna an expressionless stare.

'Do you know the nature of the documents that you arranged to have handed over to us today?'

Alessandra shrugged with an air of annoyance.

'Obviously.'

'Is the Alchemist part of the plot against the king that you claim to have information about?'

'Of the plot against the *throne*,' she corrected. 'And yes, the Alchemist is the principal instigator. The duchesse de Chevreuse is also a participant—'

La Fargue greeted this revelation without much surprise, but he hadn't heard the worst yet.

'—as is the queen,' the adventuress finished.

The old captain was visibly shaken.

'You mean the queen mother, of course . . .'

Alessandra rose from her chair, going over to the large cage and teasing one of her dragonnets by sliding an index finger between the bars.

'It's true, of course, that the queen you speak of is also

implicated,' said the beautiful Italian woman in a light-hearted tone. 'Isn't she always? But I was thinking of the other, of the reigning queen . . .'

'Of Anne d'Autriche.'

'Yes.'

La Fargue now rose in turn, pacing back and forth in front of the fireplace; and finally asked:

'These documents from the Black Claw, how did you come by them?'

'I stole them.'

'From whom?'

'By God! From one of its members . . . ! And as you can imagine, although I don't know how they learned it was me, they are most displeased about it!'

'Why?'

Sincerely puzzled, Alessandra looked at the old gentleman.

'I beg your pardon?'

'Why did you steal these documents from the Black Claw?'

'Ah . . . !' she said, finally understanding. 'Would you believe me if I told you that I dislike the Black Claw as much as you do and that, when possible, I apply myself to doing them harm?'

He approached her.

'No,' he replied. 'I would not believe it.'

She smiled and resisted the temptation to step back.

'So, why?' La Fargue insisted.

'Because I received the order to do so.'

He came closer still.

Now they were practically touching and Alessandra had to tilt her head to see the black look on her interrogator's face.

'Who was it, who gave this order?' he demanded in a grave, menacing tone.

'It came from our masters, of course, captain.'

'I serve the king of France and Cardinal Richelieu. Do you claim to do the same, madame?'

The young woman did not blink.

'I claim nothing of the sort, monsieur. Do you really want

me, here and now, to name those I am thinking of, and know that you are too?'

La Donna and the old captain both remained silent for a moment, face-to-face, he trying to probe her soul and she opposing him with the calmness of an indomitable will. They did not move, glaring at one another, barely breathing.

And someone knocked at the door.

'Captain!' called Leprat.

La Fargue hurried to open up.

'What is it?'

'The sentries in the park no longer answer to the calls,' replied Leprat. 'And the valet I sent to alert the other musketeers posted at the entrance to the domain has not returned.'

Marciac had been waiting in front of the massive Saint-Eustache church for a few moments when Rochefort finally arrived. The cardinal's henchman was accompanied by two other gentlemen, whom he asked to wait behind. Then he walked up to the forecourt alone and, not seeing the Gascon, slowly spun around, searching the darkness.

'Since when do you bring company to our meetings?' Marciac asked him, emerging from the shadows.

'Since it pleases me to do so.'

'It's contrary to our accords.'

'They are far enough off that they cannot hear you or see you. And don't speak to me of accords that you have been the first to betray.'

'Does the cardinal have any reason to complain about the success of my mission in La Rochelle?'

'No. But he still recalls that, not so long ago, you refrained from saying anything about a certain person of interest to us.'

Marciac knew that Rochefort was referring to the hidden daughter of La Fargue, who had been found and protected a month earlier by the Blades. To ensure her security, the Gascon had even entrusted her to the care of the only woman he had ever loved. Gabrielle, who happened to keep a certain establishment – *The Little Frogs*, in rue Grenouillère – where amiable young women practised the profession of satisfying the desires of generous men.

'I didn't know who she was and, therefore, was unaware of the interest that she might hold for you,' Marciac defended himself.

'And where is she, at present?'

'I have no idea.'

'But there was a time when she was hiding in Paris, wasn't there?'

'Yes,' the Gascon admitted reluctantly.

'And where was she?'

'It doesn't matter.'

Rochefort displayed a sinister smile.

'I have the notion that this girl was in a house that was quite ill-suited to someone of her sex and her age. And since you are not offering me any information, it's possible that I might have to start knocking down doors and asking questions in rue Grenouillère . . .'

Marciac's blood started to boil. His face turned red and, with a sudden move, he seized Rochefort by the collar, lifted him up on the tip of his toes, and forced him back several steps until he thumped into the church door.

'Don't you dare go near Gabrielle!' he spat. 'Don't threaten her! Don't even look at her. Forget you even know of her or, as God is my witness, I'll kill you.'

Livid, his lips twitching, Rochefort replied in a toneless voice:

'Release me, Marciac. Remember we have spectators who won't keep their distance for long if you cause trouble . . .'

The Gascon had indeed forgotten about the gentlemen who were waiting at the corner of rue du Four. In the darkness of night they would have difficulty seeing what was happening. But from their attitude, he could see that they were starting to worry.

'Will they do me an evil turn?' Marciac asked mockingly.

'It will be enough that they recognise you.'

The Gascon thought about it and then reluctantly released his grip on Rochefort.

'Don't go near Gabrielle,' he warned again, jabbing a menacing finger. 'Ever.'

And he was so wrapped up in his anger that he did not see the blow coming that caused him to topple backwards.

'And you,' hissed Rochefort, 'don't ever lay a hand on me again. Don't forget who I am, don't forget who I serve, and above all, don't forget what you are.'

Upon which, the cardinal's henchman turned on his heels and calmly walked away, rubbing his fist.

'Damn!' La Fargue swore.

Leprat had just informed him that, in all likelihood, La Renardière was being attacked.

Without sparing La Donna a glance, he left his lieutenant by the door and went to look out of the window. The garden looked deserted despite the fact that musketeers were supposed to be patrolling there. Further off, the park was a great rectangular lake of blackness, surrounded by trees as far as the eye could see. A crescent moon and some stars dispensed a paltry bluish glow over the scene.

The Blades' captain cursed under his breath.

If the enemy had overcome the sentries without a fight, by now they could be anywhere within the domain.

'It's the dracs,' announced Alessandra. 'They've found me.'

At that instant, a silhouette – with a round back and taking large strides – crossed a garden path and vanished again into the shadows. A hired blade, clearly. But a drac? A man? La Fargue couldn't say. But his instinct told him La Donna was right.

'Stay right here,' he ordered her in a tone that brooked no argument.

Snatching up his rapier in its scabbard, he buckled on his baldric as he left the room with a determined step, Leprat following in his wake.

'The chambermaid?' he asked the former musketeer.

'I am here, monsieur.'

The woman in the service of La Donna was standing in a

corner of the antechamber, near the cot on which she normally slept. Worried, almost frightened, she did not dare to move.

'Go and join your mistress next door,' La Fargue commanded her. 'Do you have the key?'

'Yes,' replied the woman showing him her bunch.

'Then lock yourselves in.' Leprat said in turn. 'And don't open the door for anyone except the captain or myself. Is that clear?'

'Yes, monsieur.'

The two men did not wait to see if they were obeyed.

They hurried down the great stairway to join Almades on the ground floor where, as a security measure, he had already extinguished most of the torches. Only a few candles remained lit here and there.

'Well?' La Fargue asked in the large front hall filled with shadows and echoes.

'They are still not showing themselves,' said the Spaniard, standing slightly back from the window through which he kept watch on the courtyard. 'But I've seen some wisps of that black mist—'

'So it is the dracs.'

'They've come to capture La Donna,' said Leprat.

'Yes. Or to kill her.'

The old captain also took up a position at a window from which he tried to take stock of the situation. The hunting lodge consisted of a small central pavilion and two wings enclosing its courtyard. The whole building was surrounded by a dry moat crossed by a stone bridge, a bridge which, unfortunately, they were too late to defend. The servant quarters lay beyond the moat, on either side of a long forecourt that stretched along the axis of the path leading to the woods.

La Fargue spared a thought for the servants housed in the outbuildings. Were any of them still alive?

'All of the windows within a man's reach are solidly barred,' Leprat indicated. 'And only the main pavilion, where we are now, is occupied. Elsewhere, the doors are locked and the rooms are empty.'

Of the three of them, he was the only one who knew the place well.

'In fact,' replied La Fargue, 'right here in this front hall is where we stand the best chance of defending ourselves, isn't it?'

'Yes. And from here we can guard the main stairs.'

'There are others. There are service stairs. And the hidden ones.'

'To be sure, but the dracs won't know where to find them. Whereas this one . . .'

In French châteaux the main staircase was always found near the entrance of the central pavilion, of which it formed the backbone.

'Then let's barricade ourselves,' decided the captain of the Blades, already pushing a bench into place. 'God only knows when the dracs will make their assault.'

Shots were suddenly fired, and the window panes by the main door shattered. The horses that La Fargue and Almades had left outside whinnied. Almost immediately, the three men heard a dull thud from above, the sound of a body falling heavily.

'Hold them back!' exclaimed La Fargue as he rushed to the staircase.

Already, other shots resounded and more musket balls came crashing into the walls.

The captain of the Blades climbed the steps two at a time, crossed the antechamber in La Donna's apartments, and ran into a locked door.

He swore, striking his fist against the panel, calling:

'OPEN UP! IT'S LA FARGUE!'

Receiving no response, he moved back a pace, lifted a knee, and sent his foot crashing against the door. It shook on its hinges without giving way. He swore even louder, took a running start, and threw himself forward shoulder first. The wood split, the lock broke and the door flew open as if it had been hit by a battering ram. La Fargue stumbled into the bed

535

chamber. But he managed to keep his balance and unsheathed his sword by reflex when he saw what awaited him inside.

The chambermaid was lying unconscious on the floor, next to the scattered keys from her bunch. At the rear of the room a wall tapestry was folded back, caught in a door that had been shut too quickly. But above all, there was a black drac who had just entered by the wide-open window.

From the yellow patterns decorating his facial scales, La Fargue identified him as the chief of the drac mercenaries who had been sent after La Donna by the Black Claw. As for Kh'Shak, he recognised the old gentleman soldier who had barred his way in Artois with surprise and pleasure.

The captain of the Guards immediately placed himself *en garde*.

His opponent smiled and, instead of a sword, brandished a pistol.

'I promised you we would meet again, old man,' he said taking aim.

The very same moment the shot rang out, the entire building was rocked by an explosion.

On the ground floor, the main door had just been blown into pieces, destroyed by the explosion of a black powder charge. Thick smoke invaded the front hall and, dazed, Leprat and Almades painfully picked themselves up from the floor, coughing amidst the last bits of debris that were raining down.

His ears ringing, Leprat thought he could hear drakish war cries. Tottering on his feet, he had just realised that he'd managed to keep hold of his pistol when he saw a silhouette outlined in the gaping frame of the doorway. He took a very approximate aim and missed his target by a fraction. The drac rushed him. Still shaken by the explosion, he was late in comprehending what was happening. And he was only starting to draw his rapier when the drac struck.

Too slow to react, the musketeer saw his death rushing towards him . . .

. . . when he heard another loud blast.

Leprat quickly recovered his wits upon seeing the drac's

head burst. His face spattered with black blood, he turned to see Danvert armed with a smoking arquebus. Other dracs were pushing their way into the building and Almades had already engaged two of them.

His white rapier clenched in his fist, Leprat dashed forward to lend him a hand.

Kh'Shak had aimed for the head and had scored a hit. But his arm had wavered at the last moment due to the explosion, so that the pistol ball had merely cut deeply into La Fargue's brow as it skidded over the bone, rather than penetrating his brain.

His hat torn away, the Blades' captain reeled. His vision was blurred and his ears rang as blood dripped down into his eyes. He thought he was going to collapse yet, somehow, he remained standing. But the floor seemed to be swaying beneath his feet.

Kh'Shak, still brandishing his smoking pistol, struggled to understand how his adversary could still be alive and on his feet, face bloodied, after receiving a ball in the middle of his forehead. Then he pulled himself together, threw his pistol away and drew his sword as he marched toward La Fargue.

The latter, half-stunned, saw the drac coming as if through a veil. He parried as best he could one, two, three successive attacks with the wild gestures of a drunken man, and attempted a riposte that the other easily countered.

The drac started to play a cruel game with him.

'You're no longer up to this, old man.'

He lunged, bypassing La Fargue's uncertain parry, and plunged the point of his blade into the captain's right shoulder. The old gentleman moaned as he retreated, bringing his hand up to the wound. The keen pain aroused him somewhat from his torpor. But the floor continued to move beneath him and his buzzing temples continued to deafen him.

'You should have hung up your sword long ago.'

Another lunge and this time La Fargue felt two inches of steel penetrate his left thigh. His leg faltered beneath his weight and almost gave way beneath him. He only just succeeded in remaining on his feet. Still retreating, he wiped a sleeve across a brow that was sticky with blood and sweat. He blinked several times. And with an immense effort of will he managed to focus on the blurred silhouette that was tormenting him.

'It's too late for regrets now, old man. Goodbye,' said Kh'Shak, as he prepared to deliver the fatal stroke to his exhausted opponent.

But it was La Fargue who attacked.

Dropping his sword and roaring like a savage beast, he rushed at the drac, grappling with him and shoving him backwards. Wide, massive, and solid, the captain of the Blades was a force of nature despite his age. And as strong and vigorous as he was, the huge drac was unable to halt the old gentleman's momentum. Benefiting from the element of surprise, the man was also powered by an overwhelming rage born of desperation. Kh'Shak felt himself being lifted off the floor. And he realised too late that La Fargue was propelling them both towards the open window.

'You old fool. You're going to—'

His teeth red with blood, La Fargue wore an evil smile of triumph and rancour as they toppled together into empty space.

With Charybdis flying ahead and Scylla right behind him, Alessandra moved away as quickly as possible from La Renardière and into the surrounding forest. After stunning her chambermaid and stealing the key to the small hidden door, she had descended a damp, narrow stairway. Then, taking advantage of the confusion that reigned at the hunting lodge, she had discreetly made her escape.

Scylla gave a raucous cry: they had arrived.

And, indeed, La Donna soon saw the clearing ahead of her where Aubusson, her friend and accomplice, was waiting with two horses he had hired that day from the master of the staging post at Dammartin.

They exchanged a long embrace.

'At last!' said the painter. 'You did it!'

'Not yet.'

'What? You're free, aren't you?'

'I shall never be entirely free as long as that sorcerer lives.'

'Don't tell me you intend to—'

'Don't worry, just return home. The cardinal's men will soon be asking you numerous, pressing questions.'

'No. I'll come with you.'

'Don't. You've done enough already. We'll meet again soon, my friend.'

And hitching up her skirt to reveal the breeches and boots she had donned before leaving her apartments at La Renardière, she mounted a horse and dug her heels into its flanks.

'Captain! Captain!'

La Fargue slowly regained consciousness. The last thing he remembered was the sound of the drac's ribs cracking as they hit the ground.

Moaning, the old gentleman discovered innumerable pains as he sat up to see Leprat descending into the moat.

'Captain! Are you all right?'

'I'll live. And him?'

He leaned on one elbow and pointed to the drac stretched out beside him.

'Dead,' replied the musketeer.

'Good. And the others?'

'Also dead. But there were only five of them. Six, with this one.'

'So there's one still missing. That's too bad . . . And La Donna?' La Fargue asked as Leprat helped him to his feet.

'She's nowhere to be found.'

At the home of the cardinal's master of magic, Agnès and Laincourt were drowsily waiting in an antechamber, one on a bench and the other in a chair, when the sound of a door being flung open roused them.

It was Teyssier, coming in search of them.

His face looked drawn, there were rings under his eyes and his hair was dishevelled. His fingers were ink-stained and in his hand he held dog-eared sheets of paper, covered with cramped writing and many crossings-out. Unshaven, he had spent the entire night studying the documents La Donna had stolen from the Black Claw.

'I need you to escort me to the Palais-Cardinal,' he said in an urgent voice. 'I must see the cardinal as soon as he wakes.'

Laincourt turned to the window.

The night was just starting to grow pale.

Dawn was breaking over Paris and the Ile Notre-Dame-des-Écailles.

Down in the cellar that stank of rotting remains, his ritual staff across his thighs, the old drac was crouched in a meditative posture. He did not make the slightest gesture and kept his eyes closed when he heard steps behind him.

'I've been waiting for you,' he said in the drakish tongue.

'Pray to your gods one last time,' replied La Donna, unsheathing a dagger.

The sorcerer stood up and faced her.

Dressed in a sturdy leather hunting outfit, she was alone. She had preferred not to bring her two small companions out of fear of being recognised at the gates of Paris. A pretty young red-headed woman with two dragonnets would not go unnoticed, and she had excellent reasons to believe that all of the cardinal's informers – although they might not know why – had received instructions to keep a lookout for her. Besides, even without Scylla and Charybdis, returning to Paris was imprudent on her part.

But Alessandra di Santi knew there was still an act to be played out in this story, before she disappeared for good.

The old drac gave her his toothless smile.

'What is it, sorcerer? Do you think I will hesitate to stab you if you stare at me? Then you do not know me . . .'

La Donna, however, was about to fall victim to her pride.

Too sure of herself, she did not see the danger coiled in the shadowy corners of the cellar, which was already creeping out to surround her. Silent and deadly, tendrils of black mist snaked towards her, licking her boots, winding around her ankles.

'Your little dragonnets, they would have sensed it—' said the drac.

'Sensed it? Sensed what?'

'This—'

The sorcerer's eyes sparkled. His fists clenched around his staff and he suddenly brandished it in the air. Instantly, the tongues of black mist rushed to attack the young woman, like a vine suddenly wrapping itself around a column. They seized her and pinned her arms against her body. Incapable of making the slightest movement, she felt herself lifted from the floor.

'I understood too late,' said the old drac. 'I realised too late that you had stopped running. I saw, too late, that you were only hiding for long enough to discover my lair . . . Indeed, how did you manage that? Your cursed little dragonnets, no doubt . . .'

He shook his staff and rattled the talismans – little bones, scales, beads, claws – that hung from it. La Donna stiffened, her body paralysed. She tried to speak, but could only manage a hiccup. Like a vice, the wisps of mist were now crushing her chest. She was starting to lack for air.

'But it wasn't enough for you to draw my warriors into a trap. Even once you were rid of them, you knew your flight would never be complete as long as I held within me that small shred of your soul which I stole from you. You needed to kill me. And that's why I was waiting for you.'

The sorcerer shook his staff again. Alessandra gave a jolt. Her eyes round with fear, she felt the black mist running fine, agile fingers over her throat towards her face, her lips, and her nostrils.

If this horror reached inside her . . .

'Dying of the sudden ranse is extremely painful, did you know that?'

La Donna gathered her last strength to tear herself away from the mist that threatened to invade her nose, her mouth, her throat, and her entire being. In vain. She gave a long painful moan in supplication. Tears welled up at the corners of her eyes.

The worst thing was that she and the sorcerer were not alone in the cellar. La Donna had seen someone slowly emerge from the shadows behind the drac's back. But why didn't he act? Why wouldn't he help her? Was he content to watch her die? Why? What had she done to deserve such indifference?

Do something . . . For pity's sake do some—

She was losing consciousness when the mist suddenly relaxed its embrace. The young woman collapsed on the dirt floor and, through a veil, saw the sorcerer frozen in shock, a blade pointing at his chest. Then the blade disappeared with a sound of steel clawing at scales and bone, and the old drac fell down dead. First to his knees. And then on his belly.

The black mist dissipated.

Coughing and spluttering but quickly regaining her wits, La Donna dragged herself backwards away from the body and the pool of blood spreading beneath it.

'Wh . . . What were you waiting for?' she finally asked, between two great gulps of air.

'I was waiting to hear the full story,' replied Saint-Lucq.

'You bastard.'

'You're welcome.'

The half-blood crouched to wipe his blade on the sorcerer's filthy, stinking rags. Then he stood up, re-sheathed his sword and, from behind his red spectacles, watched La Donna struggle to her feet, one hand seeking support from the wall.

'You'd better hurry, madame,' he said in a voice that betrayed no emotion. 'As perhaps you would like to rest for a little while, before your next appointment with monsieur de Laffemas at Le Châtelet.'

4

Rue Saint-Thomas-du-Louvre was located in a neighbour-hood that stretched from the palace of the Louvre in the east to that of the Tuileries in the west, and between rue Saint-Honoré to the north and the Grande Galerie to this south. This old neighbourhood had undergone various upheavals over the centuries, to the point of now finding itself curiously embedded in the royal precinct, after the Grande Galerie – also known as 'Gallery on the shore' – was built to link the Louvre to the Tuileries along the bank of the Seine. But whatever its changed circumstances, it had kept its mediaeval appearance. Dirty, cramped, and populous, it offered an un-fortunate contrast with the royal buildings that surrounded it on three sides.

Running north from the quays, rue Saint-Thomas-du-Louvre ended at rue Saint-Honoré, opposite the Palais-Cardinal. It took its name from a twelfth-century church dedicated to Saint Thomas of Canterbury, and had acquired a certain notoriety due to the two adjoining mansions of Rambouillet and Chev-reuse. The first was the Parisian residence of the marquise de Rambouillet, who hosted a famous literary salon there. The second belonged to the duchesse de Chevreuse, whose reputation as a lover, schemer, and woman of the world needed no further embellishment.

This evening, the duchesse was receiving guests.

Torches burned at the monument gates of her mansion, lighting up the street in the gathering dusk. Other torches illuminated the courtyard. The guests were already arriving in coaches, in sedan chairs, on horseback. But also on foot, escorted by lackeys who carried lights and who, once they reached their destination, helped their masters change their shoes or even their stockings. Groups were forming at both ends of rue Saint-Thomas. And people were almost jostling one another before the mansion itself. They conversed gaily, already pleasantly anticipating the excellent evening they would be spending. The jesting of men and the laughter of women rose from the scene, disturbing the night's nascent tranquillity.

In the courtyard, the chairs hindered the carriages as they made the turn to deliver their occupants to the front porch. Made nervous by the agitation, the horses held by their bits whinnied and threatened to rear up between their traces. Lackeys and coachmen did their best to prevent any mishaps. For their masters, it was a question of making the most noteworthy appearance thanks to the splendour of their team and the magnificence of their attire.

There was, however, one guest who — although he came unaccompanied by any servant and descended from a simple hired chair — inspired a certain amount of awe. Thin and pallid, with icy grey eyes and bloodless lips, he was dressed in the austere black robes of a scholar and did not exchange glances with anyone.

'Who is that?' some of those present asked in hushed voices.

'That's Mauduit.'

'Who?'

'Mauduit. Madame de Chevreuse's new master of magic!'

'The one they say is a sorcerer?'

Mauduit.

That was how he was known here. But he had borne and still bore many other names.

And, to a few people only, he was known as the Alchemist of the Shadows.

III

The Chevreuse Affair

The meeting took place at nightfall, on the road to Saint-Germain-en-Laye, in a hostelry whose old sign depicted a hart's head in yellow, flaking paint. The establishment had seen better days. Once a thriving business, it had suffered since a bridge had been built at Chatou to replace the ferry – which had previously been the only means of crossing the Seine in these parts. Although the bridge did not change the itinerary of those travelling back and forth between Paris and Saint-Germain, it did save time and make the stop at *The Golden Hart* less necessary.

The riders arrived at dusk.

There were four of them, all wearing great dark cloaks, wide felt hats, riding boots and carrying swords at their side. One of them was Cardinal Richelieu, riding incognito between two of his most loyal gentlemen and following the new captain of his Guards, monsieur de La Houdinière. On this expedition, however, the latter was not wearing the prestigious scarlet cape with its distinctive cross and white braid beneath his cloak. He dismounted in the courtyard, knocked on the door according to the agreed code – three times, once, then three times again – and looked around him as he waited for a response.

A wyvern screamed in the distance. Perhaps a wild one, although they were rarely found in France except in the most out-of-the-way corners of the kingdom. More likely a trained wyvern, being ridden by a royal messenger or a scout from one of the regiments assembling around Paris before setting off for Champagne, in preparation for the forthcoming campaign against Lorraine.

Someone, at last, opened the door a crack.

It was Cupois, the hosteller, who presented an anxious face with a sallow complexion, topped by a crown of red hair.

'Is everything ready?' La Houdinière demanded.

'Yes, milord.'

The hosteller had no idea who he was addressing, although he was sure he was dealing with a great lord involved in some dangerous intrigue. That, of course, worried him. But the lure of gold proved stronger than his misgivings when La Houdinière – without saying who he was or whom he served – had come by shortly before noon to inspect the place, giving strict instructions and leaving a handsome sum in advance. Cupois only knew that *The Golden Hart* had been chosen for a meeting that was at least confidential, if not clandestine, in nature.

'There are some gentlemen already waiting for you,' he said. 'They are upstairs in the largest of my rooms, where, according to your orders, I have placed a table and chairs.'

La Houdinière entered, examined the common room which was plunged into half-light and listened closely to the silence that reigned within the hostelry.

'Did they have the password?' he asked, to set his own mind at rest.

'Of course,' replied the hosteller, peeking outdoors. 'Without it, I would not have allowed them to enter.'

The captain of the Cardinal's Guards could not refrain from smiling at the notion of Cupois trying to prevent La Fargue from entering anywhere.

'Good,' he said. 'Go join your wife in your chamber and don't come back out.'

'I prepared a light meal and I—'

'No need. Go to your bed, monsieur Cupois.'

His tone was courteous, but firm.

'They're coming,' said Almades, interrupting a conversation between La Fargue and Laincourt.

Standing at the window, but at a discreet distance, he kept watch on the surroundings of *The Golden Hart*. Laconic as always, he added:

'Four riders. One of them comes in advance as a scout. I cannot make out his face.'

'Rochefort,' surmised the captain of the Blades. 'Or La Houdinière.'

'La Houdinière. He has just dismounted,' said the Spanish fencing master.

Laincourt joined him to take a look outside.

'The cardinal is waiting on his horse,' he reported. 'The other two are gentlemen from his entourage. I have met them before at the Palais-Cardinal—'

'So, no sign of Rochefort,' La Fargue concluded.

As usual he was wearing a sleeveless black leather vest over a doublet of the same red as the sash that was tied about his waist, with his Pappenheimer at his side. His close-cropped white beard was neatly trimmed, but his face was drawn, betraying the strain of the recent fight at La Renardière and his desperate fall from the window. Although he tried not to let anything show, he still experienced some pain when he moved.

'No,' confirmed Laincourt. 'No sign of Rochefort.'

'We serve the same master, he and I. And yet I must confess I always feel more at ease when I know where he is and what he is doing. He is a little like a ferocious dog. I do not like to imagine him roaming about freely in the garden . . .'

Arnaud de Laincourt nodded and then turned his head towards Saint-Lucq when the latter said:

'Perhaps Rochefort is too busy with La Donna . . .'

The half-blood was lying stretched out on the bed away from the others, in the shadows. Remaining perfectly still, hat over his eyes and fingers crossed on his chest, he had appeared to be napping until now. With Laincourt and Almades to accompany La Fargue, his presence here was useless and he knew it. But the cardinal had specifically asked that he came. He did not know why.

At the mention of the Italian lady spy, La Fargue pursed his lips doubtfully.

The Blades had been without news of Alessandra since Saint-Lucq had laid hands on her once again. They only knew that she had since been incarcerated in the Bastille and later transferred elsewhere. If monsieur de Laffemas was still interrogating her, he was no longer doing so at Le Châtelet.

'You can be certain,' said Laincourt in a grave voice, 'that La Donna has not spent more than two or three nights in a gaol cell. And if the cardinal is keeping you in the dark as to where she is being detained, it may be because she is no longer being detained anywhere.'

Saint-Lucq sat up suddenly and pivoted to perch on the edge of the bed.

'Are you saying that she is now free?' he asked in surprise, pushing his red spectacles up to the bridge of his nose.

'I'm saying I would not be too surprised to learn that she was . . .'

'And how the devil—?'

Laincourt admitted his ignorance with a shrug. But then he added:

'La Donna never plays a card without having another one up her sleeve. By returning to Paris after her escape from La Renardière, thanks to the drac attack, she knew she risked being recaptured. And no doubt she made some arrangements to protect herself in this event.'

La Fargue and Saint-Lucq exchanged a look while the cardinal's former spy remained deep in his own thoughts. As for Almades, he continued to keep his silent vigil upon the courtyard.

'They're coming inside,' he announced.

Then he looked out at the horizon where clouds darker than night were massing. He saw the first flickers of lightning from the storm which was now looming over Paris.

Leaning from a third-storey window, Marciac twisted himself around in order to expose his face to the welcome rain which, after a prolonged heat spell, was now pouring down upon the capital. Eyes closed, he smiled and breathed in deeply. The blowing wind and rumblings of thunder did not bother him in the least.

'Great God, that feels good!' he exclaimed; 'Sometimes there's nothing better than a storm . . .'

'A powerful thought,' retorted Agnès, hauling him back inside by the collar. 'Now, if you could just avoid revealing yourself to the whole world . . .'

She closed the window.

'No need to worry on that account,' said the Gascon wiping his face with a hand. 'The hosteller swore to me our man would not be back till midnight.'

He was soaked, dishevelled and delighted.

'And how does he know that, your hosteller?' asked the baronne de Vaudreuil.

Marciac shrugged blithely.

'I didn't think to ask,' he confessed. 'But he seemed particularly sure of himself on this point.'

Agnès rolled her eyes and shook her head. She was dressed like a horseman, as usual — boots, breeches, white shirt, cinched red leather corset — and had tied her thick black hair back into a long plait. At her side hung a rapier whose handsome elegance had often reserved deadly surprises for her enemies.

The thunder rolled above them, causing the window panes to rattle and the whole building's frame to creak. They were in the attic.

'There's Ballardieu too,' insisted the Gascon. 'He's watching from the street below, isn't he?'

The young woman was forced to agree:

'Yes. Ballardieu is keeping an eye on things below . . . But let's complete our task here and return to the mansion as quickly as possible, all right? In fact, we should already have finished by now.'

'Very good, madame la baronne.'

Pretending not to see Marciac's mocking bow, Agnès slowly swept her candleholder from side to side before her, surveying the bedchamber into which they had discreetly introduced themselves after bribing the owner. The room was rather shabby, as was the rest of the establishment, a very modest hostelry in the faubourg Saint-Jacques. It contained a bed, a chest, a table and a stool. Its legitimate occupant had also left behind a large leather bag.

Each of them holding a light, Agnès and Marciac got to work without conferring or hindering one another. Their mission consisted of verifying one of the few, rare pieces of intelligence that La Donna had provided to monsieur de Laffemas. According to her, an emissary of the queen mother – a certain Guéret – was in Paris to hand sensitive documents over to the duchesse de Chevreuse. Based on the spy's information, the Blades thought they could unmask this Guéret, but first they had to confirm his identity.

'What are we searching for, exactly?' asked the Gascon, kneeling before the clothing chest he had just opened.

There was more rumbling from the storm outside and the sound of the rain spattering down on the tiles of the roof resounded in the chamber. Already, drops were falling from a crack in the ceiling.

'Letters,' answered Agnès. 'Papers. Anything that proves we have located the right person. But without taking or disturbing anything. The man must not have the slightest reason to suspect that we have our eye on him . . .'

'Oh dear!' said Marciac in a strangely toneless voice, 'I'm afraid that particular cat is already out of the sack.'

Busy examining the contents of the leather bag, the young woman had only been lending him a distracted ear.

'Pardon?' she said, after a moment.

Raising her head, she saw the Gascon leap in pursuit of someone in the corridor. The chamber's legitimate occupant, no doubt. Whoever he was, they had not heard him coming over the sound of the storm and, for a few heartbeats, Marciac and the man had stared at one another in mutual disbelief . . .

. . . just before a clap of thunder broke the spell and precipitated the chase.

Recovering from her surprise, Agnès cursed, climbed over the bed and dashed out of the room in pursuit of the two men.

*

Having entrusted his cloak and hat to La Houdinière, Cardinal Richelieu – in high boots, breeches and a doublet made of grey cloth – removed his gloves and announced:

'I must be at the château de Saint-Germain within the hour, where I will be joining the king and his court. So let us be brief, monsieur de La Fargue. My escort is waiting for me in the woods a quarter league from here.'

Almades and Saint-Lucq having gone downstairs to join the two gentlemen belonging to His Eminence's suite, only four men – the cardinal, La Fargue, La Houdinière, and Laincourt – remained on the upper floor of *The Golden Hart*, in a strangely quiet and desolate room that smelled of old wood and dust. A few candles placed here and there made the shadows dance and hollowed the faces of those present. Richelieu looked even more emaciated than usual and his glance seemed more penetrating.

'What news of this plot that La Donna claimed to denounce?' the chief minister asked. 'Is there any evidence of it, according to you? And if so, what can you tell me about it at present?'

La Fargue cleared his throat before replying.

'If there is one point on which La Donna has never wavered, monseigneur, it is this one. There is a plot, and it threatens the French throne.'

'And what is its nature?'

'We still don't know. But we believe that the Black Claw is behind it.'

The cardinal gathered his fingers into a steeple before his thin lips.

'The Black Claw, you say?'

'Yes, monseigneur.'

'With the complicity of other parties?'

'Yes. That of the duchesse de Chevreuse. And of the queen, monseigneur.'

Having said his piece, La Fargue fell silent.

A hush settled around the table as Richelieu stared at him for a long moment. Laincourt tried to remain as impassive as the captain of the Blades, but the effort cost him and he detected signs of a similar struggle going on within La Houdinière.

However indirectly, La Fargue had just accused the queen of treason.

'Do you have proof of this claim?' the cardinal finally enquired. 'Not proofs concerning these complicities, but of the plot itself?'

'Not as such, monseigneur. Only the documents delivered to us by La Donna which attest to—'

'Those documents do not attest to much, captain,' Richelieu interrupted in a severe tone of voice. 'Teyssier has given me a preliminary translation to read. The documents are incomplete and very vague, even supposing that they are authentic.'

'La Donna can testify to that. Let her be interrogated.'

'Impossible.'

'Impossible, monseigneur? What do you mean?'

'The woman is no longer in our power,' said the cardinal in a voice that was too calm not to be worrying. 'After she escaped from you, during the few hours of liberty she enjoyed before being recaptured, she managed to communicate her situation to certain individuals who are very well-disposed towards her . . .'

As Richelieu spoke, La Fargue recalled Laincourt's prediction and, out of the corner of his eye, he watched for a reaction from the younger man. He was not the sort to say 'I told you so', implicitly or not. But nevertheless it appeared he had foretold matters correctly and, according to the cardinal, on the very day that Saint-Lucq had retaken La Donna into custody, an emissary from the Pope had demanded an audience with His Eminence to discuss the case of the beautiful lady spy.

'The threat was scarcely veiled,' said Richelieu. 'She was to be liberated at once, or else accused and presented to her judges. That is to say: the very members of the Parlement who would have insisted on asking questions and expressing loud protests concerning La Donna for reasons of which you are already aware. Therefore, since it was not in the interests of the king to allow a scandal, and since the support of

His Holiness could be useful to the kingdom in the near future . . .'

La Fargue nodded with a sombre face. France was merely waiting for a pretext to invade Lorraine, a Catholic bastion at the very gates of the Holy Roman Empire, which was itself being torn apart by war.

'But all this matters little in the end,' the cardinal pursued. 'Madame de Chevreuse is part of this plot, you say? Very well, there will soon be no worries on that score. In fact I can tell you that the duchesse will shortly be placed under arrest, and for proven motives.'

'Which are, monseigneur?'

'Treason,' indicated Richelieu, with a gesture of his hand to indicate that he would say no more on this subject. 'Others, just as prestigious as La Chevreuse by their birth, rank, or fortune, will be similarly inconvenienced. Special trials will be held. Sentences will be pronounced. And heads will roll.'

La Fargue frowned. He feared he was beginning to understand where all this was leading.

'Are you ordering me to give up this mission, monseigneur?'

'Nothing can be allowed to compromise the success of the matter I have just mentioned.'

'But, monseigneur—'

'It is an affair of State, captain.'

'And a plot against the king is not?'

'It is a shadowy plot, at best.'

'A plot of which the Alchemist himself is the mastermind!' exploded La Fargue.

Silence fell, heavy as an executioner's axe.

La Fargue had raised his voice and, despite being willing to pardon the old gentleman many things, the cardinal had frozen, his eyes suddenly blazing with anger. Laincourt held his breath and saw the captain of the Blades, embarrassed, inhale deeply.

'I . . . I humbly beseech Your Eminence to forgive my outburst.'

Richelieu paused until his gaze grew more peaceful and then he finally said:

'The Alchemist, yes, of course . . . That name must bring some very bad memories to mind, captain . . .'

'Indeed.'

'I therefore understand your . . . lapse. And I forgive it.'

'Monseigneur, said La Fargue in a more composed voice, 'thwarting this plot is above all a matter of protecting the king. But it is perhaps also a means of inflicting a terrible blow against the Black Claw by killing or capturing the Alchemist.'

'And it also risks compromising the fruits of some long, patient investigations into some of most eminent personages in the kingdom. All this may yet fail if you disturb the duchesse or her accomplices with your operations.'

'It is a question of neutralising the Alchemist, monseigneur. A similar opportunity may not present itself for a long time to come.'

'I am well aware of that. But you are hunting with hounds and have only just set off in your pursuit, whereas I have been laying my snares for some time now. Although you and I are not hunting exactly the same prey, you could very well end up frightening mine by tracking yours. And, to top it all, you may only be hunting a shadow.'

La Fargue was silent. What other argument could he make? Richelieu knew all the facts, all that was at stake, all the risks, all the secret realities which would lead him to take, alone, a decision that would no doubt have heavy consequences.

The cardinal granted himself another moment of reflection and then said:

'Very well, captain. Since the life of the king may depend on it, endeavour to foil this plot that threatens him. It may, possibly, lead you to the Alchemist, who is an enemy of France. If it does, you must neutralise him . . .'

The captain of the Blades wanted to thank him, but Richelieu raised his index finger to signal that he had not finished yet.

'However, I am aware that this enemy of France is also your own since the tragic events at La Rochelle. Do not let that obscure your judgement. Be prudent and discreet. Forbid yourself the slightest false step. Do not act lightly, and above all, do not commit some mistake that might irretrievably wreck the trials we are now preparing . . .'

La Fargue nodded. The cardinal, however, continued:

'That being said, I set two further conditions. The first is that you keep me informed of your projects, and of your successes as well as your failures.

'Certainly, monseigneur.'

'The second is that you transfer Saint-Lucq to my service.'

Although it left La Fargue unperturbed, this request – which was in fact an order – surprised Laincourt. But it confirmed in his mind the half-blood's unique status within the Blades. Did he really belong to them? The others seemed to consider him one of their best. However, where they willingly expressed their pride at serving under La Fargue, Saint-Lucq set himself apart and adopted the pose of an exceptional mercenary who remained with the Blades by choice, but who could leave tomorrow. Moreover, Laincourt knew that when the Blades had been disbanded, Saint-Lucq was the only member the cardinal had continued to employ on secret missions. That could not be insignificant.

'All of the Blades serve at Your Eminence's discretion, monseigneur,' said La Fargue.

'Good,' replied Richelieu, rising and accepting La Houdinière's aid in donning his cloak. 'I'm relying on you, La Fargue. But you should know that you don't have much time. The duchesse de Chevreuse will be hosting a great ball at Dampierre. The morning after this ball she shall be placed under arrest, as will all those who are implicated in her schemes, throughout France. The king desires this, so that her fall immediately follows her moment of triumph.'

The cardinal paused here, thinking to himself that this decision corresponded well with the character, at times cruel and devious, of Louis XIII. Calmly, he put on his gloves.

'One last thing, captain. The king is very attached to the success of this . . . Chevreuse affair. He has been following its slow development closely for several months now and is growing impatient. He will not tolerate seeing the duchesse escape from the arm of his justice, even if it were to occur in the course of protecting His Majesty from a plot . . .'

Before putting on his hat, Richelieu fixed La Fargue with his steely gaze and added:

'Do you understand me, captain? And are you fully aware how ungrateful kings can be?'

'*Merde!*' Marciac snarled, seeing the runaway jump from one roof to another across an alleyway.

Not knowing whether Agnès was following him closely or not, he did not slow down, took the same leap in turn and, in the dark and the wet, landed as best he could on the other side.

He swore again as he almost lost his balance.

'*Merde!*'

And then he resumed the pursuit under the pouring rain . . .

. . . hoping mightily that he was in fact chasing Guéret, the agent that the queen mother had sent to the duchesse de Chevreuse. Provided La Donna hadn't lied. Provided they had not been mistaken about the room at the inn or its occupant. Nothing was certain. On discovering two strangers searching his belongings the other man, to be sure, had not raised a hue and cry but had instead immediately taken to his heels. And now he was still fleeing as if he had the Devil on his trail, over rain-slicked rooftops in the middle of a stormy night, at the risk of breaking his neck. Frankly it was not the behaviour of a man with a clear conscience. Nevertheless. If this fellow was not Guéret, then Marciac was making a huge mistake . . .

Out of breath, soaked to the skin, his face spattered by volleys of fat, stinging raindrops, he slowed down for an instant and sought to catch a glimpse of his fugitive. He spotted his silhouette thanks to a flash of lightning. The foolhardy man had not weakened. He continued running and appeared to be taking a giant leap over a major obstacle. Feeling anger grow within him, the Gascon resumed the chase and discovered, by almost falling into it, the nature of the obstacle in question. He managed to halt himself at the last minute on the verge of empty space. This time, it was not a matter of crossing a narrow alley. Or even a street. He looked down into the shadowy well of a small courtyard.

'*Merde de merde!*' exclaimed Marciac furiously.

Going around would mean letting the other man escape. But so would waiting here for much longer.

The Gascon hesitated. He backed up a few steps, all the while cursing himself, his contrary fate, and imbeciles who scarpered over roofs during a deluge in the middle of night. He took a deep breath. Cursed some more.

And launched himself into thin air.

Windmilling his arms and kicking his legs, Marciac's leap was not a beauteous thing to behold. But it propelled him across five metres of cavernous darkness to land on the ridge of a sloping roof.

After that, things took a turn for the worse.

The roof was not only sloped but also streaming with water, that is to say, it was extremely slippery. And most of its tiles were just waiting to be dislodged.

Like a high wire artist in a gale, Marciac teetered, waving his arms, shifting from one leg to the other . . .

'Oh, *merde* . . .'

He fell onto his arse and slid down the slope, faster and faster, preceded by a cascade of tiles which came loose beneath his heels.

'*Merde-merde-merde-merde-merde-merde-merde* . . .'

And then there was only empty space.

'*MEEEEEEEEEEERDE!*'

Some worm-eaten planks slowed his fall with a crash, a thick layer of straw then cushioned it further and finally a hard bump on the floor of a stable brought matters to a conclusion. Marciac felt pain, swore in his usual manner and still very angry, rolled over on his side, grimacing.

Which he probably would not have done if he had known he was about to put his nose in a pile of . . .

'*Merde.*'

Agnès's heart leapt in her chest when she saw Marciac fall.

'NICOLAS!'

She too jumped across the small courtyard, landed with more aplomb than the Gascon and cautiously succeeded in reaching the edge of the roof.

'NICOLAS!' she called out in an anxious voice. 'NICOLAS!'

'I'm down here.'

'ANYTHING BROKEN?'

'Don't think so, no.'

'HOW ARE YOU?'

Displaying a definite sign of good health, Marciac's boiling temper rose to the surface.

'ADMIRABLY WELL!' he shouted sarcastically. 'No GASCON HAS EVER SPENT A BETTER EVENING! SO HOW ABOUT GOING AFTER THAT OTHER ACROBAT, HMM?'

Reassured, Agnès withdrew from the edge of the roof and stood up. Beneath the storm and making use of the flashes of lightning she scanned the rooftops around her, but did not see the runaway and finally picked a direction at random. She doubted she would ever be able to catch him. Even if she knew which way to go, the man now had too great a lead.

A little further on, coming around an enormous chimney, Agnès found herself looking out over a wide crossroads. The person she was looking for was not visible on any of the surrounding rooftops.

It was the end of the chase.

Regretfully, she was about to turn back when her glance fell onto the street below.

And there, dimly lit by one of the big lanterns that were left burning all night in a few scattered places in the capital, she saw the man lying unmoving on the pavement five storeys down, surrounded by a dark puddle riddled by the falling raindrops.

They rode at a walk, through the night, along the road towards Paris and the storm. La Fargue and Laincourt went ahead. Almades followed, quiet and attentive. The old gentleman had not said a word since they had left *The Golden Hart* shortly after the cardinal's departure with his escort and Saint-Lucq. He seemed absorbed in his thoughts and Laincourt chose to respect his silence. Besides, he was fairly preoccupied himself.

Around them, the darkness seemed immense and the storm rumbled in the distance like the anger of some ancient god.

'It was at La Rochelle,' La Fargue said suddenly, without taking his eyes off from the path ahead. 'Five years ago, during the siege of 1628. We were there, some of the Blades and I, the others being busy in Lorraine. We had infiltrated the besieged town in order to carry out the kind of missions that you might expect . . . .'

'Captain, I—'

'No, Laincourt. It's important that you understand. And I know you are the sort of man who can keep a secret. So don't interrupt me, will you?'

'Very well.'

'Thank you . . . For the most part, it was a matter of collecting intelligence and, by night, taking it back to our own lines. The cardinal was thus kept informed of the state of La Rochelle's defences, of the imminence and scale of relief from the English, of the true severity of the food shortages caused by the blockade, of the shifting opinion among the population and the difficulties encountered by the town's leaders. We also carried out, on occasion, acts of sabotage. And, more rarely, we eliminated traitors and foreign agents.'

La Fargue turned to Laincourt and asked him:

'But you already know all that, don't you?'

'Yes.'

Nodding to himself, the captain of the Blades shifted his position in the saddle slightly to ease the pain in his back.

'We were doing what we do best. Meanwhile, the siege was turning in favour of the royal armies after the cardinal ordered a dike built to prevent ships reaching or leaving the port . . . Then one evening, when I secretly met with Rochefort, he told me the Alchemist was in La Rochelle. Why was he there? My new mission was precisely to learn this and, if possible, to seize him. I endeavoured to do so with zeal because the Alchemist's renown, as well as the mystery surrounding him, was already immense. He was an enemy of

France and his arrival in La Rochelle had to be significant: something important was afoot . . .'

La Fargue paused in his recital of the tale and, holding back a grimace, rotated an aching shoulder. After his fall into the moat at La Renardière, Marciac – who had once almost become a doctor – examined him and determined that nothing was broken. But the captain of the Blades, as solid and tough as he was despite his age, was not indestructible and had increasing difficulty recovering from the physical ordeals he inflicted upon himself in the line of duty.

'I soon learned that the Alchemist was supposed to attend a meeting. With whom, I did not know. But I knew where and when, so I prepared an ambush. And in doing so, I walked straight into the trap that the Alchemist had set for us.'

La Fargue's glance was lost in memory for a moment.

He resumed his account:

'I am convinced, now, that the Alchemist's mission was in fact to unmask us and remove us as an effective unit in the conflict.'

'Were you under suspicion?'

'No. But the blows we struck against La Rochelle's forces would have indicated that a clandestine enemy unit was operating within the town walls . . .'

'So the Alchemist arranged for the cardinal's men to learn he was in La Rochelle, is that it? So that you would be informed in turn and make every effort to capture him.'

'Yes, that's my belief. Aware of his own value, he made himself the bait to flush us out, which he managed without difficulty. A simple, effective plan. A brilliant plan. Often, the real trick consists in making your opponent believe he's calling the tune . . .' The old gentleman slowly shook his head, as if the years had suddenly caught up with him. 'It was a disaster. One of us, Bretteville, perished during the ambush. And another, Louveciennes—'

'—betrayed you and fled. Today he lives in Spain, as the wealthy comte de Pontevedra.'

The captain of the Blades nodded gravely before adding:

'That same night, the dike gave way. Soon English supplies

and relief forces arrived in La Rochelle by sea. The king realised that he could no longer win by force of arms alone, not without beggaring the kingdom, and he commanded the cardinal to open negotiations. Richelieu disavowed us to avoid having to justify our activities during the siege; he affirmed that we were acting without orders and that he was not even aware of our existence. For the Blades, it meant disgrace. And soon the end, since the cardinal dismissed us from his service.'

'Until recently.'

'Yes. Until recently.'

La Fargue fell silent.

Laincourt followed suit, but one question continued to haunt him. A question he did not dare to ask, but which the captain of the Blades was able to guess:

'Ask it.'

'I beg your pardon, captain?'

'Your question. Go ahead, ask it.'

The young man hesitated, and then:

'How can we ever know for sure?' he heard himself wonder aloud. 'How can we know if you're pursuing this mission to avenge yourself upon the Alchemist or not? How can we know if you prefer seeking justice for yourself to serving the king and France?'

Behind them, Almades pricked up an ear.

La Fargue smiled sadly.

'You can't,' he replied.

In the faubourg Saint-Jacques, Agnès was making her way back towards the hostelry under the continuing downpour, through deserted streets sporadically lit by flashes of lightning. The young baronne, soaked and furious, walked briskly, a curl of hair dangling in front of one eye.

She soon met up with Marciac and Ballardieu. They were going in the same direction, the old soldier supporting the limping Gascon.

Ballardieu lowered his eyes upon seeing Agnès.

'Well?' she asked, directing her words at Marciac.

'Sprained ankle. Very painful . . . And the other man? Did you lose him?'

'Dead.'

'You killed—?'

'No! He fell and broke his skull.'

'So we have a problem.'

'As you say.'

The young woman turned to Ballardieu and told him in a frosty tone where he could find the body. Then she ordered:

'Dump it in the Seine. But strip it first and make sure it's unrecognisable. And keep all the clothing.'

'Yes, Agnès.'

The old soldier went about his tasks without further ado.

Taking his place, Agnès propped Marciac up and slowly, because the Gascon was heavy and could only hobble, they made their way back to the inn.

'He may not be to blame,' said Marciac.

Agnès knew he was referring to Ballardieu and replied:

'He should have warned us the man was coming. That was his job. And I'm convinced he's been drinking . . .'

The Gascon could find nothing to say in response to this. But after a few more metres in the rain, he said:

'La Fargue isn't going to be happy, is he?'

'Not in the least bit.'

They had just lost the only lead likely to take them to the duchesse de Chevreuse, to the Alchemist and to the plot against the king.

2

The rain continued after the storm and did not cease until dawn. Paris woke fresh and reinvigorated. To say that the capital was clean would have been an exaggeration; it would have required a deluge of biblical proportions to carry away the filth accumulated on its streets and to remove the foul muck clinging to its pavements. But the worst had been washed away and Parisians, upon rising from their beds, were grateful to have finally been relieved of the dust and stink of recent days. It even seemed that the cocks crowed more valiantly and the bells rang more clearly this morning, while the city glistened beneath the sun's first rays.

'Dead,' repeated La Fargue in a tone which did not bode well. 'Guéret . . . is dead.'

The garden still being soaked, they had gathered in the large fencing room inside the Hôtel de l'Épervier. The atmosphere was tense. Even those Blades who were not involved in the previous evening's fiasco were keeping their heads down. Only Almades, who had stationed himself slightly apart from the others to guard the door, seemed completely aloof.

'Yes, captain,' Agnès confirmed.

She, Marciac and Ballardieu had not had time to change from the night before. Their clothing had dried on their backs and left them looking bedraggled, not to mention their tousled hair, weary faces and obvious chagrin. Ballardieu in particular wore a hangdog look.

'How?' La Fargue demanded.

'Guéret surprised us while we were in his room,' Marciac explained.

565

He was sitting down with one bare foot resting on a stool.

'And killing him seemed like a good idea to you?'

'No!' the Gascon defended himself. 'He fled over the roof-tops. We pursued him and, unfortunately, he broke his skull in a fall.'

'Unfortunately. That's one way of putting it . . . And how was it that Guéret managed to surprise you? Was no one keeping watch?'

Agnès and Marciac exchanged an embarrassed glance. Ballardieu kept his eyes fixed on the floor in front of him.

'Yes,' said the old soldier. 'I was.'

'And you didn't see the man coming back . . .'

'It was a dark night,' the Gascon interjected. 'And with the rain, the storm—'

'—and the wine, am I wrong?' La Fargue continued relentlessly.

'No,' confessed Ballardieu. 'I just went off for a moment to buy a bottle and—'

The Blades' captain thundered at him:

'You bloody old toss-pot! Have you any idea what your foolishness has cost us?'

Ballardieu kept his mouth shut. There was an oppressive silence in the room.

After a moment, La Fargue rose and went to a window. It opened onto the wet garden, where the chestnut tree's leaves were shedding their final drops upon the old table. Hands behind his back, he took the time to regain his calm. Then, still facing the garden, he said in a quieter voice:

'Any witnesses?'

'None,' replied Agnès. 'And the innkeeper will hold his tongue.'

'The body?'

'Thrown, naked and unrecognisable, into the Seine. With the waters still high from the storm, he'll never be found.'

'His belongings?'

'His baggage and the clothes he was wearing are all here.'

From over his shoulder, La Fargue glanced at the table the young woman was pointing to. On it were placed the small travelling chest, the big leather bag and Guéret's still-damp clothing. Papers found in the false bottom of the chest were also spread out.

Leprat was already inspecting them in silence.

'There are sealed letters, a map of Lorraine and another of Champagne, false passports, promissory notes . . .' he finally announced. 'Add to that French, Spanish and Lorraine currency, and you have everything one might expect to find in the possession of a spy who, according to marks on this map, came from Lorraine and passed through Champagne to reach Paris.'

'And the letters?' asked Marciac, craning his neck to see from his armchair.

'There are three of them, all addressed to the duchesse de Chevreuse. The first comes from Charles IV, the second is from his brother, the cardinal of Lorraine, and the third is from the Spanish ambassador to Lorraine. I did not think it appropriate for me to open them.'

Nancy was the capital of the duchy de Lorraine, of which Charles IV was the sovereign. Located on the border of the Holy Roman Empire and defended by one of the most formidable fortresses in Europe, Lorraine was a rich territory much coveted by France. Relations between Louis XIII and his 'dear cousin' Charles were, moreover, execrable, the duke seeming to do everything in his power to exasperate the king and defy his authority. Twice now, royal armies had marched on Nancy to compel Charles to respect the treaties he had signed. And twice the duke had made promises that he failed to keep. Thus his palace continued to welcome dissenters, plotters and other adversaries of Louis XIII. Banished for a time from France, the duchesse de Chevreuse had been one of their number.

'And that's everything?' asked Agnès.

'My word,' replied Leprat in surprise, 'it doesn't seem such a bad haul to me . . .'

Even La Fargue looked at the young baronne with puzzlement.

Was she joking?

'To be sure,' she explained, 'these passports, maps, and letters are by no means worthless. But Guéret was sent to the duchesse de Chevreuse by the queen mother, wasn't he?'

She looked at them all intently, as if they were missing something obvious. And it was the captain of the Blades who was the first to see what she was driving at.

'In all this,' he said, pointing at the documents cluttering the table, 'there is nothing from the queen mother addressed to La Chevreuse . . .'

'Exactly. The queen mother is not going to dispatch one of her agents merely to collect a few letters in Lorraine and deliver them to the duchesse, is she . . . ? Are you sure you haven't missed anything, Antoine?'

Leprat considered the dead spy's belongings displayed before him.

'I believe so, yes . . .'

'What about the clothes our man was wearing last night?' suggested Marciac.

Agnès came to the musketeer's assistance and together they found a leather envelope concealed in the lining of Guéret's doublet. As it was closed with a strip of sealed cloth, they hesitated and looked to La Fargue for permission to proceed. He nodded gravely and they broke the wax seal.

The envelope contained a letter along with several hand-written sheets that Agnès perused, showing signs of a growing astonishment.

'It's a pamphlet,' she said. 'It's about the queen, her failure to give birth to an heir and the king's supposed intention to repudiate her on those grounds. The author claims that the king has already communicated with Rome on this matter and that he will soon be in a position to choose a new wife . . .'

All those listening gaped in disbelief.

After eighteen years of marriage Queen Anne d'Autriche was still childless. She had had several miscarriages and, for some time now, had suffered from the disaffection and indifference of her husband. Indeed, Louis XIII only rarely visited her bed. Nevertheless, the repudiation of the queen would provoke an outcry in the kingdom and a possible scandal at the royal court. But above all, it would constitute a *casus belli* with Madrid, Anne being the king of Spain's sister.

'Do you think there's any truth in it?' asked Agnès.

'Who knows?' replied La Fargue. 'But if people believe it, what does it matter?'

'This text was no doubt meant to be printed secretly in Paris,' noted Leprat. 'And then spread like wildfire.'

'In order to provoke unrest?' asked Marciac.

'Or to cause a big enough upset in Europe to embarrass the king and oblige him to renounce any such project . . .'

'And so that's it? La Donna's plot against the king?' the baronne de Vaudreuil exclaimed incredulously. 'Tell me another one!'

'No,' La Fargue intervened. 'There's something else going on. But whether its content is true or pure invention and calumny, this pamphlet is by no means innocent. I believe we have laid our hands on the package the queen mother was seeking to have delivered to the duchesse de Chevreuse.'

'And the letter probably contains special instructions to go with it.'

'Shall I open it?' asked the musketeer, holding up the missive that accompanied the manuscript.

'Yes,' ordered La Fargue.

There was, in an iron cabinet somewhere within the Palais-Cardinal, a whole collection of stolen or counterfeit seals, including that of the queen mother. Her seal could be replaced if necessary.

Leprat split the seal and unfolded the letter.

'We have a problem,' he said immediately. 'This is all in code.'

When he arrived at the Hôtel de l'Épervier, Arnaud de Laincourt saw a sedan chair leaving with Marciac as its passenger, escorted by Ballardieu. The spectacle astonished the former spy, who moved aside and bemusedly acknowledged the Gascon's wave.

'I'm going to rest my wounds at *Les Petites Grenouilles*,'

Marciac announced. 'Come and visit me there when you have a moment. I'm sure you'll receive a fine welcome!'

Laincourt watched without saying a word as the chair passed through the door and then spotted La Fargue walking briskly towards the stable, where Almades was holding two saddled horses by their bridles.

'Monsieur!' he called.

The captain of the Blades halted.

'Yes, Laincourt?'

'Could you grant me a minute?'

'It will be a short one. I have to take some documents we found in Guéret's possession to the Palais-Cardinal.'

'You captured him?'

La Fargue reflected that he would probably save time if he fully briefed Laincourt right away.

'Follow me,' he said, signalling to Almades that he should wait there.

They entered the main building by the closest door, which was that of the kitchen. The two men sat down and, having asked Naïs to leave them, the old gentleman recounted the most recent events to Laincourt. The latter listened very attentively, occasionally nodding and taking mental note of every detail.

'One thing is for certain,' he said when the captain concluded, 'this pamphlet does indeed smack of the queen mother.'

Banished from the kingdom and exiled in Brussels, Marie de Médicis, widow of Henri IV and mother of Louis XIII, was an embittered old woman still brooding over the way her eldest son had brutally evicted her from power and replaced her with Richelieu. She schemed, dreamed of revenge and placed all her hopes in her other son, Gaston d'Orléans, also known as 'Monsieur', who she hoped to one day see ascend to the French throne.

'You're right,' the captain of the Blades acknowledged.

'And this encrypted letter, could you show it to me, please?'

'Might you be able to decipher it?'

'Possibly. I used to be one of the cardinal's code secretaries.'

Laincourt took the letter that La Fargue held out to him

and ran his eyes over it rapidly. The text consisted of a single block – without punctuation or breaks in the lines – made up of symbols that were mostly borrowed from alchemy.

The cardinal's former spy smiled faintly.

'It's a very simple cipher. Each symbol stands for a letter, and that's about all there is to it.'

'You can tell all this with just a glance?' asked La Fargue, giving the young man a measuring look.

But Laincourt was already absorbed in deciphering the text.

'Perhaps certain symbols stand for frequently used words. Or certain persons. But there's nothing more complicated than that . . . And see how this sign occurs so frequently? No doubt it's an "a" or "e", if the text is in French. And you see this one, it's doubled several times suggesting that it's a consonant, an "r" or "s" or "t", for example . . .'

His eyes shining, Laincourt displayed an excitement that was unusual for this young man, ordinarily so thoughtful and reserved.

'Just a moment,' he said.

And, without waiting, he rose, went over to the chimney mantelpiece, snatched up a small notebook that Naïs used for her shopping, tore off a page, returned to his seat and with a lead pencil began to transcribe the coded letter. His eyes danced from one sheet to another while his hand wrote nimbly, as if possessed of a life of its own. With pinched lips and clenched jaws, his face betrayed his intense concentration.

'This will be easier than I dared to hope,' he said.

'Why is that?'

'Because I already know this cipher.'

La Fargue was discovering that Laincourt had hidden talents which could be highly useful to the Blades. A few minutes went by in a tense silence, broken only by the scratching of pencil on paper.

'And there you have it!' the young man declared, pushing both the letter and his transcription towards La Fargue. 'You may have trouble reading my writing, but at least you won't be late in arriving at the Palais-Cardinal.'

He was almost out of breath, but displayed no pride or even satisfaction in his work.

Smiling, the captain of the Blades sat back in his chair and considered Laincourt with the admiring and amused gaze of someone who has just been fooled by an amazing feat of magic.

'You asked if I could spare you a little of my time,' he said after a moment. 'For what reason?'

'I have a way to get close to La Chevreuse.'

'How?'

The young man then explained how the chevalier de Mirebeau had approached him with his offer, and a note that would give him entry to the Hôtel de Chevreuse.

'And you propose to make use of this note,' concluded La Fargue.

'Yes.'

The old gentleman thought for a moment, weighing the pros and cons.

'All right,' he said at last. 'But you must be very careful.'

'Understood.'

'Keep your eyes and ears open, but in a natural fashion. Remember the cardinal's orders: we must not, at any price, risk arousing the duchesse's suspicions. Don't listen at doors, peer through keyholes or ask any indiscreet questions.'

'Very well.'

'And above all, be very wary of the duchesse de Chevreuse. You wouldn't be the first person that she has led astray . . .'

La Fargue had just rejoined Almades, who was patiently waiting for him in the courtyard with their two horses, when a coach entered by the carriage gate which Guibot, hobbling on his wooden leg, had hastened to open.

'Who is that?' asked the Blades' captain. 'Did you hear the name announced through the hatch?'

'No,' admitted the Spanish fencing master. 'But it's rare to see monsieur Guibot hurry like that.'

Drawn by a smart team of horses, the vehicle halted in front of them and they understood the reason for their concierge's alacrity upon seeing the marquis d'Aubremont emerge from the cabin. A man of honour and duty, he bore one of the most prestigious and respected names in France. He was also the last friend La Fargue possessed in this world. Like the captain, he was about sixty years old with grey hair, a dignified air and precise mannerisms. He and La Fargue exchanged a warm greeting. They hadn't seen one another since the marquis had buried his eldest son.

'My friend,' said La Fargue, whose eyes sparkled with a contained joy. 'If you know the pleasure that I—'

'Thank you, my friend, thank you . . . I too am very happy to see you again.'

They had once been part of an inseparable trio: La Fargue, d'Aubremont and Louveciennes. Companions and brothers-in-arms, they fought together during the civil and religious wars that had ravaged the kingdom, and then helped the 'man from Béarn' take the French throne and become King Henri IV. Upon the death of his father, d'Aubremont had been called away by the family obligations that came with bearing a great and noble name. Twenty years later, however, the first of his sons, who had until then been a member of the King's Musketeers, was to follow Leprat and join the Blades. Endowed with an adventurous and rebellious spirit, the young man had grown distant from his father and adopted the name of a small holding belonging his mother, that of Bretteville. And it was only after recruiting him that La Fargue learned that he was the eldest son of his old friend.

'Pardon my arrival in this fashion,' said d'Aubremont. 'But I could not set down in a letter what I am about to tell you . . .'

'What is it?' asked the captain of Blades in a worried tone.

'Could we speak inside, please?'

Exhausted after a particularly active and sleepless night, Agnès went upstairs to lie down in her bedchamber. She slipped between the fresh sheets with a shiver of delight and, already drowsy, vaguely heard the sound of a coach entering the courtyard. Then she closed her eyes and it seemed to her that she had just dozed off when there was a knock at her door.

'Madame . . . Madame!'

It was Naïs, whose voice reached her from the corridor, through the fog of her interrupted sleep.

Agnès muttered something into her pillow that very fortunately was transmuted into an indistinct groan, as her words were hardly polite and certainly unworthy of a baronne de Vaudreuil.

'Madame . . . Madame . . . You must come, madame . . .'

'Let me sleep, Naïs . . .'

'You were sleeping?'

'Yes, by God!'

Timid Naïs must have hesitated, for there ensued a moment of silence during which Agnès nourished the hope of having prevailed.

'But monsieur de La Fargue is asking for you, madame! He's waiting for you. And he's not alone.'

'Is he with the king of France?'

'Uhh . . . no.'

'The Pope?'

'No.'

'The Great Turk?'

'Not him, either, but—'

'Then I'm going back to sleep.'

Agnès turned over, hugged her pillow, gave a long sigh of contentment and let a faint smile appear on her lips as she once again abandoned herself to slumber.

But she heard Naïs announce in a small voice:

'He's with the marquis d'Aubremont, madame.'

La Fargue and d'Aubremont were in the captain's private office. Having finished tying back her heavy black mane of hair with a leather cord as she dashed down the stairs, Agnès hurried to join them. She granted herself a pause in front of the door, however, to briefly check her appearance and catch her breath. Then she knocked, entered, greeted the marquis with whom she was already acquainted, sat down at La Fargue's invitation and waited.

With a small nod of his head, the captain indicated to his friend that he could speak freely.

'Madame, I have come here today seeking advice and assistance from monsieur de La Fargue, who, after listening to me, thought that you might be able to help.'

'But of course, monsieur.'

Agnès had the deepest respect for this honest and upright gentleman, a father whom fate had struck all the more cruelly since his son had been killed before they had the chance to effect a reconciliation. Like all the Blades, she felt somewhat beholden to him because of this.

'It's about my son . . .'

Agnès was surprised. Did the marquis mean Bretteville?'

'My younger son, I should say. François, the chevalier d'Ombreuse.

'Isn't he serving with the Black Guards?'

'Indeed, madame.'

The Black Guards were one of the kingdom's most prestigious light cavalry companies. The king financed them from his own private purse, although they did not belong to his military household, and he appointed their officers. These hand-picked gentlemen served the Sisters of Saint Georges, the famous Chatelaines. They formed the military guard for these nuns whose mysterious rituals, over the past two centuries, had been successful in defending France and her throne against the dragons. In their black uniforms, they protected the Sisters, escorted them and, occasionally, carried out perilous missions on their behalf.

'Here's how matters stand,' continued d'Aubremont. 'My son has disappeared and I do not know whether he is alive or dead.'

The young baronne de Vaudreuil addressed a concerned glance at La Fargue, who told her:

'Three weeks ago, the chevalier left on an expedition along with a few men from his company. It seems he was supposed to make his way to Alsace, with a possible detour into the Rhineland.'

Alsace not being French territory, Agnès thought the expedition must have been either an escort mission or a covert military operation. But even without that, the region was filled with dangers. War was raging there. Imperial and Swedish troops were contending for control of the cities while mercenary bands pillaged the countryside.

'François could not reveal more than that,' the marquis explained. 'Knowing that he was bound to secrecy, I did not ask any questions. Indeed, he probably told me more than he ought to have done . . . But it was precisely because of this that I suspected it was an important matter and one which was causing him great concern. And I understood just how accurate my suspicions were when I learned that, on the eve of his departure, François spent a long while praying at his brother's tomb . . .'

Visibly overcome by emotion, d'Aubremont fell silent.

'Since then,' said La Fargue, taking up the account from his friend, 'the chevalier has not sent any news. And as for the enquiries that the marquis has recently made of the Sisters of Saint Georges, they have yielded no results. He has received no answers. Or very evasive ones.'

'It's always the same closed doors, the same silences and the same lies,' said d'Aubremont in a voice vibrant with contained anger. 'Because I know they are lying. Or at least hiding something from me . . . But don't I have the right to know what has become of François?'

Agnès gazed deeply into the eyes of this old gentleman who had already lost one son and now feared for the life of the second.

'Yes,' she said. 'You have the right.'

'Of course,' the captain of the Blades pointed out, 'it would be fruitless to call on the cardinal . . .'

'. . . since the Mother Superior General of the Chatelaines is his cousin,' the young baronne concluded for him.

'And as for speaking directly to the king . . .'

'As a last recourse only!' decreed the marquis. 'Kings are to be served, not solicited. Besides, what would I say to him?'

There was a moment of silence.

Agnès turned to La Fargue who, without pressuring her to do anything, waited for her to come to a decision.

'Monsieur,' she said to the marquis, 'I can promise you nothing. But since my novitiate I have kept up several acquaintances among the Sisters of Saint Georges. I will go see them and perhaps I can obtain the answers you are seeking.'

D'Aubremont gave her a smile of sincere gratitude.

'Thank you, madame.'

'However, do not harbour any great hopes for I do not—'

'It would be enough to know that my son is still alive, madame. Just so long as he is still alive . . .'

Immediately after the marquis d'Aubremont took his leave, Agnès ordered a horse to be saddled for her. She would have to make haste indeed in order to reach her destination before nightfall. La Fargue joined her in the stable while André finished preparing Vaillante, the fiery young baronne's favourite mare.

'I know how much this costs you, Agnès.'

They stood side by side, watching the groom busying himself with her mount.

The young woman nodded lightly.

'I know what it costs you to resume contact under these circumstances with the White Ladies,' La Fargue continued. 'And I wanted to thank you.'

Because they dressed entirely in white, 'White Ladies' was one of the nicknames given to the Sisters of Saint Georges. They were also known as the 'Chatelaines', after their founder, Saint Marie de Chastel.

'No need to thank me, captain.'

'Of course, the marquis cannot know how great a favour you are doing him, but—'

'The Blades owe him this service at least, don't you think?'

'True.'

Out in the courtyard, one of the horses Almades still held by the bridle snorted.

'I must go to the Palais-Cardinal,' La Fargue said. 'Have a safe journey, Agnès.'

'Thank you, captain. I'll be back tomorrow.'

The duchesse de Chevreuse had been born Marie de Rohan-Montbazon.

In 1617, at the age of fifteen, she married Charles de Luynes, the marquis d'Albert. Twenty-two years older than her, at the time Luynes enjoyed the king's favours and accumulated responsibilities, wealth and honours, despite his mediocre intelligence. Soon appointed superintendent of the queen's household herself, the young, beautiful and joyful marquise de Luynes knew how to please Anne d'Autriche, who was already growing bored with life at the French court. A sincere friendship grew up between them, but the king began to turn away from his wife and he deemed that Marie had a bad influence upon her. It was true that the superintendent was by no means unsociable and willingly partook in the pleasures of life. And while her husband was promoted to duc and then supreme commander of the royal armies, she became the mistress of the youngest son of the duc de Guise, Claude de Lorraine, prince de Joinville and duc de Chevreuse. Luynes died in 1622, during the course of a military campaign in the south of France against the Huguenots when Marie was twenty years old. Exposed to the hostility of Louis XIII, she nevertheless continued her duties with respect to the queen. But one evening, while she led her friend on a run through the halls of the Louvre as a game, Anne d'Autriche fell and, three days later, she suffered a miscarriage. This tragic loss provoked the king's wrath. He blamed Marie, pronounced the young widow's disgrace and banished her from the royal court.

Defying social conventions, Marie married the duc de Chevreuse barely four months after Luynes's death. Louis XIII was opposed to their union. But the duc's loyalty, his glorious military record and his blood ties with the House of

Lorraine persuaded the king to forgive him and, shortly after, to allow the duchesse to rejoin the queen's entourage. From that position, she then embarked on one of the most notorious careers as a schemer – and as a lover – in the history of France. In the space of only a few years she pushed the queen into the arms of the duke of Buckingham and very nearly succeeded in causing a great scandal. She opposed the marriage of the king's brother, Gaston, to mademoiselle de Montpensier. She took part in a plot against the cardinal that was barely foiled and was implicated in another against the king himself. Her life was saved only by her status as a foreign princess. Condemned to retire to her country holdings, she fled to Lorraine and, without giving up any of her other pleasures, she continued to involve herself in conspiracies. After the siege of La Rochelle, England negotiated a peace treaty with France and interceded on behalf of the duchesse. She thus returned to France after a year in exile, surrounded by a certain diabolical aura, thirty years old but not ready to settle down. But she was either lucky enough or smart enough not to take part in the revolt that started in the summer of 1632 in Languedoc, which ended with the victory of the royal troops and a death sentence for the duc de Montmorency.

In Paris, the duchesse de Chevreuse lived in a magnificent mansion on rue Saint-Thomas-du-Louvre, between the Louvre and the Tuileries. Remodelled for her by one of the most celebrated architects of the day, this splendid dwelling was composed of a central building flanked by two square pavilions, from which two wings extended to frame the courtyard. The latter was closed off a by third, lower wing, which contained a monumental gate decorated with pilasters and sculptures. The lateral wings contained the facilities that were indispensable to the life any great household: kitchens, offices, servants' quarters, stables and coach houses. As for the central building, it housed the private apartments and the halls, a string of grand rooms that were used only on social occasions. To the rear, a terrace overlooked an exquisite garden.

The Hôtel de Chevreuse was a veritable palace where the duchesse gave superb parties which tended to take a licentious turn. It was also a den of intrigue into which Arnaud de Laincourt, on this very afternoon, was determined to enter.

'Come in, monsieur! Come in!' called out madame de Chevreuse in a light-hearted tone.

Laincourt hesitated for a brief instant, then doffed his felt hat and crossed the threshold of the doorway that had been opened for him.

The room into which he had been admitted was part of the duchesse's private apartments. The furniture, the parquet floor, the wood panelling, the draperies, the gilt work, the painted ceilings, the ornaments and the framed canvases were all in the best possible taste and evidence of an extraordinary luxury. The air in the room was perfumed. As for the atmosphere, it was feverish. The chambermaids and wardrobe mistresses were engaged in whirling ballet with the duchesse at its centre. Sitting before a mirror that was held out for her, she had her back turned to the door and was giving precise instructions whose results she immediately verified in her reflection. It was question of adding a hint of rouge here, a pinch of powder there; of arranging a few stray locks that did not fall perfectly; of bringing another necklace and, upon further thought, changing the earrings which simply wouldn't do.

Believing himself forgotten, Laincourt was seeking a discreet means of recalling his presence to mind when madame de Chevreuse, her back still turned, said:

'You must forgive me, monsieur, for receiving you so poorly.'

'Madame, if my visit is ill-timed—'

'Not at all, monsieur! Not at all . . . ! Stay.'

Laincourt thus remained, and waited.

Now the great matter was the perfect tilt of the duchesse's hat, the finishing touch to a ritual whose importance the young man could only guess at and which he witnessed with a certain degree of embarrassment.

'You were spoken of very highly to me, monsieur.'

'I was?'

'Does the idea displease you?'

'Not at all, madame. But since I do not know who holds me in such good esteem as to speak—'

'Well then, first of all there is the duc. But it is true that my husband looks favourably upon any who come from Lorraine as he does. You are from Lorraine, are you not, monsieur?'

'In fact, I—'

'Yes, yes . . . However, it is monsieur de Châteauneuf above all who praises your merits . . .'

Charles de l'Aubespine, the marquis de Châteauneuf, was the kingdom's Keeper of the Seals, the highest-ranking figure in the State after the king and Cardinal Richelieu.

'Monsieur de Châteauneuf is one of my most excellent friends. Did you know that?'

With these words, and after a final glance in the mirror, the duchesse rose and turned to Laincourt. He was immediately struck by her beauty, her tawny hair, her milky complexion, the flawless oval of her face, the sparkle of her eyes and the perfection of her carmine mouth. She had, moreover, an air of joyful boldness that was a provocation to the senses.

'But I must take my leave,' she said as if in regret. 'It has already been half an hour since the queen sent word that she wished to see me at the Louvre . . .' She extended her hand to be kissed. 'Come back this evening, monsieur. Or rather, no, come back tomorrow. That's it, tomorrow. At the same time. You will, won't you?'

Laincourt would have liked to reply, but she had already left him standing there.

She disappeared through a door, abandoning the young man in a cloud of powder and perfume, exposed to the some-what mocking gazes of the chambermaids . . .

Upon his return from the Palais-Cardinal, La Fargue found Leprat exercising alone in the fencing room. The musketeer was practising lunges in particular in order to limber up the thigh which had been wounded a month earlier and still remained a little stiff. Wearing boots, breeches and a shirt, he was sweating and did not spare his efforts, sometimes pressing an imaginary attack, then stepping back into position and beginning the exercise all over again.

He broke off when he saw his captain enter.

'I need to speak with you, Antoine.'

'Of course.'

'In my office, please.'

Still catching his breath, Leprat nodded, re-sheathed his white rapier and grabbed a towel to wipe the sweat from his face and the back of his neck while La Fargue went into his private office. He joined the old gentleman there as he finished putting on his doublet and, with his brow still damp, he asked:

'What is it, captain?'

'Sit down.'

The musketeer obeyed and waited. Behind his desk, La Fargue appeared to be choosing his words, before he asked:

'How is your thigh?'

'It still causes me an occasional jolt of pain, but that's all.'

'That fight with the dracs was a bit of an ordeal, wasn't it?' the captain said, only half-jokingly.

'That it was,' agreed Leprat.

A silence fell, and stretched . . .

Until finally, the captain of the Blades announced gravely:

'I have a mission for you, Antoine. A particularly dangerous mission that you will be free to refuse once I have laid it all out for you. I would understand in that case. Everyone would understand . . .'

More intrigued than worried, the musketeer gazed back with narrowed eyes.

'But first of all, read this,' said La Fargue, holding out a handwritten sheet.

'What is it?'

'The transcription of the encoded letter we found on Guéret's body.'

Leprat frowned as he struggled to read Laincourt's handwriting.

The letter began with salutations addressed by Marie de Médicis to madame de Chevreuse. Then, in a pompous style, the queen mother assured the duchess of her friendship and wished her success in all her endeavours, including 'certain affairs with respect to Lorraine'. She expressed a desire to be of assistance to her 'very dear friend' and, to that end, was placing at her disposal a French gentleman of no fortune, but 'a devoted, capable man who will know how to render you great services'. This man was in fact the bearer of the letter, Guéret, of whom the queen mother provided a fairly precise physical description. She explained that the man was being sent first to Lorraine and then to Paris, where he would wait every evening at *The Bronze Glaive*, wearing a opaline ring on his finger, as had already been agreed. The queen mother went on to describe the precarious state of her finances, of which she did not complain for her own sake, but for those who had followed her into exile. And lastly, she concluded with the usual polite formulas.

'Well?' asked La Fargue. 'What do you make of it?'

Leprat pursed his lips.

'This missive hardly deserved to be enciphered.'

'To be sure. But what does it tell us about Guéret?'

The musketeer reflected and, looking for clues, ran his eyes over the letter once again.

'Firstly, that he is an agent of the queen mother as we suspected,' he said. 'And secondly . . . Secondly, the duchesse de Chevreuse does not know him since the queen mother had to describe him.'

'Very true.'

Leprat, then, understood:

'The portrait of this Guéret could in fact be my very own . . .'

'Yes, it could.'

His chest and feet bare, Marciac lifted the curtain slightly to look down at the street without being seen. Behind him, in the bedchamber, Gabrielle had dressed again and was finishing arranging her hair by the rumpled bed. After an afternoon of passionate lovemaking and tender complicity she would soon have to take her leave of the Gascon. She was the owner and manager of *Les Petites Grenouilles*, an establishment whose young and comely boarders made their livings from an essentially nocturnal activity. Their first customers would be arriving soon.

'What are you watching for?' she asked as she placed a last pin in her strawberry-blonde hair.

Although she was beautiful, the attraction she exercised over him owed less to her beauty than to her natural elegance. She could seem cold and haughty, especially when anger lit up her royal blue eyes and a glacial mask slipped over her features. But Marciac knew her doubts, her fears and her weak points. Because she was both the only woman he truly loved and the only one he did not feel obliged to seduce. Even Agnès still had to repel his amorous assaults upon occasion.

'Hmm?' he muttered distractedly.

'I asked, what are you watching out for,' said Gabrielle.

'Nothing.'

His mind was visibly elsewhere and she knew he was lying.

In truth, she even knew what he was observing. Or rather whom. What surprised her, on the other hand, was how little time it took to arouse Marciac's suspicions. He must have been aware of something as soon as he arrived, because they had barely left the bed since then.

She wanted him to think of something else.

'How long have you been back in Paris?'

'A few days . . .'

'You could have paid me a visit sooner, rather than waiting until you were injured.'

Marciac had a bandaged ankle. It was still painful, but no longer prevented him from standing. If he didn't put too much weight on it and granted himself a good night's rest, he could be walking almost normally the following day. And there would be no trace of it at all the day after that.

'Sorry,' he said. 'I've had no free time.'

Gabrielle rose. With a sly smile on her lips, she approached the Gascon and embraced him tenderly from behind, placing her chin upon his shoulder.

'Liar,' she murmured in his ear. 'You were seen at La Sovange's mansion.'

Madame de Sovange maintained, on rue de l'Arbalète in the faubourg Saint-Jacques, a rather famous gambling house.

Now it was Marciac's turn to want a change in the subject of conversation.

'Do you know this individual, standing over there beneath the sign with the head of a dog? The one with the leather hat?'

She barely glanced at the man he was referring to.

'I've never seen him before,' she said, drawing away from the Gascon.

And then she added from the doorway:

'Get dressed and come say hello to the little frogs. They won't stop asking after you until you do.'

'I will.'

Gabrielle departed, leaving Marciac convinced that she was holding something back concerning the man in the leather hat. Peeking out at the street again, he saw the man exchange some words with a newcomer, then walk away, leaving the other man standing there.

That dispelled any doubts the Gascon might still be harbouring.

A man who stood hanging around all afternoon in the same place might be an idler or even some sort of mischief-maker. But when he was relieved at his post in the early evening, then he had to be a lookout.

Alone in his bedchamber, leaning over the basin. Leprat lifted his face dripping with cool water and observed himself in the mirror. He was bare to the waist but already wore the breeches and boots of another man who was at this very instant floating dead in the Seine. The rest of his attire – a hat, a shirt, a doublet whose lining had been re-sewn and a steel sword in its scabbard – waited upon the bed.

Leprat gave his reflection a hard stare.

He had accepted the mission La Fargue had proposed to him, that is to say, infiltrating madame de Chevreuse's clandestine schemes by passing himself off as Guéret, the agent the queen mother had sent to the duchesse from Brussels. Since he was ignorant of almost everything about the person he was supposed to replace, it was a risky business. Guéret was a French gentleman of no fortune, that much was certain. And no doubt he had followed the queen mother when, removed from power and humiliated, she had chosen to leave the kingdom. But aside from that?

Leprat, in fact, could only rely on a certain physical resemblance with the man whose identity he was trying to usurp. A resemblance which, furthermore, would not fool anyone who had met Guéret. And the musketeer knew that he would probably die under torture if he was unmasked . . .

Bah . . . he told himself philosophically, as he bent once again to splash water on his face . . . *if no one kills you today, you know what will kill you tomorrow* . . .

Upon his back, the ranse spread in a broad violet rash with a rough surface. The disease was progressing. It would one day take his life and was already weakening him, as witnessed by the wound to his thigh that was taking longer than it should to completely heal.

How much time do you have left? Leprat wondered. *And more, how much longer can you keep it a secret?*

He stood up straight and smiled sadly at his image in the mirror.

This secret that is eating away at you . . .

The expression had never been so apt.

Agnès arrived in the early evening. The abbey was located in a peaceful corner of the countryside, far from any heavily travelled roads, and was surrounded by the fields, woodland and farms from which it derived its revenues. From the vantage point of her saddle, the young baronne took her time observing the handsome buildings and the white, veiled silhouettes moving about behind the enclosing walls. The memories of her novitiate with the Sisters of Saint Georges came back vividly to her. Then she gently nudged her horse forward with her heels as bells rang out in the dusk, calling the Sisters to prayer.

She was soon admitted to wait in the cloister where she

stood alone, exposed to the curious glances and whispers from the passing nuns. She knew from experience how small a world an abbey was and how fast news travelled there. No doubt her name was circulating and it was already being murmured that she had asked to meet the mother superior. Did they remember her here? Perhaps. In any case, everyone would be wondering about the motive behind her visit . . .

Feeling quite satisfied with the effect that both her presence and her armed horseman's outfit were having, in particular on the young novices who were jostling one another to spy on her from behind some columns, Agnès forced herself to remain patient and impassive. The severe sound of a throat being cleared, however, was enough to remind the adolescent girls of their duties, before the mother superior's arrival dispersed them entirely.

About sixty years in age, Mère Emmanuelle de Cernay was an energetic woman with strong features and a frank gaze. Accompanied by two nuns who walked behind her, she gratified Agnès with a tender smile, hugged her and kissed her on both cheeks. The young woman responded with similar warmth to these displays of affection.

'Marie-Agnès! It's been so long since we have seen you . . . And your last letter dates from over a month ago!'

'The Blades have been reformed, mother.'

'Really? Since when?'

'Since about a month ago, in fact.'

'I didn't know . . . Are you still under the command of that old gentleman?'

'Captain La Fargue, yes.'

'And are you happy?'

'My word . . .' replied Agnès with a somewhat guilty smile.

'Then that's all right, that's all right . . . Just don't find yourself on the receiving end of a sword stroke that will make you regret not having taken the veil!'

'It would have to be a very nasty sword stroke, indeed, mother . . .'

The abbess took Agnès by the arm and they walked

together beneath the gallery of the cloister. Shaking her head resignedly, the old woman said:

'Intrigue. Racing about on horseback. Sword play . . . You have always loved all that, Marie-Agnès . . .'

'And the boys. You're forgetting the boys, mother superior.'

The abbess chuckled.

'Yes. And the boys . . . Did you know that the ivy on the north wall is still called "Agnès's ivy" by some of the older nuns?'

'I didn't climb it that often . . .'

'Let's say rather that you weren't caught every time you climbed it . . .'

Still talking in this relaxed manner, they left the cloister for a garden at the entrance to which the mother superior asked the two nuns trailing them to wait behind. And once she and Agnès had moved out of earshot, she confided:

'One of those two is spying on me. I don't know which one. But what can I do? The Mother Superior General continues to be suspicious of me, after all these years . . .'

Mère Emmanuelle had previously been the head of the Sisters of Saint Georges. But following some dark dealings, she had been ousted in favour of the current Superior General, who happened to be part of the Richelieu family. Since then, the Order had become a more or less blatant instrument of the cardinal's policies, to the great displeasure of Rome. The concordat of Bologna, however, had granted the king the right to appoint the recipients of the Church's major benefices in France, including the abbesses and abbots of the religious orders.

'But what can I do for you, Marie-Agnès? I imagine that you have not come to tell me that you wish to complete your novitiate . . .'

The young baronne smiled as she thought of how very close she had come to taking the veil, then she spoke of the fears of the marquis d'Aubremont, his approach to the Blades and the promise she had made to him.

The mother superior thought for a moment.

'An expedition to Alsace, you say . . . ? Yes, I think I did

588

hear something about that. Its goal, I believe, was the destruction of a powerful dragon. And as is proper in such cases, a louve was leading the hunt.'

Among the Chatelaines, there existed a small number of exceptional sisters who, thanks to a papal dispensation, were allowed to wield magic as well as the sword to fight the draconic menace. They were nicknamed the *louves*, or she-wolves, because their headquarters were located in the Château de Saint-Loup, not far from Poitiers. But also, and above all, because they were solitary and merciless huntresses. If Agnès had come close to pronouncing her own vows, it had been with the sole intention of becoming a louve herself.

'But I don't know the details of this affair,' Mère Emmanuelle was saying. 'And, in particular, I don't know what success the expedition had . . . But if you like, I can make enquiries and let you know what I discover.'

'Thank you, mother superior.'

'Nevertheless . . . Nevertheless, be very careful, Marie-Agnès. It won't take the Superior General long to learn of the reasons for your visit, and I doubt she will take a kind view of your becoming mixed up in the Order's business . . .'

In the office of magic at the splendid Hôtel de Chevreuse, in rue Saint-Thomas-du-Louvre, the man bent forward to examine the painted portrait the duchesse was showing him. Tall, thin and pale, he appeared to be about fifty-five years in age. He was wearing the black robes of a scholar and a cloth beret, also black in colour, with a turned-up, crenelated edge.

'Do you see, master?' asked madame de Chevreuse.

He was her master of magic and exercised an insidious but immense influence over her. She believed he was called Mauduit, was of Italian origin and had spent long years studying and practising the occult arts abroad. In truth, he was a dragon as well as an agent of the Black Claw.

While he studied the portrait by candlelight, the duchesse poured two glasses of a golden liqueur with a heady aroma. When he heard the clink of crystal and smelled the odour of henbane the Alchemist's nostrils flared and a gleam of longing briefly lit up his steely grey eyes, while the tip of a rosy tongue licked at his lips. But he retained control of himself, succeeded in masking a desire that was becoming a need and, with a steady hand, accepted – casually, without taking his eyes off the canvas – the glass held out to him. He dipped his bloodless lips in the liqueur and contained the shiver of pleasure that obliged him to shut his eyes.

'You will soon have to find me some more of this delicious henbane from Lorraine,' said madame de Chevreuse.

'Certainly, madame.'

'Will you tell me, someday, who your supplier is?'

'Madame, whatever would become of a master of magic who gave away his secrets?'

She smiled, rose and took several paces about the room as she gazed incuriously at the books of magic and various alchemical and esoteric objects that were on display.

Then she asked:

'So? What do you think of my find? I can assure you that this portrait is most faithful.'

The Alchemist pursed his lips.

'Precisely, madame. This young woman is far too pretty. She won't fool anyone.'

The duchesse was expecting this reaction and had prepared a visual effect. Smiling, she showed him a small piece of carton shaped like a theatre mask, which she placed upon the portrait.

'And now, master?'

The master of magic looked again at the painting and could not prevent a start of surprise.

'Admirable . . . !' he admitted. Then a shadow of doubt passed over his face. 'But her size? Her figure?'

'They are a perfect match in every respect,' madame de Chevreuse reassured him.

'As is her hair . . . And where is this marvel hiding?'

'She has been staying here, in my home, for several days now. I will present her to you during the course of a dinner I am hosting.'

'But will she be capable of—'

'I will answer for her.'

'On condition that she accepts.'

'How can one refuse a queen?'

The Alchemist gave one of his rare smiles, which always seemed cruel.

'Yes, of course . . .' he said. 'But it will still require some scheming on your part to place your protégée in the queen's entourage. How do you hope to accomplish that?'

'Through the marquis,' replied the duchesse with a hint of annoyance. 'Or through my husband the duc. We'll see.'

'Time is running short, madame. If all is not ready in time for your great ball at Dampierre . . .'

'I know it all too well, monsieur. All too well . . . Now, a little more henbane?'

Leprat had already been waiting for an hour. With an ordinary sword at his side, he was wearing Guéret's clothing and jewellery, including a ring adorned with a handsome opaline stone that he had slipped on his left ring finger. He had of course put away his ivory rapier and the Blades' steel signet ring, along with anything that might compromise his false identity. He hoped it would suffice. For although he had no doubt that the duchesse de Chevreuse was not personally acquainted with Guéret, this was perhaps not the case for all those who surrounded her and served her.

Once again, he gazed about the tavern's taproom. Sitting at the end of a table, he did not conceal the opaline on his ring finger but nor did he flash it about, to avoid trouble. While *The Bronze Glaive* was no cutthroats' den, it was not the most reputable of places. Located outside the faubourg Saint-Jacques, less than a quarter of an hour's walk from the inn where Guéret had been lodging, the establishment was exempt from the taxes and regulations that applied in Paris. Wine was cheaper here and they continued serving it after curfew every evening of the week, until midnight.

Every evening of the week, that is, except the previous evening, when the owner, having gone to Tours to bury a dead relative, had closed the tavern. Leprat had discovered this by listening to a conversation between two regulars. It explained, at least, why Guéret had returned to the inn earlier than expected and surprised Agnès and Marciac in his bedchamber. This extraordinary closure had indirectly killed him.

The difference between life and death often depends on the tiniest things, Leprat mused.

Absentmindedly toying with the opaline that served as his recognition sign, he did not react when a gentleman sat down next to him and asked without giving him a look:

'Did you have a safe journey from Flanders?'

'I've come from Lorraine.'

'Did you take pains to ensure you were not followed?'

'From Nancy?'

'The cardinal has eyes and ears everywhere.'

Leprat glanced at the stranger. He was slender and fair-haired, with a well-trimmed moustache and royale beard. He was elegantly but unobtrusively dressed in a beige doublet. And he had a friendly air.

The musketeer lowered his eyes to the gentleman's hands, who let him catch a glimpse of an opaline ring on his own index finger before he said:

'Wait a little while and then meet me around the back.'

He immediately rose and went out, after paying for the glass of wine which he had not touched.

Leprat imitated him five minutes later.

In the dark night, he had difficulty finding the narrow arched passageway that led to the rear of the tavern. He could not see a thing and was unfamiliar with the place. His instinct, moreover, told him that something was amiss. Had he already been unmasked? He thought for an instant about giving up, turning around and returning to the Hôtel de l'Épervier.

Despite everything, he decided to continue.

And was knocked unconscious the moment he set foot in the rear courtyard.

Each house in Paris had a sign. The shops and taverns had them, of course. But so did the dwellings, which was how one told them apart in lieu of numbers. These signs served to designate the addresses of both commercial establishments and private individuals: Rue Saint-Martin, where the sign of the Red Cock hangs, for example. This only applied, however, to premises belonging to commoners. Private mansions, still reserved solely to the aristocracy under Louis XIII, did not have signs. Instead they took the names of their owners, often decorated with prestigious coats-of-arms on their pediment, and that was address enough: Hôtel de Châteauneuf, rue Coquillière. Or even: Hôtel de Chevreuse, Paris.

Parisian streets were thus graced with innumerable signs in multicoloured wood that added to the capital's renown and gave it, when the weather was fine, a festive air. The subjects of these signs were varied – saints, kings of France and other sacred or profane characters; tools, weapons and utensils; trees, fruits and flowers; animals and other imaginary creatures – but showed no evidence, on the whole, of any real artistic vision or profound taste for the picturesque. For every Horse Wielding a Pickaxe or Gloved Wyvern, how many Tin Plates and Golden Lions? The most curious thing, however, was the fact that the signs for shops never evoked anything related to the nature of their business. There were no boots for cobblers or anvils for blacksmiths. Only taverns were required to distinguish themselves with a sheaf: a handful of knotted hay or twigs.

If signs served a useful purpose and brightened up an otherwise sordid urban setting, they nevertheless represented a certain hazard to the public due to the tendency of shopkeepers to give them excessive dimensions for the purposes of publicity. The ironwork that supported them often extended out a *toise*, or a measure of about two metres, into the street. Considering the width of an ordinary street in Paris, that meant signs often hung in the middle of the pavement. Added to the usual stalls and awnings, these ornaments thus hindered traffic and aggravated the crush in the most commercial streets, which were also the most heavily frequented. There were more than three hundred signs in the neighbourhood of Les Halles, and almost as many on rue Saint-Denis alone. Coaches were constantly knocking them down. Riders on horseback had to duck to avoid them. And even pedestrians often bashed their skulls on these gaudily painted wooden panels.

Usually due to distraction.

But not always.

'Hup!'

Turning round, the man saw a monkey's head diving towards him, received a blow from the sign in the middle of his brow and keeled over backwards, while the suspended panel continued its forward motion before reversing at the height of its swing.

Marciac caught it and stopped its movement.

Then he gave a calm, satisfied look at the man lying unconscious in the street at his feet, his arms spread out in a cross.

This scene took place in rue Grenouillère at the crack of dawn where, as in the rest of Paris, the neighbourhood was just beginning to wake.

Marciac returned to *Les Petites Grenouilles* on tiptoe. The house was still sleeping at this hour of the morning, since the last customers, as usual, had taken their leave late during the previous night. This suited the Gascon perfectly, as he was counting on regaining the warmth of Gabrielle's bed without her being aware he had ever left. But as he was about to take the stairs, holding his boots in his hand, he heard a voice say:

'So? How is that ankle?'

He froze, grimacing as he closed his eyelids tightly, then reopened one eye and turned his head to look through a wide-open door. He saw Gabrielle sitting alone at the kitchen table. Her face was in profile and she held her head stiffly upright as she ate, staring straight ahead of her. She had a large shawl around her shoulders and was wearing only a nightshirt, without having done anything about her hair or appearance.

She was beautiful, nevertheless.

The Gascon resolved to join her. He hated explanations and reproaches, but this time would not be able to escape making the former or receiving the latter. Reluctantly, he fell into a chair.

'My ankle is much better,' he said. 'Thank you.'

Then he waited for the tongue-lashing to start.

'Where were you?' Gabrielle finally asked.

'Out.'

'In order to exchange a few words with Fortain, I imagine.' Marciac frowned.

'Fortain?'

'The man who was watching the house. He was no longer there when I woke up. But you have reappeared. Whereas he—'

'Then you know.'

'That there are five or six men who have been discreetly watching the house these past few days? Yes, I know. The fact is, you see, I'm neither totally blind nor a complete idiot. Even the girls know something is up. The only one who hasn't realised is poor old Thibault.'

Thibault, the porter at *Les Petites Grenouilles*, was a man of absolute devotion but limited intelligence.

Marciac nodded.

'All right,' he allowed. 'But do you know who these men work for?'

'Yes. For Rochefort.'

Astonished, the Gascon studied Gabrielle's expressionless face. She still hadn't accorded him the slightest glance.

'And how do you know that Rochefort is behind all this?'

'I recognised two of his men. Including Fortain.'

'Why didn't you say anything to me?'

'I might ask you the same question. In my case, it was because I was afraid you would only make matters worse by getting mixed up in this. A strange idea, that, wasn't it?'

Embarrassed, Marciac did not at first find a reply, but then he said:

'I had to know, Gabrielle. I had to make sure that—'

'That Rochefort was watching my house? Very well. Rochefort is watching my house. So what? He can discover nothing he doesn't already know. But now that you've attacked one of his men, what will happen? Do you believe he'll let that go unanswered?'

'I'll speak to him.'

'And why would he listen to you, since he has no love for the Blades and only takes orders from the cardinal? He won't be able to resist the temptation of reaching you through me. For if you've guessed that Rochefort has become interested in me, you must know it's because of your captain's hidden daughter. Isn't it? Of course, I didn't know that when I took her in and I don't know where she is now, but what does that matter?'

Gabrielle rose, abandoning the plate of fruit and cheese which she had barely touched. She had, in fact, mostly been digging her fingertips into a quarter loaf of white bread.

She wrapped the shawl around her shoulders more tightly, walked towards the door, halted, turned round and looked at Marciac closely.

At last, she said:

'I'm going to ask you one thing, Nicolas.'

'Yes?'

'You knew. Even before you got rid of Fortain you knew that—'

He interrupted her:

'Fortain is alive. And quite well. I am not an assassin, Gabrielle. I only dragged him off to get the truth out of him.'

She had no trouble believing him.

'But even before that, you knew he was one of Rochefort's men, didn't you? And you knew why *Les Petites Grenouilles* were being watched . . .'

Marciac thought for a moment.

But however much it might cost him, he hated lying to Gabrielle.

'Yes,' he recognised, 'I knew.'

'So it wasn't even a question of making sure . . . Merely of sending a message to Rochefort. So that he would understand that you and the Blades would not stand back with your arms crossed if he bothered La Fargue's daughter.'

'La Fargue's daughter or you, Gabrielle. La Fargue's daughter or you.'

She looked at him. He was sincere.

'Yes,' said Gabrielle. 'And do you believe you have done well to protect me, today?'

She left the kitchen, went to the staircase and from there told Marciac:

'I love you, Nicolas. But I would prefer it if you did not sleep here tonight.'

She returned alone to her bedchamber.

Leprat woke up with a severe headache and a devilish thirst. He was lying in his breeches, stockings and shirt, stretched out on a made-up bed in a chamber he had never seen before. He didn't know how he came to be here, but he was sure of one thing: he had left Paris. The air smelled fresh.

The musketeer sat up and, as he rubbed his skull and the handsome bump where he had been struck, he considered his surroundings. His boots were neatly awaiting him by the door. His doublet hung from the back of a chair. His hat was placed upon a table and his sword hung in its scabbard from one of the bedposts. The room was modest but clean and quiet, plunged into an agreeable shade by the curtains that obscured the window.

As he stood, Leprat noticed that the pockets of his breeches had been turned inside out and he concluded that his boots had probably been removed to make sure he was not concealing anything inside them. That made him think of his doublet and he hastened to feel the lining. It was empty and he saw that it had been carefully unsewn. The people who had knocked him out and brought him here had stolen all the secret documents he was supposed to deliver personally to the duchesse de Chevreuse. His career as the queen mother's agent had not got off to a very good start.

Except, despite what the nasty blow to his head seemed to portend, he was neither dead nor a prisoner. If he had been unmasked, he would not have woken here in this manner. Indeed, he would perhaps not have woken at all.

A cow lowed outside.

Leprat went to part the curtains and was dazzled for a moment by the flood of light that suddenly poured into the room. Then he gradually began to make out a pleasant rural landscape, but one which failed to evoke any particular memories in him. He still didn't know where he was, except that he was looking at a corner of the countryside from the upper storey of a house located at the entrance to a village or small town. And if his day's growth of beard was not lying, he had not slept more than a night and was therefore still in France, probably not far from Paris.

But apart from that . . .

Determined to find out more, Leprat dressed and put on his baldric, finding Guéret's steel sword to be much heavier than his ivory rapier, and then left the room. He descended some stairs and emerged into a charming, sunlit garden where he found, eating at a small table beneath a canopy, the man in the beige doublet who had approached him in *The Bronze Glaive*.

The gentleman rose as soon as he caught sight of Leprat and welcomed him with an open smile.

'Monsieur de Guéret! How are you feeling? Did you sleep well?'

'Fairly well, yes,' replied Leprat, who still did not know what tack he should adopt in these circumstances.

'I'm delighted to hear that. Join me, please.' The gentleman pointed to an empty chair at his table and sat back down. 'I've just returned from Paris and finally found time to eat. Will you share this late breakfast with me?'

'Certainly.'

'I am the chevalier de Mirebeau and you are here in my home.'

'Your home, which is to say . . . ?'

'In Ivry. Paris is little more than a league from here.'

Leprat sat down at the table and discovered he possessed a healthy appetite.

'Bertrand!' called the gentleman. 'Bertrand!'

A stooped and rather dreary-looking lackey appeared in the doorway.

'Yes, monsieur?'

'A glass for monsieur de Guéret.'

'Very good, monsieur.'

And tearing a leg from a chicken, Mirebeau said:

'I imagine you have many questions. I don't know if I can answer all of them just yet, but I owe you an apology for the nasty trick we played on you last night. I can only hope that Rauvin did not strike you too hard . . .'

'Rauvin?'

'You will meet him soon. The man has a tendency to be . . . zealous about his work. And he has an excessive, indeed, almost unnatural, sense of wariness . . . In short, it's down to him that you were knocked out—'

'Knocked out and searched.'

'You realise we needed to assure ourselves that you were in fact who you claimed to be. As for the documents you were carrying, have no fear. I delivered them to the person for whom they were intended.'

'My orders were to place them personally in madame de Chevreuse's hands.'

Mirebeau smiled.

'Unfortunately, it is impossible for you to meet the duchesse immediately. But these papers needed to be delivered to her as soon as possible, didn't they . . . ? Also, there was an encoded letter inside your doublet. Do you know of its nature?'

'Not exactly, no.'

'The queen mother invites the duchess to take you into her service.'

'That much, yes, I did know. And have already accepted in advance.'

'Perfect! In that case, the duchesse's desire is for us to form a team. Does that pose an inconvenience to you?'

'Perhaps.'

'Really?' said the gentleman in surprise. 'Why is that?'

Leprat looked directly into Mirebeau's eyes.

'If I was ordered to place the documents in the duchesse's own hands, it was not merely to ensure that they arrived at their proper destination, but also to satisfy myself that no one was trying to trick me. I do not know you, monsieur. I do not know if you are in the service of madame de Chevreuse. I do not even know if you have ever met her. In fact, for all I do know, you could very well be in the service of Cardinal Richelieu . . . On the other hand, if the duchesse were to receive me . . .'

Still maintaining a smiling, friendly demeanour, the man in the beige doublet nodded calmly and then said:

'I applaud your prudence, monsieur. And I understand your concerns . . . However, considering your position, your only option is the following: to place your trust in me during the time it takes to prove yourself . . .'

'Or?'

'Or you can choose to leave.'

'Which is not likely to please Rauvin, is it?'

'Probably not.'

Agnès returned to the Hôtel de l'Épervier at the same time as Marciac. She was on horseback. He was on foot and still limped a little, carrying a bundle of his belongings on one shoulder.

'Already recovered?' she asked.

'Already cast out,' he corrected.

She nodded, the tumultuous relationship between the Gascon and Gabrielle having long ceased to surprise anyone who knew them both.

'And you, Agnès? Where do you return from?'

The young baronne de Vaudreuil jumped down from her saddle while Guibot opened up one of the doors of the carriage gate and she apprised Marciac of her approach to the former Mother Superior General of the Sisters of Saint Georges. Then, once inside the courtyard, she entrusted the reins of her horse to André and asked the old porter with the wooden leg:

'Is the captain here?'

'No, madame. He was called to the Palais-Cardinal. And this letter arrived for you this morning.'

It was now almost noon.

Agnès took the missive, recognised the seal of the Order the White Ladies printed on the red wax, opened it and read.

'Bad news?' enquired Marciac.

'This letter is from the Superior General of the Chatelaines. It expresses her wish to see me this afternoon, which amounts to the same thing as a summons.'

'Like that? All of a sudden?'

'Yes, in a manner of speaking . . .'

'Will you go?'

'I don't have a choice in the matter. But I should have liked to speak with La Fargue before going.'

'You will have to content yourself with talking to me,' said Marciac, taking Agnès by the elbow. 'Come, we'll have dinner and then I will accompany you to the Enclos.'

Laincourt had made an effort with his appearance before presenting himself for the second time at the Hôtel de Chevreuse. He had donned his most elegant doublet, found a matching pair of gloves, carefully polished his boots and stuck a new feather in his hat. His meeting the previous day with the duchesse had made a deep impression on him. She was not only breathtakingly beautiful, but her elegance, poise and nonchalant manner had disarmed him. She moved with the most natural ease in extraordinarily luxurious settings.

This time he was expected and Laincourt was immediately conducted to the terrace, where a square table had been set beneath a white cloth canopy embroidered with gold thread. There, madame de Chevreuse, looking radiant and serene, was chatting with a young girl and an older woman who, like her, was sipping raspberry water that had been cooled at outrageous expense with snow preserved from the previous winter. The young girl was very pretty, lively and very daintily attired. In contrast, the woman was grey-haired and unassuming, with a dull look in her eye.

Upon seeing her visitor, the duchesse greeted Laincourt with a bright smile and, without rising, signalled him to approach.

'Monsieur de Laincourt! Join us, please.'

He obeyed, saluting the mistress of the house first and then her guests, finding himself introduced to Aude de Saint-Avold and her aunt, madame de Jarville. Aude, who was a relative of the duc de Chevreuse, had arrived from Lorraine to be presented at the French court. Her aunt was acting as her chaperone.

'But now that I think of it,' remarked the duchesse, 'you also come from Lorraine, monsieur de Laincourt.'

'Madame, I must disabuse you of this notion. I was born in Nancy, it is true. But I am French.'

'Really? How is that possible?'

Laincourt, as was often the case when speaking of himself, became evasive.

'One of those accidents of life, madame.'

'We were speaking of the court at Nancy. Don't you think it is so much more appealing and gay than the French court?'

'I am forced to admit that it is, madame.'

The court of Charles IV in fact surpassed that of Louis XIII by far. In Nancy, at the ducal palace, the revels were almost unceasing and often licentious, whereas it was easy to grow bored at the Louvre with its austere and timid king who hated to appear in public. The duchesse thus retained an excellent memory of her stay in Nancy, where the duc had welcomed her with great pomp. Laincourt supposed she had made the acquaintance of Aude de Saint-Avold during her time there.

Aude de Saint-Avold.

As he engaged in the conversation, he had trouble taking his eyes off this young woman. She not only pleased him, she also intrigued him. She had a very charming face, with silky light brown hair, lively green eyes and full, luscious lips. Who could fail to find her ravishing? She did not even suffer from comparison with the splendid madame de Chevreuse. In her fashion, she was less beautiful but prettier than the duchesse, less seductive but more moving. And if the duchesse's confidence added a touch of triumphant arrogance to her beauty, young Aude had preserved something fragile from her adolescence, somehow both sad and carefree.

However, other than the fact that it was lovely, Aude's face attracted Laincourt's eye because he seemed to recognise it. Had he met her in Nancy? Perhaps. But her name meant nothing to him. Could the duchesse have brought Aude to Paris under a borrowed identity?

Ably solicited by madame de Chevreuse, who had no equal when it came to drawing the best out of men, Laincourt surprised himself by sparkling in conversation. He proved himself gallant, witty and humorous, finding particular pleasure in entertaining Aude de Saint-Avold, whose sincere laughter enthralled him. And so their conversation had been following a most pleasant course for more than an hour when the maître d'hôtel brought a note to the duchesse. She read it without blinking, excused herself, rose, promised to return soon and took her leave.

Laincourt's gaze followed her and he caught a glimpse of man in a black cap and black robes who was waiting for her inside the mansion.

'Who is he?' he asked.

'He is the duchesse's master of magic, I believe,' Aude replied. 'But I have not been introduced to him yet.'

Without the duchesse, the conversation lagged a little and they could not count on madame de Jarville to remedy matters: made sleepy by the heat, she drowsed in her chair. The two young people perceived this at the same time, exchanged an amused glance, and stifled mocking laughs. Madame de Chevreuse soon rejoined them, but only to say that she was going to be detained elsewhere and was entrusting Aude to Laincourt's care.

'Be good,' she said as she left them.

Which was a little like the devil warning them not to sin.

'What if we escaped?' Aude de Saint-Avold suggested with a rebellious gleam in her eye.

'I beg your pardon, madame?'

'Abduct me. Madame de Chevreuse has placed a coach at my disposal. Let's take it. And go to . . . Let's go to Le Cours!'

'To Le Cours?'

'What? Isn't that what it's called?'

'Indeed. But . . .'

Le Cours, located near the Saint-Antoine gate, was one of the most popular places for Parisians wishing to take a stroll. Rich or poor, aristocrat or commoner, all went there to promenade, seek distractions or display themselves in public. People chatted, joked or courted one another. They played hide-and-seek or skittles or pall-mall. On fine days, especially, the place was very popular. The young woman's idea was thus by no means a bad one. But Le Cours was never so crowded as on a Sunday, as Laincourt explained to her.

'Oh . . . You see how ignorant I am of all these things . . . It will take a long time to make a Parisienne of me, won't it?'

Aude's disappointment saddened Laincourt, who felt a compelling need to console her.

'But we could go to the garden at Les Tuileries,' he heard himself propose.

'Really?'

'Yes! We should definitely go, now that it's been said!'

'But . . . What about madame de Jarville?' whispered the young woman with the tone of an anxious conspirator.

'Let's leave her to her rest.'

The Enclos du Temple was a former residence of the Knights Templar located on the right bank of the Seine, to the north of the Marais neighbourhood. Ceded to the Knights Hospitaller after the dissolution of the Templar Order in 1314, this building was finally sold to the Sisters of Saint Georges during the reign of François I. It still belonged to them in 1633 and was still surrounded by a high, crenelated wall, punctuated by turrets, and defended by a massive donjon flanked by four corner towers: the famous Tour du Temple. Visitors entered the premises by means of a drawbridge and inside one found everything necessary for the life of a religious community: a large church; a cloister; a refectory and dormitories; kitchens; granaries and wine cellars; workshops; stables; gardens, vegetable plots and more extensive fields; and even some houses and a few shops. All of this contained within a mediaeval compound in Paris, on the rue du Temple, near the gate bearing the same name.

Having dined at place de Grève, Marciac and Agnès both entered the Enclos, but only the young baronne was admitted to meet the Mother Superior General. They had shared an enjoyable moment together, the Gascon regaling Agnès with comic tales of his trials and tribulations in love. He was aware that she had once been on the point of taking the veil with the Chatelaines, although he didn't know of the circumstances that had prompted her to change paths and later join the Cardinal's Blades. One thing was certain: at present, she no longer held the Sisters of Saint Georges in fond esteem and even seemed to nurture a particular rancour against the current Superior General, the formidable Mère Thérèse de Vaussambre.

While Marciac waited patiently outside, Agnès was conducted to the ancient chapter hall. The room was immense, broad, high-ceilinged and illuminated by arched windows. At the rear, a long table covered with several white cloths stretched parallel to a wall adorned with a huge mediaeval tapestry representing Saint Georges slaying the dragon. At the centre of this table, back to the wall, beneath the tapestry, sat the Mother Superior General. Tall, thin and stiff-looking, she had the same penetrating gaze as her cousin the cardinal. She was not yet fifty years of age, directed the Sisters of Saint Georges with an iron hand and had made their Order more influential than ever before.

'Approach, Marie-Agnès.'

Her hat held in one hand and the other resting on the pommel of her sword, Agnès de Vaudreuil advanced, saluted and said:

'It's just Agnès, now, mother.'

'Agnès . . . Yes. So it is. You do well to correct me,' replied the Superior General in a tone that implied the exact opposite. 'I have trouble forgetting the novice that you once were. You had so much promise! And what a louve you would have become . . . !'

Cautious, the young baronne de Vaudreuil waited silently.

'But the day will come when you will realise your destiny . . .' added the nun, as if to her herself.

Then she added in a solemn and imperious tone:

'Madame, your services are required at the side of the queen, whose suite you will join as soon as possible. You have been chosen due to your skills, as well as the abilities revealed during the novitiate which you have so unhappily chosen to neglect. However, we know that we can place our trust in you . . .'

A short while later, in the courtyard of the Hôtel de Chevreuse, Laincourt was helping a delighted Aude de Saint-Avold to climb into a coach when he felt a glance fall upon the back of his neck.

He turned around but only had time to see, at a window on the first storey of the mansion's main building, a curtain falling back into place before a thin, pallid face.

The Alchemist released the curtain and turned away from the window just as the duchesse came into his office.

'You will meet her this evening,' she promised him. 'But for now, without further delay, I can give you some excellent news: our protégée will soon be joining the queen's suite.'

'What? So quickly . . . ? How have you managed this?'

'Providence, monsieur Mauduit. Providence . . . Today, as a favour, someone asked me to—'

' "Someone"?'

'Cardinal Richelieu, through an intermediary . . . In short, the cardinal asked me to favour a distant relative of his with an introduction into the queen's entourage.'

'The king is free to appoint whomever he pleases to the queen's household. And similarly, to expel anyone he dislikes.'

'Yes, and the queen is free to turn a cold shoulder to anyone whose presence is forced upon her. And it is just such treatment that the cardinal wishes to avoid for this relative, by asking me to intercede in her favour. I believe it is also the cardinal's way of measuring my goodwill with respect to him.'

'So you accepted.'

'Of course. But, at the same time, requested that one of my own protégées be admitted to the queen's entourage. After all, I am the duchesse de Chevreuse. It would be uncharacteristic of me to give without receiving anything in return.'

'My congratulations.'

'Thank you, monsieur. And on your side?'

'All is ready. However—'

'What?'

'This relative of the cardinal, who is she?'

'How should I know?'

'A spy?'

'Without a doubt, since such manoeuvres are very much in the manner of the king, who may not love the queen but still wishes to know her every deed and gesture. No doubt to make sure she is unhappy . . .'

The duchesse's expression grew hard: she hated the king.

'This spy could do us mischief,' said the master of magic.

'In the little time between now and the ball? Come now . . . When the moment arrives, we only need to keep her apart from our . . . arrangements.'

The Alchemist, still looking concerned, fell silent.

Mirebeau did not return until the end of the afternoon.

He had left on horseback three hours previously without saying where he was going or proposing that Leprat should accompany him. The musketeer had waited in the house at Ivry with Bertrand, the chevalier's very dour-looking valet, and a translation of *The Decameron* as his sole company. He was at liberty to move about, but he preferred not to stray beyond the garden. He was perhaps being watched and did not wish to raise any alarms.

Hearing horses approaching, Leprat rose from his bed, where he had been reading, and went to look out the window of his first-storey bedchamber. He took up his rapier as he passed, placed himself to one side so he would not easily be seen and gently pushed open a window frame that was already ajar, just as two riders drew up.

One of them, still elegantly dressed in beige, was Mirebeau.

He jumped down from his mount and, calling out for Bertrand, disappeared into the house. The other man had the look of a mercenary, wearing boots, thick breeches, a leather doublet, a sword at his side and an old battered hat. Leprat guessed he must be this Rauvin of whom Mirebeau had spoken, the same man who had knocked him out by surprise in the courtyard of *The Bronze Glaive*. The man with the unnatural sense of wariness, as the gentleman had put it. And therefore someone of whom he should be particularly wary himself.

Very much at ease in his saddle, Rauvin – if it was indeed him – removed his hat long enough to wipe his brow with the back of a sleeve. Leprat caught a glimpse of a blade-like face and a balding crown wreathed by long black hair, belonging to a thirty-year-old man. The man took a jew's harp from his pocket, raised it to his mouth and made the metal strip vibrate to produce a strange melody.

As he played, he calmly lifted his eyes to the window where the musketeer stood watching him, as if to signify that he had known Leprat was there all along and could not have cared less.

Their gazes met for a long while and Leprat was filled with an absolute certainty that Rauvin represented a deadly threat to him.

'Guéret!' Mirebeau called from the stairway. 'Guéret!'

The false agent of the queen mother turned away from the window just as Mirebeau entered.

'Please get ready,' requested the gentleman in the beige doublet. 'We're leaving.'

'We?'

'You, me and Rauvin, who is waiting for us below.'

'Where are we going?'

'To a place near Neuilly.'

'And what will we do there?'

'So full of questions!' exclaimed Mirebeau in a jovial manner. 'Come now, monsieur. Make haste. Bertrand is already saddling a horse for you.'

3

Upon their return to the Hôtel de l'Épervier, Agnès and Marciac waited for La Fargue who, barely a quarter of an hour later, returned with Almades from the Palais-Cardinal.

'I know,' he said, seeing Agnès looking both angry and worried. 'The cardinal just informed me of your . . . mission.'

'Damn it, captain! What is going on . . . ? Did you agree to this!?'

'Hold your horses, Agnès. I did not agree to anything at all. As I just told you, I was summoned to the Palais-Cardinal to have this *fait accompli* presented to me.'

They were in the fencing room, where the young woman was pacing up and down.

'And you accepted this?' she asked angrily, as if La Fargue had betrayed her.

'Yes,' he said. 'Because we are the Cardinal's Blades. Not La Fargue's Blades. And even less, de Vaudreuil's Blades . . . His Eminence gives the orders. And we obey them . . .'

With a resigned air, Agnès let herself fall into an armchair.

'*Merde!*' she exclaimed.

'You will only be joining the queen's suite temporarily,' the old gentleman explained in a patient tone. 'Your sole mission will be to keep your eyes and ears wide open. It's not so terrible . . .'

'But this is simply a manoeuvre, captain. A manoeuvre!'

'That's quite possible.'

'It's damn certain, you mean! Just think for a minute! One evening I go to meet the former Mother Superior General about an affair that might very well prove embarrassing to the Chatelaines, and the very next morning I find myself

609

summoned by the current Superior General. And given an assignment where I will be unable to upset anyone. Come now! You may fool others, but not me!'

La Fargue nodded.

'It may well be true that Mère de Vaussambre wants to keep you away from certain matters. But she did not hesitate in calling upon the cardinal in order to achieve her aims: the threat against the queen could very well be real . . .'

'I don't believe that for a second.'

'But what if La Donna's plot was directed at the queen rather the king?' interjected Marciac.

Agnès shrugged.

'The duchesse de Chevreuse? Scheming against the queen . . . ? It's impossible.'

'As far as I can recall,' said Almades, who spoke so rarely that everyone pricked up their ears when he did, 'La Donna always referred to a plot "against the throne". She never said anything about a plot "against the king". We were the ones who concluded that the person of the king was under threat . . .'

'Nevertheless,' insisted the young baronne de Vaudreuil. 'La Chevreuse and the queen are sincere friends. Whenever the duchesse has been involved in a scheme, it has been against the king or the cardinal. Never against the queen.'

In this, Agnès was right.

'Be that as it may,' said La Fargue after a silence, 'there is nothing we can do. I'm sorry, Agnès, but if the Superior General wanted you out of the way, then she has succeeded.'

'We'll see about that,' declared Agnès before turning round and striding away.

'Where are you going?' La Fargue called after her.

'To find a dressmaker who can work miracles, by God! I'm going to need something decent to wear at court . . .'

After their stroll in the Tuileries gardens, Laincourt and Aude de Saint-Avold returned looking pleased with themselves and with one another, sharing a sense of being guilty of a delicious prank. They were still laughing as they descended from the coach in the courtyard of the Hôtel de Chevreuse, simply two carefree young people on a fine summer day in June. For the space of a few sunny hours, Laincourt had forgotten his mission. He had forgotten about the perils that weighed upon France, the Alchemist's plot, madame de Chevreuse's intrigues and the war being prepared against Lorraine. He had forgotten his hated profession as a spy and felt like a schoolboy.

Indeed, hadn't they just been playing truant? It was not a serious misdemeanour and the duchesse, who had boldly committed so many of her own, would no doubt forgive them. She might even be amused by their escapade, given her own fondness for the pleasures of life. As for madame de Jarville, the aunt they had been so careful not to wake, she would have to accept matters. It must be said that Laincourt had behaved like the perfect attending gentleman. Thoughtful and courteous, he had offered his arm as they strolled along the crowded lanes of the great park. Then, growing worried about the heat from the blazing sun above, he had insisted on purchasing a parasol for Aude from a hawker. The parasol turned out to be cheap rubbish and broke the moment it was opened, but the young girl laughed and held onto it as a keepsake. Finally, they drank fresh orange juice at a stand, near the pit where they saw the sleeping hydras that the queen mother had presented to the king a few years previously.

And that was all that had occurred, apart from the glances and smiles . . .

Aude de Saint-Avold was pretty, agreeable, witty and cultivated. Moreover, she was quick to wield irony with such an innocent air that she caught Laincourt by surprise several times. But above all, there was something luminous and happy about her, like a live flame, transmitted by her eyes and her smile.

Gallant to the end, Laincourt accompanied Aude from the coach to the splendid front hall of the Hôtel de Chevreuse, where the maître d'hôtel informed her that madame la duchesse was waiting for her. Laincourt then wanted to withdraw but the young woman from Lorraine implored him to stay.

'Oh no, monsieur! Don't abandon me!'

'Abandon you, madame?'

'I'm sure to be scolded for our stroll,' explained Aude, half-seriously. 'I shall tell them you abducted me and you must confirm it!'

'Madame!' exclaimed Laincourt, pretending to be worried. 'Me? Accuse myself of abducting you? I'll be thrown directly into prison.'

'Never fear. I shall arrange for your escape,' the girl whispered in a conspiratorial tone.

'Well, in that case . . .'

Thus it was on Laincourt's arm that Aude de Saint-Avold entered the salon where madame de Chevreuse was idly perusing a book on astrology. And he learned at the same time as Aude that she had been admitted to the queen's household as a maiden-of-honour. The distinction was both immense and unexpected. In the heat of her emotion, Aude forgot all about proper form and threw herself at the duchesse's feet, kissing her hands and calling her 'benefactress'. The duchesse, laughing, asked her to rise and when she was not obeyed, begged Laincourt to intervene. He helped Aude take a seat in an armchair and held her hand.

She cried, but her tears were those of joy.

'Will you visit me, monsieur?' she asked.

Arnaud de Laincourt smiled.

Maidens-of-honour were all of noble birth, lived under the watchful eye of a governess and did not appear in public except to accompany the queen on grand occasions. As for approaching them . . .

'Madame,' he said in a quiet voice, 'for that, I would have to be admitted to the queen's entourage as well . . .'

Before Aude could even begin to express her regret, the duchesse de Chevreuse announced in a playful tone:

'Bah! Consider it done, monsieur.'

Dusk was falling as the three riders came in sight of the inn. They had not exchanged so much as three words since leaving Ivry. Mirebeau, who led the way, did not seem to be in a talkative mood. As for Rauvin, he expressed his suspicious nature through silence and long stares which Leprat pretended to ignore. But the truth was that the man's hostility weighed on him. Constant and insidious, it seemed designed to play on his nerves and trip him up, and thereby provoke a confrontation. Since Mirebeau acted as if nothing was going on, the musketeer was forced to put up with it. The worst part, however, was that Rauvin – deliberately – rode last. It was his way of saying that he was keeping his eye on Leprat. And he was not the kind of man that anyone wanted to have at their back . . .

The riders stopped for a moment upon a hill.

The inn was still some distance away. Isolated, it was a former farm whose thick-walled buildings surrounded a courtyard defended by a massive gate. Right now, the two great doors remained open and there was movement in the lantern-lit courtyard. Most of the windows were brightly lit and festive sounds rose into the night: laughter, shouts, music and singing.

'Is that where we're going?' asked Leprat.

'Yes,' replied Mirebeau, urging his horse forward.

They reached the inn at a fast trot, dismounted after passing through the carriage gate and walked to the stable leading their horses by the bridle. Tables had been set up in the courtyard, along with a stage where musicians were playing. People were dancing. At the tables, the refrains were taken up in chorus, hands were clapped in time with the beat and glasses were raised only to be swiftly drained. Most of those present were soldiers, enjoying a last night of debauchery before rejoining their regiments, and here they found everything they desired: wine, drinking companions and women. There were not very many of the latter, but they did not mind being shared. Bawdy and drunk, they went from arm to arm, dancing a turn with every man, sitting on every knee, willingly allowing themselves to be rudely handled, laughing when a hand grasped their waist or a face plunged into their bosom. Anything more than that had to be paid for, however, and couples went off, out of sight from the lanterns and voyeurs, for brief fumbling embraces.

Mirebeau knew the place and was known here. Summoning the stable boy, who responded with the promptness reserved for good customers, he asked that their horses be tended to but not unsaddled.

'Keep them ready for us,' he said, giving the boy a generous tip. 'We won't be here for long.'

'Very good, monsieur.'

'This way,' he then indicated to Leprat.

'No,' Rauvin intervened. 'He stays here.'

He and Mirebeau stared at one another for a moment and then the gentleman gave in.

'All right.' And turning to Leprat, he said, 'Wait for us here, please. We'll be back soon.'

The musketeer nodded.

He had resolved to appear docile, if only to avoid giving Rauvin any opportunity to tell him to shut up and obey. He wondered whether the man was once again demonstrating his excessive sense of wariness or was simply seeking to humiliate him. But he said nothing and, from the stable's threshold, watched the two men cross the courtyard and enter the big house that constituted the inn's main building.

He thus stood waiting, pretending to watch the dancers and to be enjoying the music, while he discreetly observed the courtyard and kept track of comings and goings without anything seeming out of the ordinary . . .

. . . at least, not until he saw Rauvin come hurtling out of a first-storey window.

That evening, La Fargue, alone in his office, asked for monsieur Guibot to come see him.

'Any news of Leprat?' he asked.

'None, monsieur.'

'And of Laincourt?'

'Nothing from him, either.'

'Very good. Thank you.'

As he was leaving the office, the old porter passed Marciac who knocked on the open door by way of announcing himself.

'Yes, Marciac?' asked La Fargue.

The Gascon seemed embarrassed. He entered, shut the door behind him and sat down.

'Captain . . .'

'What is it, Marciac?'

'I have something to tell you. It's about your daughter . . . I'm not sure of anything, but I think she may be in danger.'

Having been thrown, with a tremendous crash, through a first-storey window of the inn, Rauvin landed in the courtyard under the astonished eyes of the dancers, who came to a standstill, and of the musicians on their stage, who stopped playing. He immediately ran off, as a furious-looking comte de Rochefort stuck his head out of the wreckage above.

'STOP!' shouted the cardinal's henchman, before firing his pistol.

But he missed his target and Rauvin disappeared into the darkness.

'AFTER HIM!' Rochefort ordered, and a group of red-caped guards suddenly issued forth from the inn's front door and set off in pursuit of the fugitive.

Out of instinct, Leprat had taken a step backward into the stable, and concealed himself from view.

Evidently Mirebeau and Rauvin had come here for a clandestine meeting, a meeting that Rochefort had gotten wind of and decided to attend, along with a detachment of Richelieu's men. An ambush had been set up. But if Rochefort and the Cardinal's Guards had arrived first to organise this mousetrap, they must have seen the duchesse de Chevreuse's agents arrive.

Which made Leprat wonder why he had not yet been apprehended himself.

'Don't make a move!' a voice behind him suddenly said. 'You are under arrest.'

In spite of the pistol whose barrel was now touching the back of his neck, Leprat smiled.

'You are going to be surprised, Biscarat,' he replied, extending his arms away from his body and turning around slowly.

After even a few months' service, the King's Musketeers and the Cardinals' Guards all knew one another by sight, if not by name and reputation. Leprat had earned considerable renown when he wore the blue cape, while Biscarat had been a member of the Guards for at least eight years and had achieved some fame of his own by crossing swords with Porthos in a celebrated duel.

The guard's eyes widened upon recognising his prisoner.

'You?'

There was no time for explanations, but this second of astonishment was all that Leprat required. Pushing the pistol to one side, he swiftly kneed Biscarat in the belly and knocked him out with a right hook to the head, catching the man as he fell to prevent any further injury. Then he relieved him of his scarlet cape and put it on before venturing back out of the stable.

He quickly made his way across the courtyard, beneath the lanterns, moving towards the main building of the inn.

Rauvin had fled and, under the cover of night, would no doubt evade capture, but Mirebeau appeared to be trapped. While the fate of the first man was of little concern to him, Leprat could not permit the second to be arrested. The gentleman in the beige doublet was the only means he had of becoming involved in the duchesse de Chevreuse's schemes. Leprat was thus forced to rescue Mirebeau, even if it meant thwarting Rochefort and inflicting some blows and injuries on His Eminence's Guards.

The success of his mission depended on it.

With a resolute step, Leprat approached the row of curious onlookers who had gathered before the door of the main building and, lowering his hat to conceal his eyes, he passed through them with an authoritative air.

'Make way! Make way!'

The red cape was impressive and a passage was cleared for him.

Inside, dozens of torches lit an immense hall that rose to the rafters. Twenty tables were set out on a dirt floor scattered with straw. A gallery ran along the rear wall, with a corridor and several doors on the first storey, which was accessible via two staircases that climbed the walls on either side. The hall was packed and noisy, to the point that it was impossible to be heard without raising one's voice, or to move without sidling and shouldering past people. The crowd here was the same as in the courtyard: soldiers and non-commissioned officers, prostitutes and serving wenches, plus a few debauched gentlemen. Almost everyone was on their feet protesting. The sound of a brawl coming from one of the chambers, followed by that of a breaking window and gunfire, had initially caused confusion. The appearance of the Guards in their capes and the prohibition of anyone entering or leaving the premises had then started to worry some of those present and to anger others.

Rochefort had in fact given orders to seal all the exits from the building. He was descending one of the stairways from the gallery when Leprat entered, and two guards armed with short muskets immediately took up post in front of the doors. The musketeer congratulated himself on not having delayed any longer. He didn't know how he was going to get out, but at least he had managed to slip inside without hindrance.

'Place more guards here at the bottom of these stairs!' ordered Rochefort. 'And where is Biscarat? Somebody go find Biscarat! There were three of them!'

Merely one more red cape among all the others, Leprat shoved his way through the crowd while keeping his chin down. He chose the stairs opposite those Rochefort had taken, arrived at the bottom of the steps where three guards were standing and walked brazenly past them, helped by the fact that their eyes were fixed on the angry crowd. The inn was full of soldiers and gentlemen who did not appreciate being locked inside. Emboldened by wine, some were just waiting for a chance to have a go at the cardinal's representatives, who were almost universally detested throughout the kingdom.

With the exception of Rochefort, who followed his progress with a frowning gaze, Leprat reached the gallery without attracting anyone's attention. Then he walked along the corridor where a guard was posted in front of a door.

Why keep watch on a door, unless Mirebeau was being held prisoner behind it?

Still walking with the assured step of someone who knows where he is going and who has every right to be there, while keeping his chin tucked in so that the brim of his hat concealed the top of his face, Leprat was relying on the scarlet cape to work its magic. He advanced and, at the last minute, surprised the guard by brandishing the pistol he had stolen from Biscarat. Then he forced him to turn round and roughly pushed him against the wall.

'Open the door,' he demanded.

'Impossible.'

'Where's the key?'

'Rochefort.'

Leprat cursed but did take long to reach a decision. He knocked out the guard with a blow from his pistol and then kicked open the door with his heel.

'It's me,' he announced to Mirebeau, who stood at the rear of the small room in which he had been imprisoned, blinking in the sudden light.

'Guéret?'

'Yes. Hurry up!'

Waving Mirebeau forward, Leprat glanced towards the end of the corridor.

'Good Lord! I thought you had fled—'

'I'm not Rauvin. Come on!'

The gentleman in the beige doublet was coming out just as Rochefort arrived, intrigued by this guard he had seen coming up the stairs, perhaps a little too hastily.

'GUARDS! TO ME!' he shouted as soon as he came onto the gallery. 'UP HERE!'

Leprat fired his pistol in Rochefort's direction, taking care, as he did to aim high. The pistol ball lodged itself in a beam, but caused the cardinal's henchman to retreat, which was all the musketeer had wanted. With Mirebeau on his heels, he entered the nearest chamber and the two men pushed the bed against the door before Leprat went to take a look through the window. It opened onto a section of roof by means of which the fugitives made their escape as the guards attempted to force their way into the room.

'To the stable!' Leprat cried. 'We need horses, it's our only chance!'

Mirebeau nodded.

A few seconds later, just as Rochefort ran into the courtyard with several guards, and still more were cautiously exploring the rooftops, Leprat and Mirebeau burst out of the stable at a gallop, having first liberated all the horses they found there. Spurring their own mounts and yelling like demons, they provoked a stampede, aggravated by the muskets fired at them on Rochefort's order, the furious shouts from the soldiers who saw their horses dispersing into the darkness and, lastly, by the anger of those inside the inn jostling with the guards who were still trying to prevent them from leaving. Leprat and Mirebeau, moreover, decided to take the shortest route away from the scene. Charging straight at the gate, they jumped their horses over the musicians' stage, and in doing so, carried away with them the strings of hanging lanterns. The little oil lamps broke as they fell. Trailing behind the pair of riders, they formed blazing splatters pointing in the direction of the exit, completing the panic of the other horses that had been set free. The two fugitives made good their escape, galloping flat out into the night and leaving a veritable state of chaos in their wake, as men and beasts alike ran among the scattered flames.

4

Having been warned by Marciac that Rochefort – which amounted to saying Cardinal Richelieu – was seeking to lay hands on his daughter, La Fargue had kept his fear firmly in check. But once night had fallen he retired to his bedchamber, carefully locked his door and used the flame he had brought to light some candles, filling the room with a red and amber glow.

He took out a small key which he always kept on his person and used it to open a case tucked away among his clothing, removing a silver mirror which he placed on a table in front of him. That done, he gathered his spirit, keeping eyes closed, and in a low voice uttered ancient words in a language that had not been invented by men.

The surface of the precious mirror rippled, like a pool of mercury stirred by a breeze. It ceased to send back the reflection of a tired old gentleman, replacing it with the image of the one answering his call. The mirror did not lie. It revealed the true nature of those who used it and, in this case, revealed the slightly translucent head of a white dragon.

Such was the nature of La Fargue's contact.

But what did the dragon see, when it looked back at La Fargue?

'I need to meet with one of the Seven,' said the captain of the Blades.

'Impossible,' replied the dragon. 'It's too dangerous.'

'Do whatever is necessary.'

'No.'

'No later than three nights from now.'

'Or else what?'

'No later than three nights from now. In the usual time and place.'

IV

The Dampierre Ritual

In an antechamber at the Louvre, Captain La Fargue stood looking out the window while Almades maintained a discreet guard at the door. They were waiting for Agnès, who had joined the queen's household three days previously and had not communicated with the Blades since.

Attached to the household of Anne d'Autriche, Agnès now lived in the palace and was no longer free to dispose of her time. Moreover, she knew she was being closely observed, the public manner of her arrival having aroused both curiosity and envy amongst her new peers. Although of the noblest breeding, she was nevertheless practically unknown and her sudden ascension had surprised the entire court. For two whole days, no one had spoken of anything else. It was rumoured she had been presented to the queen by the duchesse de Chevreuse, which was true. It was also said that the king had admitted her to his wife's entourage in order to initiate a reconciliation with the duchesse, which was false. Agnès's role was watch over Anne d'Autriche and to protect her if needed – a mission which the Sisters of Saint Georges' Superior General had entrusted to her with Richelieu's assent and which she was now carrying out, albeit under protest.

La Fargue turned round upon hearing the door open and saw Agnès enter. She looked very beautiful, with her hair and dress done in the latest style, her outfit including an elegant red hooped skirt, a square neckline and short puffed sleeves.

'I only have a little time,' she said as she carefully closed the door behind her.

The old gentleman understood.

'Yesterday,' he said, 'Laincourt supped at the Hôtel de Chevreuse . . .'

'I'm sure it was more amusing there than it is here.'

'No doubt. This supper, in which the marquis de Châteauneuf also took part, was given in honour of a certain Aude de Saint-Avold.'

The young baronne nodded.

'She is to be presented at court today, before joining the queen's household tomorrow. As a maiden-of-honour, I believe . . .'

'She is a distant relative of the duc de Chevreuse. She has arrived in Paris directly from Lorraine, where the duchesse no doubt made her acquaintance during her exile . . . Coming a few days after your own, this new appointment to the queen's household cannot be a coincidence.'

It was only at Cardinal Richelieu's private request that madame de Chevreuse had agreed to introduce Agnès to the queen and to recommend her. Louis XIII alone decided who was to be admitted to his wife's entourage and had occasionally used this privilege to punish her by excluding ladies she liked, claiming they exercised a bad influence over her. Thus Anne d'Autriche had learned to be wary of new faces, for she knew they had been chosen by the king and his chief minister. That was why the cardinal had sought, in this case, the good offices of the duchesse who enjoyed the queen's trust. The problem was that the duchesse had no particular desire to please either the cardinal or the king, and the fate of this little baronne de Vaudreuil was a matter of perfect indifference to her. She thus required some persuasion to become better disposed towards the idea . . .

'The duchesse,' Agnès suggested, 'might have agreed to vouch for me with the queen on condition that Aude de Saint-Avold also became a maiden-of-honour.'

'Is there anything else that would have induced the king to allow one of La Chevreuse's protégées to join the queen's suite? Especially given that . . .'

La Fargue did not complete his train of thought

They both knew that the duchesse – who never ceased to

624

plot – was on the point of being arrested as part of a general round-up of suspects which would spare neither the wealthy nor the powerful. The king had decided to strike the day after the great ball the duchesse would be hosting at the Château de Dampierre, so that her fall would come as swiftly as possible after her apparent triumph.

'What do you expect of me, captain?'

'Laincourt assures me that this young Saint-Avold is not mixed up in La Chevreuse's schemes. Nevertheless, keep your eye on her. You never know.'

Agnès sighed in resignation.

'All right,' she agreed.

'Listen, Agnès, I know you feel you are wasting your time here, but—'

'What could possibly happen to the queen here? The Louvre is swarming with the king's men, including both the Swiss Guards and the Musketeers!'

'There are dangers against which courage and steel alone do not always suffice. And it is those sorts of dangers, with respect to the queen, that worry the cardinal and the Mother Superior General . . .'

The dangers that La Fargue was referring to were dragons and their spells. And he was not mistaken in his assertion that it required more than good soldiers to combat them. It took counter-spells and fearless souls who could wield them. It took the Sisters of Saint Georges, who had been protecting the throne of France for the past three centuries.

But the Chatelaines – entrusted with Anne d'Autriche's security – were now claiming they could no longer carry out their sacred duty.

'What exactly is the problem?' the Blades' captain wanted to know.

And Agnès was regretfully forced to admit:

'It is true that the queen does nothing to make the Sisters' task any easier. You might even think she is trying to hamper them—'

'But the queen's dislike for the Sisters of Saint Georges didn't start yesterday.'

'Oh, as far as that goes, she spares the unhappy wretches assigned to her protection nothing. She gives them the cold shoulder, openly expresses her scorn and never misses an opportunity to humiliate them. From what I have been able to learn, there is nothing new there. What has changed, however, is the fact that the queen now avoids them whenever she is permitted to do so. And sometimes more. Last Friday, for example, she forbade them to accompany her to the Val-de-Grâce.'

The Val-de-Grâce, on rue Saint-Honoré, was a convent for which Anne d'Autriche had laid the first stone and was one of her favourite retreats.

'That's extremely imprudent,' commented La Fargue.

'The queen's resentment towards the White Order seems to have redoubled . . .'

'Then perhaps you are the best choice, after all. You almost completed your novitiate with the Sisters and came close to taking the veil yourself—'

'That page has been turned, captain,' the young woman said brusquely.

'I know, Agnès. I'm only asking you to trust your instincts and act for the best. You are capable of detecting things that escape the rest of us.'

Pensive for a moment, Agnès turned towards the window and then asked:

'Has Mère Emmanuelle de Cernay tried to contact me?'

Out of affection for Agnès, Emmanuelle de Cernay, formerly Superior General of the Sisters of Saint Georges, had promised to help her uncover what had happened to a certain lieutenant serving in the Black Guards. The young officer was both the son of an old friend of La Fargue and the brother of a Blade who had died in the course of a mission.

'No,' the old gentleman admitted.

'Will you let me know right away if—?'

'I promise, Agnès.'

'I must go . . . Any news of Leprat?'

'Nothing from him, either.'

'Or of the Alchemist?'

This time, La Fargue remained silent and the young woman judged it best not to press him any further.

She left.

When he arrived that afternoon, Laincourt found the Hôtel de Chevreuse in a state of upheaval. Out in the courtyard, beneath the hot sun, the servants were loading wagons with furniture, boxes, chests and rolled-up tapestries. The duchesse was not emptying the premises, but she was preparing to live elsewhere for a while. On her estate at the Château de Dampierre, as it happened.

Laincourt joined the duchesse's maître d'hôtel on the front steps, where the head servant was very busy giving orders and supervising the move. As Laincourt was now a familiar figure at the mansion the young man did not need to present himself but simply asked if he might see madame de Saint-Avold. He was informed that as she was about to go out, she was not receiving visitors. Laincourt insisted: he would wait on the terrace and only desired a short interview with her. The maître d'hôtel finally consented to this request.

'Very well, monsieur.'

And with a snap of his fingers, he summoned a lackey whom he charged with delivering the message.

Laincourt waited on the terrace, admiring the magnificent garden that stretched as far as rue Saint-Nicaise.

So, madame de Chevreuse was leaving Paris . . .

She would soon be emulated by others. As wild and welcome as it had been, the nocturnal storm that had been unleashed over the capital had merely offered a brief respite. The hot weather had resumed and, after a few days, had become an ordeal, especially with the disease and foul odours which accompanied the stifling heat. Paris had become a cesspit. Beneath a merciless sun, a nauseating muck polluted the ditches, manure baked at the stable gates, blood simmered on the pavement in front of the butchers' shops and faecal matter fermented in the latrines. This pestilence caused head-aches, nausea and respiratory disorders in weaker persons and the only effective relief was flight. Soon, as occurred each year at this time, the wealthy would begin to desert the capital. It was the season when loved ones were sent to the country or whole families emigrated, along with their baggage and servants, to some favoured retreat or ancestral castle. The king himself set an example by leaving the Louvre every summer while the palace moats were cleaned. The royal court followed suit, while more ordinary Parisians were forced to shut themselves up in buildings where the atmosphere was scarcely purer than the contaminated air outside and to wait until Sunday when they could go and breathe freely in the countryside.

'I am truly sorry, monsieur. But I can only grant you a few moments. Madame la duchesse is already waiting in her coach, ready to take me to the Louvre, and—'

Laincourt turned round and saw Aude de Saint-Avold, looking more adorable than ever in a dress he hadn't seen before. He thought she was quite ravishing, although he didn't dare say as much. But the expression on his face must have betrayed him, for she stopped speaking, smiled and blushed, her green eyes sparkling with joy.

They stood joined in silence for an instant and Laincourt resisted the desire to take hold of her hands.

'I know, madame, that you are to be presented at court today. And that you will enter the queen's household as of tomorrow. But before that, I wished to salute you and assure you of my friendship.'

'Thank you, monsieur. Thank you with all my heart.'

'I also wish to offer you a few words of advice. The royal court of France is not like the court of Lorraine. And your proximity to the queen will earn you enmity in certain quarters. Don't be fooled by false smiles, beware of hypocrites and those who aspire to a higher rank, learn to spot those who act out of self-interest and, above all, avoid getting caught up in intrigue.'

He realised that he had in fact seized her hands and that she had not withdrawn them from his grasp. She was looking at him and listening carefully, convinced and touched by his sincerity.

He stopped speaking, without releasing her hands and without her attempting to remove them.

At least, not until they heard the sound of a throat clearing: the sad-looking madame de Jarville had come in search of her niece.

Full of life and joy, Aude de Saint-Avold then took her leave with a rustling of silk.

'Farewell, monsieur! We'll meet again very soon!'

He did not reply, sure that fate had just separated them for good.

Coming from Ivry, Leprat and Mirebeau arrived in Paris by way of the faubourg Saint-Marcel. They rode side by side, at a walk, conversing in a friendly fashion.

These past few days spent together at Mirebeau's house had brought them together. On the day after the famous night when Leprat had risked his life to free him, Mirebeau had pledged his friendship, solemnly but sincerely. Leprat had initially been glad to have won the trust of the duchesse de Chevreuse's agent, for the sake of his mission. Later, he had come to like Mirebeau himself. In truth, the two men resembled one another. They were of roughly the same age, both were elder sons from noble families, and both had followed military careers: Leprat with the King's Musketeers and Mirebeau in the company of guards led by monsieur des Essarts. If life had robbed them of many of their illusions, both tried to conduct themselves as gentlemen; and lastly, as they learned exchanging confidences one night over a bottle, they had both been unlucky in love and realised, to their regret, that they would no doubt never become a father.

They smelled the capital well before they actually saw it and were soon sorry they had not chosen another route. To be sure, all of Paris stank beneath the burning sun. But Paris never stank quite so much as in the vicinity of rue Mouffetard, which they rode along with tears in their eyes. Here, the nearby Bièvre – a river that crossed the neighbourhood before plunging into the Seine – attracted various activities such as knackers' yards and tanneries which consumed great quantities of water and polluted both the river and the atmosphere.

It was therefore a relief to pass through the Saint-Marcel

gate, despite the odour of a warmed-up old latrine that prevailed within the city walls. Finally able to breathe without keeping a hand over their nose and mouth, Leprat and Mirebeau took rue de la Montagne-Sainte-Geneviève as far as Place Maubert. They crossed the small arm of the Seine by way of the Pont au Double, thus named because use of this bridge entailed a toll of a double denier. Mirebeau paid their fee. They passed before Notre-Dame cathedral, made their way through the maze of mediaeval streets on the Ile de la Cité, reached the Right Bank by the Pont au Change and ended up in front of the Grand Châtelet.

Leprat still did not know where they were going.

That morning when, after several days of idleness, Mirebeau had suddenly announced that they needed to be in Paris that afternoon, he had refused to say anything more. But he had refused in a playful manner. It was no longer a matter of distrusting Leprat, but of offering him a surprise.

A pleasant surprise.

Going along with the game, the musketeer had cherished the hope that they might be going to the Hôtel de Chevreuse to meet the duchesse. But he was forced to abandon this notion once they continued beyond Le Châtelet. Instead of going west along the quays or following rue Saint-Honoré to rue Saint-Thomas-du-Louvre, they first took rue Saint-Denis northwards, turning off once they reached the Saints-Innocents cemetery, then passed Les Halles and, keeping the Saint-Eustache church on their right, entered rue Traînée.

Mirebeau smiled as he watched Leprat out of the corner of his eye. In fact, the former musketeer had no idea of their destination until the last moment.

And it was only when they were in front of the monumental gate that he understood.

'The Hôtel de Châteauneuf?' exclaimed Marciac.

He turned to La Fargue and then looked again at Leprat, who confirmed the information:

'To the home of the marquis de Châteauneuf, yes.'

They were meeting this evening in rue Cocatrix, on the Ile de la Cité.

The place didn't look like much: a rented bedchamber beneath the rafters with cracked walls and a rough wooden floor, containing a bed without a canopy or a curtain, a clothing chest, a small dressing table, a chair in considerable need of being re-stuffed, a stained mirror and a crucifix. It was fairly wretched, but a musketeer's pay did not allow for anything better. However, the landlord was friendly, the neighbours were discreet and the street was quiet.

And Leprat felt more at home here than anywhere else.

'The truth,' he explained, 'is that Mirebeau does not belong to madame de Chevreuse or even to her husband. He belongs to Châteauneuf, who has placed him at the duchesse's disposal for her . . . affairs.'

Although night had not yet fallen, the three men had already lit a candle so they could see one another within the dark bedchamber. Leprat was sitting on his chest, La Fargue was straddling the chair backwards and Marciac was leaning against the wall with his arms crossed, next to a crookedly hung crucifix.

'Châteauneuf and La Chevreuse are lovers, as practically everyone knows,' observed the captain of the Blades. 'But what you have discovered, Leprat, is something else again . . .'

Born of a lineage that had produced several royal councillors and secretaries of state, Charles de l'Aubespine, marquis de Châteauneuf, had been the ambassador of France in Holland, Italy and England. He was reputed to be subservient to Richelieu, who, in 1630, had rewarded his loyalty and devotion by making him Keeper of the Seals. Now fifty-three years old, he was one of the most important figures in the kingdom. But he was also a somewhat ridiculous old fop who had an eye for the ladies and who, despite his age, persisted in behaving like some young Romeo.

'It would seem that La Chevreuse only likes old codgers,' observed Marciac. 'The duc de Luynes was already forty when he married her, I believe. The duc de Chevreuse was forty-four. And now Châteauneuf . . .'

'It is one thing for Châteauneuf to make the horns on the duc de Chevreuse's brow grow a little longer,' said La Fargue. 'He is not the first man to do so and, knowing the duchesse, there will be others after him. But in placing Mirebeau at La Chevreuse's disposal for her schemes, he has made himself her accomplice. And who knows what State secrets he may have let slip during their bedchamber conversations?'

'And all this has been taking place on the eve of a war against Lorraine,' added Leprat.

'Yet I thought Châteauneuf was completely devoted to the cardinal,' said the Gascon.

'No doubt that ceased to be the case the day he caught sight of the duchesse's beautiful eyes,' the captain of the Blades surmised. 'God only knows what ideas the she-devil has put in his head . . . And you may recall the ball where Châteauneuf danced all night while the cardinal lay at death's door.'

The musketeer nodded.

'It was shortly after Montmorency's execution. It was said that Châteauneuf could already see himself succeeding his master.'

'What a triumph that would have been for La Chevreuse,' Marciac noted. 'Her worst enemy dies and her lover takes his place as chief minister to the king.'

'But the cardinal did not die in the end,' said La Fargue.

'Did you actually meet Châteauneuf?' the Gascon asked.

'Yes,' replied Leprat. 'The marquis has asked me to join the group of gentlemen escorting him to Dampierre, in order to attend the ball being held there by the duchesse. We're leaving tomorrow and, since Mirebeau wanted to spend the night with his mistress, I used the same excuse to get away myself. I thought it would be more prudent if I avoided going to the Hôtel de l'Épervier, and I must confess that I've missed sleeping in my own bed . . .'

Marciac considered the bed in question, looking deeply perplexed. Even imagining one or two naked beauties lying in it, it still seemed unwelcoming . . .

A bell tolled.

Realising the time, La Fargue rose from his chair to take his leave.

'You have done very good work, Leprat. My congratulations.'

'Thank you, captain.'

'Be careful, though.'

'I will . . . By the way, was anyone injured at the Neuilly inn?'

'Amongst the Guards? Just a few bumps and bruises, as far as I know. But Rochefort is perfectly furious about the whole incident.'

'Tell him that I . . . No, on second thought, I shall reserve the pleasure of revealing the truth to him for some other day.'

The captain of the Blades smiled. He was not fond of Rochefort, either.

'Understood.'

He was the first to depart and descended the stairs while Marciac, on the landing, shook the musketeer's hand.

'Since you are supposedly spending the night with your mistress,' he murmured, 'what would you say if you and I were to pay a visit to the ladies? I know two sisters who live close by here and—'

'I'm tired, Marciac.'

'Tell yourself that it would be for the good of your mission—'

'I'll see you soon, Nicolas.'

'All right, as you wish . . . But where's your sense of duty, Antoine? This is very poor of you. And a disappointment to me!'

'Out!'

Down below, waiting in the shadowy rue Cocatrix, La Fargue found Almades who had been keeping watch. Marciac had just joined them when the captain of the Blades announced:

'I have something else to do. I'll see you both tomorrow.'

The two other men exchanged astonished looks. It was not unusual for La Fargue to leave the Gascon behind. But to separate himself from Almades . . .

633

'Captain . . .' said Marciac, attempting to intervene on the Spanish fencing master's behalf, 'Are you quite sure that—?'

'I will see you tomorrow.'

And the old gentleman went off alone.

'Let's go after him,' suggested the Gascon after a moment.

'No.'

'But it's for his own safety!'

'No,' repeated an impassive Almades.

'Well, stay then. But as for me—'

'No.'

'Since when do you give me orders?'

The Spaniard drew his sword in lieu of a reply.

'You're jesting.'

'No, I'm not.'

Marciac took a step backward and hunched his shoulders, displaying a look of wounded surprise like some scoundrel whose honesty was being placed in doubt. It suddenly occurred to him that La Fargue might not have left the two of them together in order to go off on his own, but so that Almades could keep an eye on him, Marciac, and make sure he did not try to follow his captain.

'Would you really run me through with your sword?'

'Yes.'

Back at home, Laincourt looked out the window without seeing anything.

He was lost in thought and, slowly, the blood-covered face of the hurdy-gurdy player appeared in the reflection from the window pane, above his right shoulder, as if the old man was approaching him from behind.

You're thinking about that pretty young thing, aren't you, boy? Her name is Aude.

Well, she certainly seems to be to your liking.

You might say that.

If she matters that much to you, no doubt you did well to warn her of the dangers awaiting her at the court. However . . . However, perhaps you too should be wary, of her . . .

'Me, wary of her? But why?' Laincourt asked out loud. 'On what grounds?'

He turned around without thinking.

And remembered that he was in fact alone.

Midnight.

The night was still warm when La Fargue started to cross the Pont Neuf. Around him, Paris was swallowed up in deep shadows, except for a few scattered lights here and there, fragile and distant. A thick silence reigned. One could just barely hear, rather than see, the low black waters of the Seine lapping beneath the bridge's great stone arches.

As agreed, La Fargue stopped in front of the Bronze Wyvern.

This statue stood at the end of the Ile de la Cité, where the two halves of the Pont Neuf joined at Place Dauphine. It consisted of a wyvern with spread wings, resting on a marble pedestal at the entrance to a balustered promontory that – pointing downstream from the bridge – overlooked the river. Although it was represented saddled and harnessed, the Bronze Wyvern was riderless, among all the other trials and tribulations it had undergone. A gift from the grand duke of Tuscany to Marie de Médicis, following the death of her husband Henri IV, the statue had sunk off the coast of Sardinia along with the ship transporting it. Fished out of the sea a year later, it had finally been lifted into place by the Pont Neuf in 1614. But in 1633 it had still not been mounted by anyone other than the occasional drunkard or prankster.

La Fargue walked behind the statue.

A gentleman was waiting for him, leaning on the parapet and looking out at the reflections of the moon and the stars that danced upon the inky waters of the Seine. He had a felt hat with a plume on his head and a sword at his hip, and wore a black cloak over a light grey doublet with white slashes and silver thread. He seemed to be about thirty years old, although his hair had already started to grey. He was a tall, slim and fairly handsome man, whose eyes had pale irises surrounded by a dark rim.

La Fargue halted

'Who are you?' he asked in a suspicious tone.

'I am the one who has been sent to you,' the other man replied calmly.

'I don't know you.'

'Well you're free to leave.'

The old captain thought for a moment and then asked:

'Your name?'

'Valombre.'

'Do you serve the Seven?'

The gentleman smiled.

'I serve them.'

'And are you—'

'—a dragon? Yes, I am. But unless you have a Chatelaine nun hidden up your sleeve, you will have to take my word for it.'

The jest did not make La Fargue smile and he stared at this so-called Valombre before finally saying:

'I believe you.'

'Good for you. And if we get down to business now, monsieur?'

The captain of the Blades nodded.

'I am worried,' he confessed. 'Rochefort's men are on my daughter's trail. Is she quite safe?'

'I can assure you that she is. Your daughter is doing splendidly and is out of reach of even the best of the cardinal's agents.'

'And of the Black Claw?'

'She is out of their reach as well.'

'They have immense resources at their disposal.'

'Our own are by no means negligible. Do you want to know where your daughter is?'

'No. I would be the first to be interrogated if—'

La Fargue walked several paces, turned around and raised his eyes towards the Bronze Wyvern.

'In two days' time,' he said, 'the king will have arrested his Keeper of the Seals, the duchesse de Chevreuse and all those who, with them, have plotted against the throne. The cardinal has been gathering testimonies and evidence against them for months now. It will cause a great deal of noise, no doubt about it.'

'This affair does not concern us.'

'Indeed not . . . But there's something else going on, isn't there? Something important. Something serious.'

He lowered his gaze to look at Valombre, who did not answer right away.

'Yes,' the dragon admitted at last, without any trace of emotion.

'Is the Alchemist part of it?'

'Possibly.'

'Are you not sure? Or don't you want me to know?'

'We're not sure.'

The old gentleman frowned.

'What are you hiding from me?' he asked.

'Nothing that the Sisters of Saint Georges don't already know. Perhaps you should take an interest in their secrets.'

'They seem to believe that the queen is threatened.'

'If it exists, the threat against the queen is only the beginning. But the greater danger that we fear will not spare anyone.'

2

In the Chevreuse valley, evening fell across the vast domain of Dampierre and Leprat watched from the bank of the great pond as the sunset lent its colours to the waters. Turning his back to the castle he enjoyed a moment of peace, filling his lungs with fresh air.

As they had agreed, he and Mirebeau had followed the marquis de Châteauneuf as part of his escort. It was composed of over thirty gentlemen of noble birth, each of whom attempted to outdo the others in elegance. Their presence was meant to enhance the prestige of monsieur de Châteauneuf as much as to ensure his safety. A great lord never travelled in public on his own and his status was measured by the number and rank of those accompanying him. Charles de l'Aubespine, marquis de Châteauneuf and Keeper of the Seals of the kingdom of France, could hardly ignore convention on this occasion.

The only road from Paris to Dampierre passed through the villages of Vanves, Vélizy and Saclay. It was a journey of ten leagues, which the marquis wanted to make on horseback, without resting and despite the burning sun, leaving his coach and baggage trailing behind. He was obviously impatient to reach their destination. But he also wished to make a grand entrance at the castle, where madame de Chevreuse was already waiting. So they halted at the gates to the domain for long enough to shake the dust from their clothing, refresh themselves and brush down their mounts. It was a matter of putting on a proud display. For Leprat, it allowed him to observe that Châteauneuf, despite being in his fifties and having considerable experience when it came to women, seemed as eager and anxious as an adolescent before his first gallant rendezvous. The duchesse had indeed made him lose his head.

They had arrived in the afternoon to find Dampierre swarming with busy servants and craftsmen. The paths were raked clear, the gardens were tidied, the trees were pruned and the canals were dredged. But at the heart of all this laborious agitation was the castle itself, where preparations for the forthcoming festivities would continue well into the night. The king, the queen and the entire royal court would be arriving on the morrow, the day of the ball itself. Everything had to be ready to receive them.

'It's beautiful, isn't it?'

Leprat turned his head towards Mirebeau who had come out to join him and then looked again at the sunset reflecting off the calm, shining waters.

'Yes,' he said. 'Very beautiful.'

'This domain is one of the most splendid places I know. Whatever the season, it's a veritable feast for the eyes . . .'

He broke off as a deep, mournful trumpeting almost deafened the two men.

'And for the ears!' exclaimed Leprat before they both burst out laughing.

They turned around to watch as a tarasque crossed the terrace separating them from the castle, plodding along at a slow and steady pace. The enormous, shelled reptile was pulling a train of three wagons piled with the pruned trunks of trees that had been cut down to embellish a prospect in the park. Two tarasque drivers were guiding the beast, using both their voices and their pikes. It moved forward with a rattle of the heavy chains linking its six legs to the collar encircling its neck.

Still smiling, Leprat and Mirebeau returned to admiring the view of pond, without either feeling any need to speak. Since he had discovered that Mirebeau was actually in the service of the marquis de Châteauneuf, Leprat had felt himself drawn even closer to the gentleman in the beige doublet. Now there seemed to be really little difference between them, other than the fact that they served their respective masters with equal loyalty. Life might easily have reversed their roles or allowed Mirebeau to become a member of the Cardinal's Blades. It was perhaps simply a matter of circumstances.

Leprat's gaze was drawn to an island at the far end of the pond, an island upon which he was able to make out some ruins and the silhouettes of men apparently keeping watch over them.

'What is that?' he asked, pointing his finger.

'It's the island of Dampierre. An island which isn't truly an island, since it's connected to the bank by a causeway that you can't see from here. The duc is having some pavilions built there.'

The ruins were in fact buildings being constructed.

'According to legend,' Mirebeau went on to say, 'in the time of Charlemagne there was a lord living in a black tower upon the island. He performed vile rituals there and terrorised the entire region, to the point that some valiant knights came to challenge him. Unfortunately for them, the lord was not only a wicked sorcerer, but also a dragon . . . There is, in the castle here at Dampierre, a tapestry representing the heroic combat between these knights and the monster.'

'Did they defeat the dragon?'

'Don't knights always triumph in tales?'

'And the tower? It looks like there is nothing left of it.'

'It was razed to the ground and its stones, reputed to be cursed, were thrown into the pond so that they could never be used again.'

'Legends have an answer for everything.'

'It seems that these cursed stones also gave rise to the name "Dampierre", although I know nothing of Latin . . .'

As for the musketeer, he possessed only a smattering of church Latin. He pursed his lips and the two men fell silent again.

'Enough lazing about,' Mirebeau suddenly declared. 'Come with me, we need to go to the Château de Mauvières and make sure that everything is ready there to receive monsieur de Châteauneuf's entourage.'

'We're not sleeping at Dampierre?'

'In the castle?' the gentleman asked with amusement. 'Tonight, that might be possible. But tomorrow there will be marquises in the servants' quarters, comtesses in the attic and barons sleeping on straw mattresses. Where do you think they would put us? No, trust me, we shall be better off at Mauvières. And it's close by.'

Leprat regretfully dragged his eyes from the pond and its island. He was following Mirebeau, who had set off at a brisk pace, when he heard the sound of a few notes being played on a jew's harp.

He halted, turned round and saw Rauvin in the shadows.

Mirebeau had told Leprat that the hired swordsman had escaped, but he'd not seen him since the night when Rochefort had laid his trap for them. How long had the other man been standing there, spying on them? And why had he decided to reveal his presence, if not to make Leprat understand that he was still keeping an eye on him?

As he continued plucking notes on his harp, staring directly at the musketeer, Rauvin gave a slow nod of the head.

The barony of Chevreuse had been made a duchy in 1555, as a favour to Cardinal Charles de Lorraine who had just acquired it as his holding. The seigneurial seat at the time was the Château de la Madeleine, an austere mediaeval fortress built on a height overlooking Paris and whose only real advantage was its unequalled view of the surrounding countryside. Its lack of comfort displeased the cardinal, who preferred a more elegant manor nestling in the Yvette valley barely a league away from Chevreuse. It had belonged to a royal treasurer who was obliging enough to die quickly, leaving behind him some debts and a widow who posed no objections to selling off the entire domain.

This domain was Dampierre, whose name was perhaps derived from either *domus Petri* – Peter's dwelling in Latin – or from *damnæ petræ*, meaning cursed stones. Its manor became the new ducal residence. The cardinal transformed it into a castle that was later inherited by the youngest son of the duc de Guise, who also came from Lorraine, along with the land and title in 1612. This duc de Chevreuse did not add any great distinction to the name, as opposed to the woman he wed ten years later. The famed and indomitable duchesse loved Dampierre. She stayed there often and, at her urging, her husband enlarged and embellished the property further.

However, if the domain was vast and prosperous in 1633, its castle, despite acquiring a luxurious steam bath and some other interior improvements, still compared poorly with the magnificence of the Hôtel de Chevreuse in Paris. Its roofs were covered with tiles rather than more handsome slate, while the four sides formed by its sandstone towers and pavilions enclosed a rather small courtyard, entered by means of a drawbridge leading from a forecourt lined with the castle's outbuildings.

But the main attractions of Dampierre lay elsewhere.

They included the magnificent forests in the surrounding area; the orchards and splendid flower beds arranged in the Renaissance fashion; the beautiful water-filled moats that encircled the castle and its garden; the canals feeding these moats, lined with leafy walks and bordering the main flower bed; and, lastly, the pond where one could take pleasant boat trips out to the island where the new pavilions were being built.

Pavilions which were being guarded for no reason that Leprat could see.

Mirebeau had not lied. The modest Château de Mauvières – sometimes also called Bergerac – was located just beyond the outer wall surrounding the domain of Dampierre. It belonged to a minor nobleman, Abel de Cyrano, whose son Savinien was already beginning to make a name for himself in Paris, both as a man of letters and with his sword.

Leprat waited until nightfall before slipping out of his bedchamber, which was fortunately close by the stables. He saddled a horse, and led it out of the manor before mounting and urging it forward with a dig of his heels. The summer nights were short and he had to be back before dawn.

Who would post a guard over some unfinished pavilions on an island?

Once inside the domain at Dampierre, Leprat stayed away from the paths. He entered the woods, tethered the horse to a tree and continued onward by foot. Remaining concealed, he soon found a place where he enjoyed a clear view of the island in the middle of the large pond. As he had expected, he saw men with lanterns guarding the causeway that gave access to the building site from the shore furthest away from the castle.

It would be impossible for him to cross over that way.

Leprat stripped down to his breeches and shirt, and swung his baldric round so that his rapier hung down his back. Then he took careful note of the place where he left his belongings, slid into the cold water and began swimming towards the island and its mysteries.

He had no idea who these men were or what they were doing here. During supper, Mirebeau had also confessed his ignorance, but said they did not belong to the marquis de Châteauneuf. Did they serve madame de Chevreuse, then? Perhaps. Or else some third party.

Leprat swam steadily to conserve his strength and to splash as little as possible. He drew close to the island, regained his footing once more and hurriedly climbed the bank. Then he took up position on a height where, hidden by some thickets, he was able to catch his breath while observing what was going on.

He saw more armed mercenaries guarding the building site itself, which was lit here and there by torches planted in the ground. Five pavilions had started to emerge from the scaffolding and piles of building materials. They surrounded a roof made of wooden planks. Leprat was unable to see what lay concealed beneath it, but there were mounds of earth nearby.

Had the construction project made an unexpected discovery? Or was the building work only a pretext intended to mask other activities? Whatever the case, Leprat intended to get to the bottom of the matter.

He studied the movements of the hired swordsmen before creeping forward. Quickly and silently he entered the site, tiptoed among the shadows and managed to slip beneath the wooden roof without being spotted. It sheltered a pit into which he could descend via a ramp and several ladders. The excavation of this pit had exposed the ancient foundations of a large circular building which immediately called to mind the black tower of the legend. The same black tower whose cursed stones might have inspired the name Dampierre.

The musketeer leapt into the pit and landed nimbly upon a floor of bare flagstones. There was a gap where some steps descended into the ground. They led to a very old door made of black wood which appeared to have been blocked up long ago and only recently unsealed. Its relatively well-preserved state was, upon reflection, rather astonishing. As was the ease with which it opened to reveal a spiral staircase lit by candles in a succession of niches. Leprat made his way downward with caution, counting seventy-one stone steps which took him to a level beneath the bottom of the pond. After opening another black door, he found himself in a fairly vast but empty chamber, whose vaulted ceiling was supported by rows of round columns. Here, again, a few candles shone in the darkness. The air felt damp and water dripped from the ceiling into age-old puddles.

More and more intrigued, Leprat continued his exploration. There were several doors – low and again black – on either side of the chamber. But the central aisle between the columns, illuminated by the candles set at regular intervals, seemed to indicate a path leading to an archway at the rear over which a last, solitary candle burned.

But as he stretched out a hand to draw open the purple curtain concealing the archway, he sensed a sudden movement behind him. He spun round, but only had time to see a scaly tail snaking away into the darkness. A syle. Bad news. Sometimes growing as big as cats, the carnivorous salamanders were both extremely swift and voracious. They became frenzied at the scent of blood and, when gathered in numbers, they were capable of attacking a wounded man and devouring him alive. And where there was one, there were usually others . . .

Pulling himself together, the musketeer lifted the curtain.

Having left the castle in the middle of the night, seven riders trotted forth upon the causeway joining the island to the shore of the pond. At their head was Savelda, the Black Claw's most effective servant when it came to carrying out foul deeds. Behind him rode the Alchemist, the false master of magic using the name of Mauduit and true mastermind of a plot intended to change the destiny of France forever. The third rider was in fact a very beautiful woman: the duchesse de Chevreuse, dressed as a horseman and thrilled at taking part in this nocturnal expedition. The four others were hired swordsmen who, like those guarding the island, had been recruited by Savelda to replace the mercenaries killed in Alsace by the troops serving the Sisters of Saint Georges.

The riders reached the building site and dismounted.

Only Savelda, the Alchemist and the duchesse, however, passed beneath the roof protecting the pit and disappeared down the spiral staircase. Wearing the silver-studded leather patch over his left eye, the Spaniard led the way again with a confident air. His two companions wished to make sure that everything was ready for the ceremony the following evening. He already knew this to be the case. In preparation for the last-minute inspection, Savelda had even ordered candles to be lit underground. The same candles that were at this very moment aiding Leprat's exploration.

Leprat was a musketeer.

He did not know much about draconic magic, but enough to recognise all the signs indicating a spell chamber. The drapes embroidered with esoteric patterns. The tall black candles waiting to be lit. The small table for ritual items. The lectern to support the heavy grimoire as the incantatory formula were pronounced. The altar, a large platform carved from a single block. And lastly, the pentacle engraved on the black stone floor and embossed with scarlet and golden glyphs.

But above all, there was an atmosphere of evil haunting this place. Whatever danger threatened the king, whatever the nature of the plot concocted by the Alchemist, it had something to do with this chamber which now only awaited the arrival of a sorcerer and, perhaps, a victim.

'Damn it!' Leprat muttered.

He started to feel ill.

He was suddenly very hot. His vision blurred. Dizzy, he felt his legs start to give way under him. He did not understand what was happening to him; indeed he had trouble keeping any wits at all. Then the disease eating away at his back awoke. It was as if the patch of ranse had come alive and was biting ever more deeply into his flesh. Leprat grimaced, fighting back moans of pain. In a feverish delirium of confused thoughts, he sensed that he had to leave this cursed chamber. He needed to get back to the surface and away from this place that was increasing tenfold the virulence of the ranse. He clung to this idea, concentrating on its urgency. He tottered back through the curtain. The pain lessened, but the dizziness remained. Gasping, his brow bathed in sweat, he staggered from column to column, moving in the direction of the staircase and the exit. He could barely see the way. His ears were filled with a buzzing sound and he failed to hear the party descending the steps. Sapped of his strength, he continued to stumble towards the door, which Savelda was going to open at any instant . . .

. . . when he felt a pair of arms seize hold of him and haul him away.

A gloved hand blocked his mouth.

'It's me,' a familiar voice murmured in his ear.

Saint-Lucq.

Dressed entirely in black, the half-blood with the red spectacles dragged Leprat into a dark corner just before Savelda entered. The Black Claw's agent preceded madame de Chevreuse and her master of magic. He held a lit lantern in his left hand, as the candles burning in the hall of columns did little more than point the way to the spell chamber.

Halfway to the purple curtain, Savelda slowed and then came to a complete halt. His two companions imitated him, looking puzzled. He turned around with the expression of a man who senses he has overlooked something. The leather

646

patch concealing his eye failed to mask the stain of the ranse that spread, star-like, towards his brow, his temple and his cheekbone. His fist closed about the pommel of his rapier.

'What is it?' asked madame de Chevreuse.

'I thought . . . I thought I heard . . . I don't know. Something.'

The gaze of the one-eyed man passed over Leprat and Saint-Lucq without seeing either of them. Saint-Lucq kept hold of the musketeer and had not taken his hand away from the other man's mouth. With a considerable effort, Leprat managed to control the shaking of his legs which risked betraying their presence.

'I didn't hear anything,' said the duchesse. 'Did you, Mauduit?'

'I heard nothing either, madame.'

'It must have been a syle,' Savelda conceded.

'Good Lord! There are salamanders down here?'

'This place is safe, madame,' said the Spaniard as he reluctantly moved on. 'My men have made sure of that. But down in the lower levels . . .'

The two men and the woman soon disappeared behind the curtain.

'You'll see,' they heard madame de Chevreuse promising, 'everything has been scrupulously arranged according to your instructions.'

'Let's get out of here,' said Saint-Lucq.

With the half-blood assisting Leprat, they returned to the open air by way of the spiral staircase, climbed out of the pit, slipped past Savelda's men and found refuge in one of the pavilions under construction. Sitting with his back against a large block of stone, the musketeer took his time to recover, drawing in deep breaths while Saint-Lucq kept watch over their surroundings.

'Have they come back up?' he asked after a moment.

'Not yet.'

'The duchesse was there, wasn't she? But who were the other two? I could barely see.'

'One of them was Mauduit, the duchesse's master of magic. The other one was Savelda, a Spaniard working for the Black Claw. I almost had a chance to fight him when we prevented the vicomtesse de Malicorne from summoning the soul of an Ancestral Dragon.'

'I missed all of that. I was in a gaol cell in the Grand Châtelet that night.'

'That's true . . . But what was wrong with you just now? It looked like you were overcome by a fever or by too much drink . . .'

Without mentioning the ranse, which he wished to keep secret, Leprat spoke of the spell chamber and the effect that he suspected it had on him.

'I almost fell right into the arms of our enemies. If it hadn't been for you . . .' And when Saint-Lucq did not respond to this, the musketeer prompted him, 'What were you doing down there?'

'At the cardinal's request, I have been watching Dampierre for several days now. I was intrigued by the pavilions that they were building here. And you?'

'I entered La Chevreuse's service by passing myself off as an agent of the queen mother. And, like you, I was curious about what this building site might be hiding.'

The half-blood nodded.

Leprat crouched and as his wits returned to him along with his strength, he noticed that Saint-Lucq was gloved, booted and impeccably dressed, as usual.

'You didn't get here by swimming.'

'No. I came underground. There is a passage that leads to the old cellars here. No doubt it was once used by the residents of the tower in times of siege. The entrance lies beneath a very big oak tree in the forest, not far from a stone cross that stands where two paths meet. I discovered it when following Savelda's men. Several of them came back wounded and I wanted to know why. As it happens, the tunnel is swarming with enormous syles.'

The Alchemist, Savelda and the duchesse returned to the surface. Leprat and Saint-Lucq watched them depart, along

648

with most of their hired swordsmen. The torches were extinguished. Only a handful of sentries remained.

'I better go back myself before someone notices my absence,' said Leprat.

'Well, I'm going back down. I need to see this spell chamber with my own eyes.'

'We must also inform La Fargue of our discoveries.'

'I'll take care of that. I will be in Paris tomorrow.'

'Understood.'

'Have you fully recovered?'

'Yes. Don't worry about me.'

The half-blood was about to leave when Leprat called him back:

'You saved my life, Saint-Lucq. Thank you.'

The other Blade gazed back at him from behind his red spectacles. He did not react, no doubt seeking a suitable response, to no avail.

And so he left.

In his turn, the musketeer slipped out of the unfinished pavilion. He tried to ignore the burning pain in his back, forcing himself to focus on the approaching day instead. He had lied to Saint-Lucq. He knew what was happening to him, although it cost him to admit it, even to himself.

The causeway was no longer guarded. Leprat crossed it quickly, then found his clothing and his horse in the forest. He did not spare his mount and arrived at the Château de Mauvières just as the night sky was beginning to grow pale, but before the cock's first crow. He left his horse in the stable and hurried back to his bedchamber.

But someone was watching him.

A new day dawned in Paris and, by mid-morning, the air had already grown unpleasantly warm. From all its streets, all its courtyards, all its gutters and all its ditches, the city's stink rose stronger than ever beneath the relentless sun. The sun's rays, however, did not reach sieur Pierre Teyssier's study. Behind closed shutters, His Eminence's master of magic had fallen asleep at his work table after a hard night of labour, his head resting on his forearms, snoring loudly and drooling slightly.

He awoke suddenly to what sounded very much like an altercation in the stairway outside, complete with cries and the sound of blows being exchanged. He sat up, with bleary eyes and tousled hair, to gaze with astonishment and then alarm at the individual who had just burst into the room. He was a squat, solidly-built man with white hair and a ruddy face. One could tell he was an old soldier from ten leagues off. He shoved his way past the valet who had been trying to deny him entry.

The tall, gangly young magic master rose and looked for a weapon to defend himself. He found nothing, but consoled himself with the thought that he would in any case not have known how to use it.

'Monsieur?' he asked, mustering a degree of dignity.

'Please forgive this intrusion, monsieur. But the matter is an important one.'

The valet, seeing that a conversation had been engaged, awaited the outcome.

'No doubt. However, I don't believe I know you.'

'I am Ballardieu, monsieur. I am in the service of Captain La Fargue.'

'In whose service?'

The question surprised Ballardieu. He hesitated, casting a wary glance at the valet before stepping forward, leaning over, clearing his throat and whispering:

'The company of the Cardinal's Blades, monsieur.'

Realisation finally dawned upon Teyssier.

'La Fargue! Yes, of course . . .' he sighed with both relief and satisfaction which were readily shared by the old soldier . . .

. . . but which still failed to clarify the situation.

With uncertain smiles on their lips, the two men gazed at one another in silence, each of them expecting the other to speak. The valet also waited with a smile.

Until at last Teyssier enquired:

'Well? La Fargue?'

The question woke Ballardieu from his daze. He blinked his eyes and announced:

'The captain wishes to meet you.'

'Today?'

'Yes.'

Although he tended to be taken aback by unforeseen events, Teyssier was young man of good will.

'Very well . . . Uhh . . . In that case . . . In that case, tell him that I shall receive him at a time of his convenience.'

'No, monsieur. You need to come with me. The captain is waiting for you.'

'Now?'

'Now.'

'It's just that I don't go out much.'

'Can you ride a horse?'

'Not very well.'

'That's too bad.'

An hour later, at the Hôtel de l'Épervier, Teyssier was still trying to convince himself that he had not actually been abducted. Feeling unsteady, he was finishing an ink drawing of the pentacle which Saint-Lucq had reported seeing at Dampierre and had described to him from memory. He found himself in the large fencing room, lit by the sunlight pouring through the three tall windows that looked out on the garden with its weeds, old table and chestnut tree.

Carefully avoiding the scarlet gaze of the half-blood and his disturbing spectacles, Teyssier concentrated on his sketch, which he corrected and completed in the light of his own knowledge. He could not prevent himself, however, from glancing at La Fargue who was slowly pacing up and down the room, or looking over at Marciac who was sipping a glass of wine and daydreaming as he rocked back and forth on a creaking chair. Laincourt remained outside his field of vision, but Teyssier could sense the man behind him, watching over his shoulder as the drawing took shape. Silent and expressionless as ever, Almades guarded the door. As for Ballardieu, he had left the magic master in the front hall.

In fact, as soon as Teyssier had arrived at Hôtel de l'Éper-vier he had immediately been taken in hand by La Fargue, who explained what was required of him: a drawing of a pentacle based on a verbal description.

'Do you think this is possible, monsieur?'

'Yes. On condition that—'

'Because Laincourt, who knows something about magic, claims that the purpose of a pentacle can be divined from its appearance. Is that true?'

'Certainly, but—'

'Perfect! Then let's get to work, monsieur.'

Time was indeed running short. The pentacle in question had probably been traced in preparation for a ritual that would take place that very night, during the ball being given by the duchesse de Chevreuse. And the Blades suspected this ritual of being a means, if not the ultimate end, of the plot against the king.

Teyssier, on the other hand, was growing more and more doubtful that this was the case . . .

'There was a symbol resembling the letter N, here,' Saint-Lucq was saying. 'And over here, something that looked rather like the number 7 . . . And that's about all.'

The young master of magic had recognised the two draconic glyphs recalled by the half-blood. He copied them onto the paper.

'Nothing else?' he asked.

'I don't think so.'

He made a few revisions to his sketch and then turned the sheet of paper around and pushed it across the table towards Saint-Lucq.

'So it looked like this?'

The half-blood studied the drawing carefully and then nod-ded.

'As far as I can recollect, yes.'

La Fargue ceased his pacing. Marciac stopped rocking in his chair. As for Laincourt, he straightened up with a puzzled look and said:

'There must be some mistake . . .'

'The drawing is just like the pentacle I remember,' asserted Saint-Lucq crossing his arms.

'What?' asked the old captain. 'Why would it be a mistake?'

Teyssier hesitated.

He exchanged a glance with Laincourt that confirmed the doubts and fears of both men. But still he kept silent. It was therefore the cardinal's former spy who announced:

'This pentacle is beneficial, captain. It can't harm anyone. Neither the king, nor anyone else.'

The king and his court arrived at Dampierre during the afternoon.

Louis XIII and the gentlemen of his suite rode at the head of the procession with panache, followed just behind by a detachment of musketeers. Pulled by a team of six magnificent horses, the king's golden coach followed. Then came that of the queen, and finally those of the great lords and courtiers, in order of their rank and favour. More riders in small groups brought up the rear; others trotted alongside the carriages so that they could converse with the passengers; while the most impetuous urged their mounts to prance and twirl in an effort to please the ladies who watched and laughed, bright-eyed, from behind their delicate fans.

Leaving the baggage train far behind, the parade of coaches was a splendid, joyful sight to behold, sparkling in the sun despite the dust that rose in its passage. It attracted crowds of spectators who gathered at the entrances of villages and along the roads. As it approached Dampierre, heralds spurred their horses forward to announce the coming of the king. While protocol required this, it was an unnecessary precaution. Runners had already cut across the fields to deliver breathless warnings at the castle, alarming those who had not yet finished erecting a platform, painting a fence or raking a lawn. 'The king! The king!' From the kitchens to the attic, and all the way out into the gardens, there was a great flurry of activity, with a final nail being hammered down just before the trumpets sounded.

Everything was ready, however, by the time His Majesty passed through the gates of Dampierre.

Leprat took advantage of this distraction to slip away from Rauvin, who had been breathing down his neck all morning. Although the mercenary was not following him openly, he was always somewhere in the background, no matter where Leprat went or what he did. The musketeer therefore had no choice but to carry out the tasks assigned to him by Mirebeau, who had become strangely distant. This coldness left Leprat perplexed, but he was not inclined to dwell on the matter. After all, Mirebeau must have worries of his own. For his part, Leprat had enough to think about between his mission, the danger posed by Rauvin, the underground spell chamber and the possible plot against the king. And when he wasn't preoccupied by all that, his ranse – which he knew had taken a sudden turn for the worse – continued to haunt him.

But the king's arrival gave Leprat an opportunity to take a horse and discreetly get away on his own. There were things he needed to do in the woods and, in any case, he was better off avoiding Dampierre now that the castle was swarming with blue capes. Louis XIII never went anywhere without his regiment of musketeers, all of whom knew Leprat by sight and were thus liable to unmask him.

He rode for a quarter of an hour through the underbrush before coming across a path.

What was it Saint-Lucq had told him? *Beneath a very big oak tree in the forest, not far from a stone cross that stands where two paths meet.*

If Leprat wanted to explore the underground tunnels below the ruins of the black tower that once stood in the middle of the Dampierre pond, first he needed to find the entrance to them.

The afternoon was ending when Arnaud de Laincourt crossed the Petit Pont and, with long strides, passed beneath the dark archway of the Petit Châtelet.

His surmises upon seeing the pentacle described by Saint-Lucq had been confirmed by Teyssier, the cardinal's master of

654

magic, who explained that there existed several different kinds of pentacles and, despite possible errors, omissions and guesswork, the one he had drawn was intended for a beneficial ritual. Certain features of its general design left no room for doubt in the matter.

'I can affirm to you,' he had said, 'that the person who drew this pentacle did not wish to harm anyone. In fact, in my view, quite the opposite.'

But Teyssier had been unable to say which particular type of ceremony the Dampierre pentacle was intended for. Protection, healing, benediction, rejuvenation? The sketch was too imprecise. He would have to compare it with all the others he had recorded in his grimoires and then, after careful cross-referencing, he might be able to reach a conclusion. Hearing that, La Fargue had permitted the magic master to return to his home, accompanied by Ballardieu who would remain with him until the pentacle had been positively identified.

Laincourt followed the old and very narrow rue de la Bûcherie, towards Place Maubert.

Saint-Lucq had not lingered after Teyssier's departure, saying simply, 'I'll see you this evening in Dampierre, no doubt.' La Fargue, Marciac and the cardinal's former spy had continued the discussion in the fencing room at the Hôtel de l'Épervier, while Almades contented himself with listening in. They had traded various hypotheses back and forth, trying to integrate the pentacle into a possible plot by the Alchemist and the duchesse de Chevreuse against the king. None of these speculations led anywhere. They didn't have enough facts and in the end were left with nothing but reasons to worry. Chief among them was the presence of Savelda, the Black Claw's most trusted henchman. The threat was therefore real.

Rather than continue going round in circles, Laincourt had decided to find out more about Mauduit, the duchesse's master of magic. After all, he was directly involved with the pentacle, wasn't he? Laincourt had thus gone to the Hôtel de Chevreuse, which he found almost empty and where he had learned nothing about Mauduit except that he had only recently entered the duchesse's service. The man was troubling and elusive. He was said to be a sorcerer. People tended to avoid having anything to do with him, and even the Swiss guard on duty at the mansion gate did not know his address in Paris.

After rue de la Bûcherie, Laincourt crossed Place Maubert which, at the entrance to rue de la Montagne-Sainte-Geneviève, was one of the five places in the city where prisoners were tortured and executed. Preoccupied by his mission, the young man did not even spare a glance for the gallows or the sinister wheel that was being set up on a new platform.

Upon leaving the Hôtel de Chevreuse, it occurred to him that the duchesse was fond of luxury. She only allowed herself the best, the most beautiful and the most expensive items available. Her new master of magic was, no doubt, no exception to the rule. Mauduit had probably been recommended to her or was at least fairly renowned in certain circles. The fact that Laincourt didn't recognise his name wasn't significant, since the small world of magic masters was extremely secretive.

But there was someone who was well-acquainted with this small world.

On rue Perdue, Laincourt entered Bertaud's bookshop.

An hour later, just as night was falling, Laincourt arrived back at the Hôtel de l'Épervier, out of breath. He had hoped to find La Fargue still there, but the captain had already left for Dampierre with Almades and Marciac.

'What about Ballardieu?' he asked Guibot.

'Monsieur Ballardieu has not yet returned,' replied the old porter.

'Too bad. Fetch me a horse. Quickly!'

But just then a rider entered the courtyard. It was Ballardieu. He had come from the home of Teyssier, who had finally succeeded in identifying the pentacle described by Saint-Lucq.

'You're not going to believe this!' the old soldier announced as he jumped down from the saddle.

But Laincourt did believe him.

He mounted Ballardieu's horse and left at a gallop.

As evening descended upon Dampierre, raised voices and bursts of laughter resounded in the small castle courtyard. Some Italian actors were performing, by torchlight, a lively farce which had all the guests enthralled. Even the king, who had little taste for bawdiness, appeared to be enjoying the comedy. He guffawed readily enough. Since he was normally of a dismal, brooding nature, his excellent humour astonished those observing him. It should, instead, have alarmed some of them.

La Fargue looked down into the courtyard from a first-storey window. The Italians' pranks did not amuse him. Since arriving at Dampierre he had asked to be received by monsieur de Tréville, captain of the King's Musketeers, and had communicated his suspicions to him: a plot against His Majesty was about to unfold. The two men knew, liked and respected one another. But without taking La Fargue's warnings lightly, Tréville had assured him that Louis XIII could not be in danger because an elite company of gentlemen was there to protect him. The captain of the Musketeers nevertheless allowed La Fargue to remain, on the condition that he and his Blades would not hinder Tréville's own service. He also required that they stay away from the gardens, particularly once night fell.

'My musketeers don't know you and they have strict orders. They will open fire on your men, if they do not obey these instructions.'

In the courtyard, before a painted backdrop, Arlecchino was kicking Matamoros's rear end, for vainly seeking the hand of Colombina in marriage. In a decidedly joyful mood, Louis XIII was laughing heartily at the grotesque hopping of the actor each time he received a boot to the arse. It made a sharp contrast with the attitude of the queen, seated to the left of her husband, who was forcing herself to smile and, distracted, applauded with a slight delay. She was obviously preoccupied with something . . .

'It will happen this evening,' declared La Fargue in a grave tone. He looked up at the darkening sky where the stars were beginning to come out. 'I can feel it. I know it . . .'

Tréville was reading a note that one of his musketeers had just brought him. He nodded.

'Perfect,' he said to the musketeer.

The man withdrew with a martial step and, folding up the piece of paper, the comte de Troisvilles, more commonly called Tréville, approached La Fargue and placed a friendly hand on his shoulder.

'You're obsessed with this Alchemist, my friend.'

'No doubt . . . But he is one of the kingdom's most formidable enemies. And I can sense his presence here.'

Tréville shrugged his shoulders

'I can only repeat that all the necessary precautions to ensure His Majesty's safety have been taken.'

'They may not be enough.'

'I know. There are always unforeseen events.'

Both men were haunted by the spectre of Henri IV's assassination. They remained silent for a moment and then La Fargue said:

'The queen seems worried about something.'

Tréville leaned forward to have a look.

'Indeed she does.'

Turning from the window, La Fargue went over to open the door and called in Almades who was waiting in the antechamber.

'Yes, captain?'

'Go and find Marciac. I want him to ask Agnès if the queen has any legitimate, admissible cause for concern.'

'Understood, captain.'

The Spaniard immediately complied, descending the stairs to find the Gascon, who was busy trying to work his charm on a very pretty and still very innocent young baronne. If there was little doubt that he wished for her to remain pretty, her innocence, on the other hand, was under serious threat. He was unflustered at seeing Almades, but promised the young woman that he would return, caressing her chin with his

658

index finger and grinning before going over to the austere fencing master.

'I'm listening.'

'The queen is preoccupied. Perhaps Agnès knows why.'

'All right.'

'And who is that you're with?'

'Delicious, isn't she?'

At that very instant, Matamoros finished covering himself in ridicule, the Dottore married Colombina off to Arlecchino and the play ended to considerable applause.

'Don't delay, Marciac.'

The Gascon thus hurried off, repeating his promise to the pretty young baronne as he passed, then seemed to change his mind by turning back and surprising the lady with a kiss on the cheek, before going in search of Agnès.

Thanks to Saint-Lucq's directions, Leprat located the secret passage leading to the black tower.

This edifice had long ago been taken apart stone by stone, before its very foundations were buried, no doubt so that all memory of it would be lost forever. But it had once stood in the middle of the pond at Dampierre, less than a cannon shot from the present castle belonging to the duc de Chevreuse. Legend said that a dragon sorcerer had built it and lived there. Legend also said he had worked terrible, evil magic and added that he had been finally vanquished by valiant knights. The tale might have been mostly invention, but Leprat was convinced the underground vestiges of the cursed tower had not yet given up all of their secrets.

The entrance to the passage lay in the forest, not far from a granite cross that stood where two tracks met. The way had recently been cleared to an old gate set in the brush-covered flank of a mound topped by a large oak tree. Behind the gate were stone steps, the beginnings of a narrow spiral staircase that led down into the darkness.

Leprat tethered his horse a good distance away, where it would not be spotted.

Then he approached the gate cautiously, creeping through

the underbrush, his sword in his fist. He had feared that the place might be watched, but there was no one about. However, he did see numerous boot prints scattered across the ground, no doubt left by Savelda's men when they had opened a path to the passage. And close by, at the beginning of one of the tracks, there were traces indicating that horses had been guarded here.

Leprat had brought a lantern. He lit the candle with his tinder lighter and, without re-sheathing his rapier, started down the stairs.

At the bottom he found a long corridor leading in the direction of the pond, and the island.

In the castle courtyard, the guests had watched the comedy standing behind the royal couple. Still chuckling over the antics of the players, they were slow to disperse, walking towards the salons and stairways, or lingering to converse in the light of the great torches held aloft by lackeys in livery aligned at regular intervals with their backs to the wall, standing as still as Atlases on a palace façade. Supper was due to be served before the costume ball and a fireworks display that promised to be splendid.

With a quick step that betrayed her anxiety, Anne d'Autriche regained the apartments that madame de Chevreuse had assigned to her. Accompanied by the duchesse, she was trailed by the women of her suite, including Agnès de Vaudreuil who was doing her best to keep up her role as a lady-in-waiting. She tried to be discreet, helpful and considerate, taking care not to encroach where she was not wanted. With her hair and face prettily made up, this evening she was wearing a magnificent scarlet dress with a plunging neckline trimmed with lace, a starched bodice and a hooped skirt. She knew she looked beautiful. Nevertheless, she had missed having her rapier these past few days since she had joined the queen's household. The stiletto dagger tucked in her garter was a poor substitute.

One of the last ladies to start up the great stairway, Agnès felt someone take her by the hand . . .

. . . and allowed Marciac to drag her behind a pillar.

'Do you know what's wrong with the queen?' he asked without any preamble.

'No. But she was in a very sombre mood when she woke this morning, and it has only grown worse since. In fact, she has spent most of the day in prayer.'

'Try to find out more, all right?'

'All right. Where can I find the captain?'

'He is with Tréville.'

'I'll do what I can.'

'Say . . .'

'Yes?'

'We've been seen going off together on our own.'

'So?'

'Perhaps we should kiss. To keep up appearances, of course.'

'Or perhaps I should just slap you and adjust my attire as I leave. To keep up appearances, of course.'

With a quirk at the corner of her lips, Agnès climbed the stairs as quickly as her dress and manners allowed. She passed between two halberdiers, opened the door to the queen's apartments, entered an antechamber and smiled at the duc d'Uzès, who served as knight-of-honour. Proceeding to a second antechamber, she joined madame de Sénécey, a lady-in-waiting, the elderly madame de La Flotte, a royal wardrobe mistress, and several other attending ladies, including two ravishing young women, Louise Angélique de La Fayette and Aude de Saint-Avold. All of them were waiting in the antechamber unsure what to do because, bordering on tears, Anne d'Autriche had just shut herself up in her bedchamber with madame de Chevreuse.

On learning this news, Agnès adopted a suitably serious expression, asked whether there was anything she could do to assist and upon being told there was not, she withdrew. Then she moved quickly without seeming to be in any great hurry. She smiled again at monsieur d'Uzès, left the apartments and followed the corridor as far as a small door hidden behind a curtain. She waited until no one was looking at her and then promptly disappeared through this exit. She had discovered it that afternoon, during a discreet examination of the castle's layout.

The queen's bedchamber communicated with the antechamber where the ladies of her suite gathered, but also with another small room where the duchesse would sleep tonight, a bed having been installed there for the occasion. Agnès found this room lying empty. She slipped inside and, on tiptoe, went to press her ear to the door behind which Anne d'Autriche and madame de Chevreuse were alone.

One of them was pacing back and forth.

It was the queen who, in a nervous tone, was explaining that after much reflection and much prayer she no longer wished to go through with a certain project. That it was madness and she should never have agreed to it in the first place. How could she have ever believed in the success of this enterprise? But she saw things more clearly now. Yes, she was going to renounce the whole thing.

'Madame,' the duchesse replied calmly, 'there is still time to back out. Everything will be done according to your wishes. You only need to give the order.'

'Very well. Then I am giving the order.'

'What could be accomplished this evening may never be possible again. The stars are not —'

'I don't care about the stars!'

'Are you certain you have thought this through, madame? Your Majesty's duties—'

'My duties forbid me to betray the king! As for the rest, I must place myself in the hands of divine Providence. One day my prayers shall be heard.'

'Has it occurred to you that if you renounce this project, you will still have to confess everything to the king? For the secret will come out, madame. Believe me, secrets always come out in the end. The cardinal's men are everywhere.'

'I shall beg for the king's pardon.'

'And for those who have lent you their assistance?'

'I will not allow you to be persecuted, Marie.'

'I was not thinking of myself, but of all the others.'

'How can one reproach them for having obeyed their queen?'

'Richelieu can, and he will.'

There was a silence.

Then Agnès heard madame de Chevreuse rise and take a few steps . . . A drawer was opened and closed . . . Then her steps returned . . . And the duchesse said:

'I had hoped to spare you this ordeal, madame. I'd hoped that . . . Well, look at this.'

'What is it?'

'I beg you, madame, read. And see what they have been hiding from you.'

There was a rustling of heavy silk fabric: Anne d'Autriche had just sat down. The two women remained silent, until the queen asked in a strangled voice:

'All this . . . Is it true?'

'I believe so. I fear so.'

'The king really intends to repud—'

'Yes, madame.'

The queen began to sob.

It might have been a spectral rider passing in the night.

But in fact it was a dust-covered Laincourt who was galloping on an ashen horse. He had been riding since Paris at a speed that risked killing his mount. He charged through villages, cut across fields and farmyards whenever possible, leapt over hedges, ditches and streams, taking all manner of risks. He now knew the purpose of the pentacle. And thanks to his friend the bookseller, he also knew that the master of magic serving the duchesse de Chevreuse was not who he claimed to be.

Faster, boy! Faster!

Laincourt would arrive at the Château de Dampierre within the hour.

But would he be in time?

At Dampierre, supper was being served, the queen having reappeared before anyone began to wonder about her absence.

Three tables had been set up in the castle's great hall. The high table was at the rear. The two others, much longer, faced one another and were perpendicular to the first. At these tables, the guests were seated on only one side, with their backs to the wall, while the servants waited on them from the space in the middle. Helped along by wine, the proceedings were very merry. Men and women ate with their fingers, exchanging anecdotes and jests, making fun of one another and laughing. Toasts were made, where a glass was passed from hand to hand, each person taking a small sip, until it reached the person to whom the toast was addressed. The recipient had no choice but to finish off the drink and, accompanied by cheers, eat the *tostée*, the piece of toasted bread that lay soaking at the bottom of the glass. These toasts went back and forth along the tables like playful challenges and provided an excellent pretext to become drunk. The selection of a new victim was greeted with expectant joy by all present and of course no one dreamed of declining.

Naturally the king and queen sat at the high table, in the company of the duc de Chevreuse, the duchesse and a few privileged individuals such as monsieur de Tréville and the marquis de Châteauneuf, the kingdom's Keeper of the Seals. The atmosphere was a little more formal than at the longer tables, although Louis XIII did honour to all the dishes – as was usual for him, since he had the same solid appetite as his father, Henri IV. Still looking pale, Anne d'Autriche only picked at her plate. Her eyes were a little red, causing madame de Chevreuse to worry aloud, as if on cue. The queen explained that she was suffering irritation from the heavy fragrance of a bouquet of flowers in her bedchamber. Did this little comedy fool anyone? It made the king smile, at any rate.

Retained by her duties as a lady-in-waiting, Agnès was unable to escape until halfway through the meal. Slipping out of the hall, she found La Fargue and Marciac in the dimness of an out-of-the-way antechamber. Almades closed the door behind her as soon as she arrived.

'Well?' demanded the Gascon.

Agnès recounted the conversation she had overheard between the queen and madame de Chevreuse.

'So La Chevreuse has indeed hatched a plot against the king,' concluded La Fargue. 'A plot that will unfold tonight. And the queen is an accomplice . . .'

'But what exactly is it all about?' asked Marciac. 'Are they going to make an attempt on His Majesty's life?'

'I don't know,' Agnès admitted.

'Was there any mention of the Alchemist?'

'No. But I think I know the queen's motives . . . After she and the duchesse left, I slipped into her bedchamber to look for whatever the duchesse gave her to read in order to persuade her. And I found it. It was the pamphlet that the queen mother's emissary was carrying hidden in the lining of his doublet.'

'The pamphlet that accuses the king of planning to repudiate the queen because she has not borne him an heir?' asked La Fargue.

'And claims that the king has begun negotiations with the Pope on the subject, yes.'

'So the queen has become involved in a plot against the king because she fears repudiation . . .'

'Well, yes . . .'

'But the king will never repudiate her!' exclaimed Marciac. 'Anne is the sister of the king of Spain. It would be an insult! It would mean war!'

'It is enough that the queen believes it to be true,' Agnès pointed out. 'Or rather, it is enough that the duchesse has persuaded her that it is so . . .'

The captain of the Blades nodded.

'Very well,' he said. 'I must speak to Tréville. Agnès, you must return to the queen and try not to let her out of your sight. The ball will begin soon.'

Leprat ran through a syle as it tried to scurry between his legs and, on the point of his sword, held it up to the light from his lantern. With thick red arabesque patterns running down its black back, the salamander was as long and as heavy as a

fair-sized rat. It squirmed on the sharp steel that was tormenting it, spitting and seeking to bite and claw at him rather than
to work itself free.

Filthy creature, thought Leprat as he cleared his blade with a
quick flick that sent the reptile flying.

The syle crashed into a wall, then fell to the ground with a
soft thump. It was still alive, however. In the dark, forked
tongues hissed. The sound preceded the massed rush that the
musketeer was expecting. With claws clattering and bellies
scraping against the stone, syles closed in from all directions to
devour the injured member of their own kind. The excitement of combat and the scent of blood soon produced a
predictable effect. The reptiles' scaly backs began to glow and
their furious melee, invisible up until now, became wreathed
in a faint halo. The sacrificed syle was not the only victim of
this savage frenzy. Others, wounded in turn, were attacked
and eaten by bigger and more ferocious individuals.

Leprat turned away from the carnage.

Sword in hand, he continued his exploration of the underground chambers of the black tower, chambers whose scale he
was still attempting to grasp. They were vast, perhaps immense, in any case far bigger than the two or three cellars he
had imagined he would find beneath the ruins of a mediaeval
donjon. Most of the rooms had flagstone floors with short
round pillars supporting low, vaulted ceilings. Standing empty
and bare, haunted only by the furtive movements of the syles
guarding them, and dotted with puddles that the musketeer
disturbed with his tread, these chambers had survived the
passing centuries down here in a dark, abysmal silence.

La Fargue managed to send a note to Tréville and met him
privately after the banquet. He informed him of the conversation Agnès had overheard between the queen and the
duchesse de Chevreuse, affirmed that there was no longer any
doubt that a plot was about to be sprung and insisted that the
king's security be reinforced until morning.

In vain.

'I will not increase the patrols or the number of sentries,' replied the captain of the Musketeers.

'The king's safety is under threat, monsieur.'

'Perhaps. But I cannot go against the will of His Majesty, who has demanded that my musketeers be as little visible as possible, in order to display his lack of concern over sleeping within these walls—'

'—and thereby further relax the vigilance of those he will have arrested tomorrow,' deduced La Fargue.

'Precisely. On the other hand, if the castle, for whatever reason, should suddenly be swarming with blue capes . . .'

The old gentleman nodded in resignation.

His left hand on the pommel of the old Pappenheimer in his scabbard, the other hand gripping the loop of his heavy belt, he turned to the window and lifted his eyes to the night sky.

'Besides,' added Tréville, 'the ball is about to begin. The king will open it with the queen and then, as he said he would, he will retire for the night, on the pretext that that he needs his rest before the hunt the duc de Chevreuse has organised for him in the morning . . . So the king will soon be in his apartments, with musketeers at his door and even in his antechamber.'

A musketeer entered and announced to his captain:

'A rider has just arrived. He claims to have urgent information concerning the safety of the king.'

'His name?'

'Laincourt. A former member of the Cardinal's Guards.'

La Fargue spun round.

After the ordeal of his long ride, Laincourt was trying to make himself presentable when Marciac found him in the stable courtyard. In his shirt sleeves, he was washing his face and neck with water from a bucket. Upon seeing the Gascon, he quickly dried himself with a towel and pulled on the freshly brushed doublet held out to him by a servant.

'I must speak to the captain,' he declared, giving a coin to the servant and accepting his hat in return.

'I will take you to him,' replied Marciac.

'Good.'

Grabbing his sword as he passed, Laincourt matched his stride to that of the Gascon, who asked him:

'Any news from Teyssier?'

'Yes. He finally recognised the pentacle.'

'So?'

'It is a pentacle of fecundity, employed in a ritual intended to make a barren womb fertile.'

'Are you sure of that?'

'No. But according to Ballardieu, His Eminence's magic master was positive. That's enough for me.'

They crossed the small drawbridge just as the first notes of music from the ball sounded within the castle.

As he continued exploring the ancient underground spaces beneath the black tower, sword in one hand and his lantern in the other, Leprat wondered who had built them and to what end.

They called to mind a sanctuary or refuge that might have once sheltered a community of sorcerers, or members of a heretical sect, or dragons. Who could say? The only thing for certain was that this place was no longer – if it had ever been – a peaceful haven. It was as if its walls were impregnated with an evil that weighed upon the soul. Its silence seemed haunted by painful echoes and its shadows hid lurking nightmares. And the air he breathed had . . .

Leprat suddenly realised his mind was starting to wander.

He shook his head and shoulders in an effort to gather his wits.

He could not allow these sinister chambers to take control of his thoughts. No doubt he had been wandering down here for too long. How long had it been, in fact? No matter. The musketeer deemed that he had seen enough. Besides, he noticed that the syles were starting to become dangerously bold and, to make matters worse, the flame in his lantern was showing signs of weakness.

Rather than retrace his steps, Leprat looked for stairs

leading upwards. But it was, instead, a door caught his eye: a large, black double door whose stone lintel was decorated with entwined draconic motifs. Intrigued, he approached cautiously. He listened closely and heard nothing within, then drew in a breath before pushing one half of the door open . . .

. . . to find himself in a circular room beneath an onyx dome.

Vast but empty, it was plunged in a dim amber light, coming from the glowing golden veins in the black marble that lined the floor and ran around the room in a frieze where the dome rose from the wall. The room had a large well at its centre. And four identical doors – including the one by which Leprat had entered – which faced one another in pairs as if marking the cardinal points of a compass.

The musketeer set down his now useless lantern and stepped forward, keeping his rapier unsheathed. He became filled with the conviction that the black tower had once risen directly above this dome which he examined with an attentive eye. But his thoughts were interrupted by a sound that made him turn round.

Mirebeau was aiming a cocked pistol at him.

'A fertility ritual,' repeated La Fargue after listening to Laincourt's report.

'That's what Teyssier claims. And we already knew that this pentacle was not harmful in purpose . . .'

They were in a small room adjoining Tréville's bed-chamber. The captain of the Musketeers had allowed the Blades to meet here while he watched over the opening of the ball. The orchestra was playing at the other end of the castle. They could hear the music rising through the open windows into the warm night.

'Might the pentacle be for the duchesse de Chevreuse?' suggested Marciac. 'After all, we're here in her home and it is her master of magic who—'

'She has already had six children,' Laincourt pointed out.

'No,' said La Fargue. 'The ritual is intended for the queen.

669

She has not yet provided an heir to the throne and we know she now fears being repudiated.'

'We do?'

'This evening Agnès overheard a conversation between the queen and the duchesse,' the Gascon explained to the cardinal's former spy. 'Very upset, the queen said that she wanted to renounce . . . we don't quite know what. In order to overcome her misgivings, the duchesse gave her the pamphlet that the queen mother's secret emissary had on his person. You recall it?'

'Yes. Claiming the king intends to repudiate the queen.'

'We believed this prospect was enough to convince the queen to participate in the final act of a plot against the king. An act that would take place this evening or later in the night.'

'It seems we were wrong,' concluded La Fargue.

His eyes became absorbed in thought.

Anne d'Autriche was desperate to become a mother. But the years had passed leaving her prayers unanswered and now, in addition to suffering from the king's estrangement and attacks from within his court, she faced the despicable threat of repudiation . . .

'So the queen has decided to resort to magic in order to become fertile,' Marciac reflected out loud. 'As for the duchesse de Chevreuse, she has taken it upon herself to arrange the whole matter with the aid of her new master of magic. And all this is taking place in utmost secrecy, as one might imagine. For if it were discovered that a queen of France—'

'A queen of Spanish origin, moreover,' added Laincourt.

'—was subjecting herself to a draconic ritual . . .'

The Gascon judged that there was no need to finish his sentence.

'Whatever the queen's motives,' said Laincourt, 'the king will not pardon her. In addition to other considerations, he has despised all magical arts ever since La Galigaï was beheaded for bewitching his mother.'

'Not to mention the fact that an heir born in such circumstances could only be—'

Once again, Marciac did not complete his sentence, but this time because Almades had knocked on the door and entered.

La Fargue shot him a questioning look.

'Their Majesties have just opened the ball,' the Spaniard reassured him. 'All is well.'

'And Agnès?'

'I saw her and she saw me. She did not seem alarmed.'

'Very well. Thank you.'

Almades nodded and returned to keeping track of the comings and goings in the castle.

'The king must be warned about what is afoot,' said Marciac after a moment of silence. 'But there is no plot. Only a desperate queen.'

'You're forgetting a little quickly that the Alchemist and the Black Claw are also mixed up in this,' replied the old captain. 'Last night, Saint-Lucq formally recognised Savelda in the company of the duchesse and Mauduit.'

'True, at least as far as Savelda and the Black Claw are concerned. But as for the Alchemist, we only have La Donna's word that—'

'What does it matter?' asked La Fargue, raising his voice. 'Why would the Black Claw want to help the queen have a child? Why would it favour the birth of a royal heir and thereby put an end to the divisions weakening the kingdom? And why the devil would it seek to prevent a repudiation of the queen which, if it were merely hinted at by the king, would be enough to provoke a war between France and Spain . . . ? Do you even have the beginning of an answer to any of these questions?'

'No,' admitted Marciac, lowering his eyes.

'There is a plot!' declared the captain of the Blades between clenched jaws. 'There is a plot, and the Alchemist is at its head!'

The Gascon did not reply, but turned his head away.

'Captain,' ventured Laincourt.

'What?'

'It's about Mauduit. I'm not sure, but . . . well, here's the thing. One of my friends is a bookseller and I was able to consult a very rare work that he has in his shop, of which Mauduit is the author. There was a portrait at the front of the book and . . . I know these engravings can often be misleading, captain. But this picture looked nothing at all like the man serving the duchesse de Chevreuse as her magic master.'

For a long moment La Fargue remained immobile, silent and expressionless. Could Mauduit be the Alchemist? The conviction slowly took shape in his mind, and at last he began to grasp the nature of the plot against which La Donna had warned them . . .

'The Alchemist,' he said in a grave voice, 'plans to abduct the queen.'

His pistol aimed at Leprat, Mirebeau crossed the threshold of the circular room but did not come any closer. Perhaps he feared to advance any further beneath the rock dome. Perhaps he was reluctant to step on the slabs of black marble with their strangely glowing golden veins. Perhaps he preferred to keep his distance from the man who, sword in hand, was looking him straight in the eye without blinking.

They stood about seven metres apart. The musketeer had his back to the well, the other man had the dark cellars of the black tower behind him.

'What is this room?' asked Leprat. 'What is its purpose?'

'I don't know. Just as I didn't know of the existence of these underground chambers until I followed you. Indeed, one might be surprised to find you of all people down here . . .'

Leprat did not reply.

'But considering that I am the one holding the pistol,' Mirebeau continued, 'let us agree that I shall be the one who asks the questions. All right? Good. Who are you, monsieur?'

'My name will tell you nothing.'

'Nevertheless, please satisfy my curiosity.'

'I am Antoine Leprat, chevalier d'Orgueil.'

'A musketeer?'

'Yes.'

'Nothing else?'

'No.'

'A spy, then.'

'I obey the cardinal's orders in the service of the king.'

'A musketeer who obeys the cardinal? Is that possible?'

'It is in my case.'

'And the real Guéret?'

'Dead.'

'Killed by your hand?'

'No.'

'On that point, I'll have to take your word, won't I? Since you are a gentleman, I won't ask you to relinquish your sword. But please return it to its scabbard . . .'

Leprat honoured his request.

Mirebeau looked at him sadly. He was slightly more relaxed but still had not lowered his weapon.

'What am I to do with you, monsieur le chevalier d'Orgueil?'

'As you said: you are the one holding the pistol.'

'I offered you my friendship. I offered you my friendship and you accepted it.'

'Yes.'

'You betrayed my trust.'

'I know.'

'Don't misunderstand me. I don't blame you. It was me. I made a mistake. Why didn't I listen to Rauvin's initial warnings? Unlike me, he saw right through you from the beginning. Did you know I took your side this morning when Rauvin claimed to see you returning on horseback before dawn from some mysterious errand? I thought he was slandering you out of jealousy, that he had not forgiven you for behaving better than he did on that famous night when the comte de Rochefort arrested me. After all, he fled while you stayed behind to free me. But I imagine that was just to safeguard your mission, wasn't it? And to win my trust.'

When Leprat failed, again, to reply, Mirebeau let out a desolate sigh.

'Fortunately, the friendship that I felt for you did not completely blind me. And that brings us to this . . . What am

I to do with you, monsieur le chevalier d'Orgueil? Rauvin would shoot you down.'

'You won't do that. You're a gentleman.'

'So are you. Let us settle this affair as gentlemen, then.'

The musketeer shook his head.

'I feel both friendship and esteem for you, Mirebeau. Don't make me cross swords with you . . . Besides, it would be futile.'

'Futile?'

'Tomorrow, at the break of dawn, the marquis de Châteauneuf will be arrested for treason, among other things. So will the duchesse de Chevreuse and all those who have plotted the downfall of the cardinal, or against the king. Everything is ready. The orders have already been signed and Tréville's musketeers are masters of Dampierre. His Majesty has already won the match. But you are guilty of nothing but loyally serving a master who proved unworthy.'

'What do you know about that?'

'I know you to be a man of honour, Mirebeau. Nothing obliges you to pay the price for the crimes of Châteauneuf. Nothing.'

'One is not always free to choose.'

'Châteauneuf fancied that he might one day replace the cardinal. Forgetting all that he owed Richelieu, he schemed against him. His ambition has made him lose everything. Don't accompany him in his downfall.'

Mirebeau hesitated.

'It's . . . It's too late,' he finally said.

'No!'

Leprat felt that he could persuade – and save – this gentleman.

'Leave,' he said. 'This very night. Take a horse and go without further delay. Don't let the king's justice catch up with you. And before long you'll be forgotten . . .'

Mirebeau reflected for a moment. The arm holding the pistol was no longer quite as steady as before when the point of a blade suddenly punched through his chest. He stiffened and gazed down with eyes widened in shock at the length of bloody steel which then vanished almost as quickly as it had appeared. He hiccupped, coughed up blood and gave Leprat a last incredulous look before falling to his knees, then face down against the hard marble floor.

Rapier in his fist, Rauvin stepped over the dead body and advanced, followed by five hired swordsmen.

'I do believe he would have accepted your offer,' he said. 'but I grew tired of waiting . . .'

Having opened the ball with the queen and paid her a much remarked-upon compliment, the king retired to his apartments. He had announced his intention to make the most of the game-filled forests of the Chevreuse valley, and go hunting early the following morning. He had promised, however, to watch the fireworks display that would be the high point of the evening from his window. The gentlemen who were his closest attendants, including the comte de Tréville, had followed him. And since the castle could not be taken by assault, the musketeers now reduced their watch over the area outside to mount an extremely vigilant guard at the doors, along the corridors and in the antechambers.

Arnaud de Laincourt discreetly stole a mask that he saw lying on a bench, put it on and began to mingle with the courtiers who chattered, drank and nibbled as they watched the dancers – two by two – execute a graceful choreography to the sound of the music played by the orchestra. Everyone had disguised the upper portion of their face behind a mask. But if those worn by the men were relatively sober, those of the women – matching their dresses – boasted a profusion of gold and silver brocade, plumes and ribbons, pearls and jewels. Wearing their finest attire, the royal court provided a superb spectacle that evening, beneath the gilt of Dampierre. In their display of elegant luxury and playful insouciance, the courtiers seemed completely unaware of the danger threatening them.

Laincourt tried to find Agnès.

He caught sight of her near the dais reserved for Their Majesties. Now only the queen occupied her armchair. It was impossible to approach her. She was surrounded by madame de Chevreuse and by her ladies-in-waiting, who were seated according to their rank on chairs, stools or cushions. They gossiped and laughed behind their fans, the youngest and least dignified among them pointing out the gentlemen they liked best. Among the dancers, the marquis de Châteauneuf in particular attracted much commentary, although most of it was not in praise. Watching out of the corner of his eye to see if the duchesse de Chevreuse was glancing in his direction, he exerted himself with each movement to adopt the most advantageous poses. But his age of over fifty rendered all these efforts somewhat ridiculous.

Spotting Laincourt, Agnès joined him by a window overlooking the moat and the great Renaissance flower beds among which couples strolled in search of a quiet corner.

'Did La Fargue let you know?' asked the young man.

'Yes.'

'It's now more important than ever that you remain with the queen.'

'I know.'

It was a trap.

The fertility ritual which the queen was supposed to undergo was nothing but a trap intended to lure her away, with her own consent, from the guards who watched over her. The Chatelaines' Superior General had been right: there was a plot threatening the queen. A plot in which madame de Chevreuse was a participant, acting in the belief that she was serving Anne d'Autriche's interests. A plot hatched by the Black Claw and the Alchemist, who had usurped the place of the duchesse's master of magic. A plot, lastly, whose object was to abduct the queen.

But after that?

'It will happen tonight,' said Laincourt. 'And it cannot be done without the complicity of others. That of the duchesse, certainly. But also that of most of the ladies in her entourage, whom the queen has probably won over to her cause . . . Since you are not a part of the plan, they will try to divert you at the crucial moment. Keep your eye out. And be careful.'

'Don't worry.'

'Marciac was looking for you a short while ago and could not find you.'

The baronne de Vaudreuil reflected for short instant.

'Yes. It must have been when I went to fetch the queen's jewel box. Her pearl necklace broke just after the king retired to his quarters.'

'And the queen? Where was she?'

'She was waiting in the antechamber for me to return so that we could change her finery.'

Laincourt nodded distractedly as his gaze slowly swept over the queen and her entourage.

Then he frowned.

'I don't see Aude de Saint-Avold,' he said.

Agnès turned toward the group formed by the maidens-of-honour and their governess, at the foot of the royal dais.

'You're right,' she replied.

'Do you know where she is?'

'No.'

The cardinal's former spy became worried. If Agnès – because she was a newcomer to the queen's suite – could be diverted when it came time to execute the plot, Aude was a different matter.

Like everyone else, the queen was wearing a mask.

Without meaning to, Laincourt caught her eye . . .

. . . and suddenly recognised – now looking alarmed as she realised she had been found out – the face of Aude de Saint-Avold.

'They've already abducted the queen!' he shouted as he left Agnès standing there.

Unlike Mirebeau, Rauvin had not ventured alone into the underground chambers. He was accompanied by five mercenaries whom he immediately ordered to attack Leprat.

That's one, counted the musketeer as he ran his sword through the first man to come within reach.

He freed his blade, dodged an attack, parried another and forced his opponents to retreat with a few furious moulinets.

He then returned to the *en garde* position and waited with

his back to the well which, beneath the dome, marked the centre of the circular room. The four mercenaries supposed that he was allowing them the initiative in making the next assault. They started to deploy in an arc. If the man before them was foolish enough to let them organise themselves, they would take advantage of the fact . . .

But in fact he wanted them to spread out in a row.

And to gain confidence.

So that they would lower their guard slightly.

Leprat suddenly attacked with a great shout. He deflected one mercenary's sword, stunned another with a blow of his fist to the chin, spun around as he raised his blade to shoulder height and carried through his motion by slitting the throat of the freebooter who was about to strike him from behind.

That's two.

The man staggered backwards, choking, his right hand trying desperately to staunch the wound from which blood was flowing freely, while his left hand flailed in the air, seeking a shoulder, a support, help of any kind. He finally fell backwards and lay still.

Leprat gave himself space to face a renewed attack. It was led by two mercenaries who knew how to fight a lone opponent without hindering one another. Taking a step back, and then another, the musketeer had to defend himself against two men and two sets of skills. Against two blades which he finally managed, with a single slash of his own weapon, to force away from his own body and downwards to the ground. His move unbalanced both his adversaries and made one of them particularly vulnerable. Leprat delivered a blow with his fist that caused the man to stumble forward, right into the waiting knee that lifted his chin sharply and broke his neck with a sinister crack.

Three down.

Only two mercenaries remained.

Parrying a high sword stroke from one man, Leprat pushed the other back with a violent kick to the stomach. Then he surprised the first by elbowing him in his Adam's apple and finished him off by head-butting him right in the face. His nose and mouth covered in blood, the man crumpled to the black marble floor.

Four.

The last mercenary was already charging him from behind.

Leprat spun and riposted in a single movement of lethal fluidity. He was still only halfway round and bending his knees when he blocked a vicious cut. Then he rose, letting the other man's blade slide down his own until it reached the hilt. Finally, he completed his turn by plunging a dagger he had snatched from the belt of his previous opponent into the mercenary's belly. The unfortunate wretch froze, dropping his blade and fumbling at the dagger's hilt. He collapsed after managing a few erratic steps.

And that makes five.

Out of breath, his brow shining with sweat and his eyes blazing, Leprat turned towards Rauvin and once again placed himself *en garde*.

'My congratulations,' said the hired killer as he drew his sword. 'Now it's just the two of us.'

He slashed at the air with his blade and the duel commenced.

At Dampierre, three silhouettes were crossing the duchesse de Chevreuse's private garden. Closed to guests on a false pretext, this little park adjoining the castle was now standing empty except for shadows. The trio, all wearing dark cloaks, were obviously in a hurry. They turned back several times towards the windows as if they feared being seen and hid themselves whenever the moon peeped out from between the clouds.

The one who claimed to be Mauduit, master of magic, was leading them.

'This way, madame.'

Anne d'Autriche followed him, unaware that she was placing her fate in the hands of the Black Claw's most formidable agent. She was accompanied by a chambermaid who, when the moment came, she believed, would help her to disrobe and put on the ritual garment before the ceremony that would at last let her become a mother. The young servant girl was trembling and casting frightened looks all around, but was ready to do anything in the service of her queen. Both of them were wearing black velvet masks beneath their large hoods.

At the rear of the garden, they came to a gate set in the wall.

'Be brave, madame,' murmured the Alchemist. 'The hardest part is over. Once we reach the cover of the trees, we can no longer be seen from the castle.'

He opened the gate with a key the duchesse de Chevreuse had given him and then held his hand out to the queen to assist her passage over a small wooden bridge, a sort of covered walkway that allowed strollers to cross the moat and enter the orchard.

There were armed men waiting on the other side, beneath the trees, some of them carrying dark lanterns.

'Who are these men?' asked the queen in a worried voice, but stopping herself from retreating.

'Your escort, madame. Don't be afraid.'

Anxious but still resolved to see the matter through, Anne d'Autriche nodded. She drew closer to her servant, however, and took her hand while the Alchemist exchanged a few words in a low voice with a one-eyed man whose face was visibly marked by the ranse. With an olive complexion and craggy features, the man was wearing a black leather patch adorned by silver studs over his missing eye. It was Savelda, although the queen remained ignorant of his name. Just as she was unaware that he was the henchman most valued by the masters of the Black Claw.

He finally nodded in agreement and the false magic master returned to the two women.

'All is well, madame,' he affirmed. 'However, we must hurry because it will soon be midnight. The coach that will take us to the place of the ceremony is waiting at the gate to this orchard.'

But Savelda, who was about to take the lead, suddenly froze, with the absent gaze and slightly tilted head of someone listening very intently.

'What is it now?' asked the Alchemist in an irritated tone.

Without turning round, the Black Claw's envoy lifted an imperious index finger: he demanded silence. After which, he called out softly to the three men he had left as sentries in the orchard.

There was no answer.

Savelda snapped his fingers and two of the hired swordsmen accompanying him approached.

'Go and have a look,' he said with a strong Spanish accent that drew the queen's attention.

The two men unsheathed their swords and ventured out cautiously. One of them held a lantern in his left hand and a pistol in his right.

They had not taken ten steps when they came across a dead body, while an individual emerged from the shadows beneath the fruit trees. The proud, elegant assurance of the stranger worried them only slightly less than the faint smile they detected on his lips. He was dressed entirely in black, except for the slender feather decorating his hat: it was scarlet, as were the round spectacles hiding his eyes. His left hand rested nonchalantly on the pommel of his rapier in its scabbard.

The two hired swordsmen placed themselves *en garde*. The one with the pistol aimed it at Saint-Lucq but as he continued to advance they slowly retreated until they had rejoined Savelda and the others.

The half-blood halted and brandished a pistol of his own in his right hand. In response, three more pistols pointed at him and blades were unsheathed. The queen and her chambermaid jumped, stifling startled cries. Saint-Lucq did not even blink.

'You will go nowhere with the queen,' he said in an even tone.

'Do you intend to stop us on your own?' asked Savelda with a sneer.

'I've already started to.'

'Give it up. The numbers are in our favour.'

Saint-Lucq conspicuously pointed his pistol at the one-eyed man's brow.

'If I fire, or you do, the place will be swarming with musketeers. Is that really what you want?'

'Monsieur, tell me what is going on?' the queen asked the Alchemist. 'Who is this man and why is he trying . . .'

She trailed off, shocked at finding herself ignored by the master of magic, who instead stepped forward among the swordsmen to address the half-blood:

'Then why don't you shoot? Are you afraid of wounding Her Majesty?'

'My pistol ball will not miss its target.'

'To be sure, but after that? You are familiar with the hazards of battle, aren't you?'

'I am also familiar with them,' said a voice that no one had expected to hear.

Flanked by Marciac and Laincourt to his left and right, La Fargue had entered the orchard. They had arrived from the garden, their blades already pointed in the direction of their enemies.

'And I tell you that if you harm the queen in any way,' the captain of the Blades added, 'your death will owe nothing to the hazards of battle . . .'

Defended by steep moats, the Château de Dampierre had only two exits: its guarded drawbridge and the small gate at the rear of the deserted garden. Thus the Blades had no difficulty in guessing which way Anne d'Autriche had been taken. Leaving Almades behind to gain access to the king's apartments and alert Tréville as quickly as possible, La Fargue had decided to go in pursuit of the queen without delay.

And in pursuit of the Alchemist of the Shadows.

The Alchemist now turned to the old gentleman. He recognised him and gave a twisted smile.

'La Fargue? Is that you?'

'It's me, Alchemist. Or whatever your real name is.'

'We meet at last! We almost met at La Rochelle, but . . . Ah! We both know what happened there, don't we?'

Savelda and his swordsmen had clustered round the Alchemist and the two women. Calm and resolute, they placed themselves on guard against attack from either direction. Rapiers in their hands, some of them also had pistols aimed at Saint-Lucq, on one side, or at La Fargue, Laincourt and

Marciac, on the other. They waited for an order, conscious of the fact that the first pistol to be fired would raise an alarm. The music coming from the castle would not be loud enough to cover the sound of shots. It merely drifted hauntingly through the otherwise silent orchard.

Anne d'Autriche and her chambermaid were clinging to one another in fright.

'This man has abused your trust, madame,' said the captain of the Blades. 'He is in the service of the Black Claw and is conspiring to bring about Your Majesty's ruin.'

The queen turned her worried but furious eyes to the Alchemist.

'What do you have to say, monsieur? Will you deny it?'

He shrugged.

'What good would it do?' he replied before coughing, short of breath, into his handkerchief. 'It would seem the play is over, is it not?'

La Fargue frowned.

There were four Blades. Savelda and his men numbered ten in all and they were in possession of a most precious hostage. Taking that into consideration, the Alchemist's defeatism was troubling, to say the least.

It proved unbearable to Savelda.

'Enough!' he spat.

The queen's attendant screamed and promptly fainted when the one-eyed man seized her by the wrist and roughly threw her aside. Before anyone else could react, the Spaniard was clutching Anne d'Autriche against his body, threatening to slit her throat with a dagger.

The same exclamation escaped from the lips of both La Fargue and the Alchemist.

'No!'

'I won't hesitate!' Savelda promised.

'You fool!' the Alchemist swore at him.

'I won't surrender!'

'Don't you understand? We just need to wait!'

'Wait for what?'

In the castle, the musicians ceased playing.

The silence became immense.

'Oh, Lord!' murmured Marciac as realisation dawned on him.

There was a whistling noise . . .

. . . and the first rocket exploded in the night sky.

The Spaniard's men immediately fired their pistols. The detonations cracked and balls whizzed past the ears of the Blades as they charged forwards. One of them struck Laincourt in the shoulder, halting him in his tracks. A chaotic battle broke out beneath the boughs of the trees in the orchard.

In the underground chambers of the black tower, under the dome of the room paved with golden-veined black marble, Leprat was engaged in a duel to the death with Rauvin.

And he was losing.

It had not taken him long to realise that his opponent was of a different calibre to the mercenaries whose bodies lay scattered across the luminescent floor. Like them, Rauvin had experience. But he also had talent. His strokes were quick, precise and powerful. Although driven by a ferocious hatred of the musketeer, he kept his calm.

Surprised by a thrust, Leprat was forced to step back and parry several times as Rauvin launched a series of attacks, high and low, in rapid succession. Their blades ended up crossed near the hilts and the two men circled before shoving one another away roughly, both of them nearly stumbling.

Leprat moved back, seeking room to manoeuvre.

No longer able to conceal the fact that he was struggling, he feared Rauvin would try to wear him down. His combat with the freebooters had drained him and he sensed that he had still not recovered from the worsening of the ranse that had struck him the previous day. Indeed, he wondered if he would ever truly recover. He was also wielding a rapier made of ordinary steel, which demanded far more of his wrist than the elegant ivory blade to which he was accustomed.

All things considered, the only point in his favour was the fact that he was left-handed.

It was not much of an advantage.

Rauvin attacked, obliging Leprat to step back again. But with a wide swing of his blade, the musketeer forced the other man to expose himself and landed a nasty right hook with his fist. The hired swordsman staggered. Emboldened by this success, Leprat seized the upper hand and made his opponent retreat. Rauvin quickly pulled himself together, however, feinting and slashing at face height. That stopped Leprat's momentum as he had to duck in order to avoid being disfigured.

Rauvin managed to disengage and quickly discarded his doublet which was making him uncomfortably hot.

For his part, Leprat caught his breath.

He had lost a lot of energy in this last assault and his wrist was hurting him more and more. Sweat was making his hair stick to his brow and his eyes sting.

'It looks like you're having a hard time,' observed Rauvin ironically. 'Age, no doubt . . .'

Leprat, who was approaching forty, displayed a weary smile.

'I . . . I still have some resources left . . .'

'Really? And for how much longer?'

Both remained *en garde*, circling and giving each other a measuring stare.

Rauvin suddenly delivered a cut, which Leprat parried and then riposted. After that, there was a whole series of parries and ripostes, one man retreating while the other advanced, and then vice versa as the advantage switched direction. Their soles slipped on the dark marble and the heels of their boots clattered beneath the great dome. Their blades clashed with a clear ringing sound. Their features tightened and their gaze became fixed with the strain of their efforts.

Leprat was weakening.

He wanted to put an end to matters and delivered a false attack. It fooled the hired swordsman who was expecting a flurry of strikes and had modified his guard position accordingly, exposing himself to a thrust which he saw coming too late. The musketeer lunged and scored a hit. Unfortunately he lacked reach and could not press the blow hard enough.

Nevertheless, Rauvin took an inch of steel in his left shoulder. His surprise and pain made him cry out. He stepped back in a panic, pressed one hand to his wound and watched the blood trickling down over it with astonishment.

'Hurts, doesn't it?' said Leprat.

Humiliated and furious, Rauvin launched an assault so vigorous that the musketeer could only defend himself, parrying, dodging and retreating, again and again. For too many long seconds, Leprat had to mobilise all of his strength and attention for the sole purpose of surviving, blocking and deflecting attacks that became increasingly sly and dangerous. He was being overpowered. Which was as good as saying that he was vanquished in the long run, because eventually he would make a mistake.

So he was already seeking some way out when the course of the fight took a disastrous turn for the worse.

His rapier broke.

The steel snapped cleanly and most of the blade bounced on the marble floor with a clang. It was a moment of amazement for Rauvin, and absolute horror for Leprat . . .

. . . after which the hired swordsman smiled and resumed his attack with even greater energy than before.

Leprat leapt backward to avoid a cut, quickly stepped aside to stay clear of a thrust and parried another with the remaining stub of his sword. Other desperate manoeuvres permitted him to stave off the inevitable. But he finally lost his balance and only managed to avoid falling thanks to his right hand, which reached out and grabbed the blade of his enemy. In spite of his glove, the steel cut viciously into the palm of his hand. The musketeer screamed in pain before retreating from Rauvin who stalked towards him, jabbing with his rapier, his arm outstretched. Leprat reeled like a drunkard, unable to take his eyes off the metal point threatening him. Finally, he felt his calves bump against the rim of the central well and almost fell backwards into it, in danger of being swallowed up by the shadowy void.

It was here that all strength abandoned him.

He fell to his knees and, with a confused gaze, watched Rauvin looming over him.

The mercenary was cold-bloodedly preparing to deliver the fatal blow.

So this is how it ends, Leprat thought to himself.

'Any last words?' asked Rauvin.

The musketeer somehow found the force to utter a painful snort and, in defiance, spat out some bloody phlegm.

'No? As you wish,' said the hired swordsman. 'Goodbye.'

He lifted his arms up high, both hands gripping the pommel of his rapier, holding the weapon point downwards, ready to plunge it into Leprat's unprotected chest . . .

. . . when someone said:

'Just a moment.'

Rauvin halted his gesture to glance over his shoulder . . . and saw Mirebeau.

Stunned by this development, he turned around.

It was indeed the gentleman in the beige doublet who had somehow risen from among the dead and, pale and bloody, approached with a stiff, hesitant step, his left arm held against his body and his right straining to lift his sword.

Leprat struggled to stand, leaning on the rim of the well.

'I wanted . . .' Mirebeau said to Rauvin. 'I wanted . . .'

'What?'

'I wanted you to know who was going to kill you.'

The mercenary sneered at this: Mirebeau was unable to even hold his rapier up, much less fight with it . . . But the sneer vanished when Rauvin saw the gentleman suddenly lift the pistol held in his left hand.

The gun fired.

The ball hit Rauvin in the middle of his forehead and he fell over backwards, arms extended, as Mirebeau sank to the floor in exhaustion.

Having made sure that the mercenary was quite dead, Leprat hurried over to the dying gentleman. He gently lifted his head. The other man could barely open his eyes.

The musketeer didn't know what to say. He could not utter

any words at all, with his throat constricted and tears welling in his eyes.

'Th . . . thank you,' he finally managed to croak.

Mirebeau nodded very faintly.

'A . . . A favour . . .' he murmured. 'For me . . .'

'Ask it . . .'

'I do not . . . I do not . . . want . . . to die here . . . Please . . . Not here . . .'

Beneath the trees of the orchard at Dampierre a bitter fight had ensued during the fireworks display. The Blades and Savelda's mercenaries engaged one another while dazzling flashes accompanied by loud bangs lit up the foliage before gradually fading into flickers. The changing light sculpted their faces and silhouettes as the steel of their rapiers reflected back the same light as the blood of their wounds and the feverish gleam in their eyes.

A nasty kick and a two-handed blow with the pommel of his sword delivered between the shoulder blades allowed La Fargue to eliminate his first opponent. At last enjoying a moment's respite, he looked around him at the scene revealed by a crackling bouquet that illuminated the whole sky and dispersed into thousands of multicoloured sparkles.

Saint-Lucq, having coolly shot down, at close range, one of the three mercenaries who had rushed him at the beginning of the assault, was now battling the other two with his rapier, holding his pistol by the barrel in his left hand as a parrying weapon. He did not seem to be in any difficulty, in contrast to Laincourt who, having received a pistol ball in the right shoulder, was backed up against a tree and defending himself as best he could. Fortunately Marciac had come to his aid and was fending off three men with his sword and dagger, despite a wound to the arm. The Alchemist had disappeared. But where was the queen?

La Fargue saw her.

Savelda was carrying her off towards the wooden walkway that crossed over the moat. Was the Black Claw's agent intending to reach the garden and then seek refuge in the castle? It would be like throwing himself into the wolf's jaws, but there was no time to ponder the matter.

'The queen!' La Fargue yelled, just before another mercenary engaged him in a duel. 'Savelda has the queen!'

Only a short distance away in the orchard, Saint-Lucq heard his captain's call over the explosions of the fireworks. But he also heard an order to surrender. He had just eliminated a second opponent and, keeping the point of his elegant rapier pressed to the throat of the third, he glanced over his shoulder. Some musketeers were taking aim at him . . .

Alerted by the sound of shots being fired, members of the King's Musketeers patrolling in the domain had rushed to the orchard.

'IN THE NAME OF THE KING, CEASE FIGHTING!'

La Fargue froze, having planted his sword to the hilt in the belly of a freebooter who now clung to him in a close embrace, glassy-eyed, and had started to drool a reddish foam. He allowed the dying man to sink to the ground as he freed his blade with a flick of his wrist and then looked around him.

The musketeers had already surrounded the site and, acting on the commands of their ensign, tightened their ring. They obviously intended to push everyone out from beneath the cover of the trees.

Savelda and the queen were almost at the small wooden bridge.

'THROW DOWN YOUR SWORDS AND SURRENDER!' the ensign ordered.

The fight had come to a halt but everyone present still hesitated. The threat of being shot down on the spot, however, overcame any inclination on the part of the Black Claw's mercenaries to resist further. Weakened by his wound, Laincourt was only too happy to slide down to the foot of the tree he had been leaning against . . . and then he passed out. Cautiously, La Fargue and Marciac re-sheathed their swords and slowly backed away from the musketeers, their arms extended from their bodies.

'IN THE SERVICE OF THE CARDINAL!' called the old gentleman, between two pyrotechnical explosions. 'DON'T SHOOT!'

'Who's speaking?' demanded the ensign, keeping his distance.

'Captain Étienne-Louis de La Fargue.'

'Never heard of you!'

'Monsieur de Tréville knows me.'

But something else drew the young officer's attention.

'What the . . . You! Halt! Don't move!'

La Fargue was horrified to see several muskets turn away from Marciac and him to point instead at Savelda and the queen by the bridge. Anne d'Autriche seemed more dead than alive in the arms of the one-eyed man with the ranse.

'No!' exclaimed the captain of the Blades. 'You risk killing the queen!'

'You should listen to him!' cried Savelda as he retreated up the few short steps leading to the walkway.

The fireworks' grand finale was now bursting overhead. The rockets' explosions sounded like cannon fire and, in the deafening din, no one could be certain of being heard.

'Halt, or we'll shoot!' warned the ensign.

'It's the queen!' La Fargue screamed. 'By all the saints, listen to me! It's the queen!'

He tried to take a step forward to explain. Three muskets immediately took aim at his chest and forced him to stop.

Savelda and the queen were now crossing the bridge. They would soon be out of sight.

'Musketeers, on my command!' ordered the young officer raising his hand.

'No!' yelled La Fargue at the top of his lungs.

But the order he dreaded so much never came.

Bringing the fireworks to a culmination, two immense gold and blue comets exploded at the same time as dozens of more ephemeral stars. The lights dazzled everyone except Savelda who had his back to the spectacle. The others averted their eyes, squinting or protecting them with their forearms.

It was the moment the Black Claw agent had been waiting for.

Pushing Anne d'Autriche over the railing on the left, he leapt over the one on the right. The two bodies splashed into the moat's deep waters only a second apart. That of the unconscious queen immediately began to sink.

Marciac was the first to react.

He took off running, making himself the target of a volley of musket fire, the balls buzzing past him as he dove into the moat. He vanished without it being clear whether or not he had been hit. Everyone present – La Fargue and the ensign leading the way – rushed to the edge of the steep ditch. The incandescent remains of the fireworks falling back to earth were reflected in the black waters while, at the other end of the castle, the duchesse's guests applauded the end of the display.

Unbearable seconds passed by as they all waited . . .

. . . until Marciac finally resurfaced holding the queen, who was coughing.

And therefore alive.

'Her Majesty is safe,' the Gascon announced to the dumb-founded musketeers. 'Could you lend me a hand? If you please?'

They hurried to assist him just as Almades and Tréville arrived from the garden along with more men in blue capes, the captain of the Musketeers quickly taking charge of the situation.

Unnoticed by anyone, La Fargue stood apart from the others and looked out at the orchard for a long while, hands on his hips. The queen had been saved and that was the main thing, but the Alchemist had once again escaped . . .

Then he heard that two musketeers had been found unconscious among the fruit trees and, noticing that Saint-Lucq had also vanished, he smiled.

Saint-Lucq moved through the forest skirted by the road upon which the Alchemist's coach was travelling. He had heard the horse-drawn carriage leaving by way of the gate to the orchard and since then he had been following its progress by sound, pushing aside the low branches and eating up the distance with his steady, powerful strides. Thanks to the days spent watching the Dampierre domain, he knew which route the coach would be forced to use. Right now, the road curved around the woods while the half-blood was able to take a shortcut. The vehicle would have to slow down as it approached a small bridge, and that was where Saint-Lucq hoped to intercept it.

The trees became more spaced out as the noise of the carriage came closer. Saint-Lucq realised that he was in danger of arriving too late. He picked up his pace, plunging through the underbrush and emerged from the forest, face covered in scratches, only to see the coach disappearing over the bridge.

He'd missed it!

But the Alchemist was escorted by several riders, including one straggler who was only now arriving.

Saint-Lucq seized this last chance available to him. He did not slow down, but instead adjusted his trajectory and gathered his momentum to take a flying leap from a mound close to the road. The rider never saw him coming. The horse whinnied and crashed to the earth in a great cloud of dust . . .

And stood back up, full of fright, but now mounted by the half-blood who urged it to a gallop.

Inside the coach, instinct warned the Alchemist that he was in danger. Leaning his head out the passenger door, he looked back and saw Saint-Lucq hot on his trail.

'BACK THERE!' he alerted his escort, yelling to be heard over the thunderous hoof beats and the creaking of the axles. 'A RIDER! STOP HIM!'

Then he sat back and rapidly came to a decision.

Leaning forward, he opened a compartment beneath the bench opposite him and took out a case which he placed on his knees before opening its inlaid lid. Inside was a flask containing the liqueur of golden henbane.

He would have to transform himself.

His last metamorphosis, in Alsace, had exhausted him to the point that he was still unable to regain his primal form, but even an intermediate stage might be enough to save him now. He removed the stopper from the flask and greedily emptied its contents before he was overcome by a fit of coughing, shortly followed by violent pains.

Three riders on horseback were escorting the coach, one before and two behind. Warned by the Alchemist, those two slowed down to detain Saint-Lucq who had already caught up with them. Shots were exchanged, using pistols that had been tucked into the saddle holsters. The half-blood came under fire first and responded in kind. He hit one of the mercenaries, who toppled out of his saddle. His companion fired at the half-blood in turn. The ball narrowly missed Saint-Lucq who drew closer still. The other man then took hold of his second pistol and turned to shoot, but the Blade was quicker and succeeded in lodging a ball in the middle of his brow. The mercenary fell forward and was carried off into the distance by his mount.

Seeing the turn that events were taking, the coachman screamed and was heard by the rider galloping in front. The latter drew aside from the road and, hidden behind a thicket, allowed himself to be passed by. Saint-Lucq remained unaware of this trickery. He drew abreast of the horse belonging to the first mercenary he had shot and only had eyes for the pistol remaining in its saddle holster. He grabbed the weapon as he went by and tucked it into his belt, then spurred his own mount forward.

He caught up with the coach in the long dusty cloud raised by the hooves of the horses and the iron-rimmed wheels. He drew as close as possible, reached out his arm, found a hand-hold and clambered on to the narrow platform used by the footman. He thought he could then catch his breath, but a detonation sounded and a ball smashed into the coach next to his head. Still hanging on, he turned to see the last escort rider coming up the road at breakneck speed, already brandishing his second pistol. The shot, luckily, misfired, the powder burning without exploding and the weapon only spitting out a jet of flame. The mercenary threw it away and drew his sword. Saint-Lucq did the same. A fight commenced between the two men. The half-blood only had the one handhold and one foot on the platform, and he found himself hanging halfway out over open space, at the rear of the coach whose jolting caused him to sway back and forth, thumping violently against the cabin. As for the rider, he was making wild slashes with his sword which Saint-Lucq sometimes parried and sometimes evaded by swinging a quarter turn to the left or right. But finally the half-blood struck back. Reaching out as far as he could, he planted the point of his blade into the mercenary's flank, who hiccupped and dropped his weapon in order to hold his belly with both hands. His horse slowed to a trot and then a walk, before coming to a halt as the coach vanished into the night.

Saint-Lucq replaced his rapier in its scabbard and took three deep breaths. He now needed to eliminate the coachman or at least force him to bring the carriage to a halt. Gripping the edge with both hands, he climbed up to the roof of the cabin and crawled over it face down. Unable to leave his station, the coachman tried to drive him away him with blows from his whip. Saint-Lucq protected himself with his forearm before managing to seize the leather cord and pull the whip towards him. The coachman gave it up, too busy trying to negotiate a curve which the vehicle was approaching at excessive speed. It leaned dangerously and the two wheels that lifted off the ground on one side fell back with a thump that shook both the axles and Saint-Lucq. Sliding across the roof, the half-blood caught hold at the last second and found himself once again hanging from the rear of the coach.

There were a series of thuds coming from inside the cabin and a scaly fist punched through the roof once, twice, three times, until it shattered the wood completely. Then a creature, combining the features of both a man and a dragon, emerged from the cabin, forcing a passage with the help of its muscular shoulders. More than two metres in height, it stood up straight, screaming to the sky as it unfurled huge membranous wings. Stricken with panic by the sight, the coachman jumped from the vehicle. As for Saint-Lucq, he kept his wits. He understood that he was dealing with the product of an intermediate metamorphosis. The Alchemist was truly a dragon. It remained to be seen whether it was capable of regaining its primal form. For Saint-Lucq's sake, it would be better if it couldn't.

The creature looked down at the half-blood. If its features still evoked those of the Alchemist, the reptilian eyes blazed with a primitive, bestial fire.

It roared and abruptly took flight.

A riderless horse was still galloping alongside the coach. Saint-Lucq leapt towards it, managed to grab the pommel of the saddle with both hands, hit the ground with both feet together and bounced back up to straddle the animal, which he promptly urged off the road in pursuit of the draconic creature. Seconds later, the runaway coach tipped over as it came to a bend in the road and broke apart with a crash, the team of horses whinnying as they fled.

Saint-Lucq's horse jumped a ditch, then a fence, and galloped through the fields. He kept his eyes on the creature whose scales glittered beneath the moon and the stars. He feared that he would soon be outdistanced. His horse was tired, not to mention the obstacles he was encountering on the ground. But he still had a pistol, the one he had snatched from the saddle holster as he passed and tucked into his belt.

Which meant he had one shot left.

One last hope.

Sensing it was being chased, the creature turned back and as if suspended in mid-air, it lingered for a moment, beating its wings and considering this miserable mortal determined to hunt it down. It hesitated. But a proud and ferocious instinct had already taken control of its mind, banishing all intelligent thought. It let out a great warlike scream and then dove towards the rider.

The creature and Saint-Lucq rushed at one another. The hybrid being came from above with great flaps of its wings, displaying vicious fangs and extended claws. The Blade was riding flat out, controlling his mount with his knees in order to hold the pistol with both hands. Neither of them was willing to turn aside. The creature gave another menacing scream. Saint-Lucq took careful aim. He needed to hold on until the last moment before firing.

To wait, hoping that his horse would not suddenly veer off . . .

To wait, just a little longer . . .

One shot. One hope.

Now!

Saint-Lucq pulled the trigger. For an awful instant, he was convinced it had misfired, but the gun went off just before the hybrid collided with him.

The impact was tremendous. It threw the half-blood out of his saddle and he rolled across the ground as the creature crashed a short distance away, and his horse continued its mad gallop.

Nothing moved and the nocturnal silence returned, disturbed only by the fading hoof beats of the fleeing steed.

Saint-Lucq opened his eyes, spitting out blood and dirt, and stood up painfully on trembling legs. Drawing his sword, he turned around seeking any sign of danger and almost tripped over.

He saw the form lying on the ground and limped over to take a closer look.

It was the creature who, unconscious and bleeding from a pistol ball in the shoulder, was recovering a more human appearance. As Saint-Lucq watched, its size diminished, its wings atrophied, the scales were absorbed into smooth skin and its features once again became those of the Alchemist.

The latter came to his senses and saw Saint-Lucq standing over him with a sword at his throat.

Bare-headed, Saint-Lucq was covered in dust and blood. A long lock of hair hung down before his bruised face. One of the lenses of his spectacles was missing, revealing a bloodshot draconic eye. He was struggling to remain on his feet and kept his left elbow tucked against his side to protect his damaged shoulder.

But his determination was made of the same steel as the blade of his elegant rapier.

'It's over,' he said.

*

With Leprat supporting Mirebeau's weight, the two men returned to the surface by way of the foundations of the ancient tower. They emerged from the covered pit and remained for a moment, tottering but nevertheless standing, beneath the great starry sky, enjoying the cool air and the quiet of the night. Then Mirebeau, who was having more and more difficulty breathing, coughing up the blood filling his lungs, pointed to the outer wall of one of the pavilions under construction.

'Over there,' he said. 'That would be . . . good.'

Leprat helped the gentleman walk to the spot he had chosen. He installed him against the wall, facing east, and sat down next to him.

'And now,' said Mirebeau. 'We only need . . . We only need to wait for the sun . . .'

He died a short while later.

Leprat still hadn't moved when dawn broke.

3

A few days passed before La Fargue, for the second time in less than a fortnight, paid a visit to the Grand Châtelet. Accompanied by Almades, as always, he arrived by way of the Pont au Change, whose houses aligned on either side completely hid the Seine from view and gave one the impression of travelling down an ordinary street. The two men rode at a walk, side by side, in silence. It was late morning, on a sunny day, and Paris stank more than ever.

Nothing had filtered out concerning the plot that the Blades had thwarted and – it was hoped – nothing ever would. The scandal would be enormous. Although she had obviously been unaware that she was delivering herself into the hands of the Black Claw, Anne d'Autriche was nonetheless guilty of having wanted to subject herself, unbeknownst to the king and contrary to the laws of the kingdom, to a ritual involving draconic magic. Besides, like the duchesse de Chevreuse, most of those implicated in this affair believed they were doing no evil, having persuaded themselves – out of loyalty, affection or naïvety – that they were secretly helping an unhappy and humiliated sovereign conceive an heir to the throne. Within the queen's entourage, no one knew what would have really happened if the queen had been successfully abducted by the Alchemist . . .

La Fargue and Almades exchanged a look before they passed through Le Châtelet's dark archway. La Fargue guessed what the Spaniard was thinking and waited for him to say it out loud.

Although planned for some time, the wave of arrests ordered by the king on the day following that famous night had very opportunely dominated public attention ever since. The gazettes and the gossipmongers had discussed nothing else, in Paris, in France and in the other princely courts throughout Europe.

The arrest that caused the most astonishment was that of the marquis de Châteauneuf, who was third personage of the State in his role as Keeper of the Seals. He was firstly reproached for being too eager to succeed Richelieu in the post of chief minister to His Majesty, which was often the first step on the path leading to treasonous plots. But more to the point, he was accused of confiding State secrets to his mistress, the highly suspect duchesse de Chevreuse. Some of those secrets concerned the citadels France was occupying in Lorraine. And there was also the matter of a French officer, an intimate friend of the marquis, who had been arrested recently, just before he could divulge information about the army the king was presently mustering. Thanks to the confessions of this officer, a trap had been set at an inn near Neuilly, but unfortunately it had not led to the arrest of any accomplices. Châteauneuf's guilt, however, had clearly been brought to light. He had been thrown into a prison from which he would not emerge for a long time, while others were also being dealt with by the king's justice. Convicted of having communicated State secrets, confided to her by the besotted marquis, to the duc de Lorraine, the duchesse de Chevreuse was of course one of them. But her rank still seemed to protect her, even if in truth she was skilfully negotiating the terms of her silence about what threatened to become the affair of the Dampierre ritual.

The two Blades dismounted in the courtyard of Le Châtelet and again La Fargue's eye met Almades's. This time, however, the fencing master asked:

'What do you expect from this meeting, captain?'

'I don't know,' the old gentleman admitted. 'Answers, I think.'

'Answers to which questions?'

He fell silent and the two men let themselves be led into the imposing tower that housed the prison.

Even if the duchesse managed to evade the full severity of the punishment she deserved in the Châteauneuf affair, La Fargue deemed that the greatest dangers of the Dampierre case had been averted. The queen was safe and the Black Claw mercenaries who had not been killed would never again see the light of day. To be sure, Savelda had escaped and could not be found. But the Alchemist was behind bars. As for the Blades, they had come out of the whole matter quite well. They had even acquired a new member, Laincourt, whose shoulder wound had not proved serious. Also slightly injured, Marciac was torn between two sentiments: joy at having held a queen of France in his arms and frustration at not being able to boast about it. Saint-Lucq had disappeared again and Agnès was occupied elsewhere after receiving a letter from the former Superior General of the Sisters of Saint-Georges. In the end, the captain was only worried about Leprat, who had returned from his mission looking much the worse for wear. Physically, but also mentally speaking.

At Le Châtelet, a gaoler opened a door on the level containing individual cells and stepped aside to allow La Fargue and Almades to enter. The room was cool, quite dark and sparsely furnished with a table, a stool and a bed. They found the Alchemist there, looking through an arched window defended by thick bars. As solemn and sinister as ever, he was dressed in grey, with a bandaged shoulder and his wrists bound by shackles made of a steel alloy containing draconite, the alchemical stone that inhibited the power of dragons.

The Alchemist's thin, scarlike mouth twisted into a strange smile as he turned towards his visitors.

'How kind of you to accept my invitation, captain.'

The first person to raise an alarm was a ditch digger who, looking up at the sky, could not at first believe his eyes, but then ran to the nearest village. He arrived frightened and out of breath, hammered at the door of the presbytery, and then had trouble making himself understood by the parish priest. The latter also had difficulty believing the news. The man's eyes had played a trick on him. Or he had been drinking. But other witnesses arrived soon afterwards.

They had also seen it.

They were also afraid.

The priest decided to ring the church bells.

Looking out the window of his private office, the comte de Tréville looked out over the courtyard of his mansion in the rue du Vieux-Colombier for a long while. Then he turned away and asked Leprat:

'Have you truly made up your mind?'

'Yes, monsieur.'

The captain of the King's Musketeers seated himself at his desk and granted himself a few more moments of reflection. He used this time to examine Leprat who stood at attention without blinking, with his ivory rapier at his side and his right hand wrapped in a bandage.

'Don't misunderstand me,' Tréville said at last. 'I ask for nothing more than to see you wear the blue cape once again. Indeed, no one is more worthy of wearing it . . .'

'Thank you, monsieur.'

'But I know what the Blades represent in your eyes. And I also know the respect and the friendship you have for monsieur La Fargue . . . Have you told him of your decision?'

'I shall tell him this evening, along with the other Blades.'

'It won't be easy.'

'I know.'

At the Hôtel de Chevreuse, Arnaud de Laincourt joined the duchesse on the large terrace. Still looking pale, he had his arm in a sling. As for the duchesse, she was no less beautiful or less elegant than usual, but she was alone and wore a grave expression on her face. She stood beneath a canopy that shaded chairs and a table bearing untouched delicacies: crackers, cakes, marzipans, fruit jellies, preserves and syrups. In her hand she had a liqueur glass filled with golden henbane and, from the gleam in her eye, Laincourt guessed she had already been partaking of it immoderately.

She held out her hand to be kissed and then said:

'So, you never stopped being an agent of the cardinal, monsieur de Laincourt . . .'

'No, madame.'

'Well, it's only fair, I suppose . . . In contrast to the marquis de Châteauneuf, who wanted to recruit you, monsieur de Mirebeau never believed it would be possible to win you over to our cause. He said the cardinal is a master one never ceases to serve.'

'No doubt he's right.'

'Do you know what became of him? Was he arrested?'

'Mirebeau? No. He's dead, madame.'

'Oh! That's a pity, isn't it?' said madame de Chevreuse in the same tone she might have employed to regret the loss of beautiful rosebushes killed by frost.

Laincourt did not reply and together they turned towards the magnificent garden.

'I must thank you for agreeing to visit me, monsieur. No one knocks at my door anymore, you know? All those fine people who danced at my ball and applauded my fireworks now avoid me as if I had the ranse . . . But I've long been accustomed to changes in fortune at court and I wait patiently to learn the fate in store for me. It will be exile, won't it?'

'Probably, yes.'

'And what about poor old Châteauneuf?'

'I doubt he will ever emerge from His Majesty's prisons.'

'Exile . . .' sighed the duchesse, her eyes lost in contemplation.

A lackey brought, upon a tray, a box covered with a piece of cloth. He stood there waiting patiently for his mistress to notice him.

'Ah!' she said at last. 'This is why I asked you to come see me. Take it, monsieur. It's for you.'

Intrigued, Laincourt picked up the box, but waited until the lackey turned away before opening it. It contained a letter – which was addressed to him – and a small painted portrait.

'The letter,' indicated madame de Chevreuse, 'is from madame de Saint-Avold who, for reasons you must be aware of, has been obliged to return to her native Lorraine with all due haste.'

The portrait was also of Aude de Saint-Avold. The same one the duchesse had commissioned in order to show her master of magic how much, if the upper part of her face were masked, the beautiful Aude resembled the queen: they had the same eyes, the same mouth, the same chin, the same throat.

'Please accept this gift from me, monsieur. For if I have many faults, above all I suffer from that of loving love.'

Laincourt accepted it, feeling moved.

Bells were ringing in the distance and the sound seemed to be drawing closer, but the Blade and the duchesse paid it no heed.

'Goodbye, monsieur de Laincourt. I doubt that we will meet again for a long time.'

'Goodbye, madame. But—'

'Yes, monsieur?'

'Would you agree to answer a question?'

'Is it a question the cardinal is asking through you?'

'No, madame.'

'Then I will answer.'

Laincourt took a breath and then asked:

'Why, madame? Why did you wish to help the queen to conceive a child? Your hatred of the cardinal is a secret to no one. And, for reasons that are strictly yours, you do not seem to like our king at all. And a throne without an heir means no end of pretenders and opportunists willing to scheme and rise up against your enemies. By favouring the birth of an heir apparent, you would have strengthened the throne and con- solidated Louis' reign.'

The duchesse smiled.

'You forget, monsieur, the affection I have for the queen, and how painful it is for me to see her so unhappy and so often humiliated . . . And then there was that night when, as a game, I encouraged her to run through the Grande Salle at the Louvre. If not for me, she would not have tripped against the platform. If not for me, she would not have fallen. And if not for me, three days later she would not have lost the child she was carrying. A boy, apparently . . . And while the queen forgave me, I never could forgive myself . . . So, when the man I believed to be a wise master of magic confided to me that he could . . .'

Overcome by emotion, she could not finish.

Then she exclaimed:

'Those bells are going to drive us all mad!'

To the bells ringing in the faubourgs, were now added several more in the neighbourhood of Saint-Thomas-du-Louvre.

It was both unusual and disquieting.

Laincourt lifted his eyes to the sky just as a great shadow passed overhead.

Leprat descended the great staircase in the Hôtel de Tréville when he suffered an attack. He was suddenly very hot, his vision blurred and, realising what was happening, he murmured:

'Oh, Lord! Not here . . .'

In a sweat, staggering, he bumped into a musketeer who was coming up the stairway, tried to grab hold of another and only managed to tear the man's sleeve as his legs gave way beneath him.

He tumbled to the bottom of the steps and lay there, convulsing.

A crowd gathered round him. A few men seized hold of his limbs to restrain them. They also attempted to slide a belt between his jaws to save his tongue.

'A doctor. Someone fetch a doctor!'

And while he arched his back, moaning, a black bile began to flow from between his grimacing lips.

'It's the ranse!' one man exclaimed. 'He's been stricken by the Great ranse.'

'The poor wretch . . .'

'Do you hear that?' said another. 'It sounds like the tocsin.'

Close by, the bells of the Saint-Germain-des-Prés abbey were pealing.

*

An immense, terrifying, winged shadow settled upon the prison at Le Châtelet. In the Alchemist's cell the light suddenly dimmed, while a booming roar shook the walls. Outside, all the bells in Paris were ringing.

La Fargue turned towards the darkened window . . .

. . . and saw the great black dragon that faced him, opening its menacing jaws ready to breath fire . . .

He faced it, frozen in awe.

4

The young Chatelaine who, torch in hand, was the first to enter the dark corridor was both worried and in a hurry. Behind her, Agnès de Vaudreuil seemed more assured, although all her senses were on edge too.

In coming this far, she had scrupulously respected the warnings to be cautious addressed to her by Emmanuelle de Cernay, the former Superior General of the Sisters of Saint Georges. In a letter that Agnès had found upon her return from Dampierre, Mère Emmanuelle informed her that she had been unable to discover what had become of the chevalier Reynault d'Ombreuse, the son of the gentleman who had asked the Blades for help. On the other hand, she had uncovered the identity of the sister Reynault and a detachment of Black Guards had accompanied to Alsace on their secret mission: Sœur Béatrice d'Aussaint. As well as where she could now be found. She and the baronne de Vaudreuil had undergone their novitiates together. They were friends, or they had been. Strangely, Sœur Béatrice was now being held in isolation, like a prisoner, on the orders of the current Superior General, the formidable Mère Thérèse de Vaussambre.

Advancing along the corridor on tiptoe, Agnès was led to a door. The Chatelaine guiding her looked furtively to left and right before pushing it open and then moving aside.

'Be quick,' she murmured. 'They could discover that I took the keys at any moment.'

Agnès nodded and entered.

It was an ordinary convent cell, austere and lacking in any comforts. She saw Sœur Béatrice lying on the narrow bed. Pale and with drawn features, she remained beautiful but seemed worn out. She was a mere shadow of the superb, proud Chatelaine who, early one morning in a corner of Alsace, had stood alone against a great dragon with a draconite blade in her hand and an incantation on her lips.

She was asleep.

Agnès removed the great black cloak with a hood that had hidden her head, then sat by the sleeping woman and touched her hand.

The sister opened blind eyes, filled with a glassy whiteness.

'Agnès? Is that you, Agnès?'

'Yes, Béatrice. It's me.'

'Lord be praised! My prayers are answered at last!'

'My God, Béatrice, your eyes! What happened to you?'

'It's nothing. Nothing but the price of . . . It won't last, I believe.'

'The price of what?'

'You need to know, Agnès. You need to see what I have seen!' said the Chatelaine in an anguished voice.

She wanted to sit up in her bed. Agnès gently held her down and said:

'Calm yourself, Béatrice. You need to rest. I'll come back later.'

'No!' cried out the other woman. 'Now! It can't wait . . . ! Give me your hands, Agnès.' The young baronne obeyed. 'And now, see . . . See,' she repeated in a weaker tone. 'You need . . . to see.'

Her white eyes darkened as if injected with a black liquid.

An abyss was born into which Agnès's awareness suddenly plunged.

And she *saw*.

She saw what the Chatelaine had seen that morning in Alsace when she looked into the mind of the dragon.

She saw glimpses of a future that was both terrifying and close at hand.

It was night. Panicked crowds were running through streets lit by crackling flames. Fire was raining from the sky. It was being belched by a black dragon. Or by several. Fiery blasts were striking the rooftops; dazzling columns provoked explosions of tiles; red-hot sprays fell back in incandescent particles. Screaming, terrorised people were jostling, fighting and trampling one another in their desire to flee. Some soldiers were firing their muskets futilely into the air. Human torches wriggled and thrashed horribly. The blazes consumed entire neighbourhoods and the immense conflagration was reflected in the dark waters of a river.

A river that ran past the Louvre, which had also been set alight.

Trembling, her eyes full of tears, Agnès watched Paris burn.

This book is dedicated to my father

July 1633

Night coiled itself around Mont-Saint-Michel.

Forbidding but elegant, the abbey built on the summit over-looked the immense bay that stretched out below it, still damp from the last tide and crossed by short-lived streams. A thin crescent moon floated in an ink-black sky. Just above the sands, dragonnets dove and twirled in the banks of mist, their wings tearing it away in tatters that immediately dissipated in the air.

A rider came to halt on the shore. She was young and beautiful, slender in build, with a pale complexion, green eyes and full, dark lips. Her heavy black curls were gathered into a braid that had started to come undone during her long jour-ney on horseback. She wore thigh boots, breeches and a white shirt beneath a thick red leather corset, and carried a sword at her hip. She was no ordinary rider. She was a baronne, bore the name of Agnès de Vaudreuil, and belonged to an elite unit serving at the command of Cardinal Richelieu: the Cardinal's Blades. But her past concealed other secrets, most of them painful.

One of them had brought her here.

Agnès considered the abbey for a moment, its Gothic spire and tall shadowy buildings, and the village that slumbered beneath its walls, sheltered behind solid ramparts. Having undergone various changes over the centuries, the site now belonged to the Sisters of Saint Georges, the famous Chate-laines. The mission assigned to this religious order was to protect the French throne from the threat of dragons, waging a veritable war against them. And no war could be won without possessing a strong citadel. The abbey of Mont-Saint-Michel had become the Chatelaines' citadel, and they had proceeded to enlarge and embellish it, hollowing out mysterious underground chambers beneath it and covering its roofs above with draconite – a rare alchemical stone as black and shiny as obsidian. Pilgrims ceased to visit. These days, the abbey was more often referred to as 'Mont-des-Chatelaines' than as Mont-Saint-Michel.

Referred to with a certain hint of fear . . .

Sitting straight, her hands on the pommel of her saddle, Agnès eased her shoulders slightly forward and closed her eyes. Perhaps to catch the caress of the sea breeze. Or perhaps to collect her thoughts and summon her courage. She only opened them when she heard another rider arrive behind her. She didn't turn to look. She knew who it was.

Ballardieu drew up by her side. Squat and heavily built, the old soldier presented the ruddy face of a man who had no fear of indulging in wine and good food. He had put on weight over the years and no doubt he walked with a slower step now than in his youth. But it would be a mistake to be taken in by that, for he remained a force to be reckoned with.

'No one followed us,' he announced.

Agnès glanced at him.

'Good,' she said with a nod.

With Ballardieu watching her out of the corner of his eye, she looked up at the abbey again. Her beautiful face was grave, and a curl of black hair fluttered at her cheek.

'Let's get on with it.'

She urged her horse forward.

Mont-Saint-Michel was a craggy island, surrounded by water at high tide. It was crowned by the imposing and mysterious Chatelaine abbey, while the village occupied its two more accessible sides – so accessible, in fact, that ramparts had been built to defend them. In contrast, even at low tide the western and northern sides of the island were impregnable. Here there were no walls, towers, or gates, just steep, rocky slopes that were hidden by dense trees, condemning any attackers to attempt an impossible climb.

Agnès and Ballardieu made a wide detour before

approaching the mount again from the north. They stopped in the shelter of a spur of rock on which stood an ancient chapel dedicated to Saint Aubert. They dismounted and, handing her reins to the old soldier, Agnès observed the night sky before saying:

'I must hurry . . .'

'Are you sure you would not rather—'

'Stay here and mind you keep the horses out of sight. I'll be back soon.'

'Be careful, girl. Don't make me come and get you.'

Ballardieu watched with a worried gaze as the young woman moved quickly towards an old tower that stood below the first of the rocky cliffs. This tower housed a spring that had once provided Mont-Saint-Michel with fresh water. Originally it had been accessible via a narrow stairway between high walls that descended directly from the abbey. The stairs were no longer maintained, but they were still passable. Following her instructions, Agnès knocked at the door that guarded their entry and waited.

The door opened slightly and a sister of the Order of Saint Georges peeped out warily. She was young. No doubt she had only taken her vows in the past year.

'I am Agnès de Vaudreuil.'

The sister nodded and hastily let Agnès pass. She was wearing an ample black cloak and hood over her white robe and veil. She held a similar cloak out to the baronne de Vaudreuil, and said:

'This is for you. I am Sœur Marie-Bénédicte.'

'Please don't lock the door, sister,' Agnès requested as she pulled on the loose-fitting garment.

'But I—'

'If I must make my escape on my own, I would prefer not to break my neck running into it.'

'Escape?'

'You never know, sister . . .'

Worried, and visibly pressed for time, the young Chatelaine conceded the point.

As she followed the sister up the steps, Agnès recalled her

own novitiate in the religious order. Had she really been so young, when she was forced to make the choices that would decide her future? She could scarcely believe it. And yet she had come very close to taking the veil.

The stairway was so steep it couldn't be climbed without growing short of breath. When they reached the top, a second door was unlocked and opened onto a narrow terrace looking out at the tall façade of a Gothic building that was impressive both in its size and its beauty: the church known as 'La Merveille'. The terrace served as a defensive walkway. Agnès and the Chatelaine quickly crossed it, and the baronne allowed herself to be led into the secret heart of the abbey.

Happily, there were few sentries about.

As a result, and despite her fears, Sœur Marie-Bénédicte was able to deliver Agnès to her destination without mishap. The sister opened the door at the end of a narrow archway, and followed the baronne inside after giving a last nervous glance around. They found themselves in a dark vestibule, where a burning oil lamp cast only a dim glow. The young Chatelaine lit a torch before leading them into a blind corridor.

'Here we are,' she said, halting before a door.

She looked furtively to left and right before pushing it open and then moving aside.

'Be quick,' she murmured. 'They could discover I took the keys at any moment.'

The baronne de Vaudreuil nodded and, unaccompanied, entered the austere, windowless convent cell. A woman lay sleeping on the narrow bed. Agnès had trouble recognising the beautiful face in the shadows, its pale features marked by fatigue. But it was Sœur Béatrice d'Aussaint. What ordeal could have affected her so deeply?

Béatrice and Agnès had first met and been friends during their novitiate. But Sœur Béatrice had taken the veil and even gone on to become a 'louve', or a she-wolf, as the young baronne had originally hoped to do herself. Forming an exclusive band within the Sisters of Saint Georges, the *Louves*

716

blanches, or White Wolves, took their name from the Saint-Loup convent where they were based, as well as from their military calling and their tendency to hunt in packs. Both nuns and warriors, the White Wolves rode on horseback and tracked down dragons, often armed with no more than a draconite blade and the shield of their faith. Agnès had little doubt that Sœur Béatrice d'Aussaint was one of the best.

Removing her black cloak, the baronne sat on the bed by the sleeping woman and touched her hand. Sœur Béatrice immediately opened her eyes, and Agnès was forced to bite back a gasp of surprise when she saw their glassy whiteness and realised her friend was blind.

'Agnès? Is that you, Agnès?'

'Yes, Béatrice. It's me.'

'Lord be praised! My prayers are answered!'

'My God, Béatrice, your eyes! What happened?' asked Agnès in a soft voice.

'It's nothing. Just the price of . . . It won't last, I believe.'

'The price of what?'

'You must know, Agnès. You must see what I have seen!'

The louve tried to sit up in her bed, but Agnès prevented her, gently pressing down on her shoulders and saying:

'Calm yourself, Béatrice. You need to rest. I can come back later.'

'No!' cried the other woman. 'Now! It can't wait! Give me your hands, Agnès.' The sister's fingers gripped those of the baronne. 'And now, see . . . See,' she repeated in a weaker tone. 'You must . . . see.'

Her milky white eyes darkened as if injected with a black liquid, and suddenly Agnès' awareness plunged into their abysmal depths.

And she *saw*.

It was night. Panicked crowds ran through streets lit by flames to the sound of a deafening, crackling roar. Fire rained from the sky in brief but powerful gouts, belched out by a great black dragon. Incandescent blasts struck the rooftops; the dazzling columns produced explosions of tiles and red-hot sprays of particles fell to the ground below. The city's bells were pealing in alarm. The terrorised residents jostled, fought and trampled one another in their desire to flee. Fear and panic were killing as many people as the fires and the collapsing buildings. Some soldiers were firing their muskets futilely into the air. Human torches wriggled and thrashed horribly. The blazes consumed entire neighbourhoods and the whole immense conflagration was reflected in the dark waters of the Seine as it flowed past the Louvre. The royal palace, too, had been set alight.

Paris burned, helplessly exposed to the rage of a dragon whose onyx scales glowed red and gold. It roared, spat and exulted. A single crafted jewel shone flamboyantly upon its brow. Its fire lashed out as it descended from on high to skim over the rooftops. Then it rose again with a few beats of its wings, leaving a swathe of destruction in its wake. The creature was immense and power-ful, its anger bestial. It lingered for a moment in the black skies, contemplating its work, no doubt searching for another spot to continue its ravages. Then, having found its goal, it dove back towards the flames and the horror . . .

Suddenly, the bells of Notre-Dame began to toll.

Agnès came back to her senses with a jolt.

Her eyes filled with tears and she was stunned for a moment by this shared vision which had seemed so powerful, so vivid, so real. Then the full realisation of what she had seen struck her with all its terror.

Sœur Béatrice had relinquished her grip on the baronne's hands. Her eyes had turned milky again and, having fainted, her face now expressed a measure of peaceful release: finally freed of a burden she had borne to the very limits of her strength.

'No . . . no!' Agnès exclaimed. 'Béatrice! You must explain this to me! You must!'

She took hold of the Chatelaine by the shoulders, sat her up and shook her, forcing her to respond:

'Tell me, Béatrice! What did I see? What did you show me?'

'This . . . this will come to pass,' the louve murmured.

'Who is that dragon? Where does it come from?'

'No . . . No name . . . The Primordial . . . The Primordial of the Arcana . . .'

'What? I don't understand, Béatrice. Speak sense, I beg of you!'

Struggling against exhaustion, Sœur Béatrice replied:

'The Arcana . . . Beware of the Arcana . . . and of the Heir . . . There are many of them . . . The Alchemist . . .'

'The Alchemist?'

Just then, Sœur Marie-Bénédicte opened the door from the corridor and announced:

'It's time, madame.'

'One moment,' said Agnès, without turning round. Still holding Sœur Béatrice by the shoulders, she asked her, 'This alchemist, it's the Alchemist of the Shadows, isn't it?'

'The Alchemist . . . of the Shadows.'

'It's time to leave, madame!' the young Chatelaine insisted.

'Then leave!' Agnès snapped sharply.

Turning back to the louve, who was beginning to nod off, she said, 'Béatrice, the Alchemist has been taken care of. You haven't heard, but we defeated him. He can no longer harm any—'

'The Alchemist . . . The queen . . . in danger . . .'

'No, Béatrice. Calm down. The queen is safe, I assure you. You must tell me about the black dragon. I need know what—'

'The queen . . . The Heir . . .'

'The dragon, Béatrice! The dragon!'

But Sœur Béatrice had lost consciousness again, and Agnès laid her head on the pillow before turning back to the doorway . . .

. . . to find that the young Chatelaine was no longer there.

The baronne swore and went out into corridor. It was empty: Sœur Marie-Bénédicte hadn't waited for her. Swearing even more roundly, she swept her black cloak about her and set forth. Would she be able to find the way out on her own? She reached the vestibule where the Chatelaine had lit her torch and almost ran into someone. It was the sister returning.

'Some louves have arrived,' she announced. 'Three of them. On wyverns.'

'So?'

'They were not expected,' the young Chatelaine explained anxiously. 'One went to wake the mother superior. The other two have summoned the guards and—'

She did not finish, for just then the bells began to ring.

Nagged by worry, and spurred on by his instincts, Ballardieu became convinced something had gone wrong when he saw three wyverns in white harness arrive. He was nearly halfway up the stairs leading to the abbey when he heard the bells start to toll. The old soldier picked up his pace, swearing under his breath as he climbed.

'Leave me,' said Agnès in a low voice.

Her tone brooked no argument.

She and Sœur Marie-Bénédicte had paused at the corner of a building. The bells were still ringing and the abbey was beginning to stir.

'I beg your pardon?' responded the young Chatelaine.

'Leave me here, and go back . . . Go to wherever you should be.'

'Madame, I promised Mère de Cernay—'

Interrupting her, Agnès took the nun by the shoulders and looked her straight in the eyes.

'Listen to me, sister. You have done all you can. Soon, this place will be swarming with guards. I am used to these situations and I can outwit the sentries more easily if I am on my own. Off with you!'

'Will you be able to find your way?'

'Of course,' the baronne de Vaudreuil lied. 'Now, go! Run! And thank you.'

At first reluctantly, then with a swifter step, the young Chatelaine moved away and disappeared beneath an arch.

Still hoping to leave the abbey by the route she came in, Agnès headed for the long narrow terrace at the top of the abandoned old stairway. From there, she intended to go back down to the bay and rejoin Ballardieu by the Saint-Aubert chapel as quickly as possible. The old soldier must have heard the bells and she knew him well enough to know that he would not sit still for long . . .

Avoiding a patrol that hurried past, Agnès made her way by guesswork through the maze of buildings forming the abbey. She had almost reached her goal when she made an error and climbed a flight of stairs. Her blunder allowed her to evade a second patrol which was investigating more slowly and thoroughly than the first, but it brought her to a sort of balcony from where she could only gaze helplessly at the terrace she was trying to reach. The detour saved her from worse trouble than the patrol, however, when she saw guards moving back and forth along the terrace while a figure in white – one of the louves, no doubt – gave them their orders. Armed men were already making their way down the stairway that led to the old spring.

And to freedom.

'Merde!' Agnès muttered between her teeth, thinking of Ballardieu.

Would he be able to escape? If he did, he would take the horses with him.

Determined to find her own way out, the baronne de Vaudreuil drew away from the parapet, turned around, and froze: three men had crept up behind her and now advanced in a threatening manner. Dressed in black, they belonged to the redoubtable Guards of Saint Georges, better known as the Black Guards. They were all gentlemen, all skilled swordsmen, and they protected and served the Chatelaines with absolute devotion.

The three guards drew their weapons.

'Surrender, madame,' said one, as the other two moved out to his right and left.

Sure of themselves, they had not called for reinforcements. That stung the impetuous baronne de Vaudreuil's pride, and she wondered if they knew with whom they were dealing. But their excessive confidence could be useful. Spreading open the

721

front of her cape, she unsheathed her rapier, with a blade made of the finest Toledo steel.

She placed herself *en garde*, but her wrist trembled and her eyes darted about nervously.

'Come now, madame. Give us your sword, I beg of you.'

'If you insist.'

Taking advantage of the narrowness of the balcony, Agnès attacked with a feint. She slammed a sharp elbow beneath the chin of one guard, parried the blade of the next, and fell back before the third, who lunged too far. She doubled him over with a vicious knee to his belly. The two men she had struck collapsed, one of them knocked out cold and the other not much better off. The last man standing believed he still had time to act. But the young woman turned and pressed up against him, seizing his collar. There was a click and a metallic hiss. With her thumb, Agnès had released the stiletto blade concealed in the grip of her sword. The sharpened steel sprang from the pommel and its edge now tickled at the astonished guard's throat.

'One word, one murmur, and you die. Understood?'

The man nodded.

Unfortunately, the guard she had felled with her knee was now getting up. Staggering to his feet, he took hold of the parapet and shouted:

'Help!'

All eyes on the long terrace, including the louve's, lifted to the balcony. Reacting immediately, Agnès spun on her heels and used her momentum to push the man she held toward the parapet. Surprised, he tripped and fell out into the air. He screamed briefly, clearly believing his death was at hand, but landed without too much injury on a roof two metres below.

A black cloaked figure, Agnès took flight.

The obsessive steady tolling of the bells was now mixed with the voices of the guards calling out and guiding one another. Rapier in her fist, she ran. Mont-Saint-Michel had become a net from which she had to escape at all costs. For it was not simply a matter of her freedom. She had to alert people of the terrible danger that threatened Paris. But the abbey, greatly enlarged by the Chatelaines' building and digging into the rock, was a labyrinth of passages, galleries, and narrow stairways often hemmed in by high walls. Despite her fear of becoming lost and constant dread she would run into a sentry, Agnès could not afford to slow her pace.

Bursting out of a small courtyard, she was suddenly forced to halt. A patrol was coming toward her. She turned back, re-entered the courtyard, and heard more pursuers approaching from the opposite direction. The guards would be on her in less than a minute. She dashed beneath an arch only to run into a locked door, and grimaced. She pressed her back to the wood. Was there any chance that the soldiers would pass by without seeing her? Probably not. She was cornered. There was only one question left in her mind:

Surrender or fight?

A movement caught her attention. Agnès was astonished to see Ballardieu behind the parapet of a roofed gallery overlooking the courtyard. She gave him a sign which he answered. He understood the situation and would act. She also understood and nodded reluctantly, reminding herself that it was essential she got word of her discovery out.

The patrols arrived in the courtyard from either side at the same moment. They were not solely made up of Black Guards. There were also halberdiers and several harquebusiers drawn from the village garrison. Ballardieu let the guard of his sheathed rapier scrape against the stone wall as he rubbed past it. The sound seemed involuntary and immediately alerted the armed men below to his presence.

'UP HERE! UP THERE! THE INTRUDER!'

The old soldier pretended to be startled before taking to his heels. Shots were fired and the hunt took a new course that drew the guards away from Agnès. Nevertheless, she waited a moment before abandoning her hiding-place. She listened intently, watching the shadows, and then sped away.

An idea came to her.

Her cloak flapping in the dark shadows, Agnès ran with long silent strides. Twice she had to conceal herself in a corner or recess as guards approached her, their weapons clanking and hobnailed boots clattering on the flagstones. They passed by without bothering to search, however.

Ballardieu had attracted the pack's attention and artfully kept them busy, but he could only offer the baronne a brief respite. She knew time was working against her and that the guards would soon be on her trail again, but there was still no question of descending the old stairway to the spring. Nor of going down to the village with any hope of successfully scaling its defensive wall. And even supposing she managed to escape the mount, what would she do next? Regain the mainland on foot? She was sure to be spotted and captured on the bay's immense tidal flats, especially now that all the sentries were on alert. Or be drowned in the next high tide that would come sweeping in at dawn. Its speed here at Mont-Saint-Michel was notorious. Not to mention the dangers posed by quicksand and wild sand dragonnets.

That left only the air.

That left the louves' wyverns.

The winged steeds should still be waiting on the abbey's flight platform. Supported by a solid framework, its floor jutted out from the north-eastern corner of La Merveille. It could be reached from the upper floor of the church, but also by means of a series of stairways and landings forming a permanent wooden structure that climbed the outer wall of the building.

As she expected, Agnès found a sentry at the bottom of the first flight of stairs. She quickly knocked him out and began her ascent to the platform. She took the steps two at a time, then slowed down and cautiously unsheathed her sword as she approached the top. A strong wind was howling in the night. The place seemed to be deserted, but the wyverns were there, under shelters that extended from the slate roof.

She set one foot down on the floor which, although it appeared solid, creaked like a ship's deck at sea. Suddenly, she heard the echo of distant shots. They weren't shooting at her, so they could only be aimed at Ballardieu. She hurried forward, crossing the platform, and looked down from the other side.

The view was dizzying. La Merveille's height was added to that of the mount, so the platform was perched nearly a hundred and fifty metres above sea level and overlooked the long terrace which guarded the north side of the rock, serving as a walkway for its defenders. That was where Agnès had arrived, and it was where she now saw Ballardieu running, closely pursued, with shots whistling past his ears. No doubt he had hoped to escape by the stairway leading down to the spring. But he couldn't. Cornered, he unsheathed his sword and turned, his back against the parapet. Another shot grazed him. He realised that he was finished and raised his arms wide in surrender. A Black Guard ordered the arquebusiers to cease shooting, but too late. They had already knelt to take aim and opened fire. The shots cracked out in a cloud of smoke. Hit square on, Ballardieu toppled over the wall and out into empty space.

Agnès' eyes opened wide in disbelief, a cry held prisoner in her knotted throat. Trembling, she stumbled away from the edge, back toward the centre of the flight platform.

She had just watched Ballardieu die.

Her face was livid and she fought for air, but the howling wind didn't stop her hearing:

'Now that was a useless death.'

She spun round and found herself in the presence of three Chatelaines, one of whom remained still while the other two carefully spread out to surround her. They were armed with draconite rapiers. Their heads were covered by veils and wimples, but they also wore boots and breeches beneath their white robes.

The louves.

'It's over,' said the one who had just spoken. 'Your sword.'

Her black cape flapping about her in the gusts of wind, Agnès de Vaudreuil placed herself *en garde* and, with a look full of hatred, indifferent to the outcome of a fight that she already knew to be lost, she issued her challenge:

'Come and fetch it.'

Above the abbey, three shapes had appeared in the night sky. Three white shapes, diaphanous spectres that held the glow of the thin crescent moon. Three great shapes that hovered in place, beating their wings, and seemed to waiting, watching something going on below.

The shape of three dragons.

The Chatelaines' Prisoner

1

Captain Étienne-Louis de La Fargue stood in silence before the grave. Legs slightly apart, he held his hat in both hands in front of him. He was staring down at the grey stone cross. But what did he actually see? A hint of pain flickered in his eye, like lightning in a slow-moving raincloud.

Perhaps he was praying.

Tall and broad-shouldered, he was a gentleman grown white-haired with years, but hardened by many ordeals survived, battles fought, and losses mourned. His coat and his breeches were black, as were his hat and boots. As for his shirt, it was the same dark crimson shade as his baldric and the sash about his waist, knotted over his right hip. His rapier was a long, heavy and quite sturdy Pappenheimer, a weapon which resembled this old soldier: driven by honour and duty, it was said he would rather break than surrender, and he had never broken. His patriarchal features – a grim mouth, handsome wrinkles, and a firm jaw with a closely trimmed beard – were marked by small cuts still in the process of healing, while a patch covered his left eye. His split lower lip was swollen and dark.

The captain lifted his head and his sad gaze seemed to lose itself among the rooftops of the magnificent Saint-Germain-des-Prés abbey. He was alone in the small, hushed cemetery in the faubourg of the same name. It was pleasant here, among the old stones, the ivy, and the silence. The weather was sunny, and although it promised to be another day of scorching heat, the air was still mild in Paris on this morning in July 1633.

It was a season meant for life to be relished, for laughter and for love.

Without ever appearing to, a young man kept watch over the entrance to the cemetery. Leaning against the wall by the gate, he seemed to be waiting for someone as he flipped a coin in the air, killing time. His name was Arnaud de Laincourt. He was not yet thirty years old and he had only worn the steel signet ring of the Cardinal's Blades for a short while.

A pretty young maid, who was walking jauntily past in the street clutching an empty basket, offered him a saucy glance and a cheeky little smile.

Dark and thin, Laincourt was dressed as a gentleman in a quietly elegant costume: a felt hat with the brim tilted up on one side, a slashed dark red doublet, matching breeches, a white linen shirt and top boots. With one heel placed flat upon the wall against which he slouched, he cut quite a dashing figure, his left hand resting on the pommel of a fine rapier. The crystalline blue of his eyes did not detract from his charm.

Laincourt politely saluted the young woman with a slight nod of his head.

You're good-looking, boy.

He made no response to the person who made the remark. Not just because Laincourt was the only one able to see and hear him, but because he didn't know what to reply. He, too, had noticed that women were looking at him differently.

But he was at a loss to explain why.

It's because you've gained confidence.

You think so?

To be sure! You cultivated the art of being invisible for far too long. It was becoming second nature to you. You were basking in it . . .

I was a spy.

But now, you accept the fact that people see you. And you happen to be a handsome lad. You're attractive. That's how it is.

Laincourt felt the tap of a friendly hand upon his shoulder. He glanced at the old man beside him. The old hurdy-gurdy player always appeared in this guise, dressed in rags. But his face was no longer bruised and bloody, as it had been the last time Laincourt had seen him alive. He was even smiling now, with a proud, affectionate expression that a father might bestow upon a son.

Could he be right?

Laincourt felt he had undergone a change since joining the Cardinal's Blades, the elite and secret band of five men and a woman, commanded by Captain La Fargue.

No, four men and one woman.

Or perhaps just three.

And what of that pretty young lady who occupies so many of your thoughts?

The old man pretended to be busy with his instrument.

Aude de Saint-Avold?

That's the one.

The young's man gaze grew distant.

She's gone home to Lorraine. And I doubt she will be able to return to France.

Lorraine isn't so far away.

Laincourt remained silent.

Lorraine was an independent duchy which France was preparing to invade. The French king's regiments would soon march on Nancy, the duchy's capital and a notorious hotbed of intrigue. No doubt Cardinal Richelieu would find some use for his Blades in the course of the operation. There were always opportunities for secret missions and cloak-and-dagger work in times of war.

Where is Maréchal? the hurdy-gurdy player suddenly asked.

Maréchal was the emaciated, one-eyed dragonnet that the old man used to take with him, attached to a leash, while he earned his pittance playing music in the streets. After his death, Laincourt had inherited the small winged reptile.

The young man smiled.

In his cage.

You know how he hates to be locked up—

I know. But it's the safest place for him, in these times.

Yes, the hurdy-gurdy player agreed sadly.

Then in an offhand tone he said:

Nice ring, boy. Goodbye for now.

Saint-Lucq was making his way over from the rue du Sépulcre.

Laincourt did not look, but he knew the hurdy-gurdy player had vanished.

Saint-Lucq gave Laincourt a nod as he entered the cemetery.

He was dressed entirely in black: breeches and doublet, boots and gloves, and a felt hat. Even the fine-looking basket guard of his rapier was black. A thin scarlet feather adorned his hat. It was the same colour as the lenses of the curious round spectacles that protected his reptilian eyes. For Saint-Lucq was a half-blood. Dragon blood ran in his veins, which accounted for the dark animal charm that emanated from him. Slender and supple, elegant but sinister, Saint-Lucq was a magnificent and deadly weapon.

He walked towards La Fargue and halted a few paces away, behind him and to the right. Certain that his captain had heard his approach and recognised him, he uttered no greeting but waited patiently in the sun. Almades should have been standing here, in the best spot to keep an eye on the surroundings and guard La Fargue without being intrusive. But Almades was not here. The Spaniard's tall, thin figure would never be seen again.

'He knocked three times,' La Fargue said, lowering his eyes to the grave.

Saint-Lucq did not reply.

'Just after he shut the door,' the captain continued. 'He knocked on it three times with his fist. Three times, the way he always did. In spite of the circumstances. In spite of the danger. In spite of—'

He broke off.

Almades had been his friend and his bodyguard. Exiled from Spain following some dark business, the former fencing master had already been at La Fargue's side when the Blades were formed. Silent and serious, not given to making confidences, and grim to the point of bleakness, Almades had possessed a sense of dignity that tolerated no exceptions. His only foible was that of repeating his gestures thrice. Was he saddling his horse? He tightened the strap three times. Dusting off his doublet? The brush tripled its movements back and forth. Sharpening his sword? He applied three strokes of the whetstone to one side of the blade, and then three to the other.

He couldn't help it.

'He knocked three times,' La Fargue repeated. 'He knocked three times, and then everything went up in flames.'

It had happened in broad daylight. A great black dragon had attacked Le Châtelet, the fortress in the middle of Paris whose central keep housed a prison. The bells of the French capital had pealed in alarm and those who had seen the creature passing over the city had been scarcely able to believe their eyes.

La Fargue and Almades were on the fourth floor of Le Châtelet, where the captain was visiting a prisoner in his cell. The prisoner in question was the Alchemist of the Shadows – a dragon, but one of those for whom the human form had become more natural than his true, monstrous shape. He had just masterminded a plot to abduct the queen during a ball organised by the duchesse de Chevreuse; a plot which the Cardinal's Blades had foiled. But if the queen had been saved, if scandal had been avoided, and if most of the guilty parties had been arrested or killed, numerous questions remained unanswered. And it was those questions La Fargue had intended to put to the Alchemist.

One after another, all the city's bells tolled as a great shadow passed with slow, powerful beats of its wings and settled on the keep of Le Châtelet. In a cell grown suddenly dark, La Fargue turned towards the window . . .

. . . and froze when he saw the enormous jaws opening to reveal the infernal glow deep within.

Almades reacted immediately.

With a single bound, he shoved a dazed La Fargue out of the cell and slammed the door shut behind him. The old captain nearly stumbled down the stairs before he caught himself.

'No!' he cried, spinning round as he heard Almades rap three times in quick succession on the closed door.

But the dragon was already belching its flames. The door exploded, blasted apart by a raging firestorm. A burning shockwave slammed into La Fargue, accompanied by a hail of wooden splinters. Propelled backwards, he rolled down the steps and lay stunned by a blow to the head. But the fall saved his life. Almades had known, in a fraction of a second, that there wasn't time for them both to leave the cell and still close the door.

Neither he nor the Alchemist survived.

Of their bodies, only scattered ashes and a few bones remained. Although the Alchemist was a dragon, in human form he had been no more resistant to the blast than any common mortal. With its task complete, the great black dragon had flown off, and one by one, the bells of Paris had ceased to toll . . .

As he always did, La Fargue made a rapid recovery, like a knotty old oak that only lightning could kill. He had suffered a few bruises and superficial wounds, and the doctors assured him that his eye would heal. But the pain he felt lay elsewhere, in his grief and anger, in the frustration born of impotence, and in the guilt of having survived through the sacrifice of another man.

Raising his head, La Fargue drew a deep breath.

He paused, and then turned to Saint-Lucq. His eye patch gave him an even greater air of a rough gentleman hardened by battle, but his gaze was weary.

'Still no news of Agnès?' he asked.

'None. Nor of Ballardieu.'

'I'm starting to worry.'

'Yes,' the half-blood agreed impassively.

The captain of the Blades looked down once more at Almades' grave. He remained lost in his thoughts, until his attention was drawn by a dragonnet speeding through the air above the cemetery. The little winged creatures were rarely seen at large now, as Parisians had recently begun to shoot them with slingshots, crossbows and arquebuses. Traps were set and people made sport of tormenting them, in lieu of their more distant, powerful cousins.

'We'd best be getting back,' said La Fargue, donning his hat.

The Hôtel de l'Épervier was a very austere and rather uncomfortable mansion which a Huguenot gentleman had commissioned after the Saint-Barthélemy massacre. It stood on rue Saint-Guillaume, in the faubourg Saint-Germain, not far from the large La Charité hospital. Built of grey stone, it had the unwelcoming look of a fortified manor. A high wall cut its courtyard off from the street. Flanked by a turret and a dovecote, the main building comprised a ground floor reached by a short flight of steps, two storeys with stone-mullioned windows, and an attic with a row of small dormer windows set in the slate roof. It was not an immense house, but it was efficiently arranged. The Blades had made it their headquarters, with a staff consisting of an old concierge, a young female cook and a former soldier who served as a groom.

Upon arriving at the Hôtel de l'Épervier, La Fargue, Saint-Lucq and Laincourt found the great carriage gate open and a coach standing in the courtyard. It had a superb team of horses and the coachman waiting on his seat was clean, freshly shaved and well dressed. Prestigious coats-of-arms were painted on the coach's doors.

'The marquis' carriage,' noted Saint-Lucq.

The captain nodded.

An old man was already descending the front steps as quickly as age and his wooden leg would permit. Small and thin, he had bushy eyebrows and a crown of long dirty blond hair circling his bald pate. It was Guibot, the concierge. He wore buckled shoes, a pair of dubious-looking stockings, breeches made of coarse cloth, and a shirt of yellowed linen beneath a long, sleeveless vest. Looking anxious, he tried to speak, but La Fargue cut him short.

'Give me a moment, would you?'

Just returning from the Palais-Cardinal, Marciac entered the courtyard on horseback. He leapt from the saddle and, holding the reins in one hand, he removed a sealed letter from his doublet with the other and brandished it in the air.

La Fargue seized it.

'Good news?' he asked.

'An audience,' the Gascon replied.

'At last!'

Marciac watched as the captain broke the wax seal and opened the letter. He wore a satisfied expression, but his features were drawn, his cheeks were unshaven and his hair was in disarray. His clothes were also rather unkempt, as was usually the case with him, although today he had the excuse of having spent part of the night up and about. He was dressed in a blood-red doublet, matching breeches covered in dust, a shirt with its collar hanging wide open, and a pair of worn boots. Blond, attractive, with the eye of a seducer and a roguish smile, he wore his sword with a casual grace.

'No doubt we owe this hearing to dear old Charpentier,' he explained. 'I think he took pity on us. That, or he's fed up with seeing one of us hanging about the Narrow Gallery, day and night.'

Within the Palais-Cardinal, the Narrow Gallery was a dimly lit corridor, furnished with a pair of benches facing one another between two doors, where those Cardinal Richelieu could not receive officially were forced to wait. Over the past few days Marciac, Laincourt and Saint-Lucq had each spent long hours sitting there.

'The Cardinal will receive me at ten o'clock,' La Fargue announced as he refolded the letter.

That did not leave him much time.

'Go and freshen up,' he said to Marciac. 'And get some rest.'

Then he turned towards Guibot.

'Where is he waiting for me?'

'In the main hall,' replied the concierge.

'Good. Thank you.'

'Captain?' ventured Laincourt as La Fargue was starting up the front steps.

'Yes?'

'Will you be needing me right away?'

La Fargue frowned for a moment.

'No,' he said. 'I don't think so.'

'I haven't been home for several days now, captain.'

It was true, but Laincourt really wanted to see his friend Bertaud and Bertaud's daughter, Clotilde. Jules Bertaud was a bookseller in his neighbourhood. Laincourt was always made welcome at his shop and, even if he remained oblivious to the feelings which sweet, young Clotilde had for him, he knew that both father and daughter worried if he went too long without paying a visit.

'Very well. But be here when I return from the Palais-Cardinal. God only knows what will come out of my interview with His Eminence. Is that understood?'

'Thank you, captain.'

As Laincourt went on his way and Marciac made a detour to the kitchen, La Fargue and Saint-Lucq entered the main building.

All residences of a certain social standing had at least one room large enough to hold a reception. It was called the hall, the other rooms being known as chambers and not having any specific purpose. The Hôtel de l'Épervier had such a hall, but the Blades had converted it into a fencing room where they trained, and as the place where they gathered together when they could not use the garden.

As Guibot had already informed them, the marquis d'Aubremont was waiting there. Like La Fargue, he was about sixty years of age, and was an elegant grey-haired gentleman with a dignified air, who still wielded a sword confidently and had an unwavering gaze.

When the Blades' captain entered, the two men exchanged greetings and, without further ado, La Fargue said:

'Welcome. I must tell you that the cardinal has just granted me an interview, for which I have been waiting some time now. I'm sincerely sorry about this, but I can only spare you a moment.'

He pointed his friend to an armchair, took another himself, and they sat facing one another in the sunlight from a window looking out over the garden.

'You needn't apologise,' replied the marquis. 'I did not take the trouble to warn you of my visit.'

La Fargue and d'Aubremont were not only friends, but also brothers-in-arms. They had fought together during the civil and religious war that had ravaged France, and helped Henri IV seize his throne. They had since drifted apart. Unlike La Fargue, the marquis had a name, a title, lands and a fortune to look after. All the same, their friendship had remained intact.

In the large, silent fencing room, d'Aubremont leaned forward and La Fargue did likewise, as the marquis said in a low tone of voice:

'You will have guessed what has brought me here, Étienne. But before I say anything else, I would like to offer my condolences. I'm afraid I received your letter announcing Almades' death too late, and I regret not having attended his funeral.'

'Thank you.'

'He was a brave man. A man of integrity.'

'He saved my life. If not for him—'

'What happened, exactly? Is it true, what they are saying?'

The captain of the Blades nodded sadly.

'Le Châtelet was attacked by a great black dragon,' he explained.

'In broad daylight? Completely out of the blue?'

'Yes. It came to destroy the Alchemist. It was only by chance that Almades and I happened to be there.'

'So the Alchemist is to blame for this death as well?'

La Fargue understood what his friend was trying to say and met his sorrowful gaze.

'Yes. In a manner of speaking.'

The Alchemist of the Shadows. He had been the Black Claw's agent and an old adversary of the Blades. Five years earlier, in 1628, when the town of La Rochelle was besieged by the French royal armies, La Fargue had believed they were on the point of eliminating him, but the operation had become a

738

terrible fiasco during which a Blade had lost his life. A young gentleman named Bretteville, the marquis' eldest son. D'Aubremont mourned him deeply but had never said a word of reproach to La Fargue who, for his part, was keenly aware of his responsibility for the young Blade's death.

There was a knock at the door and fair-haired Naïs, no doubt sent by Guibot, came in bearing a bottle and two glasses upon a tray. Sweet and self-effacing, she moved silently, her eyes lowered, as if she feared being noticed. She left almost immediately and La Fargue poured the wine. As brief and as discreet as it had been, the servant girl's interruption had brought the two men back to the present.

And to the reason for the marquis' visit.

'Have you discovered anything about François?' he asked.

Recently, d'Aubremont had requested the Blades' assistance in the matter of his second son, the chevalier d'Ombreuse. He served with the Black Guards of the Sisters of Saint Georges, the religious order that had defended France and the crown against the dragons for the past two centuries. The Black Guards were charged with protecting the Chatelaines whenever they weren't carrying out secret missions or military operations. But the chevalier d'Ombreuse seemed to have disappeared following a mysterious expedition to Alsace, and his father was desperate for news of him. So far all of his enquiries to the Chatelaines, as the Sisters of Saint Georges were commonly called, had been in vain.

'It's always the same closed doors, the same silences, and the same damned lies,' declared the marquis. 'I know they're lying to me. Or, at least, they're hiding something . . . But don't I have the right to know what has happened to François?'

La Fargue had agreed his friend had the right, as had Agnès. She was the one person who could help d'Aubremont, having once been on the point of taking her vows with the Chatelaines. She had reluctantly agreed to renew contact with the community which, except for a few friends, had left her with bitter memories.

'Agnès had a meeting with Mère Emmanuelle de Cernay,'

explained La Fargue as he poured another glass of wine for the marquis.

'The former Mother Superior General of the Sisters of Saint Georges,' d'Aubremont said in a hopeful tone. 'And so?'

'Mère Emmanuelle could shed little light on our affair. But as discreet as she was, the visit that Agnès paid her had an almost immediate effect: she provoked the interest and perhaps even some anxiety on the part of the present Mother Superior General, Mère Thérèse de Vaussambre.'

'And what happened?'

'You are aware that the queen detests the Chatelaines so much that she deliberately makes matters difficult for the sisters within her entourage, who are charged with ensuring her safety. Using this information, the Mother Superior General persuaded the Cardinal to assign Agnès to the queen's service: as Agnès had been initiated into certain secrets of the Order during her novitiate, she would be able to protect the queen. As she is not one of the Chatelaines, she could do so without arousing her mistrust. And in order to lend a note of urgency to the Superior General's argument, the head of the Chatelaines claimed there was an increased threat to the queen, justifying extra precautions.

'But this threat was actually merely a means of preventing the baronne de Vaudreuil from investigating further.'

'No doubt,' said La Fargue.

Privately, he thought, however, that Mère Thérèse de Vaussambre may have been killing two birds with one stone. Of course, by assigning Agnès to the service of Anne d'Autriche, she could keep Agnès away from other sensitive matters. But subsequent events demonstrated that the queen had indeed been facing a grave threat. Had the Superior General got wind of the plot that the Blades had thwarted in the days that followed?

'Be that as it may,' resumed the captain of the Blades, 'Agnès was very speedily admitted into the regular household of Her Majesty. Later, however, at the end of a course of events about which I'm afraid I can say nothing, Agnès received a letter from Mère Emmanuelle. I don't know what the letter said, but Agnès left immediately, escorted by Ballardieu. That was a week ago, and we've had no news of them since.'

'What?' exclaimed d'Aubremont.

'After François, now Agnès and Ballardieu have disappeared. Given the circumstances, I can scarcely believe it is a coincidence.'

In the modest room that he rented on rue Cocatrix, Antoine Leprat, the chevalier d'Orgueil, examined his reflection in the cheval glass that the tailor and his apprentice had left, at Leprat's request, after his last fitting. The tailor had agreed politely, with a smile that failed to mask his unease.

So Leprat had hastened to reassure him:

'You can send someone to fetch your mirror in an hour. I simply want to make sure that no further alterations are needed.'

He was lying.

Leprat was not a vain man, and he had no doubts about the cut or about the quality of the clothes he had ordered: the doublet and breeches suited him perfectly, and the shade of grey the tailor had recommended was both elegant and discreet. But as soon as he was alone, he put on a cape that he kept in a chest. Then, not without some apprehension, he turned towards his own reflection.

It was an old blue cape, with a white cross and silver braiding, which had been carefully washed and pressed. The cape of the King's Musketeers.

Standing gloved and booted in this small room that was already growing quite warm, his famous white rapier at his side, Leprat needed to reassure himself that the musketeer's uniform did not look incongruous upon his shoulders.

Not in his eyes, at least.

For being one of the King's Musketeers was no small thing. Led by the comte de Tréville, the company formed part of the king's military household. They were an elite body of gentlemen, all of whom had proved their quality through some bold action or several years of service in another corps. One did not become a King's Musketeer through favouritism. It was an honour that was earned, and even then, one had to go on proving oneself worthy of wearing the coveted cape.

The chevalier d'Orgueil adjusted his.

Admitted to the Musketeers shortly after his twentieth birthday, he had distinguished himself in their ranks before he was recruited by La Fargue. But then the La Rochelle fiasco occurred, with the death of Bretteville and the inglorious disbanding of the Blades, sacrificed by Cardinal Richelieu on the altar of political expediency. Leprat had returned to the Musketeers and had served five more years there, until La Fargue re-formed the Blades and recalled him. He had accepted out of a sense of duty, but during his latest mission he had been forced to make intolerable moral compromises. And since Tréville had sworn, many times, that the door would always be open for him . . .

Leprat took a deep breath, straightened up and gave his reflection a determined look. After long deliberations he was left with one conviction, one which held no appeal for him: he had lost faith in La Fargue's methods and would never again be a Cardinal's Blade.

La Fargue accompanied the marquis d'Aubremont back to his coach, then watched as the team passed through the carriage gate and turned into the narrow rue Saint-Guillaume.

Saint-Lucq joined him.

'What did you tell him?' asked the half-blood.

'The truth,' replied La Fargue as he walked towards the stable.

Saint-Lucq followed him.

'And?'

'And then I had to dissuade him from appealing directly to the king.'

In the warm dimness of the stable, André was already saddling two horses for them. They waited for him to finish.

'The marquis has a name, a title and a fortune,' said the half-blood, cleaning the red lenses of his spectacles with a handkerchief. 'He is a knight of the Order of Saint-Michel and the king honours him with his trust. Since this concerns his son, why hasn't he appealed to His Majesty before now?'

'Precisely because it concerns his son. The marquis is one of those men who believe that rank does not confer privileges. Asking for aid concerning his son would have been like asking for aid for himself, as a reward for his past services. D'Aubremont has too much nobility for that.'

Saint-Lucq put on his spectacles and observed:

'But it is no longer just a question of his son.'

'Indeed. So now the marquis sees fit to make use of his rank. It's no longer a favour for himself, or for a noble of similar standing, but for another person. A woman, as it happens . . .'

'That is a tribute to his sense of honour. So why convince him to do nothing?'

'Because we aren't certain of anything and I would like to speak with His Eminence first. D'Aubremont will help us as best he can, if we request his assistance.'

André led out the two saddled mounts. La Fargue thanked the groom and mounted up, immediately imitated by Saint-Lucq. In the courtyard, the air was already baking under a high, bright sun. The Saint-Germain abbey bells, in the distance, were ringing half past the hour.

'God's blood, it's hot!' murmured La Fargue, before lightly spurring his horse forward.

The stone was cool in the deep shade.

There was a metallic rattling sound in the heavy lock before the door opened with a creak that sounded like a high-pitched scream in the heavy silence. As it slowly swung wide, torchlight from the corridor illuminated an irregular trapezoid patch that gradually extended across the floor, strewn with old straw, before lapping against the rear wall. Widening further, the light finally reached Agnès, sitting in a corner of the cell. She looked up, a lock of hair falling across her weary face, and squinted painfully in the brightness.

2

The hot weather had endured for too many long days and the brief nocturnal storm that had interrupted it the previous week had brought little respite. Paris was condemned to a prolonged ordeal under the scorching sun. Along with the heat came the smell and the filth. The still air stank, aggravated to the point of nausea by the acrid odour from the cesspits, the piles of manure in the courtyards, and the latrines where a mixture of urine and excrement fermented. And then there was the Parisian muck, a vile mud born of all the rubbish and droppings which proved impossible to remove from the streets of the capital. In the heat it formed a hard crust that crumbled beneath shoes, hooves, and iron-bound wheels, becoming a dust that got everywhere, sticking to damp skin, burning eyes, irritating throats and nostrils, and invading lungs. Even the most hardened individuals suffered sickness and headaches from this pollution, and one could only imagine the damage it did to those with weaker constitutions. Every year during this season, the dust drove the well-to-do out of the city and into the countryside in search of pure air. Today, as La Fargue and Saint-Lucq were crossing the Pont Neuf on their way to the Palais-Cardinal, the king himself was preparing to move his royal court to the Château de Saint-Germain.

But was his purpose solely to flee the foul air of Paris?

Sitting behind the desk in his splendid library, Cardinal Richelieu scratched Petit-Ami's scaly skull with one fingernail. Rolled into a ball on his lap, the scarlet dragonnet sighed happily, its eyelids half-closed, while its master meditated, absently gazing at the documents before him.

There was a knock. Then Charpentier, His Eminence's old and faithful secretary, appeared in the doorway.

'It's La Fargue, monseigneur.'

'Send him in.'

Bowing, Charpentier withdrew at the same time as the Blades' captain, his hat in hand, entered with a firm martial step, stood at attention in front of the desk, and waited, left fist gripping the pommel of his heavy Pappenheimer.

He didn't move when the cardinal rose to put Petit-Ami back in its suspended cage, the dragonnet allowing itself to be shut away with obvious reluctance. Having performed this task, Richelieu did not return to his seat. Instead, turning his back to the room and to his visitor, he looked out of the window for a moment. He had a view of the magnificent gardens and the fountain that were being laid out to the rear of his palace, but his eyes were lost in the distance beyond them.

'Paris is growling,' he said. 'I can hear her. Paris is growling with anger and this heat is not likely to help. But how can we blame her?'

The cardinal fell silent for a moment, then added:

'Paris was attacked by a dragon, captain. In broad daylight, and without our being able to determine why. Furthermore, and worse, it singled out Le Châtelet, one of the symbols of His Majesty's justice and authority. Do you know what people are saying? That before leaving, it circled the Louvre three times, roaring. A final challenge, as if to add insult to injury. It's untrue, of course. But the rumour itself is significant, don't you think?'

The cardinal sat back down at his desk. La Fargue thought he looked more tired than usual, his face gaunt, skin pale and lips dry. And there was a worried gleam in his eyes.

'The people of Paris are angry because they are afraid. And, since that anger has to be directed somewhere, I seem to be their target of choice.' Richelieu smothered a small laugh. 'As far as that goes, I am no more to blame than the poor dragonnets that are being exterminated in the streets . . . But that would be of no account if Parisians were not Parisians – by which I mean, if they were not so prompt to run riot. And these messieurs who sit in Parlement, and claim to speak on behalf of the kingdom, they have no qualms about demanding measures to calm the hotheads down. I have no doubt that the very first of such measures would be to remove me from power. Which is something neither you nor I wish to happen, is it?'

The question was perhaps not entirely rhetorical.

'It is being murmured that the Mother Superior General of the Chatelaines may be soon admitted to the king's Council,' said La Fargue.

Richelieu gave him an inscrutable look, and then invited him to present his business. La Fargue proceeded to explain that he had been without news of Agnès and Ballardieu for several days, that he was growing worried, and that he was asking for permission to investigate the Sisters of Saint Georges.

'Why?' asked the cardinal with a frown.

La Fargue mentioned the other disappearance; that of the chevalier d'Ombreuse, son of the marquis d'Aubremont.

'So, the son of monsieur d'Aubremont is with the Black Guards?' Richelieu interjected.

'Yes, monseigneur.'

'I didn't know that. Continue.'

La Fargue resumed his tale, recounting how Agnès had promised to do her utmost to discover, through her connections with the Chatelaines, what had become of François Reynault d'Ombreuse. This led to the letter from the former Mother Superior General, and the subsequent hurried departure of Agnès and Ballardieu.

'Since then,' he concluded, 'there has been no news.'

'Do you know the content of this letter?'

'No, monseigneur.'

His elbows on the arms of his chair, Richelieu gathered his bony fingers into a steeple before him, and asked in a calm voice:

'What is it that you want from me?'

'First, I am asking Your Eminence to let me search for Agnès de Vaudreuil and Ballardieu.'

'And why should I do that, rather than employ you to learn why a dragon attacked Le Châtelet and killed the Alchemist of the Shadows,' replied the cardinal, betraying a dry sense of irony. 'Or assign you to some secret mission in Lorraine, where the armies of His Majesty are preparing to invade—'

'Monseigneur—'

'And those are merely the first two ideas that spring to my mind, captain.'

'Monseigneur, Almades is dead and the chevalier d'Orgueil has rejoined the King's Musketeers for good. How can I carry out any mission without Agnès and Ballardieu? If it weren't for the timely arrival of Laincourt, I would be forced to rely on just two men!'

'Marciac and Saint-Lucq. There are captains who would give their right arms to have those two . . .'

'Nevertheless, they are only two, monseigneur.'

'Why don't you recruit more?'

'Time presses, monseigneur. And the present circumstances are not propitious.'

'That's true . . . So?'

'So I beseech Your Eminence to persuade the Chatelaines' Mother Superior General to receive me.'

Before replying, the cardinal gave himself a few seconds to think, during which his gaze remained locked with the captain's.

'How are you?' asked Tréville.

'I'm fine, captain.'

'Really? You're fully recovered?'

'Fully recovered, captain. Thank you,' said Leprat.

He was lying.

Although he felt fine at this particular instant he knew he was seriously ill, and so did everyone else, ever since he collapsed at the foot of the grand stairway in the Hôtel de Tréville, with black bile on his lips and his body shaken by terrible convulsions before the eyes of all those – musketeers and gentlemen, valets and servants, traders and petitioners – who had been present that day. He had been immediately attended to and carried to a bed, while the bells of Paris pealed in alarm around him. It had happened on the very day he had come to tell Tréville that he was leaving the Blades to rejoin the Musketeers. And it had been the very same hour when the great black dragon had attacked Le Châtelet.

Leprat had the ranse; the disease believed to be transmitted by the dragons, or brought on by the noxious effects of their magic. Western physicians maintained that good health depended on the balance of four humours that suffused the body's organs: blood, yellow bile, black bile and phlegm. To these four humours, some added a fifth, called obâtre, which was peculiar to the race of dragons. According to this school of thought, the ranse was caused by the abnormal production of obâtre by a human. But this theory mattered little to the unfortunate wretches who suffered from the disease. They knew they were condemned to a slow corruption of their flesh and an irremediable fall from social grace, because death would not release them from their fate until they had been reduced to deformed, pathetic creatures; quivering idiots afflicted by incomprehensible ravings, their bodies twisted and full of ulcers, their eyes crazed, their mouths drooling and muttering as they held out their begging bowl to seek a miserable pittance.

Leprat had resolved to kill himself before that happened. But he had not reached that stage yet. To be sure, the ranse had spread across his back in a scaly violet rash threaded with black veins, which seemed at times to palpitate with a will of its own. And to be sure, he felt less vigorous than he had previously and his wounds took longer to heal. But he had only been infected for two years and could still lead a normal existence, despite the alarming nature of the fit that had so publicly revealed his condition.

A normal life, yes. But the life of a musketeer?

It was precisely this point that worried monsieur de Tréville, without his feeling able to fully acknowledge the fact.

This was the day that Leprat resumed service in the uniform of the Musketeers, and his captain had summoned him to a private interview, as was the custom in such circumstances. The two men were in Tréville's office, on the first floor of his mansion on rue du Vieux-Colombier.

'I can assure you,' said Leprat, 'that I am perfectly fit to perform my tasks, and to do more if necessary.'

Tréville, who felt a deep affection for his musketeers but tolerated no failings where their duties were concerned, gave a sincere smile.

'Fine, fine . . . Let's drink to that, shall we?'

Without waiting for a reply, he filled two glasses from a silver ewer placed on a small table, between the two windows overlooking the courtyard. They clinked, Leprat smiling while maintaining a certain reserve and that severe military posture that was second nature to him. Even without his cape he was clearly an officer. Tall, athletic, with an even gaze and a determined air, he was left-handed and thus wore his white rapier on his right. The rapier which, from pommel to point, had been carved in a single piece from the tooth of a great dragon of high rank.

'I am truly delighted to welcome you back among us,' said Tréville.

'Thank you, captain.'

'You'll see that nothing has changed. D'Artagnan is still my lieutenant. Of course, after you left, the rank of ensign you were expecting went to another man . . .'

'I understand.'

'But there are two ensigns in my company, and although I can't promise you anything the other post may become vacant soon.'

Leprat nodded.

'Good!' exclaimed Tréville, rubbing his hands together. 'If you have any other matters to attend to, do so right away. The king will be leaving soon, for his château at Saint-Germain, and we will accompany him as is proper. We depart the day after tomorrow, fully equipped. Do you have a musket, a horse and a lackey?'

'I am only in need of a lackey.'

'You can borrow one.'

Leprat saluted and Tréville insisted on accompanying him to the door, before taking him by the shoulder and saying:

'Your ranse is still new, I believe.'

'Two years.'

'Then you should know that my doctor, to whom I made enquiries concerning you, thinks that your . . . that your weakness the other day, there, at the foot of the stairs, resulted not so much from the disease as from the combined effects of fatigue and the heat . . . So it may in fact be less serious than it seems . . .'

'Thank you, captain.'

As he descended the grand stairway, Leprat smiled as he thought of the kindness monsieur de Tréville had shown him. But he also knew that he should not have succumbed to the first serious fit of this kind for several more years, and that it had nothing to do with either fatigue or the heat. Several days before this sudden fit had struck he had visited a particularly powerful ritual chamber, where he had suffered an initial malaise. He did not know how or why it had occurred, but he was firmly convinced that the draconic magic which had impregnated that forbidding place had aggravated his disease.

He could lead a normal life, yes. And perhaps even the life of a musketeer.

But only for a few months.

After that, death would come. Leprat very much doubted he would see the next snowfall.

One of the rare amenities offered by the sombre and austere Hôtel de l'Épervier was a garden that had been left in a wild state, with weeds grown tall and brush climbing the walls. A chestnut tree stood in the grounds, providing shade for an old oak table. It was never brought inside, so it looked like driftwood, with bindweed entwined around its cabled legs.

When the weather permitted the Blades liked to assemble around this table, so it was here that La Fargue and Saint-Lucq found Marciac and Laincourt chatting over a jug of cool wine. The captain dropped into a chair with a weary expression, and it creaked ominously beneath him. Without saying a word, Saint-Lucq poured two more glasses and handed one to La Fargue. The latter gave him a glance of thanks, and then sipped gravely.

As Marciac and Laincourt waited expectantly, the half-blood explained:

'We have just returned from the Palais-Cardinal.'

'And?'

'And the cardinal granted my request for an audience with the head of the Chatelaines,' La Fargue announced. 'But he was half-hearted about it, to say the least. Plainly put, he forbids us nothing, but he does not support us in making this enquiry.'

'In spite of your worries concerning Agnès and Ballardieu?'

'In spite of them.'

'Perhaps,' ventured Laincourt, 'the cardinal preferred to entrust you with another mission—'

'There was no question of that,' the Blades' captain interrupted bluntly.

A silence fell beneath the chestnut tree, where the shade was dappled with sunlight filtering through the branches. It was again Cardinal Richelieu's former spy who attempted to reopen the discussion. He did it prudently, however. For although he, like the other Blades, had been given a steel signet ring stamped with a Greek cross whose arms were capped by fleurs-de-lys, he had not worn it for very long.

'Captain,' he said, 'it has only been a few days without news of Agnès and Ballardieu . . .'

'And that's a few days too many,' interjected Marciac in a tone that made it clear that Laincourt was treading on dangerous ground.

'Certainly. But it's also less time than it would take to travel to Lyon and back. Perhaps the cardinal judged that it was too soon to become alarmed. And perhaps we should do the same . . .'

La Fargue directed a calm yet chilling glance at the young man, his expression revealing nothing of his thoughts.

Unperturbed by the growing tension, Saint-Lucq, impassive behind his red spectacles, waited for the conversation to unfold with a mixture of curiosity and amusement. Marciac dreaded the worst, however, and attempted to smooth things over.

'Arnaud,' he said to Laincourt, watching his captain from the corner of his eye, 'you've not known Agnès and Ballardieu as long as we have. Therefore you're not as attached to them as we are. Perhaps if you loved them as we do, you would share our worries.'

To which the young man replied in a steady tone:

'No doubt. But would I be right to be so worried?'

Silence fell once again, until Saint-Lucq finally made a suggestion:

'And what if the cardinal knows what lies behind all this? And what if he does not wish to give us an opportunity to discover it ourselves? Let's not forget that Mère Thérèse de Vaussambre is a relative of his, and that he helped her become the Mother Superior General.'

'No,' replied La Fargue. 'When I laid out the facts for him I mentioned the chevalier d'Ombreuse. From his reaction, I saw that His Eminence had not known that Reynault d'Ombreuse served with the Black Guards. And that is something that the cardinal would have been aware of, had he already been familiar with the affair.'

'What the cardinal knows,' confirmed Laincourt, 'he knows down to the smallest detail . . .'

The captain of the Blades reflected further and finally, reluctantly, admitted:

'Laincourt is right. The cardinal no doubt deemed it was still too soon to go to the Superior General with questions, and to risk incurring her displeasure by suggesting that the Chatelaines had anything to do with the disappearance of two Blades.'

'Well . . . presented in that light . . .' Marciac conceded. 'So when will La Vaussambre receive you?'

'Tomorrow. But I doubt that our interview will be fruitful.'

'Why is that?' asked Laincourt.

'La Vaussambre nurtures some resentment towards me. If

the cardinal supported me in this matter then perhaps I could obtain answers from her. But if we must depend on her good will alone . . .'

The door opened with a creak, and the gaoler holding the torch stayed in the doorway while the other man, always the same one, entered the cell. He was a tall man, strong and heavy, who spoke in a calm, even voice, and with a friendly tone intended to soothe. His gestures were equally gentle and careful, almost affectionate. He was one of those people who seemed to be sincerely kind, and so tended to instil in others a desire to please them in return.

Crouching down near Agnès, he discovered that she had not touched her meal and had drunk only a few drops of water. Yet he knew the stew was good, for he ate the same himself. And the water was cool and clean.

'Madame,' he said in kind reproach, 'you are still not eating. It is an unhappy thing to see you perishing in this fashion . . .'

He shook his head with a disconsolate air.

Seated on the ground in a corner, Agnès pointedly looked away from him. She was pale and thin, filthy from wearing the same clothes she had been captured in, and her long curls of black hair had almost all escaped from the remains of her braid. In her weakened state, her stomach ached and her blue eyes blazed with the sickly, savage glow of hunger. She had steadfastly refused to eat for several days. Partly because she had given in to despair, haunted by the image of Ballardieu falling backwards into thin air. But also because it was one of the few things she could still do, stuck in this cell without light or air.

'It serves no purpose to let yourself die in this manner, madame,' added the gaoler as he gathered up the full bowl and wooden spoon. 'But I will leave you the water.'

Hearing that, Agnès looked daggers at him as if he had insulted her and she kicked over the ewer standing on the floor. She couldn't bear the presence of this man, because of the kindness he showed her. She would have preferred some silent, pitiless custodian, one she could naturally hate, whose throat she could cut at the first opportunity.

And the worst thing was that, as far as circumstances allowed, he was looking after her much as Ballardieu would have done.

In a sorrowful voice, he asked:

'Come now, madame . . . Why do that?'

He did not wait for a reply, but stood up and walked to the door.

Then, in a tone betraying a certain discouragement, he said:

'We won't allow you to die, madame. I may very well receive orders to force you to eat. It would involve soup, a funnel and an oily leather tube. It's . . . It's extremely unpleasant.'

Resolute, Agnès turned her head towards the wall.

With a sigh, he went back into the corridor where his colleague had stood with the torch. He closed the door and turned the key in the lock twice, leaving his prisoner in the dark.

The night passed, and took the brief coolness with it.

The following morning, Paris woke up with the air already warm and a merciless sun blazing a path up to its zenith. A thousand hot stinks rose and, without any wind, remained there to bake all day beneath the vault of the dazzling sky.

Before noon, La Fargue and Laincourt asked André to saddle two horses. They left the faubourg Saint-Germain and crossed the Seine by way of the Pont Neuf, where, despite the heat, the traders, actors and charlatans managed to draw crowds which were almost as numerous as usual. Standing on a stool, a man was distributing pamphlets and haranguing his audience against the cardinal. It was imperative, he claimed, for the king to dismiss Richelieu and place power in the hands of the Sisters of Saint Georges, as they alone knew how to protect the kingdom from the dragons that had already begun their assault on Paris. And the man stretched his hand towards the massive silhouette of Le Châtelet where his audience could just make out, in the distance, the burnt-out remains of the central keep. La Fargue took a pamphlet which he read while continuing to ride. When he finished, he crumpled the paper without uttering a word and threw it away as they arrived at the Mégisserie quay on the Right Bank.

Travelling upstream alongside the river, the two Blades came to Place de Grève, passed in front of the Hôtel de Ville, and by way of the rue des Coquilles and then rue Barre-du-Bec, they entered the rue du Temple which they followed for its full length beneath the burning sun and slowed by the congestion of carriages and foot traffic, encroaching market stalls, deliveries, and the sporadic fights that were all common phenomena in the streets of Paris.

Finally they reached their destination, with dripping backs and damp brows under the brims of their hats. They crossed the drawbridge leading into the Enclos du Temple in silence, entering the former Templar headquarters in the heart of Paris, still surrounded by its crenelated wall, which now belonged to the Order of the Chatelaine Sisters.

Mère Thérèse de Vaussambre received La Fargue in the chapter hall, a vast high-ceilinged room, almost bare but luminous with the light streaming through the arched stained glass windows. A table stretched before the rear wall, covered in heavy white cloths that seemed to merge together and fell to the flagstone floor, beneath a large tapestry depicting Saint Georges in armour and on horseback, slaying the dragon with his spear. There was only one chair at this table, one made of black wood with a narrow seat and a tall back. And upon this chair, at the centre of the table, facing the room and the captain of the Blades as he entered, alone, sat the Mother Superior General of the Sisters of Saint Georges.

The heels of his boots ringing out in a heavy silence, La Fargue advanced with a firm step, bare-headed, his hat in his right hand and his left fist curled around the hilt of his sheathed Pappenheimer. He gave her a dignified salute, and then he waited. The cold setting for this audience failed to daunt him, but it did not augur well for the outcome of their meeting.

'It has been a long time since last we met, monsieur,' declared Mère de Vaussambre in a clear voice.

'It has.'

The Chatelaines' leader might have been forty-five or fifty years in age. Tall and slender, her expressionless face enclosed within the oval of her wimple, she wore the white robe and headdress of her Order. She was sitting very straight, her arms extended before her and slightly apart, her hands placed to either side of a letter whose broken wax seal lay scattered in scarlet pieces across the immaculate tablecloth.

'I was asked to meet with you,' she said without lowering her eyes to the missive sent to her by the cardinal. 'Speak then, I pray.'

This prayer sounded more like an order.

'I have come to request your help, mother superior.'

'My help?'

'I mean to say, the help of the Sisters of Saint Georges.'

'I'm listening.'

'Agnès de Vaudreuil is missing—' the captain of the Blades began.

But he did not finish, as he caught glimpse of the hint of a smile on the nun's harsh, thin lips.

'Do you not find it somewhat ludicrous, monsieur, that you of all people come here, asking none other than me for help, in an affair that concerns the young baronne de Vaudreuil?'

La Fargue remained silent.

'Because was it not you,' insisted Mère de Vaussambre in an even tone, 'who took her away just before she made her vows? If not for you, and if not for your Blades, Marie-Agnès would have taken the veil and today she would be sitting at my right-hand side.'

The old captain wisely chose to hold his tongue. If she continued along these lines, the conversation could only become acrimonious. And displeasing La Vaussambre was the last thing he wanted.

'If not for you,' continued the Superior General, 'Marie-Agnès would have followed her destiny. Do you have any idea of the consequences that her refusal to take her vows had? Do you know what it has cost us? And do you know what it will still cost if she does not come to reason?'

'By come to reason, you mean come to you,' La Fargue could not help himself from saying.

He immediately regretted it, seeing a flash of fury cross Mère de Vaussambre's hitherto icy gaze. But she quickly regained mastery of her emotions, aided by a welcome distraction. Having knocked, a Chatelaine entered by a small door and with muted steps in the deep silence, she slipped between the wall and the long table to whisper a few words into her superior's ear.

La Vaussambre listened before giving a nod.

Having recovered her self-control, she waited until she was alone again with La Fargue, and then said in the most formal of tones:

'So, captain, you find yourself without news of the baronne de Vaudreuil for a short while. Is there any serious reason to be worried by this?'

'I believe so.'

'You *believe*,' stressed the Superior General.

La Fargue clenched his fist around the hilt of his rapier.

'I suppose,' he conceded.

'Ah, now you *suppose*. Soon, you will *imagine* . . .'

And then, locking her eyes on the captain's, Mère de Vaussambre lifted the cardinal's letter from the table and, slowly, deliberately, she tore it in two.

La Fargue returned to the Hôtel de l'Épervier boiling with rage. He swept across the fencing room where Saint-Lucq and Marciac were waiting and vanished into the small office set aside for his personal use. Laincourt came in just as the captain slammed the door shut violently behind him.

'THAT BITCH!' they heard La Fargue yell.

In the large hall furnished with odds and ends, Marciac and Laincourt exchanged a glance, before the first man asked, 'As bad as that?' and the second replied, 'I fear so.' But the young man knew nothing more, as the Blades' captain had seethed with silent anger throughout their return trip. Sitting in profile in the deep recess of a window, Saint-Lucq turned his head towards the garden.

After a moment's hesitation, Marciac drew a deep breath, clapped his hands against his thighs, and then rose from his seat to knock on La Fargue's door.

'What?'

'It's Marciac, captain.'

'Come in.'

The Gascon obeyed.

After spending a while containing his urge to break something, La Fargue had finally removed his hat and hung up his baldric. He fell into his armchair, placed his crossed feet upon his desk, and sat there breathing heavily, his face grim and his fingers drumming an ominous beat upon the elbow rest.

'La Vaussambre made a fool out of me,' he said in a strained voice. The drumbeat abruptly ceased. 'She only received me to show me her contempt and demonstrate my impotence. She knows I can learn nothing from her unless she wants me to and she had no fear of letting me know it. It doesn't matter to her that I serve Cardinal Richelieu. Or the king. Or even if I served the Pope. Nor did it take her long to dismiss me, on the pretext that His Majesty urgently required her at the Louvre.'

'That is quite possibly true,' said Laincourt.

The young man had joined them, standing at the office's threshold while Marciac sat before the desk in the only other chair within the modest room. Saint-Lucq, whose senses were more acute than those of common mortals, could hear everything from his post in the fencing room. He had closed his eyes behind his red spectacles and looked as though he was napping.

'There is talk that Mère de Vaussambre will soon occupy a seat in the Council,' explained Laincourt.

'Truly?' said La Fargue, frowning.

'Nothing has been decided, but—'

'Then the situation is even more serious than I thought.'

'The people are afraid and the Parlement is demanding that

the Chatelaines be brought into government, as they were in the past. Some even believe they should be given the keys to the kingdom, if it would help them rid France of the dragons.'

'Right now,' interjected Marciac, 'I couldn't care less whether La Vaussambre becomes pope or sultan. What did she have to say about Agnès?'

'Nothing,' the captain of the Blades was forced to admit. 'Nor anything about Ballardieu . . . But she knows something, I'm convinced of it.'

In the adjoining room, Saint-Lucq opened his eyes a fraction of a second before Guibot came through the door to the main hall, hobbling on his wooden leg. He carried a letter which he hastened to hand over to the half-blood, who asked in return:

'From whom?'

'From a boy on a mule who just arrived,' replied the concierge. 'He said—'

'The mule spoke?' interrupted Saint-Lucq, without the slightest trace of a smile.

'No, the boy . . .' Flustered by the interruption, Guibot struggled to resume his train of thought. He looked at the half-blood with an astonished and fearful expression, and then stammered: 'He said . . . He said he was the stable boy at the *Reclining Lion* inn.'

'Never heard of it.'

'It's in Trappes.'

Trappes was a village outside Paris, where old Guibot had no doubt never set foot in his life. Saint-Lucq gave him an intrigued glance.

'It's what he told me,' the concierge explained. 'The boy, I mean,' he added, just in case.

The half-blood nodded and abandoned the game.

'Thank you.'

Realising he'd been dismissed, Guibot bowed, but then asked:

'And about the answer?'

'Thank you, Guibot.'

The old man departed, thinking to himself that the boy

759

could wait for a while, or go back to Trappes on his mule, just as he had come. After all, Guibot had other matters to attend to. And so he closed the door with a worried frown, wondering if Saint-Lucq had been jesting when he asked whether or not it was the mule who had spoken.

The letter was simply addressed to: *Hôtel de l'Épervier. Rue Saint-Guillaume. Faubourg Saint-Germain.* Saint-Lucq opened it and raised an eyebrow.

So, Ballardieu was alive.

They arrived covered in dust and drenched in sweat, on horses that were exhausted having kept up a fast trot all the way from Paris. La Fargue was the first to alight from his saddle in the *Reclining Lion*'s courtyard. Marciac, Laincourt and Saint-Lucq immediately did likewise and all of them entered the inn. If the din of their mounts' hooves had drawn the eyes of all those present to the windows, their sudden appearance brought conversation to a halt.

A man of about fifty, with a receding hairline and sagging cheeks, was wearing an apron over his full belly. Who else could he be, but the inn's proprietor?

'My name is La Fargue,' said the Blades' captain, holding up the letter that had arrived an hour earlier at the Hôtel de l'Épervier. 'Where is he?'

With a shaking finger, the innkeeper pointed to the staircase and, more generally, to the floor above where the guestrooms were no doubt located. The four men took the steps two at a time, with a clatter of spurs and a hammering of hobnailed boots that soon resounded across the ceiling. They found Ballardieu sitting in a bed behind the third door they pushed open. His head bandaged and his cheeks hidden by a villainous-looking beard, the old soldier flashed them a smile that erased the traces of fatigue from his rugged face.

They were forced to abbreviate the embraces that Ballardieu was keen to distribute all around. Then, since he was in as fine a shape as could be hoped for, despite a great weariness, a devil of a thirst, and a hunger worthy of Pantagruel himself, La

Fargue made him tell his story as he devoured an omelette, pâté, and ham, all the while emptying bottle after bottle. It was an impressive spectacle, Ballardieu having the appetite of an ogre even under normal circumstances. They finally resorted to driving away the servant girl who was bringing up more and more victuals. Softened by a smile from Laincourt, one look from Saint-Lucq put an end to her visits, and they closed the door to the room much to the regret of the curious onlookers who had crowded behind the innkeeper in the stairwell.

So: Agnès and Ballardieu had left for the abbey at Mont-Saint-Michel, acting upon a letter received from Mère de Cernay, the former Mother Superior General of the Sisters of Saint Georges. The young baronne de Vaudreuil was hoping to uncover information about a secret expedition to Alsace; the expedition that had included François Reynault d'Ombreuse, a lieutenant in the Black Guards and the missing son of the marquis d'Aubremont.

'Reynault stopped sending his father news when he embarked on this mysterious journey,' Ballardieu declared between mouthfuls.

'And this worried his father greatly,' said La Fargue. 'Especially when the Chatelaines refused to give him any explanation. Do you know who Agnès was going to meet at Mont-Saint-Michel?

'A Chatelaine she knew from her novitiate.'

'Her name?'

The old soldier thought for a moment, but then admitted:

'No, I've forgotten it.'

'Never mind. Continue.'

They had used the cover of night to carry out their operation. While Agnès secretly entered the abbey with help from an accomplice, Ballardieu had remained at the foot of the mount, in the bay, guarding their horses. But he had grown worried and finally climbed the same stairs the young woman had taken and had entered the abbey in turn.

'That was when the alarm was sounded.'

'Through your fault?' asked Marciac.

'No! But I quickly realised that the girl was in trouble.'

Ballardieu did not recount how he had deliberately diverted Agnès' pursuers towards himself, but rather jumped forward to the moment when he took a musket ball to the shoulder and had fallen into the void.

'I hope that Agnès did not witness it,' he said in a desolate tone. 'Or she will believe me dead, poor thing.'

'So you don't know what has become of Agnès?' commented La Fargue.

'Not for sure. But I believe she is being held prisoner in the abbey.' And seeing the worried glances being exchanged by his audience, he understood and protested, 'Hey now! None of that! Agnès is still alive! I would know if something had happened to her . . .'

'How?' Laincourt asked.

'I . . . would . . . know,' replied the old soldier, carefully articulating each word with a stubborn air.

'Very well,' intervened the Blades' captain. 'Let us assume that Agnès is alive and is being held prisoner at Mont-Saint-Michel. Now you, Ballardieu, what happened to you next?'

He took a great gulp of wine.

'Well, I can assure you that this abbey is very high, indeed. You simply don't realise how high it really is, until you topple over its walls.'

His fall had been painfully broken by the branches of the trees covering the north side of the mount. It was largely thanks to his bull-like constitution, and also, perhaps, to the proverbial luck of drunkards, that he did not suffer any broken bones. Nevertheless, his head had taken a brutal blow from landing on a stone. So, dazed and staggering, but also fearful that his adversaries would come after him to make sure he was truly dead, Ballardieu had continued his flight down the steep and rocky slope, braking himself against tree trunks with an unsteady hand, seizing hold of low branches, often stumbling and sometimes falling, but always rising again. Finally, he had emerged from the foliage and stepped out on the sandy bed of the bay.

'My head was spinning and my vision was blurred. But I

knew the sun had risen and that time was of essence. So I walked towards the mainland shore. Which was not an excellent idea.'

He had forgotten about the great tides. The sea water rushing back into the bay had caught up with him and the waves had first battered at his calves, and then around his waist, before overcoming his last remaining strength. Swept off his feet, he'd lost all consciousness.

'I was sure I was going to drown. But my hour had not yet struck and I was washed up on a beach, where I eventually came to my senses.'

As for what followed, Ballardieu had only scattered memories. Befuddled and almost delirious, his ears buzzing and the ground pitching beneath his leaden feet, he walked on, crushed by a terrible sun that blinded him, without any idea of where he was heading. How long did he wander?

He collapsed, only to wake in a bed.

'Some peasants found me in a ditch and brought me to their village priest. Their holy man bandaged my wounds and watched over me until I came round. I was weak and famished, but I was saved.'

Alone, he could do nothing for Agnès. Therefore he'd needed to return to Paris as quickly as possible, and without waiting to fully recover, he took to the road on the back of an old mule that the priest had kindly loaned him against the promise of future payment. For Ballardieu had lost everything during his escape: his weapons, his purse, and even his boots.

'As for my boots,' he commented, 'I do wonder if they are being worn at present by one of the peasants who carried me to the priest. But I suppose, as the saying goes, every deed deserves its reward.'

Since he had not spared it, the poor old mule had died near Trappes after an exhausting four-day journey, which Ballardieu endured on an almost empty stomach.

'And here I am. You can guess the rest . . . Now pray tell, where is that sad fellow, Almades? Did you leave him behind in Paris? And what of Leprat?

*

The Blades were soon on the road back to Paris, riding at a slow trot beneath a blazing sun. Ballardieu was on a rented horse. They remained silent, out of respect for the old soldier who had barely been able to contain his tears when he heard of Almades' death under such terrible circumstances.

'A dragon,' he muttered from time to time, with a mixture of grief and disbelief. 'Burnt alive by a dragon . . .'

At last, when they passed by the first houses in the faubourg Saint-Germain, Laincourt asked him:

'Why didn't you write to us earlier? A letter would have reached us faster than you would have . . .'

'But I did!'

'We never received anything,' La Fargue said over his shoulder.

'My first letter must have been lost . . .'

'Or else it will arrive eventually. No matter, now.'

Ballardieu urged his horse forward to draw level with La Fargue.

'We must rescue Agnès, captain. And when that's done, we must avenge Almades.'

'Believe me, Ballardieu, I will not rest until Agnès is free. But Mère de Vaussambre is hostile to us and I don't imagine we can take Mont-Saint-Michel by force.'

They were riding up rue du Cherche-Midi at a walk, towards Place de la Croix-Rouge.

'And Richelieu?' insisted Ballardieu.

'We can expect no help at all from the cardinal,' admitted La Fargue.

'What about Mère de Cernay! She feels affection for Agnès and has no fondness in her heart for La Vaussambre. Surely she will help us? She already has!'

'Do you know where to find her?'

The old soldier's expression clouded over.

'No,' he confessed. 'Only know that she cannot reside far from Paris. Agnès was not long in returning, last time she went to find her.'

'But it's simply not possible to go knocking on the doors of every convent, retreat and domain the Chatelaines possess in the region,' Marciac pointed out.

'It would take us more than a week,' said Saint-Lucq.

'And to what result, other than alarming La Vaussambre?' the Gascon added regretfully.

Upon hearing those words, a glow suddenly kindled in La Fargue's eyes.

The Gaget Messenger Service was located in rue de Gaillon, at the corner with rue des Moineaux, not far from the Saint-Roch hill and its picturesque windmills. The owner had been exercising his trade with a royal licence for several years now and was the sole agent authorised to employ trained dragonnets to carry letters to Reims or Rouen, Amiens or Orléans, and even as far as Lille, Rennes, or Dijon. The services his company provided were more expensive, but also quicker and more reliable, than ordinary post and couriers.

That evening, Urbain Gaget had a satisfied air as he stood in the shadow of the circular tower which, pierced with rows of half-moon openings, housed his carrier dragonnets. Slim and grey-haired, he was a fairly handsome man dressed in bourgeois fashion. Oblivious to the activity going on in his courtyard, he was observing the five wyverns he had recently acquired. Thanks to them he was about to expand the scope of his operations. To be sure, his business was flourishing and would continue to do so as long as he retained the royal licence protecting his monopoly, a privilege that he owed to the confidence Cardinal Richelieu had placed in him. But ministers came and went, and kings died. Moreover, Gaget was an entrepreneur at heart and his messenger business was starting to bore him, now that it had become prosperous. It was time to take on a new challenge.

Having given his instructions to the great reptiles' handlers, Gaget returned to his office, leaving word that he was not to be disturbed. But he had barely shut the door when a voice made him turn round with a start.

'Those wyverns, what are they for?' asked Saint-Lucq.

The half-blood was leaning against a wall, with his arms crossed, in a shadowy corner.

Recognising him, Gaget let out a sigh, and in a reproachful tone said:

'Good Lord! Why must you always slip in here like this? One day, you'll be the death of me!'

'I don't like knocking on doors. And do you really want people to see me knocking on yours?'

'No . . . No, of course not,' Gaget admitted grudgingly.

He sat down.

'So? What are they for, the wyverns?' insisted Saint-Lucq. 'They're new.'

'Well, since there are travellers who rent horses . . .'

The half-blood nodded: he already understood.

'But almost everyone knows how to ride a horse,' he objected. 'And even if they don't know, they can still hope that if they fall off they won't injure themselves too badly. Whereas if they find themselves on the back of a wyvern . . .'

'My beasts are the most placid to be found. They can also carry two, with my wyverneers guiding.'

'When will you start?'

'Soon. It's all in place.'

'That's good to know.'

Gaget preferred not to respond to this.

The royal licence that had made his fortune had come with certain strings attached, Richelieu having quickly seen how to make best use of this dragonnet messenger service. It sometimes involved transporting documents as a matter of urgency and with no questions asked. Or else arranging for certain items to make a quick detour by way of the Palais-Cardinal before being delivered to their final destination. Or receiving these visits from Saint-Lucq who, as he had continued to serve His Eminence after the disbanding of the Blades, had been discreetly coming here to pick up his orders.

Gaget had no doubt that sooner or later his rental wyverns would also be required to make a contribution. But he did not have leisure to dwell on this thought, as Saint-Lucq was asking him:

'How much to carry a message?'

'That depends. Where does it need to be delivered?'

'In the area around Paris.'

'The area around Paris? That's not a proper destination!'

'To be honest, there are several destinations, all of which I have listed here.'

Monsieur Urbain Gaget's eyes widened as they ran down the list that the half-blood unfolded under his nose.

'Really?' he asked, incredulous.

'Really.'

'As you wish. But my dragonnets will only travel at night. There have been too many imbeciles using them for target practice, of late.'

Gaget's first dragonnets took flight just after dusk, and numerous others followed until well after midnight. All of them reached their destinations and the next morning, in the Enclos du Temple, the comte d'Orsan requested an audience with the Chatelaines' Mother Superior General. Slender, with fine features and dark eyes, he wore the black uniform and breastplate of the company of the Saint Georges Guards, of which he was the captain at the age of thirty years. Mère de Vaussambre bade him enter immediately and was handed an unsealed letter that was not addressed to her and whose contents she read with a frown.

'Well?' she asked, raising her eyes to meet his.

'Other letters, identical to this one, were sent last night to all our convents, fiefdoms and domains throughout Ile-de-France.

The Mother Superior General read the letter a second time:

To mother superior de Cernay,
Agnès is being held prisoner at Mt-St-Michel. Help us if you can.
La F.

'Captain La Fargue must be desperate to resort to such a manoeuvre,' she observed with a half-smile. 'It's not his style . . . It's disappointing, even.'

'It's a manoeuvre which might meet with a certain degree of success, mother superior.'

'Do you think so?' Mère Thérèse de Vaussambre asked in amusement. 'Let us suppose that one of these letters actually reaches Mère de Cernay. Or that the content is simply reported to her . . . What then? What can she do? Nothing. Absolutely nothing.'

'Mother superior de Cernay still exerts a certain influence.'

'But does she have the ear of the king, as I do? Does the Parlement wish to see her seated on the Council?'

D'Orsan made a bow in her direction.

'Certainly not, mother superior . . .'

Thoughtful for a moment, La Vaussambre toyed distractedly with the unsealed letter.

'There is one aspect of this message, however, that does bother me,' she said.

'And that is?'

'La Fargue knows that we are holding Marie-Agnès. He even knows where. That is a new development which is cause for concern. Who could have told him? And what will he do when this ridiculous appeal to Mère de Cernay leads him nowhere?'

Seeing that Mère de Vaussambre was still pondering the question, the captain of the Black Guards remained silent.

'Transfer Marie-Agnès,' she ordered. 'As soon and as quickly as possible. This message is not meant for Mère de Cernay, but for me. La Fargue knows that one of his letters would reach me. He wants me to lower my guard. He wants me to believe he is reduced to placing his faith in such a foolish enterprise. But our dear captain is not one to lose his head and shoot his musket into the dark. Rest assured that at this very moment he is up to something clever. Perhaps he is even planning Marie-Agnès' escape. Now that would be much more his style . . .'

'Would he dare?'

'Oh yes. Knowing the man as I do, I think he might even succeed.'

'So where do you want us to take the baronne de Vaudreuil?'

'The Tour seems to me an appropriate place for her, from now on.'

D'Orsan hesitated a brief instant, but then bowed his head.

'As you command.'

Once she was alone, the Chatelaines' Mother Superior General went to the window, still thinking about La Fargue. She wondered what coup the old warhorse was preparing against her, thinking that he had outwitted her and regained the initiative.

She smiled.

Upon his arrival in rue des Francs-Bourgeois, Captain La Fargue found the d'Aubremont household in the midst of preparations to move. The custom was to travel with one's furnishings and, as the royal court would soon be leaving Paris, the master of the house was making ready to return to his country estate. This estate was not far from the Château de Saint-Germain, where the king retired for the season every year, away from the polluted atmosphere of the capital.

The marquis d'Aubremont received La Fargue in his private office, a pleasantly decorated room whose two windows with their small diamond-shaped panes looked out on the garden. The light shone through them, cut into crystalline patterns.

The two men exchanged a friendly handshake, before the marquis offered the captain a seat. He refused it.

'I can't stay,' he said.

D'Aubremont frowned.

'Does it have to do with our affair?'

'Yes. And more particularly, it concerns Agnès.'

'The baronne de Vaudreuil? Have you learned what has become of her?'

'We're almost certain that we know.'

La Fargue hesitated, looked towards the closed door, took hold of the marquis' elbow to draw him away from it, and said in a low voice:

'We think that Agnès is being held prisoner by the Sisters of Saint Georges, on the orders of Mère de Vaussambre. No doubt Agnès has discovered some secret. An important secret which the Chatelaines do not want revealed, and that somehow concerns your son . . . Be that as it may, Agnès lives and must be rescued.'

'I promised you my help, Étienne. The offer still stands.'

'That is precisely why I've come. Only a few days ago, I dissuaded you from using your rank to appeal to the king, did I not?'

'Yes, indeed. You convinced me to abandon the idea.'

'I was wrong.'

A short time later, upon leaving the Hôtel d'Aubremont, La Fargue met Saint-Lucq who was waiting for him in the shade of a porch. The half-blood was returning from the Temple neighbourhood, or the neighbourhood of the Chatelaines, as it was known.

'Well?' he asked.

'The marquis will help us,' La Fargue informed him. 'And on your side of things?'

'I've found a way.'

As the afternoon came to an end, Laincourt joined Marciac and Ballardieu at the Hôtel de l'Épervier. They were sitting in the shade beneath the chestnut tree, neither saying much. His hands clasped at the back of his neck, the Gascon was stretched out on the narrow bench, eyes closed, with a blade of grass in his mouth. As for Ballardieu, he was sprawled as much as one can be in a chair without falling out of it, with one arm passed over the back and one boot resting on a stool. He was getting slowly drunk on white wine. Three stoneware jugs were lying on the old bleached table, and Ballardieu was drinking from the mouth of a fourth while gazing moodily at some faraway point before him.

'Are you feeling all right?' Laincourt asked as he sat down.

The old soldier's features became animated.

'Yes, thank you.'

'I'm glad to hear it.'

'Oh, you needn't worry about me. I'm one of those people who are as right as rain after a good night's sleep.'

The truth was he was looking relatively well, with his beard now clean and trimmed, his eyes lively and his smile broad and sincere. And he still gave off an impression of strength and solidity.

'So,' he went on to say, 'it seems you're one of us, now.'

Laincourt lowered his eyes to the steel signet ring on his finger and said:

'So it seems . . .'

'I'm glad to hear it. And not simply because our ranks are thinning.'

'Thank you.'

'Almades' death. Leprat's departure . . . Do we even know why he left us?'

Laincourt shrugged.

'He's gone back to the Musketeers,' announced Marciac, still lying on the bench with his eyes closed.

'That's not a good enough reason,' objected Ballardieu.

'He's sick with the ranse.'

'All the same. Besides, if the ranse doesn't stop him serving with the Musketeers . . .'

The Gascon had no counter to this argument, so the three men fell into silence. Until Marciac declared:

'I wish that Agnès were here.'

His two companions exchanged intrigued glances.

'Obviously. As do we all,' grumbled Ballardieu, his anxiety stirring again.

'I wish that Agnès were here,' continued Marciac, 'so I could tell her how much I miss Gabrielle. Have I told you about Gabrielle, Laincourt?'

Ballardieu rolled his eyes skywards.

The beautiful Gabrielle ran a brothel in rue Grenouillère. She was Marciac's one and only true love, despite his numerous other amorous adventures.

'I believe,' replied Laincourt, 'that your female conquests

must be the only people who do not hear you talk about your mistress.'

Ballardieu was unable to restrain an amused hiccup.

Marciac rose up on an elbow and turning to the young man, enquired:

'Are you mocking me?'

'A little, yes.'

The Gascon appeared to weigh up the pros and cons, the pertinence of the mockery and its humour. And, being a good sport, he stretched out again on his back and asked:

'Have we received so much as a single reply to all those messages that emptied our war chest?'

'No word, I believe, has yet come back from the Gaget Messenger Service. And Saint-Lucq, who could best answer you on this point, seems to have disappeared.'

'You'll have to get used to the sudden and mysterious absences of our dear Saint-Lucq. That's his style . . . But sending all those letters out like bottles tossed into the sea, they're not La Fargue's usual style. It's a positively clumsy effort on his part.'

'What else could we do? We cannot attempt to free Agnès by force. Even if we succeeded, Mère de Vaussambre would complain to the king and have us arrested. And I doubt the cardinal would come to our defence, when he has forbidden us from incurring the Chatelaines' displeasure . . . Moreover, even if this is a point of law that might be disputed, it's possible that the baronne de Vaudreuil—'

'You might as well call her Agnès.'

'—it's possible that Agnès is being held for entirely legitimate reasons.'

'Pardon?' Ballardieu exclaimed.

'The Sisters of Saint Georges have the right to administer high, middle and low justice within their fiefdoms and domains,' Laincourt reminded him. 'This affair falls under their jurisdiction, before which . . . before which Agnès would have to answer several accusations.'

'Would you by any chance be a man of law?' the old soldier asked in a suspicious tone.

Lawyers suffered from a bad reputation. They were viewed as masters at splitting hairs to prolong legal proceedings and multiply the number of documents required in order to earn as much money as possible from their clients. And their reputation was, by and large, well deserved.

'I almost became one . . . But the case remains: if we act openly against the Sisters of Saint Georges, we will be dragged before their courts of justice, not those of the king.'

'Nevertheless,' decreed Marciac, 'these letters will achieve nothing other than alarming La Vaussambre.'

'Perhaps that was their purpose . . .'

'One rarely gains anything by kicking an anthill.'

'Except for ants up the breeches,' declared Ballardieu who, at the mere thought, suddenly discovered an itch in an awkward place.

La Fargue's arrival interrupted these serious deliberations.

Straddling a chair turned back to front, the captain accepted the jug that Ballardieu offered him and emptied it in three gulps. Then he wiped his mouth on the back of his sleeve, smoothed his closely trimmed beard and, for a few seconds, looked gravely at the three men who all waited expectantly for him to speak.

'I have a plan,' he said at last. 'But you will need to trust me.'

'For your eyes, madame,' he said in his gentle voice. 'It's only for your eyes.'

The two gaolers had behaved in their usual manner, the one holding the torch remaining at the door while the other entered the cell. This time, however, they did not bring her a meal. So Agnès had recoiled when the man had leaned over her.

'For your eyes, madame. It's only for your eyes.'

Despite her weakened state, she had stiffened. But she had allowed the gaoler to tie a blindfold over her eyes. He had helped her to stand and guided her out of the cell, then through a series of corridors, stairways, and doors that she could not see.

She finally understood when she emerged into the open air, and full sunlight, on a high terrace within the abbey of Mont-Saint-Michel. The cloth was thin. She could almost see right through it, in the hot, dazzling clarity of a glorious day. The blindfold was intended to prevent the light from hurting her eyes, after the long period she had spent in darkness.

'Thank you,' she murmured to the gaoler.

She immediately regretted those two words that managed to pass through the barriers of her lips and her resistance.

'Goodbye, madame.'

Other hands seized her, hands that were more brutal, belonging to a soldier. Her wrists were tied together before her. Forced to advance, she had to struggle against an instinctive urge to turn back in distress to her gaoler, who – she imagined – was watching her move away, like a helpless and miserable lover observing the departure of his beloved. She regained her self-control, guessing that the men leading her away were Black Guards. But where were they taking her? And why?

She heard the wyverns before she could make out their silhouettes. The winged reptiles waited peacefully. She was put on the back of one of them, occupying the second seat of a double saddle. She knew that these saddles had leather handles for the passenger and, having found them by fumbling blindly before her, she gripped them firmly while her feet were placed in the stirrups. A man mounted in front of her and took up the reins.

'Hold on tight,' he said.

And then the wyvern was flying.

After enduring the deep and stifling darkness of her cell, Agnès at first abandoned herself to a kind of happy exhilaration as they moved through the air, rocked by the slow beats of the wyvern's wings. Then the time started to seem unexpectedly long and, prompted by curiosity, she lifted the blindfold to her brow. The guard who was directing their wyvern saw as much when he glanced over his shoulder, but said nothing. She thought about trying something against him, but finally rejected the idea. The man wasn't armed, but there were three other wyverns escorting them, all of them ridden by members of the Black Guards with swords at their sides, and more importantly, a pair of pistols apiece in their saddle holsters.

So Agnès bided her time and lost herself in contemplation of the landscape beneath them. They were proceeding westward.

Perhaps towards Paris.

They flew until evening, when they landed in the courtyard of a large fortified abbey belonging to the Chatelaines. Although she was kept under constant watch, Agnès was allowed to wash, change her clothing, and eat. She did not refuse the meal offered to her, aware that her situation was changing and that she might soon need her strength. She forced herself not to devour her food too quickly and was careful to water her wine, out of a fear of making herself sick. No one said a word to her and she asked no questions even though there were some that were burning her lips.

The following morning, after a good night's sleep in a real bed and another light meal eaten in the deserted refectory, Agnès once again had her wrists bound and was forced to climb into a heavy wagon that resembled a large strongbox. It was in fact exactly that: a solid box made of sturdy oak covered in iron plating and mounted on wheels, used for transporting valuables. It was entered from the rear, after bending double to pass through a reinforced door equipped with two locks and a small sliding hatch. Inside, there was an iron chest riveted to the floor against the rear wall.

Agnès sat on the chest, her back to the direction of travel and facing the door that was closed upon her, plunging her into darkness. She heard keys being turned in each lock, then saw the hatch open and remain so, no doubt to allow some air and light to enter. Then the driver's whip cracked and the wagon set into motion, escorted by five guards on horseback.

A short while later, the convoy was advancing along a dusty road at a fast trot, in the harsh light of an already scorching sun.

Antoine Leprat, the chevalier d'Orgueil, was having lunch alone in a modest inn near the Hôtel de Tréville, in rue du

Pot-de-Fer. Some birds – whose fat fell in yellow drops – were cooking on a spit in the fireplace, while various soups and stews simmered beneath the lids of small black pots arranged along its outer edge. There were several tables standing before the hearth. Two rather elderly sisters, both widows, ran the establishment, cooking and serving the dishes. The atmosphere was quiet and cosy, and the clientele was mostly composed of regulars. The wine cellar was mediocre but the food was rather good. The light, as well as the noise from outside, was heavily filtered.

'May I sit down?'

Leprat lifted his nose from his plate to discover, to his pleasure, a gentleman of some forty years of age, whose handsome appearance and calm bearing indicated – without any possibility of error – that this was a great nobleman. Yet no one knew his true name, only the *nom de guerre* under which he wore the blue cape of the King's Musketeers.

'Athos!' Leprat exclaimed joyfully as he rose.

They exchanged a warm handshake and sat down facing one another.

'It's . . . quiet in here,' said Athos, taking in the humble nature of their surroundings with a steady gaze.

Leprat smiled.

'There are more charming places in Paris, and even in the faubourg Saint-Germain itself, I grant you that. But as you said, it's quiet here . . . So how did you know where to find me? I only ever come here on my own.'

Rather than reply, Athos waited for the chevalier to guess, with a faint smile on his lips, and it did not take Leprat long.

'D'Artagnan,' he concluded.

'What can I say? He may have become a lieutenant, but d'Artagnan has not changed. And he's always been intensely curious. He has to know everything. Secrets have the same effect on him as those red capes the Spaniards – one can only wonder why – like to wave in front of bulls. And you can be sure that when he saw you slipping away at noon and in the evenings, that Gascon devil couldn't resist the temptation to follow you. You must not hold it against him.'

'I don't hold it against him; besides, my habit of coming here is no great secret.'

A second glass and a new jug of cool wine were brought to the table. However, it was not one of the two sisters who served them, but Grimaud, Athos' lackey, who had been trained by the musketeer to express himself solely by means of signs and monosyllables . . . and to anticipate his master's desires.

The silent, zealous and discreet domestic then went to wait, well away from the table.

'Your habit of coming here is no great secret,' Athos said. 'But it is no mystery, either, to anyone familiar with His Majesty's Musketeers . . . You've been given the cold shoulder since your return, haven't you?'

Leprat looked at the other man, noting that he had only just returned from several days' leave of absence and already seemed to know everything. Again, no doubt from d'Artagnan. Nevertheless, the information was accurate: the company had not extended a particularly warm welcome to the chevalier d'Orgueil, despite a few brave demonstrations of friendship, and despite the trust that Tréville had clearly manifested in welcoming him back.

'I have the ranse, Athos. What else could I expect?'

'Obviously, the illness from which you suffer does not help your case. And some will now portray you as a monster they prefer to despise rather than fear. Even today, there are many who consider the ranse to be a mark of infamy. That's just how things are. You'll have to make the best of it or become a hermit . . .'

Athos had spoken in a kind, firm, steady voice, looking straight into Leprat's eyes, as if he were a doctor announcing an irrefutable and terrible diagnosis to a patient, putting aside his feelings in order to expose matters plainly, although not without compassion.

But he had not finished.

'Nevertheless, your ranse is not the main cause of your current unpopularity.' Leprat gave him a puzzled look, until the other man explained. 'Do you realise that lately you've had a tendency to don and then remove your cape? Now, most of the King's Musketeers do not care about your disease, but they cannot abide someone who rejoins their ranks by default.'

'But I haven't—' Leprat started to protest.

Athos cut him short by lifting a hand in a sign of appeasement.

'I know that. But, nonetheless, that is the impression you give. So, follow my advice and be patient. Show them that you are a musketeer and have no intention of renouncing your commission any time soon. I take it you are decided on this point?'

'I am.'

'And are you really through with the company of monsieur de La Fargue?'

'Yes.'

'Well then. Wear the musketeer's cape proudly and serve faithfully. Time will not heal your disease, but it will let you demonstrate your loyalty. And above all else, avoid getting into any quarrels that certain people may try to pick with you.'

Leprat met Athos' gaze and realised the gentleman had not given him this last piece of advice by chance.

The armoured wagon carrying Agnès arrived in Paris at the end of the afternoon.

Still surrounded by the mounted escort of Black Guards, it passed through the Temple city gate, followed the street bearing the same name, and turned left to cross the drawbridge that straddled the last vestiges of a moat around the Enclos du Temple, the Chatelaines' headquarters. It advanced a little further and finally drew up before the lofty Tour du Temple.

Removed from the darkness and the stifling heat of the sealed wagon, Agnès, with her wrists still bound, staggered slightly as she set foot on the ground. But the baronne de Vaudreuil's pride immediately gained the upper hand and, with a brusque shrug of her shoulders, she freed herself from the hands that intended to support her. Squinting painfully in the bright light, she lifted her eyes to gaze upon the tower that

778

was to be her new prison. This massive keep was one of the most secure places in the capital; so secure, in fact, that the kings of France had once deposited their treasure there. Agnès wondered if she should feel flattered to be locked up within it now.

The guards urged her forward.

Not knowing whether she would see the sun again, Agnès took in her surroundings as far as she could, gazing towards the houses neighbouring the Enclos, beyond the gardens and the crenelated wall. Some slaters were repairing the roof of one house, and a worker, no doubt intrigued by the strange-looking wagon that had just arrived, was looking in their direction. Standing, he removed his hat and wiped his brow with a red handkerchief before returning to his labour.

It was Ballardieu.

3

It was the last evening before his departure for Saint-Germain and the king wanted to spend it with the queen, along with some gentlemen from his suite. The royal couple's apartments adjoined one another on the first floor of the Louvre. Louis XIII's quarters occupied the aptly-named Pavillon du Roi, while Anne d'Autriche's were located in the southern wing of the palace; the wing overlooking the Seine. They were separated by a single door. Yet the king's visits were rare. Did this visit mean that His Majesty desired a rapprochement with his long-neglected spouse? There were those who wanted to believe it, and even some who started to dream of an heir to the French throne.

What drew particular comment, however, was the presence of Mère Thérèse de Vaussambre that evening, the Mother Superior General of the Sisters of Saint Georges. To be sure, it was not the first time that Anne d'Autriche and Mère de Vaussambre had met. But previously they had simply come into contact with each other during official ceremonies, where they were both constrained and protected by the rules of protocol. They had never exchanged more than three words unless they were obliged to and, until now, La Vaussambre had never even crossed the threshold of the queen's ante-chamber. It was common knowledge that Anne detested the Chatelaines to the point that she kept them all at a distance, even the sisters charged with her protection. This hatred had sprung from the horrid examinations the Sisters of Saint Georges had subjected her to when, newly wed, she had joined her husband in France. She had been fourteen years old at the time.

Anne d'Autriche owed her name to her mother, Marguerite d'Autriche-Styrie, the archduchess of Austria and the princess of Styria. But she was also a Spanish *infanta*, born with the name Ana Maria Mauricia, daughter of King Felipe III of Spain. And Spain was known to be particularly susceptible to the dragons' influence. So much so that, in Spain, they did not hide their true nature and some of them were even part of the high aristocracy, occupying eminent positions within the Spanish state. So it had been necessary to ensure that the future queen of France was free of all contagion, the ranse being the very least of the possible dangers that the Chatelaines dreaded. Hence the rituals they had employed to examine, throughout an entire night, the body and soul of a terrified and humiliated adolescent girl who never would forget the ordeal.

On this evening in July 1633, however, the queen made a special effort to welcome Mère de Vaussambre, which pleased the king. Only a very few knew she was paying for a mistake which, even now, remained the deepest of secrets: fearing she was sterile, Anne had turned to magic for a cure and had fallen under the spell of one of the Black Claw, a secret society of malevolent dragons. Nothing of the affair had been divulged, the main protagonists being either dead or constrained to silence . . . hence the astonishment amongst those who saw Anne d'Autriche holding out her hand to the Mother Superior General and addressing her in a kindly fashion, even if her words had clearly been rehearsed. Much repeated and discussed afterwards, these words and smiles did not fool many people. But the words were not important: the key point lay in the queen demonstrating her submission to Louis XIII, who did not linger long thereafter.

As for Mère de Vaussambre and the Chatelaines, they had won an astonishing victory.

La Fargue waited for dusk before going to the Louvre. He and Ballardieu kept their horses to a walk as they crossed the Pont Neuf and then followed the École quay, before turning into the narrow rue d'Autriche. The captain did not utter a word throughout the journey. He was worried, but still maintained the calm of a great general on the eve of battle, aware that what was about to play out – or was, perhaps, already being played out – no longer depended on him.

To be sure, the messages carried by monsieur Gaget's dragonnets had produced the desired effect: making Mère de Vaussambre bring Agnès to her headquarters in Paris. Meanwhile, the marquis d'Aubremont had agreed to provoke a major confrontation, even if it meant losing some of the king's esteem. But for the rest, La Fargue was forced to rely on the talents of his Blades, on the pride of La Vaussambre, and on luck. His plan was risky. He knew it and had not hidden the fact from anyone. Nevertheless, he felt responsible.

And rightly so.

For if this went wrong, then although he himself would not be spared, others would be the first to pay the price.

Night was falling as they landed nimbly at the foot of the wall. Saint-Lucq went first, followed by Laincourt and Marciac, the latter coiling the rope and hooking the grapple onto his belt after they had climbed the high crenelated barrier. They were in the main garden of the Enclos du Temple. With a gloved finger, the half-blood pointed to the three sentries who were patrolling the grounds, muskets on their shoulders, then indicated the door set in the inner wall, which they needed to pass to reach the Grande Tour. Laincourt and Marciac nodded.

Thanks to his dragon eyes, Saint-Lucq could see better than the others in the dark. He went first. Bent over, they reached the door in long silent strides, hugging first the outer wall, then the inner one. They huddled for a moment behind a hedge, holding their breath, but the sentry passed without spotting them, his regular steps gradually moving away from them. The door was locked, as they had anticipated, so while Saint-Lucq kept watch, Laincourt brought forth some fine tools in a leather case and, with Marciac looking on in admiration, he proceeded to attack the lock. It soon gave way. The three passed through and hurriedly shut the door behind them: another guard was approaching.

The Grande Tour du Temple was a solid square keep, flanked by round turrets at each corner, and measuring fifty metres tall. The structure was capped by a pyramidal roof surrounded by a terrace walkway. More slender and lower in height, a secondary building – the Petite Tour – was attached to the northern façade. To enter the Grande Tour it was first necessary to cross the ground floor of the Petite, where two members of the Black Guards were standing watch by the door.

The guards were quite astonished to see Marciac coming towards them, and especially to see him smiling as if it were the most natural thing in the world. This momentary distraction sufficed, before both guards felt the barrel of a pistol pressed to their temples, one to the right and the other to the left. As Saint-Lucq and Laincourt held them at gunpoint the Gascon disarmed them, throwing their swords and muskets aside, but keeping their pistols.

'If you call out, who will answer?'

'The porter.'

'Then call him.'

The man shook his head.

'Please,' Marciac insisted, jamming the barrel of the guard's own pistol into the man's nostril, to painful effect.

Standing on tiptoe, the guard rapped three times on the door.

After few seconds, someone asked:

'What is it?'

'It's me,' replied the guard. 'Louvet. Open up.'

'But—'

'Open up!'

The door opened a fraction and Marciac forced his way through, quickly subduing the porter while Saint-Luc and Marciac followed, shoving the two guards before them. The ground floor of the Petite Tour was dark and silent. Frightened, the porter was eager to tell them that the prisoner who had arrived earlier that day could be found in the basement of the Grande Tour. He went on to explain that she had been treated very well, but that did not save him from being knocked unconscious with a pistol butt. As soon as they were securely bound and gagged, the two guards were subjected to a similar fate.

'And now?' Laincourt enquired.

Marciac gave him the pistols taken from the enemy and instructed him:

'You guard the door. We'll go find Agnès.'

The young man nodded.

'Don't take too long. Time is short.'

Upon leaving the queen's apartments, the Mother Superior General of the Sisters of Saint Georges found the captain of her Black Guards in the Louvre courtyard. He immediately summoned the white coach that was waiting nearby, and Mère de Vaussambre watched her team draw up in the torchlight with a thin smile of contained satisfaction, knowing that the sight attracted surprised and envious gazes from those observing the scene. Entering the Louvre in a carriage was a rare privilege, and the fact that the king had granted it to her was a public mark of his esteem. After the welcome the queen had given her, this evening was her moment of triumph. All that was left was her admittance to the Council, and the Order of the Sisters of Saint Georges would be fully restored to its former glory. And that would happen soon.

'The baronne de Vaudreuil arrived today,' the comte d'Orsan informed her discreetly.

'Without mishap?'

'None, mother superior.'

'That's very good news. I will speak to her tomorrow and I have no doubt I can bring her back to her senses. She cannot remain deaf to the call of her destiny much longer.'

Drawn by four horses, the coach came to a halt before them. A footman jumped down to open the passenger door, while another pulled the steps down. The captain of the Black Guards presented his arm and, with his support, the Chatelaines' Mother Superior General climbed into the cabin. Then, d'Orsan having closed the door, she settled herself as comfortably as possible, closed her eyes and waited to be rocked by the movements of the coach.

In order to leave the central courtyard of this former medieval fortress that had become the Louvre, one needed to traverse an archway measuring a dozen metres in length. It ran through the eastern wing of the palace and, passing between two round towers, opened onto a drawbridge that crossed the moat. Beyond that, there was an imposing fortified gate – known as the Bourbon gate – which defended the access from rue d'Autriche. The passage was narrow, particularly dark beneath the archway, and perilous as it crossed the moat, where carriages always ran the risk of tipping over the side.

The coachman advanced at a walk. The archway filled with the echoes of hooves striking the pavement, after which the team passed beneath the raised portcullis and started over the small drawbridge. That was where a Swiss mercenary sergeant, breathless from the chase, caught up with the coach and stopped it.

'Halt!' he ordered. 'In the name of the king!'

The Tour du Temple's ground floor consisted of a great hall that gave access to a spiral staircase housed in one of the corner turrets and smaller rooms located in the three other turrets. There were a few lamps burning dimly in the silent darkness of the hall, as well as in the stairwell that Saint-Lucq and Marciac descended quietly, swords in hand. They knew the general layout of the floors above, but had no idea what to expect below. They only knew that Agnès was being held prisoner down there somewhere.

After opening a door at the bottom with only the slightest of creaks, they discovered a large chamber that resembled a cloister. Bordering a flagstone gallery, a series of columns surrounded a square space with a sunken dirt floor six steps down and a vaulted ceiling whose fan of arching curves was supported by a central pillar. The gallery was plunged into darkness, but some oil lamps shed a weak light in the middle of the room, where they could make out a table, a rack, chains and shackles, a suspended cage, and various instruments of torture.

Without consultation, Marciac and Saint-Lucq split up, the first taking the gallery to the right, and the second the one on the left. Soon, the Gascon froze and listened carefully. He seemed to hear . . . was that snoring? He turned round, seeking Saint-Lucq, but could not see the half-blood. So, alone, he approached a small door and pressed his ear to its surface. Yes, the snores were coming from within. Loud snores, the kind that only a man stupefied by drink could produce without waking himself up.

Marciac's sense of curiosity was too strong to resist.

Softly, carefully, he opened the door.

In a narrow, stinking cubby-hole, a forgotten candle was on the point of consuming itself in a saucer placed on the floor. Its flickering glow barely revealed a human form lying entwined in a blanket upon a straw mattress pressed against the wall. But it was also just enough to perceive the gleam from a ring of keys that hung from a nail near the sleeper, as well as an iron bar similar to those used by torturers to break the limbs of the poor wretches who were condemned to the Catherine wheel.

Marciac only had eyes for the keys. They had to be the prison cell keys, since the man snoring like a bear could only be the gaoler. Neither he nor Saint-Lucq had Laincourt's skill in picking locks. If they wanted to open the door to Agnès' cell quietly, they would need this set of keys.

The Gascon held his breath and entered the cubby-hole on tiptoe.

The clicking of the chain alerted him, but he perceived his danger too late and barely had time to raise his arm for protection when a syle leapt for his throat from a shadowy corner. As large and as agile as a cat, the black salamander closed its jaws on Marciac's hand. He threw it off by reflex, its sharp teeth tearing away a strip of his skin. The syle struck the wall and fell, tangling itself up in the chain attached to its neck. But it was already spinning around to attack again when the Gascon planted his rapier in its skull.

Marciac had no time to ponder who would be mad enough to keep a syle on a leash. The snoring behind him had ceased, and he turned slowly towards the now-empty mattress. His injured hand forgotten, his gaze shifted upward with growing dread to see a colossal drac, massively built, whose enormous muscles were flexing beneath his black shiny scales.

Strangely fascinated, the Gascon gulped in awe.

He had never seen a drac like this, and it wasn't his size that made him so extraordinary. Nor the yellow, pointed fangs, wet with thick saliva. Nor the sharp claws on his powerful hands. Nor even the bestial glow in his reptilian eyes.

This drac had two heads.

That explains why the snoring was so loud, Marciac couldn't help thinking.

'Uhh . . . friends?' he ventured.

The monster emitted a dull roar.

Recalled by the king just as she was about to leave the Louvre, Mère de Vaussambre was forced to abandon her coach on the drawbridge, which the coachman had already started to cross, making it impossible for him to either turn around or to back up. Leaving her captain in charge, she followed the Swiss sergeant who had been sent after her and was soon admitted into His Majesty's apartments.

Louis XIII was waiting for her with Cardinal Richelieu and a dignified gentleman whom she recognised as the marquis d'Aubremont. The cardinal was standing slightly to the rear, while the king and the marquis sat next to one another and were conversing in front of an empty chair when the Mother Superior General entered, more puzzled by her summons than worried. Louis XIII invited her to sit and apologised for having recalled her in this fashion, without respect for etiquette and at such a late hour.

'Sire, I am at Your Majesty's service,' said Mère de Vaussambre occupying the armchair provided for her.

She greeted d'Aubremont with a nod of her head, and he responded in the same manner. Then she met Richelieu's gaze, without being able to read any clues at all in his eyes.

But the king was speaking:

'I have called you before me to quickly clear up an affair which is of little consequence, but which I should like to see settled before my departure for Saint-Germain. The marquis d'Aubremont, whom you know, is one of my friends. It seems he harbours some anxiety concerning a person dear to him, someone he believes you hold prisoner.'

She turned to the marquis and, without betraying any emotion, waited.

'I'm concerned about the baronne de Vaudreuil,' he explained in a cold tone of voice.

La Vaussambre withstood his accusing glare without blinking.

So that's what it was about: with no other recourse, La Fargue had turned to his friend d'Aubremont and persuaded him to appeal to the king.

'Really?' she said.

'Do you know her?' asked Louis XIII.

'Yes, Sire. I know her. She was one of our most promising novices, but she turned away from her divine calling to enter the cardinal's service.'

Richelieu leaned over the king's shoulder and whispered in his ear:

'Agnès de Vaudreuil is one of those who, under the command of Captain La Fargue, recently served you so well, Sire.'

Louis XIII nodded.

'Mother superior,' d'Aubremont resumed, 'I have a report that says the baronne de Vaudreuil is being held against her will in a cell at Mont-Saint-Michel. Is that true?'

'No, monsieur. That is not true.'

It wasn't a lie, since Agnès was now held in the Tour du Temple. La Fargue, once again, was a step behind her.

The Superior General's nerve troubled the marquis.

'Neither there, nor in any of your other gaols?' he insisted.

'Nor in any other,' replied Mère de Vaussambre with bland assurance.

She even permitted herself to display a hint of a benevolent but saddened smile, as if to apologise for being unable to assist him, despite her willingness to do so.

Marciac burst through the small door as if he had been shot out of a cannon. He crashed into a column and fell heavily to the flagstones. Grimacing from the excruciating pain in his back, he tried to get up but failed. He lost consciousness just as he saw the drac ducking both heads beneath the lintel to emerge from his lair.

Armed with the hefty iron bar that he kept by his bed, the colossus straightened up and contemplated the Gascon, who was still breathing. Then his attention was drawn by another intruder. Saint-Lucq was advancing sideways towards him, prudently but resolutely, his rapier pointed in a straight line from its tip to his shoulder, the axis of his gaze matching that of his blade. The half-blood halted before he came into range of the iron bar. Without lowering his guard, he took three steps to one side, drawing the drac away from Marciac.

And then waited.

The monster growled and struck.

Saint-Lucq evaded the attack, then a second and a third. There was no question of parrying or even deflecting a blow from that iron bar. They were delivered with such vigour that they could easily break his sword or tear it from his grasp. Concentrating, the half-blood leapt, stepped aside, and ducked, barely managing to avoid the bar as it slashed through the air. He was waiting for the drac to tire, but he was the one growing exhausted.

Beating a retreat, Saint-Lucq left the gallery and backed into the central space of the chamber, where the equipment and instruments of torture were laid out. The colossus followed him. The half-blood attempted to take advantage of the furnishings, but if the drac was too stupid to develop a strategy or predict the dodges and ruses of his adversary, his strength and speed more than made up for the shortcomings of his bestial intelligence. Nothing could stand against him. He overturned effortlessly the torture table, swept aside a heavy brazier with the back of his hand, and struck a powerful blow at the suspended cage, which began to swing slowly back and forth. The movement temporarily distracted him from his blind fury.

Saint-Lucq chose that moment to risk it all and lunged, forgetting any notion of caution. He scored a hit, but the point of his sword simply skidded across the black scales. Even worse, as he lurched forward, an enormous fist closed around his exposed wrist, and it felt as though the drac was about to rip his arm off. Lifted from the floor by a prodigious strength, he flew towards a wall and struck it with full force. The impact knocked the wind out of him, and he dropped his rapier. His legs gave way beneath him. He tried to stand up, leaning clumsily against the stone wall. As if in a drunken stupor, he watched the drac approach out of the corner of his eye, then raise the iron bar and prepare to strike a blow that would smash the half-blood's skull. Turning to one side to disguise what his right hand was doing, Saint-Lucq seized the dagger tucked inside his boot. Perhaps he still had a chance. One. But no more than that. He waited until the last moment and made a desperate leap. The iron bar whistled past him, just before he plunged the dagger into the drac's scaly flank. And again. And again.

The drac moaned, staggered and dropped his weapon which bounced with a clear ringing tone on the flagstones . . .

. . . and then he closed his clawed hands around the half-blood's throat.

Saint-Lucq gurgled. His feet left the ground. He risked less choking to death than having his neck broken and his windpipe crushed by the fists strangling him. He stiffened his neck muscles as best he could, thrashed his legs and seized those powerful wrists, seeking to loosen their grip. He scrabbled for any hold, any weak point, any hope.

In vain.

Then a steel grapple dropped between the drac's two heads, hung for a moment against its chest, and abruptly began to be pulled up. It was the tool the Blades had used to climb over the outer wall of the Enclos du Temple, the one that Marciac had placed on his belt. The one whose rope Marciac now held.

The grapple caught in the V between the two thick necks and the Gascon, giving it a swift jerk, drove the metal hooks into the creature's throats on either side. Black blood spurted from the wounds. Releasing Saint-Lucq, the colossus tried to pull the grapple free. But Marciac had braced himself at the other end of the rope and the hooks worked themselves in deeper. The drac was pulled backwards but it refused to fall. The Gascon pulled harder, groaning as the hand bitten by the syle throbbed with pain, but he didn't give up. He heaved again, arching his back, grimacing, his soles slipping on the flagstones until the monster toppled over backward and the grapple was torn from the scaly flesh, ripping bloody shreds with it as it came loose with a sound like a chicken carcass being torn apart, when the bones and cartilage suddenly separate. A double sticky spray accompanied it.

The reptilian colossus died quickly, on his back, and the silence that returned to the devastated chamber seemed like a roar to the ears of the two breathless men.

'Are you all right?' asked Marciac after a moment.

Saint-Lucq, sitting with his back against the torture table, still needed time to recover.

'I'm all right,' he lied in a hoarse voice. He pointed with a shaky index finger. 'Over there. The . . . The door to the cells. I found it just before . . . Go look for Agnès?'

The Gascon nodded, advanced a few steps, then changed his mind and went to take the keys to the gaol cells from the two-headed drac's cubby-hole.

After all, they had earned them.

From a window in one of the older sections of the Louvre, La Fargue looked out towards the Enclos and, under the pale, bluish glow of the stars, had little difficulty in distinguishing the imposing silhouette of the Tour du Temple.

It was visible from almost anywhere in Paris and could be easily located after nightfall, thanks to the light that shone from its pyramidal roof. The light came from a big lantern containing a 'solaire', an alchemical stone that was also known as 'Bohemian stone', because only Bohemian alchemists knew its secret. The solaires – whose invention was fairly recent – shone like the brightest of flames and had only one drawback: their fabrication was both onerous and dangerous. The one in the Tour du Temple was white and, like others in Paris, it served to guide wyverns in flight. A blue one shone from the Louvre, a red one from the Palais-Cardinal and, soon, there would be a yellow one to indicate the Gaget Messenger Service.

His eyes fixed on the Chatelaines' distant beacon, the captain of the Blades waited, patient and alone.

Finally, he heard Ballardieu's footsteps approaching.

'The marquis d'Aubremont has just left the king, captain. He gave me this for you.'

'And Mère de Vaussambre?'

'The king has retained her.'

Without turning away from the window, La Fargue took the note that Ballardieu held out to him, unfolded it, and read its contents.

'She denied it,' he said, lifting his head.

And, gazing back towards the Tour du Temple, he crumpled the paper in his fist and added gravely:

'Now we can only hope they succeed.'

In the tower basement, the door that Saint-Lucq had indicated opened onto a narrow staircase, at the bottom of which Marciac found a small square room and four doors.

'Agnès?' he called. 'Agnès, are you there?'

'Nicolas? Is that you?'

'At your service, baronne.'

Thanks to the gaoler's keys, he opened the door from behind which Agnès had answered him, and freed the young woman.

They immediately embraced.

'God's blood, Nicolas! Am I happy to see you . . .'

'And I, you!'

'No doubt that explains why one of your hands is creeping dangerously close to my buttocks . . .'

'Sorry. Force of habit.'

'It's still moving down, Marciac . . .'

'The little rascal . . .'

Agnès thought it preferable to step away from the Gascon before she was obliged to break a few fingers, which would have spoiled their reunion.

'So, I did see Ballardieu on that rooftop this afternoon!'

'It was him.'

'I thought I was going mad. I believed he was dead, did you know that?'

'He's quite lively.' And showing her the way out, he added: 'Let's be off, baronne. We're not out of this yet, and time is running short.'

'You didn't come here on your own, did you?' asked Agnès as she followed him up the stairs.

'No. Laincourt and Saint-Lucq are with me.'

They found the half-blood back in the torture chamber and, as she passed, the baronne de Vaudreuil noticed the body of the two-headed drac lying in a pool of black blood.

'I see you met the master of ceremonies down here.'

'He gave us the most deplorable welcome,' replied Marciac.

They were quick to rejoin Laincourt, who, in the darkness of the ground floor, was standing with his back to the wall by the entrance. The young man had left the door ajar and was keeping an eye out for any signs of movement outside, a pistol in either hand.

He smiled upon observing that Agnès de Vaudreuil seemed to be in good health, although her face looked drawn.

'I'm delighted to see you again, madame.'

'Thank you,' she replied. 'Likewise.'

He also noticed the sorry state in which the fight with the drac had left the other two, but made no comment.

'The sentries have discovered that the little door in the garden was no longer locked,' he announced. 'You should go. The alarm will soon be sounded.'

'You're not coming?' exclaimed Agnès in surprise as she saw him step back to let them pass.

'I'll meet you where we left the horses, don't worry.'

Saint-Lucq went out first, and then he signalled Marciac and Agnès to follow him.

Laincourt closed the door behind them. He waited for long

enough to be sure they hadn't been spotted or forced to make a hurried retreat back inside the tower. Now on his own, he moved off and took the spiral staircase that rose up through one of the keep's corner turrets.

From his vantage point within the Louvre, La Fargue could not make out what took place at the summit of the Tour du Temple. Therefore he did not see Laincourt surprise and stun a sentry on the walkway. Nor see him catch the guard as he fell. Nor spread a great piece of red cloth over the lantern housing the Chatelaines' dazzling white solaire.

What he saw was the beacon at the Enclos suddenly turn red.

Like most strongholds, the Enclos was conceived to prevent invasion, rather than escapes. Having crept past several sentries unseen, Saint-Lucq, Agnès and Marciac climbed on top of a building that leaned against the outer wall and, with the help of the Gascon's bloody grapple, they soon made it to the other side. The last to straddle the crenelated rampart, Saint-Lucq looked up at the top of the Tour du Temple and saw the light of the beacon turn red: La Fargue would now know that Agnès was free.

The alarm sounded shortly thereafter, just as they rejoined André in a darkened backyard, where the Blades' groom had been waiting with their horses. There were shouts at first. Then shots were fired and the tocsin began to sound inside the Enclos.

'We have to go,' whispered Saint-Lucq.

'What about Laincourt?' Marciac protested in a low voice. 'We just abandon him?'

'That blasted tocsin will wake the entire neighbourhood, and it won't take the Black Guards much longer to send out patrols.'

'Laincourt is one of us!'

'He knew the risks.'

'We don't abandon our own, Saint-Lucq.'

'Yes we do, when the success of the mission demands it.'

'That's enough!' interjected Agnès, stopping herself from raising her voice. 'Laincourt is resourceful. He can still—'

'If he's being pursued, and if he has any brains,' the half-blood interrupted, 'this is the last place he will go. He'd be leading the whole pack straight to us.'

'Let's give him another moment,' the young woman said stubbornly.

Saint-Lucq cursed.

More detonations were heard. Curt orders were given, although their exact nature remained indistinct. But it was clear that a manhunt was under way.

'Well spoken,' murmured Marciac to Agnès. 'But all the same, you should not stay. It's too dangerous. I'll wait for Laincourt. You three should go. Laincourt and I will find you later.'

'Out of the question.'

'You don't have a choice, Agnès. Saint-Lucq is right: Laincourt knew the risks. So did we. And if we all agreed to run them, it was to liberate you. So don't let yourself be recaptured now.'

Agnès de Vaudreuil fell silent. Marciac was right, although it cost her to admit it.

She nodded sadly.

'All right,' she said. But . . .'

She didn't finish, but grinned instead as she saw Laincourt arrive with his sword in his fist, running at a steady jog and not looking particularly worried.

'What?' he asked, when he saw them all staring at him.

The king detained Mère de Vaussambre for a short while after the departure of the marquis d'Aubremont. He was courteous and attentive, seeking to end their interview on a more pleasant note than the climate of suspicion in which it had begun. Louis XIII had too great a need of the Chatelaines' support to risk alienating their Mother Superior General. Although she had not been forced to answer any accusations this evening, d'Aubremont's questions had put her in an uncomfortable position, despite the king's claim that it was 'an affair of little consequence'.

Mère de Vaussambre was not duped by this.

La Fargue had tried to compromise her and d'Aubremont knew perfectly well where matters stood. And Richelieu? Did he have any part in this? No. The trap was too crude, too clumsy, to be the cardinal's work. But what had La Fargue hoped to gain? That, in the king's presence, she would not dare deny she held the baronne de Vaudreuil prisoner?

She only understood when her coach brought her back to the Enclos.

She found the former Templar fortress in a state of upheaval, the tocsin pealing and lights at all the windows, her guards on a war footing, and even patrols out searching the surrounding streets. Men had infiltrated the Enclos. They had freed Agnès from the Tour du Temple and taken her away, leaving a dead body and several mistreated sentries behind. They had not worn masks, and one of them had been a half-blood.

'Saint-Lucq!' exclaimed the comte d'Orsan. 'It must have been the Blades.'

'A brilliant deduction,' said Mère de Vaussambre in a bitter tone.

'Mother superior, one word from you and I'll have them all arrested before dawn. Starting with La Fargue.'

'And on what grounds?'

'But mother superior!' the captain of the Black Guards protested in astonishment. 'Isn't it obvious?'

La Vaussambre remained silent.

She was in no mood to tell d'Orsan that she had lied to the king, exactly as La Fargue had known she would and had wanted her to do. How could she now accuse the Blades of liberating by force a prisoner she had just denied holding? She knew La Fargue. She knew that he would let matters rest, as long as she did the same.

Pale and simmering with frustrated rage, she ordered the tocsin silenced and the beacon restored to its original whiteness.

'And find a satisfactory explanation for all this uproar.'

La Fargue and Ballardieu left the Louvre on horseback and found the others waiting for them, also on horseback, in front of the Pont Neuf. There were smiles all around. Agnès and Marciac, above all. But Laincourt too, and even Saint-Lucq had a smirk on his face. They were relieved and happy. They were victorious.

Eyes shining with pride, their captain saluted them with a slight nod, while Ballardieu, beaming, gave the young woman a huge wink.

Reunited once more, they felt no need to say anything.

'Let's go home,' La Fargue said.

4

The dragon seated in front of the mirror had the appearance of an elegant gentleman with fine features and blond hair. He was unusually pale, his reptilian eyes shining with a dark lustre as he spoke. The mirror did not return his own image, but that of the individual he was addressing: an old red dragon whose massive scaly head, adorned with a triple bony crest, shone from the reflective surface and shimmered in the dim light. Located in Madrid, this other dragon also had a human form. But the ensorcelled mirrors revealed the true nature of those who used them.

'Do you think killing the Alchemist was a mistake?' the red dragon was asking.

'I don't know, Heresiarch.'

'I've already heard complaints . . . But the Alchemist knew the price he would have to pay. Could we have allowed him to fall into the Chatelaines' hands and taken the risk he might reveal our secrets to them under torture?'

'Certainly not. Yet—'

'The Heir can still see the light of day,' the Heresiarch continued without listening. 'Nothing can be allowed to prevent that! Nothing must impede our work!'

In front of his mirror, the gentleman remained silent. He waited until the red dragon regained his composure and then said:

'I am loyal and devoted to you, Heresiarch. However, the masters of the Grand Lodge are growing impatient. Our adversaries constantly draw attention to all the efforts and the fortunes the Black Claw has already devoted to our Grand Design. And they have no difficulty in finding willing ears to listen to them. For the moment, I have managed to minimise the extent of our failure, but—'

'It was the Alchemist's failure, and his alone!'

'Nevertheless. The Black Claw is now demanding results.'

'And it shall have them.'

'When?'

'Very soon.'

The Arcana

The day after her escape Agnès wanted to visit Almades' grave. And since she was determined to go there on her own, Ballardieu was forced to follow her to the cemetery discreetly, and to watch over her from a distance.

The day after her escape Agnès wanted to visit Almades' grave. And since she was determined to go there on her own, Ballardieu was forced to follow her to the cemetery discreetly, and to watch over her from a distance.

He knew she was grieving and he suffered as a result. Indeed, everything she felt affected him. He shared her joys and her sorrows, her doubts and her pleasures, her angers and her regrets. He could not be happy if she wasn't, and it had been that way between them ever since she was entrusted to his care, soon after her birth, by a man who was totally indifferent to the fate of his only daughter.

Ballardieu slipped behind a funeral monument when he saw Agnès walking back through the small cemetery. He heard her footsteps pass and waited for her to reach the gates before emerging from his hiding-place. But he held off for too long. Not seeing her anywhere, he cursed and had to hurry, panicked by the thought that he had no idea whether she had turned right or left in the street. He came out of the graveyard almost at a run and then halted, heart beating fast, desperately seeking a glimpse of the young baronne among the crowd thronging the city pavement.

'You just couldn't help yourself, could you?'

He managed not to jump in surprise and, composing an impassive expression on his face, turned with all the dignity of a prelate.

Arms crossed, one ankle placed in front of the other. Agnès was leaning against the cemetery wall. She was dressed like a squire, wearing boots, breeches, and a red leather corset over a white shirt, with a sword at her side. Her outfit drew glances from passers-by in the street, but she paid no heed. Bare-headed, with her long black braid draped over one shoulder, she was gazing fixedly at him.

'Excuse me?' he managed in reply.

'You couldn't help following me,' she said, drawing closer.

The old soldier, growing red-faced in the heat, feigned shock.

'Who, me?' he protested.

'What? You're going to deny it . . . ? You deny being here, at this very minute?'

He barely hesitated before answering.

'I don't deny the fact, I deny the intention. I wasn't actually following you. I was simply going to the same place as you, that's all.'

'And that's all,' mimicked the baronne de Vaudreuil. 'So what were you doing over there behind that big vault?'

'I . . . I was taking a piss.'

'In a cemetery?'

'Best place for it, doesn't bother anyone.'

She stared at him. Waiting. A trickle of sweat ran down Ballardieu's upper lip and he became aware of a wisp of hair stuck to his forehead.

'All right!' he exclaimed, suddenly stretching his arms wide in surrender. 'I was following you . . . ! So what? Can you blame me for worrying?'

'Worrying?' asked Agnès in surprise. 'Why?'

He looked warily around at the bystanders in the street and bent over to whisper in her ear:

'All of you seem to believe, and you in particular, that Mère de Vaussambre is going to accept her defeat with all the graciousness in the world. But I say she has not abandoned the idea of doing you an evil turn . . . *Ergo*, I'm watching over you.'

'"*Ergo*"?'

'*Ergo*. It means—'

'I know what it means,' Agnès laughed merrily. 'But I didn't know you spoke Latin . . . Very well, you old beast, you win. Watch over me as much as you please.'

'You won't even notice me, girl.'

'It would be the first time that ever happened.'

Shaking her head in amused disbelief, Agnès turned back to the cemetery, and as her gaze drifted towards the site of Almades' grave, hidden from her view, her smile slowly faded. Ballardieu became grim-faced as well.

'So it was a dragon that did this?' said the young woman after a moment.

'Yes,' replied Ballardieu, looking in the same direction. 'And if Almades hadn't been there, we would be grieving for La Fargue instead.'

Agnès' eyes narrowed.

'But there was another dragon there, in the room with them. The Alchemist.'

'So . . . ?'

'So . . . when did dragons start killing each other?'

In the inn on the rue du Pot-de-Fer where he had become a regular, Leprat had eaten his noonday meal alone. He was now moodily sipping *eau-de-vie* and was absently rolling a pair of dice as he kept an eye on the door. He was waiting for Athos, who was supposed to join him here when he came off duty. They would then make their way to the Louvre together, and from there the Musketeers would escort the king to his château at Saint-Germain.

It had only been a few days since Athos had advised Leprat to be patient over the cold, and even sullenly hostile, manner in which the other musketeers had greeted his return to their ranks. According to Athos, the main reproach against him was fickleness, for having doffed and donned his cape too many times. So now he had to demonstrate his loyalty. If he avoided getting into any quarrels then time would smooth over the rest. He just needed to keep his head down for the time being.

Athos was right, for the most part. But Leprat was also aware that the other musketeers looked at him differently as news of his illness spread. The ranse was eating away at both his flesh and his soul. In the long run, decades in some cases, its victims were slowly and irremediably transformed into grotesque, pathetic creatures, whose deformed bodies and tortured minds clung hopelessly to the last shreds of their humanity. But one of the disease's first symptoms was that at least some of the afflicted's acquaintances began to treat them like monsters as soon as they learned of the illness, long before that final stage was reached, and saw nothing but the inevitable and abject fall from grace. From that point on, sufferers ceased to be themselves and became merely diseased.

Became ranse-ed . . .

Antoine Leprat, the chevalier d'Orgueil, had known he had the ranse for several years now yet he had never thought of himself in those terms, as being diseased, not as long as he had kept it a secret. Now the looks he received every day reminded him of his condition and reduced him to being just that: diseased. And it wasn't just looks; there were the conversations that stopped dead when he approached, embarrassed faces, the slight gestures of recoil, and all the other more-or-less disguised, and more-or-less involuntary, signals of discomfort that were made in his presence.

His thoughts slightly befuddled, Leprat saw that his jug of *eau-de vie* was empty.

Already?

He was thinking of calling for another when the door opened. It was not Athos, but two other musketeers Leprat recognised, although neither was wearing their cape: Broussière and Sardent. The two men noticed him in turn and Broussière seemed to want to go elsewhere, but his companion obviously disagreed.

They sat down at a table.

Of the pair, Leprat was better acquainted with Broussière, Sardent having joined the King's Musketeers recently. He had never had any cause for complaint regarding the first man, but the second was one of those who were treating him badly, and doing so with increasingly boldness. Until now, following Athos' advice, Leprat had not responded to any of his cutting remarks and crude allusions. But it was becoming difficult for him not to hear them and understand the hurt they intended. Why had Sardent been behaving this way? Perhaps his spiteful hatred towards the diseased was born of fear, as was frequently the case. Perhaps he hoped, by denigrating a famous musketeer, to demonstrate that he was a better recruit to the King's guard. He was the younger son of a great lord with aspirations of adding glory to his name.

Leprat did not care to know the reasons behind the other man's animosity. But today, helped by his over-indulgence of alcohol, he was in no mood to tolerate it any longer. He knew, without the shadow of a doubt, that things would turn out badly if he stayed.

And yet he did.

The two musketeers had ordered drinks. As soon as they were served, Sardent called the girl back and asked in a loud voice:

'Is the crockery washed thoroughly, here?'

He pretended not to see Leprat giving him a black look. But Broussière noticed and seemed worried.

'Of course, monsieur. I assure you.'

The wench had started moving away to attend to other customers when Sardent asked:

'Is that truly the case?'

She turned round, looking uncertain.

'I . . . I can assure you that it is, monsieur.'

'That's enough, said Leprat in a cold tone of voice.

'Now, Sardent,' Broussière said in an appeasing tone, 'there's no need—'

'Because, you see,' his companion continued, undeterred, 'there are some people whose glasses you really wouldn't want to drink from . . .'

'I beg your pardon, monsieur?'

Leprat, livid, was on the verge of rising from his seat and only just managed to contain his anger. With a wave of his hand, Broussière dismissed the girl, who left with a shrug of her shoulders. Sardent seemed to have let the matter drop . . . when he pointed to the brim of his glass and asked:

'Is that not a trace of the ranse I see there?'

The mere mention of the disease provoked shudders of disgust among the other customers, some of whom instinctively leaned back away from their tables. Leprat stood up suddenly, and Broussière did the same as he saw the former Blade approaching with a furious step. Sardent detected the murderous gleam in the chevalier d'Orgueil's eye too late and Broussière moved to put himself between them, placing a hand on Leprat's chest.

'Leprat, please—'

But Broussière didn't complete his sentence. A sharp blow from Leprat's forehead broke his nose and made him tumble over backwards. Leprat continued to advance on Sardent. He had already unsheathed his famous white rapier. His gaze was that of a man who had decided to pin his adversary to the wall, rather than cross swords with him according to the rules.

'Messieurs!'

Leprat wasn't listening.

Sardent was scrambling to his feet and trying to draw his sword at the same time. But all he managed was to trip over his own scabbard and he lost his balance, falling among the suddenly deserted chairs behind him with a heavy crash. With the point of his ivory blade, Leprat pricked the other man's throat and forced him to stay on the floor.

Still simmering with a barely mastered rage, Leprat felt a hand calmly but firmly close about his wrist. It was Athos, who had just arrived and whose imperious call, 'Messieurs', had gone unheard.

'Get a hold on yourself, Leprat,' the gentleman said quietly.

With the air of a man waking from a bad dream, Leprat took two steps back and lowered his sword. Sardent stood up, while Broussière, his nose bleeding, struggled to rise. Athos' eyes ordered the pair to go, and they hastened to obey.

'This matter won't end here, will it?' asked Leprat.

'No, my friend, I'm afraid it will not.'

Sent out to gather news in the Temple neighbourhood, Marciac returned to the Hôtel de l'Épervier in the early afternoon. He found La Fargue and the others out in the garden, beneath the chestnut tree, sitting around the old table where they had just finished lunch. The Gascon's first act was to empty a glass of white wine. Then, drinking again and filching titbits from the dishes before Naïs cleared them away he recounted, between mouthfuls, how the Sisters of Saint Georges had managed to explain the previous night's commotion.

'The tocsin woke everyone in the vicinity. Not to mention the shots fired at Laincourt and the patrols sent out into the streets looking for us . . .'

He broke off his report to save two slices of *tarte aux prunes* from being returned to the kitchen, by swiftly placing them safely out of reach from Naïs, and her unassuming but formidable domestic efficiency.

'Go to the cellar and fill these wine jugs instead,' Agnès suggested to her gently.

'Yes,' said the Gascon. 'Go and do that instead.'

'Well?' Laincourt insisted. 'What was their explanation?'

'Dracs. Apparently some dracs tried to invade the Enclos last night. And the Black Guards, as one might expect, displayed their unceasing vigilance, bravely drove the intruders out, and then carried out a sweep of the nearby streets to make sure the danger had been entirely eliminated.'

'And why would these dracs have been trying to enter the Enclos in the middle of the night?'

Marciac shrugged.

'That remains a mystery. However, the Chatelaines are exhibiting four scaly corpses as evidence, one of them a colossus with two heads which is causing quite a sensation. People are packed shoulder-to-shoulder all the way to rue du Temple for the chance to see it.'

'I'd like to go and see it myself,' Ballardieu said in Agnès' ear.

The baronne preferred not to reply.

'I can understand the two-headed drac,' observed Saint-Lucq, 'But where did the other three come from?'

'I don't know,' Marciac confessed.

Nor did the problem seem to interest him much.

'Perhaps the Chatelaines were holding them in some

809

dungeon or other,' suggested Laincourt. 'And did away with the poor creatures to support their story.'

'Then again, there are plenty of dracs to be found in Les Écailles,' said the baronne de Vaudreuil.

Les Écailles, or 'The Scales', was the drac neighbourhood built on Ile Notre-Dame, which would later be re-named Ile Saint-Louis.

'The important thing to note here is that the Chatelaines are lying,' decreed La Fargue, as Naïs returned from the cellar with full wine jugs.

Having finished the prune tart, Marciac held out his plate to the young servant girl with a smile and a faint bow of the head. Shy Naïs took it and fled. Agnès, amused, gave the Gascon a swift elbow in the ribs as punishment for teasing the girl.

'If they're lying,' continued the Blades' captain, 'it's because they want the whole affair to end here and the truth never to come out. So we won't have to answer any accusations, as I thought. Mère de Vaussambre has too much to lose in a scandal . . .'

'But we still don't know why she was keeping you a prisoner,' said Saint-Lucq, turning to Agnès.

The previous night, after they were reunited, Agnès had told the Blades everything from the moment she set foot inside the abbey at Mont-Saint-Michel to her capture on the wyverns' flight platform. She had been there on a mission to find the son of the marquis d'Aubremont, François Reynault d'Ombreuse. A lieutenant serving in the Black Guards, he had disappeared after taking part in a clandestine expedition to Alsace. What had become of him? Was he alive or dead? Wounded? Ill? And if he was well, why did he send no word?

This was what the baronne de Vaudreuil had hoped to learn thanks to Sœur Béatrice d'Aussaint, the White Wolf who had led the expedition to Alsace, and who had been held in secret at the Chatelaines' abbey fortress on the mount.

Nothing, however, had prepared Agnès for what she actually discovered.

Still suffering from her ordeal, Sœur Béatrice had not told her how, with the support of a detachment of Black Guards under the command of François d'Ombreuse, she had tracked and almost vanquished a dragon belonging to the Arcana lodge. But she had warned Agnès of an incredible danger, when she shared a nightmarish vision of a great black dragon burning Paris to the ground. The White Wolves of the Saint Georges Order often had the gift of prescience, and the young baronne de Vaudreuil had not doubted the coming disaster was true, or that there was an urgent need to take action. Unfortunately, no further light was shed on the danger by the sister's confused ramblings afterwards, her strength exhausted. Thus there were still too many unanswered questions: Who was this dragon? Where did it come from? Why was it going to attack Paris?

And above all: when?

Her gaze becoming pained and thoughtful, Agnès returned to the crux of the matter, the vision she had seen on that fateful night:

'I saw a black dragon attacking Paris and reducing the Louvre to ashes,' she said. 'That's why the Chatelaines were holding me. They don't want me to divulge this secret, one that for her part Sœur Béatrice wanted me to learn at all costs.'

'But they couldn't have held you forever!' Marciac objected.

'They could have detained Agnès long enough,' Saint-Lucq declared coldly. 'Until the secret no longer had any importance. Or until Agnès agreed to hold her tongue about it.'

'Mère de Vaussambre has not yet given up on the idea of my taking the veil,' stressed the baronne de Vaudreuil.

'She's convinced that your destiny lies with the Sisters of Saint Georges,' said La Fargue.

'My destiny lies wherever I want it to.'

'There is one thing I don't understand,' confessed Laincourt, who was following his own train of thought. 'If your vision is prophetic—'

'It is,' affirmed Agnès. 'If nothing is done, then what I saw that night will come to pass.'

'In that case, why are the Chatelaines remaining silent? Why are they keeping this terrible prophecy a secret? Are they hiding something else, something even worse than the danger threatening Paris?'

'That's what we need to find out,' La Fargue declared.

A surprised silence followed this statement.

'Us?' Marciac finally asked. 'Why us?'

'Because someone needs to and no one else will. And because I have decided that we should.'

The Gascon felt that this last reason trumped all the others.

'So be it,' he replied.

'I have no scruples about going through the Chatelaines' dirty linen,' said Saint-Lucq. 'But the cardinal may see things in an entirely different light, under the circumstances . . .'

'The Chatelaines are powerful,' added Laincourt. 'Right now, they are in favour with the king, the Parlement, and the people, while the cardinal is more criticised than ever. Like Saint-Lucq, I doubt His Eminence will approve of our initiative.'

'That's true,' acknowledged the Blades' captain. 'That's why we won't tell him about it.'

Among his other names, both true and false, he was called the Gentleman after one of the twenty-two figures forming the Major Arcana of the Shadows Tarot. It was a tradition of the lodge to which he was proud to belong, a lodge so secret it was wreathed in a legendary aura even within the Black Claw. Like an unmentionable curse, the Arcana lodge inspired awe in those who believed in its existence and, in the remainder, an uneasy, superstitious respect. Even the powerful masters of the Grand Lodge in Madrid hesitated to call it to account for its plans, when it knew of them. As for its members, they obeyed no one but their leader: the Heresiarch.

Seated in a walnut armchair covered in Genoa velvet, The Gentleman was meditating in front of a mirror that stood on a table placed against a wall, between two large silver candelabra. His wrist lay limply on an armrest, his fingers grasping the rim of a glass filled with a golden liqueur which he swirled slowly, wrapped up in his thoughts. His blond hair was still damp from his evening bath, and he wore nothing but a pair of breeches and a shirt made of fine cloth that he had quickly pulled on over his wet skin. Tall and slim, he looked thirty years old. His features were delicate, almost feminine, and imbued with a strange, perverse charm. He was handsome, but there was something disturbing about the thrill he provoked in others.

The last rays of a flamboyant sunset still filtered through the curtains. They made the dust particles shine in the quiet dimness of his reading study, and gave an amber and purple sheen to the varnished furnishings, the lustrous woodwork, the rich tapestries, and the expensive book bindings. Stirring gently, the liquid gold in the Gentleman's glass gave off reddish shimmering glints, along with a heady fragrance.

The Enchantress came into the room.

Seeing her willowy figure approach in the mirror, the Gentleman smiled without turning round and caught her eye. She was almost naked, only wearing a pair of white stockings secured by crimson velvet ribbons. Her self-assurance and shamelessness were enough to clothe her. She was also smiling as she came towards him, slowly, splendid and sensual; the heavy curls of her mahogany-coloured hair falling to the dark areolas of her breasts. She slept or lazed about most of the day, and would only come out at night to partake in the cruel debaucheries that were her principal source of entertainment. She was of the Arcana lodge, like the Gentleman, and like him she belonged to the younger generation of dragons – the 'last-born' – for whom the outward appearance of humanity had become more natural than the draconic form.

The Enchantress leaned over the back of the armchair to kiss the Gentleman on the cheek, then came round the chair to face him, gripped the table behind her with both hands, and hopped up to sit nimbly on its edge in front of the mirror framed by the twin candelabra. A mischievous gleam in her eyes, she wormed one silk-sheathed foot between the Gentleman's knees and let it slither upwards to his groin.

He allowed her to do so without protest.

'So, what news?' she asked playfully as she started to caress him.

'I spoke with the Heresiarch last night. The Grand Lodge is growing impatient. It is anxious to see results.'

'And when was it ever otherwise?'

'Indeed. But the stakes are greater now. Our allies have become scarce, and silent. Our enemies, on the other hand, grow in numbers and speak ever more loudly. They are scoring easy points by saying that our endeavours are too costly and don't lead to anything.'

'And what do they know of our endeavours?' the Enchantress scoffed.

'Nothing. Precisely.'

'They're imbeciles. They will soon be jostling one another for the crumbs of our glory.'

'Right now, they are a nuisance which might hinder us. Who knows where their boldness may lead them?'

The Enchantress did not answer, but she did remove her foot. She stretched her hand out for the Gentleman's glass, took a deep swallow of the delicious liqueur and said:

'Don't drink too much of this nectar. You know the harm it can do.'

It was golden henbane liqueur, a popular drug amongst the idle rich. For dragons, it was the drink of choice. They relished it and sometimes indulged to the point of excess, especially the last-born. In their case, golden henbane woke long-buried instincts. It helped them reclaim their fundamental essence and, under its influence, those who struggled to assume even intermediate draconic forms were able to achieve complete metamorphoses. But there was a heavy price to pay for it. With habituation, heavier and more frequent doses became necessary, doses which could weaken, and even poison them. Numerous last-born had destroyed themselves in this manner.

Setting the glass down, the Enchantress slipped down from the table and, looking deep into his eyes, joined him on the armchair, straddling his thighs so that she knelt over him.

'But it's not those old lizards of the Black Claw who worry you, is it?' she asked him.

'No.'

'Then what is it, little brother?'

She slipped her hand between them and started to unbutton his breeches.

'The Heresiarch is not gauging the situation accurately,' he explained. 'Killing the Alchemist without consulting anyone was reckless. And waking the Primordial to achieve it was an even greater folly . . . It's as if the Heresiarch was . . . blinded by his Grand Design. He worries me and I don't know how to make him see reason.'

'Is such a thing even possible?'

'I hope so,' replied the Gentleman as he felt expert fingers slide into his breeches. 'But even the prospect of an Assembly doesn't seem to perturb him.'

'An Assembly? Who called for one?'

'The Master-at-Arms. But I suspect the Protectress was behind it. I'm convinced she is forming an opposition to the Heresiarch.'

'Meaning, against us. If the Heresiarch falls, your disgrace will follow and so will mine . . .'

'What are you trying to tell me?'

'Nothing.'

And as the Enchantress' fingers squeezed him gently but firmly, the Gentleman no longer felt a need to discuss it.

'Very well,' he said. 'But we will soon have to answer before the Arcana Assembly.'

'The Alchemist sealed his own fate,' the Enchantress reminded him.

Drawing him toward her, she made him slip his hips forward. He slumped slightly in the armchair.

'We will need to take action,' she said.

'Take action? What do you mean?'

'Later,' she murmured in his ear.

She lifted herself and eased him inside her, before abruptly sinking down upon him and arching her back with a single, great shudder.

Late that night, La Fargue joined Agnès in the stable where, unable to sleep, she was tending to her favourite horse by the lantern light. Seeing the captain enter from the corner of her eye, she continued to brush Courage, and said:

'Thank God, I did not choose him for the ride to Mont-Saint-Michel! I would have lost him . . .'

La Fargue sat on a stool.

'How are you, Agnès?' he asked gravely

The young woman stopped brushing the horse for a moment . . .

. . . and then resumed, with calm, steady strokes.

'I wasn't the one who almost lost an eye,' she said in a tone she had meant to be light.

La Fargue smiled.

He would have liked to reply that he no longer noticed the patch he was wearing, but his left eye still hurt and could not bear bright light.

'I know you too well, Agnès. There's something you're not telling us . . .'

She made no reply, but continued to brush the animal.

'If you don't want to talk about it, that's fine,' he continued. 'I just want you to know that I'm always ready to listen . . . But . . .' he hesitated. 'You were well treated, weren't you?'

'By the Chatelaines? As well as one can be, locked up in a pitch-dark cell . . . The most unbearable thing was thinking that Ballardieu was dead. And that it was my fault.'

Understanding, the old gentleman nodded.

'So what's bothering you now?'

'Apart from a dragon destroying Paris?'

'Yes, apart from that.'

Agnès put down the brush and, smoothing Courage's neck, admitted:

'I can't help thinking about what Sœur Béatrice told me. Or rather, what she tried to tell me . . . I keep trying to remember her exact words, but they were so disjointed and confused . . .'

And since La Fargue, by remaining silent and attentive,

encouraged her to continue, the young baronne said, with a distant look in her eyes:

'She said something about the arcana . . . And an heir . . . And she mentioned the Alchemist of the Shadows.'

'The Alchemist? Are you quite sure?'

Agnès shrugged.

'I wouldn't swear to that, but I have had time to ponder the whole matter. And I believe that Sœur Béatrice's expedition in Alsace was a mission to eliminate a dragon. She was a White Wolf, after all. And she had a detachment of the Black Guards accompanying her . . . Furthermore, only combat with a dragon could have caused the terrible state she was in. I think that even the vision she shared with me must have come from her confrontation with a dragon in Alsace . . .'

'And this dragon would have been the Alchemist?'

'Yes.'

'So that's why Sœur Béatrice wanted to warn you about him. Since she could not have known that we had captured him, she must have believed the queen was still in danger.'

'That's what I thought, yes.'

'But you no longer think so now?'

'I don't know,' replied Agnès, sounding annoyed with herself. 'I no longer know what to think.'

La Fargue stood up and, placing his hands on the young woman's shoulders, he waited until she looked him in the eyes before saying:

'The Alchemist is dead, Agnès.'

Uncertain, she gently freed herself from his grasp.

'I know, captain . . . And yet . . . And yet something tells me we're still not finished with him.'

2

Seated in his coach, which moved along the street at a slow crawl, with cushions wedged beneath his feet and behind his back, Cardinal Richelieu said:

'I'm hesitant.'

'I'll lead the negotiations myself,' replied Père Joseph. 'And if nothing comes of them, we will still be able to renounce the whole matter.'

'At risk of displeasing the Pope.'

'Indeed,' the Capuchin monk recognised.

Aged about fifty, he wore a plain grey habit and sandals, with a simple rope serving as a belt. He had long been the cardinal's closest advisor, his 'Grey Eminence', a figure who always operated in the shadows.

'Are we quite certain, at least, that we have squeezed everything we can out of this man?' enquired Richelieu. 'After all, he hasn't been in our hands for very long . . .'

'I believe we have, yes.'

'Has he been put to the question?'

'Yes, monseigneur. He's been tortured several times. By the Chatelaines, and on occasion even in my presence.'

The cardinal lowered his eyes to look at Petit-Ami who was curled up asleep on his knees, seemingly undisturbed by the jolting coach journey. He was fond of this dragonnet, a gift from the king. Its scarlet colour made it a rarity, but the price which His Majesty's chief minister attached to the little reptile went far beyond that.

'I would prefer to know why the Pope is so keen that we transfer this man to his custody.'

'No doubt to learn the same information that he gave us.'

'And what are we to receive in return for our prisoner?'

'Very little. But as we are in debt to Rome . . .'

The two men exchanged a long glance, before Richelieu finally asked:

'Where is the transfer to take place?'

'At the Château de Mareuil-sur-Ay.'

'Understood. You will arrange everything . . . But make sure that the game is worth the candle. And also see to it that the Sisters of Saint Georges don't get wind of this too soon. They might want to keep the marquis de Gagnière for themselves.'

That morning Antoine Leprat, chevalier d'Orgueil, paid particular attention to his appearance.

Freshly shaved, his moustache and goatee carefully smoothed, he put on a clean shirt and stockings, followed by a pair of breeches and a doublet still warm from his landlady's iron. He had polished his boots the previous evening. Nevertheless, he examined them again before putting them on, stamping his heels to make sure they fit snugly. He adjusted his baldric and added his white rapier, verifying that the sword hung at the correct height at his right hip and slid easily in and out of the scabbard. Finally, after a last glance at the handsome blue cape spread across his bed, he went out, shutting the door to his modest room where he had left everything tidy and clean behind him.

Having donned his felt hat while descending the stairs, he found Athos waiting for him below, in rue Cocatrix, at the appointed time. They saluted one another gravely before going to fetch their horses from the nearest stables. It was the start of a fine day, but neither of them was in any mood to take pleasure from it. The thought did occur to Leprat, nevertheless, that he would need to be careful to keep the sun at his back.

A quarter of an hour later, he and Athos left the Ile de la Cité by the Petit Pont.

'I would like to thank you for being at my side, Athos.'

'I am your second.'

'Precisely.'

As Leprat had expected, his violent altercation with Broussière and Sardent had not been the end of the matter. That was hardly surprising. He had broken the first man's nose and had almost impaled the second without any ado, acting in the heat of the rage Sardent had provoked. The affair was too serious to be settled in any other way but a duel and it had been decided that Leprat would confront Sardent first and then Broussière as soon as possible afterwards. The details of the first encounter were promptly agreed. It would need to take place quickly, as the more time passed the greater the risk news would leak out. Duelling was forbidden by the very royal edicts which the King's Musketeers, above all, were charged with upholding. To be sure, the king was willing to forgive them many trespasses, especially if they were at the expense of the Cardinal's Guards. But Captain Tréville could not tolerate his musketeers quarrelling and cutting one another to pieces. He would forbid the duel if he learned of it, which would leave Leprat and Sardent no alternative but to disobey him and bear the consequences. So it was best if they took their chance right away.

On the Left Bank, Leprat and Athos soon turned onto rue Galande. They crossed Place Maubert and then took rue Saint-Victor as far as the city gate of the same name. Out in the faubourg, they rode alongside the walls of Saint-Victor abbey, then those of the Royal Garden of Medicinal Plants, a vast domain which was just starting to emerge from the ground and behind which the duellists had agreed to face one another.

'There they are,' said Athos.

Indeed, Sardent, accompanied by Broussière, who would act as his second and whose nose was decorated with a large bandage, was just arriving from the faubourg Saint-Jacques by way of rue d'Orléans. They were also on horseback. Athos and Broussière saluted one another, but the other two men exchanged neither a word nor even a glance. While Sardent seemed furious, Leprat did not let his feelings show. Detouring around the site of what would one day become the famous

Jardin des Plantes, the four horsemen approached the appointed place. It seemed ideal: flat, unobstructed, and sheltered from indiscreet gazes . . .

If it were not for the fact that there was already someone there.

Seated on a large rock, the man had placed his hat upon his knee. He was wearing the King's Musketeers' blue cape with silver braiding, and was whistling as he fiddled with his horse's bridle.

His horse, tethered and placid, waited nearby.

'So?' asked d'Artagnan without raising his eyes from his task. 'Out for a ride? I like this spot very much, myself. It's peaceful here. Just right for thinking matters through . . .'

Completing his repair of the bridle, he donned his felt hat, stood up, and with an innocent smile but eyes full of gravity, he added in a casual tone:

'Unfortunately, it seems that we all had the same idea of retiring here this morning. Since I arrived first, I could insist that I stay and so oblige you to go elsewhere. But that might give you the idea that I was pulling rank, when I do like to be an amenable fellow. So, what do you say: shall we all agree to give up our present plans?'

La Fargue found Saint-Lucq helping Agnès practise her fencing skills in the main hall, watched closely by Ballardieu. Laincourt and Marciac were also present. The Gascon, who had spent most of the previous night drinking and gambling, was asleep on a chair tilted dangerously backward, his feet crossed on a window ledge. Laincourt was reading the latest issue of the *Gazette*, which was entirely devoted to an account of the dragon's attack on Le Châtelet.

Drenched in sweat, the baronne de Vaudreuil did not spare her efforts. Although she felt a need to spend her energy, she also needed to become accustomed to wielding her new sword. It was a little longer and heavier than the one she had been carrying for years, which the Sisters of Saint Georges had taken from her. And while this new one was excellently made, it was nonetheless a heavier rapier that soon tired her arm.

At the end of an exchange, Agnès suddenly lunged. Saint-Lucq parried, started a riposte but feinted and delivered a particularly treacherous thrust. Taught by the best masters, the baronne de Vaudreuil did not fall into his trap. Her counterattack was immediate and Saint-Lucq would have lost an eye had it not been for his reflexes and composure. The two fencers backed away from one another and saluted.

'Bravo!' exclaimed La Fargue.

Ballardieu wanted to applaud, a feat somewhat complicated by the paper cone filled with small cream pastries that he held in one hand, while eating with the other.

'Thank you,' said Agnès.

Putting down her sword, she reached for a towel to wipe her face, neck, and throat. She was breathless but satisfied, as if she had just had a good meal. The exercise had done wonders for her.

Saint-Lucq re-sheathed his weapon in silence.

'I have decided to trust your intuition, Agnès,' La Fargue announced. And for the others' benefit, he explained, 'Agnès thinks that we're not finished with the Alchemist yet.'

His mouth full, Ballardieu opened his eyes wide and raised an index finger to make an objection. The young woman cut him short:

'Yes, Ballardieu, I know the Alchemist is dead.'

Interested by the discussion, Laincourt closed his copy of the *Gazette*. Marciac was still asleep on his precariously balanced chair, a slight smile playing on his lips in the warmth of the sunlight streaming through the window panes. Ballardieu lowered his finger.

'But I have reasons to believe he remains one of the keys to the mystery before us,' continued Agnès.

'Reasons?' Saint-Lucq enquired.

'All right,' she conceded. 'It's more a feeling, an intuition.'

'That might be enough,' conceded the half-blood with an ease that astonished Laincourt.

'Nevertheless,' said Ballardieu after swallowing, 'the Alchemist is dead so it will be difficult to ask him . . . If only we still had La Donna in our hands!'

La Donna was an Italian adventuress who rented out her services, always excellent, as a conspirator, a spy, and a seductress. The Blades had crossed paths with her recently, when she had offered to sell to France valuable information about a plot threatening the Crown. Indirectly, this information had led to the capture of the Alchemist. But La Donna never lost sight of her own interests. Faithful to her reputation for duplicity, she had used the Blades to her own advantage before reclaiming her freedom with complete impunity thanks to the intervention of a powerful protector: Pope Urban VIII.

'Forget La Donna,' said La Fargue. 'When we arrested him, the Alchemist was serving madame de Chevreuse as her master of magic. So we know he had gained her trust, as well as the queen's. He was passing himself off as . . .'

He searched for the name.

'Charles Mauduit,' supplied Laincourt. 'Who actually exists, as it happens. Or at least, he used to.'

'Who was he?' asked Agnès.

'An itinerant philosopher and mage. The books he occasionally published were well regarded in certain expert circles. But he was known mostly through his writings, and only to the few.'

'In short,' said Saint-Lucq, 'this master of magic had a name, but no face. That made him the ideal victim, considering the Alchemist's projects. You can rest assured that the real Mauduit is dead.'

'Let us return to the Alchemist and La Chevreuse,' said La Fargue. 'Willingly or not, the duchesse was an accomplice of the man she took to be Mauduit. No doubt she knows something about him that could be of interest to us. Moreover, he could not have emerged out of the blue and, overnight, become the master of magic in one of France's greatest households. How did he introduce himself into her entourage? More to the point, who introduced him?'

The question hung in the air without a response and, excepting Marciac, all present agreed that it deserved an answer.

'Do you think the duchesse would receive you?' the captain of the Blades asked, turning to Laincourt.

The cardinal's former spy pondered the matter briefly.

'Yes,' he replied.

'Perfect. Pay her a visit and question her closely. Be skilful about it, because there is nothing we can offer her to encourage her good will. Marciac will go with you.'

The Gascon opened an eye on hearing his name spoken.

Marciac and Laincourt waited until early afternoon before going to see the duchesse de Chevreuse, as a lady of her station never received anyone before midday. They reached the faubourg Saint-Germain via the Pont Rouge, which involved paying a toll but saved them from making a long detour across the Pont Neuf and its crowds. On the Right Bank, they followed the Seine upstream before taking one of the large archways through the Grande Galerie, a long building running parallel to the river and linking the Louvre to the Tuileries palace. They travelled on foot, without fear for their boots and breeches as the scorching sun that turned Paris into a stinking oven had at least turned the perpetual muck in the streets into a hard, dry crust.

Along the way, Laincourt asked his companion in a conversational tone:

'This morning, when Agnès admitted she merely had an intuition that we should look more closely at the Alchemist, it seemed enough to convince you all . . .'

Marciac smiled.

'That's because we've learned to trust Agnès' intuitions. You will too, you'll see.'

'Really?'

'Agnès . . . You know she almost joined the Chatelaines? She would have become one of their White Wolves if she had taken the veil. That was not by chance, and . . . and well, it left her with a trace of something.'

'How is that?'

With a vague twitch of his lips, the Gascon searched for words.

'Something . . . Something inexplicable . . .'

Laincourt knew when innocent questions started to sound like an interrogation. He did not persist.

The Grande Galerie to the south and the rue Saint-Honoré to the north marked the boundaries of an old neighbourhood of narrow, miserable streets that were a blot on the landscape surrounding the Louvre. Yet it was here, in rue Saint-Thomas-du-Louvre, that the magnificent Hôtel de Chevreuse stood, the scene of elegant society parties only a few days earlier, before the mistress of the household's disgrace.

Upon their arrival, Marciac and Laincourt discovered the monumental gate to the mansion's grounds under siege. In front, a noisy throng of men and women were jostling one another and hindering traffic in the street, which only aggravated the disorder. Standing firm and impassive before them, a unit of the Cardinal's Guards in their scarlet capes prevented anyone from entering, despite protests and raised fists, while an officer tried in vain to make himself heard. Finally giving up, he ordered his men to clear the space while the great carved doors shuddered, began to open, and then spread wide. Those assembled thought they were finally being granted admittance. The uproar subsided as they retreated before the guards who enlarged their semi-circle, although elbows were out, each member of the crowd trying not to let anyone else get in front of them. But despite their hopes there was still no question of anyone entering the premises.

Slowly, ponderously, a tarasque appeared, harnessed to a train of two wagons loaded with bundles, chests, and furniture. Two handlers armed with pikes were leading the enormous, armoured reptile which, on its six short legs, turned left onto rue Saint-Thomas-du-Louvre, moving towards rue Saint-Honoré. Some lackeys escorted the convoy.

Marciac and Laincourt did not wait to see how the doors would be closed again. Some intrepid individuals were already trying sidle into the courtyard of the Hôtel de Chevreuse, where more guards were standing watch. They knew Parisians and their propensity to revolt. The heat was not helping to soothe tempers and the situation risked turning into a bloody riot if the crowd decided to attack the armed troops.

'Meeting the duchess is not going to be easy,' the Gascon observed.

Laincourt had frequented the Hôtel de Chevreuse recently. He was thus familiar with its layout, and said:

'Behind there is a large garden that stretches to the rue Saint-Nicaise. The garden wall has a small door that—'

'Do you really believe that it isn't guarded? Or that we will find it open?'

'No. You're right.'

'Let's start by finding out what this is all about, shall we?'

They took a table in a tavern close by, near a window that allowed them to watch the street and the approaches to the besieged gate.

'So what is happening at the Hôtel de Chevreuse?' asked Marciac.

The tavern was dirty, stank and only served a vile plonk. But the tavern keeper was willing enough to talk to them.

They thus learned that the king had, that very morning during his Council, pronounced the banishment of madame de Chevreuse for once more taking part in a plot against Cardinal Richelieu. Not a very distant banishment, however, since she would be assigned to residence in Touraine, at her Château de Couzières. But the news had alarmed her numerous suppliers, to some of whom the duchesse owed fortunes, and they had come seeking their money. Unhappily, except for those with special authorisations, the king had forbidden all visits to madame de Chevreuse, a measure she was probably thankful for at present.

For Laincourt and Marciac, these were ill tidings.

'There can be no doubt that the duchesse is under close watch,' said the Gascon. 'We won't be able to climb over the wall and go see her . . .'

'And time presses. She will soon be on her way to Couzières.'

'Perhaps it would be easier to reach her there, away from all the spies swarming around her in Paris.'

'Perhaps,' said Laincourt, who turned to look out the window.

It was then that he saw a spectre that had been haunting him more or less frequently, that of the hurdy-gurdy player who had been Laincourt's contact when he was still a spy for Cardinal Richelieu. Carrying his antique musical instrument on a bandolier, the old man was standing on the corner of the street and, with his finger, he was pointing at Jules Bertaud who was just leaving Hôtel de Chevreuse. Bertaud was the bookseller specialising in esoteric works who had shown a fondness for Laincourt, to the point of treating him like a favourite nephew, if not a son. Dressed in a long sleeveless vest and a crooked cap, the man was walking along, leafing through a notebook, and looking totally absorbed in whatever he was reading.

'Wait for me,' Laincourt said, abandoning Marciac at the tavern table.

Outside, he recalled his old spy reflexes and first made sure that the man he was about to greet was not being followed. Once he was convinced of that fact, he discreetly quickened his pace and caught up with Bertaud near the church of Saint-Thomas-du-Louvre which, dedicated to Saint Thomas of Canterbury, had given its name to the street. After greeting him, Laincourt drew the bookseller into the smaller rue Doyenné, on the pretext of seeking shade.

'But whatever are you doing round here?' asked Bertaud in friendly surprise.

Taking him by the elbow, the other man moved him even further away from prying eyes.

'I was going to ask you the same question, Jules.'

Bertaud frowned, looking to right and left.

'What's going on?' he asked.

'Everything's fine. No need to worry.'

The bookseller, however, was not so easily fooled.

'But it's not by accident if I cross your path near the Hôtel de Chevreuse, is it?'

'No. What were you doing in there?'

'Is it important?'

'Perhaps.'

Bertaud shrugged.

'Madame de Chevreuse desires to dispose of the books in her magic study. She has charged me with drawing up an inventory and organising the sale. There. No mystery in that.'

Those books had probably been gathered together for the most part by the Alchemist when he was calling himself Charles Mauduit and serving the duchesse de Chevreuse as her magic master. But Laincourt wished to pursue another point, and asked:

'So you have permission to come and go at the Hôtel de Chevreuse?'

'Yes.'

'Would you be able to deliver a message to the duchesse?'

Leprat, wearing his cape and with his white rapier at his side, had been waiting in monsieur de Tréville's small antechamber for more than hour. In his mansion on rue du Vieux-Colombier, the captain of the King's Musketeers had arranged two antechambers that communicated with his office by means of a different door. The 'large antechamber' was for ordinary visitors and petitioners. The 'small' was for the others.

Leprat stood at the window and passed the time by observing the preparations being made by the musketeers in the courtyard. Each of them was checking his equipment, polishing his boots, saddling his horse, having his sword sharpened on the whetstone of a passing blade grinder, making provision of victuals, greeting his friends, kissing his mistress, and accepting the gift of a ribbon or perfumed handkerchief from her. The company was making ready to depart. That evening the king would sleep at the Château de Saint-Germain and, as was proper, his Musketeers were to accompany him.

Antoine Leprat did not know where he would be sleeping. On the other hand, he had a very good idea why Tréville had summoned him: it could only be about his quarrel with Sardent.

A secretary, finally, ushered him into the captain's office. As was often the case when he had a difficult decision to make, the captain had his back to the room and was looking out the window. Old Tréville had fought at Henri IV's side before serving Louis XIII. He was a man of action who had trouble remaining seated for very long; it always made him feel he had ants crawling up and down his legs.

Leprat stood to attention and waited in silence, his hat in his hand. Although he knew he was risking dismissal, he was already preparing to refuse to offer his apologies. He would to Broussière, perhaps, because the man had unjustly fallen victim to Leprat's wrath. But not to Sardent, who had insulted him. Indeed, the affair with Sardent would inevitably be settled by a duel. By arriving first at the botanical gardens that morning, d'Artagnan had only delayed the coming confrontation between the two men, as the rules of honour dictated.

'A brawl,' said the captain after a moment. 'In an inn. Between three of my musketeers . . .' He suddenly turned round and looked Leprat in the eye. 'That's the behaviour of a common sword-for-hire and not of a gentleman, of a musketeer . . . And yet . . . And yet, I know the respect that you bear for your cape . . .'

Shaking his head with the air of a man saddened but determined to lay down the law, Tréville sat down at his desk.

'I know that this affair can only be settled by a duel of honour. I know that, but cannot allow it. You understand, don't you?'

Leprat nodded, still silent. He frowned, however. Was Tréville unaware that Sardent and he had been ready to fight a few hours earlier, in faubourg Saint-Victor?

'Moreover, if you fight this duel and win,' the old man continued, 'a friend of Sardent will pick a quarrel with you for vengeance's sake. And if you win that duel . . . Well, in short, you will wind up dead, and before you do, you will have killed or maimed half my company . . . That, too, I cannot allow.'

Once again, Leprat nodded without saying a word.

It was certain: Tréville knew nothing of his aborted duel. D'Artagnan had kept the matter secret, which was just like him. By preventing the duel from taking place through his presence, and by pretending not to be aware of anything, the clever lieutenant had acted in accordance with his rank without having to assert his authority. His ruse, moreover, relieved him of having to make a report: a way of protecting his brothers-in-arms from repercussions.

'Because it so happens,' Tréville continued, 'that I hold half my company as dear to me as I hold the entirety of your person . . .'

At this, Leprat cocked an eyebrow. Could Tréville know more than he let on? Had he chosen to save appearances in order to avoid having to take radical disciplinary measures?

Leprat hesitated, and then ventured:

'Th . . . Thank you.'

'You're welcome. So, to preserve both your person and my company, I am separating the one from the other. Monsieur le chevalier d'Orgueil, you will depart this evening on a special escort mission.'

The Illuminator arrived in Paris by the Saint-Antoine gate, beneath a blazing sun that obliged him to keep his eyes squinted.

Tall and massively built, with a large belly, he was riding a bay horse and leading a mule loaded with his baggage. He had a beret decorated with a pheasant feather on his head and a pair of worn-out, shapeless boots on his feet. His body was clothed in a dusty blue outfit. His shirt was sweat-stained beneath his open doublet, and an abundance of hair as thick and black as that of his beard emerged from his gaping collar. He was perspiring profusely. A powerful musky smell emanated from him and his breath came in muffled rasps. A *schiavone* hung at his side, a sturdy sword with a straight blade whose guard enveloped the entire hand and joined with the pommel. This Italian weapon was traditionally employed by the Dalmatian Guards of the Venetian Republic.

Leaving the crowded rue Saint-Antoine, the Illuminator took rue Saint-Paul as far as the Seine, which he followed downstream to Les Écailles.

The Scales.

Having been left in a wild state for years, the island had been adopted by the dracs who made it into their home: a damp and rotting maze of huts on stilts, rickety walkways, and dark lanes. By day, Notre-Dame-des-Écailles was a miserable village from whose depths rose a foul, marshy stink. But once night fell, Les Écailles became the beating heart of a violent, primitive culture which expressed itself by torchlight, in a moist air rich with spicy scents, and to the rhythm of sinister drums celebrating ancient rituals or punctuating warrior chants, lascivious dances, and blood-curdling tales. Here, only tribal laws and traditions held sway.

Except in the presence of a dragon.

After passing over the wooden bridge that linked Paris to Les Écailles, the Illuminator sold his mule and hired two drac slaves to carry his baggage. The trader did not negotiate with him. Usually one to drive a hard bargain, the old drac did not even dare look the Illuminator in the eye: he knew a dragon when he saw one, particularly when the dragon in question was projecting its aura of power, as the Illuminator never failed to do when in the presence of inferiors. This aura was sometimes strong enough to provoke uneasiness in humans; to a drac it was like a painful wave that resonated in the very depths of their being and woke fearful and servile instincts in them, the instincts of a race that had now been freed, but nonetheless one that had been created by the Ancestral Dragons and had been mercilessly oppressed by them.

Followed by his slaves for the day, the Illuminator rode through Les Écailles, conscious of the wary and sometimes hateful looks he attracted. He felt scorn for such reactions and pretended not to see them, but relished provoking them all the same. Proceeding at a walk and looking contemptuously down at the drac settlement, he soon crossed over a narrow canal that isolated one end of Ile Notre-Dame and delineated a closed paved quarter where a decadent community of last-born dragons had established itself. There were lurid rumours about the goings-on in this ghetto, whose mysterious dwellings were defended by sinister-looking walls and massive black doors.

At the end of a hemmed-in lane, the Illuminator arrived before one of these doors. Beneath a stone arch overhung with scarlet ivy, it presented two thick rectangular panels whose dark wood, large square-headed nails and solid iron fittings indicated their great age. The door opened slowly at his approach, revealing the courtyard of an elegant house.

The Hôtel des Arcanes, headquarters of the Arcana lodge.

There, on the bottom steps of the porch, the Gentleman awaited with a smile.

'Welcome,' he called.

Without answering, the Illuminator dismounted and exchanged a greeting with the master of the household which was far from enthusiastic. Ignoring this, the Gentleman said:

'I cannot disguise my pleasure at seeing you again, my brother.'

'It was lucky that I was in Lorraine,' replied the other dragon. 'When will the Assembly take place?'

'Soon.' And seeing the drac slaves waiting, the Gentleman asked: 'What's all this?'

'My baggage. The slaves are hired. Someone will come fetch them tomorrow.'

'Ah!' said the Gentleman in a slightly disconcerted tone. 'Have you eaten?'

'Not much.'

'Then come, I have a light meal prepared.'

On entering, the dragons passed three household servants who, pale-faced and glassy-eyed, were on their way to tend to the Illuminator's baggage, slaves, and horse.

While the Illuminator ate heartily but without showing either satisfaction or displeasure, the Gentleman kept him company, sipping a glass of golden henbane. They were alone in the luxuriously furnished salon of the Hôtel des Arcanes and spoke little: the Illuminator, when eating, obviously wanted to do just that. Once he felt full, he dismissed the lackey serving him, drank a last swallow of wine, wiped his fingers on the tablecloth, and smoothed his slightly greasy beard.

'Now it's my turn to ask,' he said, pointing a finger at the departing lackey.

This servant, too, was mute, pale-faced, with an absent look and slow gestures.

'The Enchantress' latest whim,' explained the Gentleman. 'She finds it more elegant to have human domestics. But don't ask me the secret of the potion she has them drink . . .'

'Is she here?'

'The Enchantress? Of course . . . She will be joining us for supper.'

A silence ensued between the two dragons. Their gazes crossed and locked on one another.

'The Heresiarch sent me,' the Illuminator finally said.

'Good.'

'He has charged me with a mission.'

'And that is?'

'If the Heresiarch wants you to know—'

'—the Heresiarch will tell me. Very well.'

The Gentleman did not insist.

With regard to the Heresiarch, the Illuminator displayed the loyalty of a guard dog. Whatever the Heresiarch wanted, the Illuminator would do. Without discussion, or even much thought.

'Is there anything you need?' the Gentleman asked coldly.

'Gold.'

'You shall have it. Besides that?'

'Nothing else for the moment.'

'In that case . . .'

He rose and was about to withdraw, when the Illuminator said, in a slightly raised voice, as if concluding a discussion with a final argument:

'What the Heresiarch has done, he has done for the good of the Arcana. The Alchemist's death was necessary. He had failed and was about to fall into the Chatelaines' hands. As if it were not enough that he had already allowed himself to be duped by that . . . by that Italian woman!' The dragon sounded aggrieved at the memory but quickly recovered his calm. 'No matter. But regarding the Alchemist, time was short and the Heresiarch had to act urgently. Necessity knows no law.'

And as the Gentleman continued to gaze at him without speaking, he finally asked:

'Will you support the Heresiarch at the next Arcana Assembly?'

'Does the Heresiarch doubt it?'

'If our adversaries carry the day, it may bring the Burning Sword down upon us . . .'

'Have I ever wavered?' replied the Gentleman with confidence as he turned on his heel and walked away.

But once the Illuminator could no longer see it, his expression became one of concern.

Upon their return to the Hôtel de l'Épervier, Marciac and Laincourt reported their findings to La Fargue and Saint-Lucq.

'It was only a matter of time before the king ordered madame de Chevreuse's banishment,' commented the Blades' captain. 'But when one knows how close she came to delivering the queen to the Black Claw, one can't help but think that a retreat to her château at Couzières is not such a cruel punishment . . . Nevertheless, it does not make our business any easier.'

'When must the duchesse leave Paris?' enquired Saint-Lucq.

'Very soon,' Marciac informed him.

'And for the moment, the Cardinal's Guards are keeping a close watch on her mansion, from which she is forbidden to leave . . .'

'Yes. And it's impossible to enter without the proper authorisation.'

'No visits?'

'None.'

'Letters?'

'All subject to censorship by the cardinal.'

La Fargue grimaced in annoyance.

Agnès made an entrance, returning from a long ride, while Ballardieu remained in the stable helping André with the horses.

'What's going on?' she asked.

Marciac brought her up to date.

'Argh!' she said in frustration when she knew as much as others.

'But Arnaud may have a solution,' the Gascon added.

'I know someone who is free to come and go as he pleases at the Hôtel de Chevreuse,' explained Laincourt. 'His name is Jules Bertaud, a bookseller and a friend of mine.'

'And what is this bookseller doing at the duchesse's home?' asked La Fargue.

'He is arranging for the disposal of the library in her magic study.'

'Would he agree to be our messenger?'

'I asked him and he said yes.'

'Is the man trustworthy?' Agnès wanted to know.

'I believe so.'

La Fargue scratched at his beard while he thought.

'I would prefer you to be certain,' he said.

'Bertaud is a bookseller,' retorted Laincourt. 'He is not a spy. I've known him for a long time, but I cannot answer for him absolutely.'

The old captain shrugged: the only other solution was to ask Cardinal Richelieu for a safe-conduct.

'Beggars can't be choosers . . .' he conceded finally.

'Even so, there is still a problem,' Agnès pointed out. And seeing the others looking at her blankly, she hastened to explain: 'I may be wrong, but I doubt that the duchesse de Chevreuse is able to say a word or take a step in her home without the cardinal learning of it immediately. She is most certainly being watched, discreetly but efficiently, day and night. And I would not be the least bit surprised to discover this Bertaud fellow is also being spied on.'

'You're right,' said La Fargue. Then, addressing everyone, he declared: 'We can't simply entrust this bookseller with a letter. We need to find a way he can deliver a message to the duchesse without compromising ourselves or alerting the Palais-Cardinal.'

Laincourt nodded:

'I'll think of something,' he promised.

The Bastille was built during the second half of the fourteenth century to reinforce the eastern defences of Paris. Standing by the Saint-Antoine gate, this massive fortress overlooked a bastion extending into the neighbouring faubourg. Surrounded by a large moat filled by waters drawn from the Seine, it comprised eight round towers which each had a name, such as the Tour de la Chapelle or the Tour du Puits. The towers were connected by walls as tall as they were, protecting a courtyard which was only accessible via a drawbridge which was lowered to connect with a fixed bridge across the moat. And reaching this bridge entailed traversing two outer courtyards. The first was the Cour de l'Avancée, which could be entered freely from rue Saint-Antoine and the Arsenal gardens, and contained the garrison's barracks and stables. The second outer courtyard was smaller and guarded by a gate. The Bastille governor's house was located here.

The Bastille had lost its military role during Henri IV's reign. The royal treasury was guarded there for a time. Then Richelieu rebuilt its cellars and the floors of all eight towers for use as a prison. It was a State prison, however, which meant that one could only be sent there by an order of the king, signed and sealed, known as a *lettre de cachet*. The prisoners locked away there were divided into two categories: illustrious and influential figures; and the secret enemies of France. Provided they had means, the members of the first group enjoyed fairly comfortable conditions of incarceration. The second group, in contrast, were condemned to long and anonymous solitude, without hope of a trial or a pardon.

The Masque de Fer, or the Man in the Iron Mask, was one of them.

But others preceded him.

*

In the courtyard of the Bastille, Leprat and the fifteen horse-men under his command waited patiently. Leprat was the only one to dismount, by the wagon that would convey the prisoner they were escorting. All of them were drawn from the King's Musketeers and wore the blue cape with silver braiding. They did not speak and remained in line in their saddles, grim and watchful, the butt of their muskets resting on their thighs.

Occasionally a horse became restless, but was quickly reined in.

Although it was still early evening, night had already settled within the high walls. The courtyard was silent and deserted, plunged into darkness as if crushed by the mass of grey stones surrounding it. Keys had been turned in all the locks until the following morning. All the bolts had been shot, the chains secured, and the doors shut tight. Sent back to their solitude, the prisoners knew that the gaolers would not answer their calls. The sentries who weren't patrolling the walls and towers fought with boredom in their guard-rooms, sitting around tables rolling dice. A strange tranquillity, an anxious calm, had invaded the sinister fortress. Time seemed to be standing still, which was only too true for some of the poor wretches shut away there.

Leprat did not know the identity of the prisoner he was waiting for.

He only knew that he was to accompany him to the Château de Mareuil-sur-Ay, not far from Épernay and the border with Lorraine. There, after some diplomatic negoti-ations, the man would be discreetly placed in the custody of a representative of Pope Urban VIII. Perhaps he was a Church spy that His Holiness was determined to reclaim. Perhaps he was a traitor or a fugitive criminal. Perhaps he was even an agent of a foreign power, for whom Rome was acting as an intermediary. Be that as it may, the prisoner was the object of an obscure transaction taking place at the highest level. And what would France receive in return? Another prisoner? Documents? Information? Unless the king was merely seek-ing the good graces of the Pope on the eve of a war with Lorraine – another Catholic power.

Such exchanges were not uncommon.

Indeed, based on his experience in the Cardinal's Blades, Leprat had not been overly surprised when Captain Tréville had given him his orders. And, immediately understanding what was likely to be involved, he had refrained from asking too many questions. All that he needed was information pertinent to the success of his mission. As for the rest, he preferred not to know. He had no desire to be mixed up in intrigue and politics. A musketeer again, he only wanted to serve the king with honour, fulfilling his vocation as a soldier.

Behind an officer, a unit of arquebusiers filed out from the Tour du Puits in an orderly manner. They surrounded a man dressed in boots, breeches, and a shirt, whose wrists were shackled and whose face was hidden by a mask made of leather and riveted iron, with three rectangular holes, a large one for the mouth and two smaller ones for the eyes. He seemed to be young, and was of medium height with a slender, graceful build. His blond hair fell to his shoulders. He had the bearing of a proud, refined man who had no weapons left to oppose his captors with but his pride and his scorn. He halted at the same time as his guards and waited, his head held high and his back straight.

The officer stepped forward, saluted Leprat, and took a sheaf of papers from the musketeer which he studied closely. As he did, Leprat observed and considered the prisoner. His silhouette seemed vaguely familiar, but it was the mask that intrigued him most. It was an exceptional precaution and Leprat was curious why it was necessary. Of course, it was meant to prevent the prisoner from being recognised. But why?

After declaring himself satisfied, the officer refolded the documents and returned them to Leprat. Then he ordered the prisoner to be placed in the wagon.

No doubt because they had seen more than one docile man rebel at the last moment, the solders were somewhat brusque with the prisoner who, when he was shoved, reacted as if he had received a hot poker to the shoulder and spun round. An arquebusier was already lifting his weapon, but Leprat leapt forward and interposed himself before a blow from the butt could be struck.

'This prisoner is mine,' he said. 'And he will be well treated.'

This intervention caused an angry stir among the soldiers, before their officer reminded them of their discipline.

'Thank you, monsieur,' said the prisoner.

That voice!

Squinting, Leprat suddenly recognised the eyes visible through openings cut into the mask. And he was even less likely to forget the eyes than he was the voice of a man who had coldly fired a pistol ball at his heart. Leprat remained dumbfounded while the soldiers placed the prisoner in the hitched wagon.

He realised someone was speaking to him.

'These two are for the irons,' the officer was saying, handing him a ring of small keys. 'And this one is for the mask.'

The prisoner's mask was held closed by a lock located at the rear of the skull.

Distracted, Leprat nodded as he pocketed the key ring.

'Any particular instructions?' he asked out of habit.

'None that you don't already know. But be careful, monsieur.'

'Why?'

'This prisoner, now entrusted to your care, has twice been the object of assassination attempts while under my guard. First by dagger, and then by poison. The dagger wounded one of my soldiers and the poison killed a gaoler.'

'Who wielded the dagger?'

'A madman who hung himself with his own belt before he could be interrogated. As for the poison . . .'

'I understand. Thank you, monsieur.'

'You're welcome. Good luck.'

Leprat climbed back into his saddle, placed five of his musketeers in front of the wagon, and ten behind it. Then he stood in his stirrups and, when he signalled their departure, the great courtyard rang with a loud din of hooves, creaking axles, and iron-bound wheels grinding into the paving stones.

The prisoner hidden behind the mask of leather and iron was the marquis de Gagnière, a cold and implacable killer.

Leprat had suffered the sad privilege of crossing his path recently, while on a secret mission for the king. Gagnière had laid a trap for him that a lone man had no chance of escaping, and had left him for dead after – without batting an eyelash – shooting him with a pistol at close range. Luckily, Leprat was left-handed. The ball had lodged itself in the thick leather of his baldric, which happened to fall across his chest from left to right. Shortly after that, the Cardinal's Blades had been recalled to service and confronted the Black Claw, in the person of a certain vicomtesse de Malicorne . . . and it had eventually come to light that Gagnière was her henchman. The vicomtesse had escaped. The sinister marquis had been captured and delivered to the cardinal's justice.

For Antoine Leprat to find himself escorting the marquis de Gagnière was a curious twist of fate. To crown it all, there was the possibility that he might have to risk his life to protect the man. To protect him from the Black Claw, no less! For there was little doubt the Black Claw were behind the attempts on Gagnière's life, either to punish him or to ensure his silence. Did he hide important secrets?

Leprat was only sure of one thing: the Black Claw would never give up. And there were forty-five leagues between Paris and their destination, which they would travel in a little under four days if they maintained a decent pace. The journey offered plenty of occasions for ambushes and attacks along the way.

With Leprat riding at the head, the wagon and its escort left Paris by the Saint-Antoine gate and galloped off into the night along a grey and powdery road.

When night fell, Marciac accompanied Agnès to the door of her bedchamber. They slept on the same floor of the Hôtel de l'Épervier and each had brought their own light. The Gascon, however, had no intention of retiring to his bed straight away.

'Really?' he insisted. 'Are you sure you won't come out with me to La Sovange's club?'

Madame de Sovange maintained, on rue de l'Arbalète in faubourg Saint-Jacques, a gaming house frequented by the very best society.

And by Marciac.

'No, Nicolas. Although it's sweet of you to ask.'

'I promise we'll come home early.'

'It's already late.'

'I bow to your wishes . . . But promise me that . . .'

'Soon, yes. I promise you I will.'

'Cross your heart?'

'Cross my heart. But if you want my opinion, you look like a man who needs a good night's sleep.'

The Gascon shrugged his shoulders and looked away, like a young boy caught doing something naughty.

'Sleep eludes me,' he confessed. 'I can't close my eyes without seeing Almades.'

'I know. It's the same for me.'

Marciac forced himself to smile.

'If someone had told me that I would miss his grim face so much . . . But to the Devil with this sadness!'

Pulling himself together, he opened Agnès' door for her, stepped aside to let her pass and ushered her inside with a bow and a flourish.

'Madame.'

'Thank you.'

She went in, placed her candle on a small table, and turned around to face the Gascon who remained on the threshold.

'Tell me, Nicolas . . .'

'Yes?'

'Do you know why Leprat left us?'

'Not exactly, no. He gave the captain an explanation, but I wasn't there.'

'And La Fargue, how did he take the news?'

'In his usual manner,' replied Marciac with a shrug. 'With cries, tears, and sobs. Afterwards, he wrote a poem recounting his sorrow . . .'

Agnès stifled a laugh but remained concerned.

'And you?' she asked. 'Did you speak with him?'

'With Leprat? No.'

'Do you think he would like it if I paid him a visit?'

'Perhaps. But you'll need to wait a bit. Or else go to Saint-Germain,' added Marciac. And seeing Agnès frown, he explained: 'The king has retired there, so the King's Musketeers went with him . . .'

'Oh yes, that's right . . . Well, good night, Nicolas.'

'Good night, baronne.'

Marciac closed the door and went away.

Feeling tired, Agnès undressed and freshened up. Then, turning her back to the mirror, she twisted her neck to examine the mark decorating her left shoulder. It was an old mark whose outlines had only become sharper over time. Now there could be no doubt that it was a rune or, more precisely, two runes entwined together to form one. The first signified 'dragon' and the second 'death'.

With her finger, Agnès de Vaudreuil brushed this mark which had seemed to waken recently and whose meaning she knew, although she couldn't admit it to herself. As she got into bed, she prayed for a dreamless sleep, only to have the vision of the great black dragon destroying Paris return once more to haunt her.

Upon arriving in the neighbourhood of Place Maubert that morning, Laincourt found Jules Bertaud's bookshop closed. That was hardly surprising; the bookseller rarely opened for business before noon. But his regular customers knew they could always knock on the door and peer through the shop's large front window. Bertaud was usually working in the storeroom or in some secluded corner of his shop. He would glance out and, seeing a favoured client, gesture for them to come round to the courtyard in the rear.

It was not Bertaud, however, who answered Laincourt's knock on this hot morning in July 1633, but his daughter. And rather than make him come through the courtyard, she hastened to open the door and usher him in. Clotilde was a pretty brunette with green eyes. Sixteen years old, she was totally devoted to her father and deeply in love with Arnaud de Laincourt, a fact that Laincourt alone was unaware of.

'Good morning, Clotilde. Is your father in? Could he receive me?'

'I will call him right away, monsieur.'

Thanking her with a polite smile, Laincourt began to wander distractedly about the shop, examining one book, leafing through another, without seeing that Clotilde had hesitated before leaving him, no doubt searching for something to say, before finally withdrawing reluctantly, cursing herself for being so dim-witted.

Bertaud soon came down from the first floor, where he and his daughter lived. He had his hat in his hand and the busy air of a man caught just as he making ready to go out.

'Good morning, Arnaud. You almost missed me: I was just on my way to the Hôtel de Chevreuse.'

'That's precisely what I've come to see you about. Can we talk?'

The bookseller caught Laincourt's meaning and brought him into the storeroom where no one could see or hear them. The room was dark and filled with the smell of dust and old paper.

'Yesterday,' said Laincourt in a low voice, 'I asked if you would undertake to transmit a message to the duchesse de Chevreuse. You replied yes, but I want you to know that I don't consider you bound by your answer. So, listen to me closely. I need to meet madame de Chevreuse. I must speak to her about a matter of which, unfortunately, I can tell you nothing. It must be done in greatest secret and I need to arrange a rendezvous with her. That's why I must go through you, given that you have access to the Hôtel de Chevreuse.'

'I say to you again, Arnaud, that I am willing to render you this service.'

'Don't answer just yet.'

'Are you plotting against the king?'

'No.'

'Against monsieur le cardinal?'

'No.'

'And are you acting for the common good?'

'I believe so.'

'Then that is enough for me. What must I do?'

Laincourt hesitated, and then pulled out a small book of poetry from his doublet.

'Here. Give this to madame de Chevreuse.'

'Is that all?'

'No. You must tell her: "Madame, here is the volume you spoke to me about, which I had in my shop".'

'But there was never any question of such a thing between madame de Chevreuse and me!'

'Precisely. That's how she will realise the particular worth of this book.'

'Will she accept it?'

'Without question. But if she does not, pretend that you wanted to offer it to her as a token of your admiration, but did not know how to phrase your compliment . . . But I assure you, madame de Chevreuse will take the book.'

'And after that?'

'After that, act just as you normally would. Go about your ordinary business and come home when you are finished. Neither sooner nor later than usual.'

'I don't wait for a reply?'

'Don't wait for anything. Don't change any of your habits. It's possible they are watching you.'

'"They"?' asked the bookseller in a worried tone.

'The cardinal's men.'

This reply disturbed Bertaud.

'But I thought you . . .'

'The matter is complicated,' Laincourt said evasively. 'Would you prefer to renounce this? I would understand if you did.'

'No! . . . So I just come home as if nothing were out of the ordinary?'

'Yes. If she wishes to, the duchesse will have transmitted her reply to you before then. It will either be "Yes" or "No".'

'And where will you and I meet?'

'Nowhere. If madame de Chevreuse replies yes, ask Clotilde

to wash the shop windows this evening. If no, make sure she does nothing of the sort . . . Have you understood?'

'I think so, yes.'

'Perfect.'

After leaving Bertaud's shop, Laincourt met the hurdy-gurdy player who was waiting for him and proceeded to walk along beside him.

Everything will go well, boy. The duchesse de Chevreuse will find the note you slipped inside the cover of the book and she will be at the rendezvous this evening.

That's not what worries me.

You're thinking of Bertaud.

I've compromised him. If they discover he—

There is still time for you to go back, recover the book from Bertaud and ask him to forget this whole affair. Will you do that?

No.

Well then, silence your remorse.

At the Hôtel des Arcanes, the Enchantress joined the Gentleman in the study where he kept – behind glass, set in racks, or placed on display stands – his collection of rapiers. He possessed several dozen, all of them forged by the best craftsmen of Europe. Each was worth a fortune, but that was not the main thing. Although he did not refuse to wear them, or to wield them, the Gentleman simply enjoyed the company of these lethal masterpieces. When he was preoccupied with something he spent hours, sometimes whole nights, admiring them and maintaining them in perfect condition. He would recall the memories attached to them, cherishing in particular those blades that had already taken a life, and promising the others they would shed blood soon enough.

'It seems the Heresiarch is suspicious of you,' said the Enchantress.

'Yes.'

'That's new.'

'I think the Heresiarch is suspicious of everyone right now,' the Gentleman declared calmly as he rubbed the blue steel of a

845

sharp blade with an oiled cloth. 'His Grand Design has never been so close to being accomplished.'

'Or to failure.'

'Or, indeed, to failure.'

The Enchantress slowly walked around the study, pausing before one blade, running her fingertips down another. Wearing a crimson robe, she was beautiful and bewitching, her mahogany hair caressing her pale shoulders.

'The Illuminator gave me a letter from the Heresiarch.'

'A letter from the Heresiarch? Addressed to you?'

'To me rather than to you, that's right. Which is also something new, isn't it?'

The Gentleman rose to put away the rapier whose blade he had just been cleaning. He placed it within a long chest which he closed. For a moment he remained still, reflecting, before turning back to the Enchantress.

'And what was the subject of this letter?'

The Enchantress fixed her eyes resolutely on those of her lover.

'The Heresiarch thinks that the Arcana need new blood. He asked me to admit an initiate. In my own name.'

'An initiate. As if this were the time for initiations! And who does he want you to initiate?'

'The vicomtesse de Malicorne.'

For an instant, the Gentleman thought he had misheard.

'The vicomtesse . . . de Malicorne? Are you jesting?'

The vicomtesse de Malicorne was also a dragon. And although she did not belong to the Arcana, she had been one of the Black Claw's best agents in Paris. Daring and ambitious, she had come very close to establishing a Black Claw lodge in France, something the Sisters of Saint Georges had always managed to prevent. But it was not the Chatelaines who had thwarted her, it was the Cardinal's Blades. She had failed and had emerged broken from the ordeal. Struck by the after-effects of a powerful ritual that had been brutally interrupted, she was no longer even capable of assuming the appearance that she had long made her own, that of an adorable young blonde woman.

'But she is nothing!' protested the Gentleman. 'I know the Alchemist met with her recently. She was downcast, reduced to the state of an old woman deluding herself with dreams of one day recovering her power . . . The Alchemist said she was finished.'

'He was mistaken. The vicomtesse de Malicorne can recover her strength and vitality. She can do so thanks to me, and that is what the Heresiarch wishes.'

The Gentleman gave the Enchantress a long look.

'Yes,' he said at last. 'I know you can manage it . . . But even so? Why does the Heresiarch want us to initiate Malicorne now? I'm starting to think he's losing his mind . . .'

Drawing closer, the Enchantress displayed a superior smile, the smile of someone about to deliver a major revelation.

'Do you know why the Alchemist went to see La Malicorne after her failure?'

'To put his mind at rest, I suppose. To make sure she—'

'No,' the Enchantress interrupted. 'He went to her at the Heresiarch's behest. He was worried about her . . .'

'What?'

'La Malicorne came very close to establishing the first ever lodge of the Black Claw in France. You can imagine what sort of feat that would have been, can't you? But do you believe she came so close on her own? And why was the Black Claw willing to entrust her with the Sphère d'Âme that was so essential to her plan? La Malicorne was capable and trustworthy, true enough. But to go from that to having the old masters agree to entrust her with one of their precious Sphères d'Âme?'

'No doubt in their eyes, the game was worth the candle,' the Gentleman suggested.

'And now La Malicorne has failed, now she has lost everything, now she has lost her allies but still knows numerous secrets, how is it that the Black Claw has not had her assassinated?'

'Do you mean to say . . . ?'

'Yes. She is under the Heresiarch's protection. But he is

847

doing things as he always does, and as he has always fostered her projects in the past: in secret.'

'But why?'

'You make me laugh!'

'The Heresiarch and La Mal—?' He cut himself short, shaking his head. 'No. That isn't like him. The Heresiarch has never been one to give way to passion.'

'The Inferiors say that the flesh is weak. That applies to us, too . . . Happily so. How boring things would be if we were the same cold creatures as our ancestors!'

The Enchantress gave a burst of merry laughter.

After which, regaining a straight face, she said, almost tenderly:

'But rest assured. The Heresiarch did not forget strategy when he took La Malicorne under his wing . . . Answer me this: would the old masters of the Black Claw have ever permitted one of us, one of the Arcana, to attempt to found a lodge in France?'

'Certainly not! If one of us had succeeded, we would have won far too much prestige and influence.'

'And if it had been one of the Heresiarch's protégés?'

'No. For the same reasons; they would have been destined to become one of us.'

'But by secretly favouring La Malicorne, the Heresiarch was disguising his progress. If she had succeeded, no one could have prevented her from joining the Arcana, and certainly not the old lizards in Madrid. It would have been a *fait accompli*. They'd be furious, certainly. But powerless to stop it.'

The Gentleman nodded slowly, looking thoughtful, an admiring smile on his lips.

'Clever. Very clever, even . . . Which is much more like our old serpent of a Heresiarch.'

'And his plan offered the final advantage of not compromising the Arcana if La Malicorne failed. Which is indeed what happened . . .'

'So you believe that by resuscitating La Malicorne and admitting her to the Arcana . . .'

'. . . we will accomplish what the Heresiarch wants to do,

but which he cannot. If he openly comes to the vicomtesse's rescue, the Black Claw will learn of it and realise what he has been doing all along.'

'Do you really believe the Heresiarch still feels something for La Malicorne?'

'If you ask, then you've forgotten that he continues to protect her. He must, since she is alive. Besides, can we afford to displease the Heresiarch in this matter? He wants his sweetheart? Well then, let's offer her to him.'

The Gentleman silently reflected on this.

The Enchantress, however, knew she had already won the argument. Pressing herself to him, she presented him with a little note folded in quarters and, in his ear, she said:

'She goes by the name madame de Chantegrelle and she is pining away in a convent in the faubourg Saint-Jacques, whose address is written here. I know you can find the words to convince her . . .'

Night was falling when Marciac returned to the Hôtel de l'Épervier with the news they had all been waiting for.

'The bookseller's daughter washed the shop windows,' he announced to the Blades gathered in the fencing room.

'So the duchesse de Chevreuse has agreed to my rendez-vous,' said Laincourt.

'I don't understand it,' confessed Agnès pouring a glass of wine for the Gascon. 'Or not entirely . . . If I were her, and had almost handed the queen to the Black Claw, I would be relieved to be merely banished from the royal court. I certainly wouldn't risk giving the king the slightest motive to regret his clemency.'

'That's because you're not the duchesse de Chevreuse . . . She has the taste, a true passion, for intrigue. Not to mention that boredom is probably gnawing away at her.'

'But now she knows who you really are! She knows you serve the cardinal . . .'

'Precisely,' said La Fargue. He was straddling a chair, his forearms resting flat across its back. 'That detail must have particularly piqued the duchesse's curiosity. Because she must guess that it is not by the cardinal's order that Laincourt wants to see her. If his approach was of an ordinary nature, why surround it with such secrecy? Why try to elude the spies swarming about the Hôtel de Chevreuse? Isn't he supposed to be serving the same master as they are?'

'So the duchesse has already realised that we are acting without the cardinal's knowledge,' said Marciac.

'Yes.'

'That's hardly very reassuring.'

'More than that, it's dangerous,' declared Saint-Lucq.

As was his custom, he remained slightly apart from the rest of the group, sitting in profile in the recess of one of the windows looking out at the unkempt garden with its old table and chestnut tree.

'Dangerous?' enquired Ballardieu.

'Saint-Lucq is wary of a trap,' Agnès explained to him. 'Am I right?'

The half-blood, who had been carefully cleaning his spectacles, nodded.

'La Chevreuse might want to offer the king a token of her loyalty by betraying you, Laincourt. She might pretend to agree to meet you in order to give you up to His Majesty's officers.'

Because he was a former spy and had some experience in such matters, Laincourt was forced to admit that this hypothesis was plausible.

'Yes,' he said. 'It's possible.'

'Betraying you is even doubly in the duchesse's interest,' La Fargue added. 'For the reason that Saint-Lucq has just given us, first of all. But, secondly, because the rendezvous you have proposed could easily be a ruse of Richelieu's to test her loyalty. She is too sharp-witted not to have thought of it. And so the duchesse has every reason to ensure your ruin . . .'

'I am betting that madame de Chevreuse will not resist the temptation of hearing me out,' said Laincourt. 'Furthermore, I think she even feels a certain degree of affection for me.'

'It's too risky,' decreed Saint-Lucq. 'I'll go with you.'

'No. It will depend entirely on madame de Chevreuse's

goodwill whether she answers my questions or not. We need her, whereas she has nothing to gain from helping us. I doubt that she will be well disposed towards us if she senses that we are wary of her . . .'

'That is a valid point,' admitted La Fargue gravely.

'You are taking the risk of placing yourself, alone, in the wolf's jaws, Arnaud,' said Agnès, trying to make him see sense.

'I know. But it is a risk that I must take if we are to have any chance of succeeding. Don't forget that it is not just a question of me, or of us. The only trail likely to lead us to the dragon that attacked Le Châtelet passes through the Hôtel de Chevreuse.'

'Nevertheless, be very careful, Laincourt,' La Fargue instructed him. 'You will need to elude the Cardinal's Guards, and you more than any of us know their worth.'

The tavern was located in the depths of Les Écailles, on the Ile Notre-Dame. Daylight never penetrated here and the air was stagnant and moist beneath the low beams of a ceiling blackened by the smoke from the oil lamps. The dracs who gathered in this place were of the very worst sort. Thieves, mercenaries and assassins came here to amuse themselves, drink and to seek work or opportunities for plunder.

The Illuminator abruptly released his aura as he pushed through the door.

A silence immediately fell in the large hall, which, at this hour of the evening, was packed. All eyes turned toward the dragon. Some were fearful; most were wary and hostile; a few were violently hateful. Then interest in him subsided and conversations resumed as the Illuminator, his heavy *schiavone* at his side, diminished his aura and advanced with a tranquil step.

He approached a red drac who was dining alone, eating a thick fish soup. Tall and thin, the drac was dressed as a hired swordsman, wearing an old leather doublet over a filthy shirt whose collar gaped wide open, revealing his scaly chest.

Behind him, a muscular black drac stood motionless with his arms crossed.

The red drac did not look up from his bowl as the Illuminator halted before him and threw a heavy purse on the table.

'Departure in one hour,' announced the dragon.

The drac nodded, without even pausing over his meal.

Laincourt left the Hôtel de l'Épervier on his own.

A short time later, Captain La Fargue came out in turn, but took a different route into Paris, as a magnificent summer sunset stretched across the darkening sky, the last layers of purple, red, and orange light swathing the horizon and making the scattered clouds glow.

3

After a light supper, the duchesse de Chevreuse announced that she wished to enjoy the tranquillity and cooler air of the evening, at her ease. She thus refused to be accompanied during her stroll and walked off across the large terrace on her own. Despite the tall torches that burned here and there, darkness reigned in the immense garden that, at the rear of the Hôtel de Chevreuse, stretched as far as the rue Saint-Nicaise, between the Hôtel de Rambouillet on the right and the more modest dwellings on the left. The silence was soothing in this elegant island of nature. And the air was sweet, the Parisian stink relieved by a welcome breeze.

As if weary, the duchesse sat down on a bench sheltered by the branches of a handsome elm tree, near a torch stuck in the ground. With a wave of her hand she drove off an imaginary insect, which allowed her to cast a glance over her shoulder. No one had followed her and no one seemed to be watching her from the terrace. Then she opened the volume of poetry that she had been given that afternoon by Bertaud and pretended to read.

Ten minutes later, as the bell of the Saint-Thomas church was striking the half-hour, madame de Chevreuse closed her book and took on the pensive look of someone thinking about what they had just read. While doing so, she counted to five in her head, beating the time with her index finger against the cover of the book.

After which, she pretended to resume reading.

It was the signal that all was well. Almost immediately, Laincourt emerged from the shadows. But he stayed well back, visible only to the duchesse.

853

'Good evening, madame.'

'Good evening, monsieur de Laincourt,' replied madame de Chevreuse, without raising her eyes from her book.

He could observe her at leisure and was once again surprised by her beauty. The duchesse de Chevreuse was reputed to be one of the most beautiful women in Europe and Laincourt did not doubt the truth of this, as he admired, in the warm, lively torchlight, the perfection of her profile, her milky complexion, the shine of her tawny hair, and the roundness of her throat.

Laincourt collected his wits, convinced that the duchesse was well aware of the effect she was having on him.

'I want to thank you for agreeing to this rendezvous, madame.'

'To be frank, I almost doubted that you would come. You must know the risks you are courting here.'

'Have you thought about laying a trap for me?'

She turned a page.

'I thought about it, yes. However, playing the role of an auxiliary of the cardinal's police would be more than I could bear. You guessed as much, didn't you?'

As Laincourt made no reply, the duchesse continued:

'This bookseller, monsieur Bertaud, what is he to you, exactly?'

'A friend.'

'His hand trembled quite a bit when he handed me this book. And his voiced wavered as well. I doubt that this escaped the notice of madame de Luret, who informs the cardinal when she is not reading books aloud to me. She is also quite friendly with a certain monsieur de Brussand, whose handsome air won her over.'

'Brussand? He is here?'

'Do you know him?' the duchesse asked in surprise. But then memory returned to her. 'Ah, but it's true. I forgot that you wore that cursed red cape once yourself . . . Well, monsieur de Brussand commands the guards that watch over my house and my person. Is he a friend, too?'

'He was,' Laincourt replied.

He couldn't help thinking of the look old Brussand had given him when he, Laincourt, had been accused of spying on and betraying the cardinal. He had worn the red cape of the Cardinal's Guards at the time, and the false accusations were intended to help unmask the real traitors. But Laincourt had never had the opportunity to establish the complete truth with his friend.

Once again, he found himself needing to collect his wits.

'What did you do with the note that I slipped into the book?' he asked.

'Don't worry, I burnt it as soon as I read it. Nonetheless, in future, choose your messengers more carefully.'

'Considering the urgency, I hardly had the liberty of choice. Tomorrow, you are leaving for—'

'—for Couzières, yes. Thank you so much for reminding me . . . Have you come to see me about madame de Saint-Avold?'

The question caught Laincourt unprepared.

'No,' he said.

'Aude has returned to Lorraine, did you know?' said the duchesse in a conversational tone. 'But I have a means of sending her letters. I would be happy to make sure she received one from you, if you like . . .'

Laincourt admired the ease with which madame de Chevreuse had just offered him an opportunity to compromise himself.

'No, madame. I thank you.'

'Are you no longer in love? No, monsieur. Do not protest, it's useless. Believe me, I know how to recognise love.'

'Madame, I am here on a matter of importance.'

The duchesse sighed and turned a page with a weary finger.

'Very well. I am listening.'

Laincourt explained that the Blades were investigating Charles Mauduit. The so-called Mauduit must have lied to her, at least by omission, as she had not known he was a dragon. Similarly, she was unaware he had perished during the attack on Le Châtelet.

She did, however, sense that something was amiss.

'What are you hiding from me, monsieur?'

'Pardon, madame?'

'You must be hiding something from me since, if this were only about Charles Mauduit, you would not be acting without the knowledge and perhaps even against the will of the cardinal . . .'

'By way of circumstances about which I can say nothing, madame, this affair also concerns the Sisters of Saint Georges. The cardinal is not in a position to offend them and so we feared that he would forbid us from pursuing this path.'

'So it concerns the Chatelaines. Why didn't you say so sooner?'

Evidently, the duchesse de Chevreuse shared the queen's notorious loathing for the Chatelaines. Laincourt had not known this and took careful note of it.

'Madame, you must tell me everything you know about your former master of magic.'

'What can I say? Of course I did not know he served the Black Claw . . .' The duchesse lifted her head and gazed off into the darkness. 'People had spoken highly of his knowledge. And he appeared to enjoy a certain measure of prestige among his peers. I thought he would be a suitable member of my household . . .' For the first time, she turned toward Laincourt. 'You know, I do not have much liking for magic. A little divination on occasion, but nothing more . . . It was the queen's despair, at finding herself unable to conceive, which finally convinced me that perhaps a ritual . . .'

'I wager that Mauduit suggested it to you.'

'Yes, probably.' Mme de Chevreuse pretended to resume reading. 'But he was skilful enough to make it seem I thought of it. And later, I served this monster's plans with all the willingness in the world, persuading the queen to have recourse to sorcery to enable her to become a mother.'

She spoke feelingly. Her friendship for the queen had been real and she sincerely reproached herself for what had happened.

Or what had almost happened . . .

And then Laincourt understood why the duchesse showed

no signs of any rancour against the Cardinal's Blades, or against himself. Because although their intervention had brought about her disgrace, they had saved the queen.

'Do you remember who recommended Mauduit to you?'

'Of course, but it will be of no help to you. Because she was burnt alive in the fire that destroyed her home.'

Knowing the Black Claw, this news hardly astonished Laincourt. Nevertheless, to put his mind at rest, he asked:

'Her name?'

'The vicomtesse de Malicorne.'

Laincourt fell silent, dumbfounded. Before joining the Blades, his last mission as the cardinal's spy had been to foil the vicomtesse de Malicorne's plans.

'Monsieur?' enquired madame de Chevreuse nervously.

But someone was coming.

With a simple backward step, Laincourt retreated calmly into the shadows. A lady companion of the duchesse arrived, bearing a shawl and saying the air was growing chilly. It was madame de Luret, whom the duchesse greeted rather harshly. The woman stammered an apology and quickly withdrew.

Laincourt reappeared.

'No doubt she heard us,' he said.

'Yes. This shawl was a poor pretext. You'd better go.'

Madame de Chevreuse stood up.

'One last question, madame. Were you close to the vicomtesse de Malicorne?'

'Yes. She was a friend. But she remained aloof from intrigues. If you had been acquainted with her, you would know what a charming person she was . . . Goodbye, monsieur.'

'Goodbye, madame.'

Laincourt let the duchesse leave in the direction of the terrace and the mansion, and waited long enough to spy movements in the garden. He saw a red cape passing in one place, and then a second one elsewhere.

The Cardinal's Guards were already searching for him.

Laincourt knew he was doomed if he remained where he was. So he started to make good his escape, with silent, supple steps, staying within the shadows. He wanted to flee, of course. But above all, he did not want to be seen or heard. Because if he managed to depart undetected, the duchesse could lie with relative ease. No, she had been alone. And she wasn't talking to anyone, but reading aloud. Isn't that what one does, with poetry? If he was spotted, however, others would be held accountable. Madame de Chevreuse, first of all. And perhaps Bertaud, too, who seemed to have aroused the suspicions of that cursed madame de Luret.

The Cardinal's Guards were carrying out an organised search of the garden. They tightened the noose around him, using lanterns to shed light, watching and listening for the slightest movement, the slightest sound, and they had no hesitation in hacking at the undergrowth with their swords. Fortunately, having been a member of the Guards, Laincourt knew them and knew what to expect. It was futile to hope that a simple diversion would attract all of them to the same spot: two or three would go and see, but the others would keep their positions.

He would have to be cleverer than that.

At the end of a garden path, Laincourt took time to observe and think. He estimated he had only two or three minutes before the trap closed around him. He needed to find a solution.

The pond, murmured the hurdy-gurdy player in his ear.

Of course!

Within the park, there was a large ornamental pond filled with colourful fish that the duchesse liked to admire and feed on occasion. As far as Laincourt could remember, this pond was fairly deep, deep enough that a man could hide within its dark waters. If he reached it first, he could dive in and evade the red capes coming towards him. After that, climbing the wall and jumping down into rue Saint-Nicaise would be child's play.

Laincourt hurried, hunched over, gripping his sword's scabbard in one hand and holding the brim of his hat with the other. At the corner of a well-kept flowerbed, for a moment he thought all was lost, as he held his breath and waited for a guard without a lantern to walk by. He had almost run straight into the man, but was now starting to believe that chance smiled upon him . . .

. . . until he arrived at the pond.

Which was empty.

No doubt because the duchesse was leaving, the pond had been drained for cleaning. The young man cursed. But more guards were approaching. He had to turn tail now and find another way out. They would be on him soon, very soon.

'Don't move!'

Given in a calm voice, the order had surprised Laincourt just as he was reversing course.

He froze.

'Turn round, monsieur.'

Having recognised the voice that spoke, Laincourt obeyed, but lowered his head so that, in the darkness, his face remained perfectly hidden by his hat. Because the guard who held him at bay, threatening him with a pistol, was Brussand. Brussand who had taken him under his wing when he had first joined the Cardinal's Guards. Brussand who had been so proud of Laincourt's promotion to the rank of ensign. Brussand who had felt that he had lost a son when Laincourt had been forced to give up his red cape under troubling circumstances.

'Come forward into the moonlight, monsieur. And take off your hat. I want to see who I'm arresting.'

Laincourt hesitated.

'Come forward, monsieur!'

But Laincourt could not allow himself to be taken captive, or unmasked. Either way, the Blades would be compromised and would have to explain what they were doing to the cardinal. It was bad enough for the cardinal's men to know madame de Chevreuse had met someone at night in her garden, against the express orders of the king.

But what could he do?

Kill a friend? Kill an innocent man?

'Step forward, or I'll shoot!'

Brussand. Out of all the guards present, it had to be old Brussand . . .

Laincourt sighed and took one step forward.

'Your hat, now, take—'

The guard was unable to finish his command: Saint-Lucq had come up from behind and knocked him out cold.

'Quickly,' said the half-blood. 'This way.'

It was unwise to venture out on Pont Neuf after sunset. Unpleasant encounters were frequent and there was every likelihood of being robbed, or even of winding up in the Seine more dead than alive. That night, however, a man on the Left Bank started over the bridge without a trace of fear. His name was Étienne-Louis de La Fargue, he seemed to be in a hurry, and he had the look of someone it would be foolish to trifle with. An intimidating Pappenheimer sword hung at his side.

The captain was heading for the famous Bronze Wyvern, which stood at the very tip of the Ile de la Cité, facing Place Dauphine. Going round the imposing marble pedestal, he entered the thick darkness beneath the spread wings of the statue, which depicted a wyvern saddled and harnessed for war, but riderless. There he found the person who had requested this last-minute rendezvous, leaning on the railing overlooking the black waters of the Seine.

'What is it?' asked La Fargue grumpily. 'I don't have much time.'

The other straightened up and turned round.

He was an elegant gentleman, dressed in a grey outfit beneath a black coat and wearing a felt hat with a plume. A handsome man, he seemed to be about thirty years in age but his hair was the colour of slate. His eyes were the same pale grey as his outfit, the irises ringed by a dark border.

He bore a grave expression.

'The Seven are concerned,' announced the chevalier de Valombre.

At least, that was how he had introduced himself at their first meeting. La Fargue knew nothing of him, other than the

860

fact that he was a dragon and that he also served the Guardians.

Also known as the Seven.

'And why are they concerned?

'Dragons are gathering in Paris.'

'To what end?'

'We don't know.'

'What do you know of the dragon that attacked Le Châtelet?'

'We know that it was a primordial.'

'What's that?'

'An ancient, primitive dragon. An archaic representative of what the draconic race was at the dawn of time . . . They are dangerous and savage creatures with a bestial intelligence ruled entirely by the violence of their instincts.'

'So, it was a primordial that killed Almades.'

'You can be sure that the primordial at Le Châtelet has a master who commands it. Or even several masters.'

'Such as the dragons who are now gathering in Paris?'

'We believe so.'

La Fargue nodded, and then asked:

'What do you want from me?'

Laincourt and Saint-Lucq arrived together at the Hôtel de l'Épervier. Ballardieu was sitting on the steps to the kitchen, drinking a glass of wine.

'Where is the captain?' Laincourt asked him.

'Gone out.'

'Gone out? Since when?' Saint-Lucq wanted to know.

'Less than an hour,' replied Ballardieu.

'And gone where?'

'A mystery.'

'And the others?'

'Agnès is resting. Marciac is in the fencing room.'

Laincourt and Saint-Lucq joined the Gascon inside. He had been drinking and, dishevelled, his feet crossed on the table, he was still drinking now, joylessly, alone in the dim light. His appearance astonished Laincourt. Saint-Lucq, although he never commented on it, knew of the sudden bouts of melancholy to which Marciac was sometimes victim.

'Do you know where the captain went?' the half-blood asked.

The Gascon displayed a dull-witted surprise.

'He's not here?'

Saint-Lucq cursed and walked away. Laincourt remained behind, feeling the need for a drink himself.

'So, your rendezvous with madame de Chevreuse?' Marciac enquired.

'It almost went horribly wrong,' the young man confessed. 'The alarm was raised. I could have been caught.'

'But Saint-Lucq intervened, as if out of nowhere. And he saved your neck.'

'Yes.'

'He loves doing that.'

Marciac finally noticed how shaken Laincourt looked.

'Come on, pull yourself together . . . Here, have a drink.' He filled two glasses to the brim. 'What's bothering you?'

'There will be an investigation at the Hôtel de Chevreuse.'

'No doubt. But I don't suppose it will be the first time for the duchesse . . .'

'It's not her that I'm worried about.'

'Bertaud?' the Gascon guessed.

'Yes. If they discover his part in this affair . . .'

Marciac sighed. He reckoned that he had drunk enough, put down his glass, took his feet off the table, and leaned towards Laincourt, his elbows resting on his thighs.

'Listen, my friend. Believe me, I understand you. But you're seriously mistaken if you think you can arrange a sanctuary for yourself. We all bear the burden of the intrigues we get mixed up in, and there is no way to spare those who are near and dear to us from the consequences, either. Worse, sometimes we have a duty to make use of those we love to further our aims. That can be done without their knowledge. It can be done with their willingness or not. And yes, it can lead to them being harmed. But nothing, nothing must ever prevent us from doing it . . . If that idea is unbearable to you, distance yourself from those you love once and for all. Isolate yourself. Be like Saint-Lucq . . . Or follow Leprat and leave the Blades.'

'And you? You're not Saint-Lucq, nor Leprat, as far as I know . . .'

The Gascon's face grew cloudy.

'Me? I am Marciac. I distract myself with wine, gaming, and women to forget the harm I do to those I lack the courage to leave. Choose one or another of my vices. It doesn't matter which because you will end up with all three if you follow me down the path of weakness . . .'

Just as he was delivering those words, Saint-Lucq returned, looking worried.

'La Fargue is nowhere to be found. I spoke to André: all the horses are in the stable, so he left on foot. And Guibot swears he received no letter or visit . . . It's as if he left the house suddenly, for no reason at all . . .'

'The captain is not a choirboy,' remarked Marciac as he rose to stretch. 'And he's quite capable of defending himself in Paris, even at night. Why are you getting so worked up?'

The half-blood did not answer him.

He could not find an explanation for La Fargue's absence. The captain should have been there on Laincourt's return, waiting for the result of the secret interview with madame de Chevreuse. His absence could mean only one of two things: either La Fargue was guilty of neglecting his duties by absenting himself on some frivolous errand, or he had been obliged to go out because a serious matter had arisen. Saint-Lucq could not believe the first hypothesis was true. So there was good reason to be alarmed, which Marciac would have understood if he wasn't Marciac.

Laincourt, in contrast, was also starting to wonder what was going on.

'Perhaps Agnès knows,' he suggested.

'Knows what?' asked La Fargue as he came bustling in, Ballardieu at his heels.

His arrival provoked an awkward silence, which the

863

captain did not seem to notice. But he carefully avoided Saint-Lucq's gaze as he straddled a chair and immediately asked Laincourt for his report.

The young man complied and when his account was finished, the captain of the Blades concluded:

'So, it was thanks to the vicomtesse de Malicorne that the Alchemist became the magic master of the duchesse de Chevreuse . . .'

'Yes,' said Laincourt.

'And she was the one who wanted to create a Black Claw lodge in France, wasn't she? And whose flight was assisted by the chevalier de Gagnière, on that famous night when we defeated her?'

'Yes, captain.'

'Do we know what became of her?'

'No. But it is unlikely that she still lives, because the Black Claw is rarely merciful towards those who fail. And even if she is alive . . .'

Laincourt did not think it useful to end his sentence.

'So we find ourselves at a dead end,' La Fargue said, sounding discouraged.

'I'm not so sure,' replied Marciac. 'There's still Gagnière, whom Saint-Lucq took prisoner. He must know a lot, as the vicomtesse's right arm. Let's find out which gaol he's rotting in and interrogate him.'

The idea was a good one, but they were all aware of the obstacle before them.

'We can't do any of that without the cardinal's approval,' said La Fargue. 'We can go no further without his knowledge.'

Agnès awoke a little before dawn, with a throbbing shoulder and her mind still haunted by the vision that troubled her sleep. She sat up in bed, looked towards the open window and the night sky that was becoming pale in the east, behind the Saint-Germain-des-Prés abbey bell-tower. She sighed, before getting up and, her back turned three-quarters to the mirror, examining her shoulder again. She knew what she was going to see. The elegant lines of her mark that had been pulsing with a red glow in time with her heartbeat were now growing fainter, and the pain was beginning to fade. Soon, the two entwined runes would regain their normal appearance.

Agnès straightened her shirt and went over to the window, leaning on the sill.

Looking off into the distance, her expression was grim.

She had dreamed again of the great black dragon blasting Paris, and it had such a sharp clarity that she had felt the heat of the blazes on her face, the odour of burning wood and hot ashes had invaded in her nostrils, and it seemed her ears were still ringing from the terrible noise: the roaring flames, the crash of collapsing buildings, the screams of the victims, the cavernous bellowing of the dragon. The image of that black dragon had etched itself on her mind. She only needed to close her eyelids in order to see it again, immense and powerful, triumphant in the sky of a tormented Paris, its body covered with shining obsidian scales and its brow decorated . . .

. . . with a sparkling jewel?

Agnès abruptly opened her eyes again.

She had been the vicomtesse de Malicorne and she had lacked for nothing: neither youth, nor beauty, nor wealth. And now she was madame de Chantegrelle, an old woman, a pious lady who had retired to a convent in the faubourg Saint-Jacques, resting from the last labours of an over-long life. Which was equal to saying she wasn't much of anything.

That morning, she had gone out to take a few steps in the convent's garden when she received word of a visitor. Shortly after, she met an elegant gentleman for the first time, with blond hair, regular features, and a disturbing charm. They sat side-by-side upon a stone bench and, as soon as they were alone, the stranger briefly unleashed his aura. Madame de Chantegrelle felt a delicious, electrifying thrill run through her. So he, like her, was a dragon. But a powerful and vigorous dragon, one who was not prisoner of an aging, puny body and a miserable existence.

'Who are you?' she asked.

'I am the Gentleman. I should say, rather, I am "The Gentleman Lover", since that is the full name of my arcanum. But let's content ourselves with the Gentleman. I belong to the same lodge as the Alchemist.'

'The lodge of the Arcana. So it really exists.'

'Did you doubt it?'

'Yes.'

'Soon we will have all the time we need to set you straight on that score, madame.'

'What do you want from me?'

'I have come to ask you to join us.'

'You're mocking me.'

'Not at all.'

Then the Gentleman spoke and the former vicomtesse de Malicorne listened, weighing each sentence, each word, lending an attentive ear to each intonation, each inflexion of his voice, and searching for the slightest sign of deceit or duplicity in her visitor's face. But the gentleman knew how to please and how to persuade. And she could not help being tempted by what he proposed: to reclaim what she had once been and join the Arcana lodge.

'Why choose me?' she finally asked.

'We have been observing you for a long time, madame. And, in contrast to the Black Claw, we prefer to consider what you have accomplished and what you might still succeed in accomplishing.'

'Then let us speak of the Black Claw, as you mention it. What will they say if they learn—'

'Whatever they like. The Arcana lodge is free to initiate whoever it chooses. Besides, we don't pay much heed to the old masters in Madrid . . .'

'But don't you see what I've become?'

'We have the remedy for that.'

She shot the Gentleman a look that was alight with hope and ambition.

'Truly?' she asked.

He answered her with a gentle smile full of confidence; and they spoke some more.

This time, however, madame de Chantegrelle listened little and thought much. She quickly came to the obvious decision. If she was lacking in physical and magical strength ever since the aborted ritual had nearly killed her, she had lost none of her mental acuity. She was in no position to make any demands of the Arcana, but she was resolved to set one condition.

'If I am in the state and the situation that you see before you,' she said, 'it is by the fault of a handful of men and a woman. So I should like to know: if I join you, will I have my revenge?'

And being a person who appreciated audacity, the Gentleman smiled.

'Madame, I can promise you that.'

Marciac and Laincourt accompanied La Fargue to the Palais-Cardinal. They arrived just as Richelieu was preparing to join the king at the Château de Saint-Germain and as, in the great courtyard, sixty guards in red capes, already mounted and arrayed in parade order, were waiting for the departure of His Eminence's coach. The cardinal had in fact already taken his place inside the vehicle and the Blades' captain had a difficult time gaining permission to speak with him at the coach door.

Remaining a short distance away, the other Blades also waited patiently, the Gascon holding La Fargue's horse by the bridle, while Laincourt inspected the aligned guards. He saw with satisfaction that Brussand was among them and that he seemed to be in good form, even if a bandage that no doubt constricted his skull could be glimpsed underneath his hat. From where they were standing, Marciac and Laincourt could not hear anything of what La Fargue, hat in hand, was saying to Cardinal Richelieu. But the old captain seemed to be arguing as firmly as possible. Of the cardinal, they could only see a thin, motionless hand resting upon the coach door.

'This is taking a long time,' said Marciac.

'La Fargue does not have a strong hand to play,' Laincourt pointed out.

Indeed, the conversation dragged on, forcing all those in the courtyard to endure the scorching sun. The Cardinal's Guards appeared stoical enough but their horses, standing in ranks, started to grow nervous. Impatient hooves struck the paving stones. Some mounts whinnied and shied. Otherwise, a strange silence reigned. Everyone wondered what was going on, what had delayed a departure they had believed to be imminent.

Finally, La Fargue came away from the coach with its magnificent coats-of-arms, and replaced his hat on his head. An officer gave an order. Trumpets sounded and a first squad of guards took the lead, followed by His Eminence's coach which ponderously set off, and then the rest of the escort. The procession left the courtyard and was soon travelling along rue Saint-Honoré, in the direction of the gate bearing the same name.

The great courtyard of the Palais-Cardinal suddenly appeared quite deserted.

With a stern face and a hurried step, La Fargue rejoined Marciac and Laincourt.

'We should make haste,' he said, climbing into the saddle.

Less than an hour later, Agnès was watching as La Fargue, Laincourt and Marciac carried out their final preparations in the courtyard of the Hôtel de l'Épervier: making sure their horses were properly saddled, tightening a strap here, adjusting a bit there, patting a neck and, finally, mounting their steeds. André was helping them, always observing their mounts with an expert and vaguely critical eye. On the small step that marked the threshold of her kitchen, Naïs also looked on with a worried air. Old Guibot stood beneath the archway, where he had just opened the carriage gates and was now holding one of the two massive rectangular doors.

Once all three men were ready to depart, they each saluted Agnès: La Fargue with a nod of the head, Laincourt with a sign of the hand, and Marciac with a wink. Then they left, filling the courtyard briefly with the clatter of hooves on paving stones. In rue Saint-Guillaume, they came across Ballardieu who gaped in surprise as he saw them pass by at a full trot and hastened to return to the Blades' mansion. Hobbling on his wooden leg, Guibot was already closing the gate.

Ballardieu joined Agnès in the main hall. Dressed in her usual fashion as a squire, her waist cinched by her thick corset of scarlet leather, the young baronne de Vaudreuil was pulling on fencing gloves.

'What's going on?' Ballardieu demanded to know. 'I just saw the captain and the others who—'

'Who were leaving, yes.'

'Where are they going in such a rush?'

'The cardinal was willing to allow La Fargue to meet Gagnière,' she explained. 'The problem is that Gagnière, under close guard, is en route to a secluded château near Auxerre where he will be handed over to a representative of the Pope.'

'Handed over?'

'Delivered, if you prefer. Exchanged, perhaps. Or sold. Don't ask me what Rome wants with Gagnière.'

Agnès whipped the air with her rapier, and, looking satisfied, practised a few lunges.

'Why aren't we part of the expedition?' asked Ballardieu in a sulky tone.

'Because La Fargue has no need of us. And also because I am retained by matters here in Paris . . .'

The old soldier suddenly noticed the sword that Agnès was wielding.

'Hey!' he exclaimed. 'That's your rapier!'

'None other!' enthused the young woman, saluting him as if they were about to engage in a duel.

And as if to provide final proof of her claim, she released the blade of the stiletto lodged in the grip of her weapon.

'How is that possible?'

'It was delivered this morning by one of the Chatelaines' Black Guards.'

'From Mère de Vaussambre?'

'Who else? Besides, along with my sword there was a letter written by her hand.'

'And what did it say, this letter?'

The blood in the vat was fuming. It gave off powerful, acrid, nauseating scents. Carved into the floor's stone slabs, complex pentacles gave off a red glow, as if traced by incandescent wires. Black candles burned at their points, although the melted wax ran scarlet. The air vibrated with a deep and powerful presence.

The vicomtesse de Malicorne stood naked before the vat.

Soon, the elderly madame de Chantegrelle would be no more than a detestable memory, and so would this weak, shrivelled body with its flabby flesh and spindly limbs. Even the vicomtesse de Malicorne would be forgotten. Because while she would emerge from this rebirth just as young and beautiful as before, she would also be stronger, animated by a determination that nothing and no one could shake. For now, however, she was still an old woman who waited trembling amid the intoxicating vapours, her back tense, almost arched, her chin lifted, and her eyes closed.

The Enchantress also had her eyes closed.

Kneeling on the other side of the basin built into the floor, she chanted in a low voice, absorbed in her work. Warm blood ran from her slit wrists, as if endowed with a life of its own, slipping across the stone slabs to join the darker pool that already filled the vat. A spectral form emanated from the Enchantress, which could only be detected in the shadow on the wall behind her: that of a dragon whose power, still constrained, seemed to resonate from the bowels of the earth.

The vicomtesse knew that the crucial moment had arrived.

She took one step forward, plunged a foot into the blood, and struggled to contain a moan of pleasure at the burning sensation which, like a tongue of inner fire, filled her entire being.

4

Advancing at a trot in the middle of the countryside, still several leagues from the Château de Mareuil-sur-Ay, the small column of musketeers escorting their prisoner came across a coach sitting still at the side of the road. Leprat, riding at the front, saw it first. He immediately raised a hand, ordering his fifteen musketeers and the sealed wagon they escorted to come to a halt behind him. The dust settled slowly in their wake, without a breath of wind to disperse it.

Squinting beneath the brim of his hat, Leprat studied their surroundings, pressing both hands against the pommel of his saddle, his shoulders hunched slightly forward. The journey had proceeded, until now, without incident despite his fears. After three days, he had even begun to imagine that the Black Claw had renounced any intention to do the marquis de Gagnière an evil turn, or that it remained ignorant of the fact that he was being transferred, or how, or where. But that was no reason to abandon all precautions.

A musketeer joined Leprat and drew up his mount alongside him. It was Durieux, a gentleman of thirty years with a sharp eye and an austere face who spoke little and displayed a disconcertingly deadpan sense of humour. He always had good advice. Leprat had made him his second-in-command.

'Your opinion, Durieux?' he asked.

The musketeer took time to observe the scene in his turn.

'The terrain is hardly favourable for an ambush,' he replied. 'But the ruse may lie therein.'

They were not far from the town of Épernay. The road was crossing a charming corner of the Champagne countryside, green and peaceful. The weather was superb. In the distance

871

they could see a sheepfold, but other than the coach there was no sign of a living soul.

'I'll go and see,' announced Leprat.

'Is that very wise?'

'Keep your eyes open and take command if necessary.'

'Never fear. If you should meet some misadventure, I'll make sure that someone other than Sardent writes your funeral eulogy.'

Leprat spurred his horse forward, smiling broadly at Durieux's jest, and crossed the distance to the coach at a full trot. He identified one individual as the coachman and, inside the vehicle, he could make out a shadow with whom a gentleman, leaning on the passenger door, one boot on the footboard and hat in his hand, was making conversation. The musketeer slowed and approached at a walk. Seeing him, the gentleman covered his head and advanced with a friendly smile. He was young, richly dressed, and attractive, moving with a supple grace.

'Hello there!' he hailed, raising his arm.

Leprat halted his horse, but kept one hand close to the pistols tucked into his saddle holsters. He did it with a perfectly natural air, as the gentleman gave no signs of hostility or wariness, but there were cases of murderers with even more innocent-looking faces. The true danger, moreover, could lie within the coach.

'I am Leprat, King's Musketeer. Is there a problem, monsieur?'

'A broken wheel, monsieur,' replied the other man with a strong Italian accent.

He stepped aside to point to the coach, whose left rear wheel was indeed broken. It was a very common accident, given the poor state of French roads.

'I've sent my man ahead on my horse to the next relay station,' the Italian continued to say, 'but we've been waiting two hours for him and the wretch has still not returned.'

'I fear that I cannot be of great assistance to you.'

'We are accompanying a lady of quality, monsieur. And I see that a harnessed vehicle follows you. If you could offer this lady a seat as far as the next village, one of us will remain here with the coach, while the two others could follow you.'

'This wagon, whose escort I command, is in no way suitable for a person of quality. Moreover, the only available place is next to the coachman. Even were there no question of decorum, the discomfort would be great. The sun, the dust, the jolts— '

'—are all inconveniences that I shall put up with, monsieur Leprat,' said a clear, feminine voice. 'You must remember that I am not one to be deterred by mere trifles. And furthermore, I have the feeling that we are going to the same place . . .'

Leprat then watched as a ravishing young red-headed woman descended from the coach.

A spy, a courtesan, and a schemer. Her name was Alessandra di Santi.

Otherwise known as La Donna.

III

Bois-Noir

1

The Gentleman, sitting in an armchair, was talking to the red dragon whose massive, scaly head, adorned with a set of three bony ridges, could be seen in the mirror, glimmering slightly in the dimness.

'Everything will be ready,' he promised in a grave, concerned tone.

'Good,' the Heresiarch replied with a tone of authority. 'And since that settles the final details for the next Assembly, I would like to touch on another subject with you.'

The Gentleman was immediately on edge, but he tried not to show it. Was this about La Malicorne? It would soon be two whole days and nights that the Enchantress had spent performing the ritual intended to restore the former vicomtesse's power and magnificence. She was working here, secretly, in the crypt below the Hôtel des Arcanes. Could the Heresiarch already have learned of this?

'La Donna is in France,' the red dragon announced.

The news caught the Gentleman unprepared. He needed a few seconds to gather his wits and understand what the Heresiarch was talking about.

'La Donna? But didn't the Black Claw promise to rid us of her?'

'That's what they promised, indeed. And they failed . . . So I have decided we will resolve this problem ourselves. The bitch deceived the Alchemist. She stole secrets from him that allowed Cardinal Richelieu to foil our plans. It's high time she paid the price for it!'

The Gentleman did not reply. He waited and the Heresiarch continued:

'Right now, La Donna can be found at a château in Champagne where she is taking part in the transfer of a prisoner that France holds and that Rome wants. The prisoner himself is of little consequence . . . But an opportunity like this will not present itself again any time soon. The Illuminator is already in place, and has recruited a band of drac warriors. The small number of musketeers guarding the château will not be enough to oppose them. The whole matter will be settled tonight.'

'What do you expect of me?'

'Very little. I want you to prepare the Tour de Bois-Noir for the Illuminator's return, with his dracs. They will hold La Donna in the tower for as long as necessary.'

'Just hold her?' asked the Gentleman in surprise. 'Why?'

The Heresiarch did not reply.

He waited, silent and inscrutable, until the other dragon bowed to his will.

'It shall be done, Heresiarch.'

'I am counting on it. Goodbye, Gentleman.'

'Goodbye.'

The cell door opened and Leprat, ducking his head, stepped inside. His hand on the pommel of his white rapier, he straightened up without removing his hat and allowed the musketeer posted in the corridor outside to shut the door. Low-ceilinged and damp, but clean, the gaol cell was furnished with a narrow bed, a small table, and a stool, all standing on a bare dirt floor. A bucket sat in the corner, there for the prisoner's bodily needs. The only light came from a small semi-circular opening in the wall.

'I understand you wish to speak to me,' declared Leprat.

The man he had escorted from the Bastille was sitting on the bed reading, his back against the cell wall. The leather and iron mask was still locked around his face. The prisoner closed his book and stood up politely for his visitor. There was elegance in both his gesture and in his general bearing. The marquis de Gagnière was a man of refinement and courtesy, but he was also a cold monster.

'Indeed, monsieur. I wanted to thank you for allowing me reading material.'

Leprat accepted the thanks with a curt nod of the head.

'Anything else?' he enquired.

Arms crossed, the prisoner observed the musketeer from head to foot and seemed to think.

Then he said:

'You know who I am, don't you?'

'Yes.'

'In fact, you recognised me from the moment I was entrusted to your keeping, in the courtyard of the Bastille. By my eyes, probably. And perhaps from my posture. Unless it was my voice . . .'

Leprat did not reply and watched Gagnière take a step to lean against the table.

'Do you remember your last words to me, that night in rue Saint-Denis?' asked the prisoner. 'You had just eliminated my henchmen. You were exhausted, wounded, defeated, while I aimed my pistol at you from horseback . . .'

'I told you a man of honour would dismount and draw his sword.'

'And what did I do? I shot you in the heart and left you for dead.'

Leprat nodded silently.

He had seen himself die in the service of the king, that terrible night in rue Saint-Denis.

'So you know what kind of man I am,' Gagnière continued. 'And, knowing it, you have given me no reason to complain of you during the course of our journey, while I was in your power. Another man, no doubt, would not have mistreated me – not strictly speaking. But I doubt that he would have spared me all sorts of humiliations. With you, there has been none of that.'

'I was not entrusted with the care of a man who tried to murder me in cold blood. Nor was I entrusted with the marquis de Gagnière. I was entrusted with a prisoner, and with the mission of protecting him and conducting him to a specific place. You might just as well be any other man.'

'And if we are attacked, you will defend me even at risk to your own life?'

'Yes.'

'Without regret?'

'I did not say that.'

'Do you know that the Black Claw has already tried to assassinate me, twice?'

'I know it.'

'And despite everything, you will persist in—'

'Yes.'

The prisoner took the time to appreciate this response, which he knew to be frank and firm.

Finally, he said:

'You are decidedly a most admirable man, monsieur le chevalier d'Orgueil.'

Leprat rejoined Durieux a little later, as the daylight was fading. The musketeers had arrived at Château de Mareuil-sur-Ay less than two hours earlier, where the final negotiations concerning Gagnière were to take place. They finished installing themselves and securing the stronghold, whose defence they were responsible for during the talks. Men in royal blue capes were already posted at the gate and on the ramparts.

In the courtyard, Durieux was explaining to the three stalwart fellows who usually stood guard over the château that, for the time being, they could put away their halberds, breastplates, and the single arquebus they shared. Leprat waited for him to finish, noting the skilful and courteous way he dealt with them. He could have invoked the authority his rank and his cape conferred on him, but he preferred diplomacy instead.

The halberdiers withdrew, looking satisfied.

'What did the prisoner want?' asked Durieux.

'To warn me of a danger, I think,' replied Leprat.

'Here?' Together they looked around the setting they found themselves in. 'We were much more vulnerable on the road.'

'I'm well aware of that. And yet . . .'

'Yes, I sense it, too. There's something in the air, isn't there?'

Worried, both men fell silent.

The Château de Mareuil had been built during the Middle Ages. It comprised three massive towers joined by high walls, surrounding a triangular courtyard with a keep at its heart. It was a property that had reverted to the Crown in the absence of legal heirs. A widow had previously made it her refuge, building a Renaissance-style pavilion next to one of the ramparts, which was now pierced with windows. On her death, the château had not been completely abandoned. As it was to the east of Épernay, in a wooded corner of the country-side filled with game, it had become a very convenient hunting lodge for its present owner; an old gentleman who enjoyed the king's favour. It also had the advantage of being secluded, and a full day's horseback journey from the border with Lorraine . . .

'We've finished setting up our quarters in the old keep,' Durieux announced after a moment. 'We had to do some tidying up, but we should be comfortable there. The horses are in the stable and the first watches have been posted.'

'Very good. The domestic servants?'

'People from the village. Most of them go home at night and return in the morning. They will provide a more than ad-equate service for us musketeers, but we also have to think of our guest who, as a lady of quality—' Durieux broke off when he saw Leprat's half-smile. 'What did I say that was funny?'

'Nothing.'

Leprat turned towards the Renaissance building, where Alessandra di Santi and the gentleman who accompanied her had elected to lodge, making themselves at home in the apartments belonging to the master of the château and his wife. The gentleman occupied the first, where weapons, trophies, and hunting scenes abounded. La Donna resided in the second, which was pleasantly furnished and decorated.

'Have no fear,' Leprat added with another quirk of his lips. 'I assure you that this lady can manage far more rigorous conditions than the ones she finds here.'

From a window, La Donna was inspecting the young village girls who had come to offer their services at the château. She pointed at two with her index finger and bid them come upstairs. The disappointed candidates turned away. Leprat knew who he was dealing with and had no doubt that Alessandra had selected the two prettiest and liveliest girls for her personal service. Seeing that he was looking in her direction she responded with a smile and a small wave of the hand. He replied more soberly with a pinch of his hat brim.

Durieux asked no questions.

Even so, Leprat deemed that he owed his fellow musketeer some explanations.

'I do not know who the gentleman escorting her is, but this Italian woman the Pope has sent us is an adventuress and a top-notch spy. I made her acquaintance under Captain La Fargue's command. She claimed to have knowledge of a plot and obtained the cardinal's protection in exchange for the details. As always, her motives were murky. Nevertheless, I must admit that the information she supplied turned out to be useful in a very grave affair – one I can tell you nothing about.'

Darkness was falling in the courtyard where lackeys, servants and musketeers came and went, all more or less busy.

'Is she dangerous?' asked Durieux.

'Very. Above all else, don't let yourself be taken in by that adorable face or her air of innocence. And be on your guard: she is one of those women who can't help trying to seduce men, who lives for the desire she arouses.'

From Leprat's cold manner, Durieux realised that he was speaking from experience. Then his attention was drawn by some of the village girls who had been rejected by La Donna, now standing near the château's gates and enduring – without too much resistance – the advances of two musketeers.

'Should we permit this?' he asked, indicating the joyful little group with his chin.

Leprat weighed up the pros and cons of intervening, but was not given the opportunity to reply. From the top of the château's towers, a musketeer shouted that riders were approaching at a full trot.

La Fargue, Laincourt, and Marciac arrived at Mareuil-sur-Ay in the evening. Covered in grime, they had ridden at a fast pace for two long days, over dusty roads in the blazing summer heat. They were exhausted, and had no idea if they were in time or already too late to speak with Gagnière. They were relieved when they saw the château's towers and its old walls, on top of which they spied blue capes with silver crosses.

'The King's Musketeers?' Marciac observed with surprise. 'I was expecting red capes.'

'The marquis de Gagnière is a prisoner of the king,' La Fargue noted.

A musketeer stopped them at the gate beneath the archway, beyond a drawbridge that crossed a brush-filled ditch and was rarely raised. La Fargue handed over their papers signed by the cardinal, without dismounting, and waited for the musketeer to examine them. Behind him, Marciac doffed his hat to wipe his brow.

'It's a relief to be here,' he whispered to Laincourt, who replied with an understanding smile.

'Captain?'

All eyes turned to the man who had just spoken: Leprat, who had come from the courtyard with Durieux. The musketeer on duty passed La Fargue's papers over to him, but Leprat merely glanced at them and asked:

'But what are you doing here?' And then, changing his mind: 'No, tell me later. You're a pitiful sight, all three of you, and by the look of things you've earned a rest.'

The riders were authorised to enter the château and could finally dismount in the courtyard. Leprat gave orders that their horses should be tended to and charged Durieux with finding them a place to spend the night. The old captain thanked him and, while removing his riding gloves, he caught a glimpse of a lady and gentleman at one of the windows. He did not know the gentleman, but the woman could only be Alessandra di Santi.

'Life is full of surprises, isn't it?' said Leprat watching him out of the corner of his eye. 'I'll explain everything later . . .'

The Blades spent a long while at the water trough refreshing themselves, before La Fargue and Laincourt followed Durieux into a dusty, vacant chamber within the keep where they would have to make do with straw mattresses for the night. Marciac had remained near the well, chatting with one of the pretty village girls that La Donna had engaged in her service.

Having taken the time to change his clothes, Laincourt found La Fargue and Leprat a little later in an agreeably cool room, seated at a table with a few jugs of wine. The Gascon had still not reappeared, which neither astonished nor worried anyone.

'I have informed Leprat of the essence of our affair,' the old captain announced as Laincourt entered.

While the young man took a seat and poured himself a glass of wine, the musketeer summed matters up:

'So, there's a mystery you wish to shed some light on, which has some connection to the death of the Alchemist. By investigating him, or rather the master of magic he claimed to be, you discovered that the vicomtesse de Malicorne recommended him to the duchesse de Chevreuse. La Malicorne disappeared after we foiled her plan to create a Black Claw lodge in France. So that only leaves her deputy, Gagnière . . .'

Over the rim of his glass, Laincourt shot an intrigued glance at La Fargue, who paid no attention to it. Leprat had made no allusion to the threat of a dragon destroying Paris. Was that because the Blades' captain had not told him anything about it?'

'That's right,' confirmed La Fargue. 'The cardinal has authorised us to speak with Gagnière, as long as doing so does not prevent or delay the negotiations over his fate. So we rode here post haste, in fear that these final discussions would be concluded before our arrival.'

'Those negotiations have not even commenced. Père Joseph will lead them for France and we do not expect him until tomorrow evening.'

'But La Donna is already here.'

'To be sure. But she is not here to negotiate on the Pope's behalf.'

'So what is her role?'

'To interrogate Gagnière in order to measure how much he really knows. After that, the Pope's negotiator, who will also be arriving tomorrow, will have a better idea of where he stands.'

La Fargue emptied his glass, leaned back pensively, and then gave a bleak smile.

'When one thinks,' he said, 'that less than a month ago it was La Donna answering monsieur Laffemas' questions in Le Châtelet. And now here she is, posing questions to a Black Claw agent . . .'

Leprat shrugged and said:

'My responsibilities here are limited to the prisoner's security. If you wish to speak with him, you will need to go through La Donna. At least until His Holiness' negotiator arrives.'

'I would prefer not to wait until tomorrow.'

The musketeer did not know what to reply.

'Perhaps that won't be necessary,' said Laincourt.

The two others turned toward him.

'How's that?' asked La Fargue.

'The gentleman with La Donna. I know him.'

'Signor Valerio Licini?' Leprat asked in surprise.

'That is indeed his name. A scion of one of the finest aristocratic families of Rome. But he is better known as Père Farrio.'

'A priest?' asked La Fargue.

'A Jesuit. He and I have crossed paths in the past. He is an agent of the Pope and I am prepared to wager that he also is the negotiator we are waiting for.'

'Might he also have recognised you?' the Blades' captain enquired.

'I don't know.'

'But why play this farce?' the musketeer wanted to know.

'It can be useful for a negotiator to test the waters first, to smell the air, perhaps hear things we might not have said in front of him if we knew his true identity . . . But I'm only guessing. It is not impossible to suppose that the motives of Père Farrio and La Donna are even more devious than that . . .'

Upon those words, Marciac entered the room.

Perhaps slightly more dishevelled than usual, he was in an excellent mood and had a wisp of straw in his tangled hair.

'I just ran into Durieux,' he announced. 'La Donna has invited us to sup with her this evening.'

Armed with heavy rapiers, daggers, and pistols, the dracs stood ready in the clearing, beneath the starry sky. Assassins, brigands, and mercenaries, they obeyed the orders of one of their own, who went by the name of Keress Karn. Most of them weren't much taller than him, but all of them were more heavily built than this red drac with sinewy muscles and the reflexes of a snake. Aka'rn, a colossal but silent black drac, acted as Karn's personal bodyguard.

Intelligent and devoid of any scruples, quick to be cruel, Keress Karn exercised exclusive authority over his band. He never explained his orders and they were never questioned. His cutthroats displayed a mixture of admiration and super-stitious dread towards him. Indeed, who but Karn could have persuaded them to place themselves in a dragon's service? For a drac, it was like voluntarily returning to enslavement and asking for the lash. But not a single one had challenged his decision, nor had any of them balked, later, at riding behind this dragon whose aura was so powerful that they felt, to their great shame, a servile chord vibrate in the depths of their beings. The dragon even insisted on being called 'master'. He did not mingle with them and spoke only to Karn, who was not in the least intimidated by the dragon's brutal and con-temptuous manner. The red drac then relayed his instructions to the rest of the band.

The last directive they received had been to dismount here, in this clearing.

And to make ready for combat.

So they had hitched their horses, furbished their weapons and checked their equipment as they listened to Karn explain that they would be attacking a nearby château and abducting a woman they would find there. Following those instructions, they had shared a frugal meal, eaten cold, without making a fire. Then some had addressed hurried prayers to the gods or to their ancestors, whose spirits would accompany them into battle. It was not a question of asking for protection, only of inviting an illustrious forebear to witness – perhaps – their death in combat so that glory would accrue to their lineage.

The Illuminator had, of course, observed these rituals with disdain, sitting apart from the dracs and snorting pointedly at them, when he wasn't snickering into his beard. Then he stood up, stepped forward and waited until all eyes were focused on him. In the middle of the clearing he planted the broad blade of his *schiavone* in the ground beside him and undressed completely.

He kneeled.

Was he now going to pray?

The dracs stirred, intrigued, but Kress Karn restored order and silence with a single word. He had already guessed what the dragon was about to do, having just before seen him discreetly drain a small bottle of golden henbane liqueur.

Looking rapt, eyes closed, the Illuminator began breathing more and more noisily. Then it was as if he was struck by a sharp pain. Without opening his eyes, he arched his back and suddenly grimaced. The pain seemed to go on and forced a moan between the Illuminator's clenched jaws. Soon, he was unable to contain the brusque movements of his shoulders and arms. He stood up, his brow covered in sweat, looking clumsy and shaky as his naked body changed and became covered in scarlet scales. He grew several inches in height and stifled a scream. He gained twenty pounds of muscle at the price of terrible pain. Bony growths sprouted from his suddenly knobbly spine and razor-sharp claws emerged at the tips of his rigid fingers. His face stretched forward into a snout and a pair of bestial jaws, while his eyes, turned yellow, were now divided by vertical slits.

Finally, the Illuminator – or the creature he had become – settled into his new state.

It was not a complete metamorphosis. The dragon had not

recovered its primal form, only one of the intermediate variants. But the creature that turned towards the dracs subjugated them with its air of strength, brutality, and savagery. It stared at them for a long while, as its powerful shoulders rose and fell in time with its deep, hoarse breaths and threads of thick slaver dripped from its fangs.

The dragon seized the *schiavone* planted in the ground and brandished it.

'Let's go,' it said in a cavernous voice.

Night had already fallen when, at the appointed hour, La Fargue and Laincourt crossed the Château de Mareuil courtyard heading for the signora di Santi's quarters.

'I'm still not sure this is a good idea,' said the old captain. 'After all, it was not so long ago that La Donna duped us and left us to be killed, as I hope I do not need to remind you.'

'No, captain. But we want to speak to Gagnière, which we can only do with the agreement of the Pope's representative. And we will certainly not obtain that if the signora advises against it.'

'Not to mention the fact that she probably knows more about the Alchemist than Gagnière does himself,' added La Fargue grudgingly.

'Quite true. This invitation to dine with her is an open hand La Donna is extending to you.'

'A hand, yes. Or another trap . . .'

They found Marciac and Laincourt waiting on the front steps and entered with them.

In the 'hall' of the Renaissance-style pavilion, everything was almost ready. Numerous candles were burning in holders on the walls, between the paintings and the stuffed hunting trophies, and La Donna's two village girls had just finished setting all the dishes on the table, as custom dictated, before the meal was served. Considering the place and the circumstances, La Donna had managed to prepare quite a feast: meats, pâtés, hams, cheese, fruits, creams and jams lay spread in abundance.

Embellished by several bottles of wine, this vision delighted Marciac but only aggravated La Fargue's suspicions.

'Who are they trying to dazzle here?' he grumbled.

Meanwhile Laincourt wondered what horn of plenty had supplied all this food. He told himself La Donna must have brought these victuals in her carriage and sacrificed most of her stocks to make a strong impression on her guests.

But to what end?

Alessandra di Santi soon arrived, entering on the arm of the gentleman Laincourt had identified as a Jesuit agent of Rome. Dressed and coiffed according to the latest fashion, La Donna was superb. She wore a blue satin dress that highlighted her red hair and pale complexion, and was smiling and radiant, as if enchanted to be receiving long-lost friends. Signor Licini was no less elegant, nor less courteous.

Leprat took charge of the introductions. La Donna greeted each of the Blades with a charming word and extended her hand, last of all, to La Fargue. Then, after glancing at her escort who was exchanging amiable remarks with Marciac, she whispered to the captain:

'It is Providence that sends you. We need to speak together alone, later.'

It was said in a single breath, after which Alessandra regained her smile and invited her guests to take their places around the table.

A gracious and playful hostess, she wanted La Fargue to sit on her right and Valerio Licini on her left. Then she proposed a toast, 'In honour of the captain, whose merits are never appreciated enough.' A glass of wine was filled, in which a piece of toasted bread was placed to soak. The glass was passed from hand to hand so that each guest could take a sip and, according to custom, when it was La Fargue's turn, as the one being toasted he was supposed to finish the wine and swallow the bread, cheered on by the others.

As the glass went round the table, Laincourt watched Licini.

He wondered if the Jesuit priest had recognised him as well, and had realised that his identity was no longer a secret. On meeting the cardinal's former spy's gaze, the Pope's agent removed any ambiguity by giving him a complicit nod of the head.

Laincourt concluded that they knew where they stood with one another, but was not given the chance to pursue his train of thought.

'To arms!'

The château's gate was blown away by the deafening explosion of an enormous powder charge. Spat out through the archway, a cloud of dust and debris invaded the courtyard. Fused grenades had followed and gone off, adding to the confusion.

'To arms! To arms!'

Rapiers in their fists, La Fargue and the others burst from the building where La Donna and Licini were quartered, just as the first musketeers reached the courtyard. The poor devils who had been caught in the initial explosion were staggering around in a daze, some of them wounded. But no one had time to go to their aid: sinister silhouettes were swiftly making their way through the smoke, bent on attack.

'Draaaaacs!'

While combat was engaged with Karn's band of mercenaries, La Fargue held back from the fray, trying to take stock of the situation. He looked around, wondering why the sentries had not raised an alarm prior to the explosion. His eyes lifted at the precise instant when the Illuminator leapt down from the ramparts and he tracked the path of the dragon's fall. The creature landed heavily but without harm in the middle of the courtyard before straightening with a roar. It brandished the massive *schiavone*, a detail that struck the captain.

'Leprat!' he yelled over the noise of the battle. 'Look to your prisoner! We'll take care of this monster!'

Leprat had already spotted a red drac who appeared to be directing the assault. But he nodded to the captain, renouncing his target. As La Fargue, Laincourt and Marciac deployed themselves around the scaly colossus, he ordered:

'Durieux, with me! Musketeers, stand firm!'

And he left at a run, with Durieux at his heels.

He was leaving his brothers-in-arms to fight against two-to-one odds and the Blades facing a monstrous adversary that looked capable of breaking a man's spine over its knee. But he had no choice. His first duty was to protect Gagnière, and the dracs were here to either set him free or to kill him. The Black Claw must have instigated this attack. But why would they choose to take the château by force when it would have been easier to attack the musketeers between Paris and Mareuil? Had they lacked the time to set up an ambush along the road?

Gagnière was locked up in the basement of one of the corner towers. Leprat and Durieux had to go round the big central keep to reach it, ignoring the cries and the smoke from the courtyard. They ran into a drac who was pulling his blade out of the body of an unarmed stable boy. Without halting, Leprat laid the murderer out with a blow from the guard of his ivory rapier, leaving Durieux to finish him off with his sword as he passed. The tower door was ajar. Leprat's mighty kick slammed it wide open against the wall, surprising a drac inside who turned, pistol in hand. The gun went off and Leprat felt the ball brush by him as he charged forward and hit the drac in the shoulder, almost lifting the reptilian from the ground. The musketeer brutally shoved him into the wall and stepped back. The drac had no time to recover: Durieux fired a pistol ball into the middle of his brow. The two musketeers exchanged a glance. They made a good team.

The room suddenly shook from another explosion.

A powder charge had detonated in the ditch at the foot of the tower, a good third of which collapsed outwards in a cascade of stones, wood, and ancient dust. The rest of the shattered structure groaned, creaked, and tottered danger-ously before falling in on itself. Leprat and Durieux barely had time to fling themselves back outside before the cellar was engulfed in rubble and a thick cloud of debris.

In the courtyard, the battle continued.

Three musketeers were lying in a pool of blood amongst a dozen drac bodies. Most of their comrades were wounded and only a few blue-caped figures were still fighting, but they did not concede an inch of ground. A short distance from the general mêlée, La Fargue, Laincourt, and Marciac stood against the Illuminator. They harried the dragon, attacking it from the right and left, forcing it to turn back and forth in response, always retreating before its blows to allow another to take it from behind. They had quickly realised that they could not accomplish much against this powerful and cunning creature whose scales deflected most of their sword strokes. It was a lesson they learned at great expense to themselves. The *schiavone* had sliced into Marciac's arm, while Laincourt had recklessly exposed himself to the monster's claws, which had ripped through his doublet and shirt, leaving a row of bloody stripes across his chest. As for La Fargue, with his vision restricted by his eye patch, he'd been too slow to see a reverse blow by the dragon's fist that had struck him in the temple and left him senseless for a moment. It was only a matter of time before one or another of the trio committed an even graver mistake.

A fatal one.

Covered in dust and still staggering from the aftereffects of the explosion, Leprat and Durieux were rejoining the fight when the blast of a horn resounded in the night, at some distance from the château. Immediately, the dracs broke off combat and retired in good order. The scaly monster seemed to hesitate, considering its exhausted opponents. Then with three mighty bounds it was at the top of the ramparts and, after a last backward glance, it disappeared off into the night.

Within the devastated château, those who were still standing struggled to understand what had just transpired. Then the reality of their situation set in and they rushed to the aid of their fallen comrades. Leaving Durieux to see to the most urgent cases, Leprat went to confer with the Blades:

'God's blood!' he exclaimed. 'For a moment I thought . . . Are you wounded?'

'Nothing serious,' asserted La Fargue.

The two others nodded or confirmed the same with reassuring expressions as they re-sheathed their weapons.

'Gagnière?' Marciac enquired.

'Dead . . . But what just happened here?'

Leprat turned to give an incredulous glance around the

courtyard that had been transformed into a battlefield and at the ruins of the collapsed tower.

'The Black Claw,' La Fargue said. 'Obviously, they were prepared to do anything to prevent Gagnière from being handed over to the Pope.'

Leprat nodded, thinking that although the Black Claw had been forced to employ a sizeable force to achieve its aim, their third attempt on Gagnière's life had succeeded.

'I don't know, captain,' Laincourt objected. 'The dracs managed to place the mine that brought down the tower without being seen. Why would they attack us, rather than simply set it off and kill Gagnière? Why this assault? Why all these risks and useless deaths?'

La Fargue stared at Laincourt for a long moment in silence.

Then he cursed and ran for the pavilion where La Donna had been lodging.

'What now?' wondered Marciac, following Laincourt and Leprat as they raced after the captain.

'It was a diversion!' shouted the musketeer. 'A bloody diversion!'

The Renaissance-style pavilion was filled with an ominous silence.

They found Valerio Licini's lackey lying on his stomach in a puddle of his own blood at the bottom of the great stairway.

'Dead,' said Leprat, turning him over.

The poor wretch's throat was slit.

Sword in hand and bleeding along one side, Licini himself lay across the last flight of steps before the first floor.

'He's still alive,' Laincourt pronounced after leaning down to inspect him.

They called out, conducted a rapid search of the premises, and discovered the two village girls hiding in a cubby-hole. But La Donna had vanished.

The outer wall had been pierced with windows on this side of the Château de Mareuil. One of them stood wide open to the night, next to an overturned table, torn curtains, and a single woman's shoe.

'MERDE!' swore La Fargue, driving his fist into the wall.

2

It took a day for Cardinal Richelieu to learn of the attack on
Château de Mareuil and the terrible price its defenders had
paid. It took two for La Fargue, Laincourt, and Marciac to
return to Paris and, on the third day, the captain of the Blades
was summoned to the Palais-Cardinal. That morning, it was
Rochefort who bade him enter the antechamber where Richelieu waited for him, dressed as a cavalier. The cardinal had
taken advantage of a hunting expedition organised at Saint-
Germain by the king to come back to the capital in secret,
riding full out. At forty-eight years of age and despite his
precarious health, Armand-Jean du Plessis, cardinal de Richelieu, was still an accomplished horseman. His boots were dusty
and he held a slender cravache in his gloved hands.

La Fargue presented himself, hat in hand, saluting the
cardinal with a bow and then waiting in silence. The cardinal
was standing, facing the window.

'In a few weeks,' he said, 'the king will enter Lorraine at the
head of his armies. There will be some last-minute negotiations but nothing will hinder His Majesty's inexorable march
towards Nancy. The capital of Lorraine will undergo a siege
and, very soon, the duc Charles IV will have no choice but to
capitulate . . . This intervention has legitimate motives, not
least of which is to force the duc de Lorraine to respect both
the spirit and the letter of the treaties he signs with the king of
France and then seems to . . . forget about later on. The
European powers will condemn us for this invasion but do
nothing to impede it. To be sure, some will accuse France of
wishing to annex Lorraine in order to gain a door onto the
Holy Roman Empire in Germany, and they are not entirely

mistaken . . .' The cardinal turned away from the window to catch La Fargue's eye. 'As you can see, the future is already written. And if God wills, only a few cannon will need to be fired in the execution of this necessary operation.'

A flagon of wine with a glass, a plate of biscuits and a plate of grapes stood on a tray. Richelieu took off one of his gloves in order to detach a grape from its bunch, started to bring it to his mouth, then changed his mind and put it back down.

'The only real difficulty,' he continued, 'stems from the fact that Lorraine is Catholic. And the Pope does not look at all kindly on one Catholic state making war on another, when there are so many Protestant states to make war on instead. In France, the Catholic party that hates me says as much in all its tracts, just as they oppose France being allied with the Protestant republic of the United Provinces of Holland against Spain . . .'

The cardinal fell silent for a moment, thinking to himself.

'The king will need the benevolent neutrality of the Pope when he occupies Lorraine. That is why France has been trying so hard not to displease Rome recently, and has even sought ways to please her. The marquis de Gagnière was an opportunity to do just that. Now he is dead, which is unfortunate. Even more serious is that signor Licini, otherwise known as Père Farrio, one of Rome's most zealous agents, has suffered a sword thrust through his body. Graver still, La Donna has been abducted. And all of this occurred in France, under the very noses of a full detachment of the King's Musketeers.'

'Four of those musketeers perished during this mission, monseigneur, and most of the others were wounded. The attack also took the lives of several innocent victims among the château's personnel.'

Richelieu stared at La Fargue.

Was the captain insidiously reproaching with him with only considering the diplomatic implications of this affair, while ignoring the human toll?

There was a knock at the door and Charpentier, the cardinal's old and faithful secretary, appeared.

'It's time, monseigneur,' he said.

'Already? Very well. Accompany me, captain.'

And leading La Fargue as he strode through the Palais-Cardinal, he asked:

'This creature that you and your Blades confronted, was it a dragon?'

'Yes, monseigneur. No doubt a last-born, as it was incapable of a complete metamorphosis.'

'Thank God. Are you one of those who believe the Black Claw instigated this attack?'

They descended a small spiral staircase which brought them to the ground floor.

'Who else, monseigneur? The Black Claw had an account to settle with La Donna after the affair with the Alchemist. Moreover, since she often serves the Pope, she must know secrets likely to be of considerable interest to the Grand Lodge.'

They arrived at a brisk walk in a courtyard where several gentlemen, including the comte de Rochefort, were waiting in their saddles.

'I am convinced that Gagnière's death was not the main objective of the attack,' added La Fargue. 'The Black Claw were really after La Donna.'

'I want you to find her,' said Richelieu, halting to pull his glove back on. 'It is only a matter of days before the Pope, through his ambassador, complains about this to the king. I want to be able to reply that signora di Santi is safe.'

'Monseigneur,' replied the captain of the Blades with a tense jaw, 'there is a more formidable danger than the Pope's displeasure now threatening Paris . . .'

'A danger that you affirmed had something to do with the Alchemist of the Shadows, wasn't that the one?'

'Yes.'

'Well, who knows more about the Alchemist than La Donna?'

'But who is to say whether she is still in France, monseigneur? Who is to say she is even still alive?'

'Find out.'

'How?'

Leaning towards La Fargue, the cardinal replied in a low voice:

'It is high time that your loyalty to the Seven be rewarded, don't you think? Ask them. They'll know.'

Without waiting for a reply, he joined the other riders and mounted his horse with the help of a lackey who held the stirrup for him. Then he added, just before spurring his mount forward:

'Indeed, you may be pleasantly surprised by the amount of good will that your contacts are prepared to demonstrate in this affair. Do not fail me, captain.'

And then the riders quickly filed out of the courtyard in the wake of Cardinal Richelieu.

In the garden of the Hôtel des Arcanes, the Gentleman was exercising with his sword beneath the shady vault of an arbour over which black rosebushes climbed. He practised alone, in his shirtsleeves, his hair gathered back with a leather thong.

The Enchantress observed him for a moment, admiring his feline grace and the lethal elegance of his movements. Then she approached and picked up, one after another, the three spare rapiers that the Gentleman had brought and left on a bench, comparing their weight and other qualities. He watched her do so, a half-smile on his lips. She finally chose the lightest and best-balanced of the trio. After whipping the air with the blade to loosen her wrist, she went to join the Gentleman in the shadow of the black roses.

They exchanged a fencing salute and crossed swords.

The Enchantress knew how to fight and did not seem overly hampered by her dress, lifting the heavy skirt with her left hand. She executed a series of cuts and thrusts, parried, and soon found her rhythm, gaining in boldness while the Gentlemen preserved his sang-froid and prevented their exchange from ever becoming too heated. The Enchantress soon realised that he was holding back. Without warning, she attacked with greater speed and vigour, taking the Gentleman by surprise and giving him no time to recover. She feinted and suddenly slapped him across the face with the back of her hand.

He broke off combat, retreated, and touched his bleeding lip with his fingertips, addressing an admiring and amused glance at the Enchantress. She raised her eyebrows at him in mocking defiance and placed herself *en garde*.

The duel resumed, this time in earnest.

Now, just as the Enchantress had wished, the Gentleman held nothing back. He dominated her with art, with science. He imposed his rhythm and his strength, forcing her to give way step by step. Delighted, she sensed his gaining the upper hand, knew he dominated her, handling her as he pleased. He was virile, powerful, and implacable. And when he was finished with her, he disarmed her, giving her wrist a sharp twist as he did that caused her to cry out briefly in pain. She found herself shivering with her back to the wall, under threat, completely vulnerable to the steel point that brushed against her heaving bosom pearled with sweat.

'If you kill me now, you'll never receive the gift I have in store for you . . .'

The Gentleman smiled and withdrew his sword.

'A gift?'

'Come.'

She took him by the hand and led him into the mansion.

He followed her, intrigued, and played along as she eluded him by darting up a staircase, waited for him to appear, provoked him, and then eluded him again. He saw that she was drawing him towards their bedchamber and started to realise what she had prepared for him.

'Really?' he said with a faint smile.

In his eye, there was the uncertain, happy gleam of someone who has guessed what has been offered to him just by seeing the package. Retreating before him, the Enchantress plucked a tarot card from her bodice and twirled it teasingly. He glimpsed a major arcanum card, but which one? He wasn't allowed the chance to see.

Reaching the end of the corridor, the Enchantress passed her hands behind her to open the door at her back. Following the movement, she entered and stepped aside, one arm pointing towards what lay within.

Towards the bed.

It was a splendid bed, immense, solid, made of black sculpted wood from whose canopy hung scarlet curtains attached to the columns by leather laces that often found other uses. And there, on the white sheets, a naked young blonde woman was waiting for him. She had a juvenile beauty with an adorable face, a milky velvet complexion, a slender waist and perfect curves.

She smiled, gazing at the Gentleman without uttering a word.

He remained still but was already carried away by his desire. He could not tear his eyes from her.

'Forget madame de Chantegrelle,' the Enchantress whispered in his ear. She embraced him from behind. 'Forget the vicomtesse de Malicorne.' She showed him the tarot card she had teased him with a few instants before. 'And bid fair welcome to—'

'—the "Demoiselle in the Tower",' finished the Gentleman, having recognised the major arcanum in question.

He advanced, climbed on to the bed and lay down beside the Demoiselle who offered herself to him, and he kissed her while the Enchantress unlaced her dress and joined them.

At the Hôtel de l'Épervier, the Blades conversed as they waited for La Fargue to return from the Palais-Cardinal when, guided by a blushing Naïs, Leprat joined them in the garden. He was warmly welcomed, particularly by Agnès and Ballardieu who not seen him since their departure for Mont-Saint-Michel. He seemed slightly intimidated. Perhaps it was the house, where he felt less at ease now that he had reclaimed the blue King's Musketeers cape for good. But the others treated him like a lifelong comrade and even Saint-Lucq greeted him with a nod and a faint smile.

So Leprat let Ballardieu seat him forcefully on a stool beneath the chestnut tree and was happy to clink the glass of wine that Marciac served him with those of all the Blades present. Laincourt busied himself with slicing sausage for everyone and they begged Naïs to bring more wine, bread and butter, and the remains of the ham they had started to eat the previous day.

It was almost noon.

'Firstly, what are you doing here?' the Gascon asked gaily. 'And without your cape, no less! Aren't Tréville's Musketeers at Saint-Germain, with the king?'

'Indeed. But I have been granted a leave of absence, like all those of us who were at Mareuil . . . Well, at least . . . like all those who survived . . .'

'That Durieux gave me the impression of being an excellent fellow,' noted Laincourt.

'He is,' affirmed Leprat.

'Were you close to any of the musketeers who perished there?' Agnès enquired gently.

'To some, yes.'

'How many died?'

'Six. Five fell in the battle and I learned this morning that a sixth succumbed to his wounds in the night . . . We weren't prepared,' explained Leprat, who was feeling a need to confide. 'Not for what we confronted there, in any case . . .'

'There were thirty dracs,' Laincourt explained. 'They were organised and determined, showing no mercy. They had well-made weapons and powder charges. And they knew how to fight . . . How could we have been prepared for that?'

'Not to mention the dragon,' added Marciac.

'All that just to kill Gagnière?' asked Ballardieu in surprise.

'To abduct La Donna,' corrected Agnès.

'Are we really sure about that?' objected Saint-Lucq as he leaned across the table to snag a slice of ham with the point of his dagger. 'Couldn't all of this be a ruse, more of La Donna's stagecraft? It would be just like her.'

'To be sure,' admitted Marciac. 'But why would she?'

'To escape from the Pope's supervision. To recover her freedom. To cover her tracks while she took flight . . .'

'But where would she have found thirty-odd dracs to do her bidding?' asked Agnès. 'And a dragon to command them?'

'You're right,' conceded the half-blood. 'So we must believe that, if she lives, La Donna is a prisoner of the Black Claw. I don't envy her fate . . .'

La Fargue returned a little while later, after Leprat had already left to pay his respects to the family of the dead musketeer.

'Well?' enquired Marciac.

'We must find La Donna.'

'We must?'

'By order of the cardinal.'

'How will we even start?' Agnès asked.

La Fargue hesitated.

'I'll know soon,' he said, trying to ignore Saint-Lucq's penetrating glace. 'For now, get some rest, all of you.'

They spent the afternoon in a state of torpor. Saint-Lucq went out without saying where he was going, as usual. The others remained in the dimness and quiet of the Hôtel de l'Épervier, taking shelter from the summer heat. La Fargue, Laincourt, and Marciac had been riding almost without pause for four days, and had fought hard at the Château de Mareuil. Their short night of sleep since their return had not allowed them to recover from their fatigue or their wounds, as light as the latter might be. They isolated themselves to rest, aware that they might need all of their strength again soon.

In the fencing room, Agnès read and Ballardieu dozed, until La Fargue, too worried to remain still for long without something to do, came and joined them. He sat down with a sigh and took off his patch so that he could massage his damaged eye.

'Guibot told me you received a letter from the Chatelaines' Mother Superior General,' he declared.

'Guibot talks too much.'

'He didn't mean any harm by it. It occurred to him when I asked if anything had happened here during my absence.'

'In fact, I received a first letter from La Vaussambre before your departure. And as I didn't reply to it, a second letter arrived yesterday.'

'Can you tell me what they said?'

'I can. La Vaussambre wants to see me.'

'Did she say why?'

'No.'

'But you have an idea.'

'Yes.'

'You can't keep avoiding this forever, Agnès.'

Ballardieu, who was listening, frowned and anxiously watched the young baronne de Vaudreuil. Closing the treatise on fencing she had been reading – a gift from Almades which he had annotated in his own hand – she stood up and left, saying:

'I'm going to rest a while.'

La Fargue crossed glances with the old soldier.

'When will she understand?' he asked.

Ballardieu shrugged, looking distressed.

At the end of the day, Marciac was finishing a game of patience on his bed when Guibot came to warn him that he had a visitor.

'And who would that be?'

'The vicomte d'Orvand, monsieur,' replied the old concierge.

Glad to have an excuse to be up and about, Marciac pulled on his boots, decided to do without his doublet, unhooked his rapier as he was leaving the chamber, and hastened downstairs. He was making some final adjustments to his baldric when he joined d'Orvand in the courtyard and greeted him with a broad smile.

'Good afternoon, vicomte. How are you?'

D'Orvand was like a big brother to Marciac. He worried about the Gascon, reproached him repeatedly over all the scrapes he got himself into, and then never took long to forgive him. He had often offered him room and board, paid off certain of his debts, and once had even lent him a sword when Marciac had pawned his and needed to fight a duel. While he would never stop loving him, he despaired of ever seeing

Marciac become reasonable. Perhaps he even secretly envied the Gascon's carefree attitude.

'Good afternoon, Nicolas. You look tired.'

'Not at all. So what brings you here? What do you say we go round to visit madame de Sovange? We could wager a little of your money . . .'

'Another evening. Right now, there is someone who needs to speak to you.'

'Ah?'

'Follow me, would you? My carriage is waiting outside.'

The vicomte's coach did indeed stand in the street in front of the Hôtel de l'Épervier. D'Orvand opened the passenger door and invited Marciac to embark first.

'Where are we going?' asked the Gascon.

'Nowhere.'

Intrigued, he climbed into the vehicle and found himself sitting opposite Gabrielle.

His Gabrielle.

An elegant woman, she had as much poise as she did beauty, with strawberry-blonde hair, deep blue eyes, and a calm gaze. She intimidated most men but Marciac was not one of them. He loved her completely and sincerely. In his eyes, other women didn't count, or counted very little. And never for long, in any case.

'She didn't want to come,' said d'Orvand taking a place inside the coach. 'I had to convince her to come to you for help.'

'What's happened?' asked the Gascon in alarm. 'Are you in trouble?'

'Yes,' replied Gabrielle, before correcting herself. 'Well, actually, no, it's not about me.'

Perplexed, Marciac turned to the vicomte.

'One of the . . . one of Gabrielle's protégées has disappeared,' explained d'Orvand.

Gabrielle directed a brothel located in rue Grenouillère, called *The Little Frogs*. The protégées to which the vicomte bashfully alluded were the female residents of the house.

'Who are we talking about?' Marciac enquired.

'Manon,' replied Gabrielle.

The Gascon nodded. Young, pretty, blonde, and plump: he knew perfectly well who Manon was.

'And?' he prompted.

From time to time, Gabrielle allowed her 'frogs' to take part in special evening parties at the homes of rich clients. They had heard nothing from Manon since she had gone to one of these parties.

'Didn't she have a guardian angel?' asked Marciac.

He knew that Gabrielle made sure that her protégées never went out without a bodyguard to accompany them.

'Of course she did, but . . .'

'But what?'

'What Gabrielle is reluctant to tell you,' interjected d'Orvand, 'is that she has lost most of her associates and backers of late. And even some of her best clients . . .'

' "Of late!" You mean since Rochefort has been making difficulties for her!' exclaimed the Gascon, gritting his teeth in anger. 'Gabrielle? Am I wrong?'

'I haven't come here to complain,' she retorted.

Recently, Gabrielle had rendered the Blades a service by providing refuge to a young girl being hunted by the Black Claw. This young girl was La Fargue's secret, hidden daughter, and the captain had been quick to find her another sanctuary. But this service had been enough for Rochefort to take an interest in *The Little Frogs* and to put pressure on Gabrielle in a variety of ways, including intimidation, in the hope of extracting information from her.

'But you must allow Nicolas to help you,' the vicomte insisted. 'He has experience in these matters and you know you can trust him completely . . .'

Gabrielle nodded, took a deep breath, found the courage to look Marciac in the eyes, and confessed:

'I had no choice. I resorted to Mortaigne.'

Upon hearing this name, the Gascon went rigid and pale.

A quarter of an hour later, Marciac watched the vicomte d'Orvand's coach drive away down rue Saint-Guillaume, then turn into rue des Saints-Pères. Worried, he went to find La Fargue in the small office next to the fencing room.

'Captain?' he called, as he knocked on the door left ajar.

'Come in.'

'May I sit down?'

'Please. What's the matter, Marciac?'

The Gascon reported everything he had just learned. La Fargue listened to him without interruption, and then asked:

'You and this Mortaigne, you know one another, am I right?'

'We've been associated in the past.'

'And that's all there is to it?' insisted the captain, directing a penetrating gaze at Marciac.

'No,' admitted the Gascon. 'Gabrielle was his mistress once.'

'Ah . . . But let's return to the present affair. What did he say about it? Surely he's not claiming this Manon vanished into thin air, is he?'

'According to him, the girl used this evening party to escape Gabrielle's supervision and run away with a beau.'

'But Gabrielle doesn't keep her girls against their will.'

'Indeed not.'

'So Mortaigne is lying. What kind of man is he?'

'A scoundrel. There are worse scoundrels than he, but he is a scoundrel nonetheless.'

With his feet on his desk, La Fargue gazed towards the window that looked out over the garden, now being invaded by the evening shadows. He thought for a moment, and then asked:

'Who organised the party? Who was receiving the guests at their home? Who paid for it?'

'Gabrielle did not want to tell me. Perhaps she doesn't know.'

The captain addressed him a faint cynical smile.

'I rather think she knows perfectly well who it is, and that it is a person of some importance. A person who wants their name to go unmentioned and who pays well for that privilege . . . Moreover, Gabrielle no doubt fears your provoking a disaster by going to see this man and hanging him by his feet until he tells you whatever you want to know. You have to admit it's the sort of thing you'd do . . .'

Marciac shrugged.

'Shaking the tree is not the worst way of making fruit fall out,' he said sulkily.

'But some trees are better left unshaken, and Gabrielle knows this full well.' La Fargue scratched his beard pensively. 'So what are you planning to do?'

The Gascon had already thought about the question.

'If you don't need me, I'll go talk to Mortaigne tomorrow.'

'All right. But be careful. And assure Gabrielle that we will provide all the help we can. I've not forgotten that I am in her debt.'

'Thank you, captain.'

After supper, La Fargue waited until night had fallen before going up to his bedchamber. He locked the door, put the lit candle down, and brought a small casket out of his nearly empty clothing chest. Sitting down at his table, he opened the casket with a small key that never left his person, gently lifted the lid and removed an object wrapped in cloth. It was a precious silver mirror, which he unwrapped and placed before him, next to the candle. Its flame trembled, disturbed by a breath of air from a half-open window.

And then he waited.

At the first stroke of the bell tolling the hour, La Fargue closed his eyes and, with a rapt expression, recited a ritual formula in an ancient tongue that he had learned by heart. The surface of the mirror rippled, and then it no longer showed his reflection in the dim light.

The translucent image of a white dragon's head appeared, the contours and edges of the image sparkling slightly.

'Good evening, master.'

'Good evening, captain. What is it?'

'I require your aid, at the request of the cardinal.'

'Cardinal Richelieu knows full well that the Seven do not respond to requests. What is this about?'

'La Donna had been taken by the Black Claw. I have received the order to save her, but I . . .'

'When?! When did this happen?'

'Two days ago, in Champagne. It was at the Château de Mareuil where La Donna was carrying out—'

'—a mission for the Pope, yes,' concluded the dragon.

Then, as if to himself, in a voice that combined anger and regret:

'And yet we told her not to intervene . . .'

'I beg your pardon?'

'It was far too dangerous for her to reappear so soon. But she refused to listen to us . . .'

'I don't understand,' La Fargue said, with a troubled air.

The dragon fell silent, reflecting, and finally decided to explain:

'La Donna serves us, just as you serve us.'

The old captain froze.

'Since when?' he asked.

'What does that matter? The cardinal is correct in this instance: it's absolutely necessary that she be saved. Go to the regular rendezvous tomorrow. Valombre will tell you what to do.'

The dragon's head faded and the mirror soon recovered its ordinary appearance.

La Fargue remained still, mulling over what he had just learned. So, he and La Donna sometimes served the same masters, the same cause. But whereas the rest of the time he devoted himself to serving the king of France, she hired out her talents as a spy and a schemer to the highest bidder.

. . . to the highest bidder? Really?

If she were truly the greedy adventuress that people claimed, the Guardians would not call on her services. So he had to believe that the beautiful and dangerous Italian had a moral code, after all . . .

La Fargue thought he saw a movement out of the corner of his eye.

Calmly, he turned towards the half-open window, saw nothing alarming, but got up anyway to check.

Had he imagined it?

Taking care to stand well back, he opened the window wide and craned his neck to look outside.

Nothing.

He stepped forward, leaned out, listened and looked in both directions along the deserted rue Saint-Guillaume, in search of a movement, a sound, a clue.

In vain.

La Fargue was forced to accept the evidence of his senses, but his instinct rarely deceived him. Was he simply tired? Possibly. Nevertheless, he felt a nagging doubt as he closed the window.

Clinging to a ledge just above, Saint-Lucq waited a moment before hauling himself up silently to the roof.

He had seen and heard everything.

In the most elegant and comfortable chamber of the Hôtel des Arcanes, the Gentleman, the Enchantress and the Demoiselle drowsed, naked and sated, among the sheets in disarray on the black wooden bed. The Gentleman lay on his stomach and had his back to the two entwined women. The morning light seeped through the open windows, along with the distant, soothing murmur of Paris. It was already warm outside. The remains of a fine supper, served on expensive crockery, were spread upon a table draped in red cloth.

Preceded by the pounding of his heavy tread, the Illuminator entered without knocking or waiting to be announced. He was filthy and unkempt, sweating profusely, and he reeked of the stable. He marched straight for the food, picked items from the dishes almost at random and ate them, drank, and then continued to stuff himself noisily. Although this intrusion left the Gentleman indifferent, the Enchantress did nothing to hide her exasperation. The Demoiselle was the only one to show signs of a reflexive modesty. But she caught herself before she drew a sheet over her body.

'So?' asked the Gentleman, sitting on the edge of the bed.

'The expedition was a success,' announced the Illuminator between two fat mouthfuls.

'La Donna?'

'In our custody at Bois-Noir. What are we going to do with her?'

The Gentleman shrugged.

'Sell her to the highest bidder. Or offer her to the Black Claw. The Heresiarch will decide.'

The Enchantress embraced him from behind and murmured:

'I'd so much like to amuse myself with her . . .'

'We'll see, my dear,' replied the Gentleman, turning to kiss her.

Having drunk from the neck of a flagon, the Illuminator wiped his mouth with the back of a sleeve and belched.

'Who's this?' he asked, pointing with his chin at the former vicomtesse de Malicorne.

Drawing apart from the Gentleman, the Enchantress pivoted on her knees and said:

'May I present the Demoiselle. She is henceforth one of us, or will be soon, exactly as the Heresiarch desires . . .'

The Illuminator examined the newcomer for a long moment, then snorted in disdain and turned heel.

'I'll be at Bois-Noir,' he said as he left the chamber without closing the door.

The Gentleman gave a burst of laughter and fell back on the bed, arms spread.

Both furious and taken aback, the Demoiselle stammered:

'Wh— who was . . . that brute?'

'That was the Illuminator,' replied the Enchantress, getting up to put on a vaporous garment. 'You will get to know him, but it may take some time for you to appreciate him – if you ever do.'

'He's useful,' added the Gentleman, rising in turn. He approached the table, in search of food that had not been pawed by the Illuminator. 'By the way,' he continued in a conversational tone, 'the Enchantress tells me that you have some projects of your own in mind, is that right?'

The Demoiselle rolled onto her side and propped her head on her elbow.

'I was thinking of gathering some of my former followers. I had assembled many of the servile Black Claw worshippers around me. Some of them were influential, and not all of them have been rounded up by Cardinal Richelieu's men.'

'That's probably a good idea. What do you say?' the Gentleman asked the Enchantress.

The Enchantress was dressing her hair in front of a mirror.

'It's just as well that the idea pleases you,' she replied. 'Because the Demoiselle and I have already started to put it into effect . . .'

That morning, master Guibot went to find Agnès de Vaudreuil in the fencing room, where she was practising her fencing with Ballardieu.

'Madame, someone has brought a letter for you.'

Breaking off her assault, the young woman turned towards the concierge.

And waited.

'Well?'

'Oh!' exclaimed Guibot, realising the misunderstanding. 'The bearer has instructions to deliver the letter to you in person. He asked to wait in the courtyard.'

Agnès sighed, giving the old man a curt look. Then she tossed her rapier to Ballardieu, snatched a towel as she passed and, intrigued, went to see who it was.

There was indeed a man in the courtyard. Turning his back to the front steps of the main building, he stroked his horse's mane. He wore the uniform of the Black Guards, the elite company charged with the security of the Sisters of Saint Georges.

Agnès frowned: one of the Black Guards; that surely meant another letter from the Chatelaine's Mother Superior General. But the young woman's expression went from one of wariness to incredulity and joy when the messenger turned around.

It was François Reynault d'Ombreuse, the son of the marquis d'Aubremont and younger brother of Bretteville, whom Agnès had loved in secret.

'François?' she exclaimed. 'François, is it really you?'

She fell into his arms.

'By God!' he responded. 'And who else would it be?'

A tall, handsome man, wearing his sword with an elegant air and natural poise, he was displaying a broad smile. His eyes shone, as did those of the fiery baronne, who, drawing apart from him, gave him a hard punch on the shoulder.

'Do you know how worried we all were? Your father, above all. We've been searching for you high and low, and with those cursed Chatelaines—'

'I'm well,' said Reynault. 'And I'm here. I haven't disappeared. But I was away on a mission, after which I was assigned as a guard at Mont-Saint-Michel.'

'At Mont-Saint-Michel? Recently? You mean—'

'That I was there when you so distinguished yourself, yes!'

She remembered then the astonishing kindness with which her gaoler had treated her at the abbey on the mount, and suddenly she understood whom she owed it to.

'Come,' she said. 'Come in. I'm sure the captain will be delighted to see—'

'No, Agnès,' Reynault interrupted her. 'I must leave again at once. You know these are grave times . . .'

'Ah,' said Agnès, her smile vanishing. 'So this is what brings you here . . . There is no letter, is there?'

'No. I wanted to be sure of seeing you . . . You must agree to speak with the Mother Superior General, Agnès. Please.'

The young woman reflected. Then she sighed in resignation.

'So be it. I will go this afternoon . . . But only on one condition.'

'Which is?'

'Send your father news, or allow me to.'

'I'll do that. I promise you.'

Reynault remounted his horse and Agnès watched him ride off through the carriage gate. Turning round, she saw Ballardieu standing on the front steps.

The old soldier was smiling at her tenderly.

Paris was home to a dozen courts of miracles, the enclosed areas where the communities of beggars, criminals and other marginal elements would congregate under the authority of a single chief. The most famous of these courts was on rue Neuve-Saint-Sauveur, located behind the Filles-Dieu convent and ruled by the legendary Grand Coësre. There were also the Cour Brisset, the Cour Sainte-Catherine, the Cour Jussienne, the Cour du roi François, and other more or less populated and fearsome places.

Among them, the Cour-aux-Chiens was a well of shadows and stinks, surrounded by miserable façades to which clung a tangle of rickety galleries and rotting stairways. A noisy, turbulent life thrived in the dirty and polluted air. Down below, children played, ran around, appeared and disappeared through dark alleys, the soles of their clogs stamping through the unsanitary muck. Beneath browning canvas cloths, in which the remains of past downpours of rain slowly stagnated, tables flanked by stools were occupied by men condemned to a precarious, roving existence: unemployed workers, lackeys without a master, soldiers without a billet. They drained cups of sour wine and waited to be joined by women who would urge them to drink more before dragging them away to the sordid cubby-holes where they performed their services. Some of these women did not even make the effort to come back down and instead stood at the railings above, having quickly swiped between their thighs, calling out to whoever would listen: naming their prices, boasting of their talents and mocking those who hesitated. Others, more weary or resigned, simply waited. And when no one came, they chattered amongst themselves and watched over their boisterous offspring from the heights.

At a window situated on the first floor of one of the buildings overlooking the courtyard, Marciac also observed the brats amusing themselves. Perfectly indifferent to the misery surrounding them, they charged forward with joyful cries to assault their imaginary enemies. The Gascon, behind his dark spectacles, counted nine of them entering an unlit passage in single file, by order of age and size. A snot-faced blond boy armed with a wooden sword led the charge, while a tiny girl wearing rags trotted at the rear, always out-distanced but nevertheless happy to be part of the game. A woman shouted that they were to stay within sight. In vain.

'Monsieur?' asked a timid voice.

Marciac turned his head toward the very young girl who, with lowered eyes, presented him with a glass of wine. Wearing a patched dress that was fraying at the sleeves, she was thin and pale, perhaps ill, certainly fearful. Everything about her expressed the submissiveness of a broken soul.

The Gascon took the glass without saying a word.

The girl went away. She left the door to the corridor open, and Marciac saw a drunken man struggling to retie his breeches. A dishevelled prostitute was holding him by his vest.

'You haven't paid!' she cried.

The man tried to free himself with a shove of his shoulder, but the woman wouldn't let go.

'You're not going anywhere until you've paid!'

'I did pay!'

'Not enough! Twenty deniers have never made a sol!'

With a nasty back-handed blow, the drunkard struck the prostitute in the face. She fell backward and hit the wall with her skull, bleeding from the mouth.

'There's your account paid in full.'

Then the man saw Marciac observing him.

'And you? Got anything to say?' he spat.

The Gascon gave him a disdainful look and turned back to the window.

The drunkard moved off as the woman picked herself up from the floor and insulted him, furious. Sipping his wine, Marciac waited to see him come out in the courtyard below. There, three men armed with clubs caught up with him, hit him without warning from behind, and continued to bludgeon him, egged on by the cheated prostitute. Finally, they emptied his pockets and left him bloodied on a pile of rubbish. The Gascon recognised one of the brutes: a certain Tranchelard, whom he was surprised to see here. Outside, no one did anything to stop him delivering a last blow to his dying victim.

'Sorry to have kept you waiting.'

Marciac turned to the man who had just entered the room

and was walking toward him with a smile on his face. Caught short, Marciac accepted his warm and friendly accolade before the other man released him and declared:

'I'm happy to see you again. It's been a long time, hasn't it?'

Without waiting for a reply, Mortaigne went to fill two glasses from the bottle placed on a table.

'Here's to our meeting again,' he said, handing one glass to Marciac.

Dark-haired, his chin marked by a scar that did not detract from his charm, Mortaigne seemed to be in good health but had put on weight, as far as the Gascon could judge. He was dressed as a hired swordsman, wearing a heavy leather doublet, with a dagger tucked into his right boot. His sword and baldric hung from the back of a chair.

He seemed sincerely glad to see Marciac.

'How are you?' he asked. 'I heard that you had some problems with La Rabier.'

'That matter was settled.'

'Good. She's a mean woman, that one. It's not wise to be indebted to her for long.' Mortaigne lifted his glass and drained it in one gulp, while Marciac contented himself with a mouthful. 'So . . . to what do I owe the pleasure of your visit?'

'I'm looking for one of Gabrielle's girls who has gone missing.'

Mortaigne's expression grew cloudy.

'Ah,' he said. 'Manon, is it?'

'Yes. What really happened that night? Do you know?'

'Gabrielle is making a whole story about it, but there's no real mystery . . .'

At that instant, Tranchelard and his companions went past in the corridor, bantering cheerfully with one another. Mortaigne could not see them, but he heard their voices.

'Is that Tranchelard?' he enquired.

'Yes.'

'Call him over, will you?'

'No.'

Mortaigne stared at the Gascon and then hailed his hench-man in a loud voice:

'Tranchelard!'

Coming back the way he came, the man in question ap-peared in the doorway. Tall, with long, greasy hair and a surly look, he still held the club he had just employed on the drunkard. The weapon's studs were spattered with blood and hair.

'*Patron?*'

'Did you kill him?'

'Maybe.'

'If he doesn't crawl out of here before then, dump him in the Seine when night falls.'

'Right you are.'

'That evening, Tranchelard was the one keeping an eye on things,' explained Mortaigne. Then he addressed the hench-man again: 'Marciac is a friend of mine. Tell him what hap-pened, the night that girl from *The Little Frogs* scarpered off.'

'After supper, she went up to a bedroom with a young gentleman. And in the morning, they had both disappeared. The bed wasn't even messed up.'

Tranchelard said no more.

'And that's all?' prompted the Gascon.

'Well . . . yes.'

Mortaigne thanked Tranchelard, who left.

'You see?' he said. 'There's no mystery. A young man falls for a pretty whore and carries her off, convinced that their love will overcome all obstacles. It will last until the twit discovers how much he misses his paternal allowance . . .'

The two men exchanged a long glance without blinking and Marciac recognised the gleam of a challenge in Mor-taigne's eye. The master of the Cour-aux-Chiens seemed to be saying to him: 'You've heard what I have to say. Now, either call me a liar or accept my word.'

'I'll be seeing you very soon,' Marciac promised as he left.

Mère de Vaussambre received Agnès in the large cloister of the Enclos du Temple. She waited for the baronne alone, seated on a stone bench. She did not get up, but she did close her breviary when the young woman joined her.

'Welcome, Marie-Agnès.'

'Mother superior.'

'Will you sit with me for a moment?'

Agnès sat down, ill at ease, as the Chatelaines' leader was quick to perceive.

'Calm yourself, my dear. You're in no danger here.'

'Not even in danger of being thrown into a cell in your tower keep? I seem to recall having had that experience recently . . .'

'You secretly infiltrated our sacred abbey on Mont-Saint-Michel,' retorted Mère de Vaussambre in a tone of gentle reproach. 'And rather than lay down your weapons when the alarm was raised, you had no hesitation in crossing swords with the Black Guards . . . Did you really believe that would go unpunished?'

Agnès was at loss for a reply.

'But let us forget all that, Marie-Agnès. Stop seeing me as an enemy and accept the peace offer I am making.'

'What's happened, mother superior? Why this change of heart?'

'I have never been hostile towards you, and neither have the Sisters of Saint Georges. Quite the reverse.'

'Then why do I have the feeling that you dislike me? You have never accepted the fact that I renounced taking my vows, mother superior.'

The Superior General of the Chatelaines was silent for a moment, and then suggested:

'Let's walk a little.'

They slowly paced along the lanes of the cloister.

'Your mark has awoken, hasn't it?'

'Yes, it has.'

'Don't you see that as a sign?'

'I won't take the veil, mother superior.'

'And how about your nights?'

Agnès refused to answer.

'All of the White Wolves bear the dragon's rune,' continued Mère de Vaussambre. 'But yours is different.'

'How do you know that?'

As if weary, the Superior General sighed.

'The Good Lord has singled you out, Marie-Agnès. And with each passing day, I pray you will come to understand that before it is too late. A terrible ordeal awaits you, and it is only the first, the one that will reveal if you are worthy of this destiny you so obstinately turn your back on. The destiny that you will be forbidden to fail . . .'

Agnès halted, forcing the Superior General to do likewise and turn round.

'Why me?'

'It is the Good Lord's will, Marie-Agnès.'

'I don't believe a word of it.'

'This dragon haunting your sleep, you will have to confront it soon. Do you think you will manage that on your own?'

The young woman was shaken by what she saw in Mère de Vaussambre's gaze.

She turned away.

'It's not fair,' she said.

'No, it's not . . . But this dragon is a primordial. A primitive and savage creature, extremely brutal, which certain parties have succeeded in turning into a formidable weapon. If no one opposes it, it will destroy Paris and plunge the kingdom into a storm that will devastate it. There will be misery, famine, and war.'

'Who knows about this?'

'The Chatelaines.'

'And no one else?'

'For now.'

'Why keep it a secret?'

'Because it hides another secret. One even the king does not know; one on which the fate of the entire world hangs.'

The young baronne waited.

In vain.

'No, Marie-Agnès,' the Superior General said to her with a

resigned smile. 'I cannot confide that secret to you now . . . But before you leave, grant me the boon of a favour.'

'Which is?' asked Agnès in a defensive tone.

'Speak with our new mother superior of the White Wolves. She will know how to persuade you and I think you will be glad to learn that she has recovered from her ordeal.'

Then, looking in the direction indicated by Mère de Vaussambre, Agnès recognised Sœur – or rather – Mère Béatrice d'Aussaint, who waited, smiling, with her sword at her side.

The last time they had seen one another, the Chatelaine had lain delirious on a narrow bed in the abbey at Mont-Saint-Michel.

That evening, Marciac went to rue Grenouillère. Making a cautious approach, he discreetly observed the surroundings. Not so long ago, men in the pay of Rochefort had been keeping watch over *The Little Frogs*. The Gascon had put one of them out of action, but he did not know whether his message has been received. The only sure result of his initiative had been to greatly displease Gabrielle, who knew how matters stood and – quite understandably – preferred he left Cardinal Richelieu's henchmen, as abject as some of them were, alone. Hence their most recent dispute, and their most recent separation.

Marciac did not see anyone or anything out of the ordinary, except that shutters had been recently added to the brothel's windows. He did not try knocking on the door. He went around to the back and climbed over the wall into the garden, where he found Gabrielle sitting at a small table in the shade, busy with her correspondence.

'You do know we have a door,' she said, glancing up at the Gascon. Unmoved by his appearance, she did not pause in her writing. 'We even have a porter to open it for you.'

'And how is he, dear old Thibault?'

'You can ask him when you leave. By way of the door.'

Marciac sat down on a low wall and removed his hat, fluffing his blond hair which was tangled and shiny with sweat.

'I went to see Mortaigne,' he announced.

Gabrielle put her quill down and straightened her shoulders.

'And?'

'That evening, it was a certain Tranchelard who was "keeping an eye on things", as Mortaigne put it. You know him?'

'No.'

'I thought perhaps you might have heard of him. Tranchelard enjoys a degree of renown, along with some of the other unscrupulous brutes of his type. But the last I heard, he was still part of the court of miracles in rue Saint-Sauveur. I didn't know he'd left the Grand Coësre's service. And I'm wondering why.'

'Passing from the King of the Beggars' service to that of the master of the Cour-aux-Chiens does not seem like a promotion to me . . .'

'Well put.'

'Do you think that Tranchelard might be involved in Manon's disappearance?'

'Yes.'

'And Mortaigne?'

'It's possible. I can't say for certain.'

Marciac put his felt hat back on and adjusted it to the proper angle.

'Do you believe Manon . . . Do you think she's still alive?' asked Gabrielle suddenly, with a vibrant emotion in her voice.

Her distress, which she allowed herself to reveal for the first time, moved Marciac deeply. He went to crouch beside her, took her hands tenderly, and looked up, seeking her gaze.

'The truth,' he said, 'the truth is that I don't know. Not for certain.'

'It will soon be three days and three nights, Nicolas . . .'

'Even so, we can't . . .'

On the verge of tears, but in a voice ringing with anger, she interrupted:

'If you only knew how much I blame myself!'

'It's not your fault, Gabrielle.'

'But why did I decide to rely on Mortaigne?'

'It wasn't such a bad decision. And you couldn't know Mortaigne would delegate the duty to Tranchelard.'

Gabrielle rose and drew away from Marciac.

'You're trying to excuse me,' she accused, turning her back on him.

He stood up. Embarrassed, not knowing what to say, he scratched the stubble on his cheeks and neck.

Finally, after a moment of silence, Gabrielle turned and, regaining control of herself, said:

'We can expect no help at all from Mortaigne, if I've understood you correctly.'

'No, I'm afraid not.'

'So, what do you intend to do?'

'It's time you told me who hosted this party, Gabrielle.'

'Go to the usual rendezvous point tomorrow. Valombre will tell you what to do,' the white dragon in the mirror had said.

Saint-Lucq was hiding in a porch on rue Saint-Guillaume when La Fargue came out of the Hôtel de l'Épervier, just before midnight, alone. Invisible and silent, the half-blood watched him walk away and waited until he turned into the rue des Saints-Pères before following him.

The captain walked quickly to the Seine, where he turned right on the Malaquais quay. That could only mean one thing: he intended to enter Paris via the Nesle gate. All of the capital's gates being closed at this hour, La Fargue would have to use his permanent pass signed by Cardinal Richelieu. Like all the Blades, Saint-Lucq carried a similar document. But he couldn't pass through the Nesle gate at the same time as La Fargue, nor could he afford to wait for the guards to re-open the gate for him . . .

Saint-Lucq pondered the situation for a moment, made his decision and then did not hesitate.

Retracing his steps back up rue des Saints-Pères, he quickly turned away from the river, went past the Saint-Germain-des-Prés abbey and finally presented himself at the Buci gate. His pass worked its magic, allowing the half-blood swift access to rue Dauphine. Breathing hard, for a moment Saint-Lucq thought he had lost La Fargue. But he stayed calm and spotted his captain just as La Fargue ventured out onto Pont Neuf.

The stalking resumed, more delicate than ever, as La Fargue was careful to watch for anyone tailing him and the deserted Pont Neuf offered a clear view behind. Saint-Lucq could count on the darkness as an ally, however. And his dragon eyes could see far. He gave La Fargue a long lead, wondering whether the captain would continue across the Seine or turn into Place Dauphine. But in the event, he did neither. After a last glance around him, he disappeared behind the Bronze Wyvern's pedestal, at the tip of the Ile de la Cité.

So here was La Fargue's rendezvous point with this Valombre the white dragon had spoken of. A 'regular' rendez-vous, which made the half-blood wonder when these meetings had started. Who had started them. And why. He could not bring himself to admit that his captain was a traitor . . . but he was determined to get to the bottom of all this.

Midnight tolled.

Ten minutes passed without anyone turning up. Either Valombre was late or he had arrived at the meeting point first. He and La Fargue must be in the midst of their dis-cussion. Nevertheless, Saint-Lucq rejected the idea of ap-proaching the statue to eavesdrop on them. Too risky. So he waited.

At last, La Fargue reappeared and, in a great hurry, travelled back the way he had come. No doubt he was return-ing to the Hôtel de l'Épervier. The half-blood tracked him with his eyes but did not move. Almost immediately, another gentleman wearing a felt hat and a black coat emerged from behind the Bronze Wyvern.

Surely this was Valombre.

And he was a quarry worth following.

La Fargue made haste to rejoin the other Blades. Valombre had told him where La Donna was probably being held prisoner, without being able to give definite assurances of this or guarantee she would remain there for long. So they needed to act tonight, and address any doubts or questions afterwards.

At the Hôtel de l'Épervier, the captain ordered André to saddle the horses and summoned the others to the bottom of the main stairway. Agnès and Ballardieu arrived, and then Laincourt and Marciac almost immediately after.

'So?' asked the young baronne. 'How do matters stand?'

La Fargue had refused, of course, to let anyone accompany him to his rendezvous. He had, however, announced before leaving that he might return with news concerning La Donna.

'We know where she is,' he said now. 'She's being held in an old tower, a place called "Bois-Noir".'

'I know it,' indicated Marciac. 'It's on the Seine, not far upstream from Paris.'

'Is the information reliable?' enquired Laincourt.

'As reliable as we can hope to get.'

'And where does it come from?'

La Fargue had no idea how the Guardians had discovered where La Donna was being kept. To crown it all, he could not even tell the others who had given him this piece of intelligence.

'From one of the cardinal's agents,' he lied.

But Agnès had other concerns:

'Is Alessandra still held captive by the dracs who abducted her?'

'Yes, definitely.'

There was a moment's silence, broken by Marciac after he had done the sums:

'There were about thirty of them before they attacked us, and they left ten bodies on the ground. That leaves twenty dracs, well armed and well trained. Even without counting the dragon who commanded them, that's a lot to take on.'

'There are only five of us,' Ballardieu pointed out.

'Saint-Lucq isn't here?' asked La Fargue in surprise.

'No, captain.'

'Where is he?'

'No idea,' Marciac confessed.

The Blade's captain cursed. But there was no time for that, either.

'We can't wait to see if he shows up. Make your preparations. I want to be on the move in less than an hour.'

The others hesitated for a brief instant and then nodded; whatever their reservations none of them would question their captain or his authority. Only Agnès spoke up with a suggestion:

'At the very least, allow me to fetch Leprat, captain. We'll need his sword.'

'All right. But don't take too long.'

'And I'm going to need my bag of tricks,' muttered Ballardieu.

Laincourt heard him and frowned, but understood a short while later when he saw the old soldier return with a heavy pouch full of fused grenades slung over his shoulder on a bandolier. Agnès had already mounted the first horse that André had finished saddling and called out:

'Meet us at La Tournelle gate.'

Then she dug her spurs in and left the courtyard at a gallop.

La Fargue watched her leave, still thinking about Saint-Lucq. Worried about their mission, he already sensed that the half-blood's lethal efficiency was going to be sorely missed.

After his rendezvous with La Fargue, Valombre did not leave the Ile de la Cité. He crossed the Pont Neuf, then took the Grand-Cours-d'Eau quay. His path took him alongside the dark, high walls of the Palais de Justice until he reached rue de la Barillerie, which stretched from the Pont au Change bridge to the north to Pont Saint-Michel to the south. Beyond this street lay a twisted maze of medieval streets and alleys, which Valombre entered at a brisk pace, forcing Saint-Lucq to reduce the distance separating them or risk losing sight of his quarry. The half-blood was resolved to discover exactly where the captain's secret contact was going. But his anxiety increased the closer Valombre came to the so-called Cloister neighbourhood of Notre-Dame.

The Cloister occupied the eastern end of Ile de la Cité, in the shadow of Notre-Dame cathedral. A legacy of the Middle Ages, it consisted of three streets and about forty small houses owned and occupied – in principle – by the cathedral's canons. A wall surrounded it and the area inside was only accessible through three gates. Lacking any taverns or shops, this tiny neighbourhood was much envied for its tranquillity and some of the canons had realised the profits they could make if they allowed their dwellings to be let. This practice had become firmly established and, under Louis XIII, the Cloister had more secular than religious residents.

Was this Valombre's destination?

For Saint-Lucq, the question was answered when he saw the man present himself at the gate in rue de Colombe. One minute later, the man passed through the wall into the Cloister where visitors were rare and intruders were immediately suspect.

The half-blood winced in frustration.

Should he take the risk of following the mysterious gentleman inside the Cloister? He realised this was his only opportunity to find out what La Fargue was hiding, and duly located a spot where he could climb the enclosure unseen. He landed in a garden, went over a first low dividing wall between properties, then a second, and spotted Valombre just before the man disappeared at the end of rue Chanoinesse. Saint-Lucq ran silently alongside the houses' façades but arrived at the street corner too late: the place was deserted.

Breathless but still focused on the hunt, the half-blood searched the darkness with his dragon eyes, pricked up his ears, and searched for any glow in the windows around him.

Not a trace.

He cursed – and failed to see the blow that knocked him out cold.

Of the stronghold of Bois-Noir, nothing remained but an old stone bridge, a circular wall still in fairly good shape, some ruins that had been reduced almost to ground level, and a partially collapsed keep whose bevelled silhouette was outlined against a paling sky only an hour before dawn. These isolated, long-abandoned remains stood on top of a steep hill overlooking the Seine. They could be reached by road or via a footpath. Narrow and treacherous, this footpath wound towards the riverbank in a series of switchbacks, ending at a floating landing stage where a boat was moored, with dracs already busy on board. The road climbed the far slope in a large loop leading to the old bridge, which crossed a ditch filled with brush. Down below, where the road began, a temporary enclosure had been erected to hold twenty horses grazing next to a stream. Some dracs were also camped there, but the majority of the band were within the ruins, where La Donna was almost certainly being held.

La Fargue, Laincourt, Leprat, and Marciac approached the château on the same slope as the road, but ascended by a shorter, more direct route in great silent strides, taking advantage of the darkness and only halting behind cover to catch their breaths, measure the distance travelled, and inspect the surrounding area.

'It will be daybreak soon,' murmured Leprat as he joined La Fargue behind a large rock.

The captain nodded gravely.

They had ridden flat out from Paris, with only a brief delay to scout out the terrain and evaluate the enemy's forces, but now they were running out of time. Once the sun rose, the dracs would be up and about, too.

La Fargue risked a glance up the hill. They had almost reached the foot of the walls, which had sentries posted along the top. There were some breaches by which they could pass. But to reach them would require a perilous climb.

Behind them, Laincourt and Marciac waited.

'Captain.'

La Fargue turned toward Leprat and saw that he was pointing to the landing, down below, lit by lanterns. They enjoyed a good view of the boat and the handful of dracs who were completing preparations for an imminent departure. There was a man on the landing as well: bearded and massive, with an impressive *schiavone* at his side.

'He's the dragon,' said Leprat. 'The one who attacked us in Mareuil.'

La Fargue nodded again.

'If we act quickly and effectively,' he replied, 'he might not have time to reach the château, after the alarm has been raised . . .'

'Let's hope so.'

'There are four dracs with him. We saw three more guarding the horses at the bottom of the road. So that leaves twelve or thirteen up here.'

'It gives us a chance.'

'Then let's go!'

The four men resumed their silent ascent.

'I see three,' whispered Agnès.

'So do I,' said Ballardieu. 'Two near the fire and another one, over there.'

They lay flat on the grass and were spying on the dracs charged with guarding the horses. One was seated and smoking a pipe near the dying campfire, while the second, lying still, seemed to be asleep. The third one, apart from the others, was supposed to be guarding the horses, but was in fact watching the preparations going on aboard the boat moored at the landing.

'You take care of the sentry, girl?'

'Understood. Be careful.'

'As always.'

They separated, Ballardieu heading toward the fire and Agnès making a wider detour. She went round the enclosure stealthily, taking pains not to disturb the horses, and approached the drac from behind. He had not moved and continued to gaze in the direction of the lantern-lit pontoon. She was upon in him two quick strides, clamping one hand against his mouth and stabbing him three times in the kidneys. The drac gave a stifled moan and slowly slumped, held up by the young woman.

The drac smoking a short distance away didn't notice a thing. Tired from the night watch, he was bored and sucked on his pipe, his gaze absent. A noise made him turn three quarters round, just before a pouch heavily loaded with grenades struck him beneath the chin, snapping his neck.

Killed instantly, he fell backwards as the leather bag continued its trajectory at the end of the bandolier that Ballardieu wielded with art. Its next victim was the drac who had been dozing on a blanket and who only had time to rise up on his elbows. He, too, collapsed, his temple shattered.

Satisfied, Ballardieu admired his work before collecting the first drac's pipe and blowing on the tobacco that was still burning in the bowl. Agnès and he had almost completed their mission. Their task now was to free the horses and prevent any pursuit when they fled with La Donna. In passing, the old soldier noticed that there were four blankets around the campfire.

He raised an eyebrow.

Why four?

Agnès was finishing laying out the body of the sentry she had killed when the fourth drac came out of the grove, where he had been detained by a nasty bout of the runs. Shocked, they stared at one another for a brief second.

Then it was a matter of who reacted first.

The drac had a pistol at his belt.

So did the corpse the young baronne was leaning over.

The pistol shot caught them by surprise, coming when they had already infiltrated the ruins. Leprat was silently finishing off a guard on the ramparts; Marciac was dragging a body behind a low wall; Laincourt was sneaking up on a drac who had his back turned to him; and La Fargue was progressing towards the keep, a pistol in one hand and his solid Pappenheimer in the other.

Everything suddenly accelerated.

Senses abruptly alert, the last sentry standing spotted the intruders and raised the alarm. The dracs who were sleeping woke with a start and realised they were under attack. There was an immediate stir of activity. Shouts were raised. Shots rang out and, taking advantage of what little remained of the element of surprise, the Blades hurried to do as much damage as possible.

La Fargue raced towards the keep and eliminated the drac

at the entrance with a pistol ball fired right into his mouth before kicking in the worm-eaten door. Inside, sacks and kegs were deposited in a large room from which rose a spiral staircase. La Donna was almost certainly being held on the first floor, the storeys above either no longer existing or partially destroyed.

The old captain dashed towards the steps, but was forced to beat a retreat as a huge black drac came down them, rapier in his fist. La Fargue recognised the drac even as he placed himself *en garde*: he had seen him at Mareuil, fighting beside the red drac who had led the attack. The black drac stared at the captain in return, and no doubt recognised him as well.

Combat commenced and La Fargue quickly took the measure of his formidable opponent. The drac was fast, powerful, and he knew how to fence. Right from the start, the two adversaries threw all of their strength and skill into the battle. The drac because his brutal nature drove him to it and the captain because he knew time was against him. Their blades crossed and clashed violently in a series of attacks, ripostes, and counterattacks. Neither was prepared to give way. Neither could press home an advantage.

Not until La Fargue made a mistake.

Tripping, he clumsily parried a twisting attack that tore his sword from his hand. He fell on his back, rolled to the right and then to the left to avoid two thrusts that would otherwise have pinned him to the floor, then caught the drac's ankles in a scissor movement of his legs. The reptilian tumbled, allowing La Fargue time to stand up and seize with both hands a keg, which he heaved at his opponent. It struck the drac on the brow and broke open, spilling the gunpowder within. Seeing this, the captain realised the kegs stored here were mines similar to those the dracs had employed in their assault on Château de Mareuil. But the black drac, stunned by the impact and blinded by the cloud of black powder, was already getting back up. La Fargue pounced on his Pappenheimer and, straightening, brandished it in both hands, blade forward . . .

. . . before planting it all the way to the hilt in his kneeling opponent's chest.

The drac slowly sagged and then lay down for good, arms outstretched, in a spreading pool of blood.

Out of breath, La Fargue gathered his wits before climbing to the floor above. He quickly found La Donna, who was a sorry sight to behold. She did not seem to have been beaten or particularly mistreated, but several days of captivity and fear had taken their toll. She was dirty and dishevelled, still wearing the dress in which she had been abducted. Frightened, she had her back to the wall. Her hands were bound and her eyes covered by a blindfold.

'It's me,' the captain announced.

'La . . . La Fargue?'

'Yes.'

A sudden sob shook her shoulders. La Fargue freed her of her bonds and her blindfold. Still afraid but with a gaze full of gratitude, she pressed herself against him, trembling and fragile. She thanked him in a soft whisper:

'Grazie . . . Molte grazie . . .'

'Later.' He pried her away from him. 'Can you walk? Run?'

'Yes.'

'Then follow me.'

He was already moving, dragging La Donna by the hand, when an idea came to him.

The lantern burning in the room was no longer the sole source of light, as the first glow of dawn entered through a tall embrasure oriented towards the rising sun. La Fargue approached the opening and cast a glance down below. The embrasure overlooked the steeper side of the hill, the side where the dracs at the landing had been struggling up the footpath since hearing the alarm. Led by the Illuminator, they would soon pass just beneath the keep.

'Let's go,' La Fargue said. 'Take the lantern.'

In the courtyard, among the ruins of the Château de Bois-Noir, Leprat, Laincourt, and Marciac faced odds of two or three to one. The musketeer and the cardinal's former spy were fighting back-to-back in the middle of a circle of dracs, while the Gascon was defending the top of a flight of steps.

La Fargue and La Donna left the keep at a run.

'Down!' yelled the captain.

He immediately pushed the young woman to the ground behind a low wall and shielded her with his body. The others were caught short by the explosion of the powder charges stored in the tower. The detonation was enormous, violent, and deafening. It projected stones that whistled past like cannon balls while a cloud of dust and dirt engulfed the ruins. What remained of the keep tipped into thin air and fell in an avalanche of stone, wood, and rubble that swept down and carried away the dracs climbing the steep footpath. Their screams were inaudible from above.

La Fargue was the first to pick himself up.

His ears buzzing, he saw a powdery landscape on which a rain of debris, some of it aflame, was still falling. He helped La Donna to stand. Men and dracs were also struggling to their feet around them, dazed, staggering, and no longer in any state to fight. Their gestures were slow and uncertain.

'Any injuries?' shouted La Fargue.

Leprat and Laincourt shook their heads. Marciac waved a hand. He, too, was unhurt, or at least as unhurt as one could hope for. Two riders suddenly burst into the courtyard: Agnès and Ballardieu arriving, leading mounts for the others. As the dracs were beginning to recover their wits, they made haste. La Donna mounted behind Le Fargue and the Blades spurred their horses. As a final stroke, Ballardieu covered their escape with two grenades, which he tossed over his shoulder as they left the château.

The whole band galloped down the wide looping road to the bottom of the hill. There, La Fargue ordered a brief halt, out of range of any musket fire. The expedition had almost been a disaster, but they were all still alive and La Donna had been rescued.

'Is everyone all right?' the captain asked, concerned.

They reassured him, with the exception of Marciac who was

trying to unblock his left ear by slapping the right with his palm . . .

. . . and Agnès, who was looking back in the direction of the ruins.

Dressed in the tattered remains of an outfit of clothing, a scaly creature stood at the top of the sole remaining turret. It leapt from its perch and came charging down towards the Blades.

They immediately set off again at a gallop.

The dragon had somehow survived the explosion and the keep's collapse. Worse still, anger, fear, and the threat of death had triggered its uncontrolled metamorphosis into a monster even more bestial than the one the Blades had faced at Mareuil. It was now bigger, more powerful and more compact, with arms so long that its clawed hands touched the ground when it bent its knees. Its shoulders were enormous and its spine bent into a hump where it met a neck that was as short as it was wide.

The creature came hurtling straight down the slope, taking the most direct route, then followed the road in hot pursuit of the riders. It did not run, but rather progressed by bounds with the help of its arms and legs, its body gathering itself in when it touched the ground and stretching into the air with each forward push. Its speed was extraordinary and the Blades, even at a full gallop, were losing their lead.

Agnès and Ballardieu were at the back of the column.

Without slowing down, the old soldier slid the pouch on his bandolier against his belly. He plucked out a grenade and lit the fuse from the bowl of his pipe, before letting the device fall behind him. He repeated this operation twice, but the grenades rebounded willy-nilly when they hit the earth. Only the third remained on the road, and it exploded well before the dragon reached the spot.

Ballardieu realised that he wasn't going to accomplish anything that way.

He also realised they were lost if he did nothing.

'KEEP GOING!'

Pulling hard on the reins, Ballardieu forced his mount to

rear and pivot on its hind legs. Before Agnès could react, he raced away in the opposite direction. Without thinking, she turned back as well.

Ballardieu galloped full tilt towards the dragon, which, its eyes sparkling with a savage rage, also sped up. They met just beyond the bridge that crossed over a dry riverbed. The old soldier lit a last fuse; the creature bounded for him. Their collision overturned the rider and his mount. The horse gave a whinny of pain as the two opponents rolled in the dust and tumbled down into the dry gulch, disappearing from Agnès' view. The monster was the first to rise. Foaming at the mouth, it looked about and saw Ballardieu clumsily trying to stagger away. Then the dragon saw that a strap was wrapped around its neck and felt a weight hanging between its shoulders.

Ballardieu's bag of tricks exploded and decapitated the dragon right in front of Agnès, who had jumped down from her horse and was running towards the creature, sword in her hand. She instinctively protected herself with an elbow and could not contain a grimace of disgust when she discovered what remained.

Then she turned to Ballardieu, who was standing but tottering as if drunk, with a bleeding brow and a dislocated shoulder. She realised they would not finish hearing the tale of the day when Ballardieu slayed a dragon. She gave a smile . . .

. . . which immediately vanished.

'BALLARDIEU!' she yelled, pointing her finger.

Still dazed, the old soldier looked down to see the last grenade at his feet, which had not exploded with the others. The burning fuse was just reaching its end.

The sound of the explosion drowned out Agnès' scream.

3

The riders arrived in the courtyard of the inn at a gallop. They immediately dismounted and, carrying their wounded, blood-soaked comrade, almost broke down the door in their rush to bring him inside.

'Make room!' shouted La Fargue.

He was holding Ballardieu up. Agnès, Marciac, and Leprat helped him. Together, they laid the old soldier out on the first table they saw. Laincourt and Alessandra followed them.

In the large common room, the customers had stood up and moved away from the newcomers. The innkeeper didn't know what to do, unable to tear his eyes away from the dying man, whose whole right side was one huge wound.

'Leprat,' La Fargue ordered, 'make sure there's no one following us.' The musketeer nodded and left. 'Marciac, what do you need?'

The Gascon had started to cut away the scraps of blackened clothing that were stuck to Ballardieu's raw wounds and burns.

'Water and linen. And lint for bandages.'

'Did you hear that?' La Fargue asked the innkeeper.

The man was slow to react, but he nodded and hurried off.

'And some straps!' shouted Marciac. 'Bindings, laces, anything like that!'

He needed something to make better tourniquets than the emergency ones he had already put in place.

Agnès was leaning over Ballardieu with tears in her eyes. She was whispering softly in his ear as she stroked his brow covered in dirt, sweat, and blood.

La Fargue turned to Laincourt and La Donna, and it was the captain rather than the man who spoke.

'Madame, you must leave now. You have to reach the Palais-Cardinal as soon as possible. Only then will you be safe.'

'But I can't leave you like this,' protested the beautiful spy. 'This man—'

'His name is Ballardieu.'

'It was while rescuing me that he—'

'The mission comes first, madame. Laincourt, if you please . . .'

The young man nodded and urged La Donna to turn away.

'Come madame. I will escort you.'

She started to follow him, pulled gently backward by the arm.

'Thank you,' she said. 'Thank you with all my heart . . .'

But the Blades did not care about her gratitude: one of their own was dying.

As Agnès continued to comfort Ballardieu, who probably could not hear her, Marciac murmured to La Fargue:

'I'll do my best. But he needs a surgeon.'

The captain nodded and asked those gathered in the common room:

'Is there a surgeon who lives near here?'

People shook their heads and the innkeeper, who was returning with a basin filled with the items requested by Marciac, replied:

'We are in the country, messieurs. The closest doctor lives in the faubourg Saint-Victor.'

'By the time one of us travels to Paris for a surgeon and returns,' La Fargue thought aloud, 'we could be there ourselves . . .'

'It's out of the question. Ballardieu can't ride a horse now. He's lost too much blood, it would kill him.'

'I have a cart,' offered one good fellow among those watching.

'Here.'

Squinting painfully, Saint-Lucq took the spectacles from the hand holding them out to him. He had just woken and was trying to adapt to the light. His dragon eyes saw better in the day when protected by the red lenses. The headache that had threatened to overwhelm him receded.

934

'Thank you.'

He found himself in the peaceful surroundings of a modest chamber, lying on a narrow bed. He was fully dressed, or almost; only his doublet was missing, hung on the back of a chair. His hat was on the table, beside his rapier in its scabbard, and his leather baldric.

The person who had returned his spectacles was sitting next to the bed.

Elegant, in his thirties, and with grey hair, it was the gentleman La Fargue had met in secret the previous night, and whom the half-blood had followed as far as the Cloister of Notre-Dame.

Before being knocked out.

'Where are we?'

'In my home, rue du Chapitre.'

The man saw the glance that Saint-Lucq gave his sword.

'You're not in any danger here,' he said. 'I'm not your enemy.'

'Then why did you attack me last night?'

'I did not know who you were. And after I found that out, I needed to seek advice.'

'Seek advice from whom?'

The man smiled.

'Very well,' allowed Saint-Lucq. 'Then: seek advice on what subject?'

'What should be done about you. And also, what I could reveal to you.'

Sitting up in the bed, the half-blood turned towards his host and leaned back against the wall.

'Who are you?' he asked.

'My name is Valombre.'

'That's only a name.'

'And I am a dragon.'

'That I can well believe. What do you have to do with Captain La Fargue?'

'He and I serve the same masters.'

'Explain that to me.'

'I can do that. But wouldn't you prefer to hear the truth from your captain?'

935

Saint-Lucq thought about it, probing the grey, tranquil eyes of the other man, and then said:

'Let's start with you.'

Marciac did everything he could to keep Ballardieu alive. Then the Blades transported the old soldier to Paris in the cart that had been so generously offered to them. Their patient was laid out on two superimposed mattresses, to protect him from jolts during the journey. Agnès sat nearby to comfort him, to reassure him that he would recover and that all would be well. La Fargue took the reins and the Gascon followed them on horseback. They had to halt twice on the road to tighten the tourniquets.

Upon their arrival at the Hôtel de l'Épervier, Leprat was waiting for them. He had gone ahead at a full gallop, and had found a surgeon whose services were often used by the King's Musketeers, the same doctor who had tended him when Gagnière had left him for dead in rue Saint-Denis. Ballardieu was carried into the kitchen, where he was laid out on the large oak table. Then the surgeon asked that they leave him with his patient so that he might examine him without disturbance. He had come with an assistant and had no need of anyone else. He would call if there was something they could do.

The others waited in the courtyard with Guibot, André, and sweet Naïs who was clutching her apron and flinching at the slightest sound, the smallest movement.

Finally, the surgeon came out, wiping his hands on an old rag.

'This man has already received care,' he said. 'Who ministered to him?'

'I did,' replied Marciac.

'Are you a doctor, monsieur?'

'No, but I came close to becoming one.'

'Be that as it may, if not for you, your friend would not be alive . . . Nevertheless, he is not yet out of danger. Far from it.'

'Can his leg be saved?' La Fargue asked.

'I fear not,' answered the surgeon.

At those words, Agnès turned away, seeming both upset

and furious. Leprat put an arm around her and drew her a few steps apart from the others.

'The leg is too badly damaged,' the surgeon continued with a grave face. 'It must be taken off. However . . . However, I fear your friend will not survive an amputation. He has already lost a considerable amount of blood. He is very weak. And no longer young.'

'I do not understand, monsieur,' said La Fargue. 'What do you advise?'

'The leg is lost. It must be cut off, but perhaps we might risk waiting for the patient to regain some strength before inflicting this ordeal upon him. But I stress the word "risk". For if we wait and the terrible wounds to his leg begin to spoil, your friend will certainly perish as a result.'

'So you are asking us to make a wager.'

'I am asking you to make a choice, for a friend who no longer has all his reason . . .'

Still and pale, Agnès saw the Blades' captain turn toward her.

'This decision belongs to you, Agnès,' said La Fargue. 'But if you do not want to make it, I will.'

The Gentleman dismounted in the ruins of Bois-Noir and held his horse by the bit. Without saying a word, he contemplated the smoking rubble, then the corpses that the survivors had aligned in front of a wall. There were no more than a handful of drac mercenaries still alive, and most of them were wounded. La Donna had escaped. And the Illuminator had vanished.

It was a disaster.

The Gentleman lifted his eyes towards the Enchantress who had remained in her saddle. They exchanged a long, serious, worried look, which was interrupted by the arrival of three riders.

It was Keress Karn and two of his soldiers. Filthy with dust and sweat, the red drac wore a bloody bandage on his right arm, just above the elbow.

'We found him,' the drac leader announced as he leapt down from his horse.

'Dead?' asked the Gentleman.

'Yes. In a dry riverbed, about half a league from here. We followed his tracks there.'

'Dead?' exclaimed the Enchantress in disbelief. 'The Illuminator is dead?'

Keress Karn deemed it useless to repeat himself. Besides, he considered it beneath him to answer a woman. He only spoke to the Gentleman.

Overcome by anger, the latter clenched his jaws tightly.

'Who?' he asked in a rasping voice. 'Who could have—'

'Their leader is called La Fargue,' explained the red drac. 'I recognised him. He was there at Château de Mareuil.'

'I want him to pay,' ordered the Gentleman. 'I want him to suffer, and I want him to die.'

The operation went well, and afterwards Ballardieu was carried up to his chamber. The surgeon said he was satisfied but remained cautious: he would not permit himself much hope unless his patient survived the night. He left some instructions and promised to return the following day. Then he left, taking the severed leg with him, while Naïs scrubbed the kitchen clean. The old soldier finally drifted into a deep sleep and the Blades had nothing to do but wait.

Because he knew he was of no further use to the patient and hated feeling impotent, Marciac washed, changed his clothes, and, after hastily ridding himself of the garments encrusted with Ballardieu's blood, left the Hôtel de l'Épervier while trying to persuade himself that he wasn't running away.

Besides, didn't he have other business to settle?

Exhausted but incapable of resting, he followed rue Sainte-Marguerite which ran some distance, then rue des Boucheries in the same direction, crossed through the old city wall by means of the Saint-Germain gate and ended up in the neighbourhood of rue de la Harpe. On rue Mignon, he found a taproom that was ideally located for his purposes. He stopped there, ordered a glass of *eau-de-vie* and, leaning on the counter, sipped while he kept watch on the house where Gabrielle told him the party had taken place, during which the young and pretty Manon had disappeared.

It was a big bourgeois dwelling with a solid-looking gate and a courtyard separating it from the street. Its owner was a rich and powerful man who led a discreet life. He was named Cousty, was a widower and for a long time had been the most feared judge sitting at Le Châtelet. He no longer presided there, but he was still very influential. Rumour had it that he was also mean and greedy. As proof of that, he only retained one old lackey in his service, and he beat him often.

Having finished his glass, Marciac suffered from a slight dizziness. Another man in his position would have recalled that he had not eaten since the previous day and taken remedy. Another man would have told himself that he needed to sleep and have gone home. But Marciac was Marciac, so he had another *eau-de-vie* while devising a plan. A voice inside him told him that his plan was most certainly a bad idea, but it was a voice that the Gascon seldom listened to, so that life would continue to offer him surprises. Alcohol, moreover, had a tendency to silence it.

Marciac drained a third glass and left to carry out a few errands in the neighbourhood.

Firstly, to find a pair of thick gloves.

And secondly, to buy some lamp oil.

Agnès finally fell asleep at Ballardieu's bedside.

When she reopened her eyes and straightened up in her armchair, night was falling, a candle was burning in the chamber, and the old soldier was gazing at her, his head turned to the side on his pillow.

His face was livid, with drawn features and eyes surrounded by black circles, but he smiled at her tenderly.

'Hello, girl,' he murmured in a voice still hoarse from his screams when the saw had bitten into the bone. 'So, we meet again . . .'

'You . . . You're awake? For how long?'

'No, don't fuss . . . You were sleeping so soundly I didn't have the heart to disturb you . . . And then, everything was . . . Everything was so peaceful . . .'

Agnès stared at him, incredulous, not knowing what to say,

her eyes both bright with joy and drowning in tears. Ballardieu was talking to her. Ballardieu wasn't dead. Ballardieu was there and always would be, exactly as he used to tell her when she was a small child, to reassure her.

'How is it,' he asked, 'that I'm feeling no pain?'

'You're full of golden henbane liqueur.'

'Henbane, hmm? . . . My word, it . . . it works wonders.'

'Leprat brought it. No doubt he takes it himself to soothe the pain of his ranse . . .'

'I'll need to . . . thank him.'

'I'll fetch him!' said the young and fiery baronne, jumping up. 'And the others! They're downstairs, waiting for—'

In her enthusiasm, she was almost at the door when Ballardieu stopped her.

'No, girl . . . No . . .' He raised a hand in her direction, but let it fall back on the sheet limply. 'Later, perhaps . . .'

Agnès understood and, feeling a little embarrassed, returned to his bedside.

However, instead of sitting in the armchair, she carefully sat on the bed by Ballardieu and took hold of his hand.

'I . . . I'm sorry,' she confessed, lowering her eyes.

'About this old leg?' he retorted, forcing a note of gaiety into his voice. But as Agnès would not smile, he became grave again. 'I have to believe Providence wanted me to finish my life on one leg rather than two. Of course, this is going to keep me out of some adventures, but that's not such a bad thing. I'm getting old, after all. Perhaps it's time I retired . . .'

'You?'

'Look at me, Agnès. What have I become?'

'An old beast who I love and who is still a long way from making his last trip to the stable . . .'

Moved by her words, Ballardieu smiled.

'Listen to me . . . I was a soldier, a man of the sword in your father's service. I imagined I would find glory, or perhaps fortune, on the fields of battle. Or perhaps none of that. Perhaps death. But I never imagined a different destiny from that of other warriors and hunters of fortune . . . And then your father entrusted you to my care. My life changed from the moment I laid eyes on you, but I didn't understand that to begin with, far from it. I even denied the obvious, when time passed and I became attached to you. And do you know when I finally understood?'

'No.'

'You were still very small. Perhaps four or five years old. You . . . You weren't even as tall as my sword.' Ballardieu's gaze became lost for a moment in the past. 'To make matters short . . . one day you disappeared. You simply disappeared . . . Of course, we searched for you. In the manor, first of all. Then all around, in the domain, and then even farther afield. You were not to be found, no matter how loudly we called. We beat the woodland. We sounded the pond and dragged the riverbed. All in vain. And I thought I was going to die. I stopped eating, and sleeping. And each time someone came by with news, I was torn between the hope that you were safe and the terror that they had discovered your little body lying lifeless somewhere . . . It was . . . It was a veritable torture . . . But I needed that torture to understand . . . or rather to admit to myself, that I loved you like the flesh of my flesh, and that my destiny was to protect you always.' Agnès, her eyes brimming with tears, was unable to wrench her gaze away from his. 'What I'm trying to tell you, girl . . . What I'm trying to tell you is that, sometimes, it takes us time to recognise the path that has been traced for us, and that only delays the inevitable . . . We all have a destiny, don't you see? A destiny that might be very different from the one we believe in or the one we want for ourselves. For some people, that destiny is modest. But for others, like you, it's . . . something immense . . .'

Now pensive, Agnès nodded slowly but turned her eyes away and did not answer.

'I think . . . I think I'm going to sleep for a while,' said the old soldier in a weak voice. 'You should do the same.'

The young woman stood up.

'But not in that armchair,' Ballardieu added. 'Not here . . . Go and rest in your bed.'

'The surgeon said we should watch over you.'

'Your chamber isn't far, Agnès.'

941

She hesitated, and then said:

'All right. But—'

'But what?'

'But I'm here, aren't I? How did your story end?'

Ballardieu managed a weary smile.

'Oh . . . you reappeared three days later, as suddenly as you had vanished. Marion found you: you were playing in the garden as if it were the most natural thing in the world. You were wearing the same clothes. You were clean and in good health. You were just a little thirsty, and we never found out—'

'I don't remember any of that.'

'Of course not. I told you: you were very little. A strange adventure, don't you think? And yet after that, you're surprised that I'm afraid to let you out of my sight . . .'

'Get some rest, you old beast.'

La Fargue dined alone in the garden.

Sitting at the table beneath the chestnut tree, he turned his back to the mansion and chewed without tasting his food, his gaze lost in the shadows. He was not hungry, but he knew that an empty sack could not stand upright. The darkness surrounding him was profound, barely relieved by the trembling flicker of the candle placed on the old table, which had attracted the attention of a moth.

Finally the captain realised he had company. He did not react with alarm and, still looking straight ahead, asked:

'How long have you been here?'

'Not long,' replied Saint-Lucq.

La Fargue knew that if he had become aware of the other's presence, it was because the half-blood wanted him to. Saint-Lucq, in more ways than one, belonged to the night.

'Are you spying on me?'

'I'm observing you. Who are the Guardians, captain?'

La Fargue became perfectly still, then pushed his plate away.

'I like to see who I'm talking to.'

'Very well.'

Without a sound, the half-blood dressed in black seemed to appear out of thin air. As was often the case, it was the scarlet disks of his spectacles, reflecting the light, that became visible first.

Saint-Lucq sat at the table, facing the old gentleman.

'Who are the Guardians, captain?'

'If you're asking me that question, you already know the answer.'

'I'm doing you a favour, captain.'

'A favour? You?'

'That of giving you a chance to explain yourself.'

'And since when do I answer to you?'

'Since I have served and fought and killed under your orders. Who are the Guardians?'

'They are one of the reasons why the human race has not been decimated, or enslaved, by the dragons. They operate in the shadows . . . and they watch over us. They are dragons, but they know that their time and that of their race, in this world, is drawing to a close. They believe they have no solution other than to live in accord with humans or hidden amongst them.'

'And you serve them.'

'Yes.'

'Since when?'

'Do you really not know? Valombre sent me a message about your meeting. I've been waiting for you, Saint-Lucq.'

'Since when?'

'It started five years ago. After La Rochelle.'

'Does the cardinal know?'

'He knows. He's always known. They often conceal their true intentions, but the Guardians are not the enemies of France. On the contrary, without them, the Chatelaines would not exist. You can't imagine the services they have rendered us in the past.'

'That doesn't matter to me. I want to know who I serve. I want to know who I kill for and who I might be killed for.'

Saint-Lucq stood up and walked away.

Motionless, La Fargue watched him disappear into the night, and then lowered his eyes to the table and the steel signet ring the half-blood had left there.

The Gentleman and the Enchantress returned home in the darkest hours of the night.

Having burned their dead in the ruins of Bois-Noir, they rode back to Paris at a slow walk, almost without speaking, followed by Keress Karn and the few armed dracs who had survived the Blades' attack. The Hôtel des Arcanes was brightly lit when they arrived. Surprised, they dismounted in the courtyard and exchanged puzzled, worried glances when they heard the sound of laughter coming from the garden.

They found the Demoiselle and the Heresiarch having supper together by torchlight.

The judge Cousty woke with a start when a hand gloved in thick leather was clapped over his mouth. Immediately, the man pinning him down poured a liquid on his face. It had an odour he recognised: naphta. He struggled as the lamp oil ran into his eyes and over his temples, drenching his hair and soaking his pillow. He inhaled a little of it, gagged, and almost vomited. But the hand stifling his cries was firm and the man continued to press down with all his weight. Frightened, Cousty thrashed in vain while the naphta continued to run.

When the goatskin flask was empty, Marciac threw it into a corner of the chamber and waited for the judge to calm down and submit to him. Only then did he relax his hold slightly, in order to signify to his victim that he was making the right decision. Cousty finally became still, with the sheets twisted around his naked legs. He rolled his immense, fearful eyes. His gasping breath lifted his bony chest and made greasy bubbles form at his nostrils. He squinted, trying to make out the Gascon's face in the light of the sole candle placed on a table beside the bed. He was certain he had extinguished that candle before going to sleep, as he did every night.

'I took care of your servant. So you and I are on our own, in effect. You can call out, but it will serve no purpose except to make me angry, because I hate it when people yell. Do you want me to be angry?'

The judge shook his head. The Gascon's breath stank of

alcohol and his eyes had that disturbed gleam that comes with drunkenness. Yet he seemed to be in control of himself, which made the situation even more worrying.

'That's just as well. Because otherwise, I will take that candle over there and bring the flame close to your face and hair that I've just soaked in naphta. And you know what will happen then, don't you?'

Cousty nodded slowly, convinced that he was at the mercy of a dangerous madman. Unable to move his head, his eyes strained toward the side when Marciac reached out with his free hand to seize the candlestick and brought it nearer. The judge's panic-stricken gaze tracked the movements of the flame.

'Now,' continued the Gascon, 'I am going to take my hand from your mouth. Will you be good?'

Still unable to tear his eyes away from the flame, the judge nodded. Then he breathed more freely, in both the literal and figurative sense, as Marciac withdrew his hand and moved the candle to a slightly safer distance.

The judge then recognised the Gascon's face in the light.

'I . . . I know you,' he said, out of sheer surprise.

Marciac looked at him with an extremely perplexed air.

'Firstly,' he replied, 'I strongly doubt that. Secondly, if it is true, telling me so would be an act of the greatest stupidity, don't you think? Because it might incite me to do you a very evil turn.' Cousty stayed silent. 'So let us return to the matter at hand. I am going to ask you questions and you will answer them. At the first refusal or the first lie, I will set fire to your head as if it were a big packet of tow. Have you understood me?'

Thoroughly frightened, the judge promised and he kept his word.

So much so that only few instants later, Marciac was pushing him out of the chamber and forcing him down the stairs.

'And now?' the Gascon demanded when they reached the bottom of the steps.

Cousty pointed to a recess in the entry hall, just beneath the stairs. Marciac brought him there and, without letting go, watched him press two stones at the same time on the bare wall.

A secret passage opened with a click.

'Who knows of this place?'

'No one.'

'No one. Really? Not even your lackey?'

The judge saw the slap to the back of his skull coming, but could do nothing to avoid it.

'My . . . My brothers!' he hastened to say. 'My brother acolytes know!'

'Your . . . ?' The Gascon considered the trembling, scrawny sixty-year-old man he held by the collar. Words failed him, which was rare. 'No, nothing. You go first.'

Steps spiralled downward. They descended them in the dark, before the judge opened the door to a vaulted chamber dimly lit by red solaire stones. Bare flagstones covered the floor. On the walls hung black drapes decorated with golden draconic runes, one of which was often repeated. Marciac recognised it because it featured on the banners flying over the ruins where, two months previously, the vicomtesse de Malicorne had summoned her followers to a grandiose ceremony which would have led, without the Blades' intervention, to the founding of the Black Claw's first lodge in France. It was the rune of the secret society.

Marciac shoved Cousty again, roughly. The judge tripped forward, fell down, and decided to remain on the floor. The Gascon examined the contents of the chamber slowly and carefully: the black candles waiting to be lit on their large candelabra, the diverse ritual objects, the fat grimoire on a lectern, the altar covered with a scarlet cloth.

Unmasked and vanquished, the vicomtesse de Malicorne had disappeared. More or less willing and zealous servants of the Black Claw, the supporters she had converted had been for the most part either arrested or dispersed. But it was thought that some had managed to slip through the net and that they continued to practise their 'religion', which was nothing other than a perverse cult obsessed with black draconic magic.

Cousty was evidently one of them.

'Where?' Marciac asked brusquely. 'Where is she?'

From the floor, the judge pointed a shaking finger towards the altar.

The Gascon frowned, then understood and hurried forward. He lifted up the cloth covering the altar, revealing a black wrought iron box whose sides were pierced with a few triangular holes. The box had a door with a latch. Marciac crouched down to open it and was struck by the sharp scent of urine before he made out the form of Manon, naked and trembling, her cheeks stained with tears and dirt, huddled at the bottom.

He reached out a hand to her.

'It's me, Manon. It's me. Marciac.'

Marciac had to use tender words and careful gestures to coax her out. Manon had recognised him, but the remnants of the terror provoked by everything she had been subjected to in this room, which had almost driven her mad, still gripped her and prevented her from trusting him. Finally, she rushed into the Gascon's arms and clung to him, bursting into sobs. He wanted to comfort her, but hesitated out of fear that the touch of male hands had become odious to her. He finally stretched out an arm to grab the altar cloth and wrapped it around her.

She let him.

'You,' Marciac said to Cousty over the young woman's shoulder. 'Into the box.'

Still kneeling on the floor, the judge took on a worried and incredulous expression.

'What? But . . .'

'Into that box. Now.'

'But I—'

'Don't make me force you in there.'

The Gascon's gaze was terrifying.

Defeated, humiliated, the judge obeyed and crawled into the wrought iron box on all fours. Marciac kicked the door closed and allowed the latch to fall into place of its own accord. Then he lifted Manon and carried her as one might carry a child, the young girl putting her arms around his neck and, soothed, resting her head against his chest.

In his cubby-hole, Cousty placed an eye against an air hole.

And seeing the Gascon leaving, he called out in a miserable voice:

'When will you come back to free me?'

'Did I say I was ever coming back?' retorted Marciac without turning round.

'But . . . But you must! My man doesn't know about this place! No one does! They can't even find the entrance!'

'And I imagine that you've made sure that no one can hear any screaming that goes on here, haven't you?'

'Mercy! You must come back! I'll . . . I'll die in here!'

'What a shame.'

Marciac continued to walk away at a slow but resolute pace.

'I KNOW WHO YOU ARE!' the judge shouted. 'I KNOW!'

'That doesn't worry me any more now than it did before . . .'

'I REMEMBER!' added Cousty in desperation. 'YOU WERE THERE, THAT NIGHT! YOU WERE WITH THOSE ONES WHO ATTACKED US, WHO STOPPED THE VICOMTESSE'S CEREMONY! I . . . I SAW YOU!'

Manon in his arms, the Gascon arrived at the small staircase.

'THE ENERGY OF THE DRAGON WAS DISPERSING! EVERYONE WANTED TO FLEE AND I WAS RUNNING TOWARD THE STABLE WHEN . . . IT WAS YOU!'

'So?'

'LET ME LIVE AND I'LL HELP YOU! I'LL TELL YOU EVERYTHING I KNOW ABOUT THE BLACK CLAW! I'LL TELL YOU EVERYTHING ABOUT ITS SECRET SUPPORTERS! EVERYTHING I KNOW ABOUT LA MALICORNE!'

His curiosity aroused, Marciac halted.

'La Malicorne? She disappeared without a trace . . . Goodbye, Cousty.'

'SHE HAS RETURNED! LA MALICORNE! SHE WANTS US TO CALL HER THE DEMOISELLE, BUT IT'S HER! LA MALICORNE HAS RETURNED!'

The judge believed all was lost and his voice broke down in sobs.

But Marciac was thinking.

4

Agnès had barely found the strength to remove her boots before she fell asleep. So she woke fully dressed and lying sideways on her bed. The first rays of the morning sun came in through the open window. Birds twittered and Paris was beginning to stir. Life started early in summer. It was only just past six o'clock.

The young baronne de Vaudreuil got up and stretched. Her sleep had been deep but was still haunted, as she had dreamed again of the great black dragon with a sparkling jewel upon its brow, and once again seen Paris disappear in the flames and the cries.

Worried, she leaned at her window. She closed her eyes.

Forced herself to breathe calmly.

The Hôtel de l'Épervier was waking, peacefully, along with the rest of the great city and its faubourgs.

André would soon be opening the stable doors, which always scraped at the end of their path before they touched the wall. Clip-clopping along, his wooden leg striking the courtyard paving stones, master Guibot would come out in his turn to open the gates for the first suppliers. The sound of Naïs' pretty voice could already be heard rising up the staircase: the timid servant hummed in the mornings when she thought no one was listening. La Fargue would soon be up too. It was also the hour when Marciac sometimes came home, when he had every chance – before, that is – of running into Almades who, having finished his morning exercises, would be performing his ablutions outside, barefoot and bare-chested, whatever the season. Laincourt was no doubt reading and God only knows what Saint-Lucq was doing.

And Ballardieu?
Ballardieu had just died in his sleep.
His exhausted heart had finally ceased to beat.

IV

The Primordial

Ballardieu had to be buried the day after his death. The heat prohibited any delay so his funeral was the simplest of ceremonies. It took place at a chapel, in the morning, after which the Blades carried the body to the cemetery under a dazzling sky and a white gold sun. They proceeded at a slow, steady pace, wearing their weapons, La Fargue and Laincourt on the right-hand side of the coffin, Leprat and Marciac on the left.

Agnès de Vaudreuil followed them, wearing black with scarlet gloves, a plume-less felt hat, boots, and her sword by her side. Guibot limped along heavily behind her. Next came Naïs, who sobbed and clutched a small casket against her, and André, who held the young woman by the waist and the elbow to help her walk. Even with the priest and the two choirboys leading the way, they did not make a large group. And those who moved out of the way for this meagre procession, those who watched it pass, those who doffed their hats and crossed themselves before resuming their lives without further disruption, would never know what kind of man Ballardieu had been.

After the priest left, La Fargue, Agnès, and the others gathered in the quiet of the cemetery, beneath the bored gaze of the gravediggers who waited in the shade and took turns drinking from the same bottle. All that remained was to lay the body to rest, which the Blades had decided to take charge of personally. When the moment came, Leprat, Laincourt, and Marciac watched for the sign from their captain, upon which all four set to work in silence. But as they slowly let the ropes slide and the coffin descended into the freshly dug grave, fragile Naïs broke down in sobs again. She gave a hoarse lament and, all strength deserting her, she sank to her knees and dropped her casket, which opened when it struck the ground. André helped the young servant to rise, drew her aside from the others, and did his best to comfort her. Guibot hurried to pick up the items scattered over the ground.

Naïs had felt more than friendship for Ballardieu.

At first intimidated by him, she had then been touched by the kindness and the awkwardness of this old soldier whose heart of gold could be discerned behind the cracks in his rough exterior. She had been drawn to him for precisely that reason, because he would be clumsy perhaps, but also tender and thoughtful. One night she had joined him in his chamber, slipping into his bed before taking off her shirt and snuggling up naked against him. At first, he hadn't known what to do. And since he didn't dare try anything, she had been forced to make the first move, murmuring in his ear:

'You'll be gentle, won't you?'

He was her first.

Naïs returned the following night and other nights thereafter. She offered herself to him and made love to him without saying a word, then fell asleep trustingly in his arms. She was always gone in the morning. He didn't understand it. But he respected her silence and kept the secret, although he wondered about it. Troubled, sometimes he felt guilty at the idea that he was taking advantage of her, of her youth and innocence. Did she love him? If so, she was making a mistake and would soon realise it. And what should he do in the meantime? He'd started to make her little gifts, things she would find in her chamber or on her pillow. It might be a comb, a ribbon, a brooch, or a small mirror that he had bought or won on the Pont Neuf, and usually poorly chosen because he always thought of Naïs as a child.

Nevertheless she cherished these few treasures that Guibot quickly gathered up in the cemetery and returned to her. She took the precious casket and pressed it tightly to her bosom again. Broken, docile, she let Guibot and André take her back to the Hôtel de l'Épervier.

Agnès had not even blinked when Naïs collapsed.

She stood up straight, her features pale and drawn, with dark circles under her eyes and pinched lips. She had not shed a tear or uttered more than three words since Ballardieu's passing. She had not slept, either. She was alone, prisoner of a pain that had ripped her soul from her body and slowly tore up her insides. Her gestures were slow and her gaze was distant. Everything seemed faraway, insignificant. The world no longer had colours or flavour for her. Nothing affected her except for her sense of emptiness and abandonment, except for the inner abyss on the verge of which her reason tottered.

The coffin rested inside the grave and Blades slowly backed away from it.

La Fargue saw that the gravediggers were growing impatient, indifferent to the suffering of mourners who all seemed the same to them. He waited, approached Agnès, and whispered to her:

'It's time.'

And when she did not respond, he insisted:

'It's time to go, Agnès.'

'You go,' she said in a rasping voice. 'I'm staying here.'

'These men need to do their job, Agnès. They're going—'

'I know what they're going to do!' the young baronne snapped. 'Let them go ahead, I'm not stopping them. But I'm staying here for a while longer.'

Embarrassed, La Fargue looked at the waiting gravediggers, with clogs on their feet and spades resting on their shoulders. He hesitated, then signalled to them to start work. But he remained at Agnès' side and took her arm. Consumed by an icy flame, she trembled and closed her eyes as she heard the first spadeful of earth strike the coffin lid.

When they returned from the cemetery, Agnès, still refusing to speak, immediately went upstairs to her room. Knowing she did not want to be comforted by anyone, the others went to the fencing room, where Guibot brought them wine.

'We had to put the girl to bed,' he said as he served La Fargue.

The Blades' captain nodded vaguely and waited for the

concierge to finish filling their glasses. Once Guibot left, he raised his.

'To Ballardieu,' he said.

'To Ballardieu,' repeated Leprat, Marciac, and Laincourt in chorus.

They clinked their glasses together and then La Fargue took a bottle with him out to the garden. Through the window, the others saw him sit at the table beneath the chestnut tree.

He, too, wanted to be alone.

Marciac sighed as he sprawled in an armchair, his feet crossed upon a stool. Laincourt also sat down, removed his hat and, leaning forward, hands upon his knees, he massaged his aching temples with his fingertips. Leprat remained propped against the mantelpiece of the fireplace.

A silence set in.

'I thought that Saint-Lucq would come,' Laincourt said at last.

'It's been three days since I last saw him,' replied the Gascon.

'If he'd been with us at Bois-Noir . . .'

' . . . Ballardieu might still be alive.'

'He was here the night when Ballardieu passed away,' Leprat told him. 'Guibot saw him talking to La Fargue in the garden.'

'And?'

'I don't know. The captain did not want to talk to me about their conversation.'

'Is Saint-Lucq still one of the Blades?' asked Laincourt with concern in his voice.

'The Blades!' snorted the Gascon. 'Or what's left of them . . .'

That earned him a black look from Leprat.

'What?' he said, raising his voice. 'You've put your cape back on, Saint-Lucq is nobody-knows-where with no sign of returning, and Almades and Ballardieu are dead. Count carefully: that just leaves Laincourt and me.'

'And Agnès,' corrected the musketeer.

'Agnès?' exclaimed Marciac, standing up. 'Do you know her then so little?' He pointed a finger at the ceiling. 'Do you know what she's doing up there, at this very moment? She's packing her bags!'

'You don't—'

The Gascon spread his arms and turned in a circle, as if calling on the whole world to be his witness.

'And who could blame her?' he asked. 'Don't tell me that you don't think that re-forming the Blades was a mistake.' And when Leprat didn't reply, he added bitterly: 'Gabrielle was right and I should have listened to her. Wasn't our first death enough? Did we have to bury Almades and Ballardieu, after Bretteville?'

'Marciac,' said Laincourt.

Marciac fell silent, turning round.

And saw Agnès.

'I'm leaving,' she announced. 'I . . . I won't be coming back.'

She turned on her heel and walked away.

'Agnès!' called Leprat, after a pause.

'Let her,' La Fargue said to him in a toneless voice. He stood in the doorway to the garden. 'Let her leave.'

The musketeer hesitated, cursed, and went after Agnès anyway.

He joined her in the courtyard, where she was already mounting her horse.

'Agnès!'

She looked at him patiently, both hands together on the pommel of her saddle.

But he couldn't find anything to say to her:

'Agnès, I . . .'

She gave him a sad, tender smile.

'Goodbye, Antoine. Take care of Nicolas, will you? And tell the captain that I don't blame him for anything.'

Then she turned her mount around, urged it forward slightly with her heels, and rode away at a slow jog.

Leprat stood alone in the courtyard for a moment, underneath the blazing sun. Finally, when he decided to go back inside, he passed La Fargue coming down the steps with a determined air.

'Where are you going, captain?'

The old gentleman did not stop.

'To speak with La Donna,' he replied. 'This comedy of secrets has lasted long enough.'

'But she's being held under guard at the Palais-Cardinal for her safety!' Leprat warned him as La Fargue crossed the courtyard. 'They won't let you anywhere near her!'

'Then they will have to kill me,' said the captain, without turning or slowing down.

In the park at the Palais-Cardinal, Alessandra was reading near the fountain. She was sitting in the shade, on a bench, and seemed completely oblivious to the presence of ten of the Cardinal's Guards who, stationed all around the park with rapiers at their sides and short muskets over the shoulders, watched over her. Charybdis and Scylla, her twin dragonnets, were drowsing to either side of the ravishing spy. They lifted their heads and gazed in the same direction moments before the first sounds of an argument attracted her attention.

On one of the garden paths, two sentries in red capes had stopped La Fargue. The discussion between them grew heated. Although the Blades' captain had privileged access to the Palais-Cardinal, in this case His Eminence's instructions had been quite explicit: no one was to see La Donna, not without an express order signed by the cardinal himself. But La Fargue would not hear of it. The altercation was starting to become a scuffle.

Alessandra rose with the intention of intervening before things degenerated:

'Messieurs!'

But the guards held her back and, deaf to her protests, they were quick to remove her from the possible threat, not handling her too gently in the process, which upset her dragonnets.

'Scylla! Charybdis! Be still!' La Donna ordered her small domestic reptiles.

They immediately obeyed her, ceasing to growl and flutter about as La Fargue was knocked out by the butt of a musket.

*

It did not take La Fargue long to come round, with a terrible headache.

He was lying on a bench, with La Donna applying a damp cloth to his brow.

'That was very stupid of you,' she said, when she saw that he had regained consciousness.

'I needed to speak with you.'

'All the same.'

'I achieved my goal, didn't I?'

'Because you planned to get your skull cracked open in order to see me?' she asked ironically.

La Fargue sat up and pressed the cool cloth to the back of his head.

'No,' he admitted reluctantly.

'They could have killed you.'

'Bah!' He looked around the elegant antechamber in which he found himself. 'Where are we?'

'We're still at the Palais-Cardinal,' replied the beautiful spy as she poured two glasses of white wine. 'In the chambers where I am staying . . . There was some talk of throwing you into a cell, but I prevailed upon monsieur de Neuvelle to entrust you to my custody instead, while they decide your fate. Nevertheless, you are officially under arrest on the grounds of attempting to stun one guard using the head of another. That was very bad behaviour.'

'Neuvelle?' enquired La Fargue, grimacing painfully.

'He is the young ensign commanding the detachment that is . . . that is holding me.'

'That is *protecting* you.'

'Yes. That, too.'

Alessandra returned to sit next to La Fargue and handed him a glass. Feeling suddenly tired, the old captain removed the damp cloth from his head, spread it across his thigh, took the glass, and thanked her.

'Really very stupid,' said La Donna by way of a toast.

They drank a sip of white wine together and then fell silent for a moment. Birdsong came through the open window, from the feathered creatures perched in the trees out in the park.

'We buried Ballardieu this morning,' La Fargue said, watching the yellow reflections of wine in the cut glass.

'I . . . I didn't know.'

'Less than three weeks after Almades . . .'

'I'm sorry. Sincerely.'

'They were good, brave men. Neither of them deserved to die as they did . . . And another may fall tomorrow. It could be Laincourt, Marciac, or Leprat. It could be me . . . Don't you think we've earned a few answers?' he concluded, locking his gaze on La Donna's.

Affected by his argument, she rose and went to the window. Then she returned to La Fargue, stared at him a few seconds, and nodded curtly.

'Thank you, madame,' said the captain of the Blades, rising in his turn. 'Let's start with you, shall we? The Guardians told me you serve them, just as I do.'

'That's true.'

'But you also serve the Pope.'

'Just as you also serve the cardinal. However, I work on occasion for my own benefit, unlike you. But one needs to earn a living, doesn't one?'

La Fargue did not reply to that.

'If I remember correctly,' he continued, 'you once gave me a hint of your allegiance to the Seven . . .'

'That evening at La Renardière, yes. Before everything started to move so quickly.'

'You mean: before you almost got me killed, and my men along with me, at the hands of the dracs pursuing you.'

'I was desperate, captain. I absolutely needed someone to rid me of those dracs and, above all, their sorcerer. I used you, to be sure. But it was for the common good, believe me. At the time I had information that urgently needed to be transmitted to the Pope and the Guardians.' Looking nervous, Alessandra drained her glass. She gave herself time to recover her calm. 'Besides, I don't think I was totally ungrateful for your assistance. Without me, would you have captured the Alchemist?'

'Precisely! So who was the Alchemist, exactly? And what goal was he pursuing? I no longer believe his aim was simply to abduct the queen. I also no longer believe he was acting alone.'

The beautiful Italian lady looked at La Fargue for a long moment, during which she reflected. Then, her decision made, she asked:

'What do you know of the Arcana, captain?'

Caught unprepared, he had no reply. So she led him into the adjoining room.

'Come.'

La Fargue followed Alessandra into her chamber.

There was a large cage next to the four-poster bed. The dragonnets inside stirred as soon as they saw their mistress enter, but she did not pay them the least attention. Consequently, Charybdis and Scylla watched the Blades' captain with a jealous eye.

'Look,' said La Donna, pointing at a small round table.

There were a number of illustrated tarot cards on it, next to a quill and an inkwell. Most of the cards were annotated, covered in strange inscriptions, and sometimes they were even crossed out. La Fargue leaned forward to look at them. They were splendid and bore evocative names, but he did not recognise any of them.

'These twenty-two cards form the major arcana of a tarot deck,' explained Alessandra. 'This one is a draconic tarot, however.'

The captain's gaze continued to run over the cards.

The Weaver, he read. *The Gentleman Lover, the Protectress, the Blind Illuminator, the Astrologer . . .*

'This tarot is employed in sorcery.'

. . . the Crowned Heresiarch, the Architect, the Forgetful Thief . . .

'It is primarily used for divination, of course. But there is more to it than that.'

. . . the Master-at-Arms, the Demoiselle in the Tower, the Assassin, the Immobile Pilgrim . . .

'But there are other reasons why these arcana cards interest us. Or these "blades", as they are still sometimes called.'

. . . the Alchemist of the Shadows!

'What does this mean?' asked La Fargue, placing his index finger on this last card.

'The Arcana are a lodge within the Black Claw,' explained La Donna. 'All of them are dragons and each member takes his *nom de guerre* from one of the major arcanum of the draconic tarot. The Alchemist was one of them, as was the dragon who abducted me and whom you fought to rescue me.'

'And which one was he?'

'The Illuminator.'

'So, he was this one,' said the captain, pointing to the card of the Blind Illuminator on the table.

He noticed that it was crossed out.

'Yes,' replied Alessandra as La Fargue examined the spread cards again.

'If there are twenty-two major arcana, does that mean that—'

'—that the Arcana lodge has that many members? I think so. But truth be told, I don't really know. And even if there were only ten of them . . .'

'But who are they, exactly?'

'Most of them are last-born dragons. They are ambitious, capable, prudent, determined and quite formidable. They are a force apart from the other lodges of the Black Claw. I suppose they are accountable to the Grand Lodge, but they enjoy a great deal of freedom. In fact, I think they only really obey themselves.'

'That does not sound like the way the Black Claw usually operates.'

'That's true. But the Arcana are most likely protected by their successes.'

'What successes?'

'I know that the rich and powerful always take the credit. Nevertheless, it would seem that the Arcana have been involved to a greater or lesser extent in the worst tragedies and reverses France has suffered recently.'

'Such as the failure of the siege of La Rochelle,' said La Fargue bitterly.

'Yes. Or the assassination of King Henri.'

Flabbergasted, the old captain stared at La Donna. The notion that she might be jesting crossed his mind, but the beautiful Alessandra's face remained as if carved in marble.

'The Arcana are in great danger,' announced the Heresiarch turning away from the window in the Swords study. 'The old masters of the Black Claw, who have never loved us much, are no longer willing to tolerate us. Our enemies are strong and numerous. They seek to bring about our downfall within the next month . . .'

As the Gentleman said nothing in reply, he added:

'The Council of the Grand Lodge will make a decision on this soon, but through my spies I know the matter is already settled. Our lodge will be dissolved. And if we do not submit to their ruling we will be condemned and hunted down without hope of clemency.'

Dressed as a gentleman with taste but without ostentation, the master of the Arcana looked about fifty years in age. His features were bony and severe, with prominent cheekbones, hollow cheeks, and a thin straight nose. He had a perfectly trimmed moustache and goatee. And he exuded an air of confidence and authority.

'Is it really that serious?' asked the Gentleman.

'Yes,' affirmed the Heresiarch gravely.

'The Arcana have already survived a number of cabals. Why can't we foil this one?'

'We were united then. Today, the Protectress and the Master-at-Arms plot against me and divide us. Have they not tried to approach you?'

'No.'

'Really? Perhaps the Enchantress, then?'

'Do you doubt our loyalty, Heresiarch?' the Gentleman asked coldly, feeling anger rise within him.

The two dragons stared at each other.

Narrowing his eyes, the Heresiarch scrutinised the Gentleman, while the latter seemed to challenge him to elaborate on his suspicions. Neither of them blinked, and finally the Heresiarch said:

'No, no, of course not . . . But I know that the Protectress was meeting secretly with the Alchemist, and that she had won him over to her cause.'

'I doubt that very much. The Alchemist was loyal to you—'

The master of the Arcana cut him short with a gesture of annoyance, much as one would wave away a buzzing insect . . .

The Gentleman fell silent and waited. The Heresiarch's unexpected arrival had taken him by surprise and, since then, the behaviour of the leader of the Arcana had frequently been disconcerting. He was suspicious, sometimes irritable, and alternated between sudden silences and brusque manifestations of arrogance. At first, the Gentleman had only wished to see the signs of a great fatigue. Now he was beginning to revise his opinion, suspecting something far more serious. The Enchantress, on the other hand, had immediately evoked the image of a house where just a few cracks in the façade presage an imminent collapse.

The Heresiarch took down a rapier that was prominently displayed, examined it, and said:

'Splendid. Made in Toledo, wasn't it?'

'Yes.'

'The best.'

'It's the temper of Toledo blades that is so excellent,' replied the Gentleman as if by rote. 'But I prefer Bohemian blades.'

The master of the Arcana pulled a slight face and replaced the sword. He let a moment of silence pass and then said in an even voice:

'One must grant her this much, the Protectress has very ably and very patiently woven her web. That should come as no surprise, however. The cursed Gorgon has always been opposed to the Grand Design and she has long nourished the dream of deposing me and taking my place . . .'

The Gentleman nodded.

'She is in Madrid, did you know that?' continued the Heresiarch in a casual tone. 'At this very moment, the Protectress is in Madrid to court the old lizards in the Grand Lodge, trying to convince them that she is better able to lead the Arcana and that the Black Claw would have less reason to complain if—' He did not finish. 'And all of this on the pretext of saving the Arcana from an abyss I am about to push them into!' He gave a brief burst of laughter that did not fool the Gentleman. 'An abyss,' he repeated bitterly. 'But what would become of the Arcana if the Protectress led them? Hmm? What would become of them?'

The Heresiarch's gaze took on a strange fixed stare and he added almost in a whisper:

'I would almost prefer the abyss . . .'

Once again, the Gentleman kept silent.

The other dragon slowly returned from the limbo where his obsession had taken him.

'The Guardians are plotting against us,' he said. 'The Chatelaines are hunting us, the Black Claw is abandoning us, and some of our own are betraying us. There is no more time for intrigue: if we wish to live, we must take our enemies by surprise. Will you be at my side, Gentleman?'

'I will be.'

'And do you answer for the Enchantress?'

'As I do for myself.'

'Then I will have a task for you, soon.'

'And right now?'

'Right now, we must prepare our triumph. I have not renounced our Grand Design. It would have been accomplished long ago if not for these cursed Chatelaines, but I believe it is still possible to bring it to fulfilment before it is too late. And since a ruse did not work for the Alchemist, we will resort to more . . . radical methods.'

In the chambers that Alessandra occupied at the Palais-Cardinal, La Fargue tried to take stock of the beautiful Italian spy's revelations.

King Henri IV had been assassinated on 14 May 1610, the day after the coronation of Marie de Médicis as queen of France, just when he was preparing to go to war with Spain. He had been stabbed by a Catholic fanatic named Ravaillac and – even if the Black Claw had been suspected for a time – the investigation had concluded that it was the isolated act of a madman. But could it be that the Arcana had armed and guided Ravaillac's hand? Could it be that in doing so they had spared Spain from a conflict she was poorly prepared for, and all of Europe had been dreading? The queen had been notoriously opposed to this war, and it had also displeased the Pope. Upon becoming regent of France, after her husband's death, she had immediately renounced the project. In fact, negotiations had quickly resumed between the two countries, which ultimately led to marriage between the young Louis XIII and the Spanish *infanta*.

'Don't ask me for proof, captain,' said Alessandra as if she was following the thread of his thoughts. 'The Guardians only arrived at this conclusion after careful research and patient deductions. And a few extrapolations, it is true.'

'Who else knows?'

'Who else suspects the existence of the Arcana and their schemes, do you mean?'

'Yes.'

'The Guardians, first of all. The Pope and the Chatelaines. The cardinal, for a short while now.'

'And you.'

'And me. But before you reproach me for not telling you all this earlier, you should first know that my information is recent. Moreover, for everything that concerns the Arcana, I obey the Seven in every detail and they alone decide what I am permitted to reveal to anyone.'

'You just told me that cardinal has only known this for a short while.'

'It's true.'

'Did his knowledge come from the Guardians?'

'For the most part.'

'So, what made the Guardians decide to inform him? Why now, rather than yesterday or tomorrow?'

Alessandra reflected, admiring the old captain's sagacity.

'The Arcana have been devoted, for years, to an important project they call the "Grand Design". The Guardians know nothing – or at least feign to know nothing – of this Grand Design. Perhaps the Chatelaines know a little more . . . Be that as it may, the Grand Design is on the point of being accomplished. My belief is that the Alchemist was working on it when you captured him. And I would add that I believe he was probably killed because of the things he could reveal about it.'

'Killed by one of his own?'

'Almost certainly.'

There was a knock on the door, the dragonnets became restless, and a servant announced monsieur de Neuvelle. The man himself soon appeared, wearing a red cape, his hat in his hand, and his fist curled around the pommel of his sword. He was a young gentleman, recently promoted to the rank of ensign, whom La Fargue did not recall ever having met.

He was not alone, however.

Rochefort, Cardinal Richelieu's henchman, accompanied him.

When Marciac arrived at *The Little Frogs*, Gabrielle and her charming lodgers were gardening. Contrary to his habit, he presented himself at the door and was led by Thibault into the coolest room in the house, where ordinarily these demoiselles waited for their messieurs. Through the window, the Gascon saw Manon trimming a rosebush, which seemed to amuse her and the others, who closely surrounded her and were laughing with her.

Informed of his visit, Gabrielle returned from the back of the garden, removing her gloves as she walked. But it was only once she had come inside that she untied the scarf holding in place the wide-brimmed hat, which protected her from the sun. The fierce summer heat had made her cheeks flush. She was slightly out of breath and a faint trace of perspiration beaded her brow. With a distracted air, she fixed the arrangement of her strawberry-blonde hair.

As soon as that was done, she embraced Marciac affectionately, and for once his hands did not wander anywhere.

He let himself fall into an armchair.

'We buried Ballardieu this morning,' he announced.

'My God, Nicolas! So soon?'

'The heat, Gabrielle. The damned heat.'

'But you should have warned me! I would have come. I . . .'

'It was better you stayed here, with Manon.'

Gabrielle turned towards the window and the cheerful young women who could be seen out in the garden. One of them was trying to catch a butterfly with her hat and provoking much mirth.

'How . . . How is Agnès?'

'Distraught,' Marciac said. 'Destroyed. She left the Blades.'

'I can understand that. And the others?'

The Gascon's only response was to shrug and scowl.

'And you?' insisted Gabrielle.

Marciac looked into her eyes with a pained gaze.

'Me? Me, I am weary.'

And to cut short any further expression of his feelings, he rose and went to the window.

'I have come for news of Manon,' he said.

Gabrielle joined him and, over the Gascon's shoulder, looked in same direction as he.

'She will get over her ordeal. We'll help her.'

'Good.'

'And Cousty?'

'He was taken in the middle of the night by people who do His Eminence's dirty work. We will never hear of him again.'

'So this story is over.'

'It will be when I've settled accounts with Tranchelard.'

'What do you mean?' asked Gabrielle, with the beginning of a note of alarm in her voice.

'Cousty confessed that he paid Tranchelard to look the other way, and to pretend that Manon had fled. He is as responsible as Cousty for the torment that girl was subjected to. He should pay for it.'

'No!'

Surprised, Marciac turned towards Gabrielle.

'What?'

'No, Nicolas. Enough blood has been shed!'

'Tranchelard is a scoundrel, Gabrielle. He should answer for his deeds!'

'No! There's been enough violence! . . . After you've dealt

968

with him, whose turn will it be next? Out of those who may want to avenge him? Mortaigne? The Grand Coësre?'

'But—'

'Promise me that you will not seek to harm Tranchelard!'

'Gab—'

'Promise, Nicolas! Promise!'

She had seized hold of Marciac and, with tears in her eyes, she gave him an imploring look so full of distress that it shamed him.

'Yes,' he hastened to assure her. 'Yes. I promise.'

'Truly?'

He nodded sincerely.

Then Gabrielle burst into tears and clung to him. In return he held her tightly in his arms, felt her trembling body, and inhaled her perfume.

'I promise,' he repeated, caressing her hair gently. 'I promise.'

'I have some money,' she whispered to him. 'And I've just bought a small estate in Touraine. We could live there happily if you wanted. Just you, and me, and the child I am carrying.'

Some sixty years old, Mère de Cernay had previously led the Sisters of Saint Georges. Supplanted by Mère de Vaussambre after a ferocious internal struggle, she was now the mother superior of a beautiful and prosperous abbey in Ile-de-France. She was living out her days peacefully there, without relinquishing, however, a certain degree of influence within the Order. She continued, in fact, to be widely respected and widely heeded. And consequently, closely watched.

The sun was setting when she joined Agnès, who was waiting for her near the ivy-covered dovecote where she had liked to retire during her novitiate with the Chatelaines. On her father's death, guardianship of the young baronne had been entrusted to a distant relative who had immediately given way to the temptation to lay hands on Agnès' inheritance by sending her off to the Sisters of Saint Georges, where an aunt and two or three cousins had already taken the veil. She had only recovered her wealth and her freedom several years later, on the eve of pronouncing her vows. But as fortuitous as her connection with the Order might have seemed at the time, this time spent with the Chatelaines would decide her destiny.

Mère de Cernay became concerned from the moment she saw Agnès wearing black. Then the young woman turned round and the mother superior saw her downcast expression and the tears flowing from her reddened eyes.

'My God, Marie-Agnès! What's wrong? What's happened?'

Sitting together beneath the ivy, Agnès and Mère de Cernay spoke.

Or rather Agnès spoke while Mère de Cernay listened and tried to comfort her. The young woman let herself open up and confided her feelings, releasing herself from the stranglehold of repressed pain. Without shame or modesty, she recounted all of her sorrows and doubts.

All of her anger, too.

A nearly full moon rose in the still bright sky, while sweet cooing drifted down from the dovecote. Torches were lit here and there in the great, peaceful abbey.

'Let us pray together,' the mother superior proposed at last, taking Agnès' hands. 'I know it may seem a feeble and ridiculous remedy, but it is often a real comfort.'

'No,' replied the young woman as she rose to her feet. 'No, I . . . I must go . . .'

'It's almost night. Where will you go?'

Agnès remained standing, hesitant and distressed, looking around as if the answers to her questions could be found under the ivy.

'You have felt the Call, haven't you?' asked Mère de Cernay.

Agnès gave a resigned sigh.

'Yes,' she confessed.

'Your mark?'

'Woken. Almost burning.'

'You know what that means . . .'

'What I have guessed is enough to frighten me.'

'You must not be afraid. No one should fear their destiny . . . It's Providence that sends you, Marie-Agnès.'

'A Providence that has killed Ballardieu so that there is nothing left to hold me in the secular world?' Agnès retorted aggressively.

The mother superior now rose in her turn.

'Come. Let's walk,' she said, taking the arm of this young woman who, even as a novice, had shown exceptional quality.

They were only a few steps away from the medicinal herb garden, whose paths they slowly paced.

'When I was the Superior General, the Chatelaines made a mistake,' revealed Mère de Cernay. 'An enormous mistake, and one for which I take full responsibility . . . Unfortunately, we discovered it too late, when there was no time to repair it. All we could do was to hide it. Since then, the Sisters of Saint Georges have done everything in their power to prevent their mistake leading to a tragedy . . .'

'What mistake, mother?'

'I can't tell you that because you are not a Chatelaine. But you should know you may be the one to undo it. The mark you bear signals a great destiny and . . .'

Agnès halted, obliging the mother superior to do the same and turn round to face her.

'No, mother. If I must take the veil, if I must pronounce my vows and become a Chatelaine, I deserve to know. I am so tired of secrets.'

Mère de Cernay gazed into her eyes and saw an unshakeable resolve there. She reflected for a moment longer, however, before saying:

'I suppose I should start at the beginning.'

'The beginning?'

'With the Arcana.'

On returning to the Hôtel de l'Épervier, La Fargue found Leprat waiting, who told him:

'Rochefort was here. He was looking for you.'

'I know. He found me at the Palais-Cardinal.'

'What did he want?'

'To inform me of our latest mission from the cardinal. Where are Laincourt and Marciac?'

'Laincourt is here. And there's Marciac coming back.'

The Gascon was indeed just arriving.

'I was with Gabrielle,' he announced as he joined the two others on the front steps. 'What's going on?'

'Let's go inside,' said La Fargue.

Shortly after, he addressed Leprat, Laincourt, and Marciac, gathered in the fencing room.

'As you know, Agnès has left. So has Saint-Lucq, who returned his signet ring to me. Only you two and myself remain. And you, Antoine, if you are willing to lend us a hand once again.'

'I am still on leave from the King's Musketeers,' said Leprat. 'As long as that lasts, you can count on me.'

Laincourt gave the musketeer a grateful nod and Marciac clapped a friendly hand on his shoulder.

'Thank you,' said La Fargue. 'But before you commit yourself to serving again, there are a few things you need to know.'

Then he sat and spoke in an even voice, his eyes sometimes lost in the distance, without any of the other three daring to interrupt this old gentleman who had never revealed his secrets to anyone before but was now making honourable amends. He told them how, five years earlier, after La Rochelle and the infamous disbanding of the Blades, the Guardians had approached him and persuaded him to join their service. He explained who they were and how they were trying to avoid a war between the human race and the dragons out of which no victor could emerge. He said they were known as the Seven because a council of seven dragons led them, but that the Guardians brought together numerous agents from both races – including La Donna – who operated in the shadows and were prepared to risk their lives for the common good. He confessed at last that when Richelieu had ordered him to re-form the Blades he had consulted the Guardians, and they had told him to reveal his secret to the cardinal alone. He had obeyed them, and now he sincerely regretted it.

'Sometimes honour lies in disobedience,' he concluded.

Silent and grim-faced, Laincourt, Marciac, and Leprat exchanged long glances. The Gascon realised he could speak for all three of them and asked:

'So? This new mission, what is it?'

'I believe that the Heresiarch is placing us in peril,' said the Gentleman in a worried tone.

From a window on the first floor of the Hôtel des Arcanes, he was watching the Heresiarch and the Demoiselle as they took advantage of the coolness of the evening to walk in the garden. Approaching him from behind, the Enchantress pressed herself against him and rested her chin on his shoulder.

'I think so, too,' she murmured.

'Sometimes he gives the impression he is losing his reason. He's obsessed with his Grand Design and he imagines that everyone is conspiring to bring about his downfall or that of the Arcana.'

'Which, for him, are one and the same thing.'

'I fear so. According to him, the Alchemist was betraying him in favour of the Protectress.'

'The Alchemist? That's nonsense.'

'Yet he believes it.'

'Do you know what that means?'

'That he distrusts everyone.'

'Everyone except the Demoiselle. But what else?'

The Gentleman nodded grimly before replying:

'That the Heresiarch may have killed the Alchemist out of personal motives and not because there was a danger he would reveal the Grand Design under torture . . . The Heresiarch may see clearly, however. Perhaps the Protectress does seek to supplant him. And perhaps the Black Claw has decided to dissolve our lodge.'

The Enchantress moved smoothly apart from the Gentleman.

'The masters of the Grand Lodge hate us due to their fear

and jealousy. I don't doubt for an instant that they might want our deaths . . . As for the Protectress, I don't know . . . She's not driven by ambition. So if she is plotting against the Heresiarch, it's because she's convinced that he's leading the Arcana to their doom . . .'

'The Heresiarch's plan is to deliver Paris to the Primordial's fury. That would help fulfil the Grand Design, but at what a price! The Protectress may also be right.'

'If the Heresiarch falls, you and I will not survive him. It is too late for us to turn away from him now.'

'So he has to succeed.'

'Or we need to find ourselves a way out while there's still time. What does he expect of us?'

The Gentleman looked away from the window.

'An emissary of the Black Claw is in Paris. The Heresiarch wants us to find him and kill him.'

'That's all?'

'Almost.'

'It's just as well. The less we have to do the better . . . And the Demoiselle?'

'He has given her full liberty to carry out her act of revenge. I don't know much more than that.'

'It doesn't matter.'

The Gentleman abruptly seized the Enchantress by the waist and pulled her against him.

'What do you have in mind?' he asked.

'I think we need to give the Heresiarch reasons to hope for a success. Besides, a burning city makes such a magnificent spectacle . . .'

Cardinal Richelieu was praying in the dim light of the chapel at the Château de Saint-Germain. He was alone, or at least he believed he was, until he sensed someone behind him. The exits were all guarded and no one should have been able to enter unannounced. Even so, he was not alarmed: he had been expecting the one person who was capable of eluding any security measures he might surround himself with.

Saint-Lucq was deliberately making his presence known.

He waited.

'If you were an assassin I'd be dead, wouldn't I?' asked Richelieu, rising from his prie-dieu after a last sign of the cross in the direction of the altar.

'I *am* an assassin, monseigneur.'

The cardinal turned towards the impassive half-blood and stared at him a long while.

'It has been brought to my attention that you have left Captain La Fargue's Blades,' he said. 'Is it true?

'Yes, monseigneur. For reasons that are mine alone.'

'Those reasons matter very little to me. Do you wish to leave my service?'

'No.'

'That's fortunate, because I have great need of your talents.'

Returning to Paris in the morning, Agnès thought of paying a last visit to the Hôtel de l'Épervier, to make a proper farewell to La Fargue and the others. But she renounced this idea, afraid it would weaken her resolve, and crossed the Seine via Pont Neuf, remembering that it had been Ballardieu's favourite place in all the capital. She slowly crossed the sinister Place de Grève, made her way up the long rue du Temple and rode through the fortified gate of the Chatelaines' Enclos.

The Mother Superior General of the Sisters of Saint Georges was waiting for her.

2

Three days passed without the summer heat weakening to any degree.

At night, a little coolness relieved Paris, but the heat and the stink returned with the day, as soon as the first rays of sunlight ceased to skim caressingly over the roof-tiles and started to stab down obliquely onto the streets and courtyards encrusted with dried muck. Soon, in the absence of any wind, fresh excremental stenches mixed with the staler odours of urine and dirt. Mucky exhalations rose from ditches and trenches. The smell of blood and carrion haunted the abattoirs. Acid vapours escaped from the tanneries. All of these emanations were left to slowly cook together beneath the vault of the dazzling sky, in a furnace that exhausted men and beasts alike.

Three more days passed, until that Friday evening, in July 1633, when Paris burned.

The former mansion of the marquis d'Ancre was called the Hôtel des Ambassadeurs extraordinaires. It was the property of Louis XIII, who had resided there on occasion, and now reserved it for foreign diplomats visiting Paris. The custom was to host the envoys of foreign powers as royal guests for three days following their arrival in the capital. Magnificent-looking and sumptuously appointed, the Hôtel des Ambassadeurs was ideally suited for receiving guests of distinction, and their suites. It was located, moreover, in a pleasant neighbourhood on rue de Tournon in the faubourg Saint-Germain, only a stone's throw from the Luxembourg palace.

After a final inspection of the upper storeys, Captain La

Fargue joined Leprat in the entry hall at the bottom of the main stairway.

'The sentries?' he asked.

'All of them are in place and briefed.'

'The relief?'

'In three hours.'

'Marciac? Laincourt?'

'Marciac is combing the grounds again. Laincourt was recalled to the Hôtel de l'Épervier.'

'He was recalled?'

'By a visitor. He promised not to take long.'

'All right.'

La Fargue gazed about absently, like a man trying to think of anything he might have forgotten or left undone. This evening, these walls and gilt trimmings would play host to a secret meeting whose security Cardinal Richelieu had assigned the Blades to ensure. La Donna had arranged the details, acting as an intermediary; and the most difficult issue had been finding a meeting-place. The Hôtel des Ambassadeurs had finally been agreed upon, as it was easy to guard and anonymous coaches with drawn curtains coming and going there would not attract attention. Even so, it did have some drawbacks from the point of view of security. As the Blades had quickly realised, threats could come from the neighbouring rooftops but also from the park that stretched back as far as rue Garance. When night came, they would need to increase the patrols.

'It will soon be three o'clock,' said La Fargue. 'You might as well be off to the Palais-Cardinal now.'

'At your command,' Leprat replied. 'Until later, captain.'

The musketeer departed.

At the Palais-Cardinal, he would find La Donna and one of the two guests they expected this evening. Right now the man was meeting Richelieu, incognito. He was ostensibly an envoy from the king of Spain, but in fact he spoke for the Black Claw. Louis XIII's chief minister receiving a representative of this execrated secret society was less unusual than one might think: the Black Claw was an actor on the European diplomatic and political stage, and as such, most governments had contacts with it. On the other hand, the mission that the old dragons of the Grand Lodge had entrusted to their emissary was without precedent. He was here to deliver a warning to France: that a terrible danger threatened her, and that it was the work of a handful of renegades, not of the society as a whole. Powerless to stop them, the Black Claw was nevertheless disposed to offer tokens of its good faith and wished to agree in advance to a *status quo ante bellum* in case the worst should come to pass.

The meeting planned this evening was also one of those tokens.

Both houses being located in the faubourg Saint-Germain, it was not far from the Hôtel des Ambassadeurs to the Hôtel de l'Épervier. Nevertheless Laincourt arrived in a sweat and, without taking time to refresh himself, went to find Jules Bertaud who was nervously pacing back and forth in the fencing room, where Guibot had asked him to wait.

'Arnaud!' exclaimed the small bookseller. 'At last!'

'What's happened, Bertaud?' asked Laincourt. 'I'm very busy today and can't—'

'It's Clotilde!' Bertaud said, looking very agitated. 'She's disappeared!'

'What?'

'Disappeared! My daughter has disappeared, Arnaud! She's been abducted!'

'Calm down, Jules. Calm down,' said Laincourt in a soothing voice.

With measured gestures, he sat the bookseller down, poured him a glass of water and obliged him to drink it.

'There. Slowly . . . Now, breathe . . . That's it . . . Slowly . . .'

And when Bertaud was a little more settled, he said:

'Now, tell me everything. From the beginning.'

So the bookseller told him how Clotilde had failed to return from the market that morning. He had been at the Hôtel de Chevreuse, where he was finishing the inventory of the library in the duchesse's magic study. He had therefore not been immediately alarmed that his daughter was absent when he returned home. Then, finally wondering if she had taken to bed, oppressed by the heat, he had gone to her room and found a letter, addressed to Laincourt.

'I opened it,' said Bertaud, handing him the letter with a trembling hand. 'Forgive me.'

The cardinal's former spy took the unsealed letter, observed that it was addressed to him in an unfamiliar hand and carefully unfolded it. It was a blank sheet of thick paper, which held a lock of hair. Hair that could only belong to Clotilde. Laincourt did not have to ask the bookseller if he was sure: one look into the anxious father's eyes told him all he needed to know.

'She . . . She's been abducted, hasn't she?' asked Bertaud.

'Yes.'

'Do you think she is unharmed?'

'I believe so.'

'Is this my fault? If Clotilde has been abducted, is it my fault?'

'Your fault? Where did you get that idea?' asked Laincourt.

But he was in fact unsure whose fault it was that the innocent young Clotilde had been kidnapped.

'I agreed to deliver a note to the duchesse de Chevreuse for you. Perhaps someone found out. Perhaps they want—'

'No, Jules. No . . . This is something unrelated and you must not reproach yourself for it. Look. This letter is addressed to me. Therefore I am the one they are trying to send a message to . . .'

'But who? Who? And why? . . . Oh, Arnaud, what sort of calamitous adventure have you dragged us into?'

'Who? I don't know . . . As to why, whoever has taken Clotilde means to frighten us and to cloud our judgment. No doubt they wish to draw me into a trap. Soon they will send you another message. It will be this evening, or tomorrow at the latest . . .'

Laincourt remained absolutely unflappable as he said this. Inside, the spy had taken over and was coolly analysing the situation. Clotilde had been abducted. But in broad daylight and in the neighbourhood of Place Maubert she could not have been taken by force. Not without causing a commotion. So she must have gone quietly, probably following someone she knew and had no reason to suspect.

'Someone has almost certainly abused Clotilde's trust,' said Laincourt. 'So you need to listen to me and think hard. Has Clotilde met anyone new lately? Do you know if she has made a new friend?'

'No,' replied the bookseller, shaking his head. 'No.'

'Think. It could be a beau . . .'

'A beau? No!'

'Girls don't tell their fathers everything. But you might have sensed that—'

'No! There was nothing like that . . .' The bookseller's gaze grew distant for a brief moment, and then his face took on a glimmer of a suspicion. 'Unless . . .'

'What, Bertaud?'

'There was a woman, a new client of mine, but . . .'

'Who is she?'

'A young widow who recently moved into the neighbourhood. An excellent new customer who showed a deep love of books and who seemed fond of Clotilde. Clotilde delivered books to her at home several times.'

'Her name?'

'Madame Chantegrelle. But really, Arnaud, I think you're mistaken if you think—'

'Describe her to me.'

Bertaud gathered his recollections.

'Young. Ravishing. Blonde. With sparkling blue eyes and an angelic expression. A sweet voice. An air of innocence . . . But why these questions?'

Laincourt did not reply. He wasn't even listening anymore, and had gone quite pale.

The bookseller had just described the vicomtesse de Malicorne.

Wearing a veil and dressed in the white robe of the Sisters of Saint Georges, Agnès was praying beneath the octagonal cupola of the Sainte-Marie-du-Temple church when a young sister approached her, timidly murmured a few words in her ear, and then left with soft footsteps. Sœur Marie-Agnès – she had pronounced her perpetual vows the previous day – finished her prayer. She crossed herself, stood up, and walked to the large cloister of the Enclos.

Mère Béatrice d'Aussaint was waiting for her there.

She, too, was wearing the Chatelaines' immaculate white robe. But she had a sword at her side and boots on her feet. And her robe had a tough inner lining and was slit on either side to allow riding. It revealed the cavalier's breeches she wore beneath. She also had a Latin cross and an heraldic dragon embroidered over her heart. She was dressed as a louve, a member of the Order's White Wolves, and had recently become their leader; mother superior of the Saint-Loup abbey.

Tall, beautiful, and dignified, Mère Béatrice was barely older than Agnès. The two young women exchanged a warm accolade.

'So you are one of us now, Agnès. Welcome.'

'Henceforth, it's Sœur Marie-Agnès, mother.'

'Quite right,' said Béatrice with a smile. 'Let's take a few steps together, my daughter.'

She took Agnès' arm and they walked for a moment in silence, beneath the shade of the cloister's gallery.

'I particularly wanted to greet you, Agnès. And to assure myself that you are ready.'

'It's a little late to worry about that, since that I've already taken my vows.'

'That makes you a Chatelaine. But you are not a louve. Not yet, even if you promise to become the very best of us . . .'

'Only the future will tell if that is true.'

'No. There can be no doubt about this . . .'

Agnès glanced at Mère Béatrice out of the corner of her eye and decided not to argue the point. They continued to walk with slow, even steps until the mother superior said:

'We're going to have to hasten your initiation, Agnès. You will undergo the Ordeal tonight. I have brought the Sphère d'Âme that is destined for you.'

Taken aback, the newly ordained Chatelaine halted.

'Tonight? Why so soon?'

'The truth is we have no choice in the matter. We have just learned that the Arcana have started to waken the Primordial. And you and I both know how they intend to use it. Tonight they will—'

'I'm not ready!'

'You are not as ready as you should be, but better prepared than you believe.'

'No! It's impossible! I'll never be able to—'

'There are things I know about you, Agnès, that not even you know. Trust me. You can do this.'

'It's too soon!'

'We're short of time, to be sure. But at least we know what to expect . . . Tonight, the Chatelaines will face the threat head-on. But they will all perish trying to vanquish the Primordial. They will die without you. We are still missing one louve, and that louve is you.'

Laincourt accompanied Bertaud back to his home and then went on to rue des Bernardins, where this madame Chantegrelle who so closely resembled the vicomtesse de Malicorne had acquired a house. Cautious by nature, he started by doing a little reconnaissance of the immediate area. The rue des Bernardins was close to the Place Maubert and to Bertaud's small bookshop. It was also located near the city gates of Saint-Victor and La Tournelle.

Practical if one wishes to leave Paris quickly, said the hurdy-gurdy player over Laincourt's shoulder.

The young man did not turn round and continued observing the street from the recess of a carriage gate.

You should have been on your guard from the instant Marciac discovered La Malicorne had returned. You should have known that she was planning to wreak revenge on you . . . After all, you're the one who unmasked her, just when she was about to create a Black Claw lodge in France.

A brave feat of mine that cost you your life.

Bah! You know what they say about making omelettes . . .

There's no guarantee this Chantegrelle widow is La Malicorne. There are other pretty blondes in the world. I could be mistaken.

You know very well that you're not . . . By the way, where is Maréchal?

Maréchal was the old man's dragonnet. One-eyed and utterly emaciated, it was a woeful creature to behold but the hurdy-gurdy player was very attached to it. When he died, Laincourt had inherited the reptile.

He's safe at the Hôtel de l'Épervier. I've entrusted him to master Guibot's tender care.

The young man focused his attention on the façade of the house that Bertaud had indicated to him. A ground floor and two upper storeys, with a sign representing a sleeping dragon hanging over the door. The dragon motif was very common in Paris. But knowing who was living there . . .

Laincourt wondered if La Malicorne had appreciated the irony.

The nearby Bernardins convent had given its name to the street. The chapel bell rang five times.

'God's blood!' Laincourt muttered. 'Five o'clock already.'

You're getting careless, Arnaud.

The hurdy-gurdy player's tone of voice was serious.

Retreating further into shadow, Laincourt turned towards the spectre and saw that the old beggar looked bruised and bloodied again, as he had been at the moment of his death. Lately, he had appeared to him with a dirty face, to be sure, but one that was intact.

Careless?

No one knows you're here.

Bertaud knows.

And will he go to the Blades if you're late returning?

As Laincourt did not say anything, the hurdy-gurdy player continued:

Anyway, what are you planning to do?

La Malicorne and her henchmen think they're at least one move ahead of me. According to their plans, I should be worrying myself sick while waiting for them to manifest their intentions.

They don't know that I've already started to track them down.
They may even still be in that house . . .

I doubt that very much.

Let's go and see.

No, boy! You—

But Laincourt was already leaving his hiding-place.

He soon found a way to gain access to the so-called madame Chantegrelle's house, from the rear, and after making sure that no one was watching him, he nimbly climbed over a wall and landed in the overgrown garden. There, he drew his sword before peeping through a half-closed window, which he then opened wide.

Silent and tidy, with modest furnishings, the house seemed to be empty.

Laincourt crept in noiselessly and listened. Then he explored the ground floor on tip-toe, all of his senses on alert. A flight of stairs led to the upper storeys. He climbed it and, on the first floor, a door left ajar attracted his attention. He approached and thought he heard a muffled whimper behind it. Fearing the worst, he cautiously pushed the door all the way open.

Clotilde and the Demoiselle were sitting opposite one another at a prettily set table. The tablecloth was embroidered and the crockery was delicate. The pastries sitting on the plates looked delicious. A golden syrupy-looking wine shimmered in a decanter and in two small crystal glasses. Perfectly at her ease, the Demoiselle was nibbling on candied fruits which she plucked from the crust of a piece of cake with her fingertips. But Clotilde's cheeks were stained with dried tears. Her gaze full of distress, she was fighting back sobs and sat petrified on her chair, not daring to move. Shielded by the back of her seat, a drac mercenary stood behind her with a dagger blade against her throat.

'Congratulations,' said the woman who, in Laincourt's eyes, remained the vicomtesse de Malicorne. 'You came just as quickly as I hoped you would.'

Somewhere in secret, cavernous depths, a rudimentary consciousness awoke and a reptilian eye opened slightly. The

Primordial slowly came to life and eventually heard the call which had awoken it from a distance of many leagues. The jewel on its scaly brow released a burst of light when the Heresiarch projected his mind into that of the archaic dragon. The Primordial bellowed in response to the other's presence. Then, its feet clawing over stone, it slipped into the waters of an underground tunnel leading to a black lake from which it would emerge into the evening air, before flying towards Paris.

'Any news of Laincourt?' asked La Fargue.

'No,' replied Marciac.

Daylight was already fading.

On the front steps of the Hôtel des Ambassadeurs, the two men were waiting for Leprat to return from the Palais-Cardinal with La Donna and the representative of the Black Claw. It had been less than an hour since the latter's interview with Richelieu had come to a close. His arrival under close escort was imminent and torches had been lit in the courtyard of honour in front of the mansion. Everything was ready to receive both him and the person he would be meeting here in secret.

The sound of hooves striking the dried muck approached from rue de Tournon.

'Here they are,' said the captain of the Blades.

Mounted on a black horse, Leprat was the first to enter the courtyard. Three armed horsemen followed him, then a coach without coats-of-arms and six more riders. La Fargue did not know the identity of the Black Claw's envoy, but he had no trouble recognising the one-eyed man riding just behind Leprat and commanding the escort. Armed with a solid rapier, both his clothes and his hat were made of black leather. A patch – also made of black leather and decorated with small silver studs – masked his left eye, but failed to conceal a ranse stain that spread over his cheekbone and temple. His name was Savelda, one of those who carried out various sordid and violent tasks on behalf of the masters of the Grand Lodge.

La Fargue and the Gascon exchanged a glance.

The Blades had crossed paths with Savelda on several

occasions recently. In fact, the last time he had narrowly escaped capture by them in the gardens of the Château de Dampierre after he threatened the queen's life.

First to dismount, Leprat hastened to join La Fargue and Marciac on the front steps. His expression was grave.

'That's not the worst of it,' he announced.

And the Blades' captain understood what the musketeer meant when he saw who climbed from the coach and gallantly lent his arm to La Donna.

It was the comte de Pontevedra.

La Fargue turned pale and absently took the note that Leprat was holding out to him.

'What's this?' he asked.

'It's from His Eminence, captain.'

La Fargue broke the seal, ran his eyes over the letter and returned it open to the musketeer so he could read it before passing it to Marciac.

Monsieur le capitaine,
Please do me the favour of forgetting the promise you
made the comte de Pontevedra during your last conversation
with him.
Richelieu

'What promise?' asked the Gascon.

'I promised I would kill him.'

With a face made of marble, La Fargue watched as Pontevedra climbed the steps and entered the brightly lit mansion, exchanging smiles and polite courtesies with Alessandra. Savelda followed three paces behind him.

If they were capable of vanquishing the dragons they hunted down and fought for the salvation of the kingdom of France, the White Wolves of Saint Georges did not owe their success solely to their courage and their piety, or even to the supernatural virtues of the draconite blades they wielded so boldly. They owed their success, above all, to the protection offered them by powerful entities. By departed dragons, in fact. Or rather, forgotten dragons who no longer had any physical existence but continued – sometimes for centuries – to haunt the spectral world.

Each louve associated her soul with that of a protective dragon, thanks to a ritual taught to the Chatelaines by the Guardians in the distant past. This ritual was dangerous and Agnès knew the risks she was taking when she let the heavy doors of the Hall of the Ordeal close behind her. Dressed only in a white vestment, her hair cut very short since she had pronounced her vows, she kneeled in prayer on the bare flagstones. Candles were burning in the darkness. The silence was deep, and suitable for spiritual communion. Before her, on a small wooden stand, Agnès saw a globe that seemed to be filled with a black, shifting ink whose slow swirls drew in the eye like an abyss.

A Sphère d'Âme.

A strange irony. The last time she had seen a Sphère d'Âme, Agnès had destroyed it to disrupt a Black Claw ceremony. She'd witnessed the extraordinary power contained within. A power which she would now have to confront on her own before she could be accepted by it, because it was as much a matter of dominating this spectral dragon as of winning its respect. The Ordeal richly deserved its name. It had cost some candidates their lives. Others emerged with their spirit numbed and broken. Those who passed the test successfully did not speak of it, or only to other louves, who alone could understand.

Focused on her task, determined, Agnès plunged mentally into the tormented shadows of the Sphère d'Âme . . .

. . . and felt an immense presence invade the hall.

It was as if she could feel the shadows vibrating all the way down to the bowels of the earth.

The Ordeal had begun.

Night had fallen.

At the Hôtel des Ambassadeurs, La Fargue gazed out from the torchlit terrace at the dark flowerbeds and straight paths of the great garden, where patrols paced up and down with a steady step. Alone and unable to concentrate his thoughts on any single subject, he thought about the Arcana and their Grand Design, about Laincourt who seemed to have gone missing, about the secrets of the Guards, and about the strange manoeuvres of the Black Claw and the comte de Pontevedra.

Pontevedra . . .

He had borne the name Louveciennes, and he had been La Fargue's best friend. At the time he had been a gentleman of honour and of duty. Together they had performed many brave services for the French Crown, on the fields of battle and behind the scenes of great historical events. Together they had founded the Blades at Cardinal Richelieu's request. They had carefully recruited Almades, then Leprat and Bretteville, and Marciac almost immediately after. Very quickly, the Blades had registered their first successes and gained in boldness. Then Agnès and Ballardieu had joined their ranks.

Leaning on the terrace balustrade, La Fargue heard someone approaching behind him. He glanced over his shoulder and recognised the tall and elegant silhouette of the man now known as the comte de Pontevedra. He gave no reaction, and turned his eyes back to the garden. The other joined him without saying a word and set down two glasses and the bottle of wine which he had brought out with him. He filled the glasses and pushed one in front of the captain.

The old gentleman looked at it briefly and then away.

'Surely you jest,' he said coldly. 'I would kill you if I could.'

'Yes, but you cannot . . .'

Louveciennes' betrayal had been brutal and unexpected. It had occurred during the siege of La Rochelle, in the course of a mission that subsequently ended in an appalling fiasco and the death of Bretteville. It had been a terrible blow for La Fargue: after betraying the Blades, his friend, his brother-in-arms, had fled to Spain, where he had enjoyed a dazzling ascent in his fortunes, becoming the comte de Pontevedra.

'You must return to your chambers, monsieur l'ambassadeur,' said La Fargue. 'You will be much safer than you are out here.'

'It's stifling upstairs! And Savelda is here to watch my back.'

The one-eyed agent of the Black Claw was indeed standing nearby.

'As you will. You know I would be the last person to mourn if a pistol ball fired from a nearby roof were to pass through your throat.'

With these words, La Fargue turned round and took a few steps towards the mansion, but Pontevedra called out:

'How is Ana-Lucia?'

'My daughter is called Anne. And she is well.'

'Indeed? Are you quite certain of that?'

The Blades' captain scowled.

'What are you trying to say?'

The comte de Pontevedra approached him.

'Do you know what I'm doing here?'

'You are representing the Black Claw,' said La Fargue, displaying an expression of profound contempt. 'It's not enough that you betrayed your king. You also had to betray your race.'

'Really? Am I the only one here to serve dragons?' asked Pontevedra with cutting irony. When La Fargue made no reply, he added: 'And if we're giving out lessons on morality, let's not forget which one of us seduced the other's wife, shall we?'

They had loved the same woman, although La Fargue had resisted acting on his feelings with all his might, out of loyalty to his friend.

'We loved one another, but there was only that one night,' he replied. 'One night, which Oriane and I never forgave ourselves for. Besides, you were the one she joined in Spain. With Anne.'

The two men remained silent for a moment, both prisoners of painful shared memories. Then Pontevedra spoke to Savelda:

'Leave us.'

The order took the Spanish henchman by surprise:

'My lord, I—'

'Leave us!'

Savelda hesitated again, then bowed and retired.

Pontevedra took La Fargue by the elbow and led him a few steps away. Intrigued, the captain did not resist.

'Here,' said Pontevedra, removing a leather wallet from his silver-embroidered doublet. 'I wanted to give this to you, hand-to-hand.'

La Fargue took the wallet.

'What is it?' he asked warily.

'I have resources at my disposal you cannot imagine. I know that you entrusted your daughter to the Guardians to keep her away from the Black Claw and from Richelieu's curiosity. I also know the Guardians assure you that she is safe. That's not true, and this is proof . . . You see, I don't ask you to take my word on it.'

'You do well not to.'

The captain of the Blades slipped the wallet beneath his shirt, against his skin.

Shortly after, upon returning inside, La Fargue pondered matters as he watched the comte de Pontevedra climbing the main stairs towards his quarters. Then he joined Alessandra and Leprat on the steps leading to the front courtyard. Looking worried, La Donna was clutching a note a messenger had just delivered from the Palais-Cardinal.

'Well?' asked the old captain.

'No news,' said Alessandra. 'I want to believe, but I'm beginning to think that he will not come . . .'

The person they were still waiting for, the person that Pontevedra had come to meet in secret, was none other than Valombre. The Black Claw had asked to enter into contact with the Guardians under the aegis of Cardinal Richelieu. They had insisted on the urgency of this unprecedented meeting. But Pontevedra had not deigned to explain the reason for requesting it, which had in turn complicated matters for La Donna. The Guardians were exceedingly cautious. They did not like to proceed without knowing why.

'Valombre will come if the Seven permit him to,' said La Fargue.

A rider then came into the courtyard. It was Marciac, returning from the Hôtel de l'Épervier.

'Laincourt still hasn't turned up,' he said after jumping down from the saddle. 'And it's been a few hours since he left with his bookseller friend.'

'Bertaud,' Leprat reminded them.

'Yes, Bertaud. According to Guibot, the man was frantic with worry.'

'Laincourt has no doubt gone to assist him,' La Fargue reckoned. 'But didn't he tell anyone where he was going or what he was intending to do?'

'No.'

'That's not like him,' said Alessandra gravely.

She had met Laincourt in Madrid, when he had been spying on behalf of the cardinal. She knew his qualities and held him in high esteem.

'Perhaps the bookseller is at home,' said Marciac. 'He has a shop near Place Maubert, I believe. I could pay him a visit . . .'

La Fargue cursed.

One of his men was missing and he could do nothing about it, being retained here by a secret meeting which, it seemed, might not even take place! And to crown it all, one of the participants was an individual he hated, yet was duty-bound to protect!

The captain of the Blades forced himself to recover his calm. Fists on his hips, he took a deep breath and arched his back, his face lifting to see an enormous full moon in a deep blue sky.

A window shattered just above him, showering him with sparkling debris as Savelda's broken-limbed corpse crashed to the ground at the bottom of the steps.

After a brief instant of stupor, La Fargue, Leprat, and Marciac rushed inside the building. They unsheathed their rapiers and seized their pistols as they dashed up the main stairs. Broke down the door to Pontevedra's chambers. Crossed the antechamber in a bound. Burst into the adjoining room.

Seriously wounded, Pontevedra had dragged himself over

to the bed leaving a wide trail of blood in his wake. A drac was bent over him, preparing to finish him off with a sword thrust to the chest. A second one stood near the window by which they had entered and which Pontevedra had no doubt opened to take in the fresh night air. They were armed and dressed like mercenary swordsmen, but these were no ordinary dracs: they had leathery wings, ample and powerful enough to permit them to fly.

Surprised, the first drac leaped through the window and escaped. But the Blades did not allow the second any time to react. La Fargue opened fire, then Marciac and Leprat. One pistol ball hit the winged drac in the middle of the chest. The second pierced him in the neck, and the third put out an eye and tore away the back of his skull.

La Donna arrived, but was jostled aside by the sentries who had been guarding the doors and windows on the ground floor. The room rapidly filled with agitated people. The winged drac inside was already dead. A few musket shots fired from the window failed to hit his fleeing companion, now flying off into the distance. La Fargue raised his voice to restore order while the dying Pontevedra was laid out on his bed. The captain sent the sentries back to their posts, except for two who remained at the door. Leprat helped Marciac examine the wounds of the man who – in a former life – had been one of their own. Meanwhile, Alessandra studied the winged drac. Intrigued, she picked up his rapier, looked closely at it, turned suddenly pale and dropped the weapon.

'My God!'

She ran from the room.

Marciac had just stepped back from the bed and was wiping his hands with a cloth. There was nothing he could do to save Pontevedra, as the other two already understood. Surprised by the behaviour of La Donna, he hesitated as to whether he should go after her, and gave his captain a questioning look.

'Find her!' ordered La Fargue, just before the dying man gripped him by the collar with a blood-slicked hand.

The Gascon went.

*

In the front courtyard of the Hôtel des Ambassadeurs, there were horses waiting. Alessandra had already mounted one of them side-saddle when Marciac joined her.

'Where are you going?' he asked, seizing the animal by the bit.

'The rapier. It was made of draconite.'

Draconite was an alchemical stone dreaded by the dragons. It allowed in particular the fabrication of a steel that inflicted terrible wounds on them, but gave humans no more cause for fear than the ordinary variety.

'Don't you think it strange those dracs had draconite weapons?' continued La Donna. 'Why go to all that trouble, just to kill Pontevedra?'

At that point, realisation dawned on Marciac.

Although the Black Claw's envoy was not a dragon, Valombre was. Alessandra feared that the winged dracs had been sent to assassinate him, too. Perhaps they had already struck the Guardians' representative, which would explain his alarming lateness for the meeting.

La Donna forced Marciac to release her mount and left through the carriage gate at a fast trot.

'Wait!' yelled the Gascon, climbing onto a horse.

He took off in pursuit of her.

Coughing up blood, eyes already growing glassy, Pontevedra had seized La Fargue by the collar. His fist was firm but his arm was trembling when, stammering, he tried to draw the Blades' captain towards him. The old gentleman bent down, bringing his face close to that of his former friend.

'If you're hoping for a pardon . . .' he started.

'Not . . . Not a . . . pardon,' murmured the dying man in a barely audible voice. Without releasing La Fargue, he swallowed painfully and gathered his last remaining strength. 'The . . . queen . . . The queen . . . in . . . danger . . . The qu—'

He died with the words trapped in his throat.

La Fargue had to tug on his wrist to free himself from the

dead man's grasp. He stood up and turned to Leprat with a worried expression.

'What did he say?' asked the musketeer.

'He . . . He said that the queen was in danger.'

'What? In danger now?'

'I believe so, yes. But I don't know anything about it.'

'The queen is in Saint-Germain with the king and I don't—' Leprat corrected himself: 'No, I'm wrong. The queen is not in Saint-Germain. It's Friday.'

'So where is she?'

'She's here. In Paris.'

It was a black, massive creature, which advanced across the night sky with great, steady beats of its wings.

The Primordial was flying towards Paris, and it could see the first lights of the city in the distance before it, as well as the luminous blazes of the three powerful solaires. One – white – was at the top of Tour du Temple, in the Chatelaines' Enclos. Another – red – indicated the Palais-Cardinal. A third – blue – shone above the Louvre.

The dragon with the jewelled brow felt a strange emotion pervade it: in the Arcana's magic study, the Heresiarch had just smiled.

Laincourt emerged from unconciousness and grimaced in pain.

In the dim light, Clotilde was gently dabbing his battered face with a piece of cloth torn from her dress and dampened with a little stagnant water. She looked down at him with a smiling but exhausted face, her eyes reddened and her cheeks smeared with dirt. Long locks of hair had escaped her un-ravelling chignon.

Laincourt slowly returned to full awareness.

And remembered.

Contrary to appearances, the house on rue des Bernardins had not been empty. Not only had the Demoiselle been wait-ing for him while holding Clotilde prisoner, but there were numerous drac and human mercenaries hiding in the upper storeys.

Laincourt had been disarmed.

Then, at the Demoiselle's order and before Clotilde's eyes, he had been beaten. With fists at first. Then with boots, when he had fallen and curled into a ball on the floor. And the blows had continued thereafter, methodically administered with a cold cruelty, devoid of passion or fury, while Clotilde, in tears, had begged the dracs to stop and implored the Demoiselle, who alone had the power, to put an end to the torture.

Laincourt had finally fainted.

'Where are we?' he asked, in a thick voice.

Squinting, he sat up and discovered an empty cubby-hole, damp and dusty, faintly lit by the rays of a lantern coming through a gap beneath the door.

'I don't know,' replied Clotilde. 'When you lost consciousness, they locked you up inside a chest and then put me in another. I don't know where they took us, but I think we are still in Paris. It could be . . . It could be a cellar, don't you think?'

He nodded and then rose to his feet, unable to contain a moan of pain as he did.

'Monsieur Laincourt! You shouldn't get up! You—'

'It's all right, Clotilde. Those dracs knew what they were doing. They only wanted to make me suffer and to torment you, not to do any serious damage.'

'But why?'

'Out of cruelty. And I think you can call me Arnaud, Clotilde.'

But the explanation put forward by Laincourt left the girl mute with disbelief. He availed himself of her silence to examine the door: it was solid and double-locked. There was no other exit.

'Who are these people?' Clotilde finally asked. 'Why did they hurt you? What do they want from us, exactly? And why do they . . . ? That woman. She . . . She said that you were old friends . . .'

Laincourt suddenly became aware of the full degree of

young Clotilde's distress. He came back to sit down next to her, took her hands, and said:

'Everything that has happened to you is my fault, Clotilde. I am sorry for that.'

Then, because she was looking at him in utter incomprehension, he decided that she deserved to know. He told her that he was an agent of Cardinal Richelieu. He told her about the vicomtesse de Malicorne, what she had tried to do, and how he had foiled her plans. Lastly, he explained she was now called the 'Demoiselle', but was still seeking vengeance.

'And she abducted you to get to me, Clotilde,' he confessed.

But he lacked the courage to admit that he didn't know why she was still alive. The bait was of no interest once the prey had fallen into the trap. Clotilde no longer served any purpose . . .

. . . unless the Demoiselle was reserving some refined piece of cruelty for him.

The door suddenly opened. A drac and two men burst into the room. The first struck Laincourt in the face before he had time to react. The others seized Clotilde despite her screams of terror. Laincourt tried to defend her, but a kick from a boot to his belly cut off his breath. The men dragged the girl out by force and the drac slammed the door shut behind them. He locked it with a key as Laincourt got up, staggered over, and threw himself against it in vain. His brow pressed against the wood, he hammered on the solid panel with both fists, but could only hear Clotilde crying and calling out to him for help.

'No!' he shouted. 'No! Take me! Me! Take me!'

Alessandra had been serving the Guardians for several years now. She enjoyed their confidence and knew Valombre, their representative in Paris, quite well. She liked him, had a genuine affection for him. So there was a growing fear in the pit of her stomach as she rode towards the house where the dragon dwelled on the Ile de la Cité. Sensing her fear, Marciac watched her out of the corner of his eye as they rode. He had spurred his horse forward to catch up with her at the end of rue de Tournon and had been escorting her since, without really knowing what to expect.

Having crossed the Seine via Pont de l'Hôtel-Dieu, they passed in front of Notre-Dame cathedral and were astonished to see it lit up. Surmounted by the gallery of the kings of Israel and of Judah, the three portals of the western façade were open and gave them a glimpse of intense activity within, while Chatelaines and Black Guards were assembling on the forecourt. Marciac thought there were even some White Wolves among them.

'What's going on here?' he asked.

'I don't know,' replied La Donna.

But, like him, she feared the worst.

They entered the private little neighbourhood of the canons' Cloister, to which Alessandra had a gate key.

'Valombre entrusted me with it,' she explained before the Gascon could ask.

The dragon was lodged on rue du Chapitre, not far from the old footbridge that linked the Ile de la Cité with Ile Notre-Dame-des-Écailles: a vestige of the days – before the dracs moved in there – when the canons of the cathedral still laid claim to the neighbouring island. Marciac and Alessandra found the door to the house locked but, backing up a few paces, the Gascon noticed an open window on the first storey.

'Keep an eye out,' he said to La Donna as he handed her the reins to his horse.

Then he climbed the façade with ease and slipped inside.

Increasingly anxious, Alessandra kept watch as she waited for Marciac to appear again. In the nocturnal silence she heard the murmur of religious chants coming from Notre-Dame. And wasn't that a bell tolling in the distance? A bell, which others were now answering?

Marciac opened the front door for her.

'Come inside quickly,' he said.

Hitching the horses to a ring fixed to the wall, she followed the Gascon into the house. Silent and dark, it seemed deserted.

'Nobody upstairs,' Marciac announced in hushed voice.

They explored the ground floor by the glow of the

997

moonlight that entered through the windows. They wanted to remain discreet. They did not call out, they made no light, and they almost failed to notice the badly damaged wall panel. It looked as though someone had been kicking at it about half-way up. As if they were trying to break it down.

As if it was a door.

Alessandra and Marciac understood. Exchanging a glance, they began to examine the wooden panel, running their fingertips along the frame, fishing around and finally finding the places to push and determining the correct order in which to push them. All of this took some time, but La Donna, luckily, had experience in these matters. At last, the panel slid to one side and revealed an iron door which the Gascon opened cautiously, pistol in his fist. It concealed a staircase at the bottom of which they found Valombre, lying in a pool of his own blood, lit by the dying flame of an oil lamp.

In 1621, Queen Anne d'Autriche acquired a property in the faubourg Saint-Jacques where she decided to install a community of Benedictine nuns from the Bièvre valley. Three years later, the first stone of their new cloister was laid. Thus was born the Val-de-Grâce abbey, a place where the queen experienced a tranquillity she could never find at the Louvre, hidden far from the royal court and – so she believed, at least – Richelieu's spies. She went there often and liked to stay there on Fridays, taking her meals in the refectory and lodging in a modest two-room apartment. After the Dampierre affair, the king severely reduced the liberties he allowed his wife. But he was unable to force her to give up her weekly retreats to Val-de-Grâce, even though she used them to meet in secret with her friend the duchesse de Chevreuse and to send letters to Spain with the aid of the abbess, Mère de Saint-Étienne. None of this had escaped the cardinal's notice.

La Fargue and Leprat reached Val-de-Grâce at a full gallop. If the queen was there, she was in some kind of danger. At least that was what Pontevedra had claimed before he died.

'Louveciennes only told us the queen was under threat

when he was on the very brink of death,' observed Leprat as they rode. 'Why was that, do you suppose?'

'No doubt he knew the queen was in danger, but not how imminent that danger was.'

'And he finally understood when he fell to the two assassins?'

'I think so. He must have believed that if they were attacking him now, it meant that the plot against the queen was about to take place.'

'But attacking him is the same thing as attacking the Black Claw. Who would want that?'

The captain did not reply: they were arriving and slowed their mounts.

Val-de-Grâce offered an unusual spectacle at this hour of the night. Approaching at a walk, the riders discovered the abbey lit up and the gate open. In the courtyard, numerous soldiers belonging to the light cavalry company of Saint Georges – the celebrated Black Guards – were coming and going. All of them were wearing breastplates and most of them had swords in their hands. But they were moving calmly and efficiently, without shouts or excessive haste.

'No one may enter!'

La Fargue gave his name to the sentries at the gate, showed his pass signed by the cardinal, and announced that he had a message of the highest importance for the officer in charge.

'One moment,' said one of the guards after examining the document in the glow of a lantern.

He ran off.

'Black Guards?' murmured Leprat in surprise. 'What are they doing here? They're not assigned to watch over the queen.'

'I know. And yet . . .'

The sentry was speaking with an officer in the middle of the courtyard. The officer listened to him, before turning to beckon La Fargue and Leprat forward. They dismounted and walked towards him, leading their mounts by the bridle. It was only then they recognised François Reynault d'Ombreuse.

'What's happening here?' asked La Fargue after exchanging a frank handshake with the young officer.

'We have just repulsed an assault by winged dracs. There's no merit in it, we were expecting an attack.'

'Is the queen safe?' worried Leprat.

'The queen is not here. She's being kept in safety at another location, which I don't know. You have come to warn us of a danger threatening her, haven't you?'

'Yes,' said La Fargue. 'But you knew that already. How?'

'Thanks to information secretly transmitted to the Sisters of the Saint Georges. And you?'

The Blades' captain was about to answer when a cavernous bellow made the night tremble. Together, they turned to the north, towards the centre of Paris.

There they saw the Primordial, flying in slow circles in the sky and roaring.

With rage boiling in his belly, Laincourt had resigned himself to wait. He knew that he would only exhaust himself in vain by hammering away at the door of the cubby-hole where they had him locked up. It was also useless to shout, to call out, to insult his captors. He needed to save his meagre strength so he could act when the moment came. His tormentors had neglected to tie his hands. No doubt they believed him less dangerous than he really was, an error which he was counting on being able to turn to his advantage.

For now, the hardest thing was trying not to drive himself mad imagining what Clotilde was being subjected to. That was precisely the reason why the girl was still alive and why they had been locked up together. It was so they could tear her from him, reduce him to impotence, and leave him to torment himself. La Malicorne – she would never have any other name for Laincourt – knew how to torture souls . . .

The key turned in the heavy lock.

Sitting with his back to the cubby-hole wall, Laincourt seemed listless and defeated. Even close to being unconscious:

body limp, breathing slow, head hanging, and hair before his eyes. His left hand rested inertly on the floor, palm upwards, easily visible. He was hoping to divert attention from the right hand, which lay concealed beneath his thigh, gripping a shard of pottery he'd discovered in the dust. A feeble weapon that would only allow him to strike once, but which might just slice through a jugular vein.

As long as the intended victim came close enough. And bent over.

Laincourt waited, hearing the door open with a creak and someone come inside dragging . . . a sack?

'I would appreciate it if you lent me a hand,' said a familiar voice.

Flabbergasted, Laincourt opened his eyes and discovered Saint-Lucq, dragging the dead body of one of the guards who had been posted in the corridor.

'Saint-Lucq? But how did you—'

'There's another one,' said the half-blood.

Laincourt got up and, together, they laid a second body on top of the first inside the cubby-hole. One of them had his throat cut; the other had been stabbed in the heart. All done without the slightest noise.

'Hurry up,' said Saint-Lucq.

He had posted himself on the threshold and was glancing furtively into the corridor.

'But how did you manage to find me?' asked Laincourt as he stripped one body of its sword and baldric.

'The cardinal has charged me with eliminating La Malicorne's cult. That will be achieved by the time I've finished up here.'

'By eliminating—'

'Yes.'

Laincourt stopped fiddling with his scabbard.

'Clotilde is being held prisoner.'

'The bookseller's daughter. I know, yes.'

'We have to save her!'

Emotionless, Saint-Lucq turned the blank and hypnotic gaze of his scarlet spectacles towards Laincourt.

'I thought you might say something like that.'

He offered him one of his pistols.

Valombre still lived.

Lying motionless at the foot of his hidden staircase, he had moaned when Marciac had gently turned him over onto his back, then he had regained consciousness while the Gascon examined him.

'Don't move, monsieur. My name is Marciac and I serve Captain La Fargue.'

'I know who you are, monsieur.'

'Then you also know that I am something of a doctor.'

The dragon had a deep wound at his side whose edges seem to have been eaten by acid, a sure sign that it had been inflicted by a draconite blade. He also had a broken leg and a nasty bump on his forehead.

'You have broken your femur. But I am going to take care of this wound first, before you drain yourself of more blood.'

Alessandra came back with thread, a needle, a basin of water, and cloths which she had found upstairs in the house. They would need a stretcher to lift the wounded patient up to the ground floor above, but unable to do so right away, Marciac had decided to tend to the most urgent injuries on the spot. Afterwards, they'd see about the rest.

Grimacing with pain while the Gascon sutured his wound, Valombre explained that he had been surprised by two winged dracs in his chamber, that they had attacked him, but that he had been able to escape and close the secret passage behind him. Then he had lost consciousness at the top of the steps.

'What is this room?' asked Marciac.

They were in a small hexagonal chamber, empty and bare.

'A meditation study,' replied Valombre. 'A place which is indispensable if one wishes to keep control of . . .' He searched for the right words. 'If one wishes to keep control of the dragon.'

The Gascon nodded distractedly.

'Your would-be assassins could not linger, which certainly

saved your life,' said La Donna. 'They still had much else to do.'

And then she recounted how two winged dracs – the same two, no doubt – had assassinated Pontevedra at the Hôtel des Ambassadeurs, prompting them to come and see about him. 'So they dared,' said the dragon. 'The Arcana dared to strike at the Black Claw . . .'

'And at the Guardians.'

'Unfortunately, I'm afraid that they will dare do much worse before tomorrow, madame.'

'Did you hear that?' asked Marciac, cocking an ear.

The Primordial had first flown over Paris at a fairly low altitude, making circles and bellowing. Then, as the bells of the capital joined together to sound the tocsin, the Parisians surprised in their sleep had sought to comprehend what was going on before lifting alarmed gazes towards the great black dragon which flew over their heads again and again, describing great loops in the night sky but not doing more than bellowing occasionally, its black scales gleaming in the light of the moon and stars.

The uncertainty of the population, however, did not last.

It gave way to horror when the Primordial began to belch its destructive fire, pulverising rooftops and seeding immense blazes at random across the city.

Reynault d'Ombreuse and his detachment of light cavalry left Val-de-Grâce at a fast trot. Accompanied by La Fargue and Leprat, the Black Guards rode up rue du Faubourg-Saint-Jacques as the neighbourhood became agitated, and the residents' anxiety turned to fear. The dragon seemed to be sparing the faubourgs, but for how long? Should they wait, or try to go now? Save their lives, but leave their dwellings and worldly goods behind, perhaps to be pillaged in their absence?

Reynault had had the foresight to send one of his men ahead. The troops thus found the Saint-Jacques gate open to them, but were forced to slow down nevertheless. Within the city walls, the streets were thronged. Houses were burning and the roar of fires was mingled with cries and sobs, along with the deafening din of all the city's bells pealing out at once. People deserted their homes, taking whatever they could with them. Others fought the flames with the inadequate means at hand, or tried to help their neighbours. Shouts advised the inhabitants to flee, to stay, to take refuge in the cellars, to go the churches to pray, or to run towards the banks of the Seine. Jostling became brawls. Some poor wretches were trampled. Leprat saw a woman, babe in arms, throw herself from a second-storey window of a house on fire.

They often had to force passage through the crowds.

Reynault, La Fargue, and the riders at the head of the column had no choice but to push their horses into the innocents they knocked down, the imperative being to reach Notre-Dame as quickly as possible. In this fashion, the detachment reached the Petit Châtelet, which guarded the bridge leading to the Ile de la Cité. As they were crossing the smaller arm of the Seine river, Leprat exclaimed:

'Look!'

In the sky, the Primordial was no longer alone.

Mounted on white wyverns, the White Wolves of Saint Georges surrounded it, harassing it, drawing its attention, dodging away, goading it again and again with their draconite blades. They were taking every risk to drive the creature mad. But at least it was sparing Paris as long as they kept it distracted. At least it was directing its incandescent spurts at them rather than at the city below.

Behind Reynault, the Black Guards were cheering them on.

'We need to hurry!' he ordered, breaking the mood. 'The sisters can only offer us a brief respite!'

The Ile de la Cité, too, had become a chaos of flames, cries, and terror. Making their way through the crush, Reynault and his men took rue Neuve-Notre-Dame which led straight to the cathedral and its beautiful twin towers. A row of three terraced houses was burning, and as the façades threatened to collapse into the street, the column urged their horses to pass by, braving the torrid swirls of hot coals and ash.

At last they reached the cathedral's narrow forecourt.

Men, women, children, and old people had gathered there. Seeking refuge in Notre-Dame, they had come up against a wall of Black Guards on horseback, who, impassive, with their swords at their sides and their musket butts resting on their thighs, held their mounts in place with a steady hand and would not let anyone approach the cathedral. Fear and anger on the one hand, and intransigence on the other, threatened to provoke a riot. Fists were being raised among the rancorous crowd. Two or three stones had already flown through the air.

Prudently, Reynault d'Ombreuse skirted the forecourt and led his troops alongside the cathedral to the southern entrance, or Saint-Étienne portal. This was also guarded, but as it was protected by the episcopal palace, the immediate area around it was relatively peaceful. La Fargue and Leprat dismounted with the rest of the column. They alone, however, followed Reynault inside.

Within Notre-Dame, there was a strange atmosphere of calm.

Thirty metres tall and ten spans long, the immense nave was deserted, as were the side aisles, the transept, and the crossing where four imposing pillars rose directly to the vault far above. The air seemed to be vibrating. The silence, in fact, was resonating softly with an incantation whispered with fervour by a group of kneeling Chatelaines in the choir, located behind the high altar. There was magic in their prayer. It gave off a power which set one's nerves on edge.

Discreet but vigilant sentinels, Black Guards were posted at the doors and in front the altar steps. Calling one of them over, Reynault charged the soldier with conducting Captain La Fargue before Mère d'Aussaint. But he requested that Leprat remain by his side: it was clear he would soon have need of an experienced officer.

The musketeer agreed to stay.

From the Grande Galerie, on the third storey of the magnificent western façade of Notre-Dame, Mère Béatrice d'Aussaint was watching her sisters who – as white-draped silhouettes atop white wyverns – were risking their lives to divert the

1005

Primordial's wrath. Below her, the Ile de la Cité spread between the two arms of the Seine, whose dark slow waters merged, and flowed on between the two halves of Paris. A great clamour was rising from the streets and squares invaded by crowds. Blazes had broken out everywhere. They roared, wheezed, and crackled. Some of the buildings at the Saint-Germain abbey were burning. Tall flames were flickering from the windows of the oldest section of the Louvre.

'Did the cardinal send you?' she asked upon seeing La Fargue approach.

'The circumstances did, more like it.'

'Then it's divine Providence at work.'

Side by side, they lifted their eyes towards the Primordial and the white forms that were confronting it.

'The battle being waged by your louves is doomed to failure, mother.'

'They know that. But it's only a matter of gaining time.'

'Gaining time for what?'

'For the ritual the sisters are preparing inside . . . Oh my God!'

The great black dragon had just struck a Chatelaine with a fiery blast. Burning alive in her flaming robe, she plunged from her wyvern, a long silence accompanying her fall before she vanished in the black waters of the Seine.

On Ile Notre-Dame, joyful exclamations and war cries greeted the terrible spectacle of the living torch, which fell from the skies trailing a swathe of flames. The damp and rotting alleys of Les Écailles were full of excited dracs who, ever since the tocsin had sounded, had been following the Primordial's manoeuvres. They instinctively took its side against the Chatelaines and applauded this success.

Keress Karn broke off observing the aerial combat to keep an eye on his men who, at a street corner beneath an enormous lamp, were replacing one barrel with another. Their return was welcomed with acclamations, both from dracs who were already drunk but wanted to drink some more, and from new arrivals who had been drawn by the rumour of free drink.

The first barrel had been emptied in less than an hour. The second was immediately tapped and would not last long.

Karn knew that similar scenes were taking place here and there all across the stifling maze of Les Écailles. The Heresiarch had ordered him to provide a generous flow of drac wine and that's exactly what he was busy doing. The task itself was an easy one: dracs loved this mix of wine, *eau-de-vie* and golden henbane that intoxicated them after just a few glassfuls. But Karn needed to make sure that his own men didn't touch the stuff. Although most of his band was waiting out of harm's way to go into action, those he had entrusted with delivering the barrels were susceptible to temptation. Karn himself had to avoid breathing in the fumes from the irresistible brew. To his men, he explained that they needed to keep a cool head in readiness for the forthcoming combat that night.

It was the truth, but not the whole truth.

For Karn still mistrusted the mercenaries he had hired to replace those who had fallen at Bois-Noir. The new recruits knew how to fight and to obey orders, and had no fear of dying and even less of killing. They were true drac warriors. But how would they react if they knew? What would they do if they found out the Enchantress had poured a substance that induced madness into each of the barrels? Would they accept the idea of poisoning other dracs simply to achieve the aims of the Arcana?

As for the red drac leader, he couldn't care less.

The idea of Paris burning delighted him, and now he was eager to plunder the helpless city.

Long and spacious, the cellar featured rows of columns upholding elegant vaults. Large flagstones covered the floor and the lit candles placed in large candelabra cast tortuous shadows on the bare walls. Gathered before the altar, there were thirty people reciting an incantation in the old draconic tongue. All of them were masked and draped in scarlet cloaks. All of them carried a sword. They had secretly sworn allegiance to the Black Claw and, not content with having placed their names, their fortunes, and their influence at its service, they also worshipped it in a cult whose sinister rituals induced an unhealthy fascination in them that flattered their basest instincts.

The Demoiselle was leading the ceremony.

As she chanted the words that her acolytes repeated after her, she hardly resembled the charming young person that she ordinarily pretended to be. The features of her face had become sharper, more bony and hollowed. Her eyes shone with a cold and cruel sparkle. Her tangled blonde hair fell upon her bared bosom. She seemed taller and stronger. More mature, too. But that was nothing compared to another change: below her waist, her body had formed a thick scaly tail upon which she held herself upright.

With her arms spread and her head tilted backward she undulated slightly, abandoning herself to a pleasure which was enhanced by the vapours from the decoctions of henbane which were being heated in bowls filled with red-glowing coals, placed on either side of two long, crossed daggers upon the altar. Powerful fragrances rose into the air, thick and yellow. They affected the acolytes too, and had also plunged Clotilde into a hypnotic torpor. The girl was behind the Demoiselle, bound to a stone table that was inclined to expose her to the view of all present. She was naked, and her body had been shaved and covered in painted inscriptions, and her wrists and ankles were held by leather straps.

In her ecstatic trance, the Demoiselle did not see the flasks of naphtha flying towards the gathering. She did not see them fall, burst and splatter in all directions. She only opened her eyes when one acolyte, soaking and surprised, overturned a large candelabra as he stumbled, and then suddenly caught fire. The layer of oil in which the cult members found themselves suddenly floundering was set alight. Other acolytes began to go up in flames. There was panic. The human torches screamed and struggled while the others hastily stepped away, jostling one another. Some threw off their burning cloaks, slapped on their sleeves or breeches to put out fires, threw away smoking gloves, and rubbed at their scorched hair. Meanwhile those the fire had spared stared around them without comprehension, their minds still sluggish from the golden henbane.

Saint-Lucq approached with his sword in his fist, having left two dead bodies at the door behind him.

'TAKE HIM!' screamed the Demoiselle, pointing her finger.

Having entered by a second door, two mercenaries – a drac and a human – rushed forward to meet the half-blood. Very calm and still advancing, he parried the man's attack and pierced him in the chest, withdrawing his blade just in time to avoid an attack from the drac, whom he brought down with a knee to the groin before finishing him off with another blow to the chin.

Frenzied with rage, the Demoiselle roared as her face became more brutal and scales appeared on her shoulders and throat like armour plating. She seized the two sacrificial daggers placed before her and turned to the inclined stone table. And then she roared again in fury, a prominent ridge emerging in the middle of her brow. Laincourt had freed Clotilde. The girl was having trouble standing and clung to his neck, so he held her tightly against him with his left arm while he backed up and pointed a pistol at the Demoiselle, or rather at the creature she had become.

He opened fire.

Hit in the left shoulder, the Demoiselle reeled back, but then straightened up like a reed on her scaly tail and looked in stupor at the hissing wound. The pistol ball was made of draconite. Another detonation rang out. This time, the reptilian creature arched her spine, hit in the back by a second draconite projectile. She spun round and saw Saint-Lucq aiming at her with a smoking pistol.

'FLEE!' he yelled to Laincourt. Then, giving the Demoiselle a contemptuous look, he added: 'I'll take care of this bitch.'

Blackened corpses lay on the floor, emitting a faint sound of hot sizzling grease. Only a few scattered puddles of naphtha were still burning. Among the acolytes who had not fled the scene, some drew their swords and went to attack the half-blood. Very coolly, he reversed his pistol with a flick of the wrist and grasped it by the barrel. Then he smashed in a temple, slit a throat, and perforated a heart, eliminating his adversaries in three strokes of lethal precision. The bodies collapsed almost simultaneously. The last hit the ground just as Laincourt gave a last glance backward before disappearing with Clotilde.

Saint-Lucq caught his gaze and nodded.

Foaming from the mouth, the Demoiselle had gone completely berserk. Her jaws yawned open in an uncanny fashion as she screamed at the half-blood and unleashed the full power of her aura. Its impact drove away the last remaining acolytes, who fled in wide-eyed horror, and it even forced some of the mercenaries, who had just arrived hungry for a fight, to beat a hasty retreat.

Saint-Lucq remained where he was. The dragon blood that ran in his veins made him immune to the Demoiselle's influence. Impassive and unimpressed, he raised one eyebrow behind his red spectacles and placed himself *en garde*, his black rapier in his right hand, and his pistol held like a club in his left.

Armed with the two long ritual daggers, the Demoiselle came at Saint-Lucq, her serpentine tail writhing with a scraping noise across the flagstones. A terrible duel began between them. Blows were delivered, parried, deflected, and dodged faster than the eye could see. The steel blades clanked and clashed as if propelled by a life of their own. Concentrating fiercely, the half-blood knew the slightest error would be fatal and that, in addition to the daggers, he needed to be wary of the scaly tail that threatened to knock his legs out from under him. The two adversaries were equal in the swiftness of their reflexes. They seemed to be dancing rather than fighting. They circled one another, striking to right and left, immediately riposting, advancing and retreating, never holding anything back.

And it went on and on.

Finally, Saint-Lucq decided to risk his all. He was tiring. The sweat running into his eyes was hampering him. He had to act.

Lowering his guard, he struck with his pistol, and the blow

broke the Demoiselle's wrist, forcing her to drop one of the daggers. In doing so, he exposed his side. The reaction was immediate: with her second dagger, the creature lacerated his flank. But his trap was nevertheless in place. For anyone else but Saint-Lucq would have backed off at this point, but he did not.

Instead, he promptly riposted.

And planted his rapier to the hilt in the Demoiselle's belly.

The creature froze, gurgling, transfixed by pain and horror.

Pressed up to his enemy, Saint-Lucq also waited without moving. At last, as he felt the Demoiselle growing heavier and heavier against him, he slowly turned the blade running through the body, jerked it up sharply while holding on to his victim, and pushed the creature away as he backed off.

The Demoiselle remained standing for a moment, heaped entrails falling from the gaping wound in her abdomen and hitting the floor with a flaccid noise. Then she collapsed and, giving a long strident cry, convulsed frenetically until death finally had its way.

A final shiver ran through the scaly tail.

Saint-Lucq looked at the body before slipping his pistol into his belt. Then, rapier in one fist, holding his side with the other hand, he left.

Saint-Lucq escaped without encountering any more resistance and discovered a city in distress as fires ravaged its buildings and its frightened inhabitants sought to flee. Suffering more than he wanted to admit, he leaned against a wall. He was on rue Saint-Honoré, at the entrance to rue Gaillon. The hand pressed to his flank was sticky with blood.

'Saint-Lucq!'

It was Laincourt coming back for him.

Looking very pale, Saint-Lucq straightened up.

'The girl?' he asked.

'In safety. I entrusted her to the Capuchin monks on rue Saint-Honoré.'

'Good.'

'La Malicorne?'

'Dead.'

'You're wounded.'

'I can manage.'

'Let me see.'

'I can manage!' Then, settling down a little, the half-blood added: 'We need to get to Notre-Dame. That's where everything will be decided. And I'm willing to wager that's where La Fargue will be too.'

Laincourt nodded but watched the frantic scene in rue Saint-Honoré with a worried eye. A burning house nearby fell down, throwing up great incandescent plumes and prompting cries of terror. Men and beasts knocked into one another as they scrambled away from the raining debris. Saint-Lucq understood the reason for the young man's anxiety and, with his finger, he pointed to the Gaget Messenger Service's tower.

From the Hôtel des Arcanes, the Heresiarch strove to control the Primordial. He would have preferred to ignore the armed Chatelaines that were harassing them in the air, but the great black dragon wanted to finish off the unbearable white winged creatures. They attacked it and then flitted away, sometimes inflicting a brief, stinging pain that increased its anger. The Heresiarch could not do anything about this. He was seeing the world through the eyes of the Primordial. He guided it. But he could not act against its instincts. Indeed, he ran a great risk of losing himself within the primitive meanders of the Primordial's intelligence, of being taken over by its brutal emotions and primal impulses.

It was intoxicating to be nothing more than sheer, unbridled force.

Numerous louves had already perished. Others had been forced to retreat on wounded or exhausted wyverns. Only a few remained to divert the Primordial's fury. Without them, Paris would have been one immense inferno by now, but their sacrifice had only postponed the inevitable. They would not be able keep this up much longer.

There was a jolt.

A psychic blow struck the Heresiarch just as a searing pain blinded the Primordial. The mind of the Arcana's master tottered. Dazed, he needed a moment to recover and restore the link, but he managed it . . .

. . . just before another jolt shook him again.

A drop of blood ran from his nostril.

When the great tenor bell, called the *bourdon*, of Notre-Dame tolled for the second time, once again it seemed as if the Primordial had been hit full on by a cannon ball. Driven back by the impact of the sound, the giant dragon only regained mastery of its flight after some contortions and roars. The pain faded as the deep, low-pitched note of the enormous bell diminished in the night, but the Primordial did not repeat its original mistake: it remained a safe distance away from the cathedral.

In the streets of the capital, this small victory over the dragon was celebrated with cheers of joy. But beneath the tall archways of the Grande Galerie of Notre-Dame, La Fargue asked:

'What now? Because we won't be able to stave this monster off forever, will we?'

'No,' replied the White Wolves' mother superior without taking her eyes off the great black dragon as it soared in the distance. 'No, we won't.'

The Ordeal had come to an end and there was no more time for waiting and hoping.

'Open it,' said Mère Thérèse de Vaussambre in the silence of the crypt.

A massive door stood before her.

Solemn, two Chatelaines seized hold of the rings of the heavy twin panels, turned them, and then pulled.

Slowly the door opened, without a sound, and let the light enter within.

Standing, head bowed, Agnès de Vaudreuil held something against her chest, hidden in the shell of her hands.

'Are you a louve?' asked the Superior General of the Chatelaines.

As her sole response, Agnès lifted a grave face and extended her joined hands, revealing an empty and translucent Sphère d'Âme.

In Valombre's house, Marciac climbed the secret staircase wiping his brow and rejoined Alessandra, who was observing the sky from a window. He had carefully sutured the dragon's wound and placed a makeshift splint on his broken leg.

'Well?'

'I don't see the Primordial anymore,' replied La Donna. 'It seems as though the sound of the bell at Notre-Dame is forcing it to keep its distance.'

The bourdon of Notre-Dame was indeed continuing to toll in a slow but steady rhythm.

'We must have the Chatelaines to thank for that. This must be what they were preparing earlier,' added the Gascon.

He recalled that when Alessandra and he had passed in front of Notre-Dame on their way to Valombre's home, the cathedral had been lit up and occupied by the Sisters of Saint Georges.

'Except that the dragon had not yet shown itself,' objected the young woman. 'But since the Chatelaines were certainly not there by chance, they no doubt had good reasons to believe the Primordial would strike tonight. And they were preparing for it.'

'How could they have known?'

'As for that . . .'

La Donna shrugged her shoulders, pensive. Then she turned away from the window to look at Marciac. The moonlight shone on her pretty profile and scattered silver in her red hair.

'How is Valombre doing?'

'He's sleeping. Or has fainted again. In his state, it's more or less the same thing . . . But even though he's lost a lot of blood, he'll live. Of course, he'd be better off in his bed, but I don't feel strong enough to carry him up on my back . . . Be that as it may, if you hadn't been so concerned about him, he'd be dead by now.'

While Alessandra went down to be at the patient's side, Marciac went into the kitchen to search for something to drink and a moment of calm. He found an open bottle of wine that he drained in three gulps from the neck and was starting to feel a little more at ease when he heard cries, noises, and savage laughter outside.

Intrigued, he went to have a look out one of the windows, and swore.

Bands of dracs were leaving Les Écailles across the crude wooden bridges that linked their island to the two banks of Paris, but also over the rickety and almost forgotten footbridge that led to the canons' neighbourhood, at the end of the Ile de la Cité. And even on boats, some of which capsized and went adrift, carried off by the current.

They were drunk, excited by the fires, exasperated by the din of the tocsin, exalted by the spectacle offered to them by the great black dragon in the sky. Above all, most of them were plunged into a state of madness engendered by the Arcana's wine and the drug that the Enchantress had added to it, in accordance with the Heresiarch's plans. A temporary madness, true. But a madness that blinded them, woke their warrior spirit, and revived their taste for blood. They felt a need to kill and to destroy, carry out acts of violence and satisfy their vile impulses. They brandished weapons and torches, howled war cries, burst into peals of cruel laughter.

In the Cloister neighbourhood of Notre-Dame, the pillage of the first houses in rue du Chapitre began as Marciac looked out onto the street.

Alessandra had slipped a cushion beneath Valombre's head. Sitting on the floor by the dragon in the small secret room, she heard the Gascon running down the stairs and stood up, alarmed.

'What's going on?'

'We have to go. Come.'

'Why?'

'The dracs are attacking. They're arriving from Les Écailles and plundering the neighbourhood. It's a question of minutes before they break down the door.'

'The dracs are attacking? But that's impossible!'

'Well, you can tell them that in a minute. Come on.'

He tried to grab her hand, but she would not let him.

'We can't abandon Valombre here.'

'We don't have a choice, Alessandra.'

'I won't abandon him!'

'Alessandra!'

'I'm staying here!'

Marciac cursed but refrained from commenting on the stubbornness of women. He needed to think fast and well. Of course, he could lock all three of them in here and pray that the dracs did not find the hidden staircase. But if he and La Donna had found it, why shouldn't they? And even if the looters lacked the patience to find the mechanism for opening the passage, they still had the solution of breaking in. The winged dracs who had tried to assassinate Valombre were short of time and could not make too much noise for fear of alerting the neighbours. The dracs who were coming now could do as they pleased.

'All right,' the Gascon said resignedly. 'Stay here. I'll do what I can.'

'You are leaving us?'

'I must.'

He went back up to the ground floor after waving goodbye to Alessandra, closed the iron door first and then the sliding wooden panel.

Torchlight danced behind the window panes.

Bracing himself against a large and heavy cupboard in the corridor, Marciac succeeded in dislodging it, and then pushed it against the wall with the secret passage. There he had to turn it before putting it into place. The front door of the house was already shaking from the thuds of boots. Huffing and straining, he finished the job, but exhausted, he could only check the general effect achieved: Alessandra and Valombre should be safe as long as no one thought of moving the cupboard.

Marciac left through the rear garden just as the front door gave way.

He climbed over a wall, jumped down into an alley, and in rue Chanoinesse, saw people fleeing in the direction of Notre-Dame cathedral. Dracs were breaking down the doors of the last dwellings in rue de Chapitre. Bodies were being thrown through windows to crash bloody on the paving stones. Man, woman, child, or priest, no one was spared. It would soon be the turn of the small rue des Chantres.

Marciac knew that he could not do much, except to hurry stragglers along and urge as many people as possible to flee. But there were many residents huddled up in their dwellings out of fear of the Primordial, and who were completely unaware of the new danger that threatened them. So the Gascon knocked on doors and window panes, yelling vainly over the din from the bourdon of Notre-Dame and the thousand other bells of Paris that were sounding the tocsin. Enraged by his helplessness, he thought he glimpsed a movement through a window of a house, broke down the door with a great kick, entered, and called out, warning those inside of the great danger they were in.

A small door inched open beneath the stairway and a frightened man passed his head out through the gap.

'You must leave, monsieur!' Marciac told him. 'You are not safe here!'

'But . . .'

'Are you alone?'

'No. With my wife . . . and . . . and my children. In the cellar.'

'Then they must make haste or all of you will die!' the Gascon ordered. 'And me with you,' he muttered to himself.

When he returned, the man was carrying a three-year-old boy and held a little girl by the hand. His wife followed him. She was eight months with child and had difficulty walking, breathing heavily. Marciac helped her pass through the low door.

The sound of breaking glass came from the kitchen, on the garden side of the house.

'What was that?' asked the woman in alarm.

'Quickly!' said the Gascon in a low voice.

But the little girl screamed: a grey drac marauder had just entered the room.

'Flee!' shouted Marciac. 'To Notre-Dame! Go!'

And drawing his rapier, he placed himself *en garde* while the couple and their two children escaped out into the street.

The grey drac also unsheathed his sword, and was immediately joined by another drac – this one black – who already had a sword in his fist. They advanced. Marciac retreated, overturning a table back against a wall so that it would not hamper him. The black drac was chuckling uncontrollably and his eyes, in the dimness, shone with an insane glow. The grey drac had a slightly unsteady step, but nothing more. With a kick, Marciac slid a stool towards the black drac who easily avoided it and chuckled even harder. No luck. The two dracs spread out, with the intention of obliging their adversary to fight on two fronts. Seeing this, the Gascon started to look truly worried. His guard position began to waver and the grey drac sneered . . .

At least until Marciac reached his left hand behind his back, suddenly brandished a pistol and opened fire. The drac tumbled over backward, hit in the middle of the brow. Astonished, the black drac reacted too late: the Gascon had already lunged at full stretch and planted the point of his rapier in the invader's heart.

Withdrawing his sword and backing up, Marciac looked at the two corpses.

Not a very honourable way to fight, but it was effective.

Without giving it further thought, he came out on the threshold of the house and saw that Black Guards were taking up position in the street while others were protecting the survivors' flight, aiding those who had difficulty walking, carrying those who couldn't. They were just in time: dracs were arriving from rue Chanoinesse and were immediately routed by a volley of musket fire.

Marciac recognised the officer commanding the guards.

'Leprat!'

'Marciac!'

The two men exchanged greetings.

Reynault had entrusted Leprat with keeping watch at the northern entrance to the cathedral: the Cloister portal. Realising what was happening in the canons' neighbourhood, the musketeer had decided to go to the assistance of all those who could still be saved.

'Where is La Fargue?' asked the Gascon.

'At Notre-Dame.'

'What's going on there?'

'The Chatelaines are praying, thanks to which the bell of Notre-Dame is keeping the Primordial at bay. But don't ask me any more than that. I don't understand these matters myself . . . And La Donna?'

Marciac had no time to reply.

Other dracs were arriving, with Keress Karn at their head. Neither Leprat nor Marciac knew his name, but they recognised him as the red drac who had led the assault on the Château de Mareuil-sur-Ay, when Alessandra had been abducted.

That could not be a coincidence.

Leprat gave the order to retreat and the guards abandoned the small rue des Chantres, slowly, to allow the refugees time to reach the cathedral. But then the dracs charged and furious hand-to-hand combat broke out alongside Notre-Dame, the guards falling back in good order towards the Cloister portal, where the last fugitives from the canons' neighbourhood were now jostling their way inside. Disciplined, courageous, and fighting every inch of the way, the Black Guards formed an arc in front of the portal, which gradually tightened as the survivors entered the cathedral.

Then it was the turn of the wounded, of Marciac and the rest, to enter one by one.

Lastly, Leprat and a few others retreated together into the cathedral, just as the heavy doors of the portal were closed behind them.

The siege of Notre-Dame had begun.

Fanning the night air with great beats of their wings, two saddled wyverns were flying over Paris. Above them, the sky was immense, starry and peaceful, beneath the impassive eye of a beautiful round moon. Below them the city had been thrown into fear and panic, with scenes of violence, stampedes towards the city gates, and outbreaks of rioting all across the capital. Fires burned everywhere the dragon's breath had struck. And they were spreading, flames rising with a roar like greedy, furious monsters.

His bruised face caressed by the wind, Laincourt guided his wyvern, trying not to be overcome by emotion. Or rather, by all of the emotions that were thrashing about inside him: hatred, anger, fear, revolt. He held tightly to the reins of his anxious mount and followed Saint-Lucq who was flying ahead, just as he had followed him to the Gaget Messenger Services, where the half-blood had requisitioned the two wyverns. After a few heavy, lumbering steps in the courtyard, the reptiles had taken flight. They were now carrying the two men towards Notre-Dame, whose song reached through the clouds of smoke and set off a low vibration that stirred in their guts.

Stone-faced, Saint-Lucq did not take his eyes from the twin towers of the sacred citadel.

That's where everything will be decided, he had said to Laincourt.

Everything.

Looking livid and tense, his long hair floating over his shoulders, the half-blood held his wounded flank with one hand as the glow from the great blazes below were reflected in the red lenses of his spectacles.

La Fargue and Mère Béatrice d'Aussaint had climbed to the top of the south tower of Notre-Dame, the one housing the bourdon, which – slow, low-pitched and steady – continued to ring out its protective toll.

From this terrace, exposed to the winds sixty metres from the ground, they saw the drac bands that had left Les Écailles and were now engaged in wild pillaging, starting with the Saint-Paul quay on the Right Bank, La Tournelle quay on the Left Bank, and the nearby Cloister. The mother superior of the White Wolves had sent messengers to the Louvre, the Bastille, and the Arsenal, where troops were garrisoned, alerting them to the situation. But even those who were not already mobilised to fight the fires would not be able to intervene in time. At present, the dracs were encountering no resistance and could carry out their atrocities with complete impunity, terrorising a defenceless population. Already plundered, most of the Cloister neighbourhood had been set alight and the rest of the Ile de la Cité was now under threat. Under the orders of Reynault d'Ombreuse, the company of the Black Guards was preparing to defend Notre-Dame's western forecourt. The Cloister gate on the north side of the cathedral had already been subjected to an assault by the dracs.

'Nothing will have been spared us,' said Mère d'Aussaint. 'Just when we repelled the Primordial, the riot started in Les Écailles and now we have to defend Notre-Dame itself.'

The great black dragon passed in the distance: its wide circles still keeping it well away from the cathedral bell tower. But it had not given up.

On the contrary, it appeared to be waiting.

'These riots have started just in time to suit our enemies,' said La Fargue. 'I don't know how, but the Arcana are behind them. Moreover, the dracs who attacked the Cloister portal and continue to besiege it are all well-disciplined mercenaries who are obviously following orders.'

'Orders to interrupt, at any cost, the ritual taking place inside Notre-Dame. Without it, the bell will toll in vain.'

'I agree,' replied the Blades' captain turning round. 'Perhaps you should shift some of the guards defending the forecourt and . . . Look out!'

La Fargue leapt and pinned Mère d'Aussaint to the ground as a winged drac flew past, delivering a mighty sword stroke to the empty air. As they picked themselves up and unsheathed their own weapons, five dracs landed on the terrace and, rapiers already in fists, tucked in their leathery wings.

Back to back, La Fargue and the White Wolves' mother superior placed themselves *en garde*, waiting for the dracs to make their move.

'They want to reach the bell tower,' said the Chatelaine. 'If the bell ceases to toll—'

The winged dracs attacked.

Inside Notre-Dame, as the besieged Cloister portal was being closed, the Black Guards had been quick to lead the escapees across the transept, and then made them leave by the Saint-Étienne door to seek refuge in the adjoining episcopal palace. Some of them wanted to remain under the double protection of the cathedral and the Sisters of Saint Georges, but the guards were adamant: the tranquillity of the Chatelaines at prayer had to be preserved as much as possible. Kneeling in the choir behind the high altar, the sisters had been praying for hours, their murmur haunting the empty space of the immense nave. Their fervour was such that the air seemed to vibrate, as if traversed by echoes between the slow, grave peals of the bourdon. But they were growing exhausted, to the point that some had fainted and had to be carried away.

Nevertheless they were still managing to hold firm.

As long as they prayed and the bell of Notre-Dame continued to sound, the Primordial would be forced to keep its distance from Paris.

Joining Leprat near the Cloister portal, Marciac saw his friend succumb to a bout of weakness that he alone noticed. The musketeer's legs suddenly gave way beneath him and he had to lean on a pillar to disguise his weakness. His face was pale, however, and his jaws clenched as he tried not to grimace.

Marciac took Leprat by the elbow in a gesture that might seem merely friendly, but supported the musketeer's weight as he drew him aside, beneath the first arches of the ambulatory.

'What's wrong with you?' the Gascon asked in a low voice.

'Nothing. I . . . I'm just tired.'

'Pull the other one. It's the ranse, isn't it?'

Leprat sighed. Looked away. Nodded.

Marciac understood what was happening to his friend.

'It's the ritual, it's hostile to dragons,' he said. 'It threatens your ranse which is defending itself and eating away at you. It will kill you if you stay here!'

'And where do you suggest I go? To the Hôtel-Dieu hospital next door?'

'No, Antoine, no one is asking you to—'

'At this hour, my place is here, Nicolas. Here, and nowhere else.'

Irritated, the Gascon turned away.

'Anyway,' added Leprat in a jesting tone, 'don't you think I have more to fear from a drac's sword than from the ranse, if I stay here? And so do you, by the way . . .'

Marciac did not reply.

They were near the Red portal, which owed its name to the colour of its panels. Much smaller than the Cloister portal, it gave the canons direct access to the choir. The Black Guards had barricaded it rather than defend it.

A wisp of smoke was rising from beneath it.

When he saw it, Marciac thought – too late – of the mines that had blown away the gates at Château de Mareuil.

'Down!' he yelled, pushing Leprat behind a pillar.

The blast threw the Gascon into the air.

He fell back heavily on the flagstones and, covered in dust and with blood dripping from his nostrils, he tried to get up. A high-pitched whistling filled his ears and the thump of his own heartbeat was deafening, but any sounds from outside his body were muffled. His vision was clouded and the ground beneath him seemed to sway and rock, making him dizzy. His legs like jelly, he stood with the help of a pillar and then almost slipped back to the ground. In a great blur, he saw armed dracs entering Notre-Dame through the demolished Red portal. He also recognised Leprat, advancing towards them. The mine's explosion had not spared the musketeer. His step was unsteady. He struggled to remain standing and drew his white rapier with a far too expansive gesture, like that of a drunken man. Combat was engaged as Black Guards came to the rescue. One of them jostled Marciac as he ran by.

The Gascon tripped and caught himself the best he could. The sounds of the fighting came to him from a distance, in a distorted form. For him, seconds stretched out in slow motion. He straightened, saw Leprat brandishing his sword with two hands in the midst of a confused mêlée, taking large swings with it. The musketeer was possessed by a warrior's fury. He had already taken several wounds without yielding ground and he continued to strike to the right, to the left, and to strike over and over again. Marciac wanted to come to his aid. He tried to unsheathe his rapier, took a step, then two, three, but was overcome by dizziness and fell to one knee. The immense lines of perspective within the cathedral danced, blurred, and separated above him.

Gathering his wits, he searched for Leprat . . .

And suddenly there was a great silence.

Suddenly his ears stopped buzzing and his heart stopped beating.

Suddenly icy terror stamped in his memory an image that would never leave him: Leprat had a blade planted up to the hilt in his belly and was vomiting up blood.

On the roof of the south tower, La Fargue and Mère Béatrice d'Aussaint had slain one winged drac apiece. Three remained, two of which joined forces against the captain of the Blades. Striking, parrying, riposting, at one corner of the terrace he defended the turret which housed the stairway leading to the belfry. They needed at all costs to prevent the dracs from reaching it and stopping the slow peals of the bourdon. Evading one clumsy cut, La Fargue passed beneath the guard of one of his adversaries and found the drac's chest. Then he broke off to avoid the thrust of the second drac, engaged his blade, pushed it away from the line of his body and – obeying old reflexes – projected the reptilian's body into thin air with a strong kick to the abdomen. But the creature simply deployed his wings and immediately returned to the fray, while La Fargue cursed. The drac had barely managed to set one foot back on the terrace, however, when he was struck by a pistol ball right in the middle of his forehead. It was a service rendered by the mother superior to the captain, just after she had disposed of the third drac she had been confronting alone.

'Quickly!' she said before dashing into the turret, smoking pistol in one hand and her rapier in the other.

Notre-Dame itself was under threat.

All up and down the front of the cathedral, Black Guards and louves were now desperately resisting the enemy: on the forecourt before the main façade's three portals; in the twin recesses of the gallery of the Virgin; beneath the archways of the Grande Galerie where a number of winged dracs had landed, and even on the walkway that ran across the top of the upper gallery, linking the two main towers.

La Fargue followed the mother superior and closed the door of the turret behind them, pushing the bolts home. Then they dashed down the narrow spiral staircase inside the tower housing Notre-Dame's enormous bourdon bell and the magnificent wooden frame from which it was suspended. At the bottom, a small door opened and a winged drac entered. Surprised, Mère d'Aussaint took a sword blow and backed away. La Fargue leapt to her rescue, split the drac's skull open, and pushed him back outside. But others were arriving just as the bourdon gave a deafening peal. The captain rushed towards them and forced them back along the Grande Galerie.

'Close the door!' he shouted to the leader of the White Wolves.

Mère d'Aussaint, one hand pressed over her wound, shut the door behind La Fargue, stranding him alone on the gallery. He was condemned to do or die, but the vital task now was to protect the bourdon.

Inside the cathedral, in the furious fighting between dracs and Black Guards near the remains of the Red portal, Marciac rushed towards Keress Karn as the red drac, with evil glee on his face, pulled his blade from Leprat's body. The Gascon struck with fearsome power, forcing Karn to parry and back away. But then the drac recovered and, while not managing to gain the upper hand, he ceased to retreat before the Blade's assault.

A bitter duel began.

Attacks were met with parries. Counters were followed by ripostes. The red drac knew how to fight and kept a cool head. His fencing was the kind learned on the battlefield: effective and without flourishes. Tense and focused, Marciac realised they were evenly matched. So he thought of Leprat and, careful not to let himself be blinded by anger, he drew renewed strength from the memory. His arm became the instrument of vengeance. His strokes were powerful, precise and formidable, and Karn started to grow worried. He wanted to call for help, but their confrontation had taken the two adversaries far up the ambulatory, away from the main mêlée. The red drac could do no more than defend himself. And while his moves became more and more frantic, but less and less accurate, the Gascon's never varied in their effectiveness.

At last, Marciac knew the moment had come.

Twisting Karn's blade with his own, he sent it flying away and, body stretched, he slipped the point of his sword beneath the disarmed drac's chin. Then he plunged his gaze into that of his vanquished enemy and, brusquely pushing his shoulder forward, sank two good inches of steel into the drac's throat. Keress Karn tossed his head backward and stumbled, his hand against his wound, unable to staunch the thick, heavy blood spurting out.

The Gascon watched him fall and die.

La Fargue rapidly took stock of the situation: it was not to his advantage. The dracs had taken control of the Grande Galerie and a handful of Black Guards were now retreating into the north tower. There was no one left on the side of the south tower, other than a few dead bodies and himself.

The captain of the Blades placed himself *en garde* with his back to the door, determined to sell his life dearly. He held the grip of his sword with both hands. Glared at the dracs approaching him. Took a deep breath.

And charged with a warlike scream.

He stunned the first drac with a violent blow, felled another by smashing the guard of his sword beneath his chin, brought his Pappenheimer down on a skull to the right, on a shoulder to the left, and into a belly straight ahead of him. He had taken his adversaries by surprise but their riposte was not long in coming. He was forced to parry various attacks by cut and thrust, received a wound to the arm which he did not feel in the heat of battle, followed by a blow to the head that left him stunned for an instant. He retreated, delivered two killing thrusts of his own, and then felt a pain in his thigh and a burning in his side. He withdrew again, still battling away, and felt his back bump into the tower door. At which point he knew that his moments were numbered. He squared up to his enemies, nevertheless, breathless but standing firm, his eyes sparkling and his face spattered with drops of blood.

Ready to meet his end.

Yet the dracs hesitated. The final stroke did not come.

The battle had turned in favour of the defenders inside Notre-Dame. The dracs sensed it and didn't know what to do. The fighting had already ceased out on the forecourt. Winged dracs were launching themselves into the air from the gallery of the Virgin as Black Guards arrived by way of the north tower. Pistol shots rang out, fired at the indecisive dracs in the Grande Galerie. This threat persuaded them that safety lay in flight and those who could jumped over the side and flew for safety. The others fell before pistol balls or to the swords of the guards who retook control of the gallery.

Victory seeming assured, La Fargue let himself slump down the door he had defended so well and sat on the ground, exhausted, his head bowed and his wrists resting on his raised knees.

Soon, someone approached him.

'Happy to see you again, captain.'

It was Laincourt, with a bruised face and a bloodied rapier in his fist. Even more surprising, Saint-Lucq was just behind him, busy turning over drac bodies and planting his sword in their hearts. Their borrowed wyverns had landed on the north tower of the cathedral and they had helped defend it until the counterattack came from the Saint Georges Guards.

Accepting the hand that the young man held out to him, La Fargue got up with a grim face.

'Are you wounded, captain?'

'Nothing serious. But you're a sorry sight, Laincourt.'

'La Malicorne did me an evil turn. If not for Saint-Lucq, I'd be either dead or praying I was, right now.'

La Fargue turned to the half-blood, who was gazing at him. They exchanged nods. The one said: *Thank you for being here.* And the other: *You're welcome.*

'What are your orders, captain?'

His answer was lost as the Primordial bellowed, suddenly very near.

Marciac returned to the Red portal and its corpse-strewn rubble. Having successfully defended the forecourt of Notre-Dame, Reynault had retreated back inside the cathedral. This allowed him to send a portion of his troops into the towers to retake the galleries, but also to send some of them to rescue those defending the Red portal. And so Karn's dracs were defeated and repelled. Nevertheless, the explosion of their mine and the subsequent assault had achieved the desired effect: interrupting the prayer of the Chatelaines gathered in the choir and ending the ritual that allowed the Notre-Dame bell to keep the Primordial at bay.

The defenders had won a bitter victory, then. And one which announced certain disaster.

But Marciac cared nothing for any of that.

Kneeling, he gently lifted Leprat's head and the musketeer opened his eyes slightly.

'It . . . It hurts less than . . . than it usually does,' he said in a weak, hoarse voice. 'That . . . That means it's serious doesn't it?'

The Gascon did not know what to reply.

Brushing the hair, now sticky with sweat and blood, out of his friend's eyes, he nodded and tried to smile.

'DRAGON!'

Not everyone had the reflex to dive for cover when the cry rang out.

Swooping between the twin towers of Notre-Dame, the Primordial belched fire over the Grande Galerie, taking the Black Guards by surprise. Many were set ablaze and men tumbled over the walls, screaming.

'Good God!' swore La Fargue. 'But how . . . ?'

He stood up and, incredulous, looked at the dragon now making a large loop above the Ile de la Cité. The bell still tolled, but did not seem to bother the giant creature. Evidently, the Chatelaines' magic was no longer working.

Which meant the cathedral was doomed.

'Inside!' ordered the captain of the Blades. 'Everybody inside, quickly!'

The Primordial was already coming back.

Taking their wounded with them, the guards retreated into the towers. La Fargue, Laincourt, and Saint-Lucq did the same, the half-blood closing the door at the very moment when, beating its wings slowly and hanging in the air before the Grande Galerie, the dragon sprayed it with a long incandescent burst that incinerated the dead bodies and ate into the stone like acid.

Its work done for now, the Primordial resumed its flight.

The last defenders of Notre-Dame assembled in the nave, around Mère Béatrice d'Aussaint. There were only twenty of them, including the Blades, and most of them were wounded. All of them were exhausted. They had fought, suffered, seen brothers-in-arms fall and they sensed that it had all been in vain.

They had no more doubts when the bell ceased to toll.

The Primordial was triumphant.

'We need to evacuate,' said La Fargue.

'Flee?' asked Reynault d'Ombreuse, offended by the idea.

'The Primordial is going to reduce this cathedral to ashes, and there is nothing you or I can do to prevent it.'

'The captain is right,' agreed the White Wolves' mother superior. 'We must be able to fight other battles.'

A makeshift bandage enveloped her wounded shoulder. She was pale and her features were drawn, but her gaze shone with a fierce determination. Very calmly, she thought and then said:

'We can reach the episcopal palace via the sacristy. It will keep us out of sight of the dragon.'

Reynault nodded and went to give the orders, while the mother superior took hold of La Fargue by the arm and confided:

'If you can, hold here. One hope remains.'

'I know, mother.'

Sure of its victory, the Primordial slowly circled Notre-Dame.

Intoxicated by its own power and restored liberty, it bellowed triumphantly. The Heresiarch no longer dominated it: it was as if he had been washed away, submerged by the simple and brutal emotions that guided the primitive dragon. It could indulge its primary instincts: to fly and to destroy.

The Primordial sent a few playful balls of fire that exploded across Paris, set fire to the windmills on Saint-Roch hill, and amused itself by burning the trees in the Tuileries park. But in the end, it returned to Notre-Dame. It gathered speed, aimed for the great rose-window that adorned the cathedral's main façade and, tucking its wings against its body, smashed through it in an explosion of multicoloured glass, to land heavily inside.

The Blades were waiting on the steps of the choir. La Fargue was in the middle and Laincourt, Saint-Lucq, Marciac, and even Leprat were at his sides, although Leprat, dying, could barely stand and gripped the Gascon's shoulder. They all had their rapiers in hand because they could not imagine, at this hour, perishing any other way.

Intrigued and wary, the enormous black dragon advanced with a slow, heavy step, its feet smashing the flagstones each time they struck the floor, its scaly tail lashing the rubble behind it.

It halted, stretched its neck out and lowered its head, decorated with its distinctive faceted jewel, to examine the five men closely.

The Blades did not make the slightest move.

In the silence, the Primordial's powerful breathing filled the devastated cathedral, sounding like a forge. It spent a long moment observing the pathetic creatures that were blocking its path and giving every appearance of defying it.

In a hoarse voice, it managed with difficulty:

'Wʜ . . . Wʜʏ? . . . Fᴜ . . . ᴛɪʟᴇ . . .'

'Because it is not given to everyone to choose the manner of their death, dragon,' replied La Fargue without blinking.

The idea that a being might sacrifice itself was perfectly foreign to the Primordial. It considered the five men standing before it, as if their attitude obliged it to ponder the necessity of killing them.

And suddenly the dragon turned round and moved away, with a waddle like that of a big lizard, climbed the cathedral's great organ – which it broke beneath its weight – and slithered back outside through the ruined rose-window.

Agnès stood alone on the forecourt littered with the bodies of dracs and men. She was armed and dressed as a White Wolf of Saint Georges: high beige boots whose upper folds covered her knees, lined riding breeches, a slit robe, a heavy belt that cinched her waist, ample sleeves, thick gloves, a wimple which framed her face in an oval, and a veil. She bore the cross and dragon of her order over her heart, but where the dragon was embroidered in black on the uniforms of other louves, hers was scarlet. She had drawn her sword, which she held point down, slightly apart from her body. The blade and the pommel of her sword were made of gleaming black draconite.

There she waited.

Behind her the small church of Saint-Christophe was burning.

The Primordial examined Agnès carefully without coming too near. It was uneasy. Recent experience had taught it to be wary of louves, but this one was different. It sensed an immense, extraordinary power inside her. A power that was perhaps superior to its own, although such power could not possibly inhabit a puny, frail body such as the one it saw before it.

It sensed the power of an Ancestral Dragon.

The great black dragon bellowed, and the louve did not react in the slightest.

And then it leapt.

Agnès immediately plunged forward in a roll as the dragon passed over her, and came up with her sword to slit its belly open. The draconite blade sliced cleanly through the scales and into the flesh beneath, which sputtered as if eaten by acid. Agnès stood and turned. The Primordial also spun round brusquely, with a powerful heave of its muscles. They stared at one another again, but now the louve had her back to the cathedral. The dragon was in pain. Furious, it crouched down, bellowed once more, and belched.

In a single movement, Agnès put one knee to the ground and turned her blade point down. Eyes closed, she was already praying when the flames reached her, and they parted around her like waves before the prow of a ship. The dragon persevered, breathing out a river of screaming, turbulent flames. The air itself seemed to catch fire. The corpses around her were devoured by this furnace and turned to piles of ashes that were immediately swept away. The paving stones blackened, then glowed red with the heat, and shattered. The flames striking Notre-Dame's façade rolled over the stone and exploded like the crash of fiery surf on a rocky shore.

But it was to no avail.

Exasperated and tired, the Primordial gave up. It ceased belching fire and watched the louve stand up unharmed, while the cathedral doors burned behind her. Agnès raised her eyes and looked deep into the terrifying and abysmal gaze of the archaic dragon.

It understood that she felt no fear and gave a long, mournful growl.

'Now it's my turn,' said the louve.

Abruptly spreading her arms, she cried out words of power and the air vibrated and crackled around her.

Discharges of energy shot forth around her as a white form

detached itself from her body, a white form that grew and grew, becoming immense. She was liberating her spectral dragon, summoning its power. And it reared up and deployed its wings before the increasingly frightened, mesmerised Primordial. In a trance, her arms outstretched to either side and her head tilted back, Agnès began to levitate as sparks of light whirled around her, as gusts of wind whipped her sleeves and the flaps of her robe, as the night tore open and a low roar swelled in volume . . .

And this time it was the Ancestral Dragon who belched flame.

A white fire descended upon the Primordial and submerged it in a dazzling inferno. The black dragon struggled but could not escape the blast. In its violent contortions, it smashed in the façade of one of the houses bordering the forecourt, causing the building to collapse, and with a mighty swipe of its tail it completed the destruction of the Saint-Christophe church. It screamed and moaned, a prisoner of the torments inflicted upon it by the sacred fire. And suddenly it arched its back and remained still, for the brief second it took for the jewel on its brow to explode into pieces.

The Primordial's lifeless body collapsed with a final, heavy thud.

Alone in the magic study at the Hôtel des Arcanes, the Heresiarch slumped on his back, his gaze staring and wide, and his brow split by a deep wound. Black blood ran from his nostrils and ears as he breathed his last.

All was quiet and still again on the Notre-Dame forecourt.

Agnès re-sheathed her sword.

Then, turning away from the smoking body of the Primordial she entered the cathedral through the central portal whose doors had been completely consumed by the flames, crossed the silent, devastated nave with a calm step, and found La Fargue and the others beneath the cross of the transept.

Grave, silent and still, they had gathered around Leprat who lay dead on the steps to the choir.

3

With the dawn came a fine, fresh rain.

It did little to fight the fires, but it was as though a soothing balm had been applied to the wounds of Paris. The population wanted to see it as a sign, welcoming it with hope and gratitude. Having rung a sinister tocsin the entire night, some church bells celebrated the shower with more joyful chimes.

It was still raining when Agnès found La Fargue in the courtyard of the Hôtel de l'Épervier, which had been reduced to charred and smoking ruins. The captain stared at the wreckage without really seeing it, but did not turn away when he heard Agnès approach on horseback and dismount.

'Naïs has turned in her apron,' he said tonelessly. 'André was seriously burned while saving the horses. And Guibot is dead, and buried somewhere underneath this rubble.'

The louve crossed herself.

'Paris is saved,' she said. 'Order will soon be restored in the city and we'll rebuild.'

'But the dead won't come back to life, will they?'

Agnès did not reply.

A silence settled over them.

La Fargue had not washed or changed his clothes since the night's battle. His clothing was encrusted with dirt and blood, and his face was smudged with soot. His head was bare and his wrinkles had deepened.

'What have you come to tell me, Agnès?' he asked.

'The truth. You deserve to know. The Blades have paid a heavy enough price for it . . .'

'I'm listening.'

'The Arcana's Grand Design was to seat a dragon on the throne of France. A dragon who would be born to the queen, thanks to a draconic seed planted within her, without her knowledge. They did it when she still the *infanta* of Spain, after she was promised to Louis XIII.'

'A draconic seed?'

'Her physician was a member of the Arcana. When she manifested the initial symptoms of the ranse, he performed various rituals which saved her. But he also used the opportunity to ensure that any children she carried would be transformed, becoming dragons.'

'This member of the Arcana, it was the Heresiarch.'

'Yes.'

'But weren't the Chatelaines supposed to prevent such things from happening? And besides, didn't they subject the queen to tests? Such scrupulous ones that she still nurses an enduring grudge against them?'

'Yes, indeed. But they failed to detect this seed, and when they finally realised their error, it was too late. They could not acknowledge their mistake without discrediting themselves. And what a scandal it would have created! What an insult to Spain! What a humiliation for France! It was lucky that the queen had not yet given birth to a child.'

'So the Chatelaines kept silent. And what else did they do, other than protect their secret?'

'Whatever they could . . .'

La Fargue frowned and then he understood.

'They encouraged the king's disenchantment with the queen?'

'They provoked it with certain powders.'

'And the queen's miscarriages?'

'Those children's births had to be prevented at all costs, captain. And each time, when they were examined, they revealed that the draconic transformation had begun . . .'

'The king, the queen, the cardinal, none of them know of this?'

'The cardinal knows.'

La Fargue kept silent, thinking, considering certain

mysteries in a new light. Such as the fertility ritual the Alchemist had wanted the queen to undergo, no doubt to counter the Chatelaines' manoeuvres and allow her to give birth to a child. And the assassination of Henri IV, which La Donna had told him was the Arcana's work: unlike his wife, the good king Henri had firmly opposed a marriage between his son and the *infanta* . . .

'And now?' asked the captain of the Blades. 'The Chatelaines can't deprive France of an heir forever . . . Are you going to bring about the repudiation of the queen?'

Agnès hesitated.

'We will find a solution. Perhaps we will have to be content with second-best.'

Second-best? La Fargue wondered.

Only to realise that he couldn't care less what their second-best solution was. There was almost nothing he could care about now . . . except, beneath his shirt, the leather wallet Pontevedra had given him. It contained documents about his daughter's disappearance who, to regain her freedom, had escaped the Guardians' surveillance and fled.

La Fargue had sworn to find her again.

'I have decided to move Ballardieu's body,' announced Agnès suddenly. 'I will dig him a grave at Vaudreuil, at the bottom of the garden, under a tree by the river. He liked to rest there.'

'That would please him,' said the captain. A memory came back to him. 'One day, when Ballardieu had been drinking . . .'

'Yes,' said the young woman ironically, but giving a sad smile. 'I remember that day . . .'

'One day, when he had been drinking,' continued La Fargue, 'Ballardieu told me he had spent the happiest years of his life at Vaudreuil, with you. Indeed, he made no mystery of the fact.'

Sœur Marie-Agnès de Vaudreuil nodded.

With a heavy heart and tears in her eyes, she turned to leave, leading her horse by the bridle.

'Goodbye, Agnès.'
'Goodbye, captain.'

The Gentleman and the Enchantress watched Paris from the heights of the village of Montmartre, seated on horseback and draped in large cloaks that protected them from the rain. Flames still danced here and there in the city, but mostly they could see thick columns of black smoke rising toward the low sky. After the riots, order had still not been completely restored in the capital. Refusing to lay down their weapons, the renegade dracs had built barricades which companies of the Gardes-Françaises were seizing and dismantling one by one. Drac corpses hung from every gallows in the city. And it would be unwise for those dracs remaining to leave Les Écailles for quite some time . . .

'Will we ever come back?' asked the Enchantress.

'I am sure of it.'

Laincourt brought Clotilde back home but did not stay to watch her tearful reunion with her father. As soon as the girl found refuge in her father's arms, he withdrew.

You'll miss them, won't you? said the hurdy-gurdy player walking beside of the young man.

Yes.

You can always write to them.

It would be best if they forgot all about me.

And me?

I know you're never going to leave me.

Having found La Donna and Valombre safe and sound, Marciac went to rue Grenouillère. A few houses had burned there and Gabrielle, with her frogs, was helping the owners recover anything that could be salvaged from the rubble.

Gabrielle abandoned her task when she saw the Gascon approaching. Smiling and almost crying, she walked towards him, then hurried and ran to throw herself in his arms, before breaking into gentle sobs.

'I love you,' she murmured, embracing him with all her might. 'Oh, how I love you . . .'

He smiled, exhausted but happy, and breathed in the fragrance of her hair.

'Tell me again about this estate in Touraine,' he said. 'And tell me again about this child you are carrying. I want to know what my life is going to be like.'

The next day the king returned to Paris by coach, so that he could show himself to his people and reassure them. On the way he asked:

'What was the name of that captain again?'

'La Fargue, Sire,' replied Cardinal Richelieu.

'We will have to reward him one day, won't we?'

'Yes, Sire.'

'La Fargue . . . La Fargue . . . I recall that my father had a great esteem and friendship for a La Fargue . . .'

'They are one and the same, Sire.'

And as the king said nothing more the cardinal imitated him, while reflecting on the ingratitude of princes.

Searching for his daughter, La Fargue, alone and penniless, embarked at Dieppe on 27 September 1633 aboard *La Bienfaisance*, bound for La Nouvelle-France. The adventures and events that marked his life in America remain to be told.

Marciac lived happily with Gabrielle until his heart failed him during a game of cards. He was seventy-nine years old and was teaching his granddaughter how to cheat.

A viewing was organised for Leprat at monsieur de Tréville's mansion in rue du Vieux-Colombier. For three days and three nights the King's Musketeers watched over his mortal remains. He was buried with full honours and still lies in his family's tomb at the Château d'Orgueil.

Laincourt disappeared on the road to Lorraine, and was never heard of again.

Nor was any more ever heard of Saint-Lucq.

As for Agnès . . .

4

On 5 September 1638, at the Château de Saint-Germain-en-Laye, Anne d'Autriche gave birth to twin boys in secret . . . twins who could in no way be considered identical.

Mère de Vaudreuil was immediately consulted.

'Which one?' asked Louis XIII, looking down at the two newborn babies in their swaddling clothes.

'This one,' replied the White Wolves' mother superior.

'I want him to live!' cried the queen from her bed. 'I will bear the sorrow of his being torn from me, but he must live!' she insisted between sobs.

'Madame, I have promised you this,' said the king gravely.

Shortly after, Mère de Vaudreuil galloped away into the night carrying the child.

And so the Masque de Fer was born . . .